KAGAMI

KAGAMI

A NOVEL

Elizabeth Kata

BALLANTINE BOOKS
NEW YORK

Grateful acknowledgment is made to Penguin Books
Ltd. for permission to reprint "The Sorrows of the
Deer" by Manyoshu and an excerpt from "Tanka" by
Emperor Meiji from *The Penguin Book of Japanese Verse*
translated by Geoffrey Bownas and Anthony Thwaite
(Penguin Books, London, 1964). Copyright © 1964
by Geoffrey Bownas and Anthony Thwaite. Reprinted
by permission of Penguin Books Ltd.

Library of Congress Cataloging-in-Publication Data

Kata, Elizabeth.
Kagami : a novel / Elizabeth Kata. — 1st American ed.
p.   cm.
ISBN 0-345-36874-6
1. Japan—History—19th century—Fiction.
2. Japan—History—20th century—Fiction. I. Title.
PR9619.3.K28K34 1992
823—dc20   90-93212
CIP

Book design by Debbie Glasserman

Manufactured in the United States of America

First American Edition: July 1992

10   9   8   7   6   5   4   3   2   1

*To cherished memories of times
spent in Japan*

PART I

In THE MIDDLE OF THE last century, on a high bluff overlooking the ocean and the fishing hamlet of Yokohama, stood a family house attached to a seignorial school which for several hundred years had been run according to the despotic shogunate laws that prevailed in the land.

The ancient sea pines surrounding the house on the hill and the school were like black lace etched against the sky. The people who dwelt in those two buildings were willful and passionate, kindly and patient. Theirs was a family of the times, those joyous and terrible times that saw unprecedented change in the Japan they loved.

The story of that family begins in the summer of 1845. . . .

On THE HOT, BRIGHT DAY that heralded in Renzō's seventh year he awakened early, brimming with energy. When his nurse, Honda, finally gave in to his demands about the clothes he insisted on wearing, he stood before the mirror admiring the way his hair had been swept up in tufts like little tea brushes. He liked his new hempen gown lined with crimson and sashed by a thick twine girdle, but wished he had a real sword to make him feel complete.

He knew that individual birthdays had no real significance because the entire population of Japan celebrated a communal birthday each New Year, but Renzō was determined to enjoy the day to the full.

Although he secretly admired his father, he was pleased that he was away visiting in Edo again—in all probability having his own kind of fun with that bold lady, Osen, his latest fancy so despised and gossiped about by his mother and his aunt Sumiko, who alluded to Osen as "a creature of low caste."

He was accustomed to grown-up people ignoring his presence as they expressed their thoughts and feelings freely, believing that he was always engrossed in his games and too young to understand the subjects they spoke of, and in many respects they were correct. For some time he had thought Osen was a pet animal that his father had purchased, maybe a dog, or even a monkey, but now he knew better. During his father's recent visit home, Renzō had been present when his parents had discussed Osen. His mother, her manner aloof, had exclaimed quietly, "Husband, your woman, the courtesan Osen, from all reports, is doing little to enhance your reputation. Also, although I hesitate to say this, the scandalous association is an insult to your family name."

His father had replied loudly with feigned laughter, "Must you always tug at my sleeves? Never mind. Never mind! Why not take comfort that you are my registered wife? Seemingly you and I are always to be at odds. I seldom please you. Last year you were criticizing my association with Usami, that delightful youth."

"Naturally I did not commend it." Lady Masa's voice had been tinged with ridicule. "But at least Usami is an actor of some repute."

"True, but he in no way pleased me. For the time being Osen fits my needs. My nature demands contrasts. All lovemaking demands contrasts, otherwise it cannot thrive. Come, why make my stay here so unharmonious? Please bear in mind that you no longer dwell in court circles but in a fishing hamlet, a social backwater. And remember also that I am here to request that you cease using your influence over my sister."

His mother had not dignified that outburst with so much as a glance, murmuring coolly, "Kindly take up the matter of her marriage with Sumiko. She is strong-willed and . . ."

"Nonsense . . . ," his father had thundered. "She is completely ruled by your will which keeps her tied here. Your lady-in-waiting, so to speak. My situation with the Fukuda family becomes more difficult with every passing month. I intend to brook no further female capriciousness. Have Sumiko brought here at once and send the child from the room."

Just yesterday, shortly after his father's departure from Yokohama, Renzō, his mother, and his aunt, together with a maid-servant, left the house to picnic on the beach at Hommoku Bay. The ladies wore loosely tied sashes around their cotton kimono, and the little party from the house on the hill meandered happily down the path to the fishing hamlet. The summer chorus of cicadas in the pine trees was deafening enough for the ladies to cover their ears, but Renzō, who loved the merry sound, set up his own continuous high-pitched screaming until he was ordered to stay silent.

On reaching the beach they were welcomed by the fisherfolk. The women bowed and the children, many with brother and sister babies slung on their backs, gazed curiously and shyly at the young master from the schoolhouse. With politeness and respect, sparsely clad men had adjusted their loincloths as they called cheerfully, "Perfect weather! Perfect weather today!"

"Indeed, perfect weather," his mother replied. Then, turning to him, she murmured, "Ren-chan, keep well away from the children. Several of them have skin eczema."

She spoke the truth, but he wished that she was not always quite so observant. He had hoped to talk and play with the children; but it was still enjoyable just following after the ladies. With their robes tucked up, they were gathering seashells while the waves lapped gently over their bare feet.

Banks of white clouds floated high above, and the sea was un-ruffled; only the rocking of small boats sent out ever-widening ripples. As the tide receded, women and children set to work collecting masses of velvet-smooth seaweed.

Renzō noticed that several of the near-naked youths' bodies were decorated with grotesque, highly colored tattoos. Wondering how they achieved such spectacular ornamentation, he decided to ask Aunt Sumiko, but even as he ran to her side she waved him away, saying, "Later, Renzō, later . . ." She had gone on chatting to his mother, her voice triumphant, exclaiming, "At least I have been reprieved once more and all thanks to you, older sister."

"Don't mention it. You know that my husband pays no attention to my opinions. Indeed, to the opinions of all women. Kenichi's samurai philosophy destroys within himself any feelings for the intelligence of the opposite sex."

"Sensual intelligence and sensual feeling too?"

As the two ladies laughed, mocking and merry, Renzō ran ahead of them, trying to draw attention to himself.

He joined a group of fishermen, and watched, as one by one they plunged their brawny arms deep into an immense wooden tub filled to the brim with freshly caught whitebait.

The men were bargaining, laughing good-naturedly as they made bids for the catch, while sea gulls hovered greedily overhead. Renzō, outscreeching the birds, leapt into the tub, then called out fearfully as his body sank beneath the sticky mass.

After he had been hauled from the tub by the owner of the catch, he stood by, head bent, listening to the barrage of comments around him, realizing that his behavior had lowered the price which the good man had expected to gain.

"*Dōmo, dōmo*—Ruined, squashed flat!" the man muttered ruefully as Sumiko came forward to apologize for her nephew's unrefined manners and offered recompense for the fisherman's loss.

A discussion, punctuated by many deep bows, continued for some time as the man repeated again and again, "No, no. Think nothing of it, Lady. What's done is done. Please, think nothing of it."

"Think nothing of it," an old fisherman chimed in cheerily. "Children are children. 'Tis said that even the holes by the roadside hate a boy of seven or eight years old."

Finally his aunt led him away while his mother, who had ignored the entire episode, gazed at the sky, holding a conch shell to her ear, listening to something that only she could hear.

"Strip off your garments," his aunt commanded, gesturing that he go into the sea and wash the fishy odor from his body.

It was so nice splashing about in the salty water, feeling the gritty sand beneath his feet, that he quite forgot the reason why he was there.

"Come along. That's quite enough," Sumiko ordered, but he laughed at her, boldly moving farther out from the shore. "Ren-chan, Ren-chan, you can't swim, you will drown," she warned, her voice high and shrill.

He was rescued by one of the tattooed youths who earlier had laughed so heartily at him. He lay on the sand spluttering, and the kind young maid-servant helped him on with his loincloth.

Deeply humiliated, he dawdled behind the ladies as they climbed up the steep trail toward their home. Feeling oppressed and as though he did not exist, his spirits rose high as he spied a bright green grass snake slithering through the undergrowth edging the path.

If he had known that the women had such horror and loathing for the harmless creature, he most certainly would not have caught it and hung it about his neck, shouting, "Look: *Look!* See *me*. . . ."

He was astonished at the outburst of hysteria one little snake caused. Grown-up persons were beyond his understanding. A boy never knew which way they would jump, or when, or why.

His grandfather and the dour scholars, all stoop-shouldered from so much reading and writing, dwelt in the adjoining schoolhouse. To

Renzō, they seemed scarcely human; his father especially, so seldom at home, was a man of mystery. And he fully believed that Aunt Sumiko had her cheeky monkey Zar-chan's needs more at heart than his own.

His mother, the Lady Masa, treated him with a puzzling mixture of possessiveness and indifference. When he displeased her she would remove the small folding fan tucked in her *obi*-sash and point it imperiously in his direction; those fan gestures combined with her silent glances spoke more than words could and never failed to bring him to order. . . .

Now, filled with pride and animation as he stood before the mirror on this very special birthday, he was determined to behave with new dignity.

He ordered Honda to bring him his toy sword, and, sticking it into his girdle, he strode along the dim, highly polished corridors of the rambling house and entered a ten-mat room where the family's Shinto shrine held place of honor.

For one long moment he gazed into the *kagami*, that tiny mirror of polished bronze, hoping to study the condition of his heart, to see if it was pure. He knew that grown-up people were able to do that. But all he saw was a blurred reflection of his face. He made his obeisance, careful about the quality of his expression, about the position of his hands upon the floor and about his manner of bowing during the act of reverence.

That ceremony completed, he thought he should present himself in all his glory before one of Japan's most eminent scholars, his own grandfather, Dr. Yamamoto. However, no sooner had he arrived at the entrance of the school quarters, calling out *"Gomen nasai! Gomen nasai!* Excuse me—please!,'' than the ever-present guardian of the door chided him for daring to disturb the honorable persons who had risen long before dawn and who were diligently at work.

Dismayed, Renzō stood for a moment, fingering his sword, fantasizing that it was a real weapon and that he was a grown samurai who, with one flashing action, could put an end to the impertinent servant by chopping his head from his body. But his bloodthirsty thoughts faded as he made his way toward his mother's living quarters. Even more than compliments on his unusually striking morning attire, he was in search of sustenance, for his belly was rumbling, calling to be filled with rice, hot miso soup, and crisp, pungent radish pickles.

He slid open the high wooden gate and was about to rush forward when he remembered his newfound dignity and, aware that his mother and his aunt Sumiko were glancing in his direction, he halted. The two women, still attired in their sleeping robes, sat on cushions on the veranda-platform. Their hair fell like jet-black silken skeins about their bare shoulders, and already the heat of the day obliged them to wave their fans as they murmured to each other, scarcely moving their lips, as was their habit when they were exchanging confidences.

Determined to impress, Renzō pretended to be unaware of the women's scrutiny. He spread his legs wide and with one hand on the hilt of his sword, the other shading his eyes, he gazed intently, as though lost in contemplation of his mother's garden pond.

As he gazed, he was surprised to discover just how beautiful the garden really was. The depth of the pond allowed the sky and the upper part of the tall trees on the opposite shore to be reflected in the water, thus providing an added feeling of distance. The bridge was made of naturally warped timber and cambered slightly for ease of crossing.

Renzō stood looking from the bridge into the water at the smooth movements of the brocaded carp. Those carp were his mother's pride and joy. She alone had the privilege of feeding them; always, on hearing her voice, they would come darting in her direction, leaping high from the water to receive her beneficence.

Food? His own hunger suddenly overpowered other emotions and he ran swiftly, calling fretfully, "I am hungry. Hungry, *hungry*. I want my morning meal. . . ."

At once his mother snapped her fan closed and pointed it at him. He fell instantly to his knees, bowed his head, and called politely, "Good morning, Mother! Good morning, Aunt Sumiko. Is not the weather beautiful today?"

"Beautiful indeed," Lady Masa replied. "Not so your rough ways." As though unable to bear the sight of him, she opened her rosary bag and took the beads in her hand as she intoned a prayer of homage to the glory of the lotus.

Relieved at being let off so lightly, Renzō proceeded to the kitchen quarters, where house-servants were all making a clicking music with their chopsticks as they ate their morning rice and gossiped and laughed. At his sudden appearance they fell silent, staring admiringly, astonished by his grand raiment. Even the cook, usually so crotchety, shouted, "Who *can* this handsome personage be? How fortunate it is that I have this feast of fried bean-cakes to set before him."

He devoured the tasty food, enjoying the servants' teasing praise of his person. But he frowned at the newcomer to the household, Misa, a fat twelve-year-old girl who made dreadful faces at him and said insolently, "How silly you look with your little toy sword. I could squash you flat just by sitting on you."

True, he thought, she could easily do that. He tried to put her in her proper place by pointing a chopstick in her direction, just as his mother did with her all-powerful fan. But Misa, unimpressed, merely pulled another grimace and rushed from the huge earthen-floored kitchen to unlatch the outside gates, where peddlers had arrived with their seasonal wares.

Their arrival always caused a stir throughout the house. Renzō liked them more than anyone else he knew. They were humorous, good-natured men and women who brought huge straw bags of charcoal, loads of chopped wood, and countless other mundane necessities as well as delicacies in their wicker baskets—dried persimmons, mushrooms, chestnuts, fresh flowers, fruits, vegetables—and toys. When winter was approaching, they brought straw raincoats and high-platformed wooden clogs for walking in the cold snow-slush.

He remained in the kitchen, enjoying the bustle and the bargaining and admiring the giant lobsters. Then, losing interest, he made his way to the main living room, but stopped before entering in order to eat a juicy pear he had snatched up, and then to secrete the core in the sleeve of his tunic.

His mother and his aunt, now robed and coiffed for the day, and their underlips rouged, sat smoking long-stemmed one-puff pipes as they examined goods brought by the merchant Moto San, who dealt in articles catering to womanly needs and in luxuries which only such ladies could afford.

The silk merchant had already spread his wares on the *tatami* floor, creating an orgiastic delight of color: smooth printed silks, richly embroidered brocades, patterned velvets, and air-light chiffons.

Quite often the silk merchant and his two assistants would stay on for several days, patiently awaiting the ladies' final decisions. His visits were deeply appreciated and, although he was not received as a guest, he was treated with great courtesy. In turn, Moto San, of necessity patient beyond belief, was willing to play the waiting game that was an integral part of his business.

Renzō was now on his best behavior and sat quietly, careful not to draw attention to himself. He was eager to get back into his mother's good graces as she unconcernedly observed all that was going on about her, speaking in a muted voice, obliging those around her to listen intently when she spoke.

"Tell us, Moto San," she murmured, "have you knowledge of the coming winter fashions in Kyoto?"

"Indeed, Lady Masa, I have. Underclothes, beneath unobtrusive garments, are to run riot with color, and kimono sleeves are to be slightly shorter. Yes, gentle but yet, in all, *extremely* seductive."

"And *obi* brooches?"

"Jade and coral are greatly in demand. But, Lady Masa, Edo, not Kyoto, leads fashion these days."

Wearied of such feminine talk, Renzō waited for a suitable moment to make his escape, which came when a troop of serving girls entered the room, carrying lacquered trays laden with food, hot rice-wine, and tea.

Although Lady Masa's gaze was apparently focused on the movement and bustle about her, Renzō bowed deeply in her direction before leaving the room.

Quite suddenly he remembered that it was his birthday and he felt put out, for no one had even thought to congratulate him. At a loss, he crossed the spacious hall leading to the steep stairway and made his way up the stairs to his father's private study. The wooden shutters were closed and the room was almost in darkness, but it was cool and filled with the fascinating smell emanating from the *kiri*-wood chests and from the books and boxed scrolls so neatly arranged on the low shelves that lined the room.

He liked this room and wondered what secrets he would discover if he opened all the closed doors and drawers in the chests. Pulling out one long, deep drawer, he beheld two ancient swords sheathed with silk-brocade wraps.

Renzō removed the toy dirk from his side and took a piece of blue velvet that was covering his father's writing materials on the low floor-desk. He folded the cloth around the toy and placed it with the real weapons. As he closed the heavy drawer he wondered what his father would think on finding the toy. Well, let him think what he would!

Still at a loose end, he now found himself embarking on a tour of his home. The adjacent schoolhouse and its dormitories were, of course, off limits, but here, upstairs, there were also rooms he seldom entered. As he went from each small room to the next, he slid open all the connecting partitions until finally he had created one immense chamber. He was deeply impressed as he surveyed the new *tatami* mats; white with a slight tinge of green in them, they were bordered by black tape bindings that created a dramatic effect.

After a while he entered the eight-mat room that was his aunt Sumiko's private den. On the raised *tokonoma* hung a single picture-scroll featuring three baby monkeys and beneath it stood a bronze vase with blue flowers in it. The *hibachi*, the large fire-bowl, was made of porcelain, whiter than snow and decorated with snarling, scarlet dragons. Beside the low ornate table were two purple floor-cushions and on the table lay one of his mother's fans and several tiny picture-scrolls, rolled and tied with lengths of faded cord.

Renzō plumped himself down on one of the cushions and, ignoring any feelings of guilt, he unloosed the cord of one scroll. As he unrolled the silky, yellowed parchment, he beheld amazing pictures—colored drawings portraying men and women grimacing as though in ecstasies of pain, their bodies all twisted together.

Without bothering to replace things as he had found them, Renzō left the room, disturbed by the insight into the queer tastes of grown-up folk. How could his aunt and his mother enjoy looking at such pictures? Especially his aunt. Sumiko had always entertained him with stories of brave, heroic men and women. It was Aunt Sumiko who had told him about the magnificent history of Japan, the largest, the most beautiful country in the world. She had let him know that Fuji San, the tallest mountain in the whole world, was ruled over by a goddess who bade all the flowers in the land to bloom. And there was nothing strange or ugly about that.

Outside on the wooden-railed veranda Renzō drew a deep breath of fresh air into his lungs and, forgetting that unpleasant scroll, gazed outward from the high perch.

There, beneath him, lay the fishing hamlet of Yokohama. A soft sea breeze wafted his way, sweet with the pungent scent of pine needles, and he blinked his eyes rapidly, taking in the symphony of color: so many shades of green, of morning-glory blue and of yellow field-flowers.

Far below was Hommoku Bay, from which those brawny fishermen sailed away every evening as the sun went down, to return with their catch at break of day. He envied those carefree fisherfolk, those hardy swimmers. It would be nice to become such a man when he grew up, to live among them in one of their fragile houses with a strong wife and many children—certainly *not* just one child.

His old nurse, Honda, was a fisherman's daughter, and from her he had heard many tales. He knew that no worse incident could befall a fishing boat than if a bucket should fall from it into the sea and sink; sooner or later the evil spirits inhabiting the waters would use the bucket to pour water into the vessel and founder it. He knew that a cat should always be carried on a deep-sea fishing junk, as cats had the power to repel the ghosts that frequent the ocean depths.

Although it was not yet near evening, Renzō could see the fishermen already at work on the beach. From the distance they looked small and the boats lined up on the shore resembled toys. He wished he could run down to the bay and help the men with their nets. But his mother would never allow him such freedom.

He understood that his life was extremely important to his parents; if he had an accident and died, his mother would have to produce another son from her body. Before his birth two other children, both boys, had died in their infancy. Honda had told him that his birth had given Lady Masa hours of untold agony and that she, still so young and beautiful, felt she had suffered more than enough.

He sighed deeply. Perhaps growing up was not such a good thing. His mind was filled with heavy thoughts, and even as he stood on the veranda, a bell at the monastery, on the highest hill above the hamlet, began to send out deep, sweet notes that trembled in the hot air and caused his heart to ache.

His heart? No, his stomach. He was hungry again.

Having eaten two bowls of rice, two bowls of miso soup, and every scrap of food set before him, Renzō was then taken in hand by Honda. She stripped him of his regalia and scrubbed from top to toe in the bathhouse, while croaking at him, "Be *still* while I clean you up. Why do you become so dirty so quickly? I warn you, if you don't keep yourself well bathed, you will grow hair all over your body. Do you want to look like an Ainu—an Aborigine—? No decent person wants to be in smelling distance of those hairy folk. They eat bear flesh. They are savage and wild. There, all nice and clean! Now, little master, you must scrub my aching back. Your old nurse deserves a reward."

He set to work, and as he scrubbed his nurse's back, he noticed for the first time how wizened and scrawny her body was in comparison to the smooth firmness of his mother's and his aunt's bodies.

The household bath was a communal affair, and the naked female bodies were familiar, arousing in Renzō no more interest than did the trees or the flowers. However, since seeing that scroll, his imagination had been affected and he wondered what his nurse would do if he threw her on her back and grappled with her while astride her body. Would she scream out, be terrified and angry? Would she fling her sticklike old legs into the air and cling to him, grimacing like the women in those drawings?

"I've scrubbed you enough," he shouted, and ran dripping wet from the bathhouse out into the sunlight, not caring that his mother was witnessing his wild, naked flight.

She stood on the bridge of the pond, a colorful parasol shading her from the bright glare. The silk merchant was by her side and they were admiring the carp. The new maid, fat Misa, was kneeling at his mother's feet, holding a basket from which her mistress took small balls of rice and threw them into the water calling "Koi, koi, koi . . ." For the benefit of the merchant, Lady Masa was showing how her aquatic pets actually answered when she called to them.

At the sight of her naked son she called merrily, "Ren-chan! Ren-chan, come to my side! Come hold the food basket."

As he took the basket from Misa, he pulled a hideous face at her, knowing that she could not retaliate in the presence of her mistress. Lady Masa whispered sternly to the girl, "Go at once to the bathhouse. Your body odor is unpleasant." Her head bent, Misa trotted off and Renzō, a smugly clean child, assisted his mother while the silk merchant complimented Masa on the beauty and the intelligence of her brocaded carp and also on the comeliness of her child. "A son to be proud of," he exclaimed.

Renzō straightened his shoulders and stood with his head bent humbly beneath their combined gaze. Despite her obvious pleasure, his mother murmured, "No, no, Moto San. He is a most ordinary child."

Turning to her son, she said, "Make haste, get dressed, and go to your aunt. She is waiting for you."

For the past two years Aunt Sumiko had tutored him in the arts of writing and reading and in the discipline of good manners.

She was a patient teacher. He had learned that for more than two hundred years Japan had been in a state of total isolation from the rest of the world, and that before then hosts of rapacious barbarians had caused chaos and tragedy. Since their banishment, no ugly or serious political disturbances of any kind had threatened the supremacy of the Tokugawa shogunate.

"Will the cruel barbarians ever come again, Aunt?" Renzō once asked.

"Never!" she declared. "Be assured of that. Be happy that you are a child of Japan. Enjoy this time of learning."

He was usually happy under her tutelage, but today lessons were tedious. He found it difficult to concentrate and difficult to handle his writing brush correctly.

"Must you fidget so?" Sumiko chided him. "Have you caught a fever perhaps?"

"I think I have a fever, Aunt," he lied.

She touched his forehead lightly, and laughed. "A nice cool little forehead! Come now, do it again. Treat each character with reverence."

Filled with impatience, he spent another long hour forming the difficult characters, attempting to emulate her elegant calligraphy.

"There, all finished!" he shouted. "May I go now, Aunt?"

Sumiko examined his efforts. "Disgraceful," she said. "But you have worn me out. Apologize for shouting, then put away your writing implements. No. Not like that! *Carefully* . . ."

As usual, the boy was obedient. He bowed and was given permission to go his way.

It seemed that a whole year had gone by. But the sun was still high in the sky, and everyone in the house, even the servants, was having a rest and there were no birds in the sky.

Birds! To pass the time he would visit his grandfather's aviary. Running helter-skelter toward the grove of striped bamboo, he heard the sound of a flute and he knew that the blind masseur who lived on the premises was in the grove. For forty long years he had lived in the midst of the Yamamoto family, on call to go to the school at any hour, day or night, ready and willing to massage aching muscles, to grant sleep to wearied minds and restless bodies.

When not needed the masseur hid away in quiet nooks, playing the wooden flute that was his prized possession. During the summer months he would sit in the bamboo forest that held Dr. Yamamoto's treasured collection of winged creatures.

As Renzō entered into the cool green gloom of the grove, he called out, "*Konnichiwa*—Good day to you, old man!"

"*Konnichiwa*, little master! Am I needed in the house?"

"No. Please, old uncle, may I blow music on your flute?"

"No. It plays only for me."

"I don't think that is so."

"Maybe not, but it's what I believe. Listen, this day I have composed a new melody."

Renzō, charmed that he was listening to a tune no one else in the world had ever heard, stood by, his arms folded, his expression critical. It was a cheerful tune and he asked the masseur to play it again and again until, tired of his demands, the old man tucked the instrument in his rope girdle, reached out his hand, and picked up the cane staff that was hidden in the long grass.

Renzō wondered if the old man was really blind. "Can't you see even just a little bit, old man?" he exclaimed, staring at the bleary eyes in the wrinkled, walnut-colored face.

"I have ears. I have a good nose. I have touch. I earn my rice. To *see* has no sense for me. Folk speak of light. Never have I understood that word."

"Then . . ." Renzō hesitated. "Then, all is dark to you always? You live in a dark cage, then?"

"A dark cage?" the blind man cackled merrily. "If you say so, little master, I live in a dark cage, but it is a comfortable cage. Excuse me, if you please. I wish to take my nap."

Perhaps he should leave the grove? He had no business to be there, for it was Dr. Yamamoto's retreat. The elderly scholar had a passion for the birds and fowls in the aviary. He employed a half-witted youth who wandered about the countryside with his bird-catching pole, skillfully capturing wagtails, finches, and the like. But he had explained to Renzō, "*Never* skylarks. They would pine away and die if put in a cage."

Renzō peered in between the bamboo slats at the immense enclosed area of the aviary. What a motley collection of birds it held! What havoc a fox would cause if one broke into the enclosure. Certain birds, the kites, sparrow hawks, and the one falcon, had their own compartments. The wild geese, ducks, teals, and long-legged herons had their reed-filled water pond and dwelt peaceably with other varieties, including quail, pheasants, and several bluebirds. Perched in the heights of the enclosure like an emperor surveying his kingdom was the rice-white Chinese cock. His long tail feathers resembled a waterfall and cascaded to the ground near the pond. For a while Renzō stood with his nose pressed against the smooth slats, watching the desultory swimming of the waterfowl, listening to the cheeping of small birds. But the really interesting ones, the hawks and the falcon, sat motionless—napping.

Nearby was an ancient oak tree, its leafy branches shading a lotus pond; the pink blossoms raised high above the immense leaf pads gave out a bittersweet perfume. Renzō stared down at the pink-and-green-carpeted pond, recalling the day, several years back, when he had been reprimanded by his aunt for having plucked and crushed one of the lotus blooms. "Ren-chan," she had said, "the lotus is a holy flower, the token of truth and light and purity, which displays its glory for just a few weeks." And indeed, when he had returned, the pond, once so resplendent, had become unkempt, ugly, and filled with dying stalks and leaves.

His meditations came to an abrupt end as he caught sight of a brown-speckled frog—no larger than his thumbnail—sitting on a lotus pad in the middle of the pond. He wanted it. He would capture it, as he was without a pet, having neglected to feed his finch, which had died of starvation in its cage.

It was not fair. His mother had her carp. His aunt had Zar-chan, her monkey, Grandfather had his aviary, and Father, far away in Edo, had Osen. Could he capture the frog without harming the holy flowers? Remembering his aunt's lecture, he decided to forgo a new pet and to leave the frog on the lotus pad. Instead, he climbed the wide-spreading branches of the tall oak tree.

It was nice to be up so high, looking down through the green foliage to the ground and looking up at the sky and out over the ocean. How smooth and blue the ocean was and how hard and straight the dark line that separated the sky from the sea. What lay beyond that horizon? He knew that sailors were forbidden to sail too far from the shores of Japan. In a way, maybe the entire population of the world lived in cages of a kind? He was himself a prisoner, a boy all of seven years, spending his days beneath the ever-inquisitive eyes of jailers. Women jailers at that.

How could he set himself free? He could run away, become a *rōnin*, traveling far and wide, performing tremendous acts of courage and bravery. But then his mother would again be forced to produce a new son from her body. He couldn't bear even to imagine her slender figure swollen and distorted like the maid-servant Ume, who lumbered around, complaining about her swollen legs, her aching back, as she awaited the arrival of her overdue baby.

He didn't blame the baby. Why rush to become caged up in a

world that held so many frustrations? Clambering down from the oak tree, he stamped angrily on the ground, cutting the air with his hand, shouting, "I want to be free! I want to be free, free, *free* . . ." As though scorning him, the savage-beaked falcon gave a frightening shriek that caused the other birds to flutter wildly against the bars.

As Renzō approached the aviary, time ceased to exist for him. He knew that he was about to commit a terrible deed, a crime. He also knew that he would, like all criminals, pay a high price for his wickedness. He did not care. He could not free himself. He could not free the blind man from darkness into light, but he could, and he would, free the caged birds.

His punishment was a terrible ordeal. He was alone for the first time with his grandfather, in the shadowy silence of the main study room of the schoolhouse. He could not see the elderly scholar, but he knew that he was sitting nearby, for he heard pages being turned. He smelled smoke and knew that his grandfather was using the small wooden tray containing a tiny charcoal *hibachi* which he used to light his pipe.

Sweat sprang from every pore in his skin. He bit his tongue and shut his eyes tight, strengthening his resolution to bear this ordeal. He was kneeling, absolutely motionless, holding a bowl filled with water, knowing that not one drop must spill on the age-yellowed *tatami* matting.

A lifetime seemed to go by and no sign or word of release was given. When he felt that he could no longer endure his plight, suddenly, most miraculously, the torture of his excruciating position vanished and the cramped feeling in his legs was forgotten. His head felt light. His mind had never been so clear. Without any conscious effort on his part, as though he were an observer, he saw the enactment of his deed and he saw a vision of its consequences. . . .

He had picked up a long pole, unlatched the gate, and entered the aviary. His task had been fraught with unexpected difficulties, for instead of seeing him as their savior, most of the birds had considered him to be out to harm or to kill them.

Their lack of understanding drove him into a further fury of desperation, and he ran about, opening cages, shouting instructions, and poking at the terrified creatures with the heavy pole that he brandished as though it were his father's sword.

To assist his efforts, he scrambled up a ladder and opened a wide

roof-door, shrieking with joy as many of the birds flapped their way
to freedom. Then he had plummeted to the ground, stumbled, and
fallen into the water-birds' pond, sinking to his waist in the slime
and black slush, slipping and falling flat on his face again as he
extricated himself.

Still in a fury, Renzō rushed toward the Chinese cock, screaming
out, "You! Come on down, come on down . . ." The great bird
merely ruffled his crest feathers and stared down at him, with the
reprimanding look so typical of Lady Masa. "Stupid, stupid," he
yelled. "Are you *stupid* or can't you fly?"

Attempting to help the cock in its escape, Renzō caught the waterfall of plumage in his hands and tugged hard. But the weight of
the bird as it fell into his arms sent him and the cock back into the
pond. Scrambling out, spitting evil-smelling water from his mouth,
he left the floundering bird to its fate.

By now crowds of people had gathered at the bamboo grove.
Some were laughing raucously, in amazement; others were quite
terrified, and the human voices, combined with the screeching, cack-
ling birdcalls, produced a cacophony of sound that finally brought
Renzō to his senses as he stood by, covered with black mud, helplessly awaiting his punishment.

"What *madness* . . ."

"Who *is* that wicked young rascal . . . ?"

"He resembles a savage animal. *Bring a rope.* . . ."

"But—it's the little *master*! It's Renzō. . . ."

"Is there *no end* to his mischief . . . ?"

The half-wit youth, the bird-catcher, and fat Misa lumbered about,
hollering and attempting to capture the low-flying birds. Their
crazed behavior added an atmosphere of chaotic melodrama to the
scene, and for an instant Renzō realized that he was providing an
extraordinary entertainment in the lives of these people. But at the
sight of his mother, that brief instant of pride was snuffed out.

She stood motionless and silent in the midst of the noise. He
watched as she untied the ribbons of her straw sun hat. As she held
it high, she called out, "Silence! Be silent! The master is approaching. This is not your business. Away with you."

Her command was ignored. Nevertheless, the crowd fell silent,
forming into two lines—a reception committee, agog, awaiting the
arrival of the drama's star performer.

The old scholar's voice was high and uncontrolled as he called urgently, *"Nani . . . ? Nani . . . ?"*—What goes on . . . ?" He ran straight through the bowing human aisle, then halted to survey the havoc.

Among the silent crowd, the black-robed students and tutors, their heads shaved close to their skulls, stood around their professor, waiting for his reaction.

But no one was waiting with more apprehension than the instigator of the holocaust. Renzō looked around him, shocked and bewildered; was it possible that he, with his own hands, had laid waste to that which his grandfather held so dear?

Yes, *Shiyō ga nai*—It was done. It could not be undone.

The ladies of the household had moved to his grandfather's side, also awaiting his reaction, for his attitude, his intensity, had the force of a physical agent as he raked his gaze about the horrifying scene.

Finally, ignoring the silent audience, Dr. Yamamoto hoisted up his robe. Once inside the aviary, he stepped into the pond and sank waist-deep into the water. Then he called tonelessly to his daughter-in-law, "Enough! Masa, kindly remove these onlookers. Take the child away. Bathe him."

His orders given, Grandfather proceeded, with clucking, soothing sounds, to attend to the tribulations of his floundering, mud-covered Chinese cock.

The time Renzō spent with his mother in the bathhouse had a dreamlike quality. As she ushered him into the room, she ignored the curious brigade of people. "I shall tend my son," she murmured politely as she slid the heavy wooden door shut.

In silence, she cleansed every part of his body. She, naked as he, poured many brass-bound buckets of clean, clear water over his head, then gestured for him to step into the big wooden tub. Fired by the charcoal stove beneath it, the tub was always in readiness and, even though he felt bewildered and uncertain, he took comfort as he allowed his body to sink into the watery depths.

His sudden outbreak of gulping sobs had no effect on his mother as she knelt, cleaning herself. When quite satisfied with her condition, she stepped into the tub with him and began to sing, her voice muted, and she sang a folk song he had a liking for. She had not looked at him during the song, but he knew that *she* knew he was no longer weeping. . . .

Sometime later, wearing a dark blue cotton gown tied with a yellow girdle, he was escorted by his mother to her private room.

As fragile as paper tissue, he obediently sat on a cushion close to her mirrored makeup table. She was also in a cotton robe while she sat on her floor-cushion, intent on arranging her long hair into a simple coiffure. The makeup table, the floor-cushions, and a bronze *hibachi* were the only furnishings in the eight-mat room.

Renzō gazed at the murals decorating the doors of the deep cupboards that held bedding and many other articles. The murals were boldly colored, depicting grandly robed ladies and warriors disporting themselves at an al fresco picnic.

He thought of those men and women he had seen on the scroll in his aunt's room, and then he remembered how he had carelessly left it unrolled on the table. To his consternation, he saw that the very same scroll was now in his mother's hands. *Shiyō ga nai*, he thought for the second time that day—"It is done! Nothing can change it!"

How could a day that had begun so auspiciously turn out so badly? There was his mother, examining the scroll and casting oblique glances his way. Did she know who had unfurled it? Yes. Now she was gazing straight into his guilty mind. What was happening to him? It was as though his body were on fire and he could not tear his gaze from that of his mother's.

She had not as yet applied rouge to her lower lip. She looked very young, like a girl. As she gazed, she pressed her lips tightly closed, stretching her mouth into a clandestine, mischievous smile, and shook her head from side to side. She didn't need to utter the words for him to know her thoughts. "What a rascally pair we are, you and I!"

Frightened and downhearted as he was, nothing in the wide land of Japan could have prevented him from smiling back at her, and he knew that he would never, as long as he lived, forget that moment of conspiracy and sweet accord. His mother loved him. He loved and he would love her forever.

A housemaid called from the corridor, asking for admittance. His mother, laying the scroll aside and once more examining her face in the mirror, took up her rouge brush and painstakingly applied the crimson cosmetic to her lower lip. Satisfied with the result, she bid the maid to open the door. The girl, on her knees, stated dramatically: "*Gomen-nasai*—Excuse me, please! The little master must go at once. The old master awaits him at the schoolhouse."

He felt so small, so alone as he entered the huge room. His grandfather stood holding a heavy foreign book in his hands and continued reading, seemingly unaware of Renzō's presence. Finally he put the tome down carefully and said, "So! Nails which stand out must be hammered down. Is that not so? Is that not so? Eh—eh?"

"That is so, Grandfather."

"High spirits and wicked behavior rip open graves, strew stones in the path of one's ancestors. Is that not so? Is that not so?"

"That is so, Grandfather." Oh, how frail his voice was compared with the deep-toned severity of the old scholar whose voice shot words like arrows into his head and muddled Renzō's mind until tears began to flow down his cheeks.

"What name do you bear?" the voice demanded.

His name? He stood mute. Could it be that his grandfather did not know his only grandson's name?

"Your name? What is your name?"

"Renzō, Grandfather. Renzō Yamamoto, Grandfather."

"So! Yes. An honorable name. Is that not so? Is that not so?"

"That is so, Grandfather." He was about to keel over and fall on the *tatami* matting, but he drew in a shuddering breath and managed to remain on his feet, watching and waiting.

He had no clear memory of how he was instructed to kneel: his back arched, his head erect, holding an earthenware bowl filled to the brim with water. . . .

"Not one drop must fall! *Remember, not one drop* . . ." He would never forget those words.

A long time had passed and he was still kneeling. His hands began to tremble, water spilled over the bowl's brim, and he became aware that he was no longer alone with his grandfather.

A familiar voice, that of Aunt Sumiko, filtered into his consciousness. "Father . . ." She spoke tentatively. "Night has fallen."

"What did you say?"

"The *child*, Father!"

"The child . . . ?"

"Yes. Have you forgotten?"

"Ah so! The child! Truthfully, I have been lost in my reading. Tell me, Sumiko, how old is the child now?"

"On New Year's Day Renzō will be eight, Father."

"Already! How time goes by. Tell his mother I wish to speak to her. I shall see to his future. Now, take him away."

Aunt Sumiko carried him pick-a-back through the dark, hot night, out of the school's precincts and into the home garden, past the stone lanterns where moths fluttered and night insects swarmed and buzzed their familiar chorus.

When he was at last lying on his mattress, she massaged his legs and said softly, "Ren-chan, are you hungry?"

"No, Aunt."

"A bowl of delicious noodles?"

"No, Aunt."

Gazing up at her, he saw that she was looking at him and that a fleeting smile crossed her face. "Then," she murmured, "good night. Good night, little boy."

Somewhere in the house he could hear the soft twanging tones of *koto* music. He knew that Lady Masa was plucking at the strings of her beloved harp. His mother! Was that melancholy tune her message of consolation to her son? He liked to think that it was. A wave of sleep swept all further thoughts from his mind.

Renzō was awake early. The room was dark and the heavy wooden shutters of the house were still tightly closed, as they were every night, to silence noises from the outside world.

Yesterday's tribulations no longer concerned him, and he felt remarkably energetic. He lay listening to the creaking of the unhusked rice inside his pillow; he liked those sounds that emerged as he rocked his head gently. But he did not like the snuffles and gurgles coming from his nurse's *futon*, or the stuffiness in the airless room!

All of a sudden that feeling of being caged in overwhelmed him again and, unable to stem his emotions, he climbed stealthily out of bed and crept through the dark house.

He headed back to the grove of striped bamboo and in the same way that the blind man had picked up his cane without faltering, so Renzō climbed straight up into the oak tree. A full moon helped him see his way to a high perch and then, as though in answer to a signal, the first streaks of dawn dimmed the brilliancy of the moon and the boy gasped at the sight of the phosphorescent surface of the ocean.

He watched a great junk and a fleet of smaller fishing boats loom out of the night and drift like phantoms across the silvery sea. The sails of the junk hung listlessly, and the toylike figures of the fishermen on the smaller boats were working the long sweeps as they hauled their night's catch to the beach of Hommoku.

Far off lay that mysterious, beckoning horizon. Renzō waited, until among the delicate apricot and gray blushes of the east a flash occurred and the wondrous red disc of the sun announced a day that seemed to make the world Renzō's own.

"It's a new day!" he shouted exultantly. "I am seeing a new day being born."

"Yes, a new day!" echoed his mother's voice from beneath the oak tree. "Climb down carefully, Renzō. Come, help me feed my carp. They are growing impatient."

He had not known that his mother fed her carp so early every morning. Standing by her side, holding the wicker food-basket, he felt overwhelmed with happiness.

But Lady Masa knew full well that her son's childhood was over. With extraordinary self-restraint she had conferred with her stern father-in-law, pleading that no hasty decision should be made concerning Renzō's schooling until Kenichi paid his next visit to Yokohama. But her pleading had been to no avail.

A hot flare of anger rose in her heart as she thought of her husband, that self-obsessed man, who in all probability was already in Edo, the great capital, catering to his unruly, erotic desires and not giving a thought to the son he had sired.

K ENICHI YAMAMOTO'S SPIRIT SOARED AS he gazed at the wide moats and ancient walls surrounding the Imperial Palace wherein no emperor dwelt. A handsome man with a lust for life, he was glad to be back in Japan's capital city, the country's flourishing economic center.

The overcrowded streets, the bewildering profusion of goods for sale in the stores, the theaters, bars, and numerous places of entertainment were a perfect antidote after the boredom of two weeks spent in the backwaters of his native village. Filled with a vigorous sense of masculine well-being, he hurried toward his house in Nihombashi.

He decided to take it easy for several days. Having slept with his wife, Masa, so recently, he was in no hurry to be with his mistress. His friend Fukuda likened Osen to an amorous bird of prey. Fukuda was apt to overexaggerate, nevertheless the lady's rapacious sensuality called for an inventive, energetic bedpartner. Her jealous attitude toward his wife, his domestic life, and his male friendships also called for diplomacy and patience on his part.

Merely thinking of Osen aroused a chill of resentment in him; he decided to indulge himself in a night of casual pleasure with someone else before informing her of his return to the city.

As he lay soaking in the near boiling bathwater, Kenichi luxuriated in an interlude of introspection. He enjoyed bouts of radical soul-searching; he found it amusing to chide himself for being a self-serving egotist protected by a highly polished façade.

The only person who saw through that façade was his wife, and she was of little importance. He believed that she had liquid snow in her aristocratic veins. A few days back he had reminded her that her noble, impoverished parents had been only too pleased to marry her off into the wealthy Yamamoto family.

She was a vexatious and complex creature with a sharp mind. Recently she had said to him, with some sarcasm, "You resemble a brightly flowering tree—a tree with no roots."

He had taken no offense; indeed, he quite liked the comparison and merely replied, "Is that so? Well, the more trees, the more flowers, the better in a land familiar with earthquakes and typhoons."

His scholarly father had raised him according to the precepts of Confucianism, that system of ethics based on five relationships: father and son; older brother and younger brother; ruler and subject; friend and friend, and husband and wife.

Willingly honoring his father's wish, he had married; that major obligation fulfilled, his conscience was clear.

Like the other members of his circle of married men friends, he considered that the real aim of marriage was to procreate, thereby assuring the continuity of their families, and that any other motive would simply pervert the true meaning of it. He was the father of a healthy son, a lively little fellow. There was no edict to insist that he should love Masa, and the thought that she might love him had never so much as entered his mind.

But what was this lover of fashion and pleasure doing wasting precious time in the bath! Right now he desired hot *sake* and a soothing massage before going out for a night on the town.

Kenichi opened the gate, stepped onto the crowded road, and heaved a sigh of satisfaction. As he walked through the streets on his way to the theater, he gave thanks to the gods that the Rule of the Sword no longer held such a heavy sway.

He reveled in the raciness, the excitement of the new society that was growing in Edo, the new capital. He loved the streets crowded with pedestrians, streets that became dangerous when powerful *daimyō* rode by attended by two-sworded samurai and followed by a retinue of soldiers. The populace would bow low and wait until they had passed. Getting one's head chopped off for a social misdemeanor seldom took place anymore, but it was wise to be careful.

Night had fallen and the streets were lighted with thousands of lanterns which gave out a magic glow. Kenichi loved the cries of the peddlers and the delicate sounds that wafted from the reed pipes of white-robed blind masseurs who sold relief from pain for a few small coins.

A voice hailed him, shouting cheerfully, "Yamamoto San! You there, Kenichi! *Shibaraku*—long time since we last met! Welcome back!"

The voice belonged to Fukuda, his good friend. "So, on your way to an assignation?" Fukuda asked.

He decided not to mention that he was on his way to a Nō play, hoping that his friend might offer more lively entertainment, and replied, "No. Just strolling. Glad to be back in Edo."

"That's understandable." Fukuda grinned widely. "But why take it easy? Come with me. I'm off to meet with Okura. He's at Watanabe's brothel. How about it?"

Kenichi hesitated for an instant, then muttered, "I'm not keen to meet up again with Usami."

"No fear of that," Fukuda interjected. "Usami has gone off with his new patron. Your affair with him is over, isn't it?"

"Absolutely!"

"Good! He's a money sucker. Usami would sell himself to a leper if the price were right. Did he take you for much?"

"Enough. In fact, I'm deeply involved with Osen again."

"I know. It's lunacy to fall in love with a courtesan. She will wear you out, but that's your business. Come on, you need only look. Okura tells me that Watanabe has two new boys, both untried and charming. Yes? No?"

"Well, yes."

"Excellent! Okura will be glad to see you. We three make quite a trio."

Watanabe's brothel was a splendid building, set in spectacular gardens. Its veranda-platforms jutted out over one of Edo's many canals. He catered to all tastes and was on the way to becoming an extremely wealthy man.

In theatrical circles there was great freedom of behavior, and young actors sold their favors equally to men and women. Watanabe San, however, catered exclusively to male clients, and it was not unusual for groups of Buddhist monks to patronize his premises.

His brothel was run on elegant lines, and when Kenichi and Fukuda, first checking their swords, entered the main salon, Fujiwara, a Kabuki actor of high repute, was giving a poetry reading to a large audience.

Their mutual friend, Count Okura, on sighting them, smiled, gesturing that they should join him.

Kenichi, somewhat of a poet himself, admired the actor's style. Fujiwara carried an unfurled fan which he used to punctuate his poem for dramatic effect. He wore a purple robe and the sword in his belt was in a scabbard set with glistening jewels.

"In the hills of Heguri / Sloping smooth as eightfold mats . . ." Fujiwara intoned, telling the story of the hunter, who with his bows and arrows at the ready, waited for the deer—then, there stood before him a great stag who moaned out:

> " 'Soon I must die.
> Then I shall offer my lord
> My horns as hat trimmings,
> My ears as inkwells,
> My eyes as clear mirrors,
> My hoofs as bow-tips,
> My hair as writing brushes,
> My hide as box leather,
> My flesh as mincemeat,
> My liver too as mincemeat,
> My belly as salted flesh,
> So this old servant's one body,
> Shall flower sevenfold,
> Shall flower eightfold,
> Then—praise me, praise me to the skies!' "

The two men knew the poem well and sat entranced until the end of Fujiwara's recitation, when he snapped his fan closed sharply. His audience, silent, bowed deeply from the waist as they sat on their brocaded cushions.

Fully aware of the emotions he had aroused, Fujiwara waited for the right moment. A professional actor, he was out to entertain. His audience was there before him to be entertained and now required a fillip of spice. He stood motionless. With a staccato action he raised one hand, shading his eyes as he gazed at the faces watching him expectantly. Having found the face he had been looking for, he shaded his eyes with both hands as though blinded by a sudden blaze of sunlight.

All eyes went to his target, who was one of the youths Fukuda had mentioned to Kenichi. The youth, only too delighted, aware that he was the center of attention, gazed back at Fujiwara, who immediately recited with mock passion:

> *"Handsome boy!*
> *Oh for a thread*
> *To haul him over*
> *To—my side!"*

As the youth blushed, pouting his exquisite lips, all present broke out in a barrage of bawdy, hilarious laughter, applauding Fujiwara and teasing the youth. The recital over, the audience rose to move toward the banqueting hall.

Kenichi, Fukuda, and Okura drew close together and Kenichi felt overjoyed in the midst of the relaxed, all-male gathering.

Dawn had already arrived when Kenichi and his friends staggered along the streets where crazy freaks, jugglers, and prostitutes were still active.

The fresh morning air was gradually having an effect on the trio's *sake*-laden minds, and when they arrived at the palace-moat, they lingered for a while and philosophized as only pleasantly drunken friends can. Okura exclaimed hotly, "What manner of people are we? *I* say that we are a nation of passionate, willful people who for centuries have been trained to show a smiling face to those in authority—authority meaning the point of the sword."

"I agree, I agree," Fukuda interjected. "You are correct. Our inherent courtesy has been learned at the point of the sword, my friend. Now the sword holds fear only for the careless, foolish man, but

the *courtesy* remains, our *attitude* remains the same. Nothing can
change our ways."

"Who wants change?" Kenichi gestured grandly at the peaceful
scene. "Some want to kill people they hate. Some want the rain
changed to sunny weather. Not I! I accept things as they are—
always."

"So speaks the man who lives and loves one person only—
himself," jeered Fukuda. "Come now, my friend, admit that you go
about in a positive frenzy, changing things which displease you.
Take your Nihombashi abode, for instance."

"True!" Kenichi grinned. "Let's away to it now and refresh ourselves."

The house in Nihombashi belonged to the Yamamotos' hereditary
estate. When the small edifice had been built some fifty years back,
it had stood marooned like an island on the flat terrain and was used
merely as a stopping-over place by Kenichi's father. Now half a
century had gone by and the house faced onto the longest, noisiest
street in Edo, lined on both sides with shops, business houses, inns,
and brothels.

Kenichi was forever besieged by merchants pleading to purchase
the property and offering high prices, which he consistently refused—he was sharp enough to realize that real estate values could
only escalate as time went by. There were already one million citizens in Edo and the population was steadily increasing.

All family matters were now under his control, and his father, Dr.
Yamamoto, exhausted from years of continuous study, was only too
pleased to be relieved of burdensome commercial and human problems. Once every fourth year for the past fifty years he had traveled
to Edo with the results of exhaustive study programs foisted upon
him and his students by the all-powerful, exacting shogun.

For some years now, Kenichi had taken on that onerous task,
assisted by three leading scholars from the school. He enjoyed the
stimulation of those jaunts; and in the meantime he was able to
justify his long absence from his native village by attending to commercial matters and thus managing to live the life of a carefree hon-
orary bachelor.

He was fond and very proud of his abode at Nihombashi. He had
wrought miracles and turned the ordinary little place into a modern,
enchanting home.

The house was responsible for the only companionable time in his marriage. Masa, for all her faults, possessed infallible style and good taste which he had taken advantage of by bringing her to the capital, where she had overseen the transformation of the unkempt back garden. He would always be grateful to her for her skills and for the artistry she had achieved, but he still resented the tribulations that had accompanied the process.

He had first beheld Masa on the day of their wedding which had taken place in the ancient capital city, Kyoto. Although but a girl, she had possessed a lacquered arrogance, an inborn pride, which announced to the world: "I was born to be catered to. Let others toil and labor."

The daughter of a noble clan, Masa had never passed beyond her own gate except in a sedan chair under escort. Nevertheless, she was highly educated and sophisticated beyond her years. At fourteen years of age, carefully trained in the most elaborate codes of deportment, she had shown no opposition when told of the marriage arrangements that had been made for her. Rather, she had shown the proper degree of submission. Her pleasant smile and her gentle voice had not betrayed her feelings of grief and apprehension.

She understood that the arrangements made by the marriage brokers were to be a great boon to both families concerned. Wealth from the groom's family would recoup her father's lost fortune. Her noble blood was to be an asset in the highly intellectual, well-off Yamamoto family. Her demeanor throughout the lengthy proceedings had been exquisitely regulated. Neither she nor Kenichi had ever mentioned the struggle that had taken place between them following that wedding night when he had finally subdued her and wrested a weapon from her delicate hands.

Throughout the ensuing years of her marriage, she had obeyed the codes of etiquette so deeply ingrained in her. These were codes formed by the ethics of a race that for several thousands of years had lived under strict public and private discipline. The exquisite etiquette of old-time training in the cultivated classes was inherited and as much a part of Masa as were the shape of her hands or the quality of her hair. Her way of sitting or walking, the manner of presenting or receiving a gift, so stylized but natural to her, would never change.

Masa's education included the skill of being ready at any moment to inflict her own self-destruction by performing *jigai*—piercing the throat with a dagger so as to sever the arteries in a single thrusting movement. Even in these modern times Kenichi knew that certain married women of high caste still performed sacrificial *jigai* as a demonstration of loyalty to the spirit of their husband after his untimely demise. However, Kenichi presumed that after ten years of marriage, living in the easygoing atmosphere of the house on the hill in the hamlet by the sea, Masa's ethics would have been corrupted and that it would be more likely for her to compose a satirical poem in his honor than take her life if he died before her.

Theirs was an oil-and-water marriage. He never gave a thought to the fact that she had had no say in accepting him as her husband, and that out of loyalty to her impoverished parents she had donned the white robes of a bride, a symbol of mourning, to leave the family she had loved and who had so tenderly raised her.

Certainly, she was beautiful, if one admired long, straight legs, a high-arched nose, a wide, mobile mouth. However, Kenichi's tastes in feminine beauty were different. He had no idea if his wife liked or disdained his physical appearance, although she obviously delighted in their son Renzō's looks, and the child resembled his father.

Masa's first journey from the house on the hill in Yokohama to Edo had taken on the appearance and the atmosphere of a spectacular peregrination from feudal times. Lady Masa, he had realized with annoyance, still considered herself to be a person of some importance; having agreed to travel abroad in order to renovate the Nihombashi house, she insisted on a retinue suitable for a daughter of a noble clan. She also insisted that his sister, Sumiko, accompany her on the journey, and Sumiko, in turn, insisted on taking along her pet monkey. The two highly educated women, forced to live in the isolation of a fishing hamlet, had formed a close relationship which Kenichi found irritating when he was at home. They created an atmosphere of euphoric gaiety in their quarters. They dressed up, made music, practiced classical dance, played cards and childlike games. They composed poems and wrote plays which they would recite and act out. As they sipped rice wine and smoked their one-puff pipes, they took delight in gossiping in undertones and casting oblique glances in his direction; Sumiko frequently laughed in an unseemly manner at his discomfiture.

Already eighteen and still unmarried, Sumiko was becoming a troublesome burden, and the sooner she was away from Masa's influence, the better. That journey to Edo had been Sumiko's first time away from home and Masa's first journey since her arrival in Yokohama some ten years back. To Kenichi's embarrassment, Masa had insisted on traveling the crowded highway in the old-style palanquin used on her bridal journey from the old imperial capital, Kyoto, with four bearers carrying her instead of just the two who bore Sumiko along in a light, modern litter.

The journey took two days, and instead of bedding down overnight in one of the main inns along the way, Masa had brought along a tent of blue-and-yellow-striped cloth furnished with *futon*, the pale green mosquito net she favored, conveniences for bathing and other private needs, as well as her mirrored makeup table and many black-lacquered chests containing kimono.

"Never," Masa had declared, "have I been bitten by fleas or by certain bugs which I know attack folk in roadside inns. I refuse to enter such places. So . . . ?"

Kenichi agreed to all her demands; he felt a rush of pride in having this haughty, aristocratic woman as the mother of his son. Riding his fine horse, Kenichi led the procession consisting of the palanquin and its four bearers, three litters, one bearing Sumiko and the other two the maid-servants, followed by four hired servants on foot, weighed down by immense cloth bundles slung on their backs. Sudo, that tried and true henchman, brought up the rear of the retinue, on horseback.

Masa showed no interest, surprise, or enthusiasm as they entered the metropolis, but Sumiko had cried out in wild excitement. He understood her reaction and preferred it to that of Lady Masa, whose upper-class breeding meant that she was unimpressed by the polyglot masses of Edo, and held a perfumed cloth to her nose as they passed through the bustling streets.

Finally, having settled his womenfolk into a decent inn not far from the house in Nihombashi, Kenichi breathed a sigh of deep relief and went straight to the licensed quarters, not for a time of sport and pleasure, but solely to be in the presence of females who knew their place in the order of things—females who were aware of the superiority of the male, who spoke sweetly, their eyes lowered and their manners pleasingly docile.

Apart from Masa having performed miracles in the house, he had received even greater benefits from her three-month stay in Edo. Until that time he had been on the periphery of the social circles to which his friends belonged. Count Okura's patrician parents, for instance, had never previously invited him into their family home, and Kenichi knew only too well that it was Masa's noble pedigree that had opened the doors of the Okuras' elite social circle to him. For the first time he had understood and appreciated his own father's wisdom in having taken Masa into the midst of the highly respected but definitely less noble Yamamoto clan.

On the other hand, Fukuda had enthused on discovering that his friend's wife was a blue blood, a highborn woman. The Fukudas were of plebian stock and unashamed social climbers. Fukuda's grandfather, a wily peasant, had owned nothing but his threadbare garments and had worked in paddyfields belonging to a feudal lord whose immense tracts of land had been situated on the outskirts of the then scarcely populated town of Edo.

Kenichi had heard the story of Fukuda's grandfather late one night when his friend, sake-laden, had thrown his snobbery to the winds as he described the family's rise from poverty to great wealth. In a conspiratorial manner, he pronounced, "My family owes everything we possess to a longtime dead fortune-teller who told Grandfather that he should 'go and listen to the voices of the carp in the temple pond.' Well, Grandpa, befuddled, obeyed those obscure orders, and while he stood staring into the pond, a flash occurred in his mind. To his dying day he swore that the fish had indeed spoken to him, saying, 'Young man, leave this holy place! Walk about the streets! Behold the rooftops of the houses! One day in the future you will return to this temple and sing our praises.'

"Once again he followed instructions. Wandering about the streets, gazing at the rooftops, bewildered, but with utter faith in the predictions of the carp.

" 'It was the month of May,' he told us. 'The weather was at its most glorious and huge paper carp flew from many rooftops, swimming against the blue of the sky.'

"Well, Grandpa realized that for as long as mankind existed on this earth, during the Festival of the Boy, paper carp, *millions of them*, would be purchased and flown from rooftops to symbolize the male child's ability to swim upstream against obstacles.

"He set up a factory which employed poverty-stricken youths and girls. He gave them board and lodgings and, using tough, fibrous paper patterned and painted to depict the noble fish, he went into business.

"And so, it is thanks to *my* family that most of those paper carp, with hoops thrust into their mouths to allow the wind to blow in and distend their shapes to lifelike proportions, squirm and float today in the skies over Nippon. And now, as you know, toys of all kinds are manufactured in the Fukuda factories. Millions and millions of toys."

During Masa's visit to Edo, Kenichi planned a visit to the Fukuda mansion, but Masa agreed only on the condition that Sumiko be included in the invitation.

In honor of their noble visitor, the Fukudas arranged a garden party for at least a hundred guests. In the gathering of flamboyantly dressed people, Masa stood out like a dove trapped in a cage filled with garishly colored parrots.

She was unimpressed by the treasure-filled mansion, and even more so when she was escorted by her host and his wife onto a platform projected over a sizable lake. As Fukuda senior gestured proudly at the rustic bridges and miniature islands clad with dwarf trees, and the carp in the pond at her feet, Masa drew back, her nostrils pinched, her face expressionless as the surface of the water became as if a fierce squall had struck it, while the fish in the cruelly overcrowded pond came leaping, lashing the waters into a further foam as they struggled frantically, desperate to gobble up the tidbits thrown to them.

On the way back to the inn, Masa instructed her litter bearers to break the short journey and, although irritated, Kenichi accompanied her and Sumiko into the portals of a Buddhist temple. A broad and beautifully kept walk led up to the gates; inside the religious silence was broken only by the murmured intonations of saffron-robed priests.

Against his own inclinations, Kenichi was affected by the atmosphere, which was enhanced by the bittersweet perfume of incense and by the sonorous tolling of a temple bell. A young acolyte was striking the bell with a heavy, suspended log that sent out a mellow, soulful *don-don-don*. Kenichi stood by while Masa spent some time in meditation, obviously cleansing her spirit of the vulgarity she had been forced to endure.

That evening, instead of going out with his male friends, Kenichi remained at the inn with his wife and his sister, and listened as they recited poems from among the many they had committed to memory. He enjoyed the interlude of domesticity. As if for the first time, he was impressed with the flutelike beauty and the passion in his wife's voice as she recited:

"On the road to the Palace—
Palace basking in the sun—
Men walk in their crowds.
But the man for whom I long
Is one and one alone."

For a moment Kenichi wondered if in actual fact his wife knew
and yearned for the man in the poem? Of course, his habitual emotional laziness meant that he completely ignored the very real possibility of his wife's passion being directed at him. Instead, he decided
to lighten the atmosphere with a modern poem that was creating
amusement in the tea houses; in a jocular tone of voice, he recited:

"A horse farts:
Four or five suffer
On the ferryboat."

Masa drew back as though a mongrel dog were about to attack
her. Sumiko hastily smothered her amusement and gazed at him
disdainfully. Now, suddenly bored and out of his depth, Kenichi
left the women, changed his cotton kimono for a more stylish outfit,
and went into the city in search of Fukuda, whom he finally found
at a newly opened drinking house.

Obviously overjoyed to see him, Fukuda took Kenichi aside to
inform him that his parents were deeply impressed with Sumiko and
were more than eager to have her as a member of their family.

"I'm out of my mind with delight," Fukuda had enthused. "You
know how I have shied away from marrying. My parents have spent
a veritable fortune on marriage brokers, all out to find a bride pleasing to me. Now, out of the blue, so to speak, I am doubly pleased,
for Sumiko is not only pleasing to me but *your* sister to boot."

Negotiations began. Kenichi was well aware that Sumiko was but
a cog in the wheel of family duty, that the main attraction from the
Fukuda family's point of view was the prestige they would achieve
by an association with Lady Masa, daughter of a noble family close
to the mikado.

Now, two years later, negotiations were still under way; the Fukudas were even more eager but Sumiko was stubbornly refusing
to marry. Masa, without doubt, had too strong an influence over
his sister.

Nevertheless, she had been a true helpmeet where his Edo house was concerned. Taking complete control, she had called on an army of carpenters and craftsmen and created a masterpiece. In order to prevent noise filtering into the house from the busy street, she had ordered a high, thick stone wall to be erected flush against the front of the edifice.

With ruthless abandon she had redesigned the interior of the original shabby house and replaced cheap, worn-out ceilings with fine woods. She employed an artist to design murals for the sliding partitions separating the rooms. The *tatami* mattings were of the finest quality, and all objects in the house, even the most mundane, were unique.

The garden had a formal tea house. A small bamboo fence separated the middle section of the tea garden from the inner area. On the occasion of a tea ceremony, guests left the house by passing under a wisteria trellis, then crossed stepping-stones to the inner garden, pausing on their way to use water from a stone basin to cleanse their hands and rinse their mouths.

Honored guests entered through a *shōji* and ordinary guests through a small side entrance. After finishing a simple meal with thin tea, guests would leave the tea house and rest in the moss-covered waiting area until the tea master sounded the bronze gong. Then, using the water as before, they re-entered the tea house and resumed their seats to receive the ceremonial tea.

A small hole in a granite rock to the left of the larger entrance was marked "rubbish hole," not for the disposal of actual litter but for the symbolic cleansing of the heart's selfish desires.

A stone resembling a step, in the left corner beneath the eaves, served as a hanging place for guests' swords and for their umbrellas made from the skin of bamboo shoot.

A stone lantern of the Oribe style stood beside the washbasin and the long-handled dipper. Water flowed into the basin through a bamboo water pipe; its continual flow prevented the basin from becoming a possible breeding ground for bothersome mosquitoes. Gaudy flowers were avoided in the tea house area, for they would have overwhelmed the elegant simplicity within the tea house itself.

Obviously Masa had thought only of Kenichi's pleasure, for against her own aesthetic tastes she had employed another gardener, one famous for flamboyant, conversation-making gardens. He arranged rock sculptures of the twelve horary signs used in China to represent the years. Over the years Kenichi had collected various people's thoughts on the peculiar characteristics of each of those twelve animals, and indeed, the rocks themselves had taken on individual personalities, such as dauntlessness, decisiveness, and even slyness and bawdiness.

A few small trees had been planted around the specially selected rocks, and gravel was spread evenly about the area. The high fence serving as a background for the rock groupings was made of blocks finished off with a straight line of blue roof tiles, which gave the appearance of an ancient earthen wall.

Since that time, now two long years ago, neither Masa nor Sumiko had returned to Edo, and not once had they inquired about the house in Nihombashi which had become Kenichi's citadel and a rendezvous for his chosen friends.

Late in the day after his visit to Watanabe's brothel, Kenichi and his two friends called on Nakajima, the swordsmith, an exponent of the most highly esteemed craft in the land. The sword was a sacred weapon, the living soul of the samurai, a visible sign of the proud spirit within him. Every gentleman wore two swords, just as all his ancestors had done.

Those visits to the swordsmith were always tinged with embarrassment for Kenichi and Okura. Their family clans had long, honorable pasts, but not so the newly rich Fukuda, admired by his friends for his brash, amiable character but whose precociousness was detested by the haughty swordsmith.

For two years Fukuda had been awaiting the completion of the sword he had commissioned and Nakajima Sensei still muttered beneath his breath, "No, your sword is not yet completed." Then with a courteous smile he invited Okura and Kenichi to view a priceless sword which had recently been sent to him for restoration.

Fukuda, not in the slightest bit put out, followed them into the large workshop where several smiths, wearing black caps, were in the process of tempering blades. They lingered for a while listening to the swordsmith, as he declared, "The Japanese sword will not bend! It is made of hard steel combined with soft magnetic iron. The heating in my workshop is from charcoal furnaces and the forging of one honorable blade can take over a hundred days to complete."

Fukuda interjected slyly, "Seeing that *my* sword has been in your tender care for over *six hundred days*, I must be about to receive an exceptionally fine specimen?"

"Some men are filled with wild hopes," the sword maker murmured. "Come, follow me."

He led the three men into an apartment of forty mats. It was the most prestigious sword-club room in all of Edo. Kenichi had never before entered the holy of holies, but Okura had accompanied his father, the count, there on many occasions. Members of the club would bring their special treasures with them carefully wrapped in bags of yellow cloth. The owners would draw the weapons from their sheaths, eliciting words of admiration and much erudite discussion.

The apartment's polished shelves held many volumes, all to do with the history of the sword. On the racks was a collection of weapons so valuable that no one in the land could have purchased them from the old man. He removed a sword from one of the racks. As he tenderly drew the blade from the simple sheath of *hinoki* wood, he exclaimed, "Please note how the light plays along the tempered edge. Note the oval ring at the base of the handle to afford a perfect grip. See these exquisite carvings on the discs."

Nakajima continued until the three young men, sitting in conventional positions on the *tatami* floor-mats, were exhausted. They looked for the moment, when, without causing offense, they would be free to go on their way.

At last they made their escape and proceeded with all haste to a bathhouse. There they drank themselves into the right mood for the entertainment ahead of them that night. In Kenichi's case, a visit to his mistress, the courtesan Osen. The first visit since his return to Edo.

Fukuda was sitting on the edge of the huge steaming pool that was crowded with men calling pleasantries or insults to one another. He called out to Kenichi, who was already enjoying himself in the water.

"Kenichi, don't you know that Osen's mother started out as a drifter, wearing her kimono sashed at the front? She was a common streetwalker. Don't you know that?"

"I know. Nevertheless, she now runs a reputable house. . . ."

"Ho, ho-ha! Reputable? The old horror is a spider woman. You'll never extricate yourself from her clinging web."

"I don't sleep with *her*, the mother, you know."

"I do know that and I also know that her daughter, the voluptuous Osen, has been trained by her mother, who has so successfully

groomed well over two hundred prostitutes, all of them dredged up
from the lower depths and . . ."

"Ah, Fukuda San, do I detect a note of jealousy?"

"Jealousy? Ho, ho-ha! Not at all. My vulgar background gives
me special insights where people are concerned. I don't believe that
you realize what a bitch Osen is. I tell you, my friend, you'll never
get out of her clutches."

"When the time arrives and I wish to escape her again, will *you*
bring along your sword from Nakajima, protect me with it? That
is, if you ever receive it. The sword—I mean."

Kenichi was laughing, and he grabbed at Fukuda's dangling feet.
Fukuda toppled into the water and the two friends grappled and
wrestled to the accompaniment of catcalls and cheers from the audience of male bathers.

Kenichi was nonetheless affected by the opinions of his peers. He
knew that he was being gossiped about and that they thought of
him as a man influenced by women, incapable of holding time-
honored samurai codes. He valued his samurai reputation above all
things and was determined not to lose face. Before leaving the bathhouse he suggested that he, Fukuda, and Okura, together with a
covey of choice companions, should leave the capital immediately
and travel to a hot-spring resort to stay at a newly built house of
pleasure for a few weeks.

Before his departure to the countryside, he instructed his henchman Sudo to prepare the Nihombashi house for Osen's return.

F OR TEN DAYS KENICHI STIFLED his longings for Osen. He was
helped in this by the distraction of his easygoing companions as well
as the beauty of the resort. Apart from a few humble huts of the
peasant families, the house of pleasure was the only other building
in the vicinity. Fuji San, its summit covered with permanent snow,
loomed in the distance, majestic and awe-inspiring. At certain mag-
ical moments the mountain's reflection could be glimpsed in the
limpid waters of the lake that was set like a jewel in the rustic countryside.

He and his companions rose every morning at dawn to behold
the mountain, and recited in chorus, *"Ichi Fuji, ni taka, san nasubi—*
First Fuji. Second a falcon. Third an eggplant." Fuji was the most

beautiful natural feature in the world. The falcon symbolized straightforwardness, honesty, and clean living, as the bird never fed on carrion. The eggplant was always considered to be a good omen because of its amethyst coloring.

It was said that no man could do better than to dream of Fuji San, for it was considered to be an exceedingly good omen. Although Kenichi's dreams were filled with unpleasant themes, he was able to enjoy himself. For most of each day he stripped to a loincloth and bathed in the lake, surrounded by rustling bamboos and forest trees. He and his friends relaxed in the curative waters of the natural hot spring: They streamed with perspiration and then sat on foot-high mossy pads, discussing, arguing, agreeing to disagree on innumerable subjects.

If Kenichi became even slightly withdrawn, he was pounced upon, without mercy, "Ho there! You—Yamamoto! You'd best pack up, return to Edo."

"Yes, he should. He's fast fading away."

"No wonder! Just hear that bird calling—*Osen, Osen, Osen* . . ."

"Leave him in peace, Shiro," Fukuda had called. "Realize that our brother is suffering a temporary bout of sanity."

"Certainly. Correct you are, Fukuda, and it's our duty to protect him, to keep him under our care."

"Our definite duty," Fukuda had yelled. "For our friend knows, as we all know, that just one glimpse, one sniff of his Osen, and he would be totally disarmed."

Kenichi took the teasing in good spirit, but as the days went by, his longing for Osen increased. To keep that hunger at bay during sleepless nights, he would put all thoughts of the courtesan out of his mind, and concentrate instead on certain aspects of the complex world he had been raised in.

Giri—duty! That was his father's password. Shigeo Yamamoto was now an old man of seventy and for sixty of those years he had been dominated by patterns of thought and behavior impossible to erase. His sense of duty, honor, and obligation directed every step in his life.

It was his father's fate to have been caught in the net of ever-alert government officials on the lookout for the children who showed remarkable scholarly talents. He had been snatched from his home and enrolled at the School of Dutch Learning in Yokohama. Apart from many treks to the Central University in Edo, he had remained at the school, eventually to become its headmaster.

Kenichi was unable to recall even one moment of intimacy between his parents, and after the death of his mother the only reference the old scholar ever made to his departed wife concerned certain
trees she had planted and tended. He especially admired the tremendous persimmon tree when its branches hung heavy with jewellike
fruit. "This tree, she planted the year I had our house built," he
would announce every autumn. "Kenichi, she planted that other tree
the year you were born."

His mother, Kimiko, had been a strongly built woman. She was
the daughter of a *gōnō*—a rich farmer, and the arranged marriage had
brought into the Yamamoto family a large rice-growing estate situated in Uraga.

Kenichi remembered his mother with vague feelings of regret. She
had died on giving birth to Sumiko and by that time he had been
moved from her care to live under his father's supervision in the
schoolhouse.

How bewildered he had been, aged just ten, living in the stern
atmosphere of the school. Shortly after his arrival, his mind had
become hazy, quite often blanking out, and he had believed that he
was going insane. Then late one night, while he was still at his desk,
his head throbbing and his sight blurred, he had made a momentous
decision.

Coldly and clinically, for self-preservation, he had separated his
mind into three different compartments. One for the brain worker.
One for the observer, himself watching himself, forever on the alert
to outfox his father, tutors, and the senior scholars who were always
ready to fault him, not spitefully, but for his own edification.

In the third compartment dwelt the real boy—the real Kenichi,
full of ebullient egoism, quick-witted, out to charm, determined to
escape from the career mapped out for him when the right time
came.

He had once overheard the school's oldest tutor, Suzuki San say,
"The doctor's son, Kenichi, is not to be trusted. He has the trick of
laughing at one's weakest jokes."

Jokes? Had there been moments of lightness in that school? If so,
he could not remember them. Certainly, there had been times of
great argumentation between the brilliant scholars. And there had
been times of high drama, including a suicide to which he had been
a witness.

He would never forget the cold chills that had run through his body one hot summer afternoon when a brain-fagged young student had run amok, raging through the building brandishing a dirk as he screamed his threats to kill the school's master. He remembered how he had crouched down, his breath coming in gasps, as he witnessed the terrible scene. While he watched, his father, fearless and imperious, his voice filled with contempt, had approached the berserk youth, saying sneeringly, "*Kekkō desu*—enough! *Throw down that weapon!*"

The youth had reacted to the command by plunging the dirk deep into his own breast. It had been shocking to witness blood spurting out as he stood, statuelike, puzzled, staring about the crowded room which had become so silent. Then, making no sound, he had fallen to his knees in an attitude of apology and his life so ended. "He was a weak fellow," Suzuki San had muttered regretfully. "Just a weak fellow."

On one occasion, his father had intoned, "At times I have grave doubts about your character, your trustworthiness."

"Please accept my apologies, Father."

"Apologies? I am not prepared to accept bowls cracked then mended. Kenichi, I warn you yet again. Confide in *no man* about the clandestine studies carried out here in this school. Beware of yourself. Realize that even in our elite circle there are many counterfeit men—hawks disguised as doves. You must recognize your own faults. Know, understand yourself. Have the the mirror reflect you as one without shame."

Kenichi often neglected to kneel before the household shrine and gaze into the tiny mirror it held. Such mirrors, it was said, reflected eternal purity. It did not engender vanity. Many old scholars actually carried small mirrors tucked in their sleeves so that they could contemplate themselves and examine their souls.

Kenichi, however, was not so concerned about the virtue of his spirit. Mirror-gazing gave him the satisfaction of knowing that he was a truly handsome man. He believed that he had never been intentionally cruel to anyone. He felt that his self-restraint in many areas of life deserved a certificate of merit. He was especially proud of the way he repressed his resentment at having to hide much of his scholarly work from those carefree friends he caroused with in Edo.

Amongst the present population of Japan, numbering some thirty million citizens, he was one of the few, the very few, privy to events that had occurred in the world beyond their country over the past two hundred and fifty years.

Regretfully, he was unable to commune honestly, directly, even with those most intimate to him. He was familiar with events, inventions, and names unknown to his friends and to many millions of Japanese people.

It was hard to accept that men such as Okura and Fukuda had no knowledge of the mind-bending revolutions that had taken place and were continuing to take place in the outside world. And it was equally hard to accept that such men and women had never heard of George Washington, of the American War of Independence, or of names such as Louis XVI, Marie Antoinette, Robespierre, and Napoleon. They were not even aware of the French Revolution and the tremendous social upheavals it caused. Perhaps it was even more tragic that they had no knowledge of the Industrial Revolution that had taken place in England, and about the monumental changes it had brought about in the social structure by the amazing inventions of the seventeenth and the eighteenth centuries.

In the archives of that school in the fishing hamlet were drawings of machines capable of replacing human hands, machines to improve the working and the living conditions of men, women, and children.

So much hard-kept knowledge was a heavy burden for Kenichi. He was only too aware that he was thought to be overly arrogant at times. He was. But how else could it be when his friends spoke of the new light and comfortable litters which were all the rage, and he knew so much more: that almost a hundred years earlier, steam power had been discovered and that in many lands powerful locomotives were traveling smoothly along rails, carrying passengers and goods from one location to another.

In the school's archives, translated from their original languages into Dutch, and from the Dutch into the Japanese language, were the works of Voltaire, Victor Hugo, Walter Scott, Edgar Allan Poe, and many other highly esteemed Western writers. How cruel it was that officialdom had cut the Japanese intelligentsia off from the world's rich cultures, intentionally crippling the entire nation, setting clan against clan, encouraging men to spy on and to denounce the actions of fellow citizens in a regime of secret policing of the entire population. Gradually Japan had been isolated from the rest of the world. An era of terrifying officialdom had ensued.

In many ways, even in the present time, that regime still held sway under the shogun; with the Buddhist priests holding firm in their power, and with the increasing popularity within the samurai class of Confucianism, which encouraged *bushidō*—the way of the warrior.

Kenichi, unaggressive, and loathing even the very thought of violence, had no liking for priestly men or for any religion. But, amongst countless other historical atrocities, he had been required to read accounts of those fearsome battles and dreadful bloodbaths that had taken place between Buddhists and the Christians who had at first been welcomed into the country more than two centuries before.

They, those Christians, hadn't lasted for long and as far he knew, their only legacy was the Island of Dejima. That macabre place was peopled by Protestant Dutch merchants and scholars who provided a kind of spy-hole through which the events of the world were seen, noted and utilized by the shogunate.

A—spy-hole? Kenichi was struck by a most unpleasant thought. Could it be that he himself belonged to a class of spies? Spy or no spy, how fortunate it was that he, Kenichi, was able to face the world with his compartmental detachments. For himself, he wanted no more than Edo society had to offer. He delighted in the literature of Japan written centuries ago—those diaries and poems, written mostly by women in court circles, describing their luxurious ways of life, their affairs of the heart, the light flirtations and court intrigues. He was a man who had no desire for complex matters. They had been thrust upon him. Aahh, all he wanted, all he needed was to be with that girl—Osen. . . .

On the final morning of his stay in the lakeside resort, Kenichi joined his friends as they chorused out the dawn ode to Fuji San. He was satisfied that he would be returning to Edo, confident that he had not lost face, and determined to do all in his power not merely to sleep with Osen frequently but to become her one, her only patron.

He was certain that his henchman, Sudo, would have obeyed his every instruction and that the house in Nihombashi would be in perfect order.

From EARLY CHILDHOOD, SUDO'S LIFE had been filled with anxieties
and fears, for his parents practiced a religion banned throughout the
land. Discovery would have led to imprisonment and, in all probability, to death.

So zealous were they that they would have faced death gladly
rather than deny their faith. Sudo, a frail, sweet-natured boy, had
walked on a razor's edge, making no friends at school, suffering
without complaint, and aware that he was considered to be a half-
wit by his peers because of his withdrawn, gentle manner.

He had revered and admired his parents, obeying their every wish.
Like them, he had yearned to gain further knowledge of the Christian religion they practiced so secretly, relying only on certain instructions handed down to them from their ancestors. They knew
of no other Christians in the community, they knew of no Christian
priests, and the Holy Scroll they treasured and kept hidden was
yellowed with age, and whenever they pored over it they were apt
to become puzzled by some of its contents.

When the family trio gathered together in a closely shuttered room
to partake, as best they knew how, of the Blessed Sacraments, they
whispered the holy rituals and felt deep guilt and sorrow because
they were not free to bear witness to their faith proudly and in the
open.

They knew that a Jesuit missionary, a Francis Xavier, had come to
their country way back in 1549, accompanied by his first Japanese
convert, Anjiro, whom he had met in a land called India, and they
knew that by the end of some thirty years the missionaries who
followed him had spread their religion to many of Japan's citizens.

They knew that the prime minister who had ruled until 1598 had
become suspicious of the situation and that a few years after that
time twenty-six Roman Catholic Christians, including six Francis-
can fathers, were crucified at Nagasaki and that trading by foreigners had also been restricted.

The aged family documents handed down into their care told how
matters had settled down for some time, but that when other foreigners from lands called Holland, Portugal, and England arrived in
Japan, they quarreled among themselves about trade and about re-

ligion. In the year 1614 an edict was issued for the complete aboli-
tion of the Roman Catholic religion in Japan.

Sudo's parents possessed written records of the persecutions that
followed. In the city of Shimabara alone, thirty thousand Japanese
Christians had chosen death by burning alive rather than deny their
faith.

The Sudo family had a blurred and highly romanticized idea about
Christian history since that holocaust several hundred years ago.
They practiced their secret faith alone and lived in a thatched-roof
house on the outskirts of Uraga, a coastal town some miles from
Yokohama, where they farmed rice fields that belonged to their
landlord, Dr. Yamamoto.

At the age of fourteen Sudo was accepted into Dr. Yamamoto's
school as a humble scribe. He and his parents were certain that the
Christian God they worshiped had answered their prayers by allowing him to earn his livelihood unnoticed and out of the mainstream
of life.

Sudo would never forget the autumn evening when he had returned to Uraga to visit his parents after several stimulating and
exhausting years at the seignorial school. How warmly his parents
received him. How stunned they were by the extraordinary information he relayed to them.

They sat close together, murmuring their words even though they
had no servant and their house was isolated by the surrounding rice
fields.

"Dear son," his mother whispered, "is all that you tell us really
true?"

"True. Every word I speak is true!"

"Then . . . we are not alone?"

"Not alone! Out there in the world beyond our land are many
millions of Christians."

"Millions . . . ?" she had interjected. "*Millions* of Christians? Free
to congregate openly in shrines? Free to worship our Savior?"

"Yes."

"Praise to His Holy Name! Tell us again about the great shrine
where the Christ's representative on earth dwells."

"It is in a land called Italia."

"Would that be close by to Jerusalem?" his father asked anxiously.

"Not close. Quite some distance away, Father."

"But surely it should be in the Holy Land?"

"Maybe so, Father, but it is not."

"No? Ah, well, so be it! Wife, my heart is filled to overflowing. I expected our son's first visit to be like a shower of spring rain. Now we are caught by pouring skies, by lightning flashes and thunders. So much, such startling information is muddling our minds. Prepare a feast, for is it not fitting that we celebrate?"

Before partaking of their simple meal he and his parents had bathed to purify their bodies, then, dressed in their finest garments to honor the occasion, they had knelt before the household Shinto shrine to pay honor to their ancestors, those martyrs who had walked among the thirty thousand Christians at Shimabara. Sons carrying their old parents pick-a-back and women with infants in their arms had cried out to each other, *"Don't look at the flames. Look upward to Jesus."*

His mother, unaccustomed to drinking wine, had become quite tipsy that evening of his homecoming. He and his father had undressed her and tucked her into her *futon*. But his father, a hardened drinker, had become brighter of mind and more curious. He shot questions at his son and listened intently to his replies, often raising his eyebrows and scratching at his bald pate as he expressed his amazement at Sudo's revelations.

His father knew that for some several hundred years it had been decreed that no large oceangoing vessel should ever again be constructed in Japan, and he knew of many tragic tales of sailors who, frustrated by the edict and anxious to escape such tyranny, had been foolhardy enough to sail away in frail fishing craft, never to be seen or heard of again.

Apart from the ban on practicing his inherited Christian religion proudly and in the open, the old man had no argument with the manner by which the powerful Tokugawa shogunate ruled the land.

Nippon, he had firmly believed, was sufficient unto itself; there was no need to be disturbed by rapacious foreign merchants or by knowledge or goods from the lands those foreigners came from.

"But now, here, tonight, in my home . . ." his father had exclaimed, striking both fists against his breast. "You, my son, arrive like a typhoon, telling me that throughout all these years—more than two centuries—the shogun have been conducting a steady, lucrative exchange of trade and information with the Dutch?"

"Yes," he had replied.

"*Yes* you say! What a *pitiable* reply!"

"Father," he had pleaded. "Excuse me, but I am exhausted. Soon it will be daylight and . . ."

"Never mind. Never mind, drink up. Take some refreshment. My thoughts are erupting as a volcano erupts. Tell me, is this school you work in a secret, illegal school?"

"No. Well, not exactly."

"Not exactly? *How* not exactly?"

"Well, the school, and it is one of many such schools . . ."

"Many? Surely not *many*? That, I cannot believe. How many?"

"I'm not certain, but at least fifty such establishments are scattered about the land, and certainly they must be legal because all the work done, all the translations into our language of the foreign books dealing with the sciences, medicine, mathematics, astronomy, and whatever, are sent to government officials in Edo for their perusal and used to benefit our country. Father, in reply to your question about secrecy, certainly the seignorial schools are known of in elite circles, and . . ."

"Of course, of course! Excuse my muddled mind. Gradually my clouded mind is clearing! Certain rumors, certain scraps of information which must have filtered into my head over the years, are all at once exploding into my intelligence, loud and clear. Heat more *sake* and . . ."

"Father, we *must* rest."

"Yes. Yes, but first bear with me. Compared to you with your fund of knowledge gained at the school, I see myself as a sparrow teetering on a bamboo twig, and as a sparrow, I speak to you, a young eagle. Let me tell you though, that somewhere in the back of my mind, I have known about those Dutch prisoners on Dejima Island."

"All these years you have *known of them*?"

"Yes, and also I have heard—where, when, and from whom I do not know—that strongly guarded processions at times travel the long road from Nagasaki to Edo."

"Father, it is *I* who told you of them this very night."

"Is that so? No matter! Tell me once more."

"Once more?"

"Yes, once more."

"Just once more, then! For over two centuries Dutch traders and scholars have lived on Dejima. Dutch ships arrive there bringing goods and valuable information from many lands in the outside world.

"Every four years, scholars from the seignorial school in Naga-saki, accompanied by the Dutch ship captains and certain of the Dutchmen from Dejima, and with fifty or more heavily armed guards—politely called escorts—form into a procession and make the long, tortuous journey to the shogunate in Edo. Once there, the Dutch are established in an inn at Nihombashi, where our doctors of learning are allowed to call, always in a group, to pose questions to the travelers."

"Remarkable, remarkable," his father had cried out. "Please continue . . ."

"To continue, yes, to continue, Father, I have been told by Su-zuki, one of the elderly tutors at the school, that the Japanese doctors find it an agonizingly slow and imperfect form of communication. Nevertheless, it is said that the system, alive and thriving, does, and always shall, keep our intellectuals up-to-date with what takes place in the outside world. Also, as Kenichi Yamamoto tells me, we are also greatly assisted by imported goods brought in by Dutch vessels belonging to the Dutch East India Trading . . ."

"Such as? Such as . . . ?"

"Such as telescopes, sextants, maps of the world, wondrous new inventions and, of course, most important, books. Textbooks, literature, and . . ."

"Wondrous and wonderful and so, so clever! Ah, how privileged I am to be hearing all this. Son, don't doze off! I dislike being like a dog barking at nothing. Tell me about him, the doctor's son?"

"Kenichi."

"Thank you. Kenichi. Is he also a great scholar?"

"A learned man but not as dedicated as his father. That dour old man nevertheless recently praised his son for the work he carries out when dealing and speaking with the Dutch."

"What? The young man understands and *speaks* the Dutch language?"

"He does, as do all at the school." He never failed to smile when he recalled his father's reaction as he murmured modestly, "Father, I also speak a little Dutch."

"You—you do? *You* speak another language?"

"A little. Yes."

"Speak some to me. Now, at once!"

His skill delighted and amused his father, sending him into a paroxysm of laughter so loud that his mother awakened. Leaping up from her *futon*, she called fearfully, "What . . . ? What? *Jishin*—earthquake?"

"No, no," his father had wheezed. "Come listen to our son."

His last memory of that evening was the sound of his parents laughing as he had never heard them laugh before.

Now, seven years later, as he went about directing the preparations in the Nihombashi house in readiness for Kenichi's overnight guest, Osen, Sudo was glad that he had always resisted the temptation to inform his parents of certain facts he learned during the intervening years.

Why bruise their innocence? Why tell them of the bloodshed, the burning of the Buddhist temples by those early Jesuit priests as they had gone about converting men and women to the Christian faith?

How pained his parents would be if they became aware that their ancestors had bequeathed them not just a religion of love and hope but one which also gloried in political power, in war and in bloodshed. He was glad that he had never told the old couple that in Japan other Christians such as they were living in small conclaves, also practicing their faith in secret. They would have sought their brethren out and in all probability have been put to death.

Two years had now gone by since Sudo's last visit to Uraga, and he yearned to see his parents again. He no longer had a faith of any kind and was convinced that a man's life was but a fragile, ephemeral affair. Nowadays when he clapped his hands before Shinto shrines, he did not believe that ancestral spirits hovered around him. He thought of himself as a man whose house had burned to the ground, leaving only ashes.

Sudo was no longer employed as a scribe in the Yokohama school, and for the past three years he had worked as a confidential secretary-henchman in the services of Kenichi Yamamoto, whom he accompanied on journeys and whose every order he obeyed. While staying in the house in Edo he had a room in which he could scarcely find space for his *futon* amid all the books, documents, and other important paraphernalia in his charge.

He always avoided catching a glimpse of his reflection in mirrors, ashamed of the insignificant man reflected back to him. He sometimes thought of himself as a heavily laden peddler going through life panting and sweating beneath the heavy loads he carried in his heart. At other times he thought of himself as a snail attempting to crawl to the peak of a high, snow-covered mountain and not leaving even the faintest trail to prove that he had once existed.

The heaviest burden, the most agonizing load he bore, was his passion for the courtesan Osen. That unrequited passion, he knew, must always remain mute, like a flute never to be taken up and played.

Whenever he so much as sighted Osen or heard her voice, he felt as weak as a newborn foal.

Some months ago she had come back into Kenichi's life. Sudo had been busy in the main room of the Nihombashi house when Osen, her long crimson sash trailing as she crossed the floor, glanced in his direction casually, as one would glance at a housefly.

Early one morning he had glimpsed her, her sleep-gown stripped to her waist, standing upright beneath the gauzy net that canopied the love-bed she shared with her chosen man, Kenichi. Lazily, seductively, she raised her arms, stretching them wide, yawning with sensual satisfaction. Her lover reached out and drew her down into his embrace.

That night, while working in his small room, he had heard her voice coming from the garden. "Kenichi, behold the moon!" she cried. There had been no moon, and he had crept from his room to see her standing in the dark garden holding aloft a huge round white paper lantern lit from within. "Full moon tonight," she had exclaimed, laughing. "Compose a poem for me, Kenichi."

Those stolen glimpses were Sudo's most treasured possessions. He relived and agonized over them again and again. They were dearer to him than his life's blood.

Sudo's thoughts were brought back to the present when he caught sight of the white-spotted kitten dozing in a patch of sunlight on the pale gold of the *tatami* floor. The kitten was a pet, a surprise gift for Osen from Kenichi. Kneeling, he took the creature tenderly into his arms, knowing that Osen would soon be holding it against her warm body. The annoyed kitten clawed at his face, and to his shame tears welled in his eyes. Placing the creature on the floor, he crept from the room.

To calm his ragged nerves he drank a bowl of thin tea, then went to Kenichi's bedroom to prepare the clothing his master would wear in the city later that evening when he escorted Osen to his home.

With great care he removed garments from their black-lacquered chests and arranged them on the polished wood clotheshorse.

Kenichi had chosen to wear an acid-yellow gown together with a dark blue short-coat banded in gold brocade. Sudo grimaced wryly, imagining what the elegant Lady Masa would think about such a flamboyant outfit. He was sure that one of her all-seeing, silent glances would express the thought: "Fitting raiment indeed for my husband to wear on this outrageously vulgar occasion."

Lady Masa had always been extremely kind. She never failed to inquire about his parents' health and she made sure that he was given seasonal gifts to take to them when he traveled to Uraga. How peaceful, how lovely that house on the hill in the fishing hamlet was! How gracious the ladies who dwelt there. How strange that Kenichi Yamamoto escaped from Yokohama at the slightest excuse, seldom, as far as Sudo knew, giving it a thought, and seldom mentioning Renzō, the bright-minded, handsome son he had fathered.

His meditations ended as a bustle of noise and movement told him that the master had arrived at the gate of the Nihombashi house. Sudo hurried to the entrance and went down on his knees to welcome Kenichi.

K ENICHI SHOULDERED HIS WAY THROUGH the lanterned streets of Edo. Man-borne litters, palanquins, and pedestrians crowded his way but didn't prevent him from noticing the many low-caste harlots plying their trade from the doors of certain ramshackle houses. Although filled with distaste, Kenichi was forced to grin slightly, for he himself was about to visit a brothel. As he continued on his way, he ruminated on the subject of prostitution, that thriving business conceived in ancient days, in noble and aristocratic circles when there had been no ceremony of marriage in the land.

Those now-far-distant emperors had great numbers of discarded women who were difficult to maintain in the courts. Therefore, from a practical point of view, and wisely, the women had been placed in a certain quarter in Kyoto and ordered to make their living by selling their favors to the many nobles in the city. Thus, the first licensed quarter of prostitution had been instituted in the land.

Kenichi felt that he had been born in the wrong century, for he would have reveled in living in the distant past when a samurai could sleep when so inclined, wake up at any time, either night or day, to read, compose poems, make music, make love.

In those days, emperors had been sheltered from all cares of state.

The *daimyō*, those skilled politicians, had fostered the arrangement, for it gave them freedom to go their despotic ways as they would, unchecked and all-powerful. If an emperor was foolish enough to desire more than being just a cloud-shrouded divinity, he was hastily removed and one of his sons made emperor in his place. Even these days, Kenichi pondered, the present emperor was kept in complete ignorance of affairs in his country, and naturally nothing would ever change.

He was pleased with his appearance. He was wearing two swords and was conscious of admiring glances sent his way as humble citizens stepped aside for him.

He wondered how Osen would receive him. A rumor had reached him that she knew of his deception. What valid reason could he give for not having informed her of his return to Edo? More important, he would need to placate Shiga, Osen's mother. Smart as he was, he knew that he could never outthink that woman. He could not endure the thought of a life spent without Osen. Away from her he resented, even disliked her, but no other woman had ever attracted him so much, held such sway over him. *Shikata ga nai*—There was no way out for him!

Why did life contain so many beautiful flowers with hidden thorns? He needed time in which to come up with an indisputable reason to placate Shiga, for in order to keep Osen, he must, perforce, agree to her mother's demands and keep in her good graces. Fukuda had been correct in calling her a spider woman.

O SEN'S MOTHER, SHIGA, HAD DESCENDED from a special class of harlots. Her great-grandmother had been an actress of some repute, playing male roles in the all-female Kabuki theater of those early days.

"Well," Shiga often explained to her three daughters in bitter tones, "the males took over—ousted all the females. It's ill to be born a woman. It's a man's world. From that time on all women have been banned from the stage in our country. What else was there for those actresses to do but sell their bodies?"

"Tell us again about your great-grandmother, Mumma," her daughters always chimed. "Tell us again."

"Certainly, it's a story worthy of retelling. She dressed as a male and plied her trade among Buddhist priests. That masquerade pleased them, for they preferred not to be seen associating with women. *Her* daughter followed in those footsteps, *my* mother also, but I . . . ?"

"We don't want a lecture, Mumma. We *know* about you."

"You certainly do, and now no more gossip and laziness. Agreed?"

"*Hai*—yes! Yes, as you wish, Mumma. . . ."

Over the past five years, Shiga had gained a fine reputation in the Kanda district. Businessmen of a certain class regarded her with some admiration, seeing her as a logical, sharp businesswoman, one of many who had suddenly surfaced in Edo's modern-day society.

Not only did she drag herself up from the lower depths, take herself off the streets, and open a brothel, she started a school in which she groomed young girls in the arts of prostitution. For her tuition she took a percentage of the girls' earnings when they commenced working. As her fame spread, poverty-stricken farmers registered their daughters in the school for a stated number of years. In such cases the girls were kept clothed and fed by Shiga, who treated them kindly, even generously.

She had borne three children, each one the result of a hasty few minutes spent with strange men whose names she did not know and whose faces she had not cared to glance at. During each pregnancy she had hoped for a son, but as the years went by she rejoiced that she had produced three females.

The two elder girls, Kiku and Ume, were now skilled prostitutes, but she treasured Osen, the most beautiful and tempestuous daughter; she pampered her with but one thought in mind: to find her a wealthy and preferably an aristocratic patron. Marriage was not a possibility for Osen in Shiga's mind. No family of any distinction, or even the most humble peasant family, would accept the daughter of a prostitute into their family, and Osen was not suited to live as the wife of a common laboring man. She was made for luxury, for riches, and Shiga was determined that she should get her due.

"Osen, my daughter, is second to none," she never tired of saying, and Osen's sisters agreed wholeheartedly with their mother. Osen agreed even more firmly, for she had been raised to know and to appreciate her worth.

The three girls attended their mother's lectures in the unique school and could repeat by heart the edicts laid out for the students' welfare.

Shiga's lectures to her class were clear and concise:

"The path we tread is steep and filled with hazards. Beware of your facial expressions. Never look as though a fox has entered into you.

"Always show a timorous reluctance. Males like that. They are the cocks.

"Never show fear or jealousy. Men have enough of that from their wives.

"Never distort your face by weeping. It makes for ugliness. Tears can be of value but just a few. Men like that.

"Be playful and sweetly teasing with old men. Generally speaking, they need flattery to bring them on. There are many tricks up our sleeves to please old, and, at times, uneasy young clients.

"Let every client believe that you are doing what *he* wants but do as *you* well know what to do.

"Let the client believe that he is in charge, always the cock of the roost.

"Courtesans and prostitutes gain victory when thrown to the matting, as opposed to the victory of the professional wrestler. . . ."

Her instructions concerning the techniques her girls were to employ when at work were so succinct that they claimed: "Mumma San, we often feel that you are present when we are doing our jobs!"

If a contracted girl became pregnant, she was aborted. If the contracted girls expressed desires to bear and keep their infants, they were instantly dismissed. No lies, no cheating, no outbreaks of physical brawling among the girls were allowed on the premises, and no rough, bad behavior in public either. Apart from those sternly stated laws, Shiga's girls had a relatively easy life.

Shiga was preparing for Kenichi's arrival and her mind was buzzing with plans. On his first visit to her house some two years ago, she had been interested in him and had at once set about making inquiries into his social status, his family's economic situation, and his personal character. Finally, well satisfied, she was certain that Yamamoto was the man she had been so assiduously searching for.

She had personally orchestrated Kenichi's first glimpse of Osen. His reaction had been quite startling; however, he had been made to wait and suffer until he had reached a state of desperation so intense that he was about to withdraw from the situation. At that moment, Shiga presented Osen in all her glowing perfection to him. Osen, to her mother's annoyance, had entered into the relationship much too enthusiastically, insisting that she had fallen in love with

Kenichi and that she would manage her own affairs where he was concerned. Her unprofessional behavior endangered Shiga's plans, for the girl's possessiveness and her frantic jealousies concerning Kenichi's personal and private life soon drove him away.

For several months Osen mooned about, losing weight and losing her glow. Shiga, at her wit's end, arranged to meet with the young actor, Usami, a thorough cheapskate who only too willingly accepted the monetary bribe offered in return for ending his association with Kenichi. "In any case," he laughed, "Kenichi never so much as plucked even one branch from my flowering tree."

Relieved to know that fact—for Shiga had a loathing of men who indulged in leading a bisexual life—she had spoken sternly to her daughter, and a few months ago, Kenichi had once again visited the brothel. Osen, realizing that her mother knew best, promised to play the game under her supervision. But once again the girl had been unable to subdue her turbulent emotions, and her possessiveness was evidently giving her lover second thoughts, for it had come to Shiga's knowledge that he had returned from the bosom of his family some weeks earlier.

The situation appeared to be one of disaster, but early this very morning a spindly man, Sudo by name, had arrived to announce that his master, Kenichi Yamamoto, would be calling at the Shiga establishment at ten o'clock in the evening.

Now, alone in her office, she once more went over her plans, determined not to allow the expected caller to escape from her net again. She knew that his character was flawed by certain weak spots. He was conceited; to have one's way with him it was necessary to give him only praise and adulation. She knew he would be expecting an outburst of jealousy from Osen and a threat from her mother, stating that he was not the only fish in the sea circling around the girl whom he was treating so casually.

Well, she mused, the haughty samurai was in for a shock. Her intentions were to put him completely at his ease, to confide in him and humbly ask for advice on several matters which "only a man of feeling and intelligence might graciously agree to unravel for a lone woman in desperate need of assistance."

Number one priority was her need for a more respectable dwelling. He, no fool, would realize that she was running a successful business and that no risk would be taken if she were to be given financial assistance.

Number two priority was more touchy but nevertheless not impossible to achieve. With heartfelt humility she would lay her situation before him, explaining that her daughters were alone in the world and with no male to protect and care for their welfare after their mother's demise. Could he, she would humbly plead, advise her on the delicate matter of taking a *yōshi*—an adopted son, into her pathetic little family of females? To have an adopted son, a male in the family, would be more precious to her than riches and wealth.

"My daughter Osen," she would murmur with her eyes cast down modestly, "has little or no expectations of ever becoming a wife. Such is her fate. Excuse me for mentioning this, but my daughter is at present grieving deeply, to the point of taking her own life, I fear. She has begged me to inform you now that she is unable to endure your coldness and begs to be excused from the assignation you have arranged at your home tonight."

Yamamoto was already entering her establishment, thirty minutes earlier than he had been expected. Plucking at her *obi*-sash, she noticed that her hands were shaking. Osen sat waiting in the adjoining room, arrayed more finely than ever before and listening for her signal that things had gone well. With the knowledge that her situation was about to improve, Shiga calmed her nerves. She was confident that the besotted man walking shoeless along the corridor to her shabby office would be hoodwinked by her sweet talk, and that he would not refuse to meet either of her requests. "Ah," she thought, bowing low as he stood before her. "What fools men are! How easily passion bemuses their acumen. . . ."

T WO MONTHS HAD GONE BY since the duel of wits between the elderly ex-harlot and Kenichi Yamamoto. Both had been firmly convinced of their positions, each one had achieved their own desires and had congratulated themselves happily and smugly.

Shiga's premises were now in Akasaka and her business was thriving. Her house had many small rooms, a large main salon, and a small garden on the edge of a silk-washing canal.

In order to finance those new premises, Kenichi had sold a Yamamoto property, one which he considered useless. It was a great expanse of marshy ground on the outskirts of Yokohama. He had been told that the purchaser was one of the recent class of merchants who dealt in the newfangled paper-credit system that businessmen and bankers had recently introduced into economic dealings. To his amazement, he had discovered after the deal had gone through that the purchaser was Fukuda's father, and he had remembered with amusement the story of Fukuda's old grandfather and the paper carp. He wondered if his friend's father also resorted to taking the advice of a soothsayer.

Osen was now his own woman. As her patron, he kept her where she belonged, in her own compartment, separated like a bird in his father's aviary. He had her safe in the domain of his pleasure and he had his family and his career in the domain of his major obligations. He asked nothing more of life.

He was proud of Osen's voluptuous beauty, and pleased at the way in which she conducted herself now, without tantrums or jealousies about his wife and his male friendships. His passion for her had in no way abated. She quite often spent short periods of time living with him, leaving only when her presence would have created a scandalous situation.

To his gratification, his friend Okura had intimated that his mother, the countess, and his young wife, had expressed a desire to visit his home and partake of a tea ceremony in his garden house. He had fully expected that Osen would show some sign of bitterness at being banished, but she had smiled understandingly and returned to her mother's new residence.

Truthfully, he had been glad of the respite, for although he needed the courtesan in his life, her lengthy stays under his roof became more than a little irksome. He was set in his bachelor habits and ultimately resented the presence of any woman, even Osen, as an imposition on his freedom. He would, however, always recall their reunion in the Nihombashi house. Osen was her most seductive and he spent an enthralling night, a highlight in his floating world of pleasure and sensual gratification.

Only one unpleasant event had arisen. Sudo was seized by a severe attack of illness. The doctor who was called in to attend him said that the patient was suffering an attack of nervous dysentery.

Osen, all sympathy, had knelt by the dilapidated *futon* where Sudo lay in a stupor, discussing whether acupuncture or moxa-treatment would be best for the suffering man.

Even to this day Sudo had not fully recovered his vitality. Although he carried out his duties, he appeared to be fading away. The situation was becoming serious, for without his henchman's assistance, life would present many problems for Kenichi. As he thought the matter over, he realized that he could make arrangements which would not merely benefit Sudo but also himself. He would give the man time off to visit his old parents in Uraga. That would cheer him up and improve his health, for there was no medicine better than a change of scenery. On the return journey to Edo, Sudo could then attend to affairs at the Yokohama school and also look into the matter of finding a boy suitable to be adopted by the Shiga woman.

He had already mentioned the matter to Sudo, who told of a fisherman in the hamlet who was in the last stages of that dread disease, tuberculosis. With eleven children, seven of them male, the man was scarcely in a position to quibble about any monetary proposition put before him.

And what of his own son? He had received a communication from his father, brushed by Sumiko's stylish hand, informing him that Renzō had been removed from Masa's care and was living and studying in the adjoining schoolhouse. That had been his fate as a child, and he did not envy the little boy.

Thinking of his son brought Masa to his mind, and he recalled how Countess Okura had been disappointed when she had come to the tea ceremony to find that Lady Masa had returned to Yokohama several years back.

The countess's daughter-in-law, Okura's wife, had reminded him of Masa. She also had come from a noble family close to the court in Kyoto and still followed the fashion of the married court ladies— her teeth blackened, her eyebrows shaved off.

Gazing at the young woman, he had been amazed and amused at himself, for he suddenly realized that Masa no longer followed that old-style custom. Try as he had, he had been unable to recall when his wife had made the change in her appearance. Was it before or after Renzō's birth? Was it just last year? It was not important, but it was strange to realize that he had not been aware of Masa's changed appearance. And he would never know if she had made the changes in order to appear more attractive to him, or simply in accordance with the changing times. . . .

Several weeks after the Okura ladies' visit to his home, he was invited to the home of the illustrious count. Fukuda, in his inimitable way, joshed him, saying, "So, you are taking a giant stride upward in the social world, eh! Leaping the rungs of the ladder with the agility of your sister's little monkey! Yes?"

"If you say so!" he replied. "How do you know about the invitation?"

"How? Let me just say, lives there a one who never intentionally eavesdrops? Of course *I'm* not included in the invitation. Does my hurt show? I hope not. I like to believe that I hide my misfortunes from my, may I say—my peers?"

Then, changing his mood, Fukuda mentioned that his parents were becoming impatient about the slow negotiations for his marriage to Sumiko. Kenichi once again lied, saying that his sister was greatly complimented and that very shortly a contract would be entered into.

Kenichi was determined to go ahead with the arrangements. His ears were close to the ground in economic circles and he was well aware that although the aristocracy were clinging tenaciously to the concept of their inherited, powerful positions in society, their days of glory were coming to an end. It was the monied families who would be the future aristocrats in Japan. His first visit to the Okura home had only strengthened his opinion.

He arrived at the Okura residence at the appointed hour, midafternoon, dressed in an elegantly understated manner but feeling that had Masa been with him, he would have felt more at ease. He would have preferred to present himself as a conservative samurai gentleman, complete with wife.

The litter bearers went their way, leaving him standing before a heavy postern gate set into a massive wall of dark gray stone. Through the gate and inside a small courtyard he beheld the house which stood two stories high, square, and built of time-weathered wood.

The entrance door was immediately opened and Kenichi was ushered through dim corridors into the main chamber. He was ceremoniously greeted by his host, hostess, and Okura's grandmother, who was dressed in the raiments of a Buddhist nun. Her long thin face had the appearance of one already in the spirit world.

The visit had been exhausting. The conversation was stilted, the main topic being the peculiarities of various trees and flowers.

When, after a seemingly interminable time, Count Okura suggested that everyone should adjourn to the garden and view the sunlight playing upon the moss, the idea of such a venture became as exciting as a trip to a distant star.

A flight of worn stone steps all spotted with lichens led down into a sunken area where just one tree stood, a truly patriarchal pine tree whose twisted branches spread so far from the massive trunk that the late afternoon sunlight filtering through the branches overhead dispelled any feeling of gloom in the flowerless, moss-covered ground.

Once again time seemed to come to a halt as the little group stood murmuring occasional comments concerning the distinguished tree and the aesthetic values of moss.

Kenichi always enjoyed times of social interplay, but the Okuras and their guests were not ones to indulge in clever quips. He found it difficult to recognize his friend as the sharp-tongued, licentious man-about-town. In this company, Okura moved with infinite patience, tenderly assisting his fragile, black-robed grandmother, and replying politely to any comments, *"Naru hodo! Naru hodo*—you don't say . . . Well, I never . . . Who would have thought it . . ."

He had felt more exhausted after that visit than he would have felt after several hours of judo practice, nevertheless he was confident, knowing that he had made a good impression, although he intended to give an entirely different version of the event to Fukuda.

He much preferred the atmosphere in the Fukuda household. They kept open house and gave lavish banquets and marathon poetry or play readings. Quite childishly proud of their wealth, they delighted in becoming patrons to struggling artists; and shyly shrugged away any compliments given regarding their generosity.

Although deep in his heart Kenichi despised the lowly background of the Fukuda clan, he felt that he understood Sumiko's character well enough to know that not only would she fit easily in the family circle but that she would also enjoy the new social freedoms that abounded in Edo. He decided that he would not actually handcuff his sister, but that as her brother, responsible for her welfare, he would demand that she prepare herself to be escorted to the capital by Sudo.

WHEN SUDO ARRIVED AT THE house on the hill, he brought with him Kenichi's letter, informing Sumiko, in no uncertain terms, that her marriage into the Fukuda family was a foregone conclusion. ". . . I fear too that an unhealthy attachment exists between you and my wife. Masa is the culprit. . . ."

Several nights before Sumiko's departure for Edo, the sisters-in-law spent many hours conversing intimately. Masa talked with honesty about Sumiko's future, saying, "I once felt as you are feeling. Our circumstances are strangely similar. I brought prestige into your family. You will take prestige into the Fukuda family. . . ."

"Are you defending the wisdom of my brother's choice?"

"Not defending. Accepting."

"I must accept? No. I shall not. . . ."

"Tenaciousness can be a virtue. It can also be a blemish. . . ."

"Why does our lot as women seem so unfair? Must it always be so?"

"Always? Let us not assume that time won't bring changes in social attitudes. Yes, even where women are concerned." Masa gestured that Sumiko lift up her wine cup to be refilled.

They sat facing each other, their floor-cushions drawn close to the *hibachi* as the charcoal's frail warmth competed with the chill of the autumn night. The room was lit only by a milky-white glow from the full moon shining through the paper *shōji* and, as was their habit, they smoked long-stemmed miniature pipes and ceremoniously refilled each other's thimble-size wine cups. They were experienced drinkers and *sake* affected them no more than water from a spring, merely lifting their spirits slightly and promoting good feelings and conversation.

Sumiko's brow furrowed as she sipped delicately at the hot wine. Shrugging exasperatedly, she exclaimed, "Masa, you speak of time! Attitudes! Of abstract matters. Why must things of an intimate nature always be referred to so rarely, so ambiguously, and so obliquely?"

"Why? Surely, it's a matter of taste. Good taste."

"So," Sumiko said hotly. "Complete honesty is bad taste?"

"Yes." Masa smiled. "That is, of course, except in one's own mind. Brought out into the open, why, then . . ." She mimed that earth tremors were shaking the house. "*Jishin*—earthquakes, embarrassments, and sometimes actual harm."

"Do you believe that absolutely?"

"Not absolutely, but I do believe that too intimate, too honest outpourings not only hurt, they are apt to reveal flaws in one's self."

"So complete honesty in your opinion is never good, never splendid, never liberating?"

"You are relentless."

"Yes, also resentful. To pacify me you are being hypocritical. So shall we discuss, in this last intimate time together perhaps forever, a more suitable, a more *tasteful* topic? Tell me, older sister Masa, which do you honestly prefer? The single or the double cherry blossom?"

After a brief hesitation, Masa whispered, "Sumiko, I have been grievously at fault where you are concerned."

"Never! That is not so!"

"It is so. I have taken advantage of you shamefully in my loneliness all these years. I resemble a pomegranate which when it gapes its mouth shows all that is in its heart. Contrary to what you say, I have been much too open with you, much too sincere."

"Is it possible to be too sincere?" Sumiko interjected. "My sensibilities tell me that among women, sincerity is a virtue higher than valor or prescribed obligations."

"By promoting such ideas I have harmed you," Masa exclaimed. "When you leave this secluded home, you will have to guard your tongue. Regretfully, the only advice I give you now is that you be unlike me in every way."

"My ambition is to *emulate* you. . . ." Sumiko's voice lowered as a housemaid announced from the corridor, "Mistress, I have bought the lantern you ordered."

"*Dōzo*—enter!" The two women sat in silence as the dividing doors from the corridor slid open. The girl placed an orange-colored lantern on the floor, and its glare eclipsed the soft glow of moonlight.

Masa gestured that the servant go on her way, then turned to Sumiko. "It's unfortunate that the only marriage you have witnessed has been mine. Please, Sumiko, I beg of you, don't emulate this unruly wife."

"My brother is a cold husband. I understand why you hate him."

"Hate? I hate Kenichi? Not so. I merely dislike his way of despising all vital qualities in women." A wispy smile flashed across her face as she added, "Especially mine."

"I thought you hated Kenichi."

"I hate no one," Masa murmured. "Hate is corroding, ruinous to one's character."

"What of . . ." Sumiko leaned forward, tugging at Masa's silken sleeve. "What of love, then? Do you, did you ever love your husband?"

Masa's expression hardened. As she knocked ash from her tiny pipe, she spoke harshly. "I never thought to open this compartment of my heart, but you ask for honesty, so let me tell you that on the night of my marriage day I experienced extreme physical ecstasy. My husband scorned me, insulted me for voicing my emotions. I carry that wound in my spirit."

"You will never forgive Kenichi?"

"I, he also, would find that bad taste." Masa shrugged as she continued. "Put succinctly, no marriage can succeed when both partners have aggressive characters."

"Are you advising me not to be aggressive in my marriage?"

Laughing gently, Masa murmured, "Suggesting rather that you shroud any aggressiveness with a bland agreeableness. That is, of course, unless . . ." She ceased speaking, examining the palm of one hand as though seeking to find inspiration there.

"Unless—what?" Sumiko cried pleadingly. "Understand that I'm torn by fears and uncertainties."

"Oh, it grieves me to see you fretting about situations which might never arise. I was about to say, *unless* you have the good fortune to find true companionship with your husband."

"True companionship with that vulgarian Fukuda?"

"Frankly, the idea does seem improbable. Nevertheless, all things are said to be possible. Come, hold out your wine cup."

"Yes, fill it up again to the brim. How cynical you are."

"Yes. That is so. Cynicism is cheap. I have many unpleasant characteristics. Rather than have you pine for my company when you are afar off, you must keep them in mind."

Sumiko broke into laughter and waved her empty cup, crying out, "Too late to turn me against you. Masa, you are my peerless one. Simply and honestly, I love you."

"And,"—Masa held her cup in a delicate gesture of salute—"I rejoice in your affection. How the years have flown by! I was but fourteen when I first came to dwell in this house."

"I was but a child, lonely and untutored."

"You were my one, my only delight. Unfortunately, I was too young to mother you—"

"You befriended me," Sumiko interrupted, "brought me warmth, companionship, laughter. Gifts beyond price."

"You feel like that about me?"

"I do, and more. Do you understand me?"

"Yes. Because of our unique situation, we have established a relationship such as males often achieve. Women seldom. I rejoice in it."

"I also." Then, in order to stop herself from saying more, Sumiko exclaimed, "I am suddenly hungry. Shall we have a little feast brought to us here, now and at once?"

"Great minds think alike!" Masa clapped her hands and ordered the maid to bring a light repast to the room and to replenish the *sake* supply.

After they had eaten the meal, the two women remained all through the night, talking and recalling events from the years they had spent together, away from the outside world in the primitive fishing hamlet.

Just before dawn broke, they left the house and went out into the chill autumn morning. At the end of the garden they sat down side by side, facing the sea in silence.

As the dawn slowly lit up their world, the black line of the horizon appeared and the ocean and the sky once more were visibly divided. Sitting motionless, Sumiko wondered if Lady Masa would have been shocked and angered if, rather than asking for food, she had confessed that on many a night she had yearned to share her friend's pillow. She liked to believe that Masa had felt as she had felt, but she would never know. . . .

Several days later, while bidding a sad farewell to Sumiko, Masa noticed that a recently widowed woman from the fishing hamlet was hiding a grief much deeper than her own as she watched her son leave for the capital along with Sudo and Sumiko. The boy, Yuji, was destined to become the adopted son of a family in Edo—and would thus vanish from his mother's life.

Not wishing to enter the house now that she was without her young companion, Masa remained standing on the earthen road. A bell at the nearby monastery began to toll its single note at regular intervals, and to her consternation Masa began to weep most bitterly.

THE MARRIAGE WHICH SUMIKO UNDERTOOK so reluctantly began with a complete lack of empathy between the husband and wife. Fukuda's knowledge of women, garnered over the years from prostitutes and courtesans with whom he had consorted, had in no way prepared him for the intimacies of marriage with the aloof young woman he had taken as wife.

In his easy, fun-loving way he had not considered certain important facts; that, for example, all his sexual activities had taken place with females who had served apprenticeships in the art of pleasing men. Those courtesans had employed expert sexual techniques as well as light conversation, gay repartee and all the arts of pleasant companionship to not only amuse a man but to make him feel that he was indeed a man among men.

From early manhood Fukuda had fought valiantly to achieve the aggressive attitudes expected of a samurai, all the while laughing at his own expense and dreading ostracism. Aware that his marriage into the elite Yamamoto family was the butt of many a joke among his two-sworded friends, he determined to put on a brave face and to continue with his life in the pleasure quarters in the new role of a "married" bachelor. In order to do this, Fukuda made a desperate effort to ignore the fact that his wife's stiffly compliant behavior had turned him into a disappointed, nervous wreck.

Here again he braved out the situation. One afternoon several months after the wedding ceremony, he attempted a new approach. He found Sumiko and announced to her casually, careful not to meet her gaze, "I'm off for a night of pleasure. You don't mind?"

"Not at all," she replied, careful not to meet his gaze.

"Prepare suitable garments for me," he requested, and stood by, watching as she went about the task. He saw her as a stranger, an unknown quantity, but he desperately wanted to bait her into giving vent to some criticism.

"Tell me," he asked lightly, "do you find my behavior unvirtuous?"

"Not at all."

Examining the garments which she had laid out, he said, "You consider these garments will add to my charm?"

From her gestures and her strange smile, he gathered that she gave assent to his query. "Ah, is that so! Then, would you advise that I enjoy several females tonight?"

"If you wish."

"Tell me, do you find many flaws in my character?"

"I find no flaw."

"You have no complaints, then?"

"I have no complaints."

"Not one?"

"Not one."

"Then, would you say that we, you and I, are a perfect couple?"

"That could be so."

"Could be? Not quite certain, eh?"

Realizing that he was about to tread on dangerous ground, Fukuda stopped his questions and Sumiko was glad when he went on his way.

The elderly Fukuda couple, wanting to prove their rise in the world through their son's prestigious marriage, paraded their daughter-in-law before acquaintances with such pride and sincerity that Sumiko could barely smother her feelings of embarrassment.

She had become their *hana-yome*—flower-daughter, adopted by her marriage into the Fukuda clan. Her natural family had to be forgotten; the ancestors of her new family were now her ancestors, and she made daily obeisance to them in front of the household shrine.

Raised in the seclusion and the sparse elegance of Masa's household, Sumiko was repulsed by the opulence and the vulgar show of wealth in the Fukudas' mansion. Intelligent and free-thinking, she found her new family's reliance on temple priests and soothsayers pathetically childish, but she withheld all critical comments, remembering Masa's advice—"Keep your opinions to yourself. Keep in mind the importance, the power of the unspoken word."

By keeping those opinions to herself, Sumiko developed the habit of making a slight motion of her head, always with a shadowy smile on her face. Those actions could be taken for assent or for dissent, whichever was pleasingly acceptable to any given situation.

One situation, without doubt most trying, was her mother-in-law's monthly query, "Not yet? Not yet with child?" When, after some seven months had gone by, Sumiko replied calmly, "I am with child," the elderly woman fell into a paroxysm of delight. She ran along the corridors, calling to all and sundry, shouting out the news and gathering the household members together. Sumiko, self-conscious yet innerly relieved, stood by, feeling that the expected child had very little to do with her.

Outwardly gracious and seemingly complacent, she endured the months of her pregnancy, feeling more or less a prisoner under the stern guardianship of the grandmother-to-be. Priests and soothsayers came and went, offering advice and warning of dangerous omens. After the child was born, Sumiko was exhausted, not physically, but mentally, and made no objections when the male infant was cared for and cosseted by his grandmother, with the exception of his feeding times.

Sumiko thought of herself as a stranger who dwelt in an immense inn to which unpaying guests flocked in a never-ending series of banquets and picnics in the woodlands of the estate. During those entertainments she was startled by the bawdiness of certain married women guests.

Unaccustomed to small talk, she felt that her mind was becoming stultified by the frothy, meaningless conversations flowing around her. Time and time again she yearned to be by the sea, to breathe in the salty ozone, and in these moments her heart would be consumed with desire for the life she had lived before her marriage.

In order to keep her equilibrium she made a fetish of bathing and indulged in frequent washing of her body. After rinsing, she climbed into the deep tub and drew her knees up in the fetal position, letting the water lap up to her chin. There she would stay, her mind blank, until a maid called to remind her that it was time to feed her child.

The greedy infant Yuichi aroused no maternal instincts in her. After feeding times, Sumiko was often ashamed of the relief she felt when he was taken back into the jealous arms of his doting grandmother.

Her husband no longer made intimate demands of her, and that also filled her with feelings of relief and shame. Realizing that she was trudging along a path that was leading her into a state of quiet desperation, she wrote to Masa, a long, disjointed epistle attempting to explain her situation and begging for advice. Masa's reply to that letter was brought to her by Kenichi. Although he was smugly satisfied with himself at having carried out his duty toward his sister, he was unable to forget her reproachful expression on the day of her wedding and could now treat her only with the utmost politeness and distance.

Masa's witty, exquisitely brushed letter scarcely touched on the contents of her sister-in-law's emotional outpourings; but Sumiko knew that Masa completely understood and sympathized with her problems. "Sumiko," she wrote, "isn't there one small, secluded room in your large home, wherein a busy person might at times retire to in order to refresh her spirit in solitude?"

Taking Masa's advice, Sumiko wandered along the many corridors of the mansion and found a secluded room, which she requested the use of from her mother-in-law. The latter went in haste to the nearby temple to confer with the soothsayer whose ghostly counsel she relied upon. Returning home, she informed Sumiko that the wise man not only agreed with the unusual request but that he had utilized his powers to put the idea into the young wife's head.

The fakeries of the well-paid man were as transparent to Sumiko as a shadow of the water on a pond, but she praised his wisdom while knowing full well that it would have been quite disgraceful if her first, her only request, since entering the Fukuda family, had been refused.

In the beginning the eight-mat room had served its purpose, for there Sumiko found a sanctuary where her spirits were revived. She gradually gathered there a collection of personal belongings, her *koto*—her writing materials and the chest, table and white *hibachi* decorated with crimson dragons, all of which had been brought along with her dowry from her beloved Yokohama home.

Sumiko's health improved and to her embarrassment, she realized that she was making certain surreptitious approaches toward her husband. Fukuda was nervous but he too began to court his wife. He presented her with amusing publications of books and scrolls and with simple gifts such as a dried melon gourd made into a vase, suggesting that she might care to place it on the *tokonoma* of her private sitting room.

Some days after receiving that gift, Sumiko had murmured, "This morning I arranged three purple iris flowers in that melon gourd and it gives me great delight to see them."

"Then, you admire the iris flower?"

"Highly."

"I also. For some time I've had in mind the idea of creating a garden river of iris, but I have renounced that plan."

"May I ask why?"

"Certainly. My plan was to have the garden close by your little room. You understand?" Fukuda bowed slightly, then continued. "Understand that I respect your desire for privacy. I feared that gardeners working outside your room would inconvenience you. It's of no matter."

"But . . ." Sumiko fell silent, bemused, overcome by feelings of sweet delight. She glanced at her husband, seeing him as though for the first time, not as a vulgarian, but as a sensitive, kindly man.

His gaze met and locked with hers, and for some inexplicable reason both of them broke into laughter, not from amusement but from extraordinary relief and pleasure.

"But . . . ?" Fukuda finally grinned.

"But . . . ?" she stammered. "Of what were we speaking?"

"Am I mistaken in believing you had it in mind to invite me to view those purple flowers in that melon gourd?"

For one brief moment Sumiko hesitated, then she said softly, "You are not mistaken. . . ."

From that time onward Sumiko's husband would come striding along the polished corridors on his return to the house, calling, "My wife! Where is my wife?"

The small room became their rendezvous place, where the married couple spent many hours, each one entranced by the other, lost to time and to the busy household about them. Fukuda never wearied of Sumiko's company, and in the harmonious oasis she learned to relax and to show her true self to the man whose wife she had become.

Although her attitudes toward male sexuality were tinged by her sister-in-law's sardonic outlook, Sumiko now gave full rein to her sensual desires, without fear or awkwardness, allowing her husband to believe that he was the instigator in their lovemaking. He was delighted with her praise of his amatory skills, especially as his reputation in the pleasure houses had never been that of a great lover. "My marriage to your sister," he informed Kenichi, "is a complete success."

The secluded room became a veritable love nest. In order to titillate his wife, Fukuda brought home newly published popular *shunga* books and scrolls depicting erotic variations of sexual intercourse. He remained innocent of the fact that his wife, although she had been in a fishing hamlet for the first twenty years of her life, had spent many enjoyable hours with Lady Masa studying the ancient "pillow books," those heirlooms for noble brides. "Remember," Masa had always said, laughing, "although these works were promoted mainly for their instructional matter, the pictured eroticism is, without doubt, a vicarious outlet for spinsters and for unloved wives such as I."

Sumiko quite often thought of Masa's loneliness as she reclined on the triple-tiered mattress with her husband. She rejoiced that her own fate was so different. She and her husband concentrated on pleasing the other, the more erotic the more enjoyable, and then, satiated, they would lie until she arose to prepare a light repast with hot wine. While they feasted they would gossip and laugh together, or indulge in lengthy discussion on various subjects.

He was enthralled by his wife's hitherto unsuspected intellectualism. For her part, Sumiko was shocked and yet also entranced by her husband's piratelike business proclivities. Even though they sat close together in their secluded sanctuary, they spoke scarcely above a whisper, both deeply aware that serious penalties would be put upon any individual who stepped outside the edict—*"The community, not the individual, is all-important."*

Sumiko was particularly concerned when Fukuda admitted that for several years he had been employing craftsmen, who, because of various misdemeanors, had been banished from their native villages. Fukuda was therefore contravening the law which forbade strangers to settle in any district other than their own without official permission. Such individuals, even though skilled in a special craft, had no chance of employment, for guilds representing those crafts would not employ them. Throughout Japan many men wandered from place to place, destitute and officially termed *hinin*—non-men.

Fukuda confided to Sumiko, "I have within me feelings of rebellion against many of our laws and cults. I find it pitiable that one misdemeanor alone separates a man forever from the privilege of working to earn his daily rice. Therefore, I employ quite a number of such men in our workshops."

"Your confession causes my blood to run cold," Sumiko exclaimed with astonished concern. "Certainly I admire your concepts of brotherhood, of kindliness. But I feel that you have personal gain topping your priorities. Excuse me for voicing this unwifely thought. But am I correct in my supposition?"

"You are!" Fukuda grinned at his wife admiringly. "Money," he chuckled, "is all-powerful."

"Am I to understand that money buys corruption in official quarters? The very thought shocks my sensibilities."

"*Ah—sō desuka?* Is that really so? I'm sorry to bruise your delicate feelings, but with you, only with you, it relieves me to speak brashly about the brashness of life, which everywhere is kept covered by richly brocaded façades. Come now, make a true confession. No, don't bother. I know you so well. We, you and I, although male and female, have always been discriminated against. I, because of my lowly ancestry. You, because of your sex. True—no?"

Sumiko remained silent for a long time, then her face seemed to light up and she laughed, saying, "Indeed, you know me, perhaps too well. It is true that I feel women are discriminated against. I find it strangely unjust that a male, whatever his level of intelligence, be given education in many areas; that males are not only permitted, but encouraged to revel licentiously. I think of my brother Kenichi and Lady Masa, my sister . . ." Tears seeped from her eyes as she continued indignantly. "Masa's intellect is quite on a par with his, but she lives ignored and unrecognized in a primitive village. While Kenichi . . ."

Sumiko fell silent, attempting to suppress her unseemly outburst. In a wryly humorous tone Fukuda then announced, "Also, that disgraceful man Kenichi forced his sister to marry a man she not merely *despised* but actually loathed. Ah, what a crime! He should be banished, become a social outcast himself!"

Now Sumiko was smiling. "Yes," she murmured, "but then, *you* would take him beneath your protective wing. Isn't that so? Don't reply," she exclaimed hastily. "Let me say that in reference to my marriage, Kenichi acted with a wisdom of which I believed him incapable."

Blushing, she deftly turned the conversation back to Fukuda's illegal employment of social outcasts. He insisted that apart from disobeying officialdom's stern edicts in that quarter, he believed himself to be a perfect example of good citizenship. "In every other way I serve the community. Yes, and I believe I follow its regulations with more integrity than do those high officials who accept my money and gifts for favors done. They are all fakes, resembling Buddhist monks who sit calmly chanting Sutra, apparently filled with religious zeal, but only too ready to pocket illegal cash and to enjoy the bodies of pretty youths. Yes, I would vouch for my integrity beyond that of several of my close acquaintances, men from the nobility who allow me into their prestigious circle only because of my 'vulgar' wealth."

"Surely not that last sad statement? Surely not!"

"Surely it is so. But there, I am also without virtue, for I am jealous of their inherited superiority. I have crawled to them, only too aware of my lack of character. Fukuda, always the joker! The buffoon, paying my way with sangfroid, never into their sacrosanct midst but merely on its periphery. Frankly, from my experience I know that the samurai code is but top dressing."

Fukuda, embarrassed at his outburst, flushed deeply and gazed into his wife's startled eyes as he grimaced, miming that he was about to commit suicide. Then, in a low voice, he said, "To speak disgraceful things of other men is forbidden. I disgrace *myself* in so doing." He bowed apologetically, murmuring, "Please excuse me."

Sumiko gave assent with a slight motion of her head, then said quietly, "Lady Masa once said that quite possibly time might bring about changes in social laws and attitudes. I recall having scoffed at her comments. Today I feel that great changes are already here. Are we in agreement?"

Springing to his feet, Fukuda cried out cheerfully, "Let us cease lamenting on serious matters and take our son to visit a shrine. As all good citizens should."

The family trio made their way to a nearby shrine set in large grounds. While Sumiko admired the building's pillars and eaves, richly painted with red lacquer, her husband chased after Yuichi. In a frenzy of delight the little boy had sped to the temporary booths selling toys—made in the family's workshops, to Fukuda's satisfaction.

Finally, Sumiko captured her unruly child, straightened his clothes, and gently but firmly led him before the shrine to pay obeisance.

One summer morning after a night of lovemaking, Fukuda, naked but for a loincloth, lounged on the *tatami*, eating from a bowl of buckwheat noodles. Sumiko, wearing a loose robe, knelt before the mirror, examining her face in a critical manner, murmuring, "Certainly I show the effects of a sleepless night."

"It was a *hot* night," Fukuda chortled. "Turn around, let me examine you."

Twisting her head to gaze directly into his eyes, she smiled complacently, saying, "How do I appear to you?"

"Decadent—very interesting. Aaah, no lovemaking I've had has remotely approached my times with you."

Sumiko smiled broadly and her eyes scanned the ceiling. "Are you complimenting me or yourself?"

"I refuse to answer. A superior person never needlessly exposes himself to peril! And, speaking of peril, it's rumored that your brother has taken the adopted Shiga youth to live in his house at Nihombashi."

Kenichi and his relationship with Osen was often the subject of discussion between the Fukuda couple, and Sumiko rejoined, "Let us not be too concerned. Lady Masa cares not one iota for her husband and his second household."

"Not even one iota? Well, I find that shameful. I, his friend, have his interests at heart. I fear that his generosity, his innocence, will bring about his ruin."

"Innocence? Are we discussing the same man?"

"We are. I allude to his long-standing obsession with Osen. To my mind, her motives are as strange as a cat's. Your brother has never seen through her strategies."

"Could it be that the woman has no strategies?" Sumiko left the mirror and sat close to Fukuda. "Could it simply be that Kenichi is encouraging the woman into making an atmosphere of domesticity in the house?"

"That is exactly what the cat is doing! Kenichi grows heavier, he drinks more. She encourages that—" Fukuda fell silent, and in his distress he gazed at his wife, whose lips were pursed as she fluttered her hand across a black-lacquered bowl of sweet berries. Finally, choosing the largest berry, she proffered it to him, saying, "Be easy where my brother is concerned. He is not capable of acting rashly. He has the instincts of a sky hawk."

"Sky hawk? Sky hawk! Both he and you have this queer obsession with feathered creatures. Explain it to me."

"Obsession? How you exaggerate! As to explaining, can one actually describe one's obsessions?"

"Aah, you are so sensible. Always so calm . . . Now, why are you looking so amused? Cease your laughter. Tell me!"

"Excuse my laughter, but may I suggest that in this bustling, rumbustious household even a marauding flock of wild geese would appear to be calm."

"There you go! Birds again! Tell me, what species of feathered creature does our son resemble?"

"Yuichi! A bird? Never! Quite plainly, he belongs to the world of the mischievous monkey."

"True! He uncannily resembles my grandfather. That clever old peasant who—"

"Yes, yes, so you so often say!" Sumiko interrupted hastily. "I know his story *so well.* But, are you pleased with your son?"

"So pleased I wish for one more exactly like him. Come, don't bathe yet. Shall we . . . ?"

No other child arrived, but the Fukuda couple considered themselves the most fortunate of beings and Fukuda was wont to exclaim to all and sundry, "My wife and I even enjoy the annual typhoons.

We thrill to earth tremors! We even find our atrocious child endearing."

He spoke the absolute truth from his own point of view, but Sumiko differed where her son was concerned. Small-boned, wiry, and headstrong, Yuichi held complete sway over his grandparents. They could deny him nothing, and if he were even slightly reprimanded, all he had to do was to open his mouth, scream out his rage, and they would placate him.

During his fifth year his grandparents had called in a troupe of entertainers to amuse the child. They put on a skillful show, accompanied by a huge drum and dancers imitating a pride of lions, shaking, roaring, and waving their heads.

Yuichi was fascinated and called for encore after encore until the troupe were utterly exhausted. "More, more, more," he screeched, and to his mother's shame the entertainers had been employed to remain on the estate, always ready to perform at the young master's command.

On hearing the boom of the drum, Sumiko would retreat to her sanctuary, thinking of Lady Masa and her all-powerful fan. Tears would roll down her cheeks and she felt relieved that her sister-in-law was not able to witness the unmannerly behavior of her child. Relieved also that Masa was not aware that she had grown quite stout from overindulgence at the table and that to please her husband she had taken to wearing too-colorful garments. On those occasions she would prepare her ink pad and her writing brushes, fully intending to write and beg Masa to pay a visit to Edo, but she would give up, knowing that the situation at the Nihombashi house made any such visit impossible.

When she thought of Renzō, now more or less entombed in the school's precincts, she longed to provide some relief to the monotony of his life. One afternoon while Kenichi was visiting Fukuda she sought him out. She would choose her words carefully, for he had made it plain that he resented the interest she showed in his affairs, especially those that touched on his relationship with Masa and his household in Yokohama.

She approached him when Fukuda was present, saying lightly, "Kenichi, tell me, I yearn to know, how is my nephew? Does Renzō keep strong and healthy?"

"*Hai*—yes!" Kenichi replied casually. "Certainly, he is strong and healthy."

"I fear that time and distance must be causing my image to fade from his mind. I would so much like to see him again."

"No doubt you would! However, the boy is arduously involved in his studies."

"Ah, yes, rightly so! But surely he could come occasionally to Edo?"

Kenichi stared at her, his nostrils tensed as though aware of an unpleasant odor, then he replied sharply, addressing Fukuda, "If I bring my son to visit my home in Nihombashi, will you agree that your wife will come there to renew her acquaintanceship with him?"

"You ask the impossible," Fukuda grunted, "and you know it!"

"Exactly! So, the subject is closed."

"Not so," Fukuda stated firmly. "I agree with my wife. Your son Renzō will be my guest. I will willingly escort him here. Your sister cares for his welfare. He shall stay in our home, come to know Yuichi, his cousin. And—"

"Stop, stop. . . . Put Renzō to such risk? Why, if your young rogue took a dislike to him, I fear that my son might be decapitated on the spot. No, no, I suggest that you and your wife give *all* your attention to your own child and leave me to deal with mine."

To show that he was in no way offended, Kenichi slapped his friend heartily on the shoulder, then bowing to Sumiko, he said ironically, "Sister, how nice it would be if everything in our lives were good, genuine, and beautiful. Unfortunately, my life is not quite as simple as yours. I have more on my mind than the affairs of children."

For several years Kenichi had been included in a scholarly group of advisers during conferences held by government officials, all deeply concerned about changes infiltrating Edo's society.

The peasant farmer, although in practice a poor man and heavily taxed, was becoming richer. The middlemen who serviced the wealth produced by the farmer and spent by the samurai prospered and also tended to become rich. Restricted by sumptuary laws in how they might spend their newfound wealth, they were restless and amazed by the leisure at their disposal. Throughout the great capital city many schools were springing up, schools which in the beginning had catered to lowbrow tastes in literature but which were stealthily developing into establishments run on more highly intellectual lines.

For more than two and a half centuries the Tokugawa shogun had promoted the distinctions between the classes and now that policy was at risk. Kenichi was in full agreement with plans that advocated keeping the great mass of the population from becoming too highly educated (and therefore more politically aware), by making every effort to have them look increasingly to expensive amusement and entertainment.

For many decades Edo had been known as the "city of bachelors" and prostitution had always prospered. Now, with the "new prosperity" quickly on the rise, delights which had once been the privilege of the samurai were offered to all males, regardless of class, and limited only by one's supply of cash. All houses of pleasure now fell under official dictatorship and were placed behind the fortresslike fence that surrounded the Yoshiwara district which for many decades had been the legitimate, sternly regulated brothel quarter of the city.

Nevertheless, in that artificial world of sensual pleasure there remained certain establishments—such as Watanabe's all-male brothel and those that employed the elite of the courtesan world—which welcomed only that ten percent, the samurai, over their thresholds. The favors of the witty, most beautiful, and highly accomplished women and maidens were at their disposal alone.

One winter night during a heavy snowfall, Fukuda lay, restless and bored, convalescing from an attack of bronchitis, a respiratory disease that troubled many residents in Edo. Sumiko sat by his *futon*, reading aloud from a collection of newly published poems.

All of a sudden she realized that her husband had lost interest in the readings. Laying the book aside, she said, "So, no more poetry! What now? How can I entertain you? How do you feel? Isn't it cozy, together like this, surrounded by a sea of snow?"

"Frankly, no. Unless you allow me to smoke my pipe, I fear I shall go mad."

"Then, by all means smoke to your heart's delight."

Sumiko prepared the *tabako-bon,* and after puffing at his pipe for a moment or two, Fukuda, making an amorous gesture, said suggestively, "Yes? No? Yes?"

"No, no! Not that! Not yet. You are still quite weak."

"Aah, you are right. I'm improved but still too weak for that. So then, let's just chat. I'm sure that like all good wives you have an unquenchable interest in the ways of your prostitute sisters. No matter how skillfully you pretend disinterest. Is that not so?"

"What insight you have into the feminine mind," Sumiko murmured.

"Right! Then shall I tell you of the world of the courtesan? Of life in the Yoshiwara?"

"Umm . . . I think not. Best not."

"But I wish to tell you."

"Oh, then by all means! Please tell me, not of the courtesans, but of the quarters. Can you describe that place? I mean with skill, with . . ."

"Aah, you doubt my skills. You believe I am no raconteur?"

"I doubt you not at all and in no way. Tell on."

"I shall. But first tell me how do you imagine it to be?"

"How can I imagine how it is? I can imagine nothing. I have but a practical mind. However, I must warn you that I am widely read. Classic tales of old Kyoto and the gay quarters there are well known to me."

"Such nonsense! Better never written! Now, today, in Edo, the Yoshiwara has become a place to please all the senses not only of the samurai but of the common man, and I whisper this—because of my wealth, even *such as I*!"

"To please *all* the senses? May I trust that statement?"

"You may! You may! Dare I state, even love. Yes, men come and go and many of the girls are charming. Many of them come from secret maternity hospitals run for the prostitutes by brothel owners. Some are young wives who have sold themselves into bondage to provide for their ailing husbands and poverty-stricken children. Some are apt to be caught by that rascal known as love. They write love poems. They exchange vows even though knowing that their loves are but transient affairs. And then—"

Fukuda broke off, glancing at Sumiko, who sat nursing her cheeks in the palms of her hands, her lips pursed. "You make it sound gloomy," she murmured. "Come lie on your belly. I shall massage your back. Tell me more some other time. Perhaps tomorrow."

In truth, Fukuda was not a skillful raconteur. The Yoshiwara was above all a place where gloom was unrecognized. Situated on the northeast boundary of the city, patrons entered through a single gate kept under strict guard and beyond that gate was a magnificent road bordered with cherry trees. Behind the cherry trees, elegant two-storied wooden buildings, all open to the street, displayed exquisitely robed girls—some having their hair dressed, or perhaps gazing into mirrors, some strumming musical instruments.

There were also hundreds of neat, small houses; hundreds of tea houses which served as inns; and at least three thousand registered prostitutes plied their trade day and night. At night the Yoshiwara was brightly lit by paper lanterns and teemed with customers from all walks of life. It had become a place where, for the first time in the long history of the land, peasants rubbed shoulders with artists, authors, poets, "men of the moment," in fact, every man who was interested in the pursuit of pleasure and was able to foot the bill.

For those with little to spend, there was the choice of a girl who sat on view protected by grilles of wooden bars. They were low-ranking, cheap, and easy to obtain.

To make an assignation with a high-ranking girl, one went to a tea house to be shown a "menu" of the "available," and the client would be expected to pay highly with no hesitation, to tip well and never, never to expect change. The tea house girl would take the patron over, pamper and eventually guide him to the bedchamber and the female of his choice.

Such tender, seductive treatment went to the head of many a man, and unless he were extremely rich, he was apt to ruin himself and his family. The Yoshiwara excelled at the sport of parting men from their money. Many legal wives resented the fact that an *ichiya zuma*— a one-night wife—cost so dearly and caused poor food to be served at the family table. . . .

Kenichi's affair with Osen had become a tangled web. His possessiveness had forced him to become her sole patron, but as time went by he became discontent.

In the beginning he had been pleased by her cheerful acknowledgment that she was not acceptable to certain of his friends: When he entertained she would leave the Nihombashi house until he called her back again. Then he became aware that she was showing too cheerful an attitude on those occasions; instead of rushing back to dwell under his protection, she was apt to return later than expected and moon about in a dispirited manner.

His jealousy was aroused. Not wishing to make her aware of his feelings, he changed his tactics and no longer invited guests home. The new freedoms and the new atmosphere in the Yoshiwara meant that he could meet there to commune with his friends. Together with a chosen group, his evening's entertainment would begin with a trip along the Sumida River, then a change over to ride horseback for a mile along the embankment, thence to the Yoshiwara. Sometimes they stayed there all night, rising early to return home.

Kenichi never bothered to protest his innocence when she accused him of infidelity. "If it does not trouble my registered wife, why should it trouble you?" he would mumble.

"*She* cannot be compared with me and my life of loneliness. *She* has your son to warm her heart with," Osen shrieked.

"Lower your voice. I fear that you are made of hard metal beneath that velvet skin of yours."

"How merciless you are! I have become your prisoner . . . always alone in this house."

"You are free to leave this house at any time."

That comment of his never failed to subdue Osen's rages. She knew that if she left her patron's protection the one path she could tread would lead her to the Yoshiwara, and once registered behind those walls, the regulations and the guard on the gate would combine to make her escape impossible.

In Kenichi she had a rich protector, and although she considered herself the most desirable of women, she had no intention of gambling her good fortune away. She would instantly become spry and quick-witted. "Forgive and excuse me," she pleaded after one such confrontation. "Your love is my one, my only consolation."

"Then be content. You must endeavor to be the quiet center in the whirlpool of my busy life. That is your duty."

Gracefully, she knelt down beside the *hibachi* and took up the long metal chopsticks to stir the glowing charcoal, then she blew upon it and it glowed brighter.

Although his wild passion was now over, Kenichi had no desire to indulge in sensual activities with anyone other than Osen. But he was finding that too much time spent in her company was apt to bore him. She was an uneducated, incurably light-minded woman. Life with her, apart from enjoying the delights of her body, was an unchanging diet of eating, drinking tea, drinking *sake*, and chatter, chatter, then more chatter.

Her incessant twittering was often in the background as he sat and pondered many and varied subjects. At times, and always to his chagrin, he recalled the sharp, bitter, but always stimulating hours spent in the company of his wife.

For several years his visits to the house on the hill in Yokohama had been less frequent, and during those visits he no longer shared Masa's pillow. He was slightly put out because the unspoken arrangement was apparently as pleasing to her as it was to him.

Before each of those visits he had intentions of spending time with his son, but Renzō, once so delightful, had developed into a sullen youth and Kenichi would bid farewell to Yokohama with no regrets.

Returning to Edo after one such journey and eager to be with Osen, he was informed that she was absent from the house. "Gone to the shrine," a housemaid said.

The monsoonal rains were falling in a steady downpour. "Gone out! In such a downpour?" he exclaimed.

"*Hai*—yes! Osen now goes every day. Osen cares not at all about weather conditions."

Kenichi knew only too well how much Osen disliked wind and rain. He also knew that her only reason for visiting shrines was to allow the world to see and admire her beauty, so he became deeply suspicious as he thought of Osen out in the world. Osen with some man, with a lover . . . ?

He pushed his way through the crowded streets toward the shrine, unaware of the slush and mud, with murder in his heart. He was certain that the courtesan had lied to the housemaid, or, more likely, that she had paid the servant to lie to him.

Scenes from other days flashed through his mind, one of them especially clear, of he and Osen, handsome in their finery, the cynosure of all eyes, as they strolled together one hot summer afternoon near the same shrine. But now he was not in the sunshine and not happy. . . .

She had not lied to the servant. He glimpsed her tottering along on her high wooden sandals, with a green paper umbrella held aloft, and he hastily stepped behind one of the huge stone lanterns that edged the path. After she had gone by he came out of hiding and followed her as she made her way back home. Then he made his way to a nearby tea house to calm his nerves. Yes, he pondered, the woman he could not do without was Osen. Yes, he knew with certainty that she choreographed even the most mundane events, but he found her sense of theater amusing and played along with her more than willingly. Even now, he had to admit, nights spent with her left him feeling as though they had taken a journey in a floating craft moving together in an undulating swell across a sea at times dangerously turbulent, at times peaceful.

He believed that he would never be capable of rationalizing his obsession for Osen; nevertheless, he had to find a way of ending his fear of losing her and putting an end to the jealousies which he found so disturbing. Could it be, he mused, that the old harridan Shiga might be the one to solve his problem? The idea was inspiring. He left the tea house and returned home, calling cheerfully, "I am home!"

When Kenichi finally put forward the idea of bringing Osen's mother and the *yōshi* to dwell in the Nihombashi house, Osen's features betrayed no emotions as she looked at him searchingly. He noticed that her lips had grown narrow over the last few years; strangely, that made her more desirable in his eyes.

Osen rose to her feet, removed a quilt from a wall cupboard, then fell prostrate onto the *tatami* with the coverlet pulled over herself.

Kenichi, impatient but also mystified, took up a fan and, in an effort to keep calm, he concentrated his gaze on a porcelain vase that stood on its carved stand in the *tokonoma* recess. The vase, he recalled, was an heirloom from his wife's family. Masa had brought it as part of her dowry when she had become his bride. He admired the unique shape, the slight indent in its roundness, and wondered at the daring of the artist, who, hundreds of years back, had combined peach pink blossoms against the mandarin orange of the background to create a glowing elegance.

Someone, presumably Osen, had placed a brash arrangement of flowers in the vase. The unaesthetic combination set his nerves on edge. She had no taste. But, he thought, shrugging off his criticism, that was her misfortune, not her fault. Masa, that wife of his, had taste, more than enough. Too much to please him. Was there, *could* there be such a creature as a perfect female? He thought not, and reminded himself of the saying: "A samurai should destroy within himself any feelings for women."

What kind of man was he? Here he was now, a fool, caught up in the moods and emotions of an old harlot's daughter.

"What ails you?" he shouted. "Has your brain gone soft? What ails you?"

Still Osen made no movement, no sound. Enraged, Kenichi crawled across the matting and dragged the coverlet away to stare at her face. Tears had mingled with the white paste-powder and he drew back, repulsed by the sight. But then, against his will, his passion was aroused and he fell upon her, lost to the world and all its irritations.

Some hours later he lay soaking in the bath, watching Osen, naked, engaged in washing her long eel-black hair and he wished that one of the artists who painted the girls in the Yoshiwara were present to immortalize the enchantment of the scene which he alone was witnessing.

As she stood up preparing to step into the tub, he noticed that her smooth-skinned legs were slightly crooked. The blemish pleased him just as the indent in the rounded vase had.

He smiled as she joined him in the tub and playfully entwined strands of her gleaming wet hair about his throat, as though intent to strangle him, but her face was filled with a happy, mischievous satisfaction.

"I feared you were tiring of Osen," she whispered.

"Not so. Not so," he smiled. "So then, you prefer not to have your mother and the boy live here?"

"Not that."

"Then what?"

"It's of no matter. Just . . ."

"Just . . ."

"You insist that I say?"

"Not insist, but why not say?"

Osen shook her head from side to side, biting at her lower lip. Then she murmured, "What of Kiku and Ume?"

Perplexed, he gazed at her, saying, "I don't understand?"

"My sisters! Kiku and Ume! The daughters of my mother. What of them?"

Kenichi had forgotten the existence of the old harlot's other daughters; now he recalled that Osen occasionally mentioned them and always with affection. The idea of including the two prostitutes into his plan was too macabre to consider. But, he wondered, was that really so?

"My sisters could replace the housemaids," Osen suggested calmly. "They would be industrious, truly trustworthy. Our mother will see to that."

Kenichi had an inkling that he had been mysteriously manipulated into the entire affair, but sensibly he threw that notion out of his mind. Within a month the house became a place to which he no longer dared invite even the most broadminded of his men friends.

He did not mind. It suited his convenience. The old woman Shiga and he had conferred together. He laid down stern laws and she agreed, grateful to the master of the establishment who, out of the goodness of his heart and the nobility of his character, had rescued her and her entire family and given them a life of respectability.

Sudo was astounded when Kenichi informed him that Osen's mother and sisters, together with the adopted son, young Yuji, were to stay in the Nihombashi house.

"To stay overnight?" he asked, not really believing.

"To dwell permanently," Kenichi replied casually. "The youth shall have your room. . . ." His master stared at him coldly, saying, "What ails you?"

Sudo sat open-mouthed, then he bowed his head to the floor, saying quietly, "Excuse me, please. But what of my work, my papers? My . . . ?"

"Remove them, and yourself, into the tea house. It will be more than suitable. More spacious than your present quarters."

"*Hai*—yes. Certainly," he replied. He gave no thought to the desecration of the tea house, for uppermost in his mind was the fact that he would not be banished from the place where Osen lived. He had to be near that woman who no longer ruled his life, but whose life he ruled in a fantasy world he had wittingly created. A fantasy more real than reality to him, wherein Osen, unhinged by her passion for Sudo, cheated on Kenichi, loathed his attentions, and waited only for him to leave the house. Then Osen, desperate in her desire, came creeping to Sudo's side, humbly pleading, "Take me. . . . Take me . . . make love to this poor, demented slave of love."

The fantasy now ruled Sudo's life and so powerfully that he had given up the shame he had endured when it had first crept into his consciousness. At times he would be overcome by a strange euphoria, and begin to laugh silently, his lips twitching as he beheld Osen and Kenichi together. Both of them were more or less unaware of his presence in the house and treated him not as a man, not even with disdain, but simply as a mere object.

Shabby, frail, and overworked by his master, Sudo ate leftovers and pitied those who dwelt only in the disorderly real world, for there was magic in his days, in his nights. He had no need to squander cash. No need to purchase favors from third-rate harlots. Edo's most beautiful courtesan was forever at his disposal. He, the good and faithful son, gave all he earned to his gentle parents. When he thought of them, of their goodness, their innocence, he was apt to cover his face and weep into his hands.

Secure in the knowledge that Osen was under her mother's stern jurisdiction, Kenichi felt relieved and exhilarated. His work for the shogun was not a burden, for Sudo, ever-industrious and trustworthy, did much of the detailed work; he prepared great screeds of translations from Dutch into Japanese and presented them in perfect condition, ready for his master to present to his masters.

Having housed social outcasts in his Edo dwelling, Kenichi was at times unable to suppress badgerlike grins as he wondered what his lady-wife would think of the inmates and of the place into which she had put so much thought and work. Well, he pondered, she would in all probability be scornfully amused. Nevertheless, he had made certain that articles of aesthetic value, which Masa had bought from Kyoto, were wrapped in fine cloth and placed in their individual boxes and caskets, then hidden away in safe custody.

To salve the rudeness of his actions, he provided generous amounts of cash for Osen and her family to indulge themselves in the marketplace, to purchase things which they found pleasing and to their own tastes. Of course, he cringed with embarrassment on beholding their purchases.

Little by little, Osen was becoming less interested in his comings and goings. This gratified him and, to his surprise, he began to enjoy the atmosphere of domesticity in his home. He felt benevolent as he witnessed the changes in the behavior of Shiga and her prostitute daughters, who were little by little becoming accustomed to living without having to kowtow to pimps and sell their favors in the flesh market of the Yoshiwara.

Buying Kiku and Ume out of bondage had cost Kenichi dearly, but nothing he had ever done for his mistress had given her such obvious joy. He found it fascinating to direct the course of other people's lives. And it amused him to behold Osen lording it over her sisters. It amazed him to behold the humility of those two devoted handmaidens, their adulation of the imperious courtesan.

Now, no longer a "business" woman, Shiga seemed to be an entirely changed person, the epitome of an industrious, domesticated working-class widow, dressed in dark tones as she managed the running of the Nihombashi house.

Nevertheless, Kenichi kept a sharp eye on the unscrupulous old tartar. He thought of her as a duck: on the surface calmly serene, but underwater its feet paddling like mad. . . .

The *yōshi*, Yuji, was too eager to please, but he was more than serving his purpose in the scheme of things.

Osen was greatly taken by her adopted brother; she pampered him and seldom brought up her wearisome complaint that she, Kenichi's mistress, was not as fortunate as his wife, who had a son to comfort her heart.

There were times when, hearing the youth's vibrant young voice, Kenichi's thoughts went out to Renzō. The years were flying by, and the time had come to think seriously about his son's future, especially about having him marry into a patrician family.

He believed one blunder he had made was to have pushed his sister into that unfortunate marriage with Fukuda. He deeply resented his brother-in-law's interference in his own personal life. It was no surprise that marriage into the Yamamoto family had not taken the impertinent Fukuda into the higher echelons of Edo's society, as he had hoped.

On the contrary, Fukuda's relationship with the son of the noble Count Okura had become strained. Kenichi wondered whether Fukuda realized that his unseemly comments about his happy marriage were responsible for the rift. When he recalled what a merry trio he, Fukuda, and Okura had once made, Kenichi regretted the passing of those carefree days. He disliked thinking of mistakes where his judgment had been at fault, but at the same time and with some ruthlessness, he determined to cool his own friendship with his brother-in-law. With an inordinate degree of subtle calculation, Kenichi determined that he would also let Okura know that he took a poor view of having family connections with the Fukuda clan.

His father, that weary old scholar, had once said, "Inside an arrogant man there are usually many hidden anxieties." Certainly one of Okura's characteristics was a high degree of arrogance, and, if possible, Kenichi would do his utmost to discover his friend's problems and perhaps assist in alleviating them.

One winter afternoon he sat, bored and restless, paying little attention to Osen's chatter as she crouched beside a recently purchased charcoal-burning brazier. The article was a monstrosity in his eyes, built as a low chest into which were set several drawers, with the top serving as a table. It was a common thing, suitable only for people with no taste.

He thought of various *hibachi* in the Yokohama house, some made of brass, of bronze, exquisitely carved. Some made of wood beautifully grained and others of earthenware and porcelain.

Always, when autumn set in, they would be filled to within a few inches of their brims with ash and then with overlays of calcinated oyster shell as white as driven snow heaped into a cone, with the top hollowed a little. Into that slight depression the embers of crackling, glowingly red charcoal would be placed. . . .

Now he disliked the harsh odor coming from the poor-quality fuel. He recalled that Masa insisted on using charcoal only from the wood of cherry trees, always sawed neatly into little blocks with no breaks. Her management of the charcoal and the ash, the etiquette of the *hibachi* in general, was all important to her. He recalled the way she would hold her hands over the brazier to warm them. . . .

He resented more and more the comparisons between his mistress and his wife which crept into his mind. Unwillingly, he was forced to admit that he missed certain aspects of life with Masa. He had always admired her elegance and he missed the sharpness of her mind. But, on the other hand, her cynicism always irritated him beyond the point of endurance.

Osen's voice, slightly metallic, broke into his meditations. "Do you not *agree*? Do you not also consider him highly intelligent?"

He gazed at her animated face, as though needing time to consider her questions, but in fact quite at a loss. His question was diplomatic. "You see him that way?"

"*Hai*—yes! I do," she exclaimed earnestly. "He is strong, obedient, and ambitious. Mother also hopes that you will allow him to attend a school."

So! She was alluding to Yuji! Well, he had no intention of furthering that youth's education. But he could be apprenticed in some craft. But what craft?

The boy was physically strong, certainly not good-looking, but his step was light and his hands skillful. Perhaps he could be trained as a "dresser," a backstage theater attendant?

The theater! Suddenly he became less unhappy. Life was to be lived and to the full. He would array himself and then make his way to the theater to see an afternoon performance.

The "theater" street was a mass of waving, streaming colors; the exteriors of the playhouses were bright with flags and banners that snapped in the cold breeze. With every step he took, Kenichi became more and more keyed up with excitement. He had an urge to enjoy himself, but, even more important, to meet up with Okura, who, he knew, seldom missed an opening performance of a Nō play.

The man was a purist, a devotee of Nō. Rather than the larger, more complex staging of the Kabuki theater, Okura preferred the small curtainless Nō stage projected into the audience. "Nō," Okura had once enthused, "is minute drama played at the front of a vast stage, and that stage, my friend, is the stage of Japanese history. To my mind Nō dramas are the most precious, the most elaborately poetic form of art our nation has produced."

Kenichi recalled that conversation as he settled down in his partition at the theater. With a certain smugness, he felt that fate was on his side, for as he glanced around with studied casualness he saw Okura sitting with his half-brother Shiro and Ohara, men well known to Kenichi. He knew then that his suspicions about the cooling of Okura's friendship toward him had been well founded, for in earlier days he would have been included in that brotherly group. And Okura's bow of recognition on sighting him left little doubt as to the new reserve in the relationship.

In an attempt to distract himself Kenichi concentrated his gaze on the stage and admired its unstained and beautifully polished wood.

The audience fell silent as the chorus came in and sat on the right side of the stage. Dressed in pale-toned blues and grays, the figures ceremoniously placed their closed fans on the ground before them. The fans would be opened and held only when the chorus sang. As intermediaries between the cast and the audience, the chorus were narrators, ready to report events that were taking place, to interpret the actors' emotions, and to advise them on what to do.

Now the actors were approaching along the passageway leading from the green-room and the musicians also came onstage with their instruments—just three drums, each one different, and a single flute, to be used with subtle impact to break the monotony of persistent drummings.

As always, the performance was a melodramatic court opera. At first Kenichi found himself mentally comparing the structure of the opera with the works of Western playwrights he had translated over the years, dramas strong in their dramatic construction and different indeed from Nō works, which were told as stories in high relief rather than in dramatic sequences and movement, with ghosts and priests haunting the stage, with much moralizing, all to do with *giri*—duty, the brevity of life, one's need for stoical philosophy in order to face the tragedies and misfortunes of one's existence while in human form.

By degrees Kenichi became caught up in the play; it was the tale of Unai, a pure-hearted maiden, who receives letters from two men, each declaring his passionate love for her.

Drums throbbed ominously as Unai's stern father declared that his daughter must wed the better marksman of her two suitors, thereby adding to her perplexity, for both the men's arrows pierced the same wing of the same duck—a mandarin duck—the symbol of true marital devotion.

The gentle Unai, driven to despair by the result of the trial of skill, drowned herself. The rivals, overcome with remorse and anguish, killed each other at her tomb.

Throughout the play, Matsumura, the male actor playing Unai, wore an elegant chalk-white face mask with eyebrows painted on the center of the forehead. Fans too had been used throughout the play to express various emotions, all clearly understood by those members of the audience who were devotees of Nō. Kenichi, however, was at times rather perplexed, unmoved, and more than a little relieved when the play ended. He dallied before leaving his seat, then, seemingly inadvertently, he was beside Okura, who, though lacking spontaneity in his voice, suggested that he should "come with us to the green-room. That is, if you have no other assignation?"

Elated, Kenichi accepted the coveted invitation with a suitable degree of pleasure and went backstage to sit among a chosen few in the presence of the famous actor who had played the lead role. Truly, he mused, to behold Matsumura shedding his femininity and regaining his masculinity was more titillating, more entertaining than the drama that had taken place on the stage.

However, Matsumura was quickly bored and with one slight gesture of his eyebrows he let it be known that as far as he was concerned, he had honored his admirers not exactly for too long but quite long enough.

Once out in the street, where snow was now falling thickly, Kenichi had been tempted to exclaim, "Matsumura Sensei obviously considers himself more enchanting than an avenue of flowering cherry trees." But he suppressed that unseemly comment and remarked instead, "I am honored to have been close to a man of such genius."

Clenching his teeth, one hand on the hilt of his short-sword, the other held palm upward, Okura gestured his approval of Kenichi's attitude. Kenichi now had no intention of allowing himself to be "odd man out," so he announced firmly, "I must away. . . ."

Even as he spoke, an earth tremor shook the ground, not violently, but enough to make citizens in the crowded street call, "*Jishin . . . jishin*—earthquake . . . earthquake . . ."

The four men elected to remain stoically silent, but they kept their hands tense on their sword hilts, as though in readiness to slay an impertinent stranger who had blundered into their midst.

No further tremors followed, and, as if nothing had happened, Okura said casually to Kenichi, "My father recently inquired after your welfare."

"I am honored."

"Not at all. He admires your intellect."

Kenichi gestured the compliment away, not humbly but graciously, as Okura murmured, "My father would deeply appreciate your opinion on several rare literary works he has in his possession."

No further words were needed by either man. Okura knew Kenichi fully understood that he was once again being invited to pay a call to the Okura establishment. Likewise, Kenichi was fully aware that his samurai brother's feelings had warmed toward him.

With his mind at ease he headed off alone through the heavily falling snow. On reaching the Nihombashi district he paused and stood aside with his fellow pedestrians, bowing ceremoniously as a funeral procession went by. The file of slowly moving figures was an extraordinarily poetic sight. Robed in white with touches of brilliant color, some carried lanterns that swayed in the wind, several carried masses of flowers or small bamboo cages. He knew that during the burial ceremony those cages would be opened and the caged birds would be set free.

Just for a moment he thought about his own demise, but he braced himself, bent forward against the rising wind, laughing heartily. Secure in his anonymity, he shouted, "While I live, all is a pleasure for me. . . ."

"You sound a very happy drunk, brother!" a passerby yelled cheerfully from out of the white mist. "*Omedetō*—congratulations . . ."

K ENICHI WAS EXUBERANT AT BEING back in Okura's good graces. Yet, somehow aware that he was being used, he trod softly, knowing that his noble brother's pride must in no way be bruised, but rather handled as one plucks delicate morning-glory flowers from their vines.

Rather to his amazement, Kenichi discovered that for some years Okura had maintained a second home. In a secluded house close to the Sumida River, he kept a mistress, a geisha, who was the mother of a small daughter. Okura was in no way furtive. His wife and his parents accepted the situation without even a murmur, but Kenichi was made to understand that the expenses and upkeep of the second home were difficult to meet.

Before introducing Kenichi to his mistress, Okura said, "Keiko is physically less beautiful than some men's ideals of charming womanhood. But one short hour spent in Keiko's company calms my restless nature, slakes my feelings of discontent and boredom. . . ."

On meeting the geisha, Kenichi found it easy to comprehend his friend's feelings. After a series of visits to the house he found himself envying Okura's good fortune in having the companionship of such a woman. Keiko was sophisticated and had been trained at an elite geisha school. Her talents included singing, stage dancing, the playing of various musical instruments, as well as calligraphy, painting, drawing and the composition of *haiku*. Kenichi was above all impressed by Keiko's skill in the art of intelligent conversation and of silence.

"Our relationship is not a passionate one," Okura had confided. "Frankly, I have always been repulsed by florid, passionate affairs with women. My deepest passions lie in different directions, with nature, with inanimate objects created by man."

"I understand your feelings," Kenichi had murmured. "I sympathize fully. . . ."

"I'm glad. It's good to be with you like this, speaking frankly, and at ease. You agree?"

"Absolutely . . ."

The two friends sat side by side in the sitting room of Okura's second home while Keiko attended to their wishes. She refilled their *sake* bowls and at times nodded her approval of Okura's comments, all the while displaying her pleasure and her devotion to him.

As the winter night progressed, Kenichi gently encouraged his friend to drink even more heartily than usual. He knew that a most important time had arrived in their relationship; those anxieties which his own father had said lay beneath the skin of an arrogant man were about to be brought out into the open.

In his heart the situation amused him, for all three in the cozy room were skilled at the game being played, and just as he encouraged Okura to drink heavily, so did Keiko and her patron encourage him, for they all knew that matters spoken of—no matter how intimate, how disgraceful—when men were *sake*-laden must be honorably forgotten as though never having been voiced.

During those hours Okura gave vent to the tribulations noble families were undergoing due to social changes. He voiced his scorn of the swashbuckling newly rich merchants such as Fukuda and his ilk, and bemoaned the degradation common men of wealth were forcing noble, once extremely rich families to endure. He spoke always in the abstract, never for an instant giving the impression that he or his family would accept aid of any kind.

Kenichi clearly understood that it had become his duty to relieve Okura's monetary pressures and he moved into the situation with great delicacy, curbing all displays of inappropriate frankness and making it clear that when Okura accepted the very worthwhile assistance from him, it was Okura, not Kenichi, performing the favor.

Nevertheless, both he and Okura knew that an *on*—a debt—must one day be repaid, certainly not in kind but by a repayment falling into another category. Kenichi hoped that it would pertain to his son Renzō's marriage into a high-ranking family.

As the winter season dragged by, Kenichi became more and more convinced that he had erred in taking Osen's family into his house and under his protection. He scorned himself for not having realized that the enchantment of love was, in the nature of things, evanescent, and that with the passing of time the passions of lovers must cool. To his misfortune, he had not taken that into account and was now finding it to be only too true.

Fukuda had once said, "It's lunacy to fall in love with a courtesan." Yes, but for all his erstwhile friend's rude suspicions about Osen's sly character, Kenichi believed that he was able to read her mind easily, like a book brushed in simplified characters, and just as the novelty of their combined lovemaking no longer attracted him, so, he knew Osen's passion was also abating.

New tastes and new desires were asserting themselves in both their lives. In Osen's case, the times spent in the company of her mother, her sisters, and Yuji were easygoing, filled with domestic delights and colored brightly by her knowledge that they were—all five—secure only because of her fortunate position.

He was aware that his mistress was impatient as she lay with him. She was no longer lost to desire; instead, she skillfully induced passion, just as he did. And neither of them, for their own good reasons, ever brought the subject into the open.

His own tastes were undergoing other changes. The Yoshiwara no longer attracted him; he had come to despise the place for all its artifices and its seething new, polyglot society. He admitted frankly to himself that his tastes were being influenced by Okura's mode of life, and he found the comparisons between his friend's "second home" and his own Nihombashi establishment odious.

He felt an overwhelming sense of impatience and had no doubt that before too long he would make other living arrangements. For some men, those of little feeling, the situation could be dealt with ruthlessly, but it was his principle to display a traditional reticence. It was not in his nature, he philosophized, to behave with insensitivity.

When the right time arrived, he would provide for Osen fairly and generously. Not suddenly but gently, with style. In the meantime, he would banish the troublesome matter from his mind.

Kenichi spent the month of February in a tinderbox atmosphere, dealing with official matters. A Dutch delegation had come from their prisonlike headquarters in Nagasaki to inform the shogunate in Edo that Western countries were once again on the "warpath," demanding, in polite terms, that Japan should give permission for foreign ships to be allowed anchorage off the coast when great storms arose in the Pacific Ocean. Seafarers' lives were being lost because of stern, unfriendly laws, and Japan's threat—that certain death would be the fate of sailors if they were foolhardy enough to land—was considered callous and inhumane.

Many such requests had been made over the years, but on this occasion it was plain to see that the Americans had a new, more important reason, one concerning the discovery of gold in California and its development as a commercial trading post. Wishing to trade with the recently opened ports of China and the island of Hong Kong, the Americans were desperately in need of a coaling station, and it was put forward that the most convenient place was one of Japan's islands.

Kenichi, assisted by Sudo, spent grueling hours translating letters and documents from Dutch into Japanese and interpreting, with extreme care and diplomacy, the drawn-out dialogues that took place. He was right in the center of the war of nerves between the two factions; his position was trying and the work left him mentally and physically exhausted.

Knowledge relating to affairs in the outside world was creeping stealthily into the community. But the shogun were bent on preserving the status quo, for the people were stirring restlessly beneath their despotic rule. Their aim was, by any means, to sedate the people back into an obedient state of lethargy.

Finally, the Dutch contingent, accompanied by armed guards, left the capital and returned to Nagasaki with orders to inform the impertinent Americans, and likewise the French and English would-be interlopers, that Japan's door would never willingly be opened to them. Japan was sufficient unto itself and the present-day shogun recalled, even if the barbarians did not, the trouble and carnage that had followed in the wake of their entry into Japan some hundreds of years back.

Kenichi knew that the government's blunt, behind-the-times attitudes were alienating those who dwelt in the West. But there was nothing he could do about it. In many ways, Japan as it was—a hermit kingdom—suited him down to the ground.

The foreigners he dealt with, certainly most of those Dutchmen, had rough, insensitive ways and strange attitudes on many subjects.

Many years before he had formed a clandestine friendship with a Dutch fellow by the name of Van der Linden, to whom he had endeavored to explain the Shinto philosophy. However, Van der Linden had been unable to comprehend the *kimochi*—the feeling, or that *kami*—god—simply meant a feeling of awe for superior things in nature. He had laughed at the thought of thousands of shrines set up around Japan in honor of a mountain, a unique tree, a mammoth rock. And yet he had been an authority on various aspects of history and mythology. He had presented Kenichi with his own account of

Japan's origins, in which the sun goddess and her headstrong brother became the parents of eight offspring, the first of which became an ancestor of Japan's hereditary emperors, descending to earth to rule Japan, bringing with him a sacred sword, jewels, and a mirror—those three emblems that still formed a part of imperial regalia.

On a very different, a most formidable level the Hollander had made a prediction, declaring that a time of tragedy and chaos would inevitably ensue. "Mark my words," he said. "Before this century ends there will be tragedy and chaos in this land. The government's men, so autocratic, so arrogant, know only too well that warriors clad in ancient armor, carrying spears, swords, and bows could stand no chance against the well-equipped soldiers of the West."

To Kenichi's mind the century still had a long way to go before heralding in the new. He had no wish to burden himself with frets belonging to the future. All in all, his life was very pleasant.

Van der Linden was not among the present delegation from Dejima and Kenichi never expected to come across the fellow again.

N O LONGER BOUND BY THE pangs of jealousy and love, Kenichi took on a new lease of life. With his conscience untroubled he determined to keep up appearances and to pretend that all was well between himself and Osen. He was even more generous toward her and her family and skillfully hid his disgust at old Shiga coughing, as she attempted to clear her congested lungs from the effects of winter illness.

Her condition pleased Kenichi, for it kept the sharp-eyed old woman out of the picture for the time being at least, thereby allowing him to play his game without her becoming alert to the true situation.

He felt confident that Osen was completely ignorant about his future plans, and to bolster her confidence he took to alluding to himself and his mistress as *oshidori*—a faithful mandarin-duck couple, a domesticated pair finished with the exhaustion and the excitability of frenzied, gluttonous lovemaking, more than content to live on together in a satisfying but more easygoing way.

To all outward appearances, Osen had no qualms and was busy making plans not merely for the present but well on into the future. She confided in him one cold night as they lay snugly beneath a newly purchased swansdown coverlet, saying, "In three years' time Mother achieves her fiftieth year of life. To celebrate that auspicious event, could we, do you agree, all go on a pilgrimage? Travel to the sacred shrine of Ise?"

"Why not . . . ? Why not . . . ?" he had murmured sleepily. "It is the hope of every Japanese to visit the shrines there at least once in a lifetime. You could—to give her comfort—in case she should leave this world before that time, inform her—your mother—that the *kamidana*—god shelf—in this very house is made from wood of those holy shrines at Ise."

Osen, torn between awe and the dread thought of her mother's demise, sat up, crying out, "Now, is that *so*? Now, is that *really* so?"

"Indeed it is. Does my little duck-partner not know custom demands that the shrines must be rebuilt every twenty years?"

"You must excuse me. I did not know."

"Well, now you do. Wood from the demolished buildings are cut up—into tablets—then dispensed throughout the land. Please relax and lie down again. The cold air is not exactly pleasing."

Osen's affection for, and her pride in the youth Yuji, continued to know no bounds. Although disappointed that Kenichi had not agreed to the boy attending a school, she never tired of lauding his accomplishments, praising the progress he was making as an apprentice to an acupuncturist. A diagnostician of some repute who had taken Yuji into his establishment informed Kenichi that the lad had just the right hands necessary for the practice of acupuncture.

On recalling the doctor's comments, Kenichi observed Yuji's hands and did not find them in any way superior to the hands of most Japanese people. They were agile and smooth-skinned, different indeed from the huge, clumsy hands of the Dutchmen he had been meeting with over the years. He admired the brawny strength, the long legs of those foreigners, but their hands were abhorrent to him.

Indeed, Kenichi's ambivalent attitude toward the Dutch went back quite a long way. Shortly before his marriage he traveled from Edo to Nagasaki as a junior member of a government delegation. Once there, they had crossed over a causeway to the small island of Dejima.

He had felt sympathy for the Dutch residents, who were in fact prisoners, but he had also despised them, scarcely believing that for two hundred years men had been coming from Holland who had willingly demeaned themselves, living in tiny foreign-style houses beside immense warehouses, always under guard, behind gates which were barred at sunset.

One of Kenichi's superiors had told him how Dutch ships bringing rich cargoes were diligently searched to prevent weapons and Christian books from being smuggled ashore.

The same man had sneered as he described how those shameless Dutchmen actually seemed to enjoy the treks they took to Edo, carrying with them precious information from the West concerning progressive studies in scientific, military, and political affairs. And once in Edo, they would crawl on all fours into the presence of the shogun. Then they would proceed to entertain government officials by singing queer songs and performing crazy jigging dances.

Well, certainly there was not a Japanese ever born, Kenichi was certain, who would not have preferred death to undergoing such indignities, especially in the name of trade and finance. Those Hollanders were strange beyond his understanding. Nevertheless, being the man he was, he had often chided himself about the aversion he had, not only for the outward strangeness of the Dutchmen's physical features, but also for their boorish manners. Then he would excuse himself, quite certain that those *gaijin* opinions concerning the Japanese race were not complimentary—except where females of the species were involved.

During that long trek to the school's Dutch headquarters in Nagasaki he had been shocked to learn that many of the Nagasaki prostitutes preferred submitting to their pleasures rather than to men of their own race.

One night several years earlier, just for a lark, he had purchased a painting in the Yoshiwara depicting life in just such a Nagasaki establishment. A painting with its design clearly based on that of such a couple emphasizing the foreigner's long fingernails, high, beaky nose, long curly hair, and beard and *over*emphasizing—to his mind—the man's enormous genitalia.

He had shown that work to Osen, and she had reacted not laughingly, but angrily. Instead of becoming erotically aroused as he had hoped and expected, she had become hysterical, crying out in disgust, "To see a Japanese girl so *happy* with a hairy barbarian! Too ugly! Too bad. . . ." And to his annoyance she had ripped the painting into shreds.

As winter progressed, Kenichi realized to his consternation that he had become an ungainly figure of a man.

For the past three years he had bathed with Osen in the bathroom of the Nihombashi house. For the past two years her sisters, Kiku and Ume, had usually been present to scrub his back, massage his shoulders, and tend to their sister's fastidious demands.

Osen never drew attention to his protruding belly, and her humble sisters would not have dared to. Not once had they ever addressed him directly, nor he either of them.

One morning while wallowing in the bath, his protruding stomach hidden from sight, with only his head above water, he saw the two girls as though for the first time, and once again he wished an artist were present to capture that which he alone beheld. Osen, her voluptuous body naked, sat on a low wooden stool, her shoulders plumply rounded, her breasts pear-shaped, firmly virginal. She made little murmuring sounds, instructing Kiku, who, kneeling at her feet, was busily trimming her idol's toenails. Behind her stood Ume, intent on plaiting Osen's luxuriantly long hair into one braid, threaded through with a crimson ribbon.

How strange it was, he pondered, that the three females had come from the same womb. Not one of Shiga's daughters bore the slightest resemblance to the mother. Languorously, he envisioned the men from whose seeds they had sprung.

Osen? In all probability from a man of quality, one disturbingly handsome. A man in all likelihood too intoxicated to care that he had used a common harlot in a hasty encounter . . .

Kiku—chrysanthemum, so wrongly named, fragile, pale-skinned, had most likely been fathered by an unhealthy, overworked fellow; different indeed from Ume—plum-blossom, also wrongly named. Her squat body was dark-skinned; most certainly she had come from the seed of a brawny man of the soil.

Shiga, a scavenging fowl, had produced Kiku, the albino sparrow, Ume, a dark-feathered starling, and Osen . . . ? No doubt about her! Although a hen, she had sprouted the exotic colors of a magnificent male peacock. . . .

A strange, a unique trio! They made an entertaining picture, but he had been in the hot water long enough.

Impatiently, he exclaimed, "*Kekkō desu*—enough! I have an appointment." The two girls bowed low, hastily patted Osen's body dry. As he stepped from the tub, Osen rose leisurely to her feet, holding her arms out to don the cotton garment Kiku held, while Ume stood by in readiness to attend to Kenichi's needs. . . .

Determined to regain his physical fitness before showing himself once again in the bathhouses, Kenichi began an arduous exercise program.

He bitterly resented those youthful years spent exercising his mind so much instead of his body in the manner of true samurai training. Dr. Yamamoto, that stern taskmaster, had ignored his son's wishes, exclaiming adamantly, "Sword practice! You are, always shall be a *scholar*. We scholars have no time, no right to indulge in the martial arts. Judo? Yes. It strengthens not the body alone but also the mind and the spirit of the *true* samurai. Practice judo, Kenichi, and become an expert. Learn that with bare hands any judo expert is able to conquer an opponent by dodging and awaiting the moment when his sword lunges into the void, then wresting his weapon from his hands, slinging him down, yes, to decapitate him with his own sword. You may wonder why we Japanese have not utilized those firearms brought to our land by the Portuguese centuries ago—except for hunting purposes, that is. Tell me, do you know why that is so?"

"I do, Father."

"So then—tell me."

"We consider firearms to be cowardly weapons."

"We do indeed! Why?"

"Because . . ." the young Kenichi had parrotted sulkily, "a true samurai looks his enemy in the eye and bravely conquers him."

Well, he had become a black-belt judo man, and he was confident of his prowess in that field. But now, after years of laziness, his muscles ached as he worked his body back into condition, at the judo club. However, the results were worthwhile and Kenichi called in fabric merchants and tailors, intent on arraying himself in new garments, with no expense spared.

To allay Osen's suspicions, he insisted that she also indulge herself, and for many days the main room of the house was filled with rivers of colorful fabric as the merchants unrolled their bolts of silks, brocades, velvets, and cotton cloths.

In coming to know Okura's mistress, Keiko, Kenichi was discovering "a new woman." He had never been interested in or attracted to the geisha world, for times spent in those houses were strictly asexual, costly hours. *Gei*, meaning "art" and *sha*, meaning "person," the occupation of these women was art with a capital *A*, and their exhaustive training began before their tenth year.

It was a popular, manly habit for one to move on and patronize a licensed house of prostitution after the pure delights of being in the company of elegantly robed, meticulously mannered geisha.

Kenichi likened his frequent visits to Okura's "second home" to entering into a new climate. Okura himself took on a different personality in that house; he shed his accustomed lethargy and arrogance, and together with Keiko spoke openly to Kenichi about their relationship of some seven years' standing. He explained how his father, Count Okura, had taken his son as a young man to a prestigious geisha house in order to introduce him into the "world of women," and avoid the nervous dread felt by most youths during their early sexual encounters. Visits to a geisha house, where no sex was involved, gave a young man polish and confidence before embarking on sex, which was a skill one could not master from hearsay or from books as, for instance, one could master the craft of kite-making.

"I frequented that house for many years," Okura murmured. "I scarcely noticed Keiko."

"True, that is so," Keiko agreed.

"Neither of us fell in love one with the other."

"True, that is so."

"But over the years we formed feelings of mutual ease within our hearts and achieved a wordless language of understanding." Okura folded both arms across his chest, smiled contentedly, then added, "It is still so with us."

"Yes," Keiko repeated gently. "It is still so with us. . . ."

After a lengthy pause Okura said, "After my marriage, after the birth of my legal daughter, I spoke to my father, who, with my interests at heart, made a contract with the geisha house, confirming that I should become Keiko's sole patron and protector, and . . ." Okura said emphatically, "so, I shall remain."

"How fortunate," Kenichi said solemnly, "to be so at ease, so content."

"We do have clashes of opinions," Keiko said, laughing.

"We clash all the time," grinned Okura. "On many a subject and with much enjoyment. Most women's opinions fall like flower petals, without a sound. Not so with this woman. I warn you, take care before tangling with Keiko on any given topic."

"Please, Yamamoto Sama," Keiko exclaimed. "Ignore that bold remark, *I beg of you*. Intellectually, I am but a babe. I know of and respect the honorable work you are involved in."

"You do?" Kenichi interrupted in astonishment.

"She does if she so declares." Okura laughed heartily. "I know not how, but she has ways of gleaning news and information. Remember, I warned you."

"Hmm . . . !" Kenichi, playing the game, pretended seriousness. "In truth, I'm not certain which one of you to believe."

"Both of us," cried Keiko smilingly.

"Both of us." Okura echoed her words, then said, "How time flies in good company! I must away. My wife and I are attending a ceremony this evening. Keiko, please have Rumi brought in. I wish to see her."

"Have you the time to spare?" Keiko's tone was concerned. "I know how the Lady Akiko frets when you are tardy."

"I have time. Have no concern on that score."

A nursemaid ushered in a small girl who, on seeing her father, ran straight to him, and Kenichi witnessed yet another side of the friend he had believed he knew so well. Okura obviously adored his illegitimate daughter and spent ten minutes fondling and teasing her into peals of laughter while Keiko looked on, her plain face suddenly radiant.

That evening, when he was back in the Nihombashi house, Kenichi was unable to put the pleasant scene out of his mind. Keiko, he mused, reminded him of a unique white pigeon that Dr. Yamamoto treasured greatly. To the doctor's delight, the pouter pigeon made soft, cooing sounds, like a dove. "A treasure beyond price she is," the old scholar always declared.

The four-year-old girl, Rumi, was to Kenichi's mind the most delectable child he had ever beheld. In no way had she inherited her mother's plainness, and without doubt she would develop into a remarkable beauty. Her ancestry on her father's side was noble, and Kenichi wondered whether he should mention the idea of her future marriage to his son, Renzō.

When spring arrived, Kenichi, once again slim, fit, and full of plans for his future, went about feeling as though a metamorphosis had taken place not only in his appearance, but also in his soul. Determined to gain complete freedom, and using the pretext of facilitating Shiga's recovery from her long illness, he sent her and her three daughters to stay in a hot-spring resort, one popular with small-time merchants and their women of the moment. Following the excited exodus of the women, Sudo had gone off to the Yokohama school with the results of February's laborious work, leaving Kenichi and Yuji the sole inhabitants of the house in Edo.

One spring afternoon, Kenichi, robed in new finery, traveled through the narrow, unpaved Edo streets in a litter on his way to attend a party at Okura's second home.

The entire city appeared to be one great sweep of blossoms as throngs of people prepared for the cherry-viewing festival. Everyone was dressed in their best and eager to indulge in both the spectacle of beauty and in quantities of *sake*.

From Okura's house, set on a bank of the Sumida River, Edo was like a huge sparkling jewel at night. Junks with lights at their mastheads slid silently over the purple haze of the water and echoes of laughter floated across the river from the tea houses and the shops festooned with red and orange lanterns.

While Kenichi sat with his friends on the raised veranda-platform in a state of dreamlike tipsiness, he thought he could ask no more of life. Okura and Shiro had taken him into their midst, and if memories of the happy trio he had once formed with Okura and Fukuda intruded on his thoughts, he quickly banished them.

Shiro reminded Kenichi of one who sat alone, like a rock, immovable in a receding tide. Then, at times his "climate" changed and he was reckless and disorganized but never in any way vindictive. In fact, he had been known to burst into tears publicly when hearing about the plight of other people.

As Kenichi took in the panorama of the river, the city, and the close-up images of those sitting with him, he especially admired the costumes of two young geisha whom Keiko had engaged to entertain Okura and his male guests on the festive occasion.

The two girls were as charming as nature and art allowed, delighting in their own delightfulness and ready to please. Kenichi, cleansed as he was—for the time being at least—from feelings involving sexual desires, took an aesthetic interest and enjoyment in their appearances, especially one girl whom he found daringly modern in her choice of garments and decorative accessories. Her hair, black with blue lights and gleaming where it was stiffened and gummed in intricate bands and loops, bristled with ornate jewel-tipped pins and artificial cherry blossoms. Her constant fan-fluttering displayed her arms under the winglike sleeves of her kimono, which was of heavy silk in a bewildering symphony of colors. Her long-hanging sleeves were lined with pale pink, and above her silver *obi-*

sash, one slim slip of apple-green cord showed. The all-important cord kept the immense, bulging bow of her sash firmly in its place.

Kenichi listened to the animated discussion between the girl and Okura.

"You are so correct, Okura Sama. I also dislike camellia bushes. Their flowers fall to the ground while still bright and in their prime."

"Yes, yes," Shiro interjected brusquely. "No Japanese really likes them. Much too reminiscent of the decapitation of young folk in our land."

"Exactly!" Okura agreed.

"Flowers are so important in our lives." Keiko joined in the discussion, her voice slightly mischievous. "One must have great care. To give an example, I know of one careless family who chose a *bridal* kimono for their daughter with a *hydrangea* design!"

"Oh, but surely not!" exclaimed the young geisha as though in a state of shock.

"They did," replied Keiko. "And, of course, just as those lovely flowers change their color as they fade, exemplifying inconstancy, so it was with that marriage."

"True," agreed Okura. "That marriage was a complete disaster."

"Nonsense! Complete nonsense!" Shiro exclaimed as he leapt to his feet and strode about, brandishing his arms. "I begin to feel as though I'm at a funeral! My tension is high! I must be stimulated."

"But certainly! By all means," cried Keiko, her voice comfortingly sympathetic. "Would you have a litter take you to the Yoshiwara?"

"By all means, yes," Shiro muttered as he lost his balance and stumbled over a floor-cushion. As he rose to his feet the two young geisha rearranged his disheveled garments and held him steady.

"Later, later, Shiro," Okura suggested soothingly. "Rest here a while longer."

"Yes, yes," chorused Keiko and the two girls. "Wait for just a while longer."

"If you so insist . . ." Shiro allowed himself to be seated once more. To keep him alert and amused, Keiko suggested that the two entertainers put on a titillating theatrical act, and without more ado, the girls fell to the floor and lay there prone. Then with great expertise they enacted two women to whom passionate love was being made. So clever was the enactment that those present egged the girls on, encouraging them in a ribald manner, criticizing the nonexistent males' lack of erotic skills, and when at long last, after many hilarious comments from the geisha, the two imagined males reached their climax, the girls leapt to their feet and inquired of each other, "How was it with you?"

"How was it with *you*, Ma-chan?"

"No different from usual. How was it with *you*?"

"No different from usual! No climax for us! Isn't it usually so?"

"Absolutely! Sister, let us go tomorrow to the shrine and give thanks to the Fukuda factory owners, to those makers of 'adult toys' which they make available for the unsatisfied ladies of Japan. In all probability we are all, of necessity, champions in the practice of onanism."

Their reference to Fukuda's new "adult toys" which were flooding shops in the city and the Yoshiwara aroused a storm of ironical laughter, and Shiro, his tensions soothed out, fell asleep instantly. Keiko thanked the talented girls and ordered refreshments for them. After their little feast, litters were called and the girls were escorted back to their geisha house.

Kenichi lingered on, awaiting the sunrise, and when dawn streaked the sky, he, Keiko, and Okura gazed out over the clouds of pink cherry blossom adorning the city.

"Japan," murmured Okura. "No land so beautiful."

"No land so beautiful!" Keiko echoed softly, bowing deeply in the direction of the ancient Imperial Palace.

Okura followed suit, Kenichi also, but as he bowed low he thought of the emperor, *not* in the Edo Palace but a "prisoner" in Kyoto. . . . "*Shiyō ga nai*—Nothing to be done about that!" he thought. Things as they were could scarcely be improved on as far as his own life went.

There came a bittersweet day of wind when a rain of pink petals fell over the city and the festive season was over. But the greening of the trees delighted the people too, and they went in droves to stand before the Imperial Palace to view the young willow trees reflected in the still waters of the moat. Those who were able rode out into the countryside to picnic and listen to bursts of bird song and see the first butterflies of the season. Many people composed poems about those winged creatures because one of the most popular myths of their country was that butterflies were the ghosts of people who had been cruelly treated during their earthly life.

Early one morning Kenichi joined Okura and some of their friends on such a picnic. Keiko and her daughter, Rumi, both traveled in a litter while the men rode horseback. Okura often wheeled his mount around to keep the woman and little girl company.

Attendants had gone ahead of the picnickers, carrying cushions, food, and wine as well as charcoal to be fired in readiness for the preparation of tea.

While Rumi frisked about chasing butterflies, the adults lounged at ease, enjoying the rusticity, at times silent, then alert. They began quoting and discussing famous poems, comparing those from the brushes of men with those composed by women. Keiko finally exclaimed with confidence, "Many of the most powerful masterpieces were composed by highly educated women during the tenth and the eleventh centuries."

"True," Kenichi agreed admiringly. "Allow me to take us even further back to where, in the eighth century, women composed great works. Yes, even further back to the works by the Empress Kogyoku, who left this world in the year six hundred sixty or thereabouts."

"I prefer the poetry of today," Shiro exclaimed. "For instance, listen to this:

> *"What a delight it is*
> *When a guest you cannot stand*
> *Arrives, then says to you*
> *'I'm afraid I can't stay long,'*
> *And soon goes home."*

"How perfectly that poem expresses your dour character." Okura grinned at his half-brother affectionately. "For myself, well, listen to this!

> *"What a delight it is*
> *When, skimming through the pages*
> *Of a book, I discover*
> *A man written of there*
> *Who is just like me."*

"Could there, oh, *could* there ever have been so remarkable a book written?" exclaimed Keiko with teasing laughter in her voice, and as she gazed at Okura, Kenichi was aware of the depth of her love for her protector.

OSEN AND HER RETINUE RETURNED to the Nihombashi house with their spirits dampened, for Shiga, their mother, had not responded to the therapy of the hot-spring treatments. On the contrary, she had lost weight, her digestion was troubling her, and she complained about a blurriness in her once-sharp eyesight.

Her three daughters went about in a frenzied search for assistance; they visited shrines and soothsayers, purchased high-priced advice and blessings, but to no avail. Panic-stricken, they called on the services of an old medico who gave Shiga moxa treatments—the burning of a cone of moxa powder on the patient's skin. The smell of singed flesh in the house was an odor that Kenichi found obnoxious. But he made no complaints; while in the house, he grimly followed the tried and true adage, "Bear with it! Give in! Why not lose to win!"

Having few memories of his own mother, he found the behavior and the attitudes of Shiga's daughters admirable, but difficult to understand. But once again he felt relieved at having Osen so completely distracted.

One morning, early in the oppressively humid rainy season, he caught a glimpse of Osen, her face grimaced by worry as she carried her mother pick-a-back from the house on the way to visit an acupuncturist. The sight repelled him. His former passion for the courtesan had ruled his life so strongly and for so long that he was still undergoing moments of bewilderment about his changed feelings toward her. At such times he comforted himself by recalling to mind the Buddhist proverb: "The fallen flower returns not to its branch." Yes, he mused, so it was then with a once-hot passion turned cold.

The pandemonium and the unpleasant odor of ill health that were now pervading his once delightful house drove Kenichi out into the city. However, the rain, blessed by the farming community, made the streets a quagmire of mud. Kenichi, the landlord of many rice fields, also blessed the rain but wished it would not fall so continuously over Edo.

His conscience was bothering him slightly, for Sudo had returned from Yokohama with a letter from Masa informing him that Dr. Yamamoto had suffered from the results of a severe lung infection and that the old gentleman, she felt sure, would appreciate a visit from his son. Kenichi sent a reply by special courier, assuring Masa that only the pressure of work—not the weather as her letter had suggested—was preventing him from hastening to his father's side.

While waiting for the weather to clear up, he spent his days most enjoyably in the company of Okura, Shiro, and various other brother-samurai. The group wandered around town and occasionally attended sumo contests, at which they placed bets on their giantlike favorites and sometimes won or lost sizable amounts of cash.

In truth, he had no taste for sumo wrestling. That sport, to his mind, consisted of too much preparation and anticipation, then it was all over in a flash. He much preferred jaunts to the various artists and potters, whose skills Okura was so conversant with. Kenichi, aware of his friend's worrisome financial situation, was nonplussed by Okura's readiness to pay high prices for works of art that took his fancy. He was wont to exclaim, "I like it! I shall have it!"

Although highly educated in the classics and skilled in the martial arts, the half brothers Okura and Shiro had never so much as dreamed of taking up any employment; they considered it below their dignity, coming as they did from a long, distinguished line of nobles. If either man was aware of changes taking place in society, such as merchants on the rise because of the wealth flowing into their coffers, they ignored the state of affairs with haughty aplomb.

At times while in their company, Kenichi was reminded of his wife, for their wit was as sharp as a sword blade and their comments as devastatingly honest. Like Masa too, they showed no cold malice.

However, unlike his wife, the two men held little respect for the mikado dwelling in far-off Kyoto. They also had dangerously arrogant attitudes toward the daimyō—the lords—who dwelt in their immense Edo mansions.

Certain daimyō still ruled tyrannically with small armies of war-trained samurai and soldier-farmers in their domination. They continued to disregard the statutes and to breach laws with impunity.

Kenichi had an inbuilt dread of those lords and was always careful to bow low when their processions passed. He was aware that both Okura and Shiro held him in some contempt because of his attitudes, but he ignored their scorn.

One morning, awakening with his head throbbing painfully after a night of heavy drinking, Kenichi interrupted Osen's melodramatic description of her mother's condition and shouted to her. "Be silent! Such talk disgusts me."

Osen, startled and hurt, arose from the *futon* they shared, and said with dignity, "Is that so?"

"It is so."

"So then, excuse me. Maybe, until my mother's health improves I should sleep beside her, along with Yuji and my sisters, who sincerely care about her."

"Maybe you should" was his curt response as he left for the bathhouse to indulge in a bout of professional massage. After an hour in the steamy, comforting atmosphere, both his mood and his head cleared up and he promised himself to go lightly on the *sake* bottle, no matter the circumstances.

For some time Kenichi had been looking forward to accompanying Okura on a visit to an artist by the name of Nozaka, a man whose work had recently been much acclaimed. The appointment was for that afternoon, and to kill time he returned to the Nihombashi house, stopping on his way to purchase a bonsai tree, one quite precious, its gnarled branches aglow with minute peach blossoms.

Presenting the gift to Osen, he murmured, "I hope this will cheer your mother's spirit." His mistress's face had glowed with pleasure, her beauty no less than that of the blossoms themselves.

To his relief, Kenichi arrived at Nozaka's studio precisely at the moment when two litters pulled up. Okura, resplendent in his raiment, alighted from one while Shiro, very much the worse from copious wine drinking, stumbled out of the other, announcing with cold scorn, "Already I'm yawning with boredom."

"Come along, be patient . . ." Okura coaxed his brother who was attempting to scramble back into the litter. Finally, after much altercation, Shiro was led inside the establishment and held firmly upright by his two companions.

Kenichi was embarrassed by Shiro's intoxicated state, for it was surely a great insult to the man of fame whose house they were entering. However, on meeting with Nozaka, his embarrassment melted like a snowflake on a hot plate, for the elderly artist was beaming with a wicked gaiety and welcomed Shiro, calling out cheerily, "Fortunate man to be so drunk. Lie on the *tatami*. Have a snooze. I also drink heavily. I'm forced into it. Wine bolsters up my enthusiasms. I loathe painting commissioned works, especially of late. So many clients want studies in black and white. To get fine point-tips I suck my brushes. It's a miracle I'm not completely black from all the India ink I've been swallowing. Truthfully, if I had my way, I would spend my time painting nothing but eyes. I have a passion for painting eyes. Eyes are my fetish. For the pupils I form a dull purple tone by mixing red, white, and yes, India ink. . . ."

Kenichi was intrigued and kept his own eyes on the volatile artist whose feet were clad in worn black slippers, so that he slithered about the room as he spoke, examining the contents of many small bowls, each one filled with various colored powders. Finally, he pounced on one, added a little water, and stirred the bowl's contents rapidly with his forefinger, saying, "Pardon me Okura Sama, for holding you up, but I *must* attend to this."

In one skillful slide he reached a charcoal brazier. Holding the bowl above it, he announced loudly, still stirring with his finger, "I heat so many of these substances, it's a miracle I have not stewed my finger into a soft mush."

"You should treasure your hands, Nozaka Sensei," Okura exclaimed, breaking into the artist's spiel. "I hesitate to ask, but may I and my companions have a viewing of your *kakimono?*"

Satisfied with the substance in the bowl, Nozaka placed it tenderly on a low shelf and covered it with a paint-stained damp cloth. Then, with one giant glide he crossed the room, slid open the doors, and gestured his guests into the adjoining room.

On entering the room, Nozaka at once took on a different personality; his manner was aloof and his expression absolutely blank as he gestured that the three men should seat themselves.

Nozaka moved to a nearby shelf and stood there deliberating before carefully removing a long, narrow plain wooden box from some several dozen stacked on the shelf. As the artist slid the lid open and removed a scroll, Kenichi noticed that Okura's fan had become motionless, all his attention concentrated on the article which Nozaka was slowly unfurling with infinite care.

Finally the entire work could be viewed. Against a haze of pale blue background were seven *chidori*, a species of bird said to have been born from the froth off the crests of waves. They were flying in a haphazard arrangement, their brown wings delicately outlined with chalk white, and high on the right side of the work was one splash of vermilion; Nozaka's name-stamp motif of three gingko blossoms.

No one spoke, no one moved. Then Okura murmured, "*Kekkō*

desu—it is perfect! It suits my needs." He bowed with ceremonial respect to the artist, then immediately arose in readiness to depart.

No mention was made as to price, or when the purchaser would collect the work of art. Nozaka lay the masterpiece upon a pristinely clean mat and ushered the men into his studio, where he went straight to uncover the bowl he had been so intent on, saying, "Unforgivable, I know, but please let yourselves out. This substance needs my *full* attention."

Emerging into the street, Shiro at once took command, saying to Okura, "Now that's all over! You seem more than satisfied, yes?"

"Absolutely," Okura replied. "The work is exactly what I fancied."

Okura took Shiro by the arm, saying, "Let's away to the bathhouse to relax. Yes?"

"No!" shouted Shiro. "No. I'm low in my tension. I must drink up."

"I agree. Yes, we'll all drink up, by all means. So, come along. Let's go."

"To where? Why go from here? I'm in no mood to shove slowly through these crowded streets."

Even as he spoke, the people in the street drew to each side, leaving a clear passage as the sounds of stamping feet and of voices grew louder. "*Make way* . . . Make way . . . *Make way for the mighty one.* . . ."

As though in obedience to those commands, rain poured down drenching the people, who, Kenichi included, fell to their knees. Oblivious of the mud and the slush, they touched their foreheads to the ground as a *daimyō* and his retinue approached in a slow, stately procession. The man was borne aloft in an immense, highly decorated palanquin carried by eight men and surrounded by some twenty soldier-guards in dramatic battle dress and with their gauntleted hands at the ready on their sword hilts.

Suddenly Shiro's voice rang out loud and clear, shouting, "You should go to Kyoto to play your games! Go back to the *old* capital. *Edo* belongs to the *common man!*"

A loud sigh of shock ran through the kneeling crowd. Amazed and terrified, Kenichi raised his head to see Shiro fronting the procession, his arms outstretched as though determined to halt its progress.

A guard stepped forward, his sword drawn. Shiro was instantly slain.

. . .

Even when the rainy season was over the citizens of Edo were still discussing the tyrannical slaying of Shiro. Society was divided into two factions; one claimed that the man was a disturber of the peace and had received his just deserts. The other faction muttered among themselves, declaring that Shiro, although inebriated at the time, had voiced the thoughts of the "new man." A great majority of the citizens were no longer content to smile, grit their teeth, and endure so many despotic, outdated laws and restrictions.

Kenichi belonged to neither faction. To his mortal shame he had fallen into a deep swoon on that terrible day and had never quite apprehended how he found himself back in the Nihombashi house late in the night, with Osen and her sisters hovering over his disheveled person.

Perhaps it was the unendurable shock he had received, or perhaps the drenched apparel he wore had caused him to undergo the first serious illness of his life. He lay in a state of high fever with a cruel, unquenchable thirst for several weeks. During that dark period his sleep was disturbed by nightmares that caused him to thrash his limbs and to call out, his voice hoarse with terror. His dreams were bloody and macabre and so complex that his actual memory of Shiro's russet-gowned, headless torso lying in the mud beneath the falling rain was lost to him forever.

One night during his illness he overheard Yuji's voice, high and excited, exclaiming, " 'Tis said in the city that Okura Sama and his samurai brothers took the corpse to a secret place and mourned over it for eight days. Yes, it's said they reverted to feudal funeral rites. Yes, and kept fires burning day and night, had musicians to play flutes and drums, dancers to dance. And *shinobigoto* poems to praise the dead were recited, and . . ."

That night Kenichi's nightmares were even more macabre, and in them Shiro, alive but with the face of a demon, stood unharmed in the midst of a fire, screeching with cruel laughter as Kenichi, mud-spattered and tormented, knelt on the ground holding *his* severed head in his hands, attempting to place it back on his torso, mouthing soundlessly, "I'm *alive* . . . not *dead*. . . . See, give me *time*. . . . *See,* my head is still with me. . . . Give me time to place it back where it belongs. . . ."

Following his recovery, he built a cocoon about himself, never venturing from the house. His mood was morose and he drank *sake* to blur his feelings of fear, certain that his unmanly behavior had brought about the end of his treasured friendship with Okura.

For all his effete, decadent ways, Okura considered samurai camaraderie to be all-important. Kenichi swooned whenever blood flowed, and he was certain that he had lost face forever. The thought was so painful to bear that there were times when he considered that it would be easier to end his life than show himself to the world.

Then early one morning Okura sent an emissary to the Nihombashi house, requesting that Kenichi honor him by a visit to the Okura mansion. As Kenichi perused the epistle his spirits rose, for Okura had written to say that no one had paid more honor to their deceased samurai brother than had Yamamoto San. "Others might see it from a different view," he wrote, "but I fully comprehend the breadth of sorrow, the suffering you have undergone."

In a trice Kenichi was filled with vitality and he bathed and robed himself in readiness for his journey back to respectability.

He paid no attention to Osen's chatter, for his mind was buzzing with thoughts he preferred to banish hastily. Could it be that by receiving him, Okura was now repaying that *on*—that debt? No. No, surely not in such a manner . . .

Then, could it be that Okura was once more in need of financial help and . . . ? That thought was even more insulting to his friend. . . .

If Kenichi left the Nihombashi house filled with high hopes, the Shiga women were ecstatically happy after his departure, stripping off their gowns, wearing only wraparound undergarments tied about their waists, sitting at ease fluttering fans, relishing a feast of *sushi*. "Ah—the relief!" "How good not to have a male lounging about."

"*Hai*—yes," old Shiga agreed. "Men clutter up a house. It's good to have them just come and go and so on."

"I agree," Osen said strongly. "Today I intend to relax completely and . . ."

"Not so! Not so!" exclaimed her mother. "Beautiful, seductive you may be, but pray keep in mind you are not his registered wife. Keep in mind that my life, that Yuji's and your sisters' lives are in your keeping. Depending on *his* good graces!"

"How well I know," Osen interrupted. "Have no fears."

"Fears," exclaimed Shiga. "For women such as we, fear lurks in every corner, during every moment of our lives, Osen. Even *my* blurred eyes show that your hair appears dull. That your eyebrows have need of the razor . . ."

"It is true," murmured Ume. "Sister, even as I sit here I see two small red blotches on the flesh of your back."

Horror-stricken, Osen ordered Kiku to bring her two hand mirrors, using them to study her back and shoulders. "True," she moaned. "What a catastrophe! I've been so casual of late, but he's been so ill. He's had no desire for my body."

"Call in the cosmetician," Shiga commanded. "Kiku, have we a good supply of rice powder bath-bags?"

"We have."

"Then—to the bath, Osen! You also, Kiku, and polish your sister's skin with the bags until it shines and glows."

As Osen sat by while her sisters scurried about to obey their mother's instructions, Shiga continued on, speaking sternly to her treasured daughter, saying, "When the master returns, he must see you as through new eyes. You must spend this day using *all* available resources to rebeautify yourself. I warn you. *Males* are *enhanced* by the passing years, but not so females. Are you paying attention?"

"Yes," replied Osen casually. "But beauty such as mine can scarcely be compared with that of other women. . . ."

"Enough!" cried Shiga. "Your too-confident manner turns my blood to ice even in this great heat. . . ."

As Kenichi walked through the heat of the day, his mood rose and fell in an extraordinary manner. One moment he was exhilarated and at ease, the next moment he was in the depths of depression. How, he cogitated, would Okura receive him?

To school himself into a state of calm dignity, he recalled one of his father's lectures, almost hearing the dry voice saying, "All good men, no matter the circumstances, must do their utmost to get their world back into balance. One must show stoicism. In times of pain and stress, or times tainted by embarrassments, self-control must rise to the top."

Certainly, he mused, I failed to show stoicism. So, the severe illness I have endured might have been a blessing in disguise? With that thought uppermost, he put all trepidation away and entered the gloomy Okura mansion with slightly more confidence.

Three hours later, when he departed from the Okura mansion, his step was firm and his thoughts hurtled along with a wild vitality. Okura had received him as though he had been a long-lost brother.

With the ceremonious obeisances over, Okura spoke of Shiro warmly, his expression animated and his voice enthusiastic, saying, "Let us speak of our departed brother. The dead need our affection. Their spirits take comfort and joy from sincere, admiring comments about them."

"I agree. I agree."

"But of course! Shiro, even during his childhood, had a way of taking the law into his own hands. Our brother was a true swashbuckler."

"Indeed, a true samurai."

"Yes." Okura smiled strangely, then said, "But to his own undoing, he was possessed of unharnessed angers. Do you agree?"

Not certain that agreement was being sought, Kenichi refrained from replying by refilling Okura's *sake* bowl, then he murmured, "Ah, Shiro!"

"Yes," exclaimed Okura. "He zigzagged his way through life boldly. Always too game. He had a unique obsession for the common man's welfare. Do you agree?"

"Ah, Shiro!"

"Yes. His spirit must be rejoicing in the grief, the pain, and suffering you have undergone for his sake. So ill, so gaunt, so depleted."

"Don't mention it!" Kenichi's mind buzzed busily. Was it now *his* duty to swing the conversation into a lighter circle of human feelings? If so, what should he lead with? It must be a choice which would give no offense. There was always the weather? Boring, but a topic which often led off into many and varied directions.

"Are you," he queried, his voice thoughtfully concerned, "finding the heat, the summer's humidity, oppressive?"

"Very much so! Are you?"

"Very much so!" Kenichi paused then said, "However, in the near future I'm bound for my native village."

"Is that so?" Okura reached over to refill his companion's wine cup, at the same time murmuring, "Coincidently, I, together with my friend Ohara, plan to travel in the direction of Yokohama shortly."

"Is that so!"

"Yes. We intend to visit a monastery thereabouts. One which overlooks the ocean."

"I know it well."

"How interesting! Perhaps not a pleasing thought to you, but . . ."
A faint smile crossed his face as Okura mimed that he, Kenichi, and
Ohara could travel the same road to Yokohama together.

One hour later Kenichi understood that he was to become the
third party of a new trio. He also understood that Okura and Ohara
would visit and stay, for several days at least, as his guests in the
house on the hill.

Following that visit to Okura, Kenichi returned to the Nihombashi
house overflowing with joy, to be greeted by a woman so gorgeously robed, so ravishingly beautiful, it took him several moments
to realize that it was Osen who was kneeling before him on the
purple brocaded floor-cushion, murmuring sweetly, "Welcome!
Welcome back to your home!"

How extraordinary it is, he mused as he gazed at the courtesan,
that she now affects my emotions no more than were she in fact a
picture painted on a piece of paper. Nevertheless, as the evening
wore on he accepted her attentions and enjoyed the night's pleasures
she offered. When morning arrived, he awakened feeling as though
he had partaken of a health-improving tonic.

While preparing for the sojourn to Yokohama, he was overcome
by a longing to gaze out over the immense expanse of the ocean, to
be once again in the familiar surroundings of his birthplace. At the
same time, he showed generosity and kindness to those who dwelt
in the Nihombashi house; all five inmates were completely unaware
that when the winter season arrived they would be, certainly not
put out into the storms and snow, but no longer living beneath his
roof.

Several days before their departure for the fishing hamlet, the male
trio sat together with Keiko, who was preparing ceremonial tea.
Kenichi noticed that a branch of white azalea, arranged in a bronze
vase, stood in the recess below the plover bird scroll which he had
last seen in the old artist's studio.

"It was hung for your consideration," Okura murmured. "It is
my sincere wish that you accept it."

As he politely showed his appreciation, Kenichi's stomach heaved
unpleasantly. Recalling his nightmares, he knew that he would never
be able to enjoy the work of art.

Although Kenichi had enjoyed a slight acquaintanceship with

Ohara, he knew but little of his background or his character. After spending time in the man's company, he wondered whether Okura had intentionally chosen a companion entirely different in every way from Shiro. Ohara's family background was impeccable. His gentle charm and his pleasant nature always made for good companionship. Also, he was skilled in archery, that sport wherein more importance was attached to spiritual culture than to physical exercise, as every movement was strictly ceremonious.

The son of an aristocratic Kamakura family, Ohara was also a lover of nature. He was knowledgeable but never imposed his opinions unless requested to, and those virtues, together with his ability to drink quantities of wine and become mellow rather than obstreperous, made him a delightful friend and traveling companion.

The three samurai astride fine steeds and accompanied by their individual, heavily laden servitors finally set out from Edo one morning before sunrise, eager to be on the road before traffic and pedestrians slowed them down.

Kenichi felt ten years younger—free and on the move, looking forward to introducing his peers to the pleasures of his Yokohama home, to his scholarly, elegant old father, his handsome son. He had such confidence in Lady Masa's sophistication that the thought of informing her that he was bringing two guests to stay at the house on the hill had never once entered his mind.

After some hours of travel the men dismounted to rest while waiting for their henchmen. They made their way to a nearby shrine, which was one among thousands in the land built in honor of the rice goddess.

All such shrines had stone images of foxes. That tricky creature was held in dread superstition by most simple folk, who believed that a fox had the power to enter slyly into the body of females, often through the space between the flesh and the fingernail, and to live a life of its own, separate from the unfortunate woman harboring him.

The three men strolled along the dark, hard-pressed soil pathway to the simple building where, under the heavily thatched eaves, hung a polished mirror of bronze.

Ohara commented gently, "The mirror mutely advises one to look into one's own mind. Make certain that it is as clean as a correctly regulated instinct should keep it."

"Yes, yes," muttered Okura. "However, personally looking inward, I'm more concerned by the condition of my belly. It rumbles, calling for sustenance."

"Suffer no more," Kenichi replied, laughing. "Look, the henchmen have arrived."

Some two hours after their meal, and after riding over miles of unattractive marshland, the ocean lay before their gaze and soon they entered the tiny seacoast village of Yokohama.

Kenichi dismounted and greeted the old horsesmith, who sprang forward, ready to assist the two other riders and to lead the three horses on to the sand of Hommoku beach. Old fishermen left the mending of their nets to greet the newcomers, and several women brought wooden buckets of fresh water for the thirsty animals.

Kenichi recognized one woman, and intentionally did not meet her wistful gaze, for she was the mother of Yuji, and he refused to have his mind distracted from the pleasant atmosphere of the moment.

Speaking to Okura, he explained, "We now journey on foot. Have no fear, the horses are in good hands."

"On foot?" Okura's expression clouded slightly. "How far?"

"Not far!" Kenichi, in Nō drama fashion, placed one hand on the hilt of his sword, then slowly raising his other arm, he gestured sweepingly upward toward the pine-clad hill, saying, his tone deep, "There, to that house . . ."

The following afternoon Kenichi and his two companions wandered through the monastery grounds among the maples, sea pines, and stone lanterns, where they came upon a flight of steps leading to the peak of a granite cliff that stood high over the foam-flecked waves crashing below.

A falcon and several sky hawks soared above. From time immemorial they had nested and bred their young in the area, undisturbed by yellow-robed priests who came with their prayer wheels and whirled the handles while they recited prayers locked inside the sacred prayer boxes.

Okura and Ohara stood on the peak, viewing the panorama of the fishing hamlet and the ocean beyond. They were speaking together in quiet tones and Kenichi, seeing their contentment, moved some distance off.

He was feeling overly sensitive and apprehensive, as though a wraith with mischievous intent were playing with his emotions. Impatient to discover the cause, he decided to search back over the past hours, since he and his companions had arrived, exuberant and carefree, in the fishing hamlet.

When the trio arrived at the schoolhouse, the guardian of the gate ushered the travelers into the presence of Dr. Yamamoto, who greeted them without effusiveness, saying, "Your presence here is welcome. Please consider yourselves at home."

Okura, especially, had been seduced by the mellow, otherworldly atmosphere, by the figures bent over desks, and by the strangely pleasant odor emanating from aged books and documents. He would clearly have liked to linger on, but the old scholar let it be known by bowing to the nobleman that time was pressing, and he murmured, "Please call again, sometime at your pleasure."

The trio crossed the school's austere courtyard and Kenichi slid the gate open wide, standing aside for his friends to enter ahead of him. But Okura and Ohara both stepped backward, each with a hand raised, gesturing for silence. Bemused, Kenichi peered over Ohara's shoulder and saw only his wife, who stood with her son beneath a cascade of purple blossoms. She was laughing and telling Renzō not to pluck a particular branch from the vine: "No, no. Excuse me once again Ren-chan, but not *that* branch."

"Not *this* branch! Not *that* branch! Not *this* one . . . ?" Renzō had grown tall, but his boyhood fringe was not yet shaved off. He laughed, exclaiming, "Mother, why not have me pluck just any branch at random? No . . . ? Yes? No?"

Masa was about to reply, but on recognizing her husband, she immediately bowed as Renzō fell to his knees and placed his forehead to the ground that was carpeted with fallen purple petals.

From that moment onward, Kenichi had become newly aware of his home and of the gardens surrounding it, seeing it as through the eyes of his friends, who admired the house, the elegance of the rooms, and the balconies with their uninterrupted view over the fishing hamlet and the wide ocean.

"So exhilarating," Ohara exclaimed. "Compared with the sultry atmosphere of Edo."

"I am spellbound," Okura enthused. "Here, in this house, I have the illusion that I am not earthbound but floating. . . ."

"Such grandeur," Ohara interrupted. "The dark pines and cypresses against the blue of the sky. The sparkling ocean, the sampans and small boats. Absolutely everything caught in a tenuous, all-encompassing haze of brightness. This is indeed a miraculous place."

Naturally, Kenichi was pleased by his friend's reactions, but at the same time he was rather put out that he himself had never viewed his home and its surroundings with such enthusiasm.

Masa greeted and accommodated the guests with equanimity. She gave the impression that the visit of the two men was an expected and long-awaited pleasure. She informed them that the bathhouse was at their disposal and that the midday meal was ready when they desired to partake of it.

The meal was presented with no ostentation or special bowls, plates, or lacquerware other than those in daily use. But the two guests appreciated their age and quality. Okura's quiet comment, "Ah, these Raku tea bowls!" had opened up a discussion concerning the famous potter Raku, who had begun his craft during the sixth century in Kyoto. Kenichi himself had never given a thought to those antique tea bowls, brought to his home as part of his wife's dowry.

Yes, he mused, during that meal he had not felt like the master of his own establishment, but rather a common man on the periphery, an outsider in the presence of three people secure in their aristocratic family backgrounds. The three had an inborn rapport among them.

He had glanced across the table at Renzō, who was sitting up alert, with his back straight. The bloom of childhood not yet gone, his cheeks were flushed, his eyes bright, and his manner respectful, as he replied without a trace of shyness to occasional remarks directed to him.

Sometime after the meal he had overheard Ohara saying to Okura, "To have such a son! What a joy!"

"Yes," Okura had replied. "Very unfortunate that such a splendid boy should see so little of his father. As you say, Ohara, what a joy to have such a son."

Repressing memories of that incident, Kenichi recalled how Okura had suggested, in a gallant but teasing manner, that Lady Masa, his hostess, might take him on a guided tour of the house.

Masa, "the perfect wife," had glanced at her husband as though to gain his approval, and he alone had known that her dutiful manner was ironic in the extreme.

Ohara cocked his ear and murmured, "Who plays the flute so sweetly?"

Kenichi told him of the blind masseur and of his father's aviary, and Ohara expressed keen desire to visit those caged birds. Kenichi replied, "But certainly. He, the boy, will take you there."

He noticed that Renzō, hesitating, had sent a swift questioning glance toward his mother, who had replied, her voice almost inaudible, "By all means, Ohara Sama. My husband's son has a *deep* respect for his grandfather's feathered treasures."

Her comment caused the boy's cheeks to flush, but his eyes, and his mother's eyes too, sparkled with amusement. That intimate exchange now aroused a stab of resentment in Kenichi's heart. Surely, he pondered, he was not jealous of the bond between those two?

Tossing that thought aside, he recalled the interview he had had with his father. The old scholar, retired from family responsibilities, relied entirely on his son's trusteeship and he had listened, giving his full attention while being told of the ongoing financial aid to the Okura family. He finally acknowledged Kenichi's wisdom and fully agreed that his grandson's marriage into the noble family was an acceptable idea to say the least.

"But . . ." he had queried, "Kenichi, why be satisfied with Rumi, the geisha's illegitimate daughter?"

"Because, Father," he had explained earnestly, "Okura's legal daughter, Aiko, is frail. The child's mother is Okura's first cousin, and—"

"Say no more! Inbreeding in humans, as with creatures, seldom brings good results."

"Yes. Also, Father, the Okura family's straitened circumstances means that unless a son is born to them, they are bound to adopt their future son-in-law. Which, of course, means that the legal daughter's husband-to-be will give up his own family, become Okura in name!"

"That idea incenses me. Yamamoto, Renzō must remain!"

Warily he had prevented his father from questioning him on the touchy subjects of Sumiko's debacle of a marriage, and on his own relationship with the Edo courtesan. Instead, he went on to suggest that Renzō be given time off from his studies, thereby allowing Okura to study the boy's character.

"*Sō desu na!*—I concur with the idea," Dr. Yamamoto had murmured. "But how *long* are your guests to tarry here?"

"They are to depart tomorrow afternoon, Father."

"Then, so be it! Your son, unfortunately, has the characteristics of an eagle. Or, more to the point, a falcon who resents captivity and must be forcibly, relentlessly, trained into doing his duty. Also, unfortunately, your wife is guilty of interfering with his studies. Please take her to task. Insist that she ceases interfering on matters which are none of her concern."

"Certainly," he had replied, but, recalling his own study-tortured youth, he was pleased that Masa was keeping his son's welfare at heart. His own mother, even had she lived on, would not have dared to interfere on his behalf.

Before leaving his father's presence, he had agreed to stay on for several days after the guests had departed. The doctor was greatly disturbed by the recent demands made by the Americans, and he was intent on learning of the circumstances in full from his son.

Well, certainly nothing untoward had occurred during that interview to arouse his apprehensions. On the contrary, he had felt exhilarated and many lively, entertaining hours had fled by, for he, Okura, Ohara, and young Renzō had made their way down the hillside and there, on the crescent-shaped beach, they stripped to their loincloths and swam and lazed in the sun, all four of them lighthearted, joshing with the fisherfolk. Renzō, abrim with happiness, had been allowed to borrow Okura's black stallion and ride it into the sea, the horse and boy as one, filled with unfettered energy.

Kenichi now became aware that Okura and Ohara had climbed down the cliff-top steps. From his vantage point he saw that they were taking some interest in a group of fishermen who had come to the monastery to pray for muscle strength, knowing that the annual typhoon season was fast approaching.

Ohara's voice floated up to him, exclaiming, "See how the swallows are swooping over the roof of the shrine! Surely a good omen."

A good omen . . . ? For whom . . . ? *Why* was he feeling so oppressed? Perhaps by dwelling on young Renzō's future he was oppressed by the brevity of life itself . . . ? Certainly, he mused, he was without doubt a romantic at heart, but it was not his way to indulge in feelings of abstract self-pity.

Resolving to clear his mind, he recalled the male camaraderie in the huge family bathhouse following the energetic hours spent in the outdoors. Without doubt, Okura had been enchanted with young Renzō's physical attributes, and he himself had felt a surge of paternal pride, pleased that the boy had inherited the wide shoulders and brawny arms from his paternal grandmother; a strong country woman, along with the satin-smooth hairless skin of his own mother, Masa.

Renzō was obviously enjoying the respite from his normal monotonous routine. In fact, he seemed more at ease with Okura and Ohara than with his own father. Soon, he would change that unhappy state of affairs. Yes, but for the present his mind dwelt on last evening's meal, which, to Masa's credit, had been an epicurean delight, presented with flawless style and good taste.

What a brilliant organizer that woman was! Without uttering one word, she had let the guests know by the elegant apparel she herself wore that the meal was to be a formal affair. How subtle of her to have realized that Okura, the sophisticate, would have been bored by too much countryside casualness.

A number of rooms had been opened up to form an immense apartment, one end facing onto the garden and the other looking out over the ocean. The *tatami* mats, slightly tinged with green, were stretched out across the spacious hall and precious scrolls hung in the various *tokonoma* above unique vases arranged with flowers and grasses from the surrounding countryside.

Yes, how very subtle of his wife to have included, not only Dr. Yamamoto, robed in his black silk academic raiment, but also the school's oldest, most respected scholar, Suzuki San. Young Renzō also attended the dinner party, wearing a simple hempen garment in gray with a black sash. His freshly trimmed fringe gleamed, thus exaggerating the luminosity of his beautifully shaped eyes.

To cap the affair, Masa's music tutor arrived at the house during the afternoon. Inaba, an extremely plain, elderly woman, had entertained the gathering by playing the *koto*, concentrating on themes from imperial court music.

The meal commenced in a subdued celebratory atmosphere, with Dr. Yamamoto paying Okura the highest of honors, by filling his guest's *sake* bowl when it was emptied. Okura returned the compliment and conversed with the old scholar, always bowing, saying, "Ah, is that so . . . ? Is that so . . . ?"

As the meal progressed, darkness fell and servants brought in brightly lit white paper lanterns which were doused when the moon, at its full, flooded the room and the world about the house on the hill in a wondrously soft glow.

As though on cue, the atmosphere had undergone a change. *Sake* bowls were replenished more frequently and Inaba refrained from playing the *koto*. In the congenial environment, it was natural that poetry became the subject of discussion, and after much erudite talk, the scholar, Suzuki, quoted a series of famous poems.

A moment of silence followed his impressive recitation, then Okura jokingly suggested that the youngest member present should honor the occasion by a poem to be composed on the spur of the moment.

Kenichi watched his son intently, aware of the sweet agony the boy was suffering. His eyes were on his mother's face, imploring her help, but, as though impervious to his needs, she merely examined the palm of one hand. At once, the boy stared at the palm of his own right hand and with his eyes downcast he hesitated for a moment before tremulously reciting:

> *"So round, so bright the yellow moon.*
> *My cat hides in a darkened room."*

One awful moment of silence followed his amateur attempt, then followed a combined burst of comforting, jocular laughter.

After the departure of the others, Kenichi, Okura, and Ohara settled down to enjoy a bout of heavy drinking. All three were relaxed and more at one than ever before. When dawn arrived, they beheld Lady Masa, pristinely gowned, standing on the bridge of the pond, feeding her beloved carp, accompanied by a fat young serving-maid.

The three then slept until noon, and now they were visiting the monastery, two of them obviously without a care in the world while Kenichi was, even after so much cogitation, still puzzled and still apprehensive.

While farewelling his guests from the fishing hamlet, Kenichi regretted that he was not accompanying them. Bereft of their companionship and with no desire to be put through the third degree on political matters, he decided to drink himself into a state of oblivion, for with every step he took up the steep hill his vague feelings of puzzlement increased and the persistent tolling of a bell in the monastery only increased his uncharacteristic attack of melancholia.

The garden's peaceful atmosphere calmed his ruffled spirit, and for some time he stood gazing admiringly at the persimmon tree that had been planted by his mother many years before. The dark green of the leaves and the sheen of the orange-green fruit glimmered in the sunlight as a brisk breeze caused shadows to flicker over his motionless figure.

The twang of a *koto* scale sounded and at once his mood changed to one of irritation. He quite looked forward to a wordy skirmish with his wife; it would be sensible to discuss his father's dissatisfactions concerning her attitudes toward Renzō before his mind became too bemused by the bout of *sake* drinking he was about to indulge in.

Striding along the corridors with some gusto, he reached the chamber where the music scales sounded, only to discover that it was not Masa playing the instrument but her tutor, Inaba San.

Lady Masa, the woman informed him, had gone with the serving-maid, Misa, to gather herbs that she needed for the welfare of her carp.

With some chagrin he settled down to await his wife's return, taking little comfort from the fine quality rice wine a servant had prepared and set before him. The thought came to him that never before—not even once—during all the years of his marriage had he been in the house when his wife was absent, and he was troubled by a flood of recollections concerning his relationship with Masa.

Right from the beginning he had found her to be too audacious, an irritating female, but never boring, never dull. . . .

Being in the house without her was . . . ?

It was . . . ?

With no warning—like a thief in the night—the realization came to Kenichi that Masa was the pure silk, the brightly hued thread woven in among many other coarser threads that formed the fabric of his life.

Imperceptibly, he found himself slipping toward emotions too deep for tears. Masa—he loved her.

He loved his wife. . . .

Was it a criminal offense for a man to discover that he loved his own, his registered wife? In the newly arisen love there was no itch of the flesh, no florid eruptions of passion. This newly discovered love, he knew, to his undoing, had been lying dormant for many years.

Unwillingly, unhappily, he thought back down the years to the day and the night of his wedding. How callow, how unfeeling he had been. But was *he* to blame for the agonizing embarrassments he had endured? It had been his duty to deflower the strange fourteen-year-old girl. She had been so different from any female creature he had ever come across, resembling an exotic bird raised in a climate unknown to him. Masa, that child-bride.

What a multilayered scenario his life had become. Those hateful years of brain-fagging study had stolen his youth away. Was *he* to blame that the mingled squalor and splendor of life in Edo had lured and attracted him so deeply?

Ah, there was no solace, no use in going over the past; instead, he must dwell on the future, the days, the years to come.

When he beheld Masa entering the garden followed by the serving girl, he watched his wife with his heart beating rapidly. He was overflowing with tenderness and so strongly affected by the strength of a new, unconditional love that he felt afraid, painfully vulnerable, unable to move.

Finally, Masa entered the room, glancing at him casually, saying derisively, "Ah, you miss your drinking companions! Never mind, soon you'll be back in your Edo citadel."

Her irony cut like a whiplash at his torn nerves and, avoiding her eyes, he had replied curtly, muttering, "Their visit went well. I should thank you."

"Don't mention it!" Masa replied lightly, and desperate to prevent her from leaving the room, he brought out the plover bird scroll, unfurling it, saying gruffly, "Painted by Nozaka! I was most honored when Okura Sama presented it to me as a gift. What is your considered opinion?"

Masa took her time as was her way, and then dismissed the work of art with a slight gesture, murmuring disparagingly, "Perhaps your friend lost his taste for it?"

About to admit that he concurred with her opinion, he was prevented, for at that precise moment Renzō arrived and on seeing the scroll he cried out, "How splendid!"

"So you admire it!" his mother murmured, and as the boy enthused, Masa cast an oblique, humorous glance in Kenichi's direction. That moment of combined amusement and agreement sparked off such a deluge of happiness in his heart that he almost lost consciousness.

Steadying himself, he left the room hastily and, making his way over to the schoolhouse, he informed his father that Okura was undoubtedly in favor of his daughter, Rumi, marrying into the Yamamoto family when the auspicious time arrived. Scarcely aware of his surroundings, he glibly replied to the many questions put to him by the old scholar. Finally, unable to endure the stultifying atmosphere and, knowing that he dared not trust himself to sleep beneath the same roof as his wife, who was innocent about his newly discovered love toward her, he invented an excuse that made his return to Edo imperative.

As always, his departure from Yokohama was a ceremonial affair, with his wife, son, his father, the scholars, and all the servants lined up to farewell and to wish him a safe journey.

That farewell scene was quite agonizing for him. Different indeed from the many "escape" farewells in the past. When he reached the bend in the road, he glanced back, wanting to implant Masa's and his son's images in his memory, but he could see only blurred figures. After several miles Kenichi slowed his mount to a walk and waited for Sudo to catch up with him. He needed time to gather his thoughts, to map out his plans of action. Instead of continuing to ride on, he decided to rest up for the duration of the night at an inn.

Never before had he entered such an unsalubrious place, but, ignoring his henchman's questioning glance, he ate the poor fare set before him and drank copious quantities of water. Then, unbuckling his sword, keeping it close to hand beside the shabby *futon*, he lay down.

Lying in the fetid atmosphere of the inn's dormitory, he became aware that the stranger close to his pallet had begun to retch and groan. Fearful as always of infection and illness of any kind, he arose hastily and, after buckling on his sword, prodded the sleeping Sudo awake, ordering him to pay the innkeeper for their miserable accommodation.

Relieved to be in the fresh air and once more on the move, Kenichi now felt certain that he was the master of his own destiny. He would make short work, using diplomacy, to rid himself of Osen and her family, then he would reshape his future by courting and winning his wife's love.

It was the year 1851. He was forty-three. Life stretched ahead of him, many years to be filled with never before dreamed of happiness.

Impatiently, fired with enthusiasm, Kenichi urged his horse onwards toward Edo. . . .

O N THE EIGHTEENTH DAY OF June 1853, Renzō, accompanied by Sudo, set out on his first journey to Edo. After their departure, Lady Masa sat on the platform overlooking the garden pond and let her thoughts wander, something she did more and more often. It was evening, and she had a clear image of her son at the age of seven, naked and laughing as he ran in the sunlight toward the bridge to help her to feed the carp.

Eight years had gone by since that day, and during those years she had suffered as Renzō's bright arrogance was crushed by the stern discipline of the school.

In the beginning Masa and her sister-in-law had cosseted the child during his infrequent visits to their quarters, but he had resented their attentions and withdrew into himself. He would sit and stare, a lackluster expression in his once-mischievous eyes.

When she had been deprived of Sumiko's congenial company, she had concentrated entirely on her son's well-being. Eventually, she determined upon a resolute, aggressive approach, and told him that all forms of study would not only be of interest but would reward him.

She encouraged her son to teach her about some of the subjects he was studying, and the unwilling student had become the more than willing tutor. At every opportunity Renzō would come to the house, his words tumbling out in a flood as he told her of the things he had learned.

"Stop lecturing me!" she would exclaim, laughing. "But to ease *my* mind, please read me these poems."

She understood that poetry brought him solace of a kind. And his teachings brought them closer together. In the winter months she would await the sound of his footsteps, a dry, crunching sound in the snow, and she never failed to suggest, "First, a long, brisk walk?" The outdoor exercise improved the boy's health, and she too benefited, gaining a new awareness of her body.

At thirty-seven, Masa thought of herself as an elderly woman. Her memories of days gone by were seen as if in flickering lamplight. Voices, music, sounds once recalled so clearly were now ghostly echoes.

The silk merchants no longer brought their wares to the house on the hill. Masa, a widow of two years, wore garments of a sober hue. She no longer rouged her lower lip, and she dressed her hair in a severe style.

Sometimes she recalled the exotic hothouse atmosphere of her childhood and early adolescence. Remembering the surreptitious glances she had thrown at her bridegroom during the wedding ceremony and how pleased she was that he was taller than she was, handsome, and confident, and how she had prepared herself for his arrival in the marriage chamber. Waiting expectantly, tense, listening to every sound . . .

She recalled how Kenichi had scorned her and belittled her passion, saying with disdain, "I scarcely expected a wife of noble rank to behave in such an accomplished fashion."

For the first time in her fourteen years of life she had experienced anger. Anger so hot, so burning that she had lost all sense of reason. Then, while he slept, her one thought had been to return insult with insult.

What deeper insult than to let the world know that rather than submit further to her husband's demands, she would prefer to die?

She had waited for him to wake. His amusement at seeing her, dagger at the ready to finish her own life, had injured her feelings beyond repair. With one bound he leapt on her, and a macabre wrestling match took place before he finally wrenched the sharp little weapon from her hand.

From that moment on she knew their union would never blossom, and as the years went by they had remained strangers to each other.

Masa had been greatly saddened by Kenichi's untimely death which had left her son bereft of a father. However, as time had gone by, her husband's passing into the spirit world had given her a new lease on life. She arranged her days to suit her own convenience and pleasure.

Daily, no matter the season or weather, she wandered about the gently sloping hills covered with sea pines which gave out their acrid, invigorating perfume. Even in winter, through the falling snow, she would wend her solitary way down to the crescent-shaped beach wearing her raincoat and wide straw hat. She relished the crisp, stinging air and took joy every year when she discovered plum blossoms heralding the spring. How she admired them for bursting into bloom before the snows had melted.

During the summer months she paddled in the shallow waters of

the bay, taking up and examining the perfect seashells, putting them
down each time gently, exactly where she had discovered them. She
loved the changing moods of the ocean, that lonely expanse of sea
which had distressed her so much when she came to Yokohama as
a child-bride.

It was only in autumn that she felt sharp pangs of nostalgia. She
watched the full moon in the clear night sky and smelled the chrysanthemums that grew so profusely in the area. During that season
she would luxuriate in self-pity, whispering, "How cruel! How
cruel! Was life meant to be so lonely?"

During the past winter, though, when her son's tall, muscular
figure appeared from out of the falling snow, she would plead a
false weariness. She was aware of a new restlessness in the youth,
and he had gone off, glad to be on his own. When he returned he
would sit with her and chat, as one adult to another. "Nothing so
clean, nothing so pure as the driven snow," he once exclaimed. "Can
there be anything more exquisite than the sight of snow falling
through the air above the land and the wide ocean?"

"I agree with you," she murmured. "Just now I'm composing a
play about what it's like to sit and listen to the fragile song of burning charcoal in the *hibachi*. Snow outside, two black ravens perched
on the bared branches of the gingko tree."

"May I read it?"

"But who else?" she quipped, and they laughed, knowing that
her plays and poems would never have any other readers.

She spoke only in praise about her son's late father, who had been
so seldom at home and so obsessed by the courtesan Osen.

She spoke to him about life, warning him, murmuring, "Life is
straightforward and just what one expects."

At times she mentioned his maternal family, desirous to have him
remember that he was descended from one of the noble families of
Japan. She would describe in detail the charm, the brilliance of the
court circle surrounding the mikado in the old capital, Kyoto. He
was polite but also showed signs of restlessness and would naively
bemoan the country's isolation from the rest of the world. Then she
would feel a nervous dread, afraid that he would endanger his life
if he discussed those radical thoughts outside the confines of their
home.

And she would remember how, at age twelve, Renzō had been
strongly affected by his father's tragic death.

One night, several weeks after Kenichi's visit with Okura and

Ohara, Sudo had arrived at the house in an exhausted, disheveled condition, declaring incoherently that Kenichi had been attacked by the disease cholera.

"He was suddenly so ill," he exclaimed. "In three days his life was over! His sister and her husband took charge of the hasty burial! There was no help—*Shikata ga nai!*—so sudden! So quick! What now? What now . . . ? The old woman, Shiga, and two of her daughters also died of the dread disease. What now? What now . . . ?"

Masa calmed the distressed man, then went to the school, a cloak protecting her from the typhonic wind that was raging.

There she met with further disaster. Dr. Yamamoto was struck down by apoplexy, and lay surrounded by horrified scholars who greeted her as though her presence would miraculously put things to rights.

The closest medical practitioner lived miles away in Uraga, and he would not be able to treat the doctor until the following day. For several hours she remained at the school, doing her utmost to relieve her old father-in-law who, although conscious, was unable to express his needs.

She brought about a measure of calm and common sense among the students—some many years her senior—but as the wind raged on, it was like the middle of a nightmare. She was certain that she would wake up to find that Sudo was still in Edo, with Kenichi alive, enjoying the evening in the Nihombashi house together with the courtesan whom he loved so passionately.

Eventually, content that she had done all in her power to make the doctor comfortable, she informed the scholars of Kenichi's sudden and tragic demise; she ordered them to keep the knowledge from their master for the time being. Then, with her mind on Renzō, she fought her way back to the house, buffeted by the wind, falling, rising, falling again as she stumbled through the dark gardens.

When she got home the nightmare got worse. Sudo was nowhere to be seen. She ordered a housemaid to bring Renzō to her, but the girl, backing away, called out loudly, "The young master has lost his mind."

So she searched through the house, calling, "Renzō! Ren-chan . . . Renzō . . ."

Finally, she discovered her son in his father's study. For one frightening instant she thought that it was not Renzō, but Kenichi's ghost, in the heyday of his youth, kneeling on the *tatami* in front of his father's favorite red-lacquered chest.

"Renzō . . . ?" she whispered, and, as though returning from a dream back to reality, her son opened a drawer in the chest. To her amazement, he took out a blue-velvet-covered article and raised it, holding it to his forehead for several moments. Then, replacing the article and with tears streaming from his eyes, unaware of her presence, he rushed from the house and out into the howling wildness of the stormy night.

For many years Sudo had been the lifeline between the Nihombashi house in Edo and the house on the hill at Yokohama. He was the one who had brought many letters and messages from Sumiko since she had become a member of the Fukuda family.

Over the years Sumiko's letters had become infrequent. It was mainly from Sudo that Masa learned that Sumiko had become a popular figure in the new-rich society of the capital city. Even so, in her occasional letters she always invited Masa to visit her in Edo.

After Kenichi's death, Sumiko invited Renzō too. "Is it not a sad thing that our sons, Renzō and Yuichi, should never have met?" she wrote.

Dr. Yamamoto never fully recovered from the stroke. He became vague, calling Renzō by his father's name, forgetting his son was no longer alive. The senior scholar, Suzuki San, was unofficially in charge of the school.

The old scholar's aviary lay neglected and empty except for the waterfowl, who continued to breed in the reed-crowded water pond. The lotus flowers beneath the old oak tree bloomed and faded unnoticed. The blind flute player was dead and only Fat Misa went to the striped bamboo grove to dig up the lotus roots, delicacies for the table.

Masa received a visit from her late husband's friend and companion, Fukuda, Sumiko's husband.

"Excuse me," he exclaimed apologetically, "but I feel obliged to talk with you on several matters."

Against her own will she was attracted to the man. Maybe Sumiko had influenced him? Maybe he was a man well-suited to married life and fatherhood? The levity and vulgarity she had once so abhorred in him were glossed over and she appreciated his interest in her son's affairs.

After hours of talking, Fukuda agreed that until Renzō reached an age of responsibility, no harm could come from the courtesan, Osen, living in the Nihombashi house together with her adopted brother.

"Well, I concur with you," Fukuda said. "But—with a heavy heart, for that woman, Osen—excuse me for mentioning her name in your presence—always fills me with feelings of distrust. . . ."

"But it is true," Masa had murmured, "that my late husband thought highly of that person. I prefer not to wound his departed spirit by any rude actions. Please allow the person to remain in the Nihombashi house until my son matures enough to deal with family concerns. His grandfather, my honorable father-in-law, has returned to childish things. . . ."

Fukuda returned to Edo, and from that time onward, Masa had made changes in her living style.

Sometime after Fukuda's visit Sudo arrived from Edo on a bitterly cold day, carrying a cloth bundle bearing the Yamamoto family crest. He said quietly, "Here, I have brought certain belongings of my late master. They should be here with you rather than in that house in Nihombashi."

"You are thoughtful. I appreciate your kindness," Masa replied.

She questioned him about his own plans. Bowing his forehead to the *tatami*, he replied quietly, "Thank you. Without my master, with my services no longer required at the school here, I intend to find employment in Edo."

One hour or so later, she saw him walking along the road leading to Edo, a shabby bundle slung across his frail shoulders. Suddenly he seemed like a weary traveler deeply in need of succor. Remembering his faithful service, she hastened to him and said, "Sudo San! Sudo San, one moment! One moment if you please. I am in need of your help."

For the past year Sudo had been living in her home, spending his time industriously at his desk in her late husband's study, keeping it as Kenichi had kept it.

She took to doing certain light household chores in between her study periods, then she played the *koto* or wrote her plays. But she was always on the lookout for a visit from Renzō, more and more disturbed by the boy's attitudes.

There were times when he threatened to run away to escape the rigors of his studies. "I have no control of my own life," he would mutter. "I am like a prisoner, caged in. When I was a child I longed to know what lay beyond the horizon. Now I know that out there a world exists with countries ruled by governments allowing free expression to man's creativity. We in Japan are living in the dark ages.

"Sometimes I feel that I am going mad. Am I to spend my life trudging back and forth from this hamlet to Edo, as my father did? Is that *my* fate?"

He no longer took solace from poetry or from the hours spent talking with her. She would sit by, patiently, never rebuking him, realizing that his life was too tame.

She was filled with a mixture of pride and fear, dreading that she would become like the mother in the poem, who prayed to the gods to watch over her son, a runaway gambler, crying out, "Oh, never let him lose a game. . . . Keep watch over him! Never let him lose a game. . . ."

So she had made arrangements for Renzō to travel to the capital with Sudo, hoping that the vitality of Edo, and being with his aunt Sumiko would curb his anger and dissatisfaction. . . .

On that June evening in 1853 Fat Misa lumbered in, interrupting her meditation, shouting as if she were in another room, "Lady, Lady, time for your evening rice!"

"Later," she murmured. "I shall dine later."

It had taken some time for her spirit to calm again. Ignoring the swarms of insects, the vicious mosquito attacks, she gave thought to the preparations for Renzō's return to the hamlet and for the most important festival of the year, *Obon*, the Festival of the Dead.

When the thirteenth day of July arrived, the house on the hill, like every house in Japan, would be swept and garnished, the lacquer trays would be covered with choice offerings of food; and they would be covered too by the holy leaves of the lotus. Fresh water would be provided and precious cups filled with tea to welcome the invisible guests—family members who had departed this life.

Throughout Japan fires would be kindled on the seashore, by lakes and rivers; torches would be lit and lanterns would glow to guide the returning spirits to the shrines in their beloved homes.

Not yet of that spirit world herself, she became aware that pangs of hunger were overriding her thoughts.

Lady Masa rose gracefully from the floor-cushion and entered the house to partake of the evening meal.

Somewhere, someone was playing a flute. "Out of tune . . ." she murmured. "Never mind, never mind! Such is my life, out of tune and lonely, here in this out-of-the-way fishing hamlet."

She shrugged and then clapped her hands twice, signaling that she was ready to eat her meal.

As she sat beneath the diffused glow of the paper lantern, Masa had no premonition of the earthshaking events that were soon to take place, events that would not only affect her own life, but the civilized world itself.

NOTHING HAD EVER DISAPPOINTED RENZŌ Yamamoto more than his arrival at Edo.

For some years his favorite pastime had been the study of treasured documents; of paintings, drawings, and maps in the school's archives of certain capital cities in the Western world. Countless stolen hours had been spent poring over architectural wonders: magnificent Houses of Parliament, great palaces, spired cathedrals, wide boulevards.

Edo, Japan's major city, was nothing like those pictures of Paris, London, or Rome. The streets were unpaved and narrow, the low buildings, most built of wood, were uninspiring.

To his horror, the city was reminiscent of his grandfather's aviary, divided as it was into hundreds of separate districts fenced in by high wooden stockades. Each stock was guarded by stern officials who, Sudo informed him, demanded identification before allowing citizens to pass from one district to another after sunset.

He could not believe that this was the metropolis his father had loved so much. "Was it always like this?" he shouted to Sudo as the unlikely pair guided their mounts slowly through the overcrowded noisy streets on their way to the Fukuda residence.

"Worse" was Sudo's shouted reply. "Gradually, it is improving."

"There is a *terrible* stench in the air."

"Naturally. Over a million people dwell here. One million citizens crowded together naturally pollute the air. Just think about it!"

He realized that many of the bullock-drawn carts crawling through the streets were carrying human waste, taking their odorous cargo out into the countryside, where it would be used to fertilize the land.

Suddenly, he felt distressingly homesick. He longed to be back in the clean, sweet air of his native village. In the fishing hamlet, the children were clean-skinned, but here, in Edo, he was shocked to see many small boys and girls with sores and snotty noses.

He rode onward, looking neither to the right nor the left, certain that before the week was over he would be back in Yokohama.

Sumiko's pride in her nephew knew no bounds. "Was there," she inquired of Fukuda, "ever so charming, so handsome a youth?"

"Never!" he had agreed. "Frankly, I've quite fallen in love with him."

"It's no wonder! He so resembles his mother."

"Not in the least," Fukuda exclaimed. "He is his father's son in every way."

"I beg to differ. Ren-chan smiles and casts enchanting glances just like Masa."

"Hmmm . . . then we must protect him or he will be taken hostage to the Yoshiwara. Maybe you should warn him of his seductive mannerisms. But I see him quite differently. He has the makings of a lady-killer."

"Enough! He is but a youth! Ah, you can't imagine how I have *yearned* to have him by me once again."

"You think not?" Fukuda grinned widely, exclaiming, "Scarce a day has gone by over all the years of our marriage without—"

"I know, I know. How I must have irked you."

"Occasionally, yes. But now he is here and already his influence has turned our son into quite an acceptable housemate. Have you noticed?"

"Indeed! But I fear that Yu-chan is becoming rather a nuisance. He gives his cousin no respite."

"Nonsense! Renzō obviously enjoys admiration."

Fukuda spoke the truth. Renzō was positively wallowing in his first taste of being a social success.

After some hesitations he had easily swallowed the edifying fact that he himself was handsome, intelligent, modest, charming, altogether delightful. . . .

He gloried in having not only an aunt but also an uncle and a cousin, a lovable little boy who clung to him, calling proudly to all and sundry, "Look, look! See my Yokohama cousin! I love him. He is *mine*."

"Yokohama cousin" became his sobriquet in the grand mansion set behind high stone walls.

The house on the hill in the fishing hamlet was nothing compared with this palace with its stylized gardens and huge expanse of natural forest which lay in the district alluded to as Yoyogi.

His aunt Sumiko, once a slim, quiet young woman, was now stout and self-confident. She no longer lectured him like a child, but gazed at him with admiration and asked his advice on many matters. He gave his opinion with the aloof dignity of a scholar.

He never lost an opportunity to address his aunt's husband as Uncle. Having an uncle was an entirely new experience, and this one plied him with gifts, and escorted him about the city when it was aglow with thousands upon thousands of gaily colored lanterns.

Perhaps he had not actually grown in stature since arriving in Edo, but without doubt he was quite some inches taller than his jolly new uncle and many of the grown men in the city. He came to enjoy elbowing and politely jostling as he pressed his way through the crowds, each person, he felt certain, happy but not quite as happy as himself.

His mother had instructed him to take his credentials and the gift she had prepared to the home of Count Okura. On the third day after his arrival he traveled there in a litter.

Before setting out, his aunt had examined him critically, finally saying, "Ah, Ren-chan, you could not look more *pleasing*. Now that your boyhood fringe has gone, I behold a samurai! Remember that your mother, Lady Masa, is *more* noble than the family you are presently to be with. Go proudly!"

The night after that ceremonious visit, he had lain sleepless beneath the mosquito net, listening to the steady breathing of his young cousin, Yuichi, who insisted on sharing his luxuriously wide, soft pallet.

He felt that in some insidious way he had been utilized by Okura.

In that dour old house he was completely at ease. The people there mirrored the mannerisms and the speech of his mother, and he had responded in kind.

The old count, his health delicate, had nevertheless insisted on escorting him to view an ancient pine tree, saying, "Some years ago your now-departed father stood beneath this tree."

That mention of his father had torn open a part of his heart he preferred to keep closed tight. Checking his tears, he had bowed reverently and as he returned to the house he imagined that he was treading in the footsteps of the father he had loved but had known so little.

Okura had greeted him in the most friendly way, recalling the

pleasant time which he and his friend, Ohara, had spent some years
before in the Yamamoto household, "A never-to-be-forgotten pleasure," he had murmured, and then he had expressed his regret that
the pressures of life had prevented him from enjoying the company
of Fukuda, saying, "May I entrust you to relay my respects and
good wishes to your aunt's husband?"

But at this information his new uncle had gazed at him blankly
for some moments and then, to Renzō's astonishment, Fukuda had
begun to laugh, his shoulders hunched up, his head shaking from
side to side. His aunt also shook her head and finally said to her
husband, "What am I to make of that?"

"Make of it what you will," Fukuda had replied, grinning widely.
"Just this morning my mother informed me that her soothsayer had
prophesied that Yuichi, her treasured grandson, would one day
marry into the nobility. Ho, ho, ho, ho . . ."

His aunt, completely at a loss, had gazed at her husband for several moments and then, turning her gaze upon Renzō, murmured,
"Ren-chan, by any chance did you meet with Okura's little daughter, Aiko?"

"No, Aunt," he replied.

After leaving the room he heard sounds of hilarity as they burst
out laughing.

The flamboyant clutter of the art objects in his aunt's home attracted
Renzō. He had little trouble in separating the dross from the gold
and he wished that Lady Masa could be there to see the collection
of Fukuda's original works of art.

Several paintings made him grin as he recalled the day when he
had run amok in his grandfather's aviary. Those pictures of men and
women he had discovered in his aunt's room had distressed him
then, but now he viewed erotic works calmly and with an admiringly critical eye.

To his delight, strongly against his aunt's wishes, Fukuda had
taken him—dressed more stylishly than his mother would have approved of—to visit the infamous Yoshiwara district.

"Tut tut!" Fukuda had scolded his wife. "We go to look, not
touch."

Here, Renzō thought exultantly, is the place, so bright, so full of
flowers, music, and song, my father loved so dearly. Here, every
girl is silk-clad, beautiful, and happy. Here, every man is trouble-
free.

Aware of admiring glances thrown his way, especially by male revelers, he kept close to his escort, but when Fukuda led him into one of the finest houses, his heart beat uncomfortably fast. He had no wish to even speak with the gorgeously robed women who laughed and clapped their hands in teasing approval of him as he followed Fukuda through many rooms and then out onto a wide veranda where two brocaded cushions had been placed in readiness for them.

Deliciously pretty girls fluttered about, bringing tasty dishes and bowls of steaming hot tea which both he and Fukuda partook of with relish. "Soon the parade will commence!" Fukuda said. "The onlookers are gathering."

Certain that he would awake to find himself back at his floor-desk in the school, being prodded from this dream by old Suzuki San, Renzō gazed down, overcome by curiosity and excitement.

The wide thoroughfare below was lined with men accompanied by their chosen female companions. The men chattered, flirted, laughed as he had never imagined grown males would do.

Then they were hushed, obviously awaiting some special event.

Renzō leaned farther forward to behold the first of the many parades he was to witness during his lifetime. There was never one like this, the ceremonial "Graduation Parade of *Shinzō*" for "newly made" courtesans.

Here they came! There they went! Hundreds of young girls pigeon-toeing along on high black clogs.

The sleeves of their kimono trailed to the ground.

Their bulging *obi*-sashes were tied in front instead of the back.

Their faces were chalk-white, their lips vermilion, their hair dressed high, gleaming black, decorated with jeweled stickpins.

The courtesans were divided into distinct groups. The colors and patterns of their raiment announced which house they belonged to. "See," Fukuda murmured. "Each group is followed by their sponsoring *oiran*—the madams who have trained them through their years of apprenticeship."

"Yes, yes, Uncle. I see."

"Every fan, Renzō, every lantern in this graduation parade comes from *my workshops*."

"Your—workshops . . . ?"

Without thought, Renzō spoke in a derogatory tone. He swiveled around to stare at Fukuda, recalling a time in his childhood when the very name of the man who was entertaining him so kindly had been the embodiment of vulgarity. As though reading his thoughts, Fukuda stared back, his eyebrows raised at the embarrassment that was causing his young companion's face to flush. Then, in a businesslike tone, he said, "Life's a comic affair! Come, Renzō, be easy. With me you must never be embarrassed, never afraid. Understood?"

Renzō smiled with relief, and for the first time Fukuda saw that in some respects the youth resembled Lady Masa.

Sumiko had been at a loss on discovering that Sudo was expecting to stay in her household. He was not exactly a guest and certainly not a servant. But Lady Masa had instructed him to guard her son during his first journey away from home and her instructions had to be honored.

"How exactly should we treat Sudo?" she asked her husband.

"Treat him?" Fukuda had just finished his morning rice and was at work with his ivory and gold toothpick.

Resisting the words *"Must* you do that?" Sumiko murmured, "Yes. Please advise me."

Rinsing clean his black-lacquered chopsticks with hot tea, Fukuda placed them in their box, then said wryly, "Why not bed him down in a nice room? A very nice room. Strange, withdrawn chap. He won't trouble anyone."

But Sudo did trouble Renzō, who thought of his father's henchman as a hunting dog, ready to sniff out the tracks of his young charge in the great, dangerous city.

That visit to the Yoshiwara had brought back memories of his father and his mother's scathing remarks about the courtesan Osen.

He knew that his father had cared deeply for that mysterious woman. He had once come upon a collection of poems, beautifully brushed by his father's skilled hands, and when he had read them he put them away carefully. He hoped that his mother would never read those poems—it was plain that her husband had loved the courtesan.

One of the poems had read:

> *With my wife I*
> *Share a pillow of ice*
> *Duty!*
> *Ah—Osen . . .*

His adolescent heart had been torn in two. He loved his mother but surely he should also respect the woman whom his father had loved so deeply?

Now, in Edo, he determined to inquire into the courtesan's whereabouts. Perhaps Sudo could help. But Sudo denied knowing anything, and muttered contemptuously, "Who knows? Such women drift from man to man."

Certain that he was lying, Renzō took his problem to Fukuda, who frankly admitted that the courtesan and her adopted brother were living in the Yamamoto Nihombashi house. "It's common knowledge," he said.

"It is?"

"It is." He hesitated, then said, "Your mother, Lady Masa, accepts the situation."

"My mother? She knows that?"

"Yes. Leave well enough alone, Renzō. Keep away from such things until you know how to deal with them. Understand?"

"Yes," he had replied, but he went without permission from the mansion and made his way through the city, inquiring of passersby as he went. Finally he stood in front of the house at Nihombashi, completely at a loss, his heart thumping.

He could scarcely believe that the street which his father had spoken of with such enthusiasm was this dirt road lined with booths and shops, and filled with crowds of people.

Renzō was jostled until his back was pressed against the strong, high fence of the house. Dripping with perspiration, and overcome with guilt, he wished that he had obeyed Fukuda's injunction to leave things alone.

Just as he made up his mind to walk away, a gate in the fence slid open and a woman stepped out on to the roadway. A litter pulled up in front of the house. Several men, seeing her, called out admiringly, "Ah—Osen! Osen! Osen . . ."

A brawny youth erupted into the street and assisted the gorgeously arrayed courtesan into the waiting litter. He gave instructions to the porters in a brisk voice.

The litter moved off and the youth gestured at Renzō in a vulgar manner that he should be on his way.

After some time he had gone, but his heart was beating fast.

He had been hotly aroused by the sight of the ravishingly beautiful courtesan, the love of his own father's life, and it was enough to overwhelm him with almost unendurable shame.

He felt that not only had he eaten of forbidden fruit but that he understood his father's obsessions for Osen ... Osen so mysteriously seductive ...

On his way toward the district of Yoyogi he entered a Shinto shrine to cleanse his spirit.

Resuming his journey, Renzō was halted by a crowd of citizens, each of whom shoved and elbowed his own way to the front of the crowd. Feeling more confident, he finally forced his way through until he could see a bold placard pasted to a wall. It read:

DOWN WITH THE TOKUGAWAS WHO STAND BETWEEN US AND OUR EMPEROR.
SOCIETY MUST BE REFASHIONED.

Fighting his way back through the crowd, Renzō fled. He was overwhelmed by fear and by a strange excitement.

For several years Fukuda had belonged to a secret group out to undermine the power of the Tokugawa government.

The rumblings of discontent among the intelligentsia and the businessmen of Edo and other large cities in the land were growing deeper, spreading wider. One slogan of the swordless movement was "Oh to die for the emperor."

Fukuda, in truth, had no intention of dying for anyone, let alone the emperor, but he resented these despotic, crippling laws in the social and business world and willingly helped to print antigovernment banners and placards which were then illegally posted throughout Edo and the countryside. Naturally, he kept his wife from knowing of his nefarious, radical actions.

As Renzō made his way home, Fukuda, clad in a red loincloth, lounged on the *tatami* in his wife's room, enjoying the sultry July afternoon.

With his head resting on a furled cushion, he watched Sumiko going through the intricacies of robing herself and he grinned as she ordered a serving-maid not to pull so tightly at her *obi*-sash, saying to the girl, "I want it *much* looser. You pull too tightly."

"Does she ...?" he chortled. "Or is it that you grow plumper?"

"I must admit that is so." She placed a closed fist between the sash and her billowing breasts to show the maid the exact tension she required and said, "Is my plumpness displeasing to you, then?"

"On the contrary! Our lovemaking prospers as does our iris garden."

As the maid left the room the husband and wife gazed out through the open *shōji* to view the harvest of flowers.

They were especially enamored of the yellow iris. The blooms had achieved quite regal dimensions and now measured some ten inches across the petals. And there were the other colors: the white, blue, the purple varieties and the tall-standing green spears soon to burst into bloom.

Sumiko remembered the early days of their marriage. Her eyes were bright, as though she were about to cry, and as Fukuda gazed at her he murmured teasingly, "So then—you *admire* the iris flower?"

At that moment they heard Renzō's excited voice calling out, "*Gomen nasai*—May I enter?" Disconcerted, Sumiko requested that her nephew should wait a moment and then swiftly tidied the hastily discarded garments lying in disarray by the *futon*; she placed a wad of used tissues in the wicker rubbish basket. Cleaning her hands with a twisted damp towel, she swooped upon a book of erotic pictures which she and her husband had been emulating to the best of their ability.

She slipped the book beneath the *futon* as Fukuda laughed and said, "I have never seen you so flustered! He is not a little boy any longer!"

"I know. I know," Sumiko whispered. "But I am his *aunt!*" Then she caroled, "Enter! By all means, Ren-chan, please come in."

Disheveled, dripping with sweat, Renzō entered and flopped down on the *tatami*, crying out, "In the city I saw posters. Radical *antigovernment posters*, and . . ."

"Yes, yes. Calm yourself," Fukuda said admonishingly. "What a country bumpkin you are! For several years all sorts of posters and placards and banners have been seen in public places, denouncing the government."

"But what a risk! Put up by whom?"

"Just let us say by invisible hands." Fukuda muttered, "Changes are in the air, and . . ."

"But such radical slogans advocate anarchy, *revolution*."

"Enough. Enough," Sumiko whispered, her voice tinged with horror. "It is a *lovely* day. The sky is *blue*. We live in *peace*. Our land is *happy*. Such talk darkens my spirit."

"Talk of blue skies, happiness, and peace *brightens* my spirit," Fukuda said complacently.

"I was alluding to Renzō's talk of anarchy and revolution," Sumiko said on her dignity. "Revolution means bloodshed, and . . ."

"Bloodshed! Perhaps. But not *all* radical movements are composed of crazed sword-swingers. Calm down. Stop fussing. We are not simpletons. Not blind. Not fools. If radical slogans are needed to battle for a more reasonable way of life, I applaud them. The two-sworded ones must realize that an unsworded majority now regards the power of the shogun as too tyrannical to endure. In addition . . ."

To Renzō's astonishment, his aunt suddenly burst out laughing. "Oh, how I admire your modernity! Your rhetoric, your knowledge of political and business matters. But . . . but . . ."

"But what?" Fukuda was extremely put out by her levity.

"Just . . ." Sumiko, laughing, gestured that her husband's scant attire was scarcely in keeping with his pontifical lecture and then left the room.

Fukuda adjusted his brief undergarment and stared aggressively at the youth whose samurai father had irreparably broken a glowing friendship some years before.

The boy—Kenichi's son—was gazing at him, his eyes wide and expectant, and pleading, "Uncle, please continue, explain things in more detail. Your words set my mind on fire."

"Is that so? Well, excuse me from continuing the discussion. I resent being cross-examined. I have no intention of losing my head."

Renzō, deeply embarrassed, even more deeply hurt, whispered chokingly, "Do you believe that I, *Kenichi's son*, would ever betray your confidences?"

Fukuda hesitated, then said in a light tone, "Let me just say, old fears never die. No common man should ever trust a samurai."

Unbidden, disdain flooded Renzō's being. Turning away he said coldly, "So? Then—best you keep your silence." When he turned around, Fukuda had left the room.

Filled with shame, he sprang to his feet and went into the long corridor, calling urgently, "Uncle! Uncle . . ."

A door slid open and Fukuda, tying a black sash about a hastily donned cotton gown, poked his head out and said calmly, "Is the house on fire?"

"No. May I enter?"

"Why not, why not? Come in. Close the door."

Renzō, without humility, said, "I apologize to you."

"For what?"

"You know."

"Ah—that!" Fukuda shrugged carelessly. "Insults roll off my back like water from a duck's plumage. However, I accept your apology. We human beings are so complicated, yet we can't stop rain from falling or wind from blowing. It will always be so. Come, let us bathe together, as your father and I so often did in days now gone by."

In the clear, hot bathwater, Fukuda was unable to prevent himself from wondering how the youth would act if he were put to the test. He also wondered what action Renzō would take if he were to discover that his late father's henchman, Sudo, was the author of some of those radical posters that were flooding Japan's cities and countryside.

Fukuda had a sharp mind, sharp as the point of an arrow, and even though radicals were beating their drums he believed that those muffled sounds were barely heard in government circles and that the great majority would continue to bow down before the ceremonial ruthlessness of the shogun, who was clever enough not only to allow political activists to indulge themselves but actually encouraged them.

He had no intellectual pretensions but an ability to find his way around things. For instance, the law stating that "should a quarrel or dispute occur, one shall not unnecessarily meddle in it," went deeply against his grain. He had spent his entire adult life breaking laws he disagreed with.

For years his spirit had been poisoned by the arrogant attitudes of men, who, he knew only too well, had been attracted to him because of his wealth.

Even now he was willing to take up that broken relationship with the son of Count Okura because the connection could be beneficial to his son Yuichi's future.

After Renzō's visit to the Okura residence, he had made inquiries about the financial situation of that noble family. He learned that they were selling off family heirlooms and were heavily indebted to merciless moneylenders.

Before too long he would generously help the poverty-stricken family out of trouble. Okura would be innerly shamed but he would accept assistance and, in the time-honored way, he would one day make repayment. By adopting Yuichi into the aristocratic clan, Fukuda hoped. He had no scruples about having his son marry and change his name if it would better his life.

In many ways he admired the brilliant shogun strategies, but he believed that they neglected one powerful weapon—money.

His own grandfather had risen from serfdom, just one rank above scavengers who earned their meager supply of rice by tanning the hides of dead animals.

The old man's son had become a despised merchant, who, in spite of his newly gained wealth, had bowed down beneath sumptuary laws, laws that regulated the way in which he and his family dressed their hair, clad their bodies. Laws that regulated the cash they could spend on weddings and funerals.

The policy of keeping merchants in their inferior station was crumbling slowly. His own mode of life proved that. With daring, skullduggery, and bribery, he had purchased undreamed of freedoms and a luxurious way of life. Nevertheless, he was convinced that many decades would grind by before the almighty power of the sword would be replaced by the power of money.

But as his wife had just said, it was a lovely blue-skied day.

From that day Renzō turned his thoughts toward home.

His heart would thump when he recalled the trauma of seeing Osen. He was unable to rid himself of the thought that he had offended his father's spirit and the person of his mother.

He realized what a profound influence his mother was in his life and he longed to be with her once again in the clear air of the fishing hamlet. Much to his astonishment, he missed the discipline of the school, and was bored by the froth and bubble of life in the Fukuda household, where he had to show enthusiasm for entertainments which were given for his pleasure.

Although the unhappy episode with his uncle had ended well, he was aware that Fukuda's old mother resented her grandson's affection for his newly found cousin. He believed that the woman actually hated him and did not know how to deal with the situation.

He had spoken to his aunt, but she had merely leaned her head to one side and said in a genial tone, "Don't mind her, Ren-chan. I always think of my mother-in-law as a *stork*."

"A stork! Why?"

" 'Tis said that those birds can live on for a thousand years. Need I say more?"

He realized that Sumiko's life was not all honey and springwater. He made up his mind to devote his time to her, as an *on*—a payment for the love and devotion she had given to him during the years of his early childhood.

Sumiko showed her delight when he let her know that for the

rest of his visit he desired nothing more than to be in her company. As the days went by, he spent hours and hours with the merry-hearted woman.

Sumiko confided to him that she suffered from claustrophobia in the crowded, barricaded districts of Edo and in the heavily wooded estate surrounding the mansion.

"Can you imagine," she commented ruefully, "that the magnificent cryptomeria, and the glorious gingko trees you are admiring once prospered many miles away from this place? They were uprooted, carried here to this garden on bullock-drawn carts, and replanted just to please my father-in-law's fancy. What do you make of that?"

"Hmm . . . a fiasco!"

"Absolutely! We are agreed!"

Taking Yuichi with them, they went deep into the woodland to picnic and to view the tailless, pink-cheeked little monkeys who scampered about jabbering one to the other while Sumiko shouted to her small son, "When a girl, I had a little pet monkey. I loved it dearly. . . ."

One had to shout to be heard over the sounds of cicadas and frogs. Renzō was relieved to journey to the estate's stables.

As he admired the horses, wishing that he could take his pick from among the finely bred animals, Yuichi cried out proudly, "Yokohama cousin, all these nags belong to me!"

"Is that so!" Sumiko cried. "Now, who told you that?"

"My grandmother. She also told me that her soothsayer says that I will live in a palace."

"Did she now!" Sumiko's eyes blazed angrily. "Yuichi, you must not believe such things. Soothsayers say things just to make folk feel happy. Not true things."

"Is that so?" The child gazed first at his mother, then at Renzō. "Do you believe this, Cousin?"

"I have no doubt," Renzō replied. "Leap upon my back, Yu-chan. Pretend I'm a horse." With the child clinging to his back he galloped about, adding his own laughter to the ringing laughter of the child while Sumiko looked on, shouting her approval and encouraging his antics.

That same afternoon a courier arrived at the Fukuda house, bringing an exquisitely brushed invitation card from the old Count Okura requesting the pleasure of Sumiko, her son, and her nephew Renzō's company on the following day, and stating that a garden party was

to be held to commemorate the one hundredth year of a much-
revered family tortoise.

Fukuda had treated the invitation casually, merely advising his
wife not to curb their son's rather too lively manners. "Let him run
wild if he so wishes," he grinned. "The Okuras know that he is his
father's son."

Perhaps it had been Sumiko's stern admonishments, perhaps it had
been his grandmother's priest's advice given to the unruly child on
how best to conduct himself. But without a doubt no small boy
could have behaved more charmingly than had Yuichi on that calm,
hot July afternoon.

Not so the seven-year-old Aiko, granddaughter of the noble
count. She was so fraily built that one feared a puff of wind might
blow her away, but she was so precocious and so bold that Renzō
found it difficult to believe that she had come from the womb of
her mother, a willowy woman, cold-eyed, svelte, who scarcely uttered one word, remaining almost as stationary as the centurian tortoise during the entire proceedings. Meanwhile, her daughter ran
about in a demented manner, nursing a small, bulging-eyed dog
under one arm and laughing in the rudest way whenever a guest
spoke to her.

On arriving back at the Fukuda mansion, Sumiko exclaimed
proudly, "Yuichi, our son, behaved so nicely. I was unable to fault
him."

"What of Aiko, the Okura child?" Fukuda queried. "Is she
charming?"

"Anything but! She resembles a scrawny chicken. Need I say
more!"

"Please don't," Fukuda replied. "Did Yu-chan take to her?"

"He was *openly, blatantly* terrified of her. And . . ."

"Once again, say no more." Fukuda went into one of his hunched-
shouldered fits of silent laughter, and when through it he said, "Do
you know that I was terrified of you in those early days of our
marriage?"

"I most certainly did not know that. Were you really?"

"Not really, in fact, not at all. You know how I like to tease you."

Turning to Renzō, he said, "Well, tomorrow is your last day with
us. How time flies! Be frank, how do you wish to spend tomorrow?
I am at your command."

"Kind, generous, thoughtful as usual," Sumiko murmured. "Don't
you agree, Ren-chan?"

"I do, Aunt, with sincerity."

"Naturally!" Sumiko smiled at her nephew affectionately, and addressed her husband in an urgent tone, saying, "I have the intention of stealing into the city tomorrow morning with my nephew. I have a problem. I need advice and support from him."

"Really! May I inquire, humbly, about your problem?"

"Certainly. It is to do with a gift I wish to send to Masa."

"Ho, ho! *Quite* a problem! I shall be more than delighted to pay for it. Go with free and happy hearts. Ah, as I shall not be needed, I shall attend to business affairs some distance off in Uraga. I will be away all night and return the following morning in time to bid you farewell, Renzō."

Renzō awakened slowly, lying with his eyes closed, recalling that this, the eighth day of July, ended his stay in Edo. Early the following morning he would be riding on his way back to Yokohama. He smiled, pleased that his vacation was so soon to be over.

Some hours later two litters carried him and his aunt away from the house through the narrow, crowded streets of the metropolis which had so disappointed him and which he now had come to dislike more than ever.

After dismissing the litter porters, Sumiko began her search for the gift he was to carry back to his mother.

"What to choose? No easy task," Sumiko moaned. "Her taste is infallible."

"Mother's tastes are simple, Aunt."

"Exactly! So simple they are one above sophistication. For days I have considered and considered but no inspiration comes to me. Perhaps—an *obidomê*—a brooch?'

"As you wish."

"A *flat response*! No. Then—perhaps a brocaded sash?"

"Umm . . . my mother robes in the garments of a widow, Aunt."

"But of course. Really, I can scarcely imagine that. Masa and I took such delight in choosing our raiments. Ren-chan—inspiration! A carp!"

"You think so?" Renzō spoke dubiously, but Sumiko was fired with enthusiasm and tottered along on her high, modern footwear, skillfully edging her silk-clad body through the bustling pedestrians. Her companion followed closely, wondering how he was to arrive back in Yokohama with a fish still in a reasonable condition.

"Here, in here." Sumiko almost yodeled her instructions to him as she entered a tiny curio shop, empty but for the proprietor, who sat like a buddha, dressed immaculately and seemingly lost to the common world about him.

With no hesitation Sumiko brought him back to reality, calling politely, "We regret disturbing you, Ishikawa San. Thank you for many past attentions over the years. Today I search for a *netsuke*—one of a carp."

For the following two hours Renzō sat bathed in sweat while his aunt went through the ritual of purchasing a little carving, an ornament with many uses: to be worn above the girdle to hold in place one's tobacco pouch, as an ornamental button, or just as a treasure to fondle, to admire and love.

During the proceedings tea was taken. One by one dozens of *netsuke* were brought out and placed on a black velvet pad to be discussed in detail. As though time had ceased to exist, Sumiko gave her full attention to the carvings. Carvings of frogs, cheeky badgers, minute human figures, musical instruments, rats, bears, and so on, but to Renzō's distress and impatience not a single fish.

More tea was taken. Then Ishikawa San resumed his buddhalike stance for some five minutes and finally, as though struck by an original thought, produced the desired *netsuke*, carved with exquisite detail from jade of a rare dark green hue, jade so clear, so smooth to touch that Sumiko smiled with happiness.

As they emerged from the little shop Sumiko pleaded with Renzō anxiously, saying, "Tell me, was my instinct right?"

"Absolutely!" He spoke with feeling, and his opinion would have been identical even if his aunt's instinct had led her to purchase a sack of charcoal, or a wild pig, and he made a resolution that never again would he undertake a shopping expedition with any female person. Never had he felt so exhausted, so clammy, and so bored.

To his consternation, Sumiko admitted that she was once again in need of his advice. Clutching at his arm as though in need of support, she moaned, "Renzō, for days now I have suffered extreme pain. Will you advise me?"

"But I know little of illness, Aunt."

"Of course and fortunately. But what of courage?"

"Please explain a little more."

"I fear that I must sacrifice a tooth."

"How can *I* assist you?"

"Just by keeping your eye out for a sign proclaiming that a dental expert dwells within."

"Must it be done today, Aunt?" Renzō's stomach was twisting and turning. "Wiser perhaps, to let the tooth cure itself. No?"

"*Obviously*, you have never suffered toothache."

"True. Ah, then fortunately, over there is a tooth doctor's sign. I shall await you out here."

"You intend to desert me, then?" Sumiko gazed at him, her eyes brimming with unshed tears, and he saw that her right cheek was swollen.

"Never let that be said," Renzō replied with a newfound gallantry. Filled with nervous dread, he followed the suffering woman in to a large booth and was astonished to see some twenty or so youths squatting on the floor busily endeavoring to pull nails out of bits of board using their forefingers and thumbs.

Their master came forward, smiling and bowing politely. Noticing Renzō's interest, he gestured to the youths, exclaiming, "My apprentices."

"My tooth no longer aches," Sumiko cried out. "How *fortunate*! Come, Renzō, let us go on our way."

The dentist, however, was obviously skilled in dealing with liars and cowards, and before a pair of hands could be struck together three times, Sumiko was seated on a shabby cushion, her mouth opened wide. Before Renzō had time to turn his horrified gaze away from the grisly scene, the dentist, using his thumb and forefinger, pressed once on her gum, and was holding the offending tooth in his hand, saying proudly, "Now, no more pain! Please rinse your mouth with this salted water. Tomorrow the swelling will go."

To Sumiko's extreme pleasure, she was no longer suffering but rather filled with pride, and announced, "I made not a whimper! Not *one*!"

"You were extremely courageous," Renzō murmured. "Now let us make our way home. You had best rest awhile."

"No indeed! Let us not rush headlong back to duty. I have a yearning to eat grilled eel. Are you not hungry?"

Clearing his mind of boredom and impatience, Renzō smiled into the eyes of the woman who had played such an important role in his life, exclaiming merrily, "Literally, I starve! Aunt, after our eel feast, could we not attend a theater performance of some kind?"

"Why not, why not?" Sumiko's eyes glinted with pure joy. "This will be a day which we, you and I, shall always remember. You agree?"

"I most certainly agree, Aunt."

Entering beneath the hanging banner with its bold white characters proclaiming that only the finest, the freshest eels in Edo were
to be relished, Renzō and Sumiko sat on floor-cushions facing each
other across a low, scrupulously clean unstained wooden table in the
little eating house.

Being the only customers, they received full attention from
the chef's wife, who kept up a running commentary concerning the
weather, the joy of being alive—privileged to live in not only the
largest but also the most beautiful country in the entire world. And
how delightful it was to have such pleasant, illustrious folk patronize
her humble premises.

Having completed her spiel, she brought bowls of steaming hot,
fine quality tea and delightfully designed plates holding portions of
crisp, bright red watermelon to the table. While partaking of the tea
and the fruit, Sumiko's and Renzō's appetites were titillated by the
delicious smell of eel filets marinated in soya sauce, sugar, and wine,
being cooked by the master of the establishment.

"Shall we," Sumiko suggested, "also indulge ourselves with just
one bottle of *sake*?"

"Why not?" Renzō replied with studied casualness. As the meal
got under way the couple were wafted into a sweet haze of clandestine intimacy, induced not only by wine, but also the cozy atmosphere.

With the air of conspirators, they expressed feelings usually kept
in one's innermost heart. Sumiko confessed that although fortunate
in her marriage, there were times when she was filled with painful
nostalgia, when she longed to be once more back in the house on
the hill, beside the ocean. "Truly," she confessed, "my *heart* lies
there, and so it shall always be."

Renzō, rather in the manner of his scholarly grandfather, declared
that in no way was one's pathway through life meant to be easy,
saying in a melancholy tone, "You have my deepest sympathies. I
myself lead a life most extraordinarily complicated."

"Already, at your age! To be aware that even the most beautiful
of flowers wither and fade? Ah, my heart quite aches for you. Shall
we order just one more bottle to cheer our spirits?"

"I shall do so immediately!" Renzō clapped his hands together
twice. After the small porcelain bottle was brought to the table, he
revealed that curiosity had urged him to seek out the Nihombashi
house which he had heard so much about from his now-far-off
childhood days.

"Interested in the house from an *architectural* point of view?" Sumiko queried solemnly.

"Truthfully speaking, I must admit—no."

"*Naru hodo*—I understand! Then . . ." Sumiko caressed her swollen cheek tenderly before inquiring tentatively, "Then, was it that you just wished to revive memories of *Kenichi*?"

"Once again, no. Truthfully speaking, Aunt, I had a craving to . . ."

Blushing deeply, Renzō fell silent and stared at Sumiko in a rather belligerent manner, to which she responded by murmuring, "Please be easy. *Nothing* shocks me." Sighing deeply, she continued. "Whether one likes it or not, one is attracted by one's devious longings and desires. Is that not so?"

"Then . . ." Renzō muttered between clenched teeth. "You find it not unseemly, not scandalous, that I wished to see *her*?"

"On the contrary. Understandable and logical. *Did* you?"

"I *did*. I saw her."

Renzō concentrated on pouring the dregs of the *sake* bottle into the tiny bowl which Sumiko held out to be replenished. Staring at him intently, she whispered, "So, is *she*, the courtesan, really seductive beyond belief?"

Suddenly aware of finding himself in a perilous situation, Renzō straightened his back, and speaking strongly and firmly, said, "Inadvertently, I caught but a *glimpse* of her."

"Yes, and . . . ?"

"And," he stated even more firmly, "she appeared to me to be about as seductive as, well, as this now-empty *sake* bottle."

"Now, is that so?"

"Yes."

"Vulgar?"

"Most."

"In no way erotically ravishing?"

"In no way."

"A street-cat creature?"

"A perfect description."

"Ah-ha . . ." Sumiko murmured triumphantly. "My husband is seldom mistaken. *Always*, he has alluded to *that* woman as a feral creature."

Renzō's heart skipped several beats as he gazed at his aunt, saying nervously, "Aunt, please tell no one that . . ."

"Say not one more word!" Sumiko interjected understandingly.

"Let us agree to keep silent on the subject. Let us now sally forth to have our spirits lightened by the skills of conjurors and acrobats."

Fortified by the wine, having taken of delicious food, and quite intoxicated by the comforting experience of having divulged their most secret feelings one to the other, Renzō and Sumiko made their way through the bustling, narrow streets with the confidence of longtime city dwellers.

Finally they passed beneath crimson pillars and into the grounds of a shrine.

"But . . ." Renzō cried, "must we tarry here? I want *entertainment!*"

"Exactly!" Sumiko uttered. "And here we shall find it. Have confidence. Come, first let's pay obeisance."

They hurried across the immense paved courtyard to the main building, where they washed their hands and rinsed their mouths with clear cool water, rather too hastily for the white-robed, high-capped priests who cast frowning looks in their direction.

On passing a woman crouched by a bamboo cage filled with small, scrawny birds, Renzō backstepped, crying out, "Aunt, I *must* free these birds from this miserable small cage."

"By all means! Poor creatures." Sumiko stood by while Renzō used all his small cash, handing coin after coin to the shabby old fortune-teller who, on receiving each donation, set some thirty birds loose one by one, into the air. The old dame chuckled delightedly, crooning, "Ah, young master, your kindly act will bring you *great* rewards."

Wanting no reward, Renzō exclaimed to Sumiko as they hurried onward, "Frankly, I have no faith in such superstitious nonsense. How about you, Aunt?"

"Absolutely none," Sumiko exclaimed. "It's well known that the gods guard the pure of heart, but, Ren-chan, bear with me. . . ."

Now it was Renzō who stood by while Sumiko purchased a paper prayer strip attached to a string which she tied to the branch of a huge tree, its low spreading branches almost completely covered with both fresh and badly tattered dangling paper bequests to the gods.

Rushing toward Renzō, Sumiko declared in a slightly embarrassed tone of voice, "Just for a lark I hung a prayer to promote patience within myself. Being a woman, I do have certain problems."

"Like . . ." Renzō suggested brazenly, "a mother-in-law. No?"

"Exactly!" For no reason they could clearly understand, the couple broke into a chorus of hysterical laughter, not caring that such unseemly behavior was making them the center of attention.

"Ah," Sumiko finally cried out, "there is nothing like laughter to bolster friendship! I find that mirth elevates my spirits to a lofty plane. How about you?"

"Absolutely, Aunt." With a burst of eloquence Renzō went on to say, "Much more so than religion, to be frank with you. Now, even more so after having witnessed scenes of poverty in this metropolis."

"Poverty! Really? Excuse me, but I lead such a secluded life on the estate. Never mind! Look, over there! The theater booth! Let us hasten on in a mannerly style."

"Yes. Good manners are without doubt the religion of our people, so *you* always instructed me. Do you remember the lecture you once gave me about the holy lotus flower, Aunt?"

Once more they were overcome by a burst of uncontrollable hilarity which continued as they checked their footwear before entering a large low-roofed marquee to join the audience of mannerly men, women, and children sitting in rows on cushions before a slightly raised, carpeted platform.

No sooner had they seated themselves than the entertainment commenced. A troupe of gaily clad acrobats performed incredible feats, leaping, somersaulting, spinning, twisting, and turning as though they had no bones in their bodies.

Fans swished, the audience sighed their approval. Never having seen such a performance, Renzō was enthralled, and rather put out when Sumiko prodded his side and hissed, "Don't look now! But to your right, three rows to the front . . . No, no, don't look now!" Again came a prod, "Yes, look now!"

Following her instructions, Renzō saw Okura sitting with a woman and a small girl who were obviously on familiar terms with Okura.

Glancing at Sumiko, he saw that her lips were moving slightly. He inclined his head to hear her say, "So, it *is* true! I've heard rumors! Geisha mistress! Illegitimate daughter! Be mannerly. Understand? As far as Okura Sama is concerned, *we*, you and I, are not here. Understand?"

During the tricks of a conjuror and the brilliant act of a juggler Renzō cast surreptitious glances in the direction of Okura's group. He was charmed by the girl-child, who at times twisted her head, allowing him to see her pert profile. Then, losing interest, he gave his full attention to the star act of the performance.

A black velvet backdrop unfurled itself from the roof of the marquee. The illustrious conjuror, Chudo, appeared as though from nowhere. A slim, spare man, he was robed in the style of dress once assumed by courtiers during the golden age of the Heian period many centuries before.

Unseen musicians played a gentle, seductive melody and straightaway Chudo produced a scrap of white paper out of thin air and twisted it into the form of a gigantic butterfly.

He threw the butterfly into the air, then, with an amazing sleight of hand, produced an opened fan that he wielded so cleverly that the paper butterfly, taking on a life of its own, wheeled, dipped, and hovered as though fluttering over a field of flowers in the sweetness of a spring morning.

The butterfly alighted on the edge of Chudo's fan, then rose again, its wings quivering tremulously as it flew high above the conjuror's headdress and finally came to rest gently on the floor. Just a scrap of paper.

A great sigh of appreciation mixed with regret rose from the audience. After one long bow, Chudo left the stage and the audience rose to leave.

Emerging from the marquee and while waiting in line with those intent on retrieving their footwear, Renzō's emotions oscillated between regret and guilt. He was not quite willing to admit that the entrancing butterfly had been merely a scrap of twisted paper—an illusion.

He also despised himself for having spoken so disparagingly to his aunt about Osen, that enchanting woman. Osen, who had been so beloved to his father. With a very real pang of grief he realized that he had wounded his father's spirit and that one day he would have to repent and make amends.

Glancing at his aunt, he became aware of her punctiliously solemn expression and he understood that just as she had carefully avoided an embarrassing confrontation with Okura and his "second family," so she was now intent on regaining a dignified and proper pattern of behavior with him, her nephew. He accepted the fact, with some regret, that their combined episode of intimate companionship was over, never to be forgotten but remembered as he would always remember the insouciant flutterings of a creature conjured up by a magician.

In no way repentant, Sumiko was exhilarated and clutched at the material of her kimono, raising it discreetly just several inches in order to ease the hobble-style walk which the garment demanded, for she was eager to pass the barricades dividing the districts before sunset.

As she and Renzō entered the crowded thoroughfare, suddenly, without warning, the everyday atmosphere was shattered. Warriors in full battle dress rode helter-skelter into the street, brandishing their weapons, shouting, "Invasion . . ."

"Invasion . . ."

"Ships of evil mien are at our shores . . ."

"Death to all barbarians . . ."

"Invasion . . . Invasion . . ."

Terrified citizens scattered, attempting to protect their lives as the disorderly, maddened warriors rode onward, spreading the dire tidings and stirring up pandemonium. . . .

Many hours later, their garments torn, their minds even more disheveled, Renzō and Sumiko arrived back at the Fukuda mansion to find that hundreds of citizens had forced their way into the grounds and into the house itself, seeking refuge from the holocaust of terror that was erupting throughout the city of Edo.

The secluded estate had become a veritable madhouse. Shouts and screams resounded as people ran about, terrified, weeping, clinging to one another, while the sonorous voices of monks and priests explained to the gods that "black ships of evil mien, yea, evil vessels, sailing against the wind are said to be at our shores. . . ." They called on the deities to bring forth a god-wind to blow those dastardly barbarians away from the sacred shores of Nippon.

Certain optimistic folk, including Fukuda's old mother, screamed out, declaring to those who would listen, " 'Tis but a tale of *wicked goblins* . . ."

"Rest assured, 'tis but a tale of evil tricks played by the wicked sea-serpent."

"Rest assured! Do we not all know that fishermen from time to time behold ghostly apparitions rising up out of the ocean?"

Sumiko, desperate to find her child but unable to force her way into the house, cried, "Ren-chan, go and find Yuichi. Bring him to me."

One long hour later, Renzō discovered his small cousin in Sumiko's sitting room, lying in a wall cupboard, sound asleep.

He dragged the still-sleeping child from the cupboard and struggled back to Sumiko, who, weeping tears of relief, clasped Yuichi against her bosom, crying out, "Why . . . ? Why are we being so cruelly punished?"

Even as she spoke, a meteor flashed through the sky, its wedge-shaped crimson tail brightening the darkness in a weird incandescent glow, adding terror to terror, and all those present, some screaming, some moaning, fell as one to their knees, moaning, "It is the end. . . ."

"Why are the gods so angry?"

"Where now shall our beloved ancestors go?"

"It is the end. . . . It is the end. . . ."

Kneeling, both hands covering his face, Renzō became aware that a firm hand was prodding at his shoulders. He gazed up into the face of Sudo, at the same time crying out to him hysterically, "Can all this be true . . . ? Is this night to be the end . . . ?"

"Pull yourself together," Sudo reprimanded the frenzied youth. "Remember your schooling! Rise up! Come with me."

"To go where?"

"To see history in the making. Do as I say. Now!"

The servitor had become the master. Renzō resembled a puppet controlled by a puppeteer as he followed Sudo away from the isolation of the Fukuda estate into the vortex of a city in turmoil.

Roped together for safety's sake, Renzō and Sudo struggled their way through the nightmarish atmosphere of the metropolis.

Edo's tidal waves of panic arose, fell, rose again, as rumors spread, telling not only of an invasion to the sacred shores by wicked earthly beings, but of one more awful, of an "invasion" by angry gods.

The clatter, the shouts of armored foot soldiers, the pounding hooves of war-horses, and the loud cries of brightly robed firemen pushing their carts melded in with the incessant tolling of temple bells and the terrible *don-don-don* of shrine gongs. Men, women, and terrified children shrieked in panic as they ran, not knowing where they should go and many of them searching hopelessly for lost family members.

Flames from fires which had been kindled along the rivers and the waterfront lit up the macabre scenes, and the flickering glares aroused further panic. Crazed citizens attempting to enter the already overcrowded temples and shrines were crushed underfoot and received no assistance from the monks and priests who were intent only on informing the gods that "disaster has struck our sacred land. . . ."

Just before dawn broke, Renzō and Sudo, bedraggled and exhausted, arrived at the waterfront, where they fought their way to the top of a crowded, tottering lookout tower. Speaking for the first time, Renzō clutched at Sudo's frail shoulder, whispering, "Sudo San. Explain! Tell me. . . . Tell me what goes on?"

For some moments Sudo remained silent as he craned his neck toward the dark ocean, then he said, "Put simply, a flotilla of American warships stands at anchor in the bay at Uraga. Put simply, we are in for a period of shocking humiliation. Put simply, I believe that our isolation from the rest of the world is about to end."

With a spine-tingling surge of excitement, Renzō recalled the day when he had freed his grandfather's birds from their cages.

He recalled the many times he had gazed out toward the dark line dividing the ocean from the sky, and he recalled his longing to know what lay beyond the mysterious horizon.

"Don't you understand what I am telling you?" Sudo muttered harshly.

Wildly flamboyant visions flashed through Renzō's mind, visions of traveling far away to see for himself the wonders of the modern world he knew so little about. Visions of his own country no longer closed up. Visions of an entire people freed from the power so ruthlessly wielded by the despotic, self-appointed generalissimos for hundreds of years.

Gazing downward, he saw crazed citizens lugging cartloads and buckets of mud, working like maniacs in the glare of the fires, calling out, their voices hoarse, "Death to all barbarians" as they went about the building of a puny mud fortress.

"Don't you understand what I have told you?" Sudo repeated even more harshly.

Renzō raised one hand and gestured toward the horizon, then he replied quietly, "I understand."

LATE IN THE AFTERNOON FOLLOWING that day and night of chaos, the governor of Uraga halted a contingent of bemused, terrified

Dutch nationals who, under heavy guard, arrived at the besieged town from Edo on the way back to their headquarters in the distant city, Nagasaki.

On sighting the gun-spiked American vessels anchored off shore, and seeing the thousands of heavily armed Japanese warriors setting up camps in the area, shouting exaltingly, "Death! Death to all barbarians . . ." the Hollanders expected at any moment to have their heads swordslashed from their torsos. However, their fears were allayed for the time being when a governor's aide, outwardly calm, although obviously stressed, ordered that they should be detained and kept under heavy guard for their own protection.

The helpless foreigners were quick-marched to a strongly barred room to await their fate. Not one man had any hope of surviving the oncoming battle, for even though modern firearms had the power to make the bravest of warriors bow down in abject servility, this was Japan, a land of aggressive, highly trained militarists, each one passionately convinced that it was his duty to die for Nippon, the sacred land.

When dawn arrived, another government official entered the overcrowded, airless room and requested a proficient interpreter—only one. Immediately, a man stepped forward, exclaiming, "I, Jan Van der Linden, am proficient."

He acted not with bravado but with desperation. He suffered from claustrophobia and felt that he would prefer to die in the open rather than in a closed room behind bars. Once outside, he drew gusts of fresh air into his lungs as armed guards led him through streets where with fanatical, crazed energy, preparations were being made to do combat with the invaders. As he walked through the milling crowds of citizens and armed warriors, Van der Linden was convinced that a holocaust of bloodletting was about to take place.

As though oblivious of the anchored American warships, small-armed Japanese crafts were being rowed hither and thither over the sunlit water, while on land men, women, and children dragged cartloads of mud and sacks of stones to bolster up the town's crumbling fortifications under the instructions of inexperienced men.

Stentorian shouting came from the camps of warriors engaged in setting up high cloth screens emblazoned with the crests of their clans, as they prepared for battle. Every temple bell rang out, adding to the apprehension Jan was feeling in the tinderbox atmosphere of the once-peaceful town.

He was shoved through milling groups of sword-brandishing warriors who on sighting him shouted blood-chilling slogans:

"Kill all intruders . . ."

"Death to all barbarians . . ."

"Death to all traitors . . ."

Arriving at the governor's unpretentious residence, the Dutchman was led into a four-and-a-half-mat room furnished with a low table and one floor-cushion. He was then left alone, wryly wishing that he were a religious man, able to gain solace by prayer, but being a realist, he compelled himself into a state of calm by dwelling on the events that had led him to this place at this time of terror and uncertainty.

Van der Linden, now forty, recalled how excited he had been when aged twenty he had been offered a posting to Japan as a clerk in the Netherlands Trading Company. While traveling Japanward, he had imagined that he was going to an exotic land, one where the white man would be held in respect. But those dreams and expectations had turned to ashes and gradually the rot had set in once he was incarcerated on the island of Dejima.

The wily Dutch company's headquarters in Holland, intent on placating their isolated employees, sent luxurious goods to better their lives. They received free cigars, spirits of every kind, clothes, musical instruments, and, to Van der Linden's pleasure, books and manuals.

The even more wily shogun government had, with their uncanny insight into human nature, made certain that the desires of the flesh were catered to—male and female prostitutes were permitted to have dealings with the Dutch residents.

Yuri, one of those harlots, had become Van der Linden's woman. He had been inexperienced, inhibited, and shy. She had been experienced, uninhibited, and adventurous, more than willing not only to endure his clumsiness but to take him high into ecstasies of sensual passion. Their relationship continued and she had twice borne his children.

Bribery and corruption were rampant in Dejima, and thus his two daughters had dwelt on the island for some years, along with those children sired by other inmates. Then, out of the blue, they had all been taken away, leaving much heartbreak and anger. The children's fate was unknown. Yuri, herself bereft but helpless, had bowed her head, saying, "It is said they have been taken far away to live in a country called Macao. Nothing can be done."

He had suffered grief and resentment, but time had dulled those emotions. He had studied the Japanese language, understood its complexities, and had become so proficient that his services were forever in demand. This, his most recent expedition to the shogunate in Edo, had been but one of many.

Even though he traveled under heavy guard and endured extreme humiliations while in the capital, those long journeys through Japan's countryside had relieved the "closed-in" times of panic he often experienced walled up on Dejima. . . .

An overwhelming feeling of nausea brought Van der Linden's mind back to the present. About to stand up in order to relieve his cramped stomach and legs, he stoically remained seated as the door slid open. Accustomed to the arrogance of Japanese officialdom, he was not prepared for the cordial greeting he received from the governor's aide into whose presence he was ushered.

The aide, a stocky man, spoke gravely: "We appreciate your cooperation, Van der Linden San. An onerous situation has arisen. Abrupt changes in society are dangerous. Changes must be always constructive and gradually made. May I presume that you agree? I allude to your willingness to collaborate. You understand?"

Not fully understanding, Van der Linden nevertheless gestured in the affirmative, whereupon six men entered the room. They listened as the aide informed them in a staccato manner that after prolonged anxieties, and much soul-searching by the governor and his colleagues, a barge had carried local officials out to board the American flagship. He ended by stating, "We Japanese were treated most courteously while on board."

He explained that the American squadron's leader, Commodore Matthew Calbraith Perry, Commander of the United States Naval Forces, Special Ambassador to Japan, had played the role of an omnipotent Being whose visage was not to be looked upon lightly. He had not appeared, but had let it be known that he "intended" to come ashore. He let it be known that he had come on a "friendly mission," bringing letters from the President of America which were to be delivered to the emperor, the ruler of Japan.

"Let me report," the aide continued, "that our delegation acted with dignity while on board. We were proffered and accepted a beverage called champagne and quaffed it down, at the same time not hiding the fact that we were fully aware why the intruders had come from America. These American warriors of the sea have arrived here with a deep knowledge of our country.

"We let it be known that we will be pleased to welcome the high and mighty commodore ashore, showing him every courtesy. We beseeched that we should be given time to make suitable preparations for an auspicious reception. This was agreed to. . . ."

Falling silent, he stared into space for a short interval, then with an abrupt turn of his head he gazed at the Dutchman, saying quietly, "Until your services are required, certain arrangements have been made for your security."

Exhausted, Van der Linden tried to quell his rising panic as he was escorted to a servant's cottage on the grounds of the residence. He was convinced that a cunning trap was being prepared to "welcome" the American invaders.

He spent the remainder of that day and the following night in the company of an old woman. She expressed no amazement at her "guest's" fluent use of her language as she bustled about the stifling hot room, bringing the Dutchman snacks to eat, while she chatted about the weather, not once alluding to the sounds of pandemonium in the area.

She displayed no interest in the soldiers who stood guarding the house, and on learning that the foreigner had no family of his own, she bowed in a regretful manner, murmuring, "Sad, sad! I pity you. . . ."

When dawn arrived, he offered her his gold cigar case in payment for her enforced hospitality. With innate dignity she refused the proffered gift saying, "Gokigenyō—Please travel life happily and safely."

Escorted back to the outside world, Van der Linden saw that the number of troops in the vicinity had greatly increased and the spectacle which met his eyes discouraged any hopes for a peaceful confrontation. Along the sandy beach and surrounding the entire area stood thousands of warriors garbed in ribbed leather and iron armor. Behind them was the mounted cavalry wearing spike-horned helmets, flanked by standard-bearers holding aloft battle-worn crimson pennants. Swords were sheathed but hands were twitching at the ready for action.

Looking around him, he was aware of their sullen, smoldering anger, and wondered what the eventual death toll would be. He was certain that he himself had but a short time left to live.

The overall silence was more spine-chilling than the battle cries had been, and the screeching of the gulls played havoc with his taut nerves. Never before had he comprehended the true meaning of the word *alone*.

As he was marched toward a recently erected marquee that served as the audience hall, his habitual dislike for many things Japanese changed into admiration for the undeniable artistry of the hasty preparations that had been made. The interior walls of the hall were hung with lengths of violet silk gathered together by thick cords of rose-pink hues. Richly carved chairs commandeered from Buddhist temples were placed on a raised dais carpeted with red felt and magnificent arrangements of azaleas were placed about the chamber. To his perplexed mind the place exuded a beautiful, a peaceful atmosphere.

Then, once again, he became convinced that the pretty arrangements were but one part of the overall cunning trap. But then, as the governor's aide came forward to greet him most politely, he felt that maybe at long last the prevailing regime of the shogun might be about to bow to the inevitable.

The aide, now robed ceremoniously, instructed him to keep himself in readiness when—and if—his services as an interpreter were to be called upon, and he had but a few moments to take in the sight of the functionaries seated on the dais, including two dignified, middle-aged men, both gorgeously dressed in garments of brocade elaborately embroidered with gold and silver thread.

Ushered from the hall, he stood to attention, gazing outward across the water where the American squadron was at anchor.

One, two, three hours elapsed.

No movement on the warships.

No movement on land.

No sound except for the cries of the gulls . . .

Then Van der Linden watched spellbound as American cutters carrying some three hundred men approached the landing pier. He shuddered as American cannons boomed out a thunderous salute. A wave of movement swept through the ranks of mounted warriors, as they struggled to control the terror of neighing horses and their own wrenched nerves.

Star-spangled American flags fluttered on the cutters. Officers, marines, and sailors detailed for the day's ceremonies were resplendent in their pristine uniforms. Music played by a band on one of the cutters was martial, yet macabrely cheerful.

A drawn-out moan of protest seeped from the throats of some ten thousand humiliated Japanese warriors as Commodore Matthew Perry landed. Tall, dignified, expressionless, he marched, back erect, head topped by a high-plumed hat. Preceding him were two gold-braided ensigns carrying highly polished wooden caskets. The commodore, flanked by two stalwart black men, moved steadily forward toward the audience hall, followed by his retinue, all marching in step to the persistent drumrolling and the band music.

No violence occurred.

On reaching the audience hall, the Americans halted. The band and drumrolling ceased. Two Japanese officials bowed low, very low. Drawing the silken curtains aside, they gestured that the commodore and his attendants should enter.

With an abrupt hand salute, responding to the bows, the Americans entered the edifice. The curtains were closed.

Outside that conference chamber there was silence but for the cries of gulls.

For the remainder of his life Van der Linden was to feel that he then lived through an eternity of time. However, just twenty minutes had gone by before those closed curtains had once more been drawn aside.

The band struck up as the "visitors" emerged. With brisk military precision the Americans marched to their cutters and returned across the sparkling blue waters to board their great vessels. The commodore left behind the dread information that he would return again to Japan, in February the following year, with a larger squadron, expecting to conclude an amicable treaty.

"So," Van der Linden wondered, "so, can it be that Japan's closed door has at last been pushed ajar?"

Ignorant about the fate of his colleagues and not daring to make inquiries, he was escorted back to Edo and once there, was told that his services would be required as a translator until further notice.

The clothing and personal possessions he had been traveling with were brought to him. He was provided with pleasant quarters, and when his services were not required he was given permission to move about the city accompanied by two young guards.

Edo was the heart of a newly arisen society. The steady beat of that heart was felt beneath the façade of conformity as the citizens hustled and bustled, going about their business. Van der Linden saw them to be good-natured people and he would have walked among them unguarded without fear for his person.

It was astonishing to see shops and booths in the capital selling fans, banners, lanterns, and model toys depicting those "mysterious ships of evil mien," in a humorous, colorful manner, and, depicting even more grotesquely the figures and visages of the American intruders, especially those of the two stalwart black men who had attended the commodore and who were thought to have had their bodies painted especially for the occasion.

The city Edo was ugly, but the cheerful citizens, the bright banners, the flowers, gave it a certain charm that relaxed him. He became accustomed to having artists sketch him, tailors scrutinize his apparel, fingering the lapels of his jacket, its buttons, and muttering, "Interesting, very interesting . . ."

Months had gone by, then, accordingly, in February 1854, the American squadron sailed into the Gulf of Edo. The frosts and winds of winter added to the tensions of the Japanese officials who straightaway boarded the flagship, requesting that the commodore should return to his former anchorage in Uraga. They informed him that bitter political feelings were running high in the capital and that the "visitors' " safety could not be vouched for.

The great commodore firmly declined, but after many conferences and much parley, he finally compromised, agreeing that he would conduct negotiations at an anchorage abreast of the fishing hamlet of Yokohama.

Van der Linden, hustled off to the hamlet, watched as the American squadron steamed into Yokohama Bay, where at the anchorage there was just sufficient room for the whole squadron of nine ships that had taken up their position in a menacing line of battle.

On shore, Japanese warriors, flag bearers, and musicians were lined up, outwardly obedient, inwardly agonized. Their emblazoned coats of armor, glistening lacquered headgear, and crimson pennants made a picturesque scene beneath the clear blue of the winter sky.

Seventeen American guns boomed out in a salute to Japan's "emperor" as Commodore Perry's barge touched the shore, and when the band struck up and the splendidly outfitted contingent marched toward the newly built audience hall, American howitzers commenced firing a salute of twenty-one guns.

To Van der Linden's disappointment, he once again was not present to interpret during the many conferences which were carried out between the commodore and the high-ranking Japanese officials.

As the days went by, and while the Japanese conferred on how to circumvent the American proposals put forward, the crowd of onlookers increased. Only by using physical force could the Japanese authorities have prevented the intermingling that took place between the citizens and the barbarian interlopers.

To Van der Linden the Americans were anything but barbarians. Never had he imagined that men could be so at ease during a time of such stress. They were exuberantly healthy, so spic-and-span and, without exception, courteous under extremely complex circumstances.

Try as he would, the Dutchman could not rid himself of a latent fear that at any moment a blood-shedding disaster was about to take place. He could not believe that Japan's fight-to-the-death warriors would endure such nerve-wracking humiliation, and he dreaded their vengeance.

Despite his fears he determined to show a cheerful mein when called upon to act as an interpreter, working in tandem with a young lieutenant who was boyishly impressed with his fluency in speaking the Japanese, English, and Dutch languages. The young man had no interest in anything Japanese, except for currency, asking if the Japanese gold *koban* coin actually had pure gold content, saying that he was eager to take a necklace of coins back to Baltimore as a gift for his sweetheart, but only if the coins were of pure gold.

When the delivery of gifts intended for the emperor was brought ashore and exhibited to the people, such a highly charged eruption of excitement and curiosity burst forth that the atmosphere changed to that of a festival. As he moved about in the milling crowd, Van der Linden found himself laughing convulsively and shouting out encouragement together with the lieutenant and the Japanese onlookers as they watched elderly officials squatting on and clinging to the roof of a miniature steam-driven locomotive which was put into operation on a circular track of rails. With no inhibitions, men, women, and children pressed forward pleading to have the experience of being twirled around at the terrifying rate of some seven or so miles an hour.

Intense interest was aroused by a telegraph outfit that was set up. Citizens stood by for hours, watching, mystified while cadets extended the wires in a direct line at buildings a mile apart. When finally communication was set up, pandemonium broke out as the onlookers learned that in an instant of time messages were being conveyed from building to building. Dignitaries and all and sundry stood in line pleading with the Americans to work their magic again and again, murmuring among themselves, "*Omoshiroi*—interesting beyond belief."

"How admirable! How amazing . . ."

"Yes, but above all, how cheated we have been all these long years locked away from all these remarkable, useful inventions . . ."

"Yes, so I feel. Personally, I'm filled with resentment. . . ."

"I also. So, these pleasant, clever men are savage barbarians? Nonsense. Absolute nonsense. . . ."

"Yes. I feel so fooled. *Nothing* hurts more than ignorance. . . ."

Boarding one of the American ships, Van der Linden was taken aback to see how the Japanese functionaries and their attendants went mooching about, peeping into the muzzles of guns, handling the ropes, looking here, there, everywhere, making notes on mulberry-bark paper with their cakes of ink and fine brushes, indulging their curiosity to the limit. They seemed completely at ease and not at all in awe of the Americans, who as usual behaved in the most polite manner at all times.

Knowing the irksome Japanese custom of dragging out negotiations, Van der Linden was in no way surprised when many days went by before a treaty satisfactory to both parties was signed.

Hour after hour, day following day, the two factions worried on, each one determined to outwit the other. In the end a sanguine Commodore Perry became the victor, and celebratory banquets were given both onshore and aboard the ships.

Courtly thanks were made to the Americans for their gifts to the "emperor." In the "emperor's" name, a haul of glorious gifts was presented in return for "the pleasure of the President of the United States of America."

Following the gift presentations, Van der Linden as an interpreter attended a banquet on board the flagship. It was a sumptuous affair, where champagne flowed freely, arousing unrestrained conviviality. The Japanese dignitaries took the lead in proposing toast after toast, shouting loudly and enthusiastically so as to be heard above the music of the bands which played cheerful celebratory tunes.

Satisfied that the treaty had been signed and delivered, the intrepid commodore then proceeded with a party for some miles into the country, wanting to see the scenery and to meet the inhabitants. Charmed by the scenery and favorably impressed by the people and the tidiness of their dwellings, he instructed the Japanese officials to cease from interfering with his rights to mingle freely. Most unwilling, the Japanese officials obeyed his orders.

The Americans appeared to have no knowledge of, or any interest in the internal rumblings which were gathering force between different political factions in the land. Van der Linden had come to believe that the Americans were not aware that the "mighty emperor" was but a powerless Being tucked away in Kyoto, or, that it was the powerful shogun-run government to whom they were paying such honor.

Following the departure of the Americans, Van der Linden was astonished to be set free with no instructions as to how he should support himself.

Unaccustomed to freedom, he was at a loss. Nevertheless, glad to be alive, he began to revel in the unexpected time of liberation, and after those many closeted years spent on Dejima Island, he began to feel at his ease. He roamed about, conversing with the country folk, who saw him as a token man; they called him "Jan San" and invited him to stay in their tiny houses and huts and share their food.

These peasant folk were so hospitable that Van der Linden never lacked a night's lodging and never paid for it. But as the months went by, things changed when ships brought other foreigners to the port. Men from many lands, out for what they could get, aroused disgust and fear in the little community as their harbor frontage of Yokohama was transformed into a rough boomtown.

Soon Japanese merchants on the make arrived from Edo, setting up booths and shops, charging high prices for cheap goods, inveigling the foreign merchants and seamen to purchase secondhand kimono, garish hair ornaments, poor quality lacquerware, even terrified baby bears attached to chains.

Before too long, an immense "pleasure house" was built on the edge of the marshlands. It was erected hastily by the enterprising government as a resort for the Westerners, who had been more than willing to indulge in the pleasures of the flesh, to "buy" a girl for their personal use if they so wished, never questioning the price.

Liquor shops sprang up and drunkenness was rife. It seemed to Jan Van der Linden that his paradise was becoming a nightmarish town, and gradually his Japanese acquaintances had begun to avoid him. Without their hospitality he was homeless. Forced into selling his meager personal possessions in order to exist, he lost weight and before too long his garments became ragged, his hair and beard long and unkempt.

One blustery autumn day he left the foul-smelling, crowded harbor area to walk several miles along the coast to the Bay of Hommoku.

On reaching the crescent-shaped beach, he gazed upward to the pine-clad hills. At the sight of a large building on the top of one hill, at once a memory stirred in his mind.

Vaguely, he recalled a Japanese scholar of the Dutch language, whom he had met on several occasions in the past. That handsome, pleasant fellow had spoken of a seignorial school which he had been trained in. He had spoken of his home in a fishing hamlet, Yokohama, describing it in a colorful manner, explaining that it looked out over the ocean.

Van der Linden was unable to recall the man's name. Nevertheless, as though directed by another power, he made his way up the narrow, winding track and on reaching the entrance of the largest building a distant monastery bell began to chime most sweetly. Suddenly he remembered that the scholar's name was Yamamoto. Kenichi Yamamoto, the son of the school's master.

The school building was shuttered and silent. Down at heart, he pushed open a postern gate and passed into a stylized, extraordinarily beautiful garden.

Standing on a fragile, curved bridge was a woman who, on seeing him, became rigid, staring at him, her face set and cold.

Aware that his unkempt appearance terrified her, he bowed deeply, speaking courteously as he explained that he was an acquaintance of the scholar Kenichi Yamamoto and was desirous of meeting with him once again, adding with humility, "I am at starvation point, sorely in need of advice and assistance."

The woman, obviously still fearful, called out flutingly, "Renzō ... Renzō ..." and a youth came rushing from the house. ...

PART II

RUMI YAMAMOTO'S SERVING-MAID, KENKO, was relieved that the onerous task of assisting her mistress to don Western attire had been completed without too many complaints and scoldings.

She wondered why a woman who possessed so many kimono, *obi*-sashes, and rich accessories chose to wear such complex, uncomfortable garments. She sighed at the thought of having to tidy up the shambles that had been created. "Shall I now go to prepare your footwear, young mistress?" she asked humbly.

"Umm . . . ? What . . . ? Oh—my shoes! No, no, Misa can attend to that. Kenko, go to the street and hail a ricksha. Please don't dawdle. Time is passing."

When Kenko had left the room Rumi stood before the long beveled mirror, critically examining her image. Twisting sideways, she admired her silhouette. The blue taffeta bodice continued into a point on her stomach beneath which a dark purple sheath-skirt decorated with a mass of frills fell to the floor continuing on into a short train. Beneath those garments she wore a Cranfield bustle, imported from London, a cleverly contrived contraption with a wire spring that folded up when its wearer was sitting or lying down, to resume its proper shape upon rising.

Her luxuriant hair was arranged in a series of plaits tied back into a bun and a small pillbox hat trimmed with a tuft of white feathers tilted perkily over her forehead.

Not quite satisfied with her appearance, Rumi became aware that her mother-in-law, Lady Masa, was gazing into the room through the partially opened sliding doors. As usual, the older woman's expression was enigmatic, but there was a glimmer of amusement in her voice as she said, "So, you are finally dressed, Rumi. What trials you undergo. Old age has its compensations."

"Really?" Rumi replied smilingly. "I hope I live long enough to discover that for myself. Mother, I admire your good taste, so tell me, does this hat clash with my bodice?"

"Better perhaps the one with violet clusters and veil?"

"Exactly!" While making the change, Rumi chattered on, speaking quickly as was her habit, saying, "Mother, I regret that you refuse so many invitations. Afternoon receptions at the French legation are so stylish. My sister, Aiko, told me that her mother-in-law might be present. Evidently Aunt Sumiko is herself again. How embarrassing it was for her family having her believe that she was fox-haunted. Aiko tells me that the old lady went about with a peculiar animal expression, holding her hands up like paws."

"Never mind. Sumiko has recovered from her ordeal."

"True! Aiko told me that Yuichi pampered his mother. Also, that he paid a veritable fortune to an exorcist who stayed on in the house for a month, demanding fine food and foreign wines which he gobbled and quaffed between sessions of praying and reading from ancient Buddhist scripts."

"Is that so?"

"Yes. Such nonsense. Aiko's husband is superstitious beyond belief, but I *personally* considered Aunt Sumiko to be a most logical woman."

"Sumiko still grieves for the loss of her husband. Grief has no logic."

"You think so? Mother, excuse my frankness, but I can't help feeling that Aunt Sumiko should have been somewhat relieved by her husband's passing into the spirit world."

"Relieved?"

"Yes, relieved! Poor old man, there he would stand, beating a tattoo on his chest." Rumi mimed the action while continuing on, deepening her light voice, speaking excitedly, exclaiming, "Behold me—*Fukuda*! My eyes were the first to see those black warships at Uraga. Ho-*ho*, was I scared? Just let me say that on the following morning, when I crept from the hut in which I had been hiding, my curiosity took over. *What did I do?* I inveigled a fisherman to row me, also my two artist employees, way out across the water. Yes, ho-ho, out to the great ships. From high decks the American invaders looked down, admiring our bravado as our frail craft bobbed on the choppy waves. Until too seasick to continue, my artists sketched away. *Ho-ho*, and before the week was up our shops did a roaring trade selling goods depicting strange ships and the hook-nosed, hairy-faced barbarians. *Ho-ho-ho* . . ."

"You are quite an accomplished mimic, Rumi," Lady Masa interjected.

"Is that a reproach? If so, please excuse me. I intended no unkindness. Fukuda Sama was a nice old man, but is it not true that his illness affected his reason?"

"Unfortunately, sadly, yes."

"So, surely Aunt Sumiko found it tiresome, always hovering over an old man who gabbled out ridiculous tales, reliving the past."

"Tiresome! Reliving the past . . ." Lady Masa, about to continue, fell silent, closing her eyes for a moment, then, removing a fan from her sash, she pointed it toward the direction of the front entrance porch, saying quietly, "Here comes your maid. Your ricksha has arrived. Rumi, please give my regards to all. Please, return home soon and safely."

"I shall, Mother. Kindly excuse my not farewelling you as I should and as I wish, but my bustle is not made for floor-kneeling."

"I understand. *Asonde kudasai*—Please enjoy yourself."

Returning her daughter-in-law's bow, Masa stood by watching Fat Misa kneeling at Rumi's feet to assist her with the intricacies of buckling on foreign shoes before sliding open the entrance door of the house which led out to the paved Tokyo street where a man-pulled ricksha stood waiting.

For ten years Masa had lived in the family house in Nihombashi. She disliked the place intensely but accepted her situation, obeying her son's dictates when he informed her that his young wife yearned to live once more in the capital she had been born in and which she knew and loved.

Speaking rather haltingly, Renzō asked, "Does the plan disturb you unduly, Mother?"

"Not in the least," she murmured untruthfully. "Are you intending to build a house there?"

"Build! No. Mother, surely you recall that we have a family house in Nihombashi?"

"*That* house?"

"Yes. It shall be refurbished—modernized, a second story built. Mother, the district has changed. No more trashy little shops in our street but newly built Western-styled buildings. The old house now stands between a three-storied English bank and a two-storied edifice belonging to an American shipping company. And—"

"Enough!" She interrupted him gently, then even more gently she murmured, "Renzō, I have no reservations where any of your plans are concerned. Surely you know that. I have but one query to make. Need I state it?"

"No. I understand. It concerns the woman who has occupied the house these last years?"

"Quite true. So . . . ?"

"So—that one—in the house at Nihombashi shall be given shelter here in this Yokohama house. It must be so. It is my duty to care for her welfare. For the sake of my father's spirit, I . . ."

"Enough!" she once again interrupted. "Please be free to make your arrangements."

Renzō made his arrangements and she was swept along in their wake, likening herself to an outmoded barge towed by a fast-moving steamship.

Following Rumi's departure from the house, Masa made her way to her private quarters, one ten-mat room on the ground floor, which opened out onto a miniature garden. Seating herself on a cushion, she saw her grandson, Shinichi, aged ten and as straight as a dagger, standing on a moss pad gazing down intently into the fish pond.

She loved him dearly, but no boy had greater proclivities for mischief than he. "Don't disturb my *koi*, Shin-chan," she called, and she flashed him a smile as he leapt up guiltily.

"I am just—looking," he said placatingly. "Never again would I catch one of your fish and feed it to Neko."

"I'm glad to know that. Where *is* your cat?"

"Neko is gone. I'm wondering where. Old Misa told me maybe *you* chased it away, Obā-chama, to punish me. Did you?"

"Certainly not. Neko will come back. Cats always do. Now, please be more careful. Don't stamp about like that on the moss. Walk carefully. Come, I shall read you a story."

"No. I must find Neko. . . ."

As he rushed off, Masa called, "Come back. Remember your manners."

The child halted and made a brief, sharp bow in her direction, then, grinning widely, he ran from the garden, yelling, "Neko, Neko, Neko . . ."

Once more alone Masa felt that she should bring up with her daughter-in-law the subject of her grandson's unmannerly ways. But why disturb family harmony? Better by far to keep one's innermost thoughts unspoken. Voicing them could cause unpleasantness such as that which existed in the Fukuda household, where Sumiko and her daughter-in-law were in a perpetual state of warfare—Sumiko, always defeated, while Aiko, the victor, went her way triumphantly. At times Aiko behaved outrageously, appearing in society wearing European male apparel, clad in narrow, pinstripe trousers, wearing a jacket cut away at the waist with short tails, a high top hat on her head. She would stride about carrying a gold-topped walking stick, exclaiming, "I *prefer* to dress this way. I refuse to have *my* person squeezed into wired armor. If my husband has no objections, why should his mother—or anyone?"

"But that is not so, Masa," Sumiko had confided, tearfully. "Yuichi lives in fear of his wife's acid tongue. Masa, I envy you. Rumi is so malleable, so pretty."

"That is so," she had replied. She had not confided in Sumiko about her own daughter-in-law's faults. Truthfully, she had little in common with Rumi, so apt to become churlish if criticized even slightly.

If given a choice, she would have preferred Aiko as a family member, but one made the best of things. At times she wondered if a woman had ever existed who felt that any female was worthy of being her son's wife. She thought not.

Sumiko's son, Yuichi, had a promiscuous nature, inconstant, sharp, full of witty sayings, and a talent for getting his own way in the world of business. Different indeed from her own son, Renzō. Yet the two men were closer than brothers.

She found their companionship admirable but not the way they rushed headlong, ruthlessly determined not only to Westernize themselves, but the country itself. They actually applauded when gracious, ancient buildings and houses were demolished to be replaced by brick monstrosities that people entered wearing their street footwear.

Admittedly, she herself enjoyed traveling in the trains that snaked their way along iron rails, and she appreciated the convenience of communicating by telegraph.

Above all, she rejoiced that the mikado had taken his rightful place, dwelling with his empress in the Imperial Palace, yes, as an emperor honored by diplomats from many lands, granting them audiences, entertaining them at splendid banquets and receptions, accepting toasts from those representing Queen Victoria of England, the king of Persia, the presidents of America and France, among other rulers.

One of the highlights in her uneventful life had been to witness the young emperor's arrival in the capital. The city's officials and citizens had gone through months of crazed activity preparing for that auspicious day which had begun the "Enlightened Government of Brilliant Rule."

Rarely had she been so emotionally moved as on that chilly sunlit

November day, when she had witnessed the royal procession
streaming along, resembling a slowly flowing river, glowing gold,
silver, crimson, and all colors of the rainbow.

Sunlight had lit up the sheen of the escorts' silken garments as
they surrounded the emperor's domed-roofed, black-lacquered palanquin topped by the magnificent golden phoenix. The palanquin
had glittered brightly as it was carried forward, high upon the
shoulders of its honored bearers, each one garbed in yellow brocade
and wearing grotesque medieval head ornaments.

Sometime later, Renzō had told her that although eminent foreigners had been impressed by the exotic pageantry, they had been
scornful, insulting to the extreme, about the Japanese troops bringing up the rear of the grand procession.

"Is that so?" she had murmured. "Renzō, I also thought them to
be unkempt, clumsy in their ill-fitting Western uniforms. You did
not find them so?"

"Truthfully, yes I did. Mother, it's all so embarrassing. We are
tragically behind the times."

"Take care, Renzō, not to develop an inferiority complex. Was it
not *you* who recently made a quote, saying with confidence, '*The
city Roma was not built in one day*'?"

"Yes." He had grinned at her, then he had spoken seriously, saying, "Now that old fears, old enmities, are being done away with,
before too long we will become less ill at ease, more accustomed to
foreign protocol."

Well, Renzō had been correct. Gradually, things were improving.
Foreigners in Japan were no longer offensively alluded to as barbarians. Recently, an official manual had been widely circulated, entitled
"Seventeen Subjects of Inquiry As to the Means of Washing Away
the Shame of our Country in Regard to Foreign Relations."

The manual had been pounced on, studied avidly, and it was rumored that when His Royal Highness, the Duke of Edinburgh, the
son of Queen Victoria, had come on an official visit, not only had
he enjoyed himself immensely, he had *praised* the manner of the hospitality offered to him. When back in his own land, he had spoken
of the "chat" he had held with the mikado which had taken place
in a "wondrously lovely waterfall pavilion. . . ."

She, Masa, had read with great interest that the English duke presented the mikado with a diamond-studded snuffbox, a token from
his illustrious mother, the queen.

Masa's thoughts were broken into by the sight of Shinichi's cat slinking toward her fish pond. She shuddered involuntarily and rose hastily to drive the creature away.

Settling herself down again, she was embarrassed by the animosity the cat always aroused in her. She had a tenderness toward all living creatures. Why then did she wish that Neko would run away and return no more?

Ten years ago when the family had arrived in Edo—no, she must accustom herself to calling the capital Tokyo—a very old cat firmly entrenched on the premises of the Nihombashi house had given birth to a litter of kittens. Rumi had insisted on keeping one, Neko, as a pet.

Naturally she, Masa, had made no objections, but apart from worry about the welfare of her brocaded carp she believed that the animal stared at her insultingly, as though to say, "My green eyes see things *you* cannot see. My peaked ears hear ghostly voices *you* cannot hear."

Could it be, she wondered, that Shinichi's pet had descended from a cat that had belonged to, had been fondled by the courtesan whom Kenichi had loved so passionately?

Try as she would, she was unable to prevent herself from imagining the erotic scenes that must have taken place between her husband and the harlot, Osen. These fabricated scenes mortified her spirit. Nevertheless, she felt that the very air of the house was unfriendly to her. Of late she was cast down by feelings of despair, overcome by negative emotions.

As a young girl she had been torn from her childhood home. As an aging widow she had been torn from the home in Yokohama which she had learned to love and where she had made a life that pleased her. Now, here in Nihombashi, she felt so cramped, her individuality crushed.

Certainly, she had been severely perturbed when those invading American warships had arrived at Uraga. Yes, and how terrified she had been also when the tall, gaunt Dutchman Van der Linden had appeared so suddenly in her garden. Although certain that he was out to molest her, she had remained outwardly calm. Fortunately so, for the man, with no evil intent, had come to the house on the hill, not only hoping to renew his acquaintance with Kenichi, but in great need of succor.

She had given him shelter in the schoolhouse for a short time, but now it was rumored that the Dutchman had gone off to live in a place called Macao.

Masa had seen Yokohama turn into a degraded shantytown, and then, gradually, into a splendid port city.

During those early days it was disturbing to have riotous foreign men riding roughshod about the countryside, hunting and shooting waterfowl and foxes. They used to tramp their way up the hillside and boldly enter through the gates of the Yamamoto property.

The port city had grown up by the harbor and on the surrounding marshlands several miles away from the beach of Hommoku. She had rejoiced in those circumstances. When Westerners built small dwellings along the beachfront, it had not offended her sensibilities too deeply. Masa had enjoyed strolling about, surreptitiously examining the foreigners' houses and the inmates, interested to see their clothing, especially their underwear hanging out to dry on lines strung up in their gardens. Such extraordinary garments!

Naturally, she had kept herself aloof from those newcomers, but having learned that one small, ugly building was not a dwelling but a Christian chapel, she had been unable to restrain her curiosity and had entered the shrine.

How cold and unimpressive it had been; no decorations, no color, no incense burning, no chanting monks in impressive robes.

But, on the other hand, the German missionary Dreyer, and his wife, had come forward at her entry, not bowing, but thrusting their hands forward. At a loss, she had tentatively stuck her own hand out. First, the man had grasped and clutched it, shaking it up and down again and again. Then his wife had performed the same act.

Masa had been horrified by the intimacy of their actions. But her heart had gone out to the kindly couple, both so eager to find another convert to their faith.

They had not converted her. In fact, their converts had been so few that after several years had gone by, with great common sense they had turned the ugly little chapel into an eating house, converting great numbers of Japanese people not to Christianity but to the delights of pork, sauerkraut, and apple strudel. The Dreyers had become rich. Their eating house had expanded and grown famous.

She still found those hand-shaking salutations too intimate, although she accepted them as an intrinsic Western custom, in no way so loathsome as was their custom of placing one's mouth on the other's cheek. To be subjected to performing such an outrageous salutation scarcely bore thinking of. The two cultures coming together so suddenly had caused many problems, many misunderstandings. One needed to bolster one's sense of humor, to discipline one's feelings. Everyone made mistakes. Westerners ridiculed the way people removed their street footwear before entering a train's carriage, quite often leaving their clogs on the station platform while the smoke-belching locomotive sped away.

Above all, Japanese people disliked being ridiculed. Throughout history ridicule had been considered to cause too much pain for it ever to be endured. But foreign ways were entering the native community and long-established ethics were disintegrating. Recently, during the Cherry Blossom Festival, she had been meandering along with ease in her heart while viewing the pink-hued clouds of blossoms. She and Sumiko and their daughters-in-law, all, apart from Aiko, robed in flowered silk kimono. Suddenly, they were accosted by a woman tourist, one of the many who were now flocking into the land, arriving in steamships, only too willing to purchase fake antiquities sold to them at disgracefully high prices by shameless Japanese shopkeepers. The foreign tourist woman had purchased a black cotton jacket decorated with bold Japanese characters advertising a firm that removed human waste from people's dwellings.

Obviously startled by the sight of a young Japanese woman swaggering along in foreign male attire, the woman had most politely requested Aiko to translate into English the characters on the back of her jacket.

Aiko had obliged, and to Masa's astonishment, the woman had not been upset. On the contrary, she had smiled and gone on her way, still wearing the jacket, while Aiko and Rumi exchanged wide, conspiratorial grins.

"How peculiar Westerners are," Sumiko had murmured. "Look, see how folk are laughing at her. Has she no pride?"

"I told her," Aiko had exclaimed scathingly, "that the characters read—'Beautiful is my fragrance.' "

Sumiko and Rumi had laughed hilariously, but she had not been amused.

Why was she spending her days spinning a web of unhappiness about herself? She must adapt to the foreign influences that had struck so deeply into many aspects of her life.

Just as she had learned to subdue longings for her early life in the old capital, Kyoto, so, now she must learn to subdue her nostalgia for the clean, salty air of Yokohama. She must cease thinking of *that* woman Osen now living in the grand old house on the hill. And she must cease mourning the loss of her lovely garden.

As she gazed despondently out at her present little garden, Fat Misa entered the room, shouting, "Shall I light incense sticks, Older Mistress? The lavatory cleaner has arrived. The air begins to stink."

"Please do," she replied and, watching the clumsy woman lumbering about, she recalled that her grandson had alluded to the servant as "*Old* Misa."

Misa—old? And what had Rumi said before leaving the house? Something about the stupidity of living in the past? How strongly young folk resented talk of the old ways, old customs! The young accept new ways and new customs with enthusiasm, and rightly so, for the wild passions and the fires of revolt had been extinguished. The young could not possibly comprehend the anguish felt by old samurai whose swords lay unpolished—the insignias of their manliness lying rusting from disuse. The carrying of swords had been forbidden. Many samurai, loyal to their creed, had died by their own hands, a time-honored custom that had always been followed in cases of hopeless trouble. In loyalty, many wives had also committed suicide. Numerous new-thinking men were assassinated, others had broken down from overwork.

Masa remembered so much. Too much . . .

Feudalism had not ended without dissent and bloodshed. Even though her country had been opened up to the rest of the world, and even though the power, the value of Western armaments was fully understood, the shocks to ancient traditions had been overwhelming. Throughout the land two factions had arisen. The most powerful, threatening to take up arms, preferred to die in battle against their brothers rather than to bow in humility before the arrogance of the barbarians. "Bow down? Never never!" had been their clarion cry.

Sumiko's husband, Fukuda, belonging to the second faction, was adamant in declaring that the time had arrived for the nation to wake up. Not only to *bow* before the threatened invasion, but to pounce on and take every opportunity of equipping the country with knowledge of Western commerce and education in all forms. "We must not suffer the indignity of *enforced* foreign occupation," he had insisted. "The door must be opened wide—*pushed wide by us.*"

Well, the door had been opened—wide. Perhaps too wide. Too suddenly, Masa thought.

During the past three decades a continuous stream of ships had arrived at Japan's ports and they continued to arrive, off-loading droves of Christian missionaries, mobs of businessmen, adventurers, and, unfortunately, confidence men and tricksters. Englishmen were employed in the construction of railways and telegraph and, most astonishingly, in the organization of the country's first navy. Military officers from France trained the country's soldiers in modern tactics. German nationals assisted with modern systems of local government, also with medical science. American experts supervised the system of postal service and agricultural arrangements and introduced their system of education, which, to old-time students' amazement, included lengthy vacations.

From Masa's point of view, too many old rules and regulations were done away with as though they had never existed. These days, she seldom dwelt on the past, but when she did it was difficult to realize that His Imperial Majesty was, at the time of Commodore Perry's arrival, but a child of one year, hidden away in a puppet-court in the ancient city of Kyoto.

To her delight and gratification, when the capital, Edo, had been renamed, Tokyo, the boy emperor had been brought out of seclusion and the Meiji Era, the Age of Enlightenment, had begun.

Nowadays, the emperor's undoubted enthusiasm for Western ways was sweeping throughout the land. His court and those in high echelons of society were encouraged to wear foreign garments, to build Western-style houses, and to partake of beef and ice cream and a myriad other delicacies which had been introduced by travelers from other climes. Many embassies were sent to the West. Japanese students of all ages, and from all walks of life, were attending schools and universities in various lands. Citizens of means were being motivated to travel abroad, and recently her precocious grandson had taken to parroting off a Royal edict in his sweet, treble voice; testing her memory, Masa recited very softly . . .

"If it is to be our benefit to change, let it be done quickly, on a grand sweeping scale. When the time comes, when an agreement must be made, it is important to get the right agreement, no matter how complex, how challenging. The top priority must be to think ahead, to move forward."

"Think ahead . . . move forward!" Yes, wise advice, Masa reflected. The acrid fragrance wafting from burning incense sticks was causing her eyes to water. Or so she preferred to think.

Moving out into the garden, she examined the damage her grandson had caused to the patch of emerald-green moss surrounding the tiny fish pond. Thoroughly depressed, she murmured, "I have lived too long and in vain. . . ."

Shinichi came running toward her, the cat in his arms. In one hand he held a letter and was calling, "A letter from London for you! May I have the English stamps, please?"

Immediately, her spirit was buoyed up. The letter was from Renzō.

Rescuing the gaily stamped envelope, she smiled at the boy, saying, "So—Neko did come home. That's nice for you. Yes, Shin-chan, you may have the stamps, later."

On the day following the arrival of Renzō's disturbing letter, Masa decided to call a ricksha and tour about the capital, hoping to calm her mind before paying a visit to Sumiko.

Bowling along a wide, paved road, she settled back, pleased that the ricksha runner was young and stalwart. Masa had quickly adjusted to the transition from litters to the large-wheeled ricksha, and she enjoyed spinning along in the open air.

It was said that two million persons were now dwelling in Tokyo and that one could travel some fifteen miles in two directions without reaching the surrounding countryside. Even so, apart from the few broad main roads, the place was still a positive maze of narrow streets and lanes bordered by countless small shops and dwelling houses, but it was orderly, a city wherein a person could travel without fear of molestation of any kind.

Over the years, some palaces of the once dreaded *daimyō* had been ruthlessly torn down or converted into government buildings. The one she was passing now had become the University of Tokyo. There were no longer any more semi-secret schools, and she was glad of that. It was painful to recall how Renzō had suffered beneath the stern rule of his grandfather, but the old scholar had only been doing his duty. She hoped that his spirit was not too uneasy because of the new ways.

Japan had now adopted the European calendar, but she continued to follow the old one, still relying on seasonal changes.

No longer did harlots and courtesans tie their *obi*-sashes in front to be publicly known for what they were.

It had been advised that women who could afford to should wear European clothing. Well, she had no intention of doing so.

For no obvious reason her runner brought the ricksha to a halt, and as though he had all the time in the world at his disposal, he stood staring at a newly built Christian church made of brick, topped by a slender spire pointing skyward. She found the spire aesthetically pleasing, but the young man was gesturing toward it in a derogatory manner. Apparently relieved at having expressed his opinion, he took up the shafts of the vehicle and sped onward.

She recalled how the Dutchman Van der Linden had spoken to Renzō about a group of Japanese citizens, some three hundred people, who had come forward after the arrival of the Americans. All of them had admitted that their families had been practicing the Christian faith in secret for several hundreds of years. Masa could not help but admire such integrity.

The ricksha was approaching the Imperial Palace and Masa was reminded of the "order" she had received earlier that year to attend the first reception of the empress, for the wives of American and Russian diplomats.

She had been overwhelmed by the honor. In the throne room, standing on the sidelines, scarcely breathing, she had beheld Their Imperial Majesties receiving the foreign ladies and actually shaking hands with them.

Following the drawn-out, gracious formalities, immense gold screens had been put to one side and armchairs of crimson and blue brocade had been lightly wheeled into the carpeted, elegant chamber.

She had been reluctant to waste her gaze upon the gathering of stylishly dressed European women, each one unique, with hair of various colors, several, surely most unfortunately, red-hued.

Masa's attention had gone straight to the mikado, so young, so noble, attired in purple silk, with an overdress of white and with long, flowing sleeves. The empress's hair had been drawn back from her forehead and fastened with ribbons. Her oval-shaped face was white-powdered, her lips painted vermilion. In her robe of shimmering brown silk and crimson overdress wrought with pure gold, she might have stepped from an ancient court painting.

The auspicious ceremony had been conducted in an atmosphere of extreme cordiality. When finally the signal for departure had been given, the emperor and empress had farewelled the diplomats' wives in the European manner and young Japanese maidens had come forward to carry the trains of the foreign guests.

That was the only recognition which Masa, as the daughter of an aristocratic Kyoto family, had received from the palace. She expected no other. She understood that the honor had been given, not to her as an individual, but as a solace to the spirits of her noble ancestors. *Kekkō-desu*—It had been more than enough.

Once again the ricksha came to a stop. Masa descended to the ground and joined the throng of citizens who were bowing in reverence before the royal residence. Then, having made her obsequies, she informed the ricksha runner that she wished no further delays.

Visiting the Fukuda home was always an ordeal. She was appalled by the mansion's front façade, said to be a true example of a Tudor manor house. She was always discomfited at being asked to give her opinion, saying lightly, without revealing her distaste, "I find the house—interesting." Frankly, she was not in favor of imitations of any kind.

Even the garden surrounding the mansion clashed with the building. She had greatly admired paintings depicting English-style gardens with green lawns and with a riotous splendor of colorful flowers. Here there was no lawn; the lofty cryptomeria, pine and maple trees, were surrounded by swept gravel, creating a dour atmosphere, not tranquil or conducive to meditation.

In random fashion, elaborate stone carvings of deer, storks, and tortoise stood before the imitation English façade of the house. And even more distressingly out of place were two ancient stone lanterns guarding the entrance of the residence.

On entering the house, Masa was once again struck by the conviction that no man in Japan had more determination to Westernize his home than Yuichi Fukuda. Moving hastily past many rooms, each one richly carpeted and overcrowded with massive European furniture, she was relieved when at last she entered Sumiko's hideaway, the room decorated in traditional Japanese style.

The *shōji* were wide open, capturing the perfume-filled air. An ornate iron kettle spouted out a tiny spiral of steam from its raised perch above the charcoal that burnt merrily in a well-remembered white *hibachi* decorated with snarling red dragons.

"How peaceful," Masa murmured. "Truly, Sumiko, in this room I feel so at home. I . . . ."

"You do? Then I'm pleased for you," Sumiko interjected as tears seeped from her eyes. "Personally, this room now fills me with sadness. How could it be otherwise? Ah, Masa, if you but knew of past intimacies enjoyed here, you would understand. Since my husband's departure from this world, I understand the true meaning of melancholy. . . ."

"You have all my sympathy."

"Sympathy—yes. Certainly. But not understanding. Never mind. I must not burden you with my tribulations. Masa, how does my appearance strike you?"

Gazing at Sumiko, who appeared a picture of health, Masa weighed her words carefully before saying, "Perhaps, a little fragile? Have you no appetite? Are you unable to sleep at night?"

"No desire for food. Every night I toss and turn. How could it be otherwise in this house? If you had my problems, you might understand, but your life is so uncomplicated, so trouble free."

Masa, having arrived with several burdensome problems and most desirous to discuss them, decided to bide her time to give Sumiko a chance to air her complaints.

The camaraderie between the two women remained firm, but for some years they had indulged in occasional arguments.

Flooded with warmth toward Sumiko, she spoke softly, saying, "Please be free to confide in me."

"Thank you. But first I shall order a repast. Lobster *osashimi*, perhaps? Bean curd soup, perhaps, and *sake*?"

"Perfect. That is, if those delicacies tempt your sad belly."

"Probably not, but that is of little matter."

Masa picked daintily and ate sparsely as Sumiko tucked into the midday meal with relish and drank numerous bowls of *sake*.

The meal over, the maid gone, both women fluttered their fans while Masa murmured, "Now, confide! What, for instance, is your main, your most pressing problem?"

"Masa, older sister, need you ask? Aiko, my son's wife, has become a controversial figure in Tokyo society. The very word *propriety* has no meaning to her. She is a devotee of the exotic. She despises my conservative opinions. She is uncompromising. Her character is enigmatic."

Masa smiled to herself, recalling those distressed letters that she had received many years ago from Sumiko about *her* mother-in-law.

"Masa, her air of superiority bears no description. Her insolence is *untenable*. . . ."

"But she has many virtues. She is not vindictive, not malicious, or given to the sulks. . . ."

"Excuse me for interrupting. *Most* maliciously Aiko goes out of her way to flaunt her aristocratic background."

"Excuse *me* for interrupting, but I have always been perplexed. It was my understanding that Yuichi was to be adopted into the Okura clan."

"True."

"So?"

"So, he flatly refused. His father, my husband, agreed. Briefly, Masa, Yuichi is intent on receiving a peerage in the future." Gesturing that Masa come closer, Sumiko spoke without moving her lips, saying, "The Fukuda business concerns are myriad. My son intends to draw them all together beneath one roof, so to speak. Into a corporation. You understand?"

Repressing her true emotions, Masa took her time before replying, "Not fully. Sumiko, Count Okura's spirit must surely be bruised by having no adopted son bearing his name. Was he aware of the situation?"

"No. As you know, he and his entire family, but for Aiko, were wiped out during the earthquake in 1854. Aiko had no dowry."

"Is that so?"

"That is so. Unfortunately, Count Okura had indulged himself to an incredible degree, collecting art treasures, borrowing and spending wildly. Unfortunately, his priceless treasures were destroyed along with his house, which Okura had sold to my husband. Count Okura died a pauper."

The room was suddenly all too quiet, and in the stillness the two women sat fluttering their fans rhythmically.

Finally, Sumiko broke the silence, murmuring, "Believe me, Masa, I do not agree with certain new moralities that have been forced upon our people."

"Is that so?"

"That is so. Nevertheless, I rejoice that my son does not suffer the indignities *his* father endured, so cruelly insulted by his two-sworded samurai so-called friends. Count Okura, and yes, *Kenichi*, my own brother, being but two of them."

Overcome by her emotions, Sumiko cried out, "My husband was so sensitive, such an *endearing man*. Was he not always kind, sympathetic toward Renzō, to you yourself?"

"He was. On many occasions. His character was to be admired. Your marriage to him was auspicious."

"Absolutely. Different indeed from yours to my brother. Different indeed from my son's union. That is a tragedy."

"Come now, Sumiko, surely *tragedy* is too strong a word?"

"Not so. Aiko has no wifely virtues. She goads Yuichi beyond the endurance point. She, like her father, spends money recklessly.

Then she accuses Yuichi of being newly rich. She has given him no child as yet. She embarrasses him in society. They argue violently."

"Why, then, does he not divorce her?"

"He refuses to do so."

"Could it be that he takes pleasure in Aiko's bullying ways? That could be so. Yuichi, even in childhood, was pandered to by his grandparents. And his father and you seldom reprimanded him either. Is that not so?"

Sumiko stared at her sister-in-law as though seeing her for the first time; holding her breath, then speaking deliberately, she said, "Masa, your version of my son's character amazes me. Never has he failed to answer the clarion call of duty. While *your* son, Renzō, has spent the years of reconstruction meandering about the world, enjoying the gaieties of New York and London, Yuichi has remained at home, head down, dealing with high-level Western businessmen, often outwitting them. Not once has he indulged himself, taken time out to visit foreign lands. He has valiantly sacrificed himself for the good of his country."

"Excuse *me*, Sumiko, but I am amazed at *your* version of Renzō's character. Astonished that you, who know of his study-tortured youth, of the way he was inducted into working as an interpreter, forced to travel the countryside year after year in the company of foreign invaders, at times caught up in bloody skirmishes between the battling factions. Forced into his manhood too early, but always with integrity, working for the good of his country. Giving his all. Yes, then because of his scholarship, he was included in the embassies sent to America to study Western thought processes. Absent from home so often, away from his wife, his son. Ah, Sumiko, how little you know of Renzō's difficult life."

"Please excuse me."

"Certainly. We, you and I, have always given each other the privilege of saying clearly what we feel and think."

Sumiko stirred uneasily, avoiding Masa's eyes as she murmured haltingly, "Truthfully, on my side, not always."

"Is that so?"

"Yes. Not so with you, Masa, dear sister?"

Again flooded with warmth toward Sumiko, Masa spoke gently, saying, "Perhaps that is so, but we have been so close, so intimate. And today I wish to confide to you that my central concern is with Renzō. Yesterday I received an epistle from him from London."

"He is in good health, I hope. How I yearn to see him once again."

"He did not mention his health." Masa gazed at Sumiko, her expression indecisive, then, speaking firmly, she said, "His letter held hints of financial problems. Much to my shock and, I frankly admit, to my anger."

"Can it be possible that Renzō has inherited Kenichi's love of gambling! If so, how tragic! I understand your anger."

"Sumiko, my anger is not directed to my son but to *your* son." Gesturing for silence, she continued, her voice brittle. "Are you aware that, apart from the old house in Yokohama, the house in Nihombashi is all that remains of the rich Yamamoto estate? Are you aware that the rice fields, the huge marshlands, once Yamamoto property, now belong to the Fukuda clan? That the European buildings which have been constructed on those Yamamoto marshlands now belong to your son's business corporation? *My* son must now search for ways to earn a livelihood for his family."

"Not so! Not so, Masa. There is no need for him to *work*. Yuichi cares deeply for his cousin. Always, he will shelter Renzō."

"Yuichi? Shelter *Renzō*? Neither my son nor I have any intention of becoming 'cold-rice' relatives. The very thought of Renzō beholden to your son's benevolence is anathema to me. He will not become a henchman caught up in the intrigues, the dishonesties of trade."

Masa ceased speaking and gazed at Sumiko, who sat as though paralyzed, her hands raised, dangling limply from her wrists.

"Sumiko," she exclaimed briskly. "Are you about to perform foxily again? Or," she quickly added, "are you perhaps a little tipsy?"

Immediately and most guiltily Sumiko clasped both hands against her bosom, lowering her eyes.

"You realize, of course," Masa murmured, "that I was not in the least concerned when the exorcist was called in to treat you. I fully understood your need to draw attention to yourself."

Sumiko took her time before answering. "Frankly, I'm *relieved* to know that you understand. I could think of no other way to gain Yuichi's full attention."

"Again, I understand, but ...." Masa snapped her fan closed, pointing it toward Sumiko. "But—" she continued, "surely you felt quite ridiculous?"

Once more Sumiko took her time before answering. "Frankly, most ridiculous." Staring at her sister-in-law, her eyes glimmered mischievously.

Masa's stern expression changed to one of amusement. Then, about to laugh, she cried out, "What—what is that peculiar sound I hear?"

"Aiko is making it. On a piano."

"How—how *loud, discordant*. Surely the instrument is out of tune? My senses are being violated."

"Ah, maybe now you realize why at times the eccentricities of my daughter-in-law drive me into acting as I do? No? For hours she bangs her fingers upon the keys quite deranging my mind. Could you endure in silence, with dignity?"

"I could not! Sumiko, if she persists, a tutor must be called in to . . ."

"She already has a tutor. A man, a *foreigner*, a *Russian*. He comes daily. Here, *to my home*. She, Aiko, is forever practicing."

Masa listened intently, then exclaimed, "The music now sounds quite different. . . ."

"The Russian tutor now plays the instrument. You find it pleasing?"

"I do. Most. Sumiko, take instructions yourself."

"I, from the foreigner . . . ?"

"Why not? You are skilled on both *samisen* and *koto*. So why not on the piano? Not only could it be interesting, but, more important, some empathy might be aroused between you and Aiko. Surely Yuichi would be delighted. No?"

"My gratitude knows no bounds. Masa, I shall consider the idea. How brilliant you are."

"Not at all. Not in the least. Remember, Sumiko, I also am a mother-in-law."

"Ah, yes, but Rumi is so dovelike. *Your* life is so uncomplicated. So . . ." Sumiko, realizing that she was treading on dangerous ground, rose up, saying briskly, "All of a sudden I feel spry, positively girlish. Masa, shall we go together and gather strawberries. . . ."

At home in Nihombashi, Masa removed her footwear and, after the traditional ceremony always performed when entering one's home, she informed Misa that she wished to take a bath.

When at last in the deep tub, with the clean, hot water lapping up to her chin, her thoughts dwelt on her son. Renzō's letter had distressed her, but she was far more anxious about the difficult task he would have in dealing with his cousin Yuichi's offers of assistance.

Yuichi fukuda was living through times when a man's personal life was of secondary importance compared with the confusion in a land undergoing a period of transformation beneath the rule of the imperial government, with its determination to industrialize rapidly in order to make up for those centuries of lost time.

Yuichi, with his bloodhound proclivities, was interested in every facet of society. It had become his policy to employ and to keep a sharp eye on young men who had spent some years abroad studying economics along with other Western vocations. Some, their time abroad completed, returned home converted to the Christian faith.

In his opinion, some of those conversions reeked of fakery. Yuichi had made it his business to seek out and confer with several missionary men and their wives in the community.

Unfailingly accompanied by an interpreter, he had listened to enthusiastic preachings concerning the sinfulness of mankind and the eternity of agony one would endure unless one "gave up all worldly pleasures . . ."

"Then," he had inquired, "if I, Fukuda, give up sin, all worldly pleasures, after my death—what?"

He had been astonished by the fervor, the shining face of the missionary who had informed him that if he died as a Christian, he would live somewhere high above the sky, in a heaven where no work would be required of him. He would dwell forever in a heaven of perpetual peace.

"*Naru hodo*—Is that so?" he had replied.

The very thought of living throughout eternity under such circumscribed circumstances was untenable. He had been relieved to depart from the American missionary's home which was handsomely furnished with Japanese artifacts. Beneath the foreign couple's indisputable enthusiasm he had detected elements of condescension toward Japan and most things Japanese.

On the whole, the entire affair had left him with a sour taste; nevertheless, he had made it his duty to send a sizable amount of cash to the couple, to "assist in furthering your good works in my country." One never knew what the future held in store. Also, without doubt various Christian groups were carrying out valuable works, opening schools and hospitals, not only in Tokyo and

Yokohama, but also in country districts. Yes, every coin had two sides.

Shortly after that confrontation with the missionaries, he spoke about it with no little wit while in the company of his mother and his wife. His mother was indignant to hear the missionary's family believed that all children were "born in sin."

"Yuichi, I sincerely hope that you informed them that we, that all *Japanese folk* are born pure as the driven snow," she exclaimed.

"I did, Mother, I did," he lied, laughing.

Aiko had also laughed, then she had gone on to say that she was deeply attracted to music played on a great organ which had recently been brought from Germany and placed in a newly built church in Tokyo. "I find such music stirs my spirit," she had said. "I intend visiting the cathedral whenever so inclined."

"Best not," Sumiko cried out reprovingly. "You might be snared into their trap. Your husband must forbid you."

"You think so?" Aiko inquired with false sincerity.

"I certainly do." His mother glanced at Yuichi expectantly.

"Well . . . ?" Aiko stared at him daringly. "You forbid me?"

Trapped, he gestured toward her abruptly, intentionally knocking over his bowl of steaming tea, and during the ensuing confusion Aiko shrugged indifferently.

Rather than object to his wife's liking for Western music, he encouraged her interests and gladly paid for the instruments she requested and for the various tutors who came to his home.

Her fetish for wearing male attire embarrassed him, but wisely, he made no objections. He was powerless and would remain so unless a palliative was found to end the charade his life had become.

When she had first appeared dressed in pinstripe trousers, top-hatted, swinging a cane, he had agonized, believing that Aiko was out to belittle his manhood, but the very thought had shamed him, for he knew that there was nothing malicious in her character, and in a way he was proud of her, for she went her haughty way with undeniable style and panache.

Yuichi, now chairman of the family business, sat facing the group of men who held managerial positions in the company. He never let it be known that he secretly relished having men with noble backgrounds in his employ.

On this occasion he had put forward the idea of opening branches in Shanghai and in New York. His announcement had aroused tremendous enthusiasm, but the dialogues were becoming drawn out and annoyingly repetitious.

With one abrupt gesture he let it be known that the conference was over, and after saluting each man with the exact quality bow each deserved, he was finally alone to relax and listen to the bell-like trilling of the cricket whose fragile bamboo cage stood on his European-style office desk.

Sighing regretfully, he thought of his departed father, that humorous, radical person who had dared to step out of his "common man" background, welcoming the opening of Japan's doors to traders from the outside world. He had not considered industrialism as a Western priority, proclaiming, "If they, the foreigners, can do it, we can do it. It's as simple as that. Administration? Follow Confucius: *'When engaged in administration, be like the North Star. As it remains in its one position all the other stars surround it.'* " His father had been fond of quoting Confucius and, to the best of his ability, following his doctrines, especially: *"The great man does everything to help the poor but nothing to enrich the rich."*

His father had not feared the barbarian invaders. Intuitively, he had known that America, desperate to stake a claim in Asia for political and commercial gain, presented no threat to the Japanese people as a whole.

He had been proved correct. Ignoring the country's internal revolts and skirmishes, he had gone about preparing to trade with the foreigners when the time was ripe.

In 1859, when less than a hundred newcomers were living in the unsavory port at Yokohama, he had set up dozens of tiny booths there selling wares to them at no profit, but, as he had expected, when the influx of foreigners began arriving at the newly opened port, the Fukuda business had boomed beyond all expectations.

Having been a mere child during those tremulous times, Yuichi had learned much about those early years from his cousin Renzō, who had been a member of a grand embassy which the then-ruling shogun had dispatched to Washington in 1860 to exchange ratification.

"It was a tremendous experience," Renzō had exclaimed. "Truly, I felt like a falcon, unhooded and unchained, even though I resented being stared at as though I were a circus freak, dressed as I was like all the delegates, carrying two swords, wearing silk robes. But, on the whole, we were received with true American cordiality and considered exotic enough to have one of America's leading poets, Walt Whitman, write of us:

> *"Over the Western sea hither from Niphon come,*
> *Courteous, the swarth-cheek'd two-sworded envoys,*
> *Leaning back in their open barouches, bare-headed,*
> *impassive . . .*

"Impassive? Leaning back?" Renzō grimaced. "What a misstatement! I, as a humble interpreter traveling with a group of nobles—all of them intent on learning and observing—was kept so busy translating and keeping records, I returned home on the point of exhaustion. . . ."

The Yamamoto's henchman, Sudo, had been hurt to the quick at not having been included in that embassy. No one had recognized the daring work he had carried out against the tyranny of the shogun. Embittered, he blamed Renzō, and turned his face in a new direction, joining the Fukuda clan, to become a conscientious employee. He now held a position in the corporation, but for all his success, he lived like a hermit. Unmarried and uninterested in society, Sudo seemed wary, unwilling to show his inner feelings. Yuichi wondered about Sudo's early years. In all probability, the man's life had been fraught with difficulties.

In all truth, "the child was father to the man." His own name was now mentioned in reverent awe among his many employees for he had learned to exude an aura of imperiousness, not only tricking them but tricking himself.

During Yuichi's childhood, his every whim had been gratified; nevertheless, he had been a frightened little boy pretending to ignore the chaos around and about him in the adult world. He had lived through invasion, through a devastating earthquake, cholera, and smallpox epidemics. Not altogether an untroubled period of time. He had come out of it outwardly unscathed, but his spirit was deeply scarred and he had tricked himself to rely on the many foolish superstitions fed to him by his adoring old grandmother. His memories of her were growing pale, but he still treasured the tiny bamboo cricket cage she had purchased for him from a vendor in one of her beloved Buddhist shrines. That original chirping insect had aroused a passion of tenderness in his five-year-old heart. On awakening

one morning to find it curled still and cold, he went into a paroxysm
of grief, which flared into a tantrum.

The old woman quieted him down, declaring sternly that his pet
had not passed into the spirit world but was merely suffering a
condition that would be easily cured.

He crouched by the cage as the soothsayer came in, with all his
mystical trappings, ordering that Yuichi bow his head while he
mumbled incantations. Hey, presto, the cricket not only recovered,
it grew larger, trilling its song more merrily than ever before.

"This illustrious cricket must not perish," the old man said. "It
protects the little master. Call me next time it has a spasm. I shall
once again cure its malady."

After the third visit of the soothsayer Yuichi clearly understood
that new crickets had been placed in the cage but he pretended otherwise and would rejoice, saying, "I could not live without my
cricket." Even now, in his manhood, he kept replacing the dead
insects, and pretending that his first little darling still lived on, protecting him, his family and his business interests.

The childish trick worked for him, but then, it was his policy
never to change a system unless a better one could be thought of.

Tricking himself was no problem, but tricking others was a hazardous business, especially in matters concerning his marriage. It
was regrettable that his mother had little liking for her daughter-in-
law. But Aiko brazenly turned a cold shoulder to Sumiko's criticisms. She was secure in her aristocratic background, her manner
supercilious and frosty. But Yuichi knew only too well that beneath
his wife's cold exterior lay a volcanic heat that could erupt into
flames and destroy him if he made a wrong move.

Shortly before their marriage had taken place, Yuichi decided to
confide in his father, to tell him of his tragic physical predicament,
but his father had merely laughed, saying, "Nonsense, nonsense!
Marriage will soon remedy that little matter. Your problem, Yuichi,
comes from too much frolicking in the pleasure houses."

"Not so, Father," he exclaimed. "True, I have spent much time
with courtesans, yes, even with the lowest of harlots but never once
have I achieved a climax. In desperation I have put my problem to
acupuncturists, to soothsayers, but all to no avail. Father, I am
impotent. Marriage is out of the question. Please, support me, Father. . . ."

"Nonsense, nonsense! You are *my* son. Your *mother's* son. Our union could not bring forth such a weakling. Trust me. Marriage will do the trick."

For once, his father had been mistaken. Filled with anguish, he had stood watching his bride's palanquin being lowered to the ground before the entrance of his parents' great house. His blood had run cold on sighting the tall, stylish maiden he was taking to wife. He knew she would have been instructed as every Japanese bride was instructed: *"Look into the shrine's mirror every day. If scars of selfishness or pride are in your heart, they will grow in the lines of the face. Watch closely. Be strong like the pine, yield in gentle obedience like a swaying bamboo, and yet, like a fragrant plum blossoming beneath the snow, never lose the gentle perseverance of loyal womanhood."*

Well, for some ten years their union had survived, Aiko a virgin wife, undaunted, bending like a swaying bamboo to her situation. And she was strong like the pine; the epitome of loyalty; enduring her mother-in-law's bitter complaints at not having grandchildren, or at least one grandson.

On their first night together Yuichi had deepened his voice and muttered, "Our life together stretches far into the future. I see that you are weary. I understand. Tonight, rest yourself."

"Weary—I? Not in the least."

"Is that so?" Never had he felt so belittled, so desperate. He had gazed at her and she had gazed back, her eyes questioning, groping to understand.

Then finally, "Is it that you find me repulsive?" she queried casually, as one would ask a person if he found the soup too cold.

Speechless for a moment, unable to drag his eyes away from hers, he muttered, "It's not that."

"Not?"

"Yes. Not that."

"Then, tell me, is it that you . . . Then, can it be that your patron saint is *Monju?*"

He, Yuichi, a homosexual? If only he could reply in the affirmative.

"By your expression, I think that it is not so," she said firmly. "Then, is it that you love a courtesan passionately, and . . ."

"It's not seemly that you question me so. Please rest yourself."

"Excuse me, but I question everything. I am practical. You may think me shameful, but I have looked forward to experiencing my first sexual encounter. Not as a foolish girl in love with love, but with interest. So . . . ?"

"So . . ." he lied. "Unfortunately at present, I am suffering a slight ailment. I hesitated to tell you."

"An—ailment?"

"*Hai*—yes."

"A *body* ailment?"

"Yes."

"Where?"

"Need you ask?"

"Oh—*there!*"

"Yes."

"I understand. Thank you for clearing the situation. So—please rest yourself, husband."

Reprieved, he crawled onto the bridal-*futon* and to his amazement Aiko sped about in the dim lamplight, mussing up her bridal accoutrements, mussing up her stylized hair, exclaiming in laughter, "I want no gossipy servants spreading rude rumors about *my* wedding night."

Finally, she lay down beside him and all through that sleepless night he had wondered at the character of the girl he had married. He dreaded the future and envied the blissful sleep Aiko was enjoying.

Never again had that subject of his "ailment" been mentioned. For ten years he and his wife presented themselves to the world as a conventional married couple. They shared the same room, took their baths together, played chess, card games, went about in society together, prayed before the family shrine.

He was always wary, she, nonchalant, doing as she pleased, impervious to all criticism. At times, the atmosphere would be tense as they lay side by side during sleepless nights while Aiko directed subtle insults his way. Her comments struck their mark like poisoned arrows as she intentionally spurred him on to quarrel with her, but in a peculiar way those antagonistic clashes relieved their tensions, strengthening, not weakening their union. "Your wicked tongue bears no description," he would shout.

"Have a care," she would retaliate. "I merely prune a few branches. Easily, I could chop the whole tree down." Following those interludes, so therapeutic, their inner frustrations done away with, they were peaceful once more, all anger banished.

Over the years Yuichi kept searching, hoping to find a way to end his impotency. Now he no longer expected to find a cure. Even if a miraculous cure were to be found, he could not even remotely imagine he and Aiko attempting any form of sexual intercourse. The thought itself was incestuous.

At times he saw that she wore a forlorn expression and filled with dread, he would fret, wondering if she had fallen beneath the spell of love for one of the many eminent men in their large circle of acquaintances.

On one occasion, highly suspicious, but treading softly, he said, half jestingly, "Aiko, why so dreamy, so forlorn? Are you in love?"

"I am," she snapped. Then, seeing his fright, she continued, her tone self-derogatory, "Aiko loves Aiko. Surely you know that! You must. Night after night, year after year you have heard me panting my desires. Known that *Aiko* was loving *Aiko*." With false humility she cried out, "Tell no one, husband. Don't slander my reputation. I would find such gossip unendurable."

"Your life is truly unfortunate."

"Not so. I like steering my own craft, so to speak. Look to your own life. Have no frets for mine."

Not only had she become as a sister, a friend, she was his savior. Divorce Aiko? Never, never.

Yes, but what of children? Children were what marriage was all about. Of late his anxious mother frequently brought up the matter of adoption, but Yuichi Fukuda wanted no stranger inheriting *his* name, *his* wealth.

He wanted a child from Aiko. A child with the blood of *his* clan running through its veins. But his tragic deficiency made that as impossible as writing on water.

As though struck by lightning, he sat rigid, not daring to breathe, his mind aflame, shamed by the loathsome notion he had conjured up. He must dismiss the improper thought from his mind. It was taboo, against all rules. Yes, but he had thought of it and as time went by the macabre idea of having a surrogate father for his child would not be repressed. His own mother, Sumiko, had once been a Yamamoto. Yuichi had her blood in his veins. The same blood as Renzō, who was soon to return home from Japan as a man with financial and career problems. Ever since becoming aware of those problems he had made up his mind to shelter his cousin and to take him into the Fukuda Corporation. Never, for one moment, had he conceived of the possibility of Renzō owing him an *on*—an obligation.

But without doubt Renzō *would* feel obliged to return those obligations one day and in some form.

Renzō? Aiko . . . ?

Ah, how carefully, how softly he would have to tread. There was nothing he would not do to achieve his purpose. And he always got what he wanted.

Japan's capital city, Tokyo, would have astounded Kenichi Yamamoto had he been able to return from the spirit world in human form. Edo, once so dear to his heart, had undergone many changes, not only physically but in the attitudes and the manners of the people who dwelt there.

Not far from the Imperial Palace were the compounds of foreign legations with their national flags flying proudly on high poles. The inmates rode through the newly paved streets in splendid carriages, employing Japanese servants in their homes, and in sporting clubs, ball games called cricket, croquet, and tennis were played.

Many foreigners had fallen in love with Japan's natural beauty, with the gentle charm of ancient temples, the cleanliness and the politeness of the people.

On the other hand, there were many who looked down their noses at Japan and all things Japanese, sending disparaging letters back to their homelands, reporting:

"It's a land of depravity. . . ."

"The Japanese are people without any deep emotions. . . ."

"The Japanese hate us. Don't be taken in by their impassive façades, it's all a fake. . . ."

"Ignore the smiling, the bowing and scraping. It's all a tricky cover-up. . . ."

Nevertheless, neither faction was averse to purchasing unique articles, both old and newly made, by the hands of Japanese artisans, usually at cheap prices, delighting in their bargains and proudly exhibiting them to jealous compatriots, crowing triumphantly, "I bought this treasure for a mere song. . . ."

In Japan's native community an unbridgeable gap separated the younger generation from those who had reached adulthood before the arrival of Commodore Perry. There were tensions between them. Young people—the moderns—admired Western ways, attempting to emulate them with unswerving dedication.

Elderly people who had suffered beneath the despotic rule of the shoguns were apt to glamorize those times and yearn for old days, old disciplines.

The swordsmith Nakamura's once-hallowed Sword Club was

now a restaurant popular among the foreign community and internationally minded Japanese epicureans who went there to enjoy a new and delectable red-meat dish, *sukiyaki*, prepared in vessels on top of glowing charcoal braziers. It was a dish unfailingly accompanied by rice wine, pipingly hot and tantalizingly intoxicating, causing good humor without headaches.

If old Nakamura's ghost haunted the *sukiyaki* restaurant, he must surely have wondered if he had done the right thing by leaving his residence standing instead of turning it into a pile of ashes before taking his voluntary departure from the world.

If Count Okura's aristocratic spirit wandered amid the restaurant's revelers, he alone would have known that one night, some twenty years back, the great chamber had been filled with an eerie silence when the swordsmith, robed in a garment woven by his wife, entered, bowing to those present. Then, seating himself and with stylized, leisurely movements allowing his garment to flow down, carefully fixing the flowing sleeves of his robe tight under his knees in order to prevent him from falling backward in an ignoble, unseemly manner . . .

Count Okura and those others who had been present—a chosen few—had watched as the old man took up the sharp dirk, one fashioned by his own hands, to stab it into his body on the left side below his waist, drawing it unhurriedly across to the right, then thrusting deeply into the wound, cutting upward.

He had made no moan, no sound of any kind, and as he had withdrawn the weapon, Count Okura, his *kaishaki*—his "more than friend"—had leapt up from his crouching stance, and using the old master's most precious sword he had performed a coup de grâce, swiftly freeing the man's spirit.

The bright lights, the odors of cooking, hair pomades, the cloyingly sweet perfumes worn by females at the eating tables, and the loud buzz of talk and spurts of laughter would have disturbed those now-departed-men's spirits, for in their memory it was a chamber lit by altar candles, acrid, bittersweet. A memorial honoring certain men who had preferred death rather than living on to endure the unendurable . . .

Ueno Park, once the private property of a powerful shogun, was now open to the general public, who came to meander in its tranquil beauty and to view the five-storied pagoda and the great pond with a tiny islet in its center where the goddess Benten was enshrined.

One midsummer afternoon, after having viewed those points of interest, Aiko and Rumi, together with Shinichi and Aiko's aged attendant, Yuki, made their way through the sight-seeing crowd toward a vermilion-painted bridge from which a deluge of wisteria plunged downward to a pond amassed with many-hued water lilies.

The two young women were intent on being photographed by an American camera expert who, with his paraphernalia, was ready to produce images of those who stood in line eagerly awaiting their turn to have him work his skill.

A great number of Japanese citizens were garbed in Western-style garments, but many stared with polite astonishment at the sight of a Japanese woman striding along in male attire, swinging a gold-topped ebony cane. Two European males coming face-to-face with Aiko stopped in their tracks, both grinning, one with his eyebrows raised, saying loudly, "Shades of George Sand—Japanese version! What ho! What next . . . ?"

Aiko, whose English was fluent, ignored their impertinence, but as she moved onward she wondered who George Sand might be and she was determined to find out.

While awaiting their return in the long queue, Rumi kept a sharp eye on her energetic son as she chatted in a desultory fashion, saying quietly, "Aiko, older sister, is it not a pity that cameras are not able to capture the beauty of color. You agree?"

"Hah . . . Yes, but I'm not one to fret about the impossible. Rumi, when our turn comes, let us ignore the photographer's command that we should smile."

"By all means! I agree it's more comely to be immortalized wearing a thoughtful expression. Aiko, I wish to be captured together with you. I should not have worn a kimono. I shall look old-fashioned."

"Not so. You look charming. As usual. Now, tell me, when is your husband expected home?"

"Soon. In September. Isn't it miraculous that steamships make it so speedy to reach Japan from England?"

"So—yes! How long has he, Renzō, been absent from his homeland?"

"I'm not quite sure. Maybe already two years? Certainly he will scarcely recognize his son."

"True! Shin-chan continues to sprout up like a well-watered bamboo. How closely he resembles his father."

"He does. I'm hoping our next child will be a daughter and resemble me."

"How can you wish for a daughter? Sons always have a prior claim with their fathers."

"Oh, not so. My father—*our* father, Aiko—delighted in his daughters."

"Are you speaking of the now-departed Count Okura?"

"Aiko, please don't be flippant. Not about our father."

"Flippant? Not so. Father never once showed interest in me, and, come to think of it, neither did my mother."

"Is that so? I'm sad to know that."

"Don't be. In no way am I jealous of the affection our father had for you."

"I'm glad to have you say so. Jealousy must be a terrible torment. I have never experienced it. For instance, Lady Masa, my mother-in-law, is convinced that *she* has prior claim on my husband. I just find it a little *vexing* that Renzō writes great screeds to her and mere notes to me, his wife."

"Really? Lady Masa doesn't allow you to read those lengthy epistles?"

"She does, but I seldom bother. I find them dull, all to do with architecture, scenery, and, yes, tombstones. Renzō once wrote about spending an entire day in an ancient London church, reading inscriptions on tombstones and—"

"How mournful."

"Yes, he is given to fits of strange behavior, but he has a vigorous, bright personality on the whole."

"That's good. You look forward to his return, then?"

"Admittedly, the thought excites me. Daily life in the home is so dull. His mother is totally absorbed in herself. *My* mother, Keiko, is different, so lively. I long to see her, quite desperately so."

"What prevents you from so doing?"

"Frankly, her social background. You do understand?" Rumi glanced at Aiko inquiringly. "Do you not?"

"Umm . . . Yes. Why don't you assert yourself and visit your mother?"

"I'm essentially unassertive."

"You should force yourself. Much better than harboring secret resentments toward Lady Masa. Personally, I admire her!"

"I'm afraid you don't really know her. Aiko, merely one of her cold glances is enough to deter me from following my own wishes. Truly, she becomes more high and haughty with every passing day."

"You should ignore her. Certainly, she is never condescending to *me*."

"But . . ." Rumi murmured, "Your parentage is impeccable. I wonder if people in other countries are so class conscious?"

"Without doubt, maybe even more so." Aiko's voice had a distinctly cutting edge as she continued, saying, "Every land has its indigenous aristocratic culture. Always, there will remain an invisible dividing line in class structure."

"Ah, *your* tone now rebuffs me. Aiko, have *you* scorn for my parentage?"

"Not the slightest whiff. Again, I say, assert yourself. Does not Renzō come from provincial stock on his paternal side?"

"He does. His paternal grandmother was from a farming clan. Ah, Aiko, always you lift my spirits."

"I do?"

"You do," Rumi said, smiling. "There is no doubt on that score. Hmm . . . yes, I *shall* arrange to visit my mother. Her circumstances are now humble."

"Where does she dwell?"

"In Kamakura, on Ohara Sama's, our patron's, estate. But surely you must know that? What a kindly man Ohara Sama is."

"Indeed he is. Rumi, the thought occurs to me that sometime, maybe next year, we could travel to Kamakura and pay homage to Ohara Sama."

"Brilliant idea. Yes, and visit my mother as well."

"Your—mother? Umm . . . yes, certainly. Yes, you could also see her. . . ." Aiko, suddenly impatient, exclaimed, "I abhor this standing in line. I no longer feel like being photographed. Rumi, excuse me, but please call your son to your side. See, look, he is over yonder, together with Yuki. . . ."

"You are leaving? But we have waited so long. It seems a pity . . ."

"I wish to leave. Please excuse me. . . ."

After leaving Rumi, Aiko made her way up a long flight of lichen-covered steps that led to the high parapet overlooking the park. She moved swiftly, lithely, unaware of her attendant's heavy breathing as the woman padded along laboriously in her wake, a sharp stiletto hidden in her sash, a weapon she would have used without a second thought against anyone out to harm the noble lady.

Yuki was always puzzled by Aiko's curious character and never gave up hope that her spirit would calm down, thereby ending the constant stream of bickerings and arguments between them.

She fully believed that the gods had made her responsible for Aiko's well-being. She had cared for her since the hour of her birth, and it had been she who rescued her charge from among the ruins of the Okura mansion which had collapsed during the earthquake in 1854. She had come upon Aiko, bruised and disheveled, screeching, "Not dead . . . not dead . . . *He must not be dead*. . . . He must not be dead. . . . I must find, *I must rescue him*. . . ."

Naturally, Yuki had believed that her charge had been alluding to her father, but, on coming across the crushed, blood-covered body of Count Okura, the child had scarcely glanced at that tragic figure, but continued searching and screaming. Finally she had discovered the lifeless form of her pet dog.

Over the following years Aiko felt no pangs of conscience about her absence of feelings concerning the demise of her parents. They had been two distant strangers in her life. Her dog had loved her. The death of her pet had meant the end of love.

Yuki had escorted her, sometimes pick-a-back, sometimes on foot, trudging through the devastated capital with its ten thousand dead, then, farther on through Yokohama, farther to the town of Kamakura, and to the gates of Ohara's large estate.

Bowing, with her face to the ground, the nursemaid had moaned. "Here I have brought to you the daughter of Count Okura. Of all the noble family, only she now remains. . . ."

Ohara, that kindly man had straightaway taken the orphaned child into his home, and Aiko had lived in his protection until her fifteenth year, when her marriage to Yuichi Fukuda had taken place.

The marriage, Ohara carefully explained, had been arranged many years back by Count Okura, who had been deeply obligated to the Fukuda family, having accepted many favors from them.

Well versed in the tyrannous world of obligations, Aiko had made no objections. Also, she clearly understood that Ohara's wife would be relieved to rid herself of further responsibilities toward the girl she had raised with every care but without affection.

Her marriage to an impotent male, a man from the merchant class, had proved to be a fiasco. Then had come the stunning shock of discovering that her husband's cousin, Renzō Yamamoto, had taken to wife not merely a pretty girl but one who was the illegitimate daughter of Count Okura, her own half sister.

Standing on the parapet gazing out over the spacious parklands, Aiko shuddered to remember that time of discovery. She felt that she had been ridiculed.

During those years spent on the Ohara estate in Kamakura, she had been casually aware of a woman, a geisha, who dwelt with her daughter in a cottage on the estate. On many occasions she had seen the mother and daughter walking together, both robed a little too flamboyantly for good taste as they meandered through the town's peaceful streets.

Although conscious of their surreptitious, curious glances, never once had she evinced interest in the female duo. They were commoners. She was an aristocrat. The matter began and ended there.

Her anguish came not from the knowledge that her father had kept a second family. Recalling her cold, stern-visaged mother, she understood and concurred with his arrangements, but having learned that the geisha and her daughter had known all along that she, Aiko, was the count's legal daughter—that the Ohara family had also known—she had become furious and filled with an icy disdain.

However, with no intentions of adding to the complexities of her life, she had sensibly gone out of her way to accept her half sister courteously, and as time had gone by, a certain rapport had developed between the two young women.

She admired Rumi's charmingly crooked smile and her barrage of light chatter was often amusing, but when her half sister spoke with maudlin regret about the loss of the father who had cherished her so tenderly, Aiko, the rightful, the unloved daughter, always made a hasty escape, filled with emotions too overwhelming to keep hidden.

Aiko lit one of the slim European cigars she had recently taken a liking to, and as she smoked she stared into space, her nerves on edge, discontent, thinking of herself as a being who had been born imprisoned in a gloomy dwelling, wandering endlessly through dim corridors, into shuttered rooms, always with the hope of sliding back a door to discover someone waiting for her, someone not only to love her but whom she could speak to without hypocrisy and express the tumultuous passions she was forced to subdue.

Bitterly, she envisaged herself as a stunted tree meagerly watered, bearing no fruit or flower. For the first time, she understood that voluntary suicide held a great attraction. If life were not pleasing, why not end it? She shrugged that grim thought away and flung her cigar butt to the ground, glaring at Yuki, who picked up the object, muttering, "It's not good to follow the rude ways of the barbarians."

"Is that so?"

"*Hai*—yes, that is so."

" 'Tis said that the emperor smokes cigars."

" 'Tis not said that the Imperial One throws rubbish to the sacred ground of our land."

"True. He, the emperor, is fortunate. He has no impertinent servants."

"To dare speak like this. What sticks in your craw? My belly rumbles. May we not now return home?"

"Go if you so wish." Aiko stared at the strongly built woman defiantly. Just as defiantly, Yuki stared back. Then, muttering grumpily, she squatted down to await her mistress's pleasure, mumbling a stream of complaints about certain person's liking for the vulgarity of the barbarians who trod about the city so brazenly. In Yuki's opinion, the foreign women flaunted themselves, clinging to the arms of males as surely only a harlot would. These women laughed with their mouths wide open and wore street footwear in dwelling places.

Her very own mistress not only followed certain barbarian ways but flaunted herself, outrageously wearing tight trousers and other hideous foreign apparel in public.

Yuki had lost face because of Aiko's brazen ways. Servants in the Fukuda household seldom missed an opportunity to poke fun at her. For years she had spent cash buying prayers at shrines, prayers all to do with the hoped-for birth of Aiko's child. Why, she wondered, were the gods so unwilling to answer those prayers?

Now her mistress was ready to leave; suddenly and all in a hurry she was striding down the steep flight of steps. Yuki rose up to follow.

. . .

Aiko knew that Yuichi lay awake in the hot, airless room but, determined not to indulge in altercation of any description, she breathed rhythmically, feigning sleep.

Night never came softly to her; it came like a savage flood of black water swamping her in its cold depths, making her acutely aware of the loneliness of her life. She wondered what it would be like to be desired, to be fulfilled, and because she would never know, she felt a deep compassion for herself. Maybe in life one was born either lucky or unlucky. If that were so, there was little she could do but accept her fate and make the best of things by following new trends to an even greater extent.

But how? Already, she was expert in Japanese arts considered suitable for women. Already, she was a member of an exclusive international club, able to play tennis and croquet.

She liked and felt quite at ease with certain patrician ladies in the foreign community. Especially her English friend Lady Marjorie Coomber from the British legation. She admired her determination to understand and to speak the Japanese language. In many ways, the Englishwoman reminded her of Lady Masa.

At times, she encouraged Rumi's mother-in-law to speak of life in the old capital, Kyoto, telling how as a young girl she had accompanied members of the court, all of them riding along in highly decorated ox-drawn carts with their splendidly arrayed outriders. They would dawdle through the wide streets, sail on the lake, drink wine flavored with petals of the chrysanthemum flowers, view the moon, and listen to the music of lute and harp.

"How beautiful. How free you were," Aiko exclaimed.

"Yes. Beautiful, free also, but, in retrospect, I realize that the prevailing tone was extremely formal. . . ." Lady Masa gazed at her thoughtfully, then she said, "One does tire of trivial amusements; however, with the rarest of exceptions, it is impossible to prevent intelligent persons from leading a fulfilled life. Do you not agree?"

Well, Aiko had agreed, but even in her wildest imaginings, Lady Masa could not understand how it felt to lie beside one's husband, year after year, not as lovers but as strangers.

Even a woman as experienced, as sophisticated as Lady Masa would find it difficult to unravel the tangled skeins of such a sterile union.

How difficult their lives were. She was willful, while Yuichi, apart from the curse nature had laid upon him, made grave breaches of etiquette. She lacked excitement in her life. He had excitement in the business world. They indulged in heated discussions, but of late she had found those squabbles boring.

Aiko sighed deeply.

"You are awake?" Yuichi asked, his voice alert. Making no reply, she continued breathing quietly, and it came to her mind that if she confided in Lady Masa, that wise woman, fully explaining that Yuichi was unable to sire a child, not merely with his wife but with *any* female, then with great diplomacy Lady Masa would maybe influence her sister-in-law to encourage Yuichi to adopt a son.

If only Yuichi would finally agree, then much of the tension would go from their lives. Oh, why was her mind always in turmoil?

"Are you awake?" Yuichi queried once again.

So, unconsciously, she must have sighed. Remaining stubbornly silent, she wondered what thoughts were running through her husband's head. She had sympathy for him but more for herself.

The burning stillness in the room was broken by the chirping of the caged cricket close by her husband's *futon*. How desperately lonely she was. Yes, and how lonely Yuichi must be feeling.

Dawn was still a long time away. "Are you awake?" she murmured.

"No," he replied whimsically, "but, as you know so well, I enjoy nothing more than talking in my sleep."

"Talk on, then."

"On what subject?"

"That's up to you."

"Not so. You broke the silence."

"True. Well . . ."

"Yes? Well—what . . . ?"

"So, yes, well, let me think. Ah, yes! Today I went with Rumi to Ueno Park to be photographed."

"Is that so? When will you receive the results of the work?"

"Never."

"Never?"

"I wearied of waiting. I more or less ran off, and left Rumi."

"Typical of you."

"Are you suggesting that I am ill-mannered?"

"Not suggesting—stating. Was it not rude to leave your sister alone in a public place?"

"Her son was with her."

"He is but a *child*." Yuichi broke into a false fit of coughing, a habit he had acquired when he became displeased or trod on dangerous ground.

Aiko, playing the game, inquired lightly, "Have you caught a chill?"

"That could be. But maybe not. Tell me, how do your piano lessons progress?"

"Hopelessly."

"How so?"

"My tutor, Kochetov, informed me that not only are my hands too delicate to manage the instrument but that I am tone deaf."

"Ignore the Russian barbarian. Employ a new, a more accomplished teacher."

"Far from being a barbarian, Kochetov is the most accomplished of pianists, also a man of propriety. I admire his honesty. He has advised me to expend my energies in other directions."

"For instance?"

"He suggests that I coax my rich husband to become a patron of the newly formed Academy of Foreign Music which the government has some enthusiasm for."

"Does the idea please you?"

"It does."

"Then, it also pleases me."

"Thank you."

"Don't mention it! By the way, my cousin Renzō returns home shortly."

"So I believe. His wife speaks with some pleasure about that."

"She does?"

"Yes, why should she not?"

"Hmm ... Well, in all probability that firefly lady is unaware, innocently unaware, that the fortunes of my samurai cousin are at a very low ebb."

"Is that so?"

"That is absolutely so."

"Excuse me, but do I detect a note of triumph in your tone?"

"Possibly."

"How unedifying. I believed that you admired Renzō greatly."

"I do. But my plebian background causes me to relish having once-haughty men from the two-sworded class in my employ. Bowing low, and ..."

"Excuse me once again, but are you expecting Renzō Yamamoto to place his proud face flat on the *tatami* at your feet?"

"No. Ten thousand times no. I have every intention of smoothing his path without the slightest strain on his dignity. By the way, do you admire him?"

"Not particularly. I find him handsome, good-natured but rather conceited. . . ."

"Not so."

"Not handsome, not good-natured?"

"Are you out to irritate me? He is not *conceited*. Now, his father, my mother's brother, Kenichi, was the epitome of a conceited man. He—"

"Must we go back into history? That was a most trying habit of your honorable father. He—"

"Take care what you say! My father was a most honorable man, which is more than can be said for certain persons' fathers. . . ."

"What are you hinting at? No. Don't trouble to answer. I agree with you. But for *my* father's extravagances I would not be lying here beside you, nor living in this monstrosity of a house, nor enduring your mother's insults, her—"

"Enough. But no, please continue. What a virago lies beneath your cool exterior. Let us take up the subject once more of Renzō's return. So, you find him handsome, good-natured. So, you do in truth admire him. I'm glad. Without fail we must welcome him home warmly. Do all in our power to smooth his pathway. I intend to call upon your services."

"My . . . services? Please remember that you are not sitting behind your all-powerful desk at your place of business."

"I meant no offense."

"Then, none taken." Aiko yawned widely, covering her mouth with one of her slender hands. "How stuffy, how dark this room is. My English friend, Lady Marjorie, tells me that she sleeps at night with the windows wide open. How refreshing that must be. How delightful to gaze out and upward, see the stars, the moon."

"Tonight, there is no moon."

"How prosaic you are." Once again Aiko yawned. "I no longer feel like wasting my breath talking with you."

Lying awake, staring into the blackness, quick tears filled Aiko's eyes just as they had when she ran down the hazardous steps descending from the parapet recalling that brief span of happiness in her early childhood.

How futile it was for a woman of her age to harbor and nourish moments of past anguish about the death of a dog.

"Go away little ghost," she murmured. "Stay away . . ."

"What . . . ? What did you say?" Yuichi asked uneasily.

Twisting her head sideways in his direction, Aiko spoke gently, saying, "When a child, I had one friend. Only one. A dog."

Abruptly, Yuichi called out triumphantly, exclaiming, "I recall it! A bulging-eyed little monster! I recall how you clutched it in your arms, running around like a crazy child. You really frightened me that day."

"I did?"

"You most certainly did."

"Hmm . . . I'm glad. Glad I scared you."

"You were such a rude, nasty child. Yes, you scared me."

"And now?"

"Still, at times, yes, I fear you."

"Don't fear me. Fear for me."

"What? What are you insinuating?"

"Absolutely nothing."

"Your tone implied otherwise. I detest your innocuous remarks. Your haughty attitudes."

"Yes. Both you and your mother find me too haughty. . . ."

"Must you always bring my mother into our conversations?"

"Conversations?" Aiko broke into a burst of hysterical laughter. "Ah, well, dawn is yet a long time off. Converse on. Converse on . . ."

As the hours dragged by, Aiko became more and more depressed, knowing that there was no bridge to cross the river that swirled with its dangerous undercurrents between her and her husband. . . .

L ITTLE MORE THAN TWO DECADES had passed since the veil of obscurity shrouding Japan had been blown away. Not all, but many barriers had fallen and Japanese trading vessels steamed over the oceans of the world. The *Osaka Maru*, one such ship, built in England and purchased by the Japanese government, had been on the high seas for several weeks carrying a large cargo toward the coast of Japan.

Before leaving Portsmouth, the vessel's master, Captain Okuno, had been pleased to welcome aboard one paying passenger, Renzō Yamamoto, an experienced drinker with whom he could exchange tales when mealtimes came around. He liked Yamamoto and regretted that he would have little more of his company, for in twenty-four hours his ship would be anchored in the busy harbor of Yokohama.

Renzō leaned on the ship's rail, his cherished English pipe grasped in one hand. His hair was blown by the wind and he shivered slightly, for the last of the sunlight was gone and he was feeling less exhilarated about returning home.

In maturity, he was a singularly engaging man, with the endearing quality of taking a true interest in people. He was always ready to smile and his manner was confident. He knew that although life brought changes, feelings remained the same—that although storms rocked boats, they seldom sank them.

Caressing the smooth bowl of his pipe, he wondered why he was now feeling so crestfallen. He was not too concerned by the plight of his present doubtful financial situation. He was no fool, but all the same he was a man with heavy responsibilities, a family man with dependents relying on him for their welfare. Attempting to bolster up his enthusiasms, he thought of his young son, Shinichi, neglected by his father just as he had been neglected by his own father, Kenichi. He was determined to have the boy understand that he was cherished.

He thought of his wife, Rumi. Truthfully, he scarcely knew her. Rumi, so matter-of-fact, somehow managed to chill his heart, but she was gentle, malleable, and in all probability—it was to be hoped—she had depths which in time he would discover. Perhaps he might even grow to love her? Ah, yes, but was that possible? Feelings remained the same.

His mother, Lady Masa? She was the rock, the steadfast one, and yet he feared that she was discontent, living as she was in the Nihombashi house, in all probability haunted by the ghosts of her husband and the woman with whom he had been obsessed.

That woman Osen! Even now, so many years later, that one glimpse he had had of her, so inscrutable, so beautiful, made him feel guilty and uncomfortable. Her image was implanted in his mind, epitomizing sensual desire. He thought of her as a full moon hidden in a lustrous mist, forever young, robed in garments aglow with color, always mocking him, ruining his affairs with other females.

He knew that if he should see the courtesan as she now was, an elderly woman, his obsession would fade away, but he held on to his memory, luxuriating in it with nothing to put in its place. No matter what the future held, he was determined not to go near his childhood home on the pine-clad hill in Yokohama while Osen was alive and dwelling there.

Anger surged within him when he thought of Sudo, who had left him in the lurch to join the Fukuda clan instead of remaining with him as a faithful henchman should.

Yuichi, his cousin? Always so eager to assist him in every way. Yuichi, so wealthy, a prominent man in Tokyo's business world. Yes, he would have quite a battle on his hands, not a violent but a painful one when he informed Yuichi that he intended to make his own decisions about his future without accepting any further assistance.

He had always been baffled by his cousin's wife, Aiko, and for some unknown reason he had always avoided meeting her eyes, disliking the stony cynicism of the young woman. Unseductive and built like a youth, she was obviously incapable of producing children. Yuichi must be deeply enamored of his wife, but surely if she remained barren he would divorce her and marry a buxom young girl to bear progeny, sons to inherit his wealth as well as to continue the family line. Such as it was. Such as it was? Ah, yes, once again those unchanging feelings! Yes, once a samurai, always a samurai.

A seaman came to his side, bowing casually, saying, "Ship's master is awaiting your presence in the eating room."

"*Ah—sō ka!*—Is that so?" he replied, and pocketing his pipe he walked along the deck. The thought of food and whiskey buoyed up his spirits and he felt a sudden rush of longing for things European. . . .

During adolescence Renzō had been tossed into a world of political upheaval, tension, bickering, and jealousy. With no father, no worldly-wise patron, he had eventually become a tag-end man, traveling about Japan working as an interpreter for the Americans, then for the British, who had more or less overshadowed the Americans due to the latter's horrendous Civil War.

He had been included in a Japanese delegation to America. But his work was always that of a humble translator, a mouthpiece. Always working on tasks far below his intelligence level, he had accustomed himself to hide his disappointments, smiling in a congratulatory manner when men of lesser talents had been given interesting and important positions.

Little by little he had lost any enthusiasm or desire to join in the wild rush forward in the new Age of Enlightenment which had become a period of rapid and often unexpected change, involving not only men of integrity with brilliant minds but also self-appointed experts out to further their personal welfare.

A number of students from the defunct schools were making names for themselves in Japan's literary world, but Renzō, because of his dislike for all scholarly work, came to envisage himself as an eagle with clipped wings. In a dispirited manner, he had drifted with the flow, traveling about Japan, always the translator, rarely at home with his family.

Then Lady Masa, saddened by her son's lack of self-esteem, spoke to Ohara, and that kindly man agreed that Renzō deserved some reward for the grueling years of work he had carried out with integrity. "I sympathize with your son. His future appears bleak. He needs to be uplifted, given some relief from work connected with his scholarly skills. Even so, Lady Masa, it must not be forgotten that Renzō has seldom been able to spend time with his wife. He scarcely knows his child."

Lady Masa agreed, then murmured, "Unashamedly, Ohara Sama, I am convinced that Renzō's family life will not flourish unless he is given a reprieve. If given the opportunity of spending several years in London, his mind, and his emotions too, would be refreshed. On his return home I feel that he would be sought after to fill a position worthy of his talents. Do *you* not agree?"

Ohara agreed warmly, and with diplomacy he arranged a London posting based on Renzō's fluency in the English language. So, Renzō was posted to London. The appointment, although not apparently so, was merely that of a caretaker, where tact and a degree of firmness was required to prevent an effete, aristocratic young diplomat, Moto, from causing social faux pas in European society.

Moto's posting to London was a flagrant example of nepotism, but his mother was dear to the empress's heart.

Many prominent personages who had figured in the earlier scenes of the extraordinary national drama following the arrival of Commodore Perry were living in the twilight zone of enforced retirement, in some cases having been replaced by persons with little or no ability to play serious roles in the task of modernizing Japan.

Generally speaking, the government carefully examined the propensities and qualities of men who were sent abroad to fill diplomatic posts, to study the sciences and various Western skills, but jealousy was rife, and certain aristocratic young men accustomed to having their own way and desirous of seeing the world were given permission to "look into certain matters and to report on them."

Usually those "matters" were of no importance, but problems arose when a man such as Moto, accustomed to having the common people bow low before him, was unable to forgo his colossal egotism on finding himself set down in the midst of teeming American and European cities as a foreigner not conversant with the language—a foreigner stared at and at times ridiculed and deeply perplexed by being alluded to as a "Japanese, a man from Japan." Japan? But—he came from *Nippon*. The very word Japan was strange to his ear and unwieldly to his tongue.

Despite his dislike of Moto, Renzō understood his feelings and, knowing that it would be to his own advantage, he became his face-saver, advising him to relax and make the best of the disappointing situation.

With no hesitation, the neurotic young man gathered a small coterie about himself, a group of dilettantes who slept most of the day and played Mah-Jongg through the nights.

The large, pleasant hotel room which Renzō occupied was one in the suite designated to Moto, and he became accustomed to hearing the click of dice, the rattle of tiles, and explosive cries of *"Pung—kong—chow . . ."*

The simplistic exercise of writing succinct descriptions of English table manners, of how to dress, to behave courteously in various levels of English society was but child's play.

Renzō had little to do but follow his own whims. . . .

When Renzō arrived in London in the spring of 1875, it was the year that heralded in Queen Victoria's thirty-eighth year on the throne. Napoleon Bonaparte was long dead and gone, indeed seldom mentioned, and England was intent on putting her skills and energies into becoming a mighty, free-trade nation.

The grandeur of this metropolis had compensated for the overwhelming disappointment Renzō had suffered when, as a callow youth, he had ridden through Edo accompanied by Sudo. Straightaway he fell in love with the vast, teeming citadel.

Utterly seduced by the free-for-all atmosphere and with little or no work, Renzō plunged headlong into the gaieties of international society. He became an avid theatergoer, bewitched by the make-believe of musical comedy, applauding performances until the palms of his hands burned hot.

Already proficient in English, his scholarly training had given him a sharp ear and he soon discovered not only many subtleties of the rich language, but also its charm when it was spoken by those who were highly educated. He employed a tutor, and before many months went by, he was enunciating every word correctly, with style, thereby arousing a degree of jealousy among his Japanese colleagues—but, fortunately, not with Moto San, who after having mastered a dozen or so well-worn clichés together with formalities concerning greetings and farewells, had exclaimed petulantly, "*Kekkō-desu*—enough! I dislike not only the *language* but the *people*. I dislike the *food*. I shall pine away unless I am able to bathe my body as I am accustomed to so doing."

Renzō managed his daily ablutions using the perfumed soap, the basin, and water ewer in his bedroom most happily.

He was entranced by mansions fronting onto wide, clean streets; by garden squares, green-lawned, aglow with flowers where prim nursemaids aired their small charges and where stylishly dressed men and women aired their well-groomed, pampered dogs. He felt quite certain that his father's spirit was sympathizing with him as he spent extravagantly at tailoring establishments in Savile Row and at jewelers' shops in Bond Street, outfitting himself handsomely. Renzō's two large wardrobes bulged with his Western apparel. He had a special liking for English topcoats, also for sporting garments, especially for skintight riding breeches and fine leather boots. He frankly admired the prepossessing, well-proportioned image his pier glass reflected, and he had a hazy memory of himself when a child, staring into a mirror, not quite satisfied because a sword had been needed to enhance his costume. He seldom ventured outdoors minus one of the many elegant walking sticks he possessed, or one of his black cloth umbrellas.

By the beginning of his second year in London, Renzō had gained a sparkling reputation. He was a sought-after guest at dinner tables, where, faultlessly garbed, smelling just faintly of cologne, he conversed skillfully, flirting lightly with bare-shouldered, richly gowned women, entertaining them and answering their questions about the mysterious land, Japan.

"Tell us, Mr. Yamamoto, you play no cricket in Japan?"

"Unfortunately, no. But football? Yes."

"Football! Played in Japan? Now, is that so?"

"Yes, indeed! Way back in the year 905 it was already a popular outdoor sport for gentlemen and was played by kicking a leather ball. The aim being to prevent it from ever touching the ground. Yes, football, archery, and fencing have played important roles in Japan's sporting culture."

"Please tell on, Mr. Yamamoto."

Nothing loath, Renzō spoke of the nobility's love of horse racing, gambling, and cockfights, describing events in colorful, humorous terms, telling how from ancient days ladies had enjoyed watching boat races and betting on the outcome. How during winter months ladies played games in the snow, built snow mountains and rolled snowballs.

"So entrancing, Mr. Yamamoto. Tell us about Japanese females. Here, in England, we have the impression that they are docile to the extreme, always kept in the background."

"I regret having to disillusion you. Let me just say that the ladies of Japan are known throughout the land as flowers with iron stems."

"Charming, charming!"

Although his reputation as a man-about-town and a ladies' man prospered, Renzō never for one instant stepped over the bounds of light flirtation.

He realized that Westerners' sexual indulgences differed greatly from those in Japan, where sex and sensuality were considered to be aspects of "human feelings" and should be allowed to have their sway.

Standing on the sidelines, looking, listening, and hearing rumors, he believed that many of his newly made English acquaintances indulged their sexual appetites in secretive, even hypocritical ways, but, as secrecy and hypocrisy were also aspects of "human feelings," he accepted the morality of the land he was dwelling in without criticism. Nevertheless, accustomed as he had been to patronizing strictly administered brothels in his own country, he had been shocked by the rafts of females—many pathetically young—who walked the streets of London, plying their trade, naming their price. He saw them as defenseless, pitiable creatures. Never once had he been tempted to indulge himself with one of those unfortunate females. Occasionally, he purchased the services of women in a bordello that was popular with men from the Japanese community in London, but the women in the establishment appeared to have had no training, no idea how to captivate their clients before the sex act took place. For all its lush atmosphere and high price, the bordello had a musty odor that offended his fastidious nature.

After discovering that several of his colleagues had contracted a disease there, he made up his mind that he would take care of his virility by attending to his needs as he had when a youth, alone, by himself, on his own *futon*. He treated the procedure as a required health measure, even though at such times he was haunted by the memory of that one provocative glimpse he had had of his father's mistress, Osen, and he would liken himself to one who lighted a candle with another's flame and he believed that it would always be so.

Never before had he felt so liberated. He escaped at every opportunity from the company of his colleagues, most of whom lived a ghettolike existence, speaking nostalgically of Japan and things Japanese.

Renzō thought of his time in London as an unexpected gift from the gods. He liked and admired the English people. Their air of aloofness pleased him, as did their capacity to laugh with good humor at their own foibles. He soon realized that beneath many a cool exterior, the English people had proclivities for the exotic and the erotic, so he felt a deep empathy with many of them.

Unexpectedly Renzō became involved in a titillating relationship with a married woman, one Hilda Turton, who had told him that her grandfather had made a mighty fortune from his dealings with the African slave market. "I quite idolize the old rapscallion," she had declared brazenly.

"You do?" he had queried tentatively.

"Should I not?"

"Well, I would not. No offense, I assure you, Mrs. Turton."

"No offense taken, *Renzō*." She stared at him, not haughtily but rather in the manner of an accomplished courtesan. After recovering from the shock of hearing her use his given name in so intimate a way, he was excited and from that moment on a duel of wits began between them.

One afternoon while strolling with a group of friends beneath the autumn-tinted trees in Hyde Park, Hilda gestured that she wished to have a moment's tête-à-tête with him. Obligingly, Renzō drew close and without preamble she said in the most matter-of-fact tone, "Renzō, always, *without fail*, when I want something, I get it."

"You do?"

"Yes—always. Without fail."

"Really? No matter the cost?"

"Cost has never concerned me."

"Then you are to be envied by lesser mortals such as I." Gazing at her contemplatively, he said lightly, "Where is this talk leading?"

"To my bed, dear samurai. Where else? Put succinctly, I am bored. I want a new, an exciting experience." Shrugging, she gazed at him provocatively. He moved away from her a little and gave her a swift, penetrating glance, which she returned in kind.

"So, I have shocked you? You are shocked that I want you?"

"Not at all. Not in the least. Allow me to say that the very *thought* of providing you with a new experience delights my heart." Renzō laughed as he locked gazes with the blue-eyed, beautifully groomed woman whose husband was so near by. Still laughing, he said in a warm, firm voice, "Hilda, you *can't have me.*"

"I can't?"

"Absolutely—not!"

How he had admired the sound of her laughter ringing out so clearly, reminding him of his son's laughter when the child had received an unexpected gift.

The English, he mused, were without doubt the most delightful of all people, their sense of humor was a real pleasure for him.

From that day onward he and Hilda built up a platonic friendship based on matters completely unsensual. This was a new experience for both of them, a friendship in which they talked, laughed, confessed their faults and weaknesses to each other. When in her company he was apt to recall the interlude he had enjoyed one day away back in the past, when he and his aunt Sumiko had sat together in a small eating-house savoring grilled eel and drinking rice wine.

Hilda confessed that her father had "sold" her to her elderly husband, an impoverished man with a noble lineage. Snapping her fingers, she said angrily, "Hubert, my husband, loves only my money. I am but a piece of property to him. Since the day of our marriage he has been obsessed by his newly gained wealth. I despise and loathe him."

"That's understandable," Renzō had said. "Hilda, I personally would prefer to be a pauper than a man who sleeps with an abacus beneath his pillow, keeping track of money and possessions."

"Bite your tongue in shame, Renzō. Don't make me cross. Your thirst for spending money is never quenched. Confess. Does your wealth come from your wife's family? No, don't answer, but, tell me, are you in love with her?"

"My wife, Rumi, is a woman as fragrant, as pretty as a plum blossom."

"So . . ." she mocked, "so, you don't love her."

"I am deeply attached to my wife."

"My God—attached! What bastards men are! Cold, unromantic, unfaithful. Truly, it's hell being a woman."

Later on Renzō was taken aback to learn that the females in England were little, if any, better off than were their sisters in Japan. Daughters of wealthy merchants were often married off to impoverished English nobles. Women had no vote, no say in politics of the land. On marriage, their property became that of their husbands. He found them, all women, worthy of his sympathy, but he was pleased to have been born a male.

Mention of Rumi had jolted his conscience, and he requested Hilda's assistance and her advice on the purchasing of gifts, giving her his wife's measurements, saying, "Please spare no expense. Choose garments à la mode. Everything . . ."

"From the skin up?"

"Yes," he boldly declared. "From the skin up."

Hilda's comments alluding to his spending sprees in no way jolted his conscience. His life had been one of austerity, one with no opportunity of pandering to any desires he might have had. He was, he comforted himself, Kenichi's son. His father had always indulged himself and he could follow suit, he convinced himself. He spent with abandon and sent home for funds to the Fukuda business firm that had managed the affairs of the Yamamoto's estate following Kenichi's death.

On receiving news of his uncle Fukuda's death, Renzō was saddened and quite unable to think of life in Japan without the living presence of that unique, colorful man. Then, with a newfound cynicism, he decided to cease grieving and get on with the carefree time he was enjoying.

At every opportunity, Renzō would roam about the city, delving into the historical backgrounds of monuments, mansions, palaces, bridges, and parks.

Having grown up in the doctrine of the power of the sword, he was acutely aware of how important a part that weapon had played in the drama of English history, honored as it was on the tombs of crusaders, lying beside their effigies, some of cold, pure marble, others, and more to his liking, carved from fine wood of oak trees. His loathing of the myriad executions that blotted Japan's history was somewhat tempered on learning that English justice had also been stained by the axing of many heads to suit political purposes.

On the other hand, he was charmed by flower-filled window boxes, by chimes of clocks and the joyous carillon of bells that rang out on Sundays, calling citizens to the exotic Christian shrines they worshiped in.

The poverty that abounded in the metropolis did not scandalize him, and gradually he learned to ignore street beggars who stood by, mouths agape, watching him, along with other fortunate folk, stepping from their carriages to enter marbled porticoes of mansions in Belgravia and Park Lane—residences aglow with lights in readiness for musical evenings, for diplomatic soirees.

Renzō attended one entertainment after another. At concerts and balls he wore silver-buckled pumps and gloried in the giddy whirl of the waltz.

At times he became uncomfortably aware that he was being cold-shouldered by his fellow countrymen. Gossip ran hot about his flamboyant behavior, but he tossed off any feelings of embarrassment, sadly aware that before too long he would return home to Japan and take up the responsibilities of family life.

Then, one sweet day in April he received a letter from Tokyo. The epistle was not brushed, but written with a pen, on paper headed Fukuda Corporation, and signed by none less than Sudo. He informed Renzō that his request for further funds which would enable him to purchase a custom-built carriage in London and then to have it shipped to Japan, was considered to be unseemly.

The letter had continued on in businesslike terms, stating that following the demise of Fukuda Senior, it had come to notice that the once-rich Yamamoto estate had dwindled away, leaving only the Nihombashi and Yokohama houses and school buildings. As neither of those properties engendered any profit, it must be clearly understood that since the demise of Kenichi Yamamoto, Fukuda Senior had—with benevolence and with pleasure—supplied funds from his own purse for the upkeep of his good friends, the members of the Yamamoto family. The situation, it must be understood, now posed a number of difficult questions. Questions which, without doubt, would be dealt with pleasantly and with common sense at a later date. Meanwhile, the president of the Fukuda Corporation, Yuichi Fukuda, had every good intention of carrying on his father's interest in the welfare of his cousin's family. Nevertheless, it was important to state, within reason . . .

Renzō's pride received such a blow that he was left in a state bordering on dementia.

Striding back and forth in his room, unaware of the blood that was seeping from his lower lip which he had bitten into so cruelly, he yearned to be back in Japan, his father's sword in his hand, unsheathed. . . . His honor had been ripped away in one fell swoop. The honor of his ancestors. The honor of his son. He had no redress. Who was to blame . . . ? Useless, more than disgraceful to lay blame on his father. Never that—never, never, or on that good man Fukuda.

He, Renzō, fool of fools, incompetent, ignorant of financial dealings. He alone was to blame.

Striding back and forth, back and forth, he contemplated suicide but immediately dismissed such a facile escape. What of his son, Shinichi? Living on, growing to manhood with no pride in his father. Never, never.

Lady Masa, his mother . . . ?

Merely thinking of his mother brought him a measure of calm. All at once he felt as though she were actually in the room with him, her features enigmatic, pointing her all-powerful fan in his direction, saying derisively, "Life is a drama that calls for careful balancing. If a samurai's sword becomes rust-covered from neglect, strong endeavor will make it bright and gleaming once again."

He ceased his pacing to stand still and rigid, oblivious to the world about him as his mind went back to one far-off day when as a child he had caused havoc in his grandfather's aviary.

He recalled the torture he had endured, kneeling, holding that bowl abrim with water. . . . *"Not a drop must spill,"* the old scholar had admonished. *"Not one drop . . ."*

He recalled the succor of having his body sink into the enfolding comfort of warm bathwater. Then, clean, sitting in Lady Masa's room, he had understood that his mother loved him, that he loved her. . . .

Remembering, just remembering the pride and elegance of his mother caused his blood to run cold as he envisioned her impov-

erished, cast down, like a flower nipped by frost, her pride defaced. . . .

Once again anger engulfed his mind. Was he, Renzō Yamamoto,
expected to bow down, express gratitude to the vulgar Fukuda clan?

Never! Of all human emotions, forced gratitude was the most
debasing. He had no intentions of being overwhelmed by this unexpected misfortune. Unwittingly, carelessly, and ignorantly, he
found himself tied to obligations that must be met.

At present, far from home, he was in a position wherein he could
neither go forward nor backward. Time would move forward. In
four months he would be back in Japan.

For the present, his duty was to remain free of anger. To be self-
disciplined, not to gratify his feelings of fury by writing a scathing
letter to Yuichi Fukuda. He would write to him politely, gently
lampooning his own lack of training in the world's marketplace,
adding that nevertheless, he was filled with zeal, anxious to obey
rules that from time immemorial had mapped out the code of samurai ethics.

He would then write to his mother, explaining the situation in
frank terms, honoring her commonsense attitude to life and assuring
her that he had confidence not only in making reparations for
"favors unwittingly received" but also in keeping the Yamamoto
family's banner unstained.

Try as he did to discipline himself, that obnoxious letter was seldom absent from his thoughts. Then after several days passed he
became attuned to the situation that had been thrust upon him, accepting it as one more holocaust in his life.

He believed that man's fortune was mysterious. That a day filled
with joy was often followed by one ruled by grief and trouble. That
when misfortune occurred, one moved forward to meet it head-on,
never allowing it to engulf him. So, he determined, his duty was to
move forward.

With grace and diplomacy he withdrew from the social whirl.
Those frolics had become but a parody. Half humorously, half
grimly, he accepted that his spending spree was over. With no social
engagements to fulfill, and given his unpopularity in the Japanese
community in London, time hung heavily on his hands. The future
was seldom far from his thoughts. He was filled with impatience,
eager to return to Japan, to search for ways wherein he could repay
debts and support his family, by his own endeavors. There were
moments when his courage deserted him, when he was overcome

by a sickening feeling, dreading the very idea of having to return to the lonely confines of a scholarly life. But he had no training, no skills for anything else.

Regaining lost courage, he allowed his mind to fly off in other directions, but all to no avail. The unedifying thought of becoming involved in the world of business was always dismissed, not only because of its vulgarity and chicanery, but also because he was aware of his pitiable ignorance. His long and rigorous education and work had left him alienated from the competitive Japanese society of the day.

He was forced to look at the world anew but he had lost his dreams and hopes. And to heighten his confusion, he became overwhelmed by homesickness, a yearning for Japan, for things Japanese. As a stranger in a strange city, he took to wandering through the streets of London, always immaculately dressed, but with his spirit in tatters.

Late one afternoon, as he was walking along Bond Street, he paused to glance casually through the open door of an antique shop and was stirred by the bittersweet odor emanating from its interior like a ghostly incense from days long gone by.

Acting on impulse, he entered the establishment, fascinated by the sight of rare objects gathered together from both Europe and the Orient.

A number of men and women were wandering about in the cleverly lit showroom, speaking in hushed voices as they examined valuable articles. He thought it pleasing, if slightly odd, that the tall, good-looking young man, presumably in charge, showed little interest in those who were viewing the merchandise.

Renzō's attention was drawn toward an extremely beautiful youth accompanied by an elderly man. They were gazing into a glass case filled with tiny trinkets. He recognized them to be a homosexual couple and was amused by the petulant manner of the youth, who was exclaiming, "I am *enamored* of it, Gerald. I want it. It's so naughty. So enchanting. Just see how divinely his tiny balls are carved . . ."

Renzō was about to move politely out of earshot, when, as though having received a signal, the proprietor approached the couple. Renzō stood watching as the case was opened and a minute age-yellowed *netsuke*—the carving of a badger—was removed. A transaction took place and he was staggered by the high price that was paid.

All at once the sluggish waters of his mind began to run like a swift river, clean and invigorating. He felt that Kenichi, his father, was by his side, saying, "I might have seemed thoughtless and inconsistent, but not so. I have left you a rich inheritance of artworks, a veritable treasure chest. Renzō, just open the lid."

The following three hours were among the most illuminating hours of his life. After having conferred with the young man, Arthur Bixby, Renzō had been guided through the shop, up the stairs and into the brightly lit living quarters of the establishment's true proprietor, Mr. Victor Caswell.

Victor Caswell, some ten years senior to Renzō, was not merely overweight but frankly fat, and like many fat men he possessed the charm of a baby. There was a ringing quality to his voice and, despite his rotundness, he dressed like a dandy, being deeply interested in fashion. He also had an insatiable interest in people and a seemingly bottomless fund of knowledge about antiques.

Although garrulous, Caswell did possess the art of listening when being spoken to. "I consider myself to be a man of vision, Mr. Yamamoto," he had said. "I never judge a book by its cover. My background is bourgeois. I have a passion for the old, the rare, but above all, I am a man of business. May I say that I like your proposition. May I say that from this moment onward I'm more than willing to accept your proposals. So far, it has proved difficult to obtain articles of undoubted authenticity from your mysterious country. The demand is never-ending. Unfortunately, many objects that have come into my hands have not been authentic. I sell them in my other establishment, one in Malta Street in Soho. Are *you* familiar with Soho?"

"Not as *yet*, Mr. Caswell."

"Ah—I *like* that statement. You soon will be, Mr. Yamamoto. Allow me to refill your glass. This sherry soothes one's palate into ecstasies. . . ."

So it was that Renzō entered the world of business. His only qualm concerned his mother's distaste of the world of commerce, but that matter would have to be dealt with in the future.

In the meantime, the tempo of his life quickened as he strutted into the realms of business as though to the manner born. Never for one instant could he have imagined how dramatically his actions would affect the lives of many people. If, by chance, a soothsayer had crept to his side to whisper, "Renzō Yamamoto, in the casket of the Hours / Events deep hid / Wait on their guardian Powers / To raise the lid," he would have shrugged casually, carelessly, and gone on his way.

Following his meeting with Victor Caswell, Renzō went through his luggage in search of articles that might be of interest to the Bond Street dealer, and he had been astonished at the Englishman's reactions and delighted by the amount of ready cash that flowed into his pockets.

He rejoiced that he had not followed his own inclinations before leaving Japan. Had he done so, he would not have bothered to take along the extra trunk his mother had packed tight with articles familiar to him: "It is possible that your spirit might yearn for solace as times goes by. Also, the brocades, scrolls, and lacquerware would make suitable 'thank you' gifts to foreigners who, I hope, will make you welcome in their land."

Apart from articles which bore the family crest, Renzō sold all his booty to Victor Caswell. He was enthusiastic and confident as he chatted to the dealer about the collections of treasures he owned back in his own country.

"You possess a veritable king's ransom," Victor had chortled. "But what of the future?"

"The future?"

"Yes. When, finally, your coffers are emptied. What then, 'Prince Yamamoto'? From where will come fresh supplies?"

Renzō was at first taken aback, but then said decisively, "In all truth, Mr. Caswell, my mind has not as yet taken that aspect into consideration."

"Well, I go by my intuitions," Victor exclaimed warmly. "And I see a rosy future. Now, tell me about Japan's weavers, potters, painters, and masters of lacquerware. Remember, we must deal only with the genuine. Our market here, as in America, is already being flooded with quantities of trash coming out of Japan. . . ."

Seldom a day went by without Renzō's paying a call to Victor Caswell's living quarters above the shop in Bond Street where he dwelt with his plump, sweet-voiced wife. The spacious living room was uncluttered, even sparsely furnished, and its polished floors were covered with finely woven, fringed Persian rugs.

One wall was given over to a collection of small paintings alluded to by Victor as "my precious, my self-indulgences. Ah, torture me on the *rack* if you desire to torment me, but *don't* harm my Monet or my Manet. See how light actually emanates *from* them!"

"But galleries, the Louvre included, don't hang them," young Bixby interjected dourly. "Critics have nothing but insults for the efforts of your rebel French artists."

"Dear boy, don't *mention* bourgeois gallery men and critics. They, I swear, suffer from paralysis of the mind."

Conceding defeat, Bixby turned to Renzō and said, "The French have taken to raving for the works of your Japanese artists. Victor tells me that you possess original Hokusai and Utamaro and Shuncho works."

"I do, Mr. Bixby. Also scrolls and books, many depicting life in the courtesan world and that of the geisha. Many are exotic and many, I fear, are too erotic for public exhibition in London."

"Stop! No so *loud*, Mr. Yamamoto!" Victor exclaimed with mock terror. "Walls have ears. Arthur, what an unexpected bonanza has come our way! Mr. Yamamoto, the growth of censorship in England has created a *tremendous underground market* for erotic works. Beneath the prudish façade of our society, erotica flourishes! You are not aware of that?"

Renzō's immediate thought had been one of amusement, but he said, "I *have* become aware that a sense of reticence in certain areas exists here."

"I," Bixby announced firmly, "have a decent sense of reticence, Victor. . . ."

"Then, away with it, dear boy!" Victor interjected. "Let sunlight filter into your dark, hypocritical mind, and—"

"Hypocritical—I?" Arthur Bixby spoke more firmly. "Victor. You slander me."

During the early stages of his acquaintance with Arthur Bixby, Renzō often wondered why the upper-crust young man was working in a shop as a salaried employee. Indoctrinated from childhood, Renzō could instantly place persons into the various classes of society they belonged, and he had not been surprised to learn that Bixby was the son of an English peer.

"Unfortunately for young Bixby," Victor Caswell had confided, "he was the second son. After his father's death, the title, the family fortune—such as it is—went to his older brother, Robert. Too bad, eh?"

"It is the same in my country," Renzō had replied. "In Japan, Arthur would be known as Master Cold Rice. Big brother always gets served first."

"Well, it's a poor custom. Bixby's only hope of maintaining the style to which he was born depends on his finding a wealthy bride, and perhaps enduring a loveless marriage."

"It would be exactly so in my country, Mr. Caswell."

With some aplomb, Arthur Bixby had ignored Victor Caswell's instructions that he "hop to" and escort Renzō to his other establishment. Several days later, intent on furthering his knowledge in the realms of business and artistic expertise, Renzō went alone toward the quarter of London known as Soho.

Wending his way along the noisy, crowded street, he became aware of tantalizing odors floating out of small, shabby eating-houses wherein swarthy-skinned folk spoke Greek, Italian, and other languages of which he had no ken.

Filled with elation, he roamed onward until he finally came to Malta Street, and there, on the corner was a sprawling, ramshackle building embellished with a red signboard, reading:

CASWELL'S EMPORIUM
GENUINE ANTIQUES
BARGAINS GALORE

On entering the premises, he had liked the bazaarlike atmosphere of the indoor marketplace with stalls set up, all a higgledy-piggledy colorful disorder of goods for sale, each stall with its own proprietor noisily intent on gaining the attention of those who milled about on the lookout for bargains and out to barter.

Looking the place over, Renzō beheld Victor Caswell, dressed as usual in fashionable mode, wearing a monocle and with top hat stuck rakishly on his head and carrying the stout, gold-handled cane he used to assist his ponderous body. He hailed Renzō with delight, taking his arm, leading him from stall to stall, introducing him as "Prince Yamamoto from Japan. One close to the family of the great tycoon . . ."

Helpless as a fly caught in the web of a great spider, Renzō squelched his feeling of embarrassment. Recalling the way his old nurse, Honda, had bullied him, he gave no resistance, at the same time slightly resenting the man's hold on his body, while Victor, unaware of such fastidiousness, kept up a stream of comments all to do with the fakery of the goods on sale, exclaiming, "As dealers, we must learn to spot a fake *instantly*. . . . This bargain basement is *chockablock* with faked, misattributed works, and not

228   KAGAMI

only *this* place. London *abounds* in knaves and thieves. Same in Tokyo, eh?"

"Absolutely not!" Renzō had replied firmly.

"Nonsense! Human nature is the same everywhere. Let me warn
you never to purchase goods brought to you by genteel, shabbily
dressed folk. Make it your policy to send 'em off to other venues.
Buying stolen goods causes untold problems. . . ."

"Are you suggesting that the worthy, the honest, must suffer because of dishonest persons?"

"I am. I am. Sad but true. Come, enough of this. Let's away for
a chop, a pint of ale. How do you like my Soho premises? Not
exactly respectable but very prosperous. Frankly, Yamamoto, *nothing* is more *respectable* than prosperity. Frankly, *I* was not born with
a silver spoon in my mouth. Now, am I correct in assuming that
you were? That all of a sudden it has been snatched from your gob?
Ah—don't answer. Pardon my indelicacy . . ."

In some ways, Victor Caswell reminded Renzō of his old uncle,
Fukuda. He found his idiosyncrasies intriguing; he admired his uncanny knowledge and saw him as a shrewd man. On the contrary,
he found young Bixby uninteresting and paid little attention to him.

Somewhat to Renzō's amusement, Arthur Bixby invited him to
his family home, an austere mansion, where he met Arthur's brother,
Sir Robert, and his wife, Lady Bixby. They, having but recently
returned from five years spent in India, appeared to be incapable of
accepting the fact that their Oriental guest understood English even
though he spoke it with skill and confidence.

Renzō, his amusement once again aroused, secure in his samurai
pride, behaved in a charming, understated manner, sympathizing
with Bixby every time his sister-in-law spoke at length describing
the luxurious life which the British enjoyed while living in the colonies and of their heavy responsibilities, saying how grateful the
natives of heathen lands should be for "blessings bestowed upon
them by us, the British."

"Yes, we British have bestowed many blessings on our colonies
and on other foreign countries," Sir Robert proclaimed. "Your people, the Japs, must be benefitting greatly, Mr. Yamamoto." Turning
to his brother, he exclaimed in a measured, kindly voice, "Arthur,
is Mr. Yamamoto fully comprehending?"

Bixby cleared his throat uneasily and replied, "Mr. Yamamoto's
understanding of our language is quite remarkable."

"No, no. Not all," Renzō murmured, "but I struggle on. . . ."

When he and Bixby left Brunton Street, the young man attempted to apologize, saying, "My brother's closed mind has always embarrassed me."

"Not at all. Not at all. Traditions go deep in *all* ancient cultures. Certain Japanese traditions embarrass me. If it so happens that you should ever visit my country, Mr. Bixby, you would find great similarities."

The young man made no reply, for at that moment a streetwalker accosted the two men. On seeing Renzō at close quarters, the gaunt-faced woman drew back, startled, muttering, "My gawd, what's this? A Chink . . ." Horrified, she scuttled away into the shadows.

"This is indeed an evening of dread embarrassment," Bixby stammered.

The reserved young man was now genuinely upset. To put him at his ease, Renzō remarked placidly, "Scarcely a female likely to cause a man to succumb to the temptations of the flesh."

"I agree. I agree."

"In my country, the world of prostitution is quite congenial. Ah, once again let me encourage you to visit Japan. Our courtesans could but enchant you."

"Really?" Arthur Bixby's manner became distinctly withdrawn. "Mr. Yamamoto, with respect, could we speak of less trivial matters?"

"I'm unable to resist saying that in no way do I consider delights of the flesh to be—trivial. In all honesty, Mr. Bixby, do you?"

"In all honesty—I do not. But I consider those *delights* to be private."

"So—then, let us on to vital issues such as freight on board, etc., etc. I've much to learn and little time. Why waste precious moments dwelling on the unmentionable!"

Despite himself, the young man burst into laughter, exclaiming, "You must consider me pompous to the extreme."

"Not so. I find you to be, *omoshiroi*—interesting. Yes—most interesting . . ."

However, Renzō was in fact overcome by boredom. He bade Bixby farewell and returned to his quarters, where, before retiring, he made a list of gifts to purchase for those he would soon be with in his homeland. He was particularly pleased with his choice for Lady Masa, for he knew his mother would treasure the gilt-edged, suede-covered volume of hand-painted English roses.

. . .

After Renzō had made his farewells to all his other friends in London, Victor Caswell declared, "Now, my friend, our final moments must be devoted to business matters. Agreed?"

He realized that Victor Caswell was paying a great tribute to him when he exclaimed with infectious abandon, "Between you and me there has been forged a bond of trust. I haven't the slightest idea why, but I feel that fate himself is directing us."

"Is that so?" Renzō asked, reaching out to steady his ponderous friend as they walked along Bond Street for the last time together. "Frankly, Victor, my meeting with you and Bixby has been so auspicious. So . . ."

"Forget about young Bixby," Victor chortled. "Bixby is not our kind. He has no vision. Well, if he does, he certainly hides it behind the impenetrable mask of his upper-crust family background. When a moneyed lass comes his way, he'll be off like a shot. Yes, they're a poor lot, Bixby's family."

Victor laughed. "Lend me a hand again, Renzō. I must lose weight. Any magic Jap remedy for that? I mean, of course, without giving up food and grog?"

"Unfortunately, no."

"Pity! Ah, here we are. By the way, tell me, have you ever noticed the aroma that emanates from the shop?"

"Yes. That tantalizing fragrance was what first enticed me into your premises."

"Good! Good! I must order more sticks of that magic incense. . . ."

Neither Victor Caswell nor Renzō Yamamoto would ever know that their conversation had been overheard by Arthur Bixby, who had been walking close behind them, not eavesdropping, but out of politeness not interrupting the older men.

His pride was badly hurt at hearing himself and his family discussed in such a rude manner.

To the best of his ability, he assisted in the arrangements for Renzō's departure. When the last day in July arrived, the Englishman stood watching the Japanese cargo vessel, the *Osaka Maru*, steam slowly away. At that moment he had no idea of the drastic changes life held in store for him.

On the third day of September in the year 1878, Renzō arose before dawn. The *Osaka Maru* was due to anchor at Yokohama harbor soon after daybreak, and he leaned over the rust-encrusted rails to breathe in great gulps of the sweet, balmy air.

The sails of junks hung listlessly, and on the sampans were the half-nude figures of the fisherman working the long sweeps, laughing, and shouting to one another.

He watched, scarcely breathing, and as the red disc of the sun arose and sunlight came creeping over the far-off hills, he beheld the pristine glory of snowcapped *Fuji San*. Renzō was home. How *could* he have stayed away so long?

When Renzō arrived back in Japan, it was to find that the country was preparing the ground for constitutional government. Radical changes were taking place in the judicial and administrative systems, in the currency, and in the organization of both the army and the navy.

During his absence, mandatory military service for able young males had been introduced, as well as compulsory universal education throughout the land, for females and males. Her Imperial Majesty, the empress herself, had become the patron of one school for girls, and it was widely accepted that in order to create a fine nation, the education of girls was of a high priority.

Railways and new roads were being spread farther throughout Japan, and citizens who had never so much as dreamed of leaving their native villages were now traveling far and wide.

Having come from London, it was strange to be in a city where the phonograph and telephone were arousing great interest, and lectures were given on those intriguing inventions, and it was amusing to hear Japanese versions of "Home Sweet Home," and "Shall We Gather at the River," among many other English songs being sung by children and by adults in all manner of places. But a feeling akin to great pity melded in with Renzō's love for his country. It seemed as though having awoken from a deep sleep much too late in the day to fulfill obligations, that right throughout society there was deep consternation. An anguish of a kind never experienced, even dreamed of, arousing a sense of euphoria colored with the knowledge that to keep abreast in the powerful tide of modernization, strength beyond endurance would be needed.

But, obviously, the bridge between Japan and the United States was becoming sturdy. General Grant, the eighteenth president, had visited the country with his wife and had been received by the emperor and empress. The illustrious American couple had been guests of honor at a soiree given by Prime Minister Sanjo, and on that occasion the Great Hall in the newly built College of Engineering was filled with two thousand splendidly dressed men and women, their combined voices, it was said, had resembled the sound of waves roaring onto a shore.

Renzō had little interest in such affairs. He resolved to give his all to the new area into which he had entered.

Never would he forget the flurry and excitement caused by his arrival at the Nihombashi house. Unable to sleep, he lay wide-eyed, overcome by feelings of claustrophobia. The house seemed to have shrunk. He, the master, felt like an intruder.

Lady Masa appeared to have aged, to have lost her innate imperiousness, and his young son most obviously looked upon him with some suspicion, actually asking hopefully, "Will you be going away again soon, Father?"

"No. No, I'm home to stay," he had replied, smiling.

"You mean—forever?" The apprehension in Shinichi's voice had aroused a burst of embarrassed laughter, and although the child had recovered himself, saying, "That will be nice," Renzō felt that his son resented his presence in the household where he had been cock of the roost in the ménage of women.

Rumi, certainly even prettier than he remembered her, expressed no interest in hearing about his experiences. She chattered on happily, reporting snippets of local gossip, speaking of people he had never met. Then, finally, she accepted him into her bed with a bland serenity.

Now, lying beside his sleeping wife, his heart was disturbed, filled with strange yearnings. Was he to live out his life longing for a woman he was never to meet! Well, surely it was so for most men.

How mistaken he had been moving his family away from Yokohama to live in this house in Tokyo. He had never liked the capital. His son should be growing up in his ancestral home. In that house on the pine-clad hills overlooking the beach of Hommoku. How vividly he recalled his mother sauntering along the water's edge with his aunt, their kimono tucked up to reveal their red petticoats.

Those vanished years! Wryly, he thought of how he had resented and had fought the austere severity of the shogun regime. Even the short train journey from Yokohama to Tokyo had reflected the decline of its authority. New freedoms were encouraging rough manners. It seemed as though vulgarity was replacing gentility.

His future? During his wife's light, artless chatter, there was the mention of a much sought after post at Keiō University. "Ohara Sama was much pleased to recommend you," Rumi exclaimed, smiling.

Glancing at his mother, he realized that she expected a pleased response from him. He hid his feelings, determined to sidestep any questions concerning his plans.

Here he was, back home. Restless, overcome by burdensome thoughts, worrying with no results. He needed a strong drink.

Lady Masa was in no way startled when she heard her son's voice murmuring from the corridor, "Mother . . . ?"

"Come in," she replied, "So good to have you home."

In the soft glow of the floor lamp, Masa appeared to be untouched by the frost of her years as she rose up from her *futon* to slip a purple *haori* coat over her sleeping robe. And as his gaze followed the graceful movements of his mother, he listened to the delicate sound of bamboo leaves rustling against the closed shutters. Seating himself, Renzō said, "Mother, I am in need of a drink. . . ."

"Understandable! I shall summon Misa at once."

"Please don't. I prefer whiskey to *sake*."

"Ah . . ." Lady Masa murmured. "I often thought of you on the high seas. Truly, I expected to find you energetic, but you appear sadly lethargic."

"Hmm, yes. I'm not as yet accustomed to being on dry ground. In a few days my body will adjust."

"I'm relieved to hear that. Thank you for the many letters you wrote me. Each one so intriguing, so colorful. Renzō, do you regret that the thrill of living abroad has come to an end?"

"In some respects, yes. In some respects, no."

They sat in silence, each one examining the other, and hiding their deepest emotions. He was distressed by the colorless tone of her voice and wondered what thoughts were passing through her mind as she sat so upright, staring emptily at her hands.

Finally, he muttered, "Family reunions, no matter how pleasant, are exhausting to one's emotions."

"True," she replied in a low voice. "Especially so for one who returns back home to shoulder problems and heavy obligations instead of bright, welcoming banners. Is that not so?"

"Not so altogether." He spoke firmly, saying, "Mother, no matter how difficult our financial situation, the moon goes on shining. I recall you once saying that to fully enjoy moon-viewing, there must be clouds. Now, excuse my abruptness, but I've many things to explain. The years are slipping by like a swift river. When I was young the world seemed eternal. I want you to understand my plans."

"Is that so?" Lady Masa's voice was tinged with amusement. "You speak so poetically. I shall try to understand but you must speak frankly. Tell me, Renzō, what shall you do, then? Already I've gathered that you have no desire to accept the teaching position which Ohara Sama has put forward. Correct?"

"Correct."

"So . . . ?"

"So, I have made other arrangements." He avoided her eyes, saying in a conciliatory voice, "I admit that when I received *that* letter from the Fukuda Corporation, I was devastated. It was a whip shaking at my face. For days I was perplexed, wondered how one could cook rice when no rice was left. You understand?"

"I understand."

"Then, as though struck by a flash of lightning, I realized that my father had left his family a rich inheritance. Aware of that, I entered into the world of business."

He stopped speaking, seeing that her eyes were dark with foreboding. "Forgive my brashness," he said. "I have shocked you."

"Shocked me?" Lady Masa gestured that he should allow her time before she continued. "Shocked me?" she repeated. "Yes, for more reasons than one. My mind is flashing with confusion. How could it be otherwise? A rich inheritance, you say? But the family estate has been frittered away! You have entered the business world, you say? How could that be? You are a *scholar*! You have no experience, no expertise in commerce circles. I sense danger and I find it unendurable to have you so downgrading yourself."

"All this is not exactly flattering," he remarked harshly as though to no one in particular.

"Cautionary notes must be sounded. I fear the pitfalls ahead. . . ." As though unable to bear even the thought of those pitfalls, Masa bent her head low, whispering, "But, so be it. You must go your own way."

"I appreciate your concern." Renzō sensed that his mother was greatly concerned and hurt too. Yet he felt obliged to make his plans clear and he continued on, describing the shop in Bond Street and Victor Caswell. "A true friend, a trusted, knowledgeable dealer . . ."

Finally his mother interrupted him, not with words but by refilling the bowl before him from the near-empty whiskey bottle and he knew that she was performing a simple but clearly understood act, accepting the situation with grace.

"Thank you!" he exclaimed. "I was in need of your approval."

"My admiration also. I give it not in flattery. Suddenly my spirit has become strangely exhilarated. New vistas open up before me. The very thought of my entering a convent is now quite ludicrous."

"A convent? You—a nun? Really, Mother?"

"Such was my intention. To relieve you of one burden at least. Now there is no need. Renzō, I'm enthralled to learn that an appreciation of our country's art has burst upon the Western world."

"You no longer feel that this is a step downward—socially?"

"*One* step?" Lady Masa exclaimed airily. "Nonsense! A positive flight of steps downward. However, your approach is certainly unique. The dissemination of Japanese art throughout the world is commendable." Masa sighed deeply, looking far away as though across the world to foreign lands. "I find that in no way unedifying. Perhaps it's the air of the new age which has been causing me to pine for a time of action. Perhaps, unconsciously, I've been preparing myself for radical changes in my spirit. My life has been so cloistered. I'm woefully ignorant of the world of trade. Renzō, as you advance into it, you must take care never to show contempt for old ways and traditions. Never throw precious luggage into the mud while traveling . . ."

As Lady Masa paused in order to renew her breath, Renzō stared, astonished by her lack of reticence as she spoke on, her voice a mixture of sternness and laughter. "Allow me to say, Renzō, that I rejoice knowing that at last you have freed yourself from the fetters placed upon you these many years."

Masa rose and padded across the *tatami* that had been renewed in honor of Renzō's return. He sat watching as she pushed the wooden shutters aside and turned to face him, gesturing outdoors, and murmuring in a mischievous voice, "Renzō! Look—a new day!"

"Yes," he replied gently. "A new day . . ."

Still feeling that he was treading the ship's deck, and in spite of the whiskey he had consumed, Renzō attempted to walk steadily along the dim corridors of the house. He felt deeply relieved but suspicious of the uncharacteristic enthusiasm his mother had shown toward his plans for the future. He liked to believe that she had been sincere, but he was doubtful.

Rumi had no intention of allowing her husband to blame her for the domestic inconveniences he complained of immediately after his arrival back. When he exclaimed with no little irritation, "My garments are in a crushed, disgraceful condition," she advised him to have copious Western-style wardrobes built.

When he showed dissatisfaction in the laundering and upkeep of his clothing, she advised him to employ a valet, saying, "The household servants are uneducated females. Your new garments mystify them. Truly, you appear to hope for miracles." Wardrobes were built. A valet was installed.

His demand that he begin each day with an "English breakfast" aroused terrible consternation in the kitchen quarters. After a series of mornings of complaints, Rumi murmured calmly, "Now, if you *must* have eggs, crisp bacon, golden brown toasted bread spread with butter and imported marmalade, perhaps you should undertake the preparation of that delectable foreign meal yourself—with your own hands."

Much to her and to his own astonishment, he accepted the challenge, thereby even further terrifying the household staff, who crouched nervously at the ready to obey his slightest order. All three servants burst into tears one morning as he berated them because the cow's milk he required had turned sour. The unseemly domestic episode had come to a stop when Renzō beheld his young son standing by with a cynical expression on his handsome face, watching his father with the supercilious air of an experienced stage director dealing with an amateur actor whom he might dismiss at any given moment.

He longed to win the affection of the boy, who continued to treat him as a stranger, with overstated respect, and in a disconcertingly unchildlike manner, gazing through rather than at him.

Shinichi attended a school run by American missionaries, and he appeared to be gripped by a mania for study. Without doubt he had become prey to the American spirit of rivalry and was keen to be included among the bright children who were sailing off to the United States to attend preparatory schools before entering colleges and universities there.

"I find my son too highly strung," Renzō complained to Rumi.

"I dislike his overly bold ways and I find his preoccupation with study quite unnatural."

"Your mother tells me that our son has inherited his great-grandfather's intellectual aptitudes," Rumi replied placidly. "He is a born scholar. Are you not pleased, even *proud* that he resembles Yamamoto Sensei?"

"Certainly, he resembles that scholar, but I have the feeling that my son wants to *punish* me."

"Is that so?" Rumi merely smiled. "Well, in his innocence he feels that you've neglected him these many years. Just give him time. Are you blaming *me* for the faults you find in your son?"

"Not at all," he exclaimed with false sincerity. "Your advice is sensible."

From that time onward, he treated Shinichi in an affectionate, slightly joshing manner in the hope that the boy would relax and that a stronger, more congenial bond would gradually develop between them.

Renzō did not want to become so engrossed in financial matters that he had no time for the pleasures of social life. He fully subscribed to the proverb, *"Only a fool forgets to play. Soon he'll get stomach disorders and die."*

He hoped to build up his family's assets little by little, and any resentment he had harbored against the Fukuda family faded from his mind. He met with Yuichi over lunch and his resilient attitude proved to be a perfect foil for the undercurrent of tension that Yuichi faced him with, saying, "Renzō, greatly to my distress, my mother, your aunt Sumiko, tells me there is a rumor that you and I are not exactly on good terms. Now—please allow me to explain that unfortunately couched letter. . . ."

Stopping himself from laughing right in Yuichi's face, Renzō merely exclaimed heartily, "Mothers have a tendency to interfere in their sons' affairs. We should ignore their gossip."

Yuichi was more than willing to listen to Renzō's personal plans once he clearly understood that his cousin had no intention of accepting a position in the Fukuda Corporation.

"But," Yuichi exclaimed finally, "nevertheless, allow me to assist you in your project."

"Thank you. However, my ideas are modest." Renzō's tone was one of mock humility. "Under your influence I could find myself in the perilous situation of becoming truly rich. Also, frankly, we both know that in all probability I must always remain indebted to you. Enough is enough. Is that not so?"

Yuichi responded with a grin, muttering, "Who knows what the future holds! Who knows? Yes, it could be that my future welfare might depend on *your* aid."

"Call on me at any time." Renzō laughed heartily. Gazing at his cousin through hazy blue cigarette smoke, he added, "But—not for financial aid, eh?"

"There are needs other than financial ones in a man's life." Yuichi fell silent and Renzō departed slightly bothered, knowing that Yuichi was in need of something but not brave enough to make a request.

In all truth Renzō would have gladly accepted his cousin's advice, for he was woefully ignorant about current practices of trade and commerce. Above all, he required a man skilled in accountancy and with an understanding of banking. He knew of no such person. From early years he had lived the life of a nomad, unable to form close, brotherly friendships such as those his father had achieved. He thought of approaching his one-time patron, Ohara, but that ethical samurai had received him coldly when he had traveled to Kamakura to announce his return home and to pay his respects.

Without doubt the reputation he had gained as a maverick among his Japanese colleagues while in London had followed him back home and was clearly working against him.

Although not too distressed, he realized with a thoughtful wince that he would have to search in other directions in order to obtain the assistance he needed to succeed in his money-making ventures.

Tokyo's Akasaka district was a seedy area that catered mostly to the needs of the common folk, but millions of people from all classes came to the district all year round to visit a temple enshrining a miniature statue of Kannon, the goddess of mercy. Legend had it that many centuries back, two young men fishing in the nearby Sumida River found the tiny image while hauling in their catch.

Fronting the temple was a gigantic caldron of burning incense, ready for worshipers to cup the smoke and massage parts of their bodies, thereby cleansing their spirits and dispelling ailments. The temple's interior glowed with lavish gold plating, soft lighting, and precious paintings, but one never saw the highly revered figurine, for the temple's first priest, Shokai, ordained it "a hidden image," never to be seen by the human eye.

Renzō had taken to frequenting this tawdry district which reminded him of Soho, in London. Quite often as he strolled about he thought of Victor Caswell, wishing he could behold the marvelous array of secondhand wares of sale in booths and pawnshops. Among the polyglot collection of traditional garments, hand-painted kites, fans, and boxed scrolls, many objects of real antiquity were on view, and to Renzō's amazement, swords, highly decorated and forged by time-honored methods, were on sale at pathetically low prices.

The sight of those dishonored weapons hurt his spirit in an inexplicable way and he instinctively purchased them, not with any intent to resell or make any profit, and as time went by a goodly collection of swords piled up in the Yokohama warehouse he had rented for storage purposes. He had the vague idea of returning the swords to their rightful owners, at the same time knowing that it was impossible, for the family crests had been painstakingly removed by shamed, poverty-stricken warriors.

One morning as he idled along, followed closely by his new valet, Rin, who was lugging several of the swords he had just purchased, Renzō's attention was caught by a man walking toward him, also carrying several swords. The man stopped suddenly, staring intently, then exclaimed, "Yamamoto! So, can it be you?"

Halting, Renzō gazed back and gradually recognized the man. "So," he had replied, "Nakasone! Can it be you?"

Rin stood by like an obedient dog as the two men inconvenienced passersby hailing one another with enthusiasm. Renzō was especially pleased, for some instinct told him that this meeting had been arranged by fate.

Later that evening, Renzō recounted the morning's episode to his mother. Both were secretly relieved that Rumi was spending the night at the Fukuda residence in order to assist Aiko in the musical evening she was arranging.

"Mother, Nakasone's background is impeccable, but like many nobles, he has fallen on hard times. His father never recovered from the difficult years of the Restoration. Sadly, he took his life and his wife valiantly followed him."

"Tragic indeed." Masa bowed her sympathy.

"Yes. Nakasone is now alone in the world."

"Surely by this time he must have married and produced a family?"

"Not so. He is not attracted to women."

"Ah," Masa murmured. "Certain of your father's samurai brothers were so inclined. Renzō, I was interested to learn that foreigners
consider the Way of Manly Love not merely degenerate, but pun-
ishable by the laws of their lands."

"True." Renzō smiled. "Who told you that?"

"Aiko. She is extremely *au fait* with the ways of the *gaijin*."

"Could it be that Aiko is inclined toward the Way of Womanly
Love?" Renzō grinned. "I find her strange, to say the least."

"Really? Personally—whatever her predilections—I like Aiko immensely." Lady Masa held out her cup to be replenished. "But
please inform me further about the meeting with your old acquaintance. You went together to the Tsukiji Hotel—that dreary edifice—
and . . . ?"

"Yes. And—spoke together for several hours. Nakasone told me,
without embarrassment, that all he owned were the clothes on his
back, that over the years he had sold all his family possessions. The
swords he was carrying—his own and his honored father's—were
to be sold also. For all his outward composure, I sensed an urgency
and a bitterness in my old colleague."

Renzō broke off speaking in order to relight his cigarette, and
Lady Masa's mouth was tight with disdain as she murmured, "There
is much hidden desolation in the land these days."

Renzō inhaled smoke deeply into his lungs, coughed, then gestured that he agreed with her. "After quaffing numerous glasses of
French brandy, Nakasone admitted that as far as he was concerned,
life was a parody under the New Rule of the Restoration. I understood him only too well. Like myself, he spent his early years as a
student at one of the other Schools of Dutch Study. Then, like myself, he was utilized by the shogun in the humble capacity of translating, interpreting, sent hither and yon, year after year, away from
family. We both trailed in the wake of the confident newcomers to
the land, attempting to obey their orders, along with those of the
government. We were caught up in situations quite beyond our
comprehension. . . ."

At that moment, Renzō became aware that his mother was gazing
at him, smiling her mischievous, tight-lipped smile. He grinned,
saying, "Hmm . . . that burst of self-pity has refreshed my spirit.
Excuse my childishness."

"Giving vent to inner feelings in your mother's presence needs
no apology."

"Thank you! I was certainly carried away. Now, to continue. Nakasone is no ordinary man. He is shrewd, intelligent, and ambitious. He informed me that during his two compulsory visits to the United States, he came to admire American business methods. For several years now he has been studying the intricacies of commerce and banking as well as the Western patterns of thought in general. He has approached many newly formed business houses in Tokyo, only to be insulted. He admitted to feeling very bitter indeed."

"Understandable."

"Absolutely. However, I was faced with an awkward situation. When I, with some delicacy, offered to help him, there was a distinct cooling between us."

"Again—understandable."

"Yes. I hastened to inform him of my new venture. Of my partnership with Victor Caswell. Then, with the utmost sincerity, I suggested that he join with me in the enterprise. Truly, he then became so animated he let forth a battle cry of exaltation! We laughed uproariously, ignoring the glances cast our way by the others in the hotel. Mother, to sum up, a great burden has been lifted from my shoulders."

"I'm profoundly moved," Masa responded. She sat searching about the room as though in need of inspiration. "Chance meetings are apt to bring about drastic changes in lives. I feel that you two men have everything to gain and nothing to lose." Holding out her empty cup, she murmured, "I wish to pay tribute to the gods for the gifts they give."

As Renzō replenished the tiny vessel, he said, "Tribute to my father also? Only his wisdom makes all my plans possible."

"To—your father also . . ."

No one could have detected a certain element of cynicism beneath the impenetrable mask Masa wore as she drank from the cup.

COOL AUTUMN SUNLIGHT FILTERED THROUGH the small garden of the Nihombashi house, and a brisk wind blew in sudden gusts, as though determined to rid the small maple tree of its crisp scarlet leaves.

A year had passed since Renzō's return, and Lady Masa was entertaining Aiko, who had arrived unexpectedly, wearing a soft-hued kimono, her manner both ceremonious and apologetic as she exclaimed, "Excuse this too casual call, Aunt Masa."

"Please—don't apologize! Your visit delights me."

"Truly I'm not disturbing you?"

"Not in the least."

"I'm glad. I was hoping to find Rumi at home. I wish to congratulate her. She is well?"

"Extremely so. She hopes for a daughter."

"So she has told me. And Renzō?"

"He also desires a daughter. But without doubt, if a male child arrives, we will all welcome him joyfully."

"Naturally!" Aiko pressed a clenched fist against her lips for an instant, then murmured, "Would it offend if I smoked a cigarette?"

"No indeed. I'm told they soothe one's spirit."

"They do. Will you not try one?"

"Hmm—yes. Please instruct me. But first allow me to order refreshments. What shall it be? Tea? Sweet bean soup?"

"Not the latter. I find it cloying."

"I also. Then tea, but perhaps *sake*? Or shall we quaff a portion of the whiskey my son sets such store by?"

" 'Tis said that whiskey should be quaffed only after the sun has gone from the sky," Aiko said laughing. "So—let it be *sake*."

The two women sat facing each other across the low cherrywood table that was so highly polished it reflected their slim-wristed hands moving above its surface.

The room echoed with Aiko's laughter as Masa undertook the task of learning to smoke the cigarette, saying after several delicate coughs, "Most enjoyable and less troublesome than the one-puff pipe."

"I agree, but, Aunt, please hold the cigarette upright, otherwise the nicotine in the smoke will stain your fingers."

"Thank you. You are a fine instructress. May I ask who taught you?"

"My friend, Lady Marjorie Coomber, an English lady. We have become quite intimate and speak freely of many things. Perhaps I should not confess this, but I find it more enjoyable talking with friends than with members of my household. Does that shock you?"

"It would if you do not consider me as a friend."

"Thank you!" Aiko bowed deeply. "I have always feared that you find me too audacious."

"Audacious, yes, but charmingly so." Lady Masa raised her tiny *sake* cup in a salute. "Tell me more about your friend. I have not as yet met an English person. My son thinks highly of all things pertaining to England."

"So I have heard. Strangely enough, my friend, Lady Marjorie, is related to an Englishwoman whom your son knew while he was in London."

"Is that so? How extraordinary."

"Yes. The world grows smaller, does it not! Quite dangerously so in some ways. Well, perhaps not dangerous, nevertheless rumors are apt to follow one across the wide oceans of the world in these days of modern travel and communication. My friend, Lady Marjorie, quite yearns to become acquainted with Renzō, whom her friend alludes to in her letters as 'my dear, handsome samurai, Renzō Yamamoto.' Certainly I despise gossip, but I'm tempted to believe that Rumi's husband might have been a little more than friendly with my friend's friend, Turton San."

"If so," Lady Masa murmured, smiling, "one thing is certain—that English lady must be a delightful person. My heart goes out to her in gratitude."

"How broadminded you are." Aiko gazed at her companion with admiration.

"You think so? Naturally, Aiko, I rejoice when life is kind to him. And Renzō's life has not been exactly easy."

"I regret to hear that, but I envy your son." Once again Aiko placed a clenched fist against her lips, and Masa glanced at her with some concern.

Finally, she said gently, "Aiko, you are not well? Perhaps the *sake* . . . ?"

"Not that." Aiko's eyes were suddenly abrim with tears. Lowering her hand, she spoke harshly, yet so softly that the older woman was forced to lean closely toward her. "Not that," Aiko repeated. "Aunt Masa, to be honest, I knew that Rumi was absent from the house. It was you I hoped to see today. Truly, I need your advice and help."

Mystified, Masa gazed mutely into the eyes of the distressed young woman. "If it's in my power, I shall help you," she said firmly.

"How can I begin?" Aiko spoke in a staccato manner. "There is no child in the Fukuda home. . . . Yuichi's mother accuses me of barrenness. . . . Yuichi refuses to adopt a child. . . . Will you not influence his mother? Encourage her to influence Yuichi into taking a *yōshi* into the family to bear his name. His problem can be solved only by adoption. Aunt Masa, am I making myself clear?"

"Truthfully, no." Masa spoke in a comforting tone, as though to an agitated child, for she realized that something was gravely wrong with the highly strung young woman. "Certainly adoption is a matter to be treated warily. For me to apply duress on Sumiko could be fatal. . . . Aiko, am I to understand that your despair comes from the thought of Yuichi divorcing you?"

Aiko's glance swept from side to side, and she shuddered before replying. "No. He and I are an ill-assorted couple, but it's not that." She paused, then said in a bitter tone, "I care little about myself."

There was a short silence, then Masa spoke firmly, saying, "I'm even more nonplussed. Aiko, would it not simplify matters to go through a divorce? Then for Yuichi to remarry if he is so adamantly against adopting a son."

"Taking a new wife, taking *ten* new women to his bed would only worsen his situation." Aiko's voice was colorless, and Masa waited patiently for her to continue.

Finally, so disturbed that she was straining to keep her voice low, Aiko said, "Aunt Masa, this is altogether too difficult to explain. Please understand that although our marriage is a farce, I care deeply for my husband's feelings."

"Most obviously so."

"Yes, I care deeply, but as a *friend*. Or, more to the point, as a *sister*. Now am I making myself clear?"

"No. I'm still quite at a loss."

"So? Then I must explain with uninhibited frankness?"

"If you so wish. If you feel you must."

"I dread the thought of betraying my husband. But, for his own sake, for his family's welfare, he *must* adopt a son. The stark truth is . . . Yuichi is impotent. Even after ten years of being his wife I remain a virgin. Not from choice, or any physical fault in me." Aiko straightened her back and looked directly into the older woman's eyes defiantly, as though challenging her to deal with the situation as she would, and smiling with apparently contemptuous pride in having spilled out the bitter, humiliating tale.

They sat gazing one to the other while Masa digested the information. Her mind was slightly off balance, for she had always seen Yuichi Fukuda as a henpecked husband. Now she realized that for all his bravado, there was an element of deep emotional insecurity in his makeup and she sympathized with his misfortune as one would naturally sympathize with any male in a society where it was obligatory to sire children, and preferably male.

Eventually, she said, "Is there no remedy for his ailment?"

"Unhappily not."

"Aiko, it would be a flagrant blunder for me to interfere in this delicate matter. Most courteously, I must decline. But . . ." she continued, "I believe that good sense should be applied where emotional matters are concerned."

"So," Aiko queried, "you agree that Yuichi's unwillingness to adopt is irrational?"

"I do. You have never reproached him?"

"Not directly. Certainly we battle on many subjects. But . . ." Aiko waved her hands helplessly.

"Of course not. You would not be so undiplomatic. Now, I dislike conjuring up memories to do with my own married life, but . . ." A wry, fleeting smile crossed Masa's face. "Aiko, I was about to say that Kenichi, Renzō's father, always gave me the impression that he relied upon male friends when he needed advice."

"Unfortunately, my husband has many male acquaintances but no intimate friends that I know of."

"Unusual to say the least."

"Yuichi is completely engrossed in the world of business. He distrusts other men. I have no wish to belittle him but he is fundamentally insecure. He is *so* class-conscious. . . ."

"Umm . . ." Masa gave an understanding wince. "Like his father, Fukuda, he hides an animosity toward the samurai behind a bold façade?"

"Exactly!" Aiko grinned slightly. "He also despises my haughtiness, but what can I do?"

"It is inborn in you." Masa's tone was conspiratorial, and the aristocratic women exchanged an understanding glance. Choosing her words carefully, Masa said, "Your husband, I believe, still has a deep affection for Renzō. With your permission may I confide this problem to my son. . . ."

"No, no, no," Aiko cried out, interrupting the older woman without apology. "Yuichi would know that I had betrayed him."

"Not so," Masa replied patiently. "I would speak only of Yuichi's unwillingness to adopt." In an acid tone she exclaimed, "Naturally, *as a male*, Renzō would be sympathetic, and convinced that *you* are at fault. I know enough about the nature of the male species to be convinced on *that* point."

"You think so?"

"I know so. So—have I your permission?"

Aiko sat in silence, as if paralyzed, then she murmured, "Excuse me, please, but my mind has stopped working."

"I understand." Masa knew instinctively that the young woman was regretting having confided in her, and to put Aiko's mind at rest, she murmured, "Then be easy. Just remember that I am your trustworthy confidante. Always here . . ."

Truthfully, she was relieved to let the matter rest and, wishing to end Aiko's visit on a light note, she murmured, "Recently, my grandson informed me that the American children at the school he attends believe that babies are brought to households, already dressed, carried in the beaks of storks."

Aiko was smiling faintly. "Ah," she exclaimed, "if only that were so, the Fukuda household would ring with the laughter of many children. . . ."

After the young woman's departure, Lady Masa noticed that the maple tree in the garden had been stripped of all its leaves and that the cat, Neko, was dashing about in a demented fashion, as if it were his duty to leap upon and subdue the wind-tossed leaves.

She no longer felt animosity toward the cat. She was feeling curiously content with life, living essentially in the present and relieved beyond measure at the way Renzō was facing the economic burdens that had been so unexpectedly foisted upon him. Before many months had gone by, in addition to Nakasone, he had employed a number of other people, who considered him not merely as an employer but as their savior.

On the surface Masa was careful to show only a mild interest in her son's affairs, but secretly she was inordinately pleased that he involved her and felt that she could have made a mark in the marketplace were she not so advanced in years.

It had taken only three shipments to London to empty the coffers of Kenichi's rich collection. The monetary reward had been great, but in order to fulfill further commitments, sizable amounts of that income had been spent on purchasing heirlooms from various families of the samurai class who had fallen on hard times.

Rumi displayed no interest in her husband's new mode of life, but during one of her chattering sessions she casually mentioned her mother's collection of garments left over from her career as a geisha. "All so rich, so exotic. Silks, velvets, brocades so gorgeously patterned. Jeweled pins. Fans, ancient umbrellas . . . Ah, yes, it was my great pleasure to dress myself up. Truly, my girlhood was so carefree. . . ."

"Is that so?" Renzō said, his manner disinterested. But Masa was strangely moved by the note of nostalgia in the young woman's voice and, rather to her shame, she sensed that Keiko's souvenirs could prove to be of some monetary value to Renzō.

Rumi prattled on gaily about her beloved mother. "Both she and my father called me their 'little pony.' Certainly not because I ran swiftly, but because my jaws were never still. 'Tis said that when a child, I had the habit of talking *continuously*. Yes, even in my sleep. Well, so Mumma often told me. . . ."

"She told you truly," Renzō broke into his wife's patter, smiling in her direction but with his mind obviously on other matters. Then, in a changed voice, he turned to his mother, saying, "Victor Caswell was enamored of that classic Nō mask we sent him. He is more than eager to have any number. The more the better."

"Difficult," Masa had replied. "They are such rare treasures."

"Hmm . . . yes. No theater will part with even one, no matter the price offered."

"Nō masks!" Rumi clasped her hands together. "My father, the count, had a passion for Nō drama and a fetish for collecting those gargoylelike masks. Frankly, they scared me. Even now, *if* I had the joy of visiting with *my mother*, I would be scared to look at those devilish masks. However, Mumma admires them greatly and declares that my father honored them above all of his treasure trove. He . . ."

"But, Rumi, surely Count Okura's art collection was destroyed by the fire following that horrendous earthquake?" Masa inquired with gentle persistence.

"Not so. Not completely all," Rumi replied placidly. "The masks stored in my father's 'second home' escaped that holocaust. Mumma has many of his treasures in her humble Kamakura dwelling. . . ."

As though envisioning her mother, Rumi murmured, "Excuse me for expressing my opinions, but I find it more than disgraceful— especially in these modern times—that my mother is still considered as a social outcast."

"An outcast?" Renzō, hiding his true feelings, said breezily. "Absolute nonsense. Is that not so, Mother?"

"Why, yes," Masa replied aloofly. "Rumi, the highway to modern-day life is but newly open. If you so desire, you have my full permission to visit with your mother."

KEIKO, THE EX-GEISHA, WAS BORN into a middle-class family in Hiroshima, a peaceful city situated at the point where the River Ota enters the Inland Sea of Japan, a city linked closely with Miyajima, the Island of Light, which rises from the bay opposite.

She spent her adult life hearing people pay their homage to Fuji San, but Keiko believed that Miyajima held pride of place. During her early childhood, it was her father's habit to awaken his family early and have them behold the night's mists dissolving in the shafts of sunlight around the island that appeared too beautiful to be real.

Her father had explained to his children that Miyajima was so sacred a place that births or deaths were forbidden on its precincts. In case of a sudden death, the corpse would be hastily removed, and if by chance a child arrived in the world unexpectedly, the mother would be sent from the island to undergo a purification ceremony lasting thirty days.

During Rumi's childhood she had preferred stories of Keiko's family life to traditional folk tales. "No, no," she would demand, "tell me again about the big birds, those cranes who lived on Miyajima."

Keiko would say, "Certainly! Truly, Rumi-chan, those cranes were taller than most men. Such wonderful creatures . . ."

"And they ate fish from your hands?"

"Yes. Gobbled them up."

"And did pigeons really fly down from the eaves of the temple and sit on your shoulders?"

"They did, the deer roamed about, so gentle and tame, licking salt from the granite rocks."

"Now tell me about the little house in Hiroshima."

"Oh, it was not so little. We had five airy rooms set behind my father's shop. . . ."

"Oh, yes! Tell me again about that shop."

"My father was a very revered apothecary. Many people came to the shop for medical advice. He would provide them with medications made from herbs that had the power to cure many kinds of pains. . . ."

She never told Rumi how tragedy had struck her household during an epidemic of cholera, leaving her orphaned and bereft of her two brothers. It was clear that unhappiness of any kind was abhorrent to Rumi. Accordingly, Keiko had always made light of the lonely years she spent as an apprentice in the geisha school, and of her time working in Edo.

To her dying day she would be mystified and never cease praising the gods for the miracle of ordaining that the devastatingly handsome, noble Count Okura should choose her above all other women to share so important a part of his life.

But, so it had been. Ten years of childhood happiness. Twelve years of artifice as an entertainer. Eight years, each one filled with warmth, pride, and delight in the Edo house, as a second wife, the mother of her man's adored child. Then tragedy once more, followed by those eight years living with Rumi in Kamakura on Ohara's estate, as she nurtured and watched her daughter blossom into full beauty.

Then sadness and loneliness had descended once again; for more than ten years, Keiko had lived completely alone, considered unworthy of acknowledgment by the family into which Rumi had married. Never for one moment had Keiko felt animosity toward members of the Yamamoto family. She was a sensible woman and accepted the situation with pragmatism.

When the day finally arrived for Rumi to leave the little Kamakura house, Keiko bid her farewell cheerfully, but when night fell she prepared two sleeping *futon* instead of just one and she stayed awake all night, praying that her daughter would be accepted graciously into the Yamamoto family.

All at once, the mistress of the Ohara mansion changed her attitude toward the "geisha woman" and the kindly master of the household, Rumi's patron, appeared to forget Keiko's existence, no longer providing for the upkeep of the little cottage hidden away in a corner of his estate.

Grateful for the roof over her head, she had eked out a meager existence employing her skills as a seamstress, making Western-style handbags from the richly brocaded material of her treasured *obi-*

sashes, and, after having gained permission to set up a booth by the entrance of the modern Kamakura Hotel, she sold her wares to foreign tourists for a mere pittance.

Always immaculately groomed and robed in dark kimono, she soon became a respected booth-keeper. The ever-curious tourists liked her alert, easy manner and admired her handiwork; before too long Keiko was able to exchange greetings with her customers in their native tongue, laughing cheerfully with them when they laughed at her self-taught English.

Her complete lack of self-pity enabled her to take joy in other people's happiness; nevertheless, her heart ached when she beheld family groups walking together. But rather than dwelling on her loneliness, she bore no grudges and kept herself busy, especially enjoying the steady stream of chatty letters brushed by the hand of her daughter. Keiko always replied to those epistles, exaggerating her success as a booth-keeper and describing in humorous terms the activity she witnessed around the hotel.

Then all at once the tempo of her life changed. Late one afternoon she arrived at the cottage, somewhat taken aback on seeing a suave, elegantly costumed man standing nearby. She stopped to bow politely, murmuring, "Fine weather," but he did not go on his way as she expected.

Returning her bow, he remained, gazing at her in a questioning manner and, as though hypnotized, she had gazed back, her mind spinning.

He was a stranger. But why then was he so familiar to her?

Suddenly he smiled and it was as though the gallant Kenichi Yamamoto stood before her, returned to life. . . .

Rumi's mother and Renzō found an instant rapport. Sitting with her in the shabby but neat cottage, he was reminded of his aunt Sumiko, also of Hilda Turton, for Keiko appeared to be a curious mixture of those two other women. The atmosphere she generated was cozy, yet spiced with poignant sensuality. He liked his wife's mother immensely, and as they spoke together he was overwhelmed on discovering that she had known his father.

"Ah—Kenichi," she said as she smiled. "No man was *ever* more charming. *No* man had a greater love of life than your honored father."

"You knew him so well, then?"

"I knew him well. I admired him greatly. He came often to the second home of Count Okura and always charmed us with his gaiety."

Ignorant about so many aspects of his father's life, Renzō felt that he had stumbled upon treasures beyond price as Keiko described in colorful terms the woodland picnics and happy gatherings Kenichi had taken part in.

"All so long ago," Keiko cried out, not with sadness but with joy, and he listened, his eyes alight, as their feelings for Kenichi drew them together.

While Keiko bustled about preparing hot *sake*, and as tasty a meal as she could from her poorly stocked larder, Renzō was filled with embarrassment as to how he could approach the subject of the late Count Okura's ancient Nō masks.

Before too long the sky would be darkening. The last bright shafts of sun in the room struck a glass bowl containing tiny translucent fish.

As Keiko knelt to pour *sake* into the cup he held out, he said, "I've been admiring your small aquarium."

"Thank you! I'm fond of my fish. It calms one's spirit to watch them swim."

"True. They move so gracefully."

"Sadly, they have a tendency to die. . . ."

"I advise you to procure a larger bowl."

"Excellent advice." Keiko bowed, and as Renzō spoke on he believed that no other woman had ever been so charmed by, and so intent on, his every word. He overlooked the years of stringent training Keiko had gone through, learning the art of pleasing men. After two short hours she had not only a complete understanding of Renzō's financial situation and his entry into the world of antiques art dealing, but when he casually mentioned the late count's collection of Nō masks, she instantly understood why he had appeared for the first time on her doorstep.

Not for an instant did Keiko resent his intentions; instead, she entered into the game with tact and spoke quietly and knowledgeably of Japanese artists throughout the ages.

With the utmost diplomacy—recalling Kenichi's scandalous passion for Osen—she refrained from mentioning certain artists who had deified courtesans of the Yoshiwara in Edo. "Count Okura," she murmured finally, "greatly admired the works of Nozaka, who delighted in the delineation of plover birds. . . ."

Keiko hesitated for a moment, then said gently, "For some years,

I have used only this one room as living quarters. . . . The remaining three are stocked from floor to ceiling with treasures collected over many years by your wife's honored father. Not all, for naturally his main collection was kept in his family home, where everything was destroyed, as you are no doubt aware."

"Yes. Such a tragic loss."

"Tragic?" Keiko's eyes were downcast. "A loss but not tragic when compared with the loss of . . ." Rising, she murmured, "How quickly night has come. Excuse my neglect. I shall light the lantern and heat more *sake*, and then, if it is not too bothersome, you might care to see those masks. . . ."

Renzō's visit to Kamakura was the first of many. Before the month was out, Keiko's house no longer harbored the salvaged art collection, and instead of her roadside booth, she was in charge of a curio shop within the Kamakura Hotel itself. The shop was gaining fame among foreign tourists, for it sold only genuine articles, most of them crafted by local artists.

When Renzō first put the idea to her, Keiko protested. "Thank you, but I must refuse. Please excuse me. I fear I should fail in managing such a shop."

"Nonsense, nonsense. You are a born businesswoman." There was such a ring of authority in his voice, she at once agreed, and when one rain-drenched day Renzō arrived at the hotel accompanied by a young woman stylishly robed in Western-style garments—it took several moments before Keiko realized that her beloved daughter was back in her life.

Kekkō desu—more than enough! Yes, more than enough and almost too much happiness to endure . . .

Kamakura's reputation had been blotted by countless dramatic incidents, by massacres entailing the loss of thousands of lives. It had withstood the ravages of tidal waves, of earthquakes too, but as Keiko and Rumi strolled along the road skirting the glistening sands of the bay, they gave no thought to far-off times of battles and blood-drenching. The high sloping hills burned with the crimson of maple leaves. Fresh sea breezes wafted in from the purple haze of the Pacific as curling waves raised crested manes before dashing on to the glistening sand.

Leaving the road, the two women walked together in a magnificent garden where lawns of moss and lotus ponds were dominated by the immense bronze statue of Buddha, whose expressionless eyes symbolized the extinction of mankind's earthly desires.

"This is a holy place," Keiko said. "Many years ago I came here with your father. We traveled from Edo, I in a litter carrying you in my body. The count was on horseback, accompanied by his retainers. It was springtime.... Your father and I together stood here, where you and I now stand. Together, we entered through the door cut in the bronze lotus-petals on which the great Buddha sits. Together, we climbed the interior ladder up into the noble head, wherein we prayed to the goddess of mercy who is enshrined there."

"Really? Were your prayers answered?"

"I believe so."

"A dubious reply! For what did you pray?"

"For the welfare of the child conceived by our love."

"Then your prayers were answered. . . . How times have changed. Those days must have been so romantic. My husband would be highly amused if I suggested we should undertake such a pilgrimage. Renzō is definitely turning his back on old traditions. You know that our son attends a school run by Americans? A Christian school."

"You are displeased about that?"

"Not at all. Few things displease me. My husband is so easygoing. Ever since his return from England, the atmosphere in our home has become less strained. My mother-in-law appears in no way mortified at having her son involved in business enterprises."

"Her attitude is amazing, to say the least. But she is right, one must move with the times. I quite revel in having become a successful businesswoman! Rumi, you must have been inspired."

"I—inspired? In what way?"

"How else but in suggesting that your husband involve me in his business ventures?"

"The idea came not from me but, I suspect, from the noble Lady Masa herself."

"Is that so?" Keiko glanced at her daughter intently. "Do I detect an undercurrent of malice in your voice?"

"Yes," Rumi replied without amusement. "How could it be otherwise? I have never enjoyed being treated in a condescending manner."

"Ah, so has it been like that? I'm sorry. I believed your life to be truly pleasant."

"I've always been aware of unspoken criticisms, aware that certain of my mannerisms are considered to lack elegance but, fortunately, I manage to hide my hurt feelings."

"Hiding hurt feelings is an insidious business. It damages one's self-esteem."

"That's not true with me. But, I shall always be thought inferior to my half sister, Aiko, in my mother-in-law's opinion."

"Ah, how sad! Does Aiko also scorn you, then?"

"Not openly. Never. She is always pleasant to me. There is a mysterious quality about Aiko. One moment she is hard, the next moment wistful. She resembles sunlight on the snow."

"Truthfully, you dislike her?"

"Not so. I dislike her sense of superiority. I envy her indestructable elegance but, on the other hand, I like her immensely. Also, I feel sorry for her."

"You have a generous nature. I'm glad. But why should you feel pity for your half sister?"

"It's difficult to explain. At times Aiko gives me the impression that she is treading her way carefully through a dark forest."

"Rumi, be especially kind to Aiko. I have never so much as spoken to her, but she deserves your sympathy. Frankly, the only fault I ever found in your noble father was his lack of interest in his legal daughter. He gave all his paternal love to you."

"Yes, my childhood days spent in the Edo house beneath your care and my father's affection were perfect. And because of those joyous early days I am now strong in my spirit."

"It relieves me to hear you say that you know you were loved as a child by both your parents. It would relieve me even more to have you say that your marriage is not a loveless affair. Please speak frankly. Your husband appears to be an extremely kindly man."

"He is. No woman could have a more kindly husband. Renzō has never displayed any interest in eroticism, or in other women either, during the time when he has been living at home. What he does when he is away is no concern of mine." Rumi's eyes were bright with amusement. "So perhaps I do not really love him in the full meaning of the word, because I am not jealous?"

"Not so," Keiko said mildly. "You are my true daughter and never *once* did I feel jealousy toward your father's legal wife."

"But," Rumi exclaimed derisively, "my father *chose* to be with you. *His* wife was foisted upon him as *I* was foisted upon Renzō. In all probability, my father's official wife was madly jealous of *you*. No?"

"Hmm . . ." Keiko chuckled. "Elderly and stout as I am, Rumi, I am not unaware of the fact that even today I'm capable of arousing jealous glances from the wives of certain mature men who purchase goods from me at the hotel's shop!"

"You are skilled in the art of pleasing men. Perhaps once a geisha always a geisha?"

"Exactly." Keiko and Rumi smiled understandingly. As they left the sacred garden, Keiko announced firmly, "Now, I beg of you, Rumi, please be careful not to offend Yoshikawa San. He is extremely temperamental, but I find his work is more attractive to foreigners than that of other potters in the district. . . ."

The old potter sat at his wheel wearing only a loincloth, and sweat ran from his body as he sliced off a lump of clay and slapped it on his throwing wheel, spinning it rapidly while his fingers and spatula went to work hollowing, narrowing, shaping it. Then, with one smooth movement he cut it loose from the wheel with a piece of wire and beckoned the two women to follow him to the drying shed.

Keiko took out her fan, wielding it energetically, for the heat from the kilns was causing beads of perspiration to blemish her heavily powdered face. "Thank you, Yoshikawa, *Sensei*," she murmured cheerfully, "for giving us so much of your time. But may we now see the articles you have readied for me?"

He looked at her closely, a slight sneer twisting his lips, and grunted, "No interest in the craft, eh?"

"Not so," Keiko cried out apologetically. "*Most* interested. Just fearful of stealing your precious time."

Sometime later Keiko and Rumi were ushered into Yoshikawa's showroom, a pristine apartment furnished starkly with one low table and brocaded sitting cushions. "Please relax," he muttered, then faded in a wraithlike manner from the room.

"Really," Rumi exclaimed severely, "the old man insists on being courted as though he were a god of some kind."

"Not so loud," Keiko warned. "*All* artists have a godlike quality. *Time* has no meaning for them."

Finally, the old potter returned, almost unrecognizable, dressed formally in his crested black silk gown and his manner that of a spry businessman. He was followed humbly by three young apprentices, each one carrying a number of little boxes which they placed on the *tatami* with great care, then, with even more care they opened the boxes slowly while their master viewed every article with the eye of a connoisseur. As though seeing his own handiwork for the first time, he would exclaim, "Now, *this* piece I must have for myself. Now, *this* vase is without peer! I must have it for myself."

Rumi sat by, regarding her mother's tolerant attitude with admiration as Keiko made comforting cooing sounds of agreement. Even though she had commissioned every article, she knew that if the old craftsman decided not to carry out the contract, she must graciously bow to his decision.

She and the potter had an inherent distaste for written contracts, together with a deep understanding of the observance of legal niceties. They were adept at playing those games which were such a spicy part of daily life, and when at last the transaction between them had been concluded to their combined satisfaction, they both felt triumphant and revitalized.

The inordinately lengthy proceedings left Rumi tired and cross, and as she and Keiko left the potter's premises she said petulantly, "Mumma, are you obliged to go through such nonsensical games time and time again?"

"Nonsensical?" Keiko laughed cheerfully. "It's just the Japanese way!"

"Well, maybe it's a good thing that our Japanese ways are being disturbed by new trends. And, Mumma, speaking of new trends, I who suffered *untold agonies* while giving birth to Shinichi, will produce this child I now carry without one *twinge* of discomfort."

"How can that be?" Keiko stood gazing worriedly at her daughter.

"Mumma, you have obviously not yet heard of chloroform. The doctor at the newly built American hospital in Tokyo has kindly explained the miraculous medication to me. He, Dr. Parker, is to deliver my child, and—"

Keiko was shocked. "*He* . . . ?" she whispered. "*He, a foreigner, a man*, will deliver your child? Oh, surely not!"

After Rumi's explanation, Keiko glanced up at the white clouds skimming across the sky, and declared, "*Without doubt*, many foreign ways are wonderful beyond my comprehension. But, Rumi, little pony, is it really a safe procedure?"

" 'Tis said that the illustrious Queen Victoria of England herself favors and praises the use of the miraculous substance. Need I say more?"

"Say no more!" Keiko's sudden smile then changed to a frown, and she added softly, "Rumi, my only advice to you is that you

educate your children to the best of your ability, and as they grow
up make certain that they do not forfeit our true Japanese ways."

"I shall do my best," Rumi murmured casually. "But, Mumma,
many of our ways are considered queer, even degenerate, by foreigners in the community."

"Maybe so," Keiko replied sternly. "Those outsiders probably do
find us complex folk, but, Rumi, *we must keep our own identity*."

"I agree. I agree," Rumi replied politely. "Mumma, over there is
a ricksha. Please hail the runner."

"But it's only a short walk to the hotel. Some fifty or so steps."

"Too long and too many for my comfort."

In NAKASONE, RENZŌ HAD DISCOVERED not only a true friend but a
colleague who freed him from the harassments of dealing with mundane duties, while he sought out rare objects with the aplomb of an
experienced antiquarian and gathered fresh interests and much enthusiasm from the steady flow of correspondence sent by Victor
Caswell.

In one letter Victor wrote: *"A measure of good fortune has fallen
upon our mutual friend, Bixby, in the form of a sizable inheritance bequeathed to him by a late, unlamented spinster aunt. Rumor has it that he
has gone off to see the world before settling down to marry and raise a family
of his own ilk. One hopes that travel will broaden his outlook. Personally,
I doubt that. Now on to more important matters. Lacquerware is much in
demand. Especially those marvelous pieces so richly decorated in gold. More,
please . . ."*

Renzō reviewed his life with satisfaction, smugly pleased at the
money that was flowing in with so little effort on his part. Regardless of his poor reputation at the Office of Foreign Affairs, he was
a popular, much sought after person in Tokyo's thriving international society, and he was proud of his pretty wife, on whose
Western-style clothing and jewelry he spared no expense.

Mainly because of Rumi's affection for her half sister, he was a
frequent visitor at the Fukuda mansion, always careful to mask his
distaste of the house with its overwhelming display of wealth. The
only two rooms he felt at ease in were the music room with its
parquet floor, collection of Chippendale chairs, and the grand piano,

and, even more to his taste, Sumiko's calm, *tatami*-floored nest which held so many warm memories.

Perhaps it was the Westernization of his cousin's home that induced him to make some changes in the house at Nihombashi. Relying on Lady Masa's advice the house and its garden now had the appearance and the atmosphere of a traditional Japanese home. He liked returning to it; it was as though he dwelt in two different worlds, one bustling and modern, the other reminiscent of life before the intrepid American, Commodore Perry, had arrived in Japan.

Fat Misa had passed on into the spirit world, replaced by an expert cook who ruled the kitchen and kept two serving-maids on their toes at all times. A competent nursemaid was installed to care for Etsu, the baby daughter so adored by her father that he often wondered how he had managed to exist, believing that he was more or less content, before her arrival.

Etsu, a small replica of her mother, wrought a miraculous change in Shinichi. When he first hovered over the infant he exclaimed tenderly, "No boy ever had so delightful a sister. Never. I'm certain of that. I'm so glad Et-chan resembles mother."

"Hmm . . ." Renzō grunted. "So—you wouldn't like her so much if she resembled your father, then?"

Suddenly the boy broke into a smile and gazed at the infant, saying, "We, you and I, Et-chan could have no better father." Renzō knew that he had finally gained his son's trust and affection.

Nakasone was an impressive figure of a man. Broad-shouldered and heavily muscled, his sturdy appearance belied his gentle disposition. His aquiline features revealed his good breeding. At ease in the company of friends, his eyes sparkled with good humor but, when angered, they darkened beneath their heavy brows, advising that he was not a man to be taken lightly.

Renzō thoroughly enjoyed his friendship and was relieved that it made no call upon him to pay visits and carouse with female inmates of the Yoshiwara.

The two men were completely relaxed in each other's company; they frequented bathhouses and occasionally left the city to ride horseback along country roads.

As they galloped together, they shouted in warriorlike voices to each other before returning to a rustic inn where, after bathing, they played chess and talked on many subjects deep into the night.

One night, much the worse from a lengthy bout of whiskey drinking, Renzō was moved to exclaim, "Truly, Nakasone, feeling, without sensuality, such as exists between us, is a gift from the gods."

"I agree. I relish the fact that you in no way feel threatened by me and my kind of sensuality. Hold out your cup."

"Thank you! Yes, just one more before we take off to sleep. By the way, are you involved with anyone at present?"

"Yes. A pleasant young man. A student who was in need of a patron. He's presently installed in my home but he hopes to be accepted next year at an American university."

"So? You are bound to miss him when he departs."

"Not at all."

"Not at all?"

"It's not in my nature to be carried away in my affairs." Nakasone broke into a laugh. "Frankly, I despise sentimentality."

"I also." Renzō rose to his feet and swayed as he exclaimed nervously, "Ah, a slight earthquake . . ."

"Not so," Nakasone remarked ironically. "You are drunk. To bed, to sleep is the sensible thing to do. But, by the way, unburden yourself. Are *you* presently involved?"

"Yes," Renzō lied unashamedly. "Merely a light affair. Like you"—he grinned—"it's not in my nature to be carried away. . . ."

"So, you mock me?" Nakasone pulled a fearsome grimace, and the two men fell about laughing uproariously as they staggered off to their rest.

In truth, Renzō was caught up in an affair so passionate and fraught with danger that he felt like a fragile ship at sea riding fearsome storms. There were times when he cursed the situation. Every aspect of his life had been so auspicious when the summer season had begun, but he had felt restless, in need of some challenge, some excitement.

The thought of entering into a casual, well-conducted relationship with a young, fetching girl was attractive, and with that thought in mind he visited the Yoshiwara one afternoon. During that visit he had paid a high price for the services of an intelligent, witty girl skilled in the sensual arts of arousal and intent on insuring her client's enjoyment.

Without doubt she had succeeded in certain ways; however, the girl's professionalism and her artificial gestures were displeasing to him. Then, to further his discomfiture, immediately after his climactic release his gaze rested upon a painting hanging in an alcove.

"Are you seeing a ghost? Are you ailing in some way?" the dulcet voice of the prostitute murmured.

"Not ailing," he replied stiffly, then added in a teasing manner, "Nor do I believe in ghosts . . ."

He spoke truthfully, nevertheless the painting of a flamboyantly costumed courtesan brought back so vividly that one glimpse he had had of Osen, that his mind became dazed.

After that dislocating experience, he forsook any thought of returning to the Yoshiwara and decided to concentrate entirely on his family, friendships, and on his successful business ventures.

The last thing he expected was to be suddenly gripped by an overwhelming passion. In fact, never before had he felt more content than on that hot July morning when he accompanied his entire family in a hired carriage from Nihombashi to attend a garden party at the Fukuda mansion at Yoyogi.

"How this area has altered," Lady Masa murmured regretfully. "Yuichi's father was so proud of his huge woodland estate."

"Skilled financier as he was, he would but applaud his son's business acumen," Renzō replied cryptically. "This land was destined to be encroached on by the increasing sprawl of the city. It's not considered seemly these days to have large estates. Yuichi has kept more than enough for family purposes."

"Surely my uncle Yuichi never owned all this land?" Shinichi asked his father, frowning severely.

"He did," Renzō said with some irony. "He still owns much land in other areas. If you're interested in details, ask your uncle to tell you about them, and about his old ancestor who was able to commune with fish in temple ponds."

"Enough of such unseemly talk," Lady Masa reprimanded Renzō with a wry smile.

"Are you saying I must not question my uncle, Grandmother?" Shinichi asked even more sternly. "Why should I not?"

"No reason why not, but question him politely, and certainly not about his possessions. Kindly remember your age."

"Yes." Renzō grinned at his son. "You are not as yet a full-fledged professor. Come, Shin-chan, smile. Look, see how happy your sister is. . . ."

He reached out and took his daughter in his arms, cuddling her close as the carriage passed through the gates, then along the graveled driveway of the greatly diminished Fukuda family estate.

The garden party that was to be a turning point in Renzō's life had been arranged by Sumiko, who, on hearing that many foreigners gave parties to celebrate their individual birthdays, had at once declared, "What a splendid custom! The idea appeals to me. From this year onward I shall celebrate my own birthdays."

"Guests bring gifts to the person whose birthday it is," Aiko remarked with the boyish grin which her mother-in-law disliked so intensely.

"So . . . ?" Sumiko pondered. "So . . ." she repeated. "I consider that custom to be most vulgar."

"Then—no party?"

"A party—yes." Sumiko's voice was triumphant. "But, *I* shall present gifts to all invited. What do you think of that idea?"

"I consider it charming and, with your permission, I shall enter into the spirit of the occasion with enthusiasm."

If Sumiko had declared, "I shall present food to my guests spiced with poison," Aiko would have responded the same way, casually and without thought, for she had become deeply concerned about Yuichi, whom she believed was teetering on the edge of madness. She was finding it more and more difficult to conduct herself normally.

Her fears had arisen one winter afternoon while she, Sumiko, and Yuichi were sitting together in the cozy atmosphere of her mother-in-law's room. They sat around the *kotatsu*—the covered firepit in the floor—and the ancient heating system induced feelings of intimacy that were enhanced as they gazed through the open windows at the snow drifting over the outside world.

The harmony of the occasion was shattered when Sumiko, speaking as though to no one in particular, exclaimed, "I've received an epistle from Ohara Sama in which he mentions that a tragic event has occurred, leaving orphaned a delightful boy, aged but six years. Ohara Sama finds it his duty to place the boy as *yōshi* in a suitable family. He seeks our assistance and advice on the matter."

Sumiko busied herself replenishing Yuichi's cup with the air of one skilled in the expertise of diplomacy, then she added, "Yuichi and Aiko, you, with *so* many acquaintances, must know of a family who could express interest. We owe so much to Ohara Sama for his kindness over these many years. It behooves us to assist him in this delicate matter."

Her nerves jangling, Aiko stared at Yuichi as he said jovially, "Personally, I have no such family in mind. Have you, Aiko?"

"No . . ." Aiko replied in a restrained voice. "I have no such family in mind."

"Pity!" Yuichi commented cheerfully. "Now, Aiko, have you spoken to my mother of the auspicious report to us after the thorough examination and the treatments you are receiving under the skills of Dr. Sugimoto?"

Having never so much as heard of the doctor, she could only stare at her hands in embarrassment and confusion.

"Ah," Yuichi chuckled, "I see that you have not as yet confided the excellent news. Mother, allow me to explain. . . ."

Even more befuddled, Aiko sat by while her husband spoke enthusiastically of Dr. Sugimoto, who had recently returned from the city of Vienna, where he had furthered his expertise in dealing with the problems of women. After many consultations, Yuichi recounted, the doctor had informed Aiko that her barrenness could, and *would*, be remedied under his care.

Sumiko, also bewildered but enthralled, listened eagerly as her son told of a world-famous foreigner, Sigmund Freud, of whom Dr. Sugimoto had become a dedicated disciple. "Professor Freud," Yuichi enthused, "is convinced that barrennesss is often the result of female hysteria, that hysteria is of physical origin, and that *ideas* can actually produce *changes* in the physical body. It's now accepted that certain disturbances in a child's mental and sexual growth are responsible for drawbacks during her or his adult life. Dr. Sugimoto declares that Aiko's childhood—so sadly disturbed—has built up a blatant case of neurosis within her. Her inbuilt anxieties and lack of self-esteem prevent her from achieving pregnancy."

At that juncture, Sumiko was forced to exclaim, "But Aiko has *never* showed a lack of self-esteem. To the *contrary—*"

"Ah-ha . . ." Yuichi interrupted triumphantly. "Exactly. She cleverly hides her true view of herself. Hence, her problem. Now, is it not excellent news that her prejudiced view is undergoing changes under her treatment of psychoanalysis? Seriously, Mother, have you noticed no change in Aiko's attitudes of late?"

Sumiko pursed her lips tightly and leaned forward. Aiko, repulsed, drew back as her mother-in-law stared into her face and finally murmured flatly, "I find no change. Frankly, Yuichi, this

Freud San's reputations smells strongly of those fake soothsayers in whom your grandmother put such trust."

"Not so—absolutely *not so*, Mother. A new realm of medical science has arrived." Turning to Aiko, Yuichi spoke as though to a retarded child, slowly and encouragingly, murmuring, "You have utter confidence in Dr. Sugimoto's treatments, have you not?"

In her extreme embarrassment, Aiko's face flushed crimson. Making no reply, she stared blankly at Yuichi, who smiled at her understandingly and said, "No call to be so shy. Mother, just see how she still hides her true emotions. Aiko, ring the bell. I'm in need of hot *sake*. Mother, rest assured that before too long you shall be cradling a grandchild in your arms."

Stupefied, Aiko rang the small bronze hand-bell to summon a servant.

That night, lying in the dark room beside her husband, Aiko berated him, finally exclaiming hotly, "I find you quite horrible. Yes, and worse—I find you *pathetic*."

"Now, is that so?" Yuichi replied pleasantly. "I've been branded in various ways but never before have I been branded pathetic. I must object. By the way, tell me, how *do* you feel about the treatments you are undergoing?"

"Cease this foolish game. Out of respect for your mother I remained silent, but, Yuichi, my patience is at a dangerously low ebb. You know of your own condition. Know that you are your *own* liability. Or, can it be that your mind is sorely affected?"

"Must you speak so rudely?"

"Excuse me, but yes, I must. Truly, I suffer for and with you, Yuichi."

"And—find me pathetic?"

"Yes . . ." Aiko now spoke softly, a note of pleading in her voice. "There is but one solution to our problem. Time is passing. I beg that you at least *consider* adopting the boy whom Ohara Sama has put forward for your consideration."

"No." Rising up, Yuichi lit the *andon* and in its frail light he sat cross-legged on his *futon*, gazing directly into Aiko's eyes, saying quietly, "For the first and for the last time, shall I tell you why I have no plan, no intention of adopting a child?"

"Yes, but speak the truth and seriously."

"I shall. Pay heed. Plainly put, I dislike your sometimes cruel and capricious nature, and the way you grab at what you want from life with the insensitive egotism of an aristocrat. But, for all that, yes, and *because* of all that in you, *it's your child I want.* I cannot, I shall not, accept any other child into my family." Yuichi snuffed out the light and lay down.

Aiko, quite frightened for his sanity, lay quietly, not knowing what to say. Finally she whispered, "But, you know, we *both* know, that what you want is quite impossible."

With an edge of anger in his voice, Yuichi ground out, "It is not impossible. *It is not.* Take your time. Consider the matter. You are no simpleton. I rely upon you, absolutely. Please, no more talk of it. Good night. Please allow me to sleep. Good night!"

Some two hours later, overcome with curiosity and emotion, Aiko whispered, "Are you awake?"

"Yes."

"Is there such a person as that Dr. Sugimoto you spoke of?"

"There is. Hearing of his reputation, I went to him for treatments."

"And . . . ?"

"And . . . found him to be but a quack doctor of the first order. Now, allow me to sleep. . . ."

From that time onward Aiko found it difficult to think along normal lines. She took to watching Yuichi with the detachment of a doctor, anxious about her patient's mysterious ailment. She not only fretted about his mental state but came to realize how she had come to care for the man she had dwelt with for so many years.

As the winter turned to spring, then to summer, seldom an hour would pass without Aiko silently repeating those harshly ground out words:

"It is *not* impossible. . . ."

"It is not. . . ."

"Take your time. Consider the matter. . . ."

After months of pondering, the only conclusion she was forced to admit horrified her more than her darkest imaginings. Her spirit was filled with such disgust that she hastened to a shrine to gain purification; however, she likened that unsuccessful visit to the one Yuichi had paid to the so-called quack merchant, Dr. Sugimoto.

Hoping to provide her husband with at least a modicum of solace, she adopted a more gentle, obedient attitude toward his mother. She valiantly stifled feelings of embarrassment and irritation when that woman gazed at her expectantly, asking her every moon, "Not yet? Not as yet with child?"

"Not as yet," she had replied on the morning of Sumiko's birthday celebration. "No. Not as yet . . ."

Never since the loss of her husband had Sumiko felt so refreshed and satisfied. The great day had arrived and everything was worked out to the last detail, if not without some tribulations and subtle decision making.

The guest list she presented to Aiko and Yuichi for their consideration had finally been whittled down from fifty-two to a mere fifteen: the five members of the Nihombashi house, Ohara Sama, his wife, their two sons and their wives, along with the three children of that family. And, of course, Yuichi and Aiko.

Ticking the guests' names off one by one on his fingers, Yuichi exclaimed, "Fourteen so far. May I ask who the fifteenth person is to be?"

"Who else but myself?"

"But, of course . . ."

The gifts had been decided upon after much deep consideration. Both Sumiko and Aiko agreed that rich, flamboyant presents would be unacceptable to the spirits of the recipients; instead, pure crepe-silk *furoshiki* had been chosen. Light, flowered designs for the ladies; dark hues for the gentlemen. And for each child, there was an entrancing wood carving of an animal.

"At last," Sumiko cried out triumphantly. "All fifteen gifts have been purchased."

"Fifteen? For whom is the extra gift?" Yuichi inquired.

Blushing but slightly, Sumiko murmured, "Unseemly perhaps, but I have also bought myself a present. Yuichi, and Aiko you also, please follow me. . . ."

As the trio walked single file along the corridors toward Sumiko's sitting room, Yuichi and Aiko were startled on hearing a most peculiar voice. When the door was slid aside they beheld a great white, yellow-crested bird who greeted the intruders to his new domain by hopping about frantically, squawking, *"Hello Cocky . . . hello Cocky . . . hello Cocky . . ."*

Above the raucous sound Sumiko called out proudly, "A talking bird! I find him quite irresistible. Is he not a wondrous creature?" Kneeling before the low perch, she encouraged her pet, repeating his words, mimicking his voice as the husband and wife looked on, fascinated, but nevertheless somewhat dismayed.

Eventually Yuichi exclaimed, "From whence did he come?"

"Well you may ask!" Sumiko cried out. "Ah, how my honored father would have delighted in Cocky. He is a cockatoo bird. He comes from a wild land, far away, called Australia. He was brought here by a foreign seaman along with a covey of other parrots. That Australian mariner of the high seas sold his booty to a bird merchant on the Ginza. Excited customers queued to make purchases and *arguments* actually broke out among us. With no humility, I raised my voice and offered the vendor ten times the amount he was asking and . . ."

Pausing to catch her breath, Sumiko gestured triumphantly as though to the entire world. "I now own this unique, this remarkable bird! Hello Cocky . . . hello Cocky . . . hello Cocky . . ." she croaked. "Hello Cocky-chan . . ."

"How much did you pay?" Yuichi inquired with curiosity, but also with admiration.

Sumiko smiled victoriously as she named the price with some pride, and Yuichi, grinning at Aiko, said, "I've paid less for a highly bred horse. . . ."

Soon after his arrival at the garden party, Renzō wondered if his aunt was conscious that she had created a "masterpiece" of an occasion. The party took place some distance from the house, in a wide, secluded area of flat ground beneath the spreading branches of oaks and ancient pines, which provided shade from the sun's glare but allowed glimpses of the sky through the different green foliages.

Farther on but unseen, flowers growing in the summer's heat announced their presence by wafting a confusion of sweet perfumes to combine with the clean, sharp aroma of pine needles.

All the guests were at ease in their cool cotton kimono. The three Ohara boys and Shinichi, accustomed to wearing the more constricting Western-style school uniforms, now wore loose-fitting calf-length robes of brightly colored cloth. They scampered about, taking special delight in drawing up water from the depths of an ancient well, and as they drank from bamboo cups, they called out, "So cool! How sweet this well water is."

Carpenters had been called in, and under Sumiko's stern supervision they had erected two low-railed platforms of unpainted wood. The floor of the larger one was covered with freshly woven matting of a creamy hue and was furnished with foot-high tables and a scattering of purple- and violet-colored sitting-cushions. A short distance away, a similar but smaller platform provided a stage for musicians, and the two flute players piped on tirelessly while the old drummer used his bamboo whisk with skill and panache. The trio played requests and accompanied those who chose to break into song whenever the mood so took them.

Various songs sung by mature members of the party aroused feelings of nostalgia, even to the point of tears, as the older guests regretted that the children present were hearing the melodies and the words for the first time.

"Sad," old Ohara had been moved to cry out. "It is our *duty* to keep these songs alive. Singing has always been a part of our everyday life."

"True," his wife murmured. "Most Japanese children can carry a tune before they learn to talk. . . ."

"That's so," Ohara broke in politely. "Singing is also associated with work. For instance, those singsong cries used by tradesmen to identify themselves and their wares . . ."

Ohara was interrupted by the arrival of a frail old man, a paid entertainer who stood on a mat gesturing with his fan as he recited the tragic tale of a deer pleading for praise before a huntsman killed it. For all the weakness of the man's voice, his audience was impressed and Yuichi murmured to Ohara, " 'Tis said that this actor, Fujiwara, was quite famous in his day."

"He was indeed. I, and *your* honored father, also Renzō's father, Kenichi, and Count Okura, too, held him in high esteem. He performed frequently at Watanabe's famed male brothel."

"Is that so? Thank you for telling me. How I wish my father were present here today." Yuichi, moved to tears, sat by thinking of his father, that dear, unpredictable man. . . .

His spirits were revived as a group of garishly robed acrobats catapulted into the garden, exciting the children with their spectacular twisting and somersaulting to the accompaniment of their shouts and rhythmic drum beating.

As suddenly as they had appeared, the troupe bowed low to the assembled guests, and then departed. It was as though their performance had been just a figment of the imagination.

"I suggested to them that enough would be enough," Sumiko announced. "Ah, I was correct as usual. The servants are approaching."

The feasting, the al fresco banquet, had begun. *Sake* cups were filled and hot tea was quaffed, along with the delicacies exquisitely served on unique dishes that had been stored away for many years.

Gradually, the atmosphere changed to one of easygoing enjoyment, then to one where hilarity took over among much teasing and clever quips.

Renzō was slightly intoxicated; he ordered Etsu's nursemaid to place the child by his side, and announced loudly, "See this little one! Look about, she is the only female child in this covey of children." Using his own chopsticks, he fed the little girl tidbits, scorning the nursemaid's whispered suggestion that her small charge would probably suffer from so much rich food.

"Nonsense!" He gestured the girl away, at the same time glancing at his wife for her opinion, but Rumi was also tipsy and merely shrugged, saying with a laugh, "Do as you will with the child!"

Shinichi, however, approached his father and frowned as he took the child up, exclaiming, "Et-chan, Et-chan, come with big brother. You and I shall drink nice water from the well."

Renzō, scarcely conscious of the event, joined in a conversation between Aiko and the two Ohara brothers, who were discussing the charms of traveling abroad. Breaking into the conversation with no apology, he remarked emphatically, "As for me, no city could better London. I quite fell in love with it. . . ."

"I beg to differ," Ohara Senior said adamantly. "*Paris* is the queen city of the world, Yamamoto San. Renzō, *you* fell in love with London? Not only was *I* in love with Paris, but *Paris* was in love with *me.*"

"No, no! How drunk are you, Father," his young son cried out. "Her name was *Mimi*—not Paris, *n'est-ce pas?*"

During the barrage of laughter no one laughed more heartily than did the wife of the man who had so loved the French girl Mimi. "I had the privilege of accompanying my husband on his third and most recent visit to France," she exclaimed. "Naturally, he did not introduce *me* to his Mimi-chan, but if she possesses the chic of many Parisian women, then, must I not admire his good taste?" As another outburst of laughter quite drowned out a solo being played by one of the flautists, she gestured toward Aiko, and said loudly to her husband, "It is *my* opinion that Aiko would arouse much admiration if seen strolling along a Paris boulevard. No?"

All eyes were directed to Aiko, who accepted the attention with cool aplomb.

"Without doubt" was the emphatic reply. "French men, and women also, would be bound to stop in their tracks, exclaiming—*'quel délicieux ministre plénipotentiaire!'* "

Rumi alone was in no way amused. She rose hurriedly and left the platform as if to confer with Shinichi, who had climbed on to a pine branch with Etsu in his arms and was perching there as though intent on keeping his sister out of danger. Rumi gathered up Etsu and rejoined the group. At once, Yuichi grasped the child and she nestled close to him as he cooled her hot cheeks with a damp hand towel.

Observing him, Aiko leapt to her feet, announcing urgently, "The time has come for action! Come, everyone, shall we not dance?"

"Yes. Yes, by all means." Sumiko rose from her cushion with the energetic actions of a young girl and called to the musicians, "Kindly play *'Chakkiri Bushi,'* " adding in a slightly lower tone, " *'Picking the Tea Leaves from the Plants'* is a jolly song for dancing. Masa, it was such a favorite of ours. Remember . . . ?"

As the musicians struck up the lively melody, even Shinichi forgot his dignity and joined the circle of dancers, following their actions, flinging his arms skyward, pacing and stamping, singing exultantly, *"Yoi, yoi—yoi . . . yoi . . ."*

No one danced and sang more energetically or more skillfully than Sumiko, Masa, Ohara, and his elderly wife. It was they who called for tune after tune, and it was they who loudly instructed younger members of the party in the intricacies of steps and movements.

"Arms *higher*, more *curved*, Renzō," Sumiko admonished. "Yuichi, like this! Like *this*! Watch *me*. . . ."

"No, no, Aiko," called Masa. "Follow your sister. See how skilled Rumi is. . . ."

"Yes, follow me, Aiko," Rumi cried, laughing. "My mother the geisha taught our dear father this one. It's a Hiroshima dance . . ."

The musicians played on, the dancers danced, shouted, and sang in a joyous spirit of innocent abandonment. Then, one by one they left the circle in various stages of exhaustion.

Following the dancing interlude, some of the guests sat on the platform, wielding fans, silent and content, others meandered about the grounds, alone, or speaking in desultory tones to companions.

Renzō, more than contented with every facet of his life, stood alone, smoking his pipe. Leaning against the trunk of a giant pine

tree, he smiled complacently on hearing his son's voice ringing out
from the nearby tennis court.

Yuichi's wife's voice rang out commandingly. "Hit the ball *over*
the net, Shin-chan—not *into* it. . . ."

"No, no. Grip the racket's handle *lower down*. . . ."

He saw that Sumiko, overly stout and puffing quite heavily, was
hastening toward the old well, accompanied by his mother. Both
women were speaking animatedly and laughing together.

His sense of pleasure was heightened as Yuichi approached him,
carrying two crystal tumblers, waving a bottle of imported whiskey,
and calling, "Renzō, Cousin, join me in this most civilized drink?"

"With pleasure! You hold the tumblers, I shall do the honors."

"As you wish. Pour generously. So much infectious gaiety and
nostalgia has weakened me."

Obeying instructions, Renzō smiled warmly, saying, "So with
me. But the further I advance into life, the better it becomes. Certainly, on a day such as this neither of us has reason to complain or
to shed tears. You must agree?" Saluting Yuichi with his tumbler,
he drank deeply.

Yuichi, about to reply, changed his mind as Aiko appeared, carrying Etsu and holding a boldly patterned paper parasol. As she
left the glare of the sun, she exclaimed with some relief, "Ah, Et-
chan, how cool, how nice it is here in the shade . . ."

Suddenly aware of the two men beneath the pine tree, she halted
and Yuichi went to her, taking the child into his arms and remarking
in a teasing voice, "Aiko, Aiko! Your hair and your attire are in a
shambles. With whom have you been wrestling in the heat? No
matter. Don't answer. Come with me to Renzō. Your arrival is
timely. I need your help."

After a moment's hesitation spent attempting to neaten her hair,
she followed her husband, murmuring somewhat impatiently, "Well,
what is it, then? A matter of such importance that it cannot wait?"

Teasing even more, Yuichi replied, "In my opinion, yes. My
cousin has just declared that I have no reason to complain, or to
shed tears." Pausing, shifting Etsu into a more comfortable position,
he added, his eyes glistening with amusement, "Please, Aiko. Tell
him how I weep into my pillow every night. And—*why* I weep."

Renzō gazed admiringly at his daughter and concentrated on producing smoke circles from his pipe. He was bored and completely
uninterested in Yuichi's nonsensical carryings-on, but said casually,

half-humorously, " 'Tis said that most rich men are apt to weep for fear of losing their possessions."

"Not I! My tears come filled with the brine of sorrow. Aiko kindly mops them up after having wrung my pillow dry. Explain to my cousin, Aiko, how he can relieve me of my sorrows. Explain how he *should*, how he *could*, oblige me."

Renzō, struck by the mention of obligations, glanced sharply at Yuichi, his suspicions quickly diminishing on realizing that his cousin was merely playing a game, a game that was acceptable because of his intoxicated condition. Removing his pipe from between clenched teeth, he bowed with mock ceremony, first to Aiko, then to Yuichi, exclaiming, "Tell me, then! So, what *should*, what *could* I do for you? Whatever—it will be my pleasure."

"Thank you!" Now Yuichi's shoulders were shaking with laughter, and Etsu, delighted by his merriment, laughed also, pounding a tiny fist against his cheek as he pronounced, "You, Renzō, could— and should—present me with one of your children."

"Which one shall it be?" Renzō quipped. "My son Shin-chan? My daughter Et-chan? Regretfully, I must refuse. . . ."

"Sad, sad! I thought as much. Nevertheless, I won't despair. Kindly give thought to the matter. . . ."

Still laughing, Yuichi walked away, taking Etsu with him.

Highly amused, Renzō leaned against the rough bark of the pine, aware of the sun's leisurely descent but scarcely conscious of the woman who had remained standing beneath the tree. Then, glancing at her with a mixture of rancor and curiosity, he wondered what was going on in her mind. What lay beneath that cold surface as she stood there clutching the furled parasol as though not sure what to do with it? Never before had he been alone with his cousin's wife, and he found it difficult to break the silence between them. Bracing himself, he said politely, "Your husband, my cousin, is a great prankster."

Her lips shaped the words, "You think so?"

He had some difficulty in restraining his impatience toward the aloof young woman. Irritated, he said with some irony, "May I relieve you of that parasol? You hold it as though it were a fearsome weapon."

At once Aiko dropped the article to the ground. About to reach down and retrieve it, Renzō remained stationary, confused, and overcome by conflicting emotions, gazing intently at her downcast face, feeling as though the two of them were alone in the world, both of them vulnerable and waiting for something extraordinary to happen.

Instinctively, he knew that his feelings were shared by the woman who stood poised as though ready to take flight. . . .

Impossible thoughts flooded his mind. He was so ripe, so ready for a light affair. So aware of time passing.

But she, Aiko, was his cousin's *wife*. His wife's *sister* . . . So many major, formidable barriers between them . . . Guilt-ridden, torn between feelings of overpowering excitement and decency, he sought to put an end to the deplorable situation.

As though having read his thoughts, Aiko stooped and picked up the furled parasol. The spell was broken and she turned from him to move away.

Involuntarily, he uttered a short sharp sound of protest, and she halted, motionless, her back toward him. Then she turned to face him and looked directly into his eyes. Her expression was so challenging, so provocative, it sent a wave of passion through his being. He felt as if he had been struck by an overpowering force.

"Aiko . . . Aiko . . . ?" he repeated her name urgently. She did not speak, but her unuttered words, the darkening of those eyes gazing into his, sufficed to ravish him. Time stood still. Then once more she turned from him, walking away in a leisurely fashion while he remained standing in the shadows of the tree, affected so profoundly that the world about him seemed to be swaying softly.

From that day onward as the summer season continued, Renzō existed in a state of limbo, ignoring talk and newspaper reports describing the gigantic strides Japan was so rapidly taking toward Westernization.

Yuichi Fukuda and his compatriots were deeply aware of the attitude of the world around them, especially aware that China and other Asian countries looked on with suspicion as Japan strode toward industrialism. They clearly understood that urgent economic and social demands called for diplomatic skills in many quarters where amity on international levels had to be obtained.

Many seemingly unspectacular reforms also aroused Yuichi's interest because he realized that they were changing the face of the country. The eating of red meat was weakening Buddhism's hold on the people, and the miracle of vaccination was conquering the dread scourge of smallpox.

Money from many sources was now flowing into his coffers.

Photography was one. It had become so popular that scarcely a person existed whose likeness had not been taken and framed. Countless thousands of them had been taken by the now famous, cheaply priced Fukuda cameras, and encased in popular Fukuda-style cherrywood frames. Photographs of family members before their deaths were considered treasures beyond price and added a new dimension every year to *Obon*, the festival during which the beloved one's spirits returned to behold themselves portrayed in picture form before household shrines.

Inwardly yearning for praise and recognition, Yuichi had been gratified when an imperial edict had created a Senate and House of Peers. He had no political ambitions but went out of his way to favor and to assist senators who would remember him when high honors and titles were to be handed out to citizens of worth.

Unlike his wife, Yuichi had little interest in those thousands of foreigners who were now living in Japan.

Quite a few of them had decided to stay on as permanent residents, and among those were a number of male homosexuals who found a haven in the midst of people whose morality accepted all human feeling as a natural part of life. Able to relax without fear of blackmail, shame, or punishment by the law, those men, mostly highly educated, taught in tertiary institutions and established small, charming homes, employing "Boy Sans" willing to oblige their employers' whims. In some cases, men of good families achieved long-lasting relationships with males of their own class.

Those bachelors formed a valuable social nucleus, and were sought after by hostesses in need of that extra man at dinner parties. They also served as escorts for women who were widowed, or alone while their husbands were away traveling. In the case of Lady Marjorie Coomber, an indefatigable hostess, the homosexual bachelors were a valuable source of partners for her at the many entertainments she attended.

Sir John Coomber, elderly and good-natured, gave his youthful wife a free rein. He arose each morning on the stroke of five to go about his own life and was fully occupied working with several dedicated Japanese scholars, translating the subtleties of Japanese poetry into the English language.

Her husband's diplomatic career had taken Lady Marjorie to live in India, Australia, and China and, in each of those lands, her completely unprejudiced nature meant that she took on cargoes of friendships—people with whom she corresponded on a regular basis, always hoping to meet with them again. "If not in this world, my dear one," she would write, "then without doubt, in heaven."

Now, in Japan, she was making new friends of all nationalities. Among her many activities, she presided over a "ladies' reading circle" which met once a month to discuss the literary works of Oscar Wilde and other modernists whose writings she admired.

Before coming to Japan, her English friends had told her that Japanese women were downtrodden creatures. It was not so from her point of view; her friendship with Aiko Fukuda had proved that.

Aiko had arrived one afternoon to the reading circle bringing with her a brocade-bound book, announcing casually, "Books such as this play a significant part in basic education in Japan," adding with her gamin grin, "If any deprived wife is present here today, she might receive inspiration from the work."

The exquisitely illustrated book on pornography was literally pounced upon. At first the ladies suppressed their enjoyment, but soon there were gales of laughter from the seven women present, all of whom had grown up with the puritanical mores of the times, which had prevailed in their own lands.

"But, how outrageously *intriguing* . . ." Mable Langston finally exclaimed. "I'm certain no such book exists in my native America."

"My entire *body* is ablush!" Mrs. Collins, the elderly wife of an English cleric in Tokyo, took a small magnifying glass from her reticule, intent on examining one of the most explicit illustrations in detail. Then she murmured, "Ah-ha . . . ! My dear husband could be in for a surprise or maybe three tonight. . . ."

The ladies' responses took Aiko aback, for she had brought the book along hoping merely that it might bring a lighter mood to the serious discussions.

EVER SINCE SUMIKO'S GARDEN PARTY, Renzō had been furious with himself, at times wondering if he was a conceited fool to believe that Aiko had in fact sent that burning invitation his way. The next moment, he would be convinced that he had not been mistaken.

Quite at a loss, he was unable to carry out his work conscientiously. Thoughts of Aiko were a constant distraction, and there were nights when he lay awake, keeping Rumi from sleeping while he encouraged her to speak of her sister, which in all innocence she

did, being only too happy that her husband was so interested in—
as she assumed—the intimacies of her daily life.

Never before had he been so conscious of his own body. He
scented himself after each bath and dressed with even more care than
usual, causing Nakasone to remark scathingly, "What a dandy you
have become."

"Not so!" was his tactiturn reply.

His emotions had become too confused, too strong to suppress
properly, and as a result he would sit brooding, his expression so
dour that both his wife and his mother were concerned for him.

One evening, attempting to cheer him, Rumi described a small
Japanese-style house which Lady Marjorie Coomber had had built
in the grounds of her Tokyo residence. He sat staring glumly as his
wife enthused, "Truly, you should see it, Renzō. Lady Marjorie is
eager to meet with you. Are you aware of that?"

He shrugged the question off and was about to make his escape,
but changed his mind and listened intently as Rumi rattled on to
Masa. "My sister, Aiko, was responsible for the design and the de-
cor of 'The Folly,' as Lady Marjorie calls it. She says jokingly that
the little house might become a rendezvous for her and her many
lovers."

"A remarkably frank statement," Masa said, somewhat shocked.
"That is, if the English lady was *not* joking."

"Oh, I'm sure it was a joke. No lady could be a more devoted
wife, so Aiko tells me, and she would know, for seldom a day goes
by without she and Coomber Sama meeting."

"Is that so," Renzō grunted. "How do they fill in their time?"

"How . . . ? In countless ways. Following the inspiration of
America's forward-thinking Mrs. Bloomer, they indulge themselves
in the pastime of cycling. . . ."

"They do?" Lady Masa's voice held a tinge of envy.

"They certainly do, Mother. Yes, daringly wearing midcalf blue
serge skirts which reveal ankle-length trousers. Their heads topped
by smart straw boaters, they pedal along the country roads for
hours. . . ."

"What courage Aiko has," Lady Masa put in.

"True," Rumi agreed. "She has never minded being gossiped
about. They attend concerts, go on shopping sprees. And . . ." Rumi
said, turning to face Renzō, her tone more than a little teasing, "you
may not have noticed, but I, your wife, was absent from home for
three days last week disporting myself along with my sister and her

friend at the Hot Spring Resort. The English lady was transported with joy. Actually, Aiko and I had a joke between us saying that the *gaijin* was becoming more Japanese than we Japanese."

"I'm convinced that I'd dislike the Coomber woman intensely," Renzō responded scathingly.

"Maybe so, but you'll never know, will you? You refuse all her invitations, even though she yearns to meet with you, being related to Hilda Turton, that lady whom you knew so well in London."

Masa, aware of a tinge of resentment in her daughter-in-law's voice, said, "Rumi, please tell us about your experiences at the resort. Both of us would like to hear. Is that not so, Renzō?"

"Yes. Yes, why not entertain us?"

"I've no wish to bore you with my chatter."

"Your chatter never bores. Tell on . . ." Renzō encouraged his wife, and Rumi, her eyes sparkling, gave free rein to her acting abilities, exhilarated at having an interested audience.

"Well . . ." she began in her light, silvery voice. "After reaching our destination in the mountain district, we three intrepid females were carried farther upward in bamboo litters hung on a single pole. Coomber Sama, due to her weight, had *three* bearers instead of two. Personally, the swaying of the litter caused me some nausea, but the *gaijin* definitely enjoyed the swaying and the perils of the journey.

"After settling down in the rustic inn, we changed into *yukata*. 'So free a garment,' our friend declared. 'No corset to torture me . . .' " Rumi mimed Lady Marjorie's delight. "She was enchanted by the maids who rushed to oblige us even before we clapped our hands for service. She likened the maids to *butterflies*. At that, I told her in no uncertain terms that we Japanese females considered butterflies to be emblems of inconstancy and that it was insulting to be thought of in that light. . . ."

"How did she react to your scolding?" Masa asked with interest.

"With complete understanding. Indeed. She entered into every activity with genuine enthusiasm. She did not hesitate to strip naked, to bathe in the steaming pool, even when a group of rollicking rustics arrived, some never before having seen a foreign female. Was Coomber Sama embarrassed when those men, women, and children gathered about examining, splashing, laughing, yes, even touching her rosy white skin?"

"Well, *was* she embarrassed?" Renzō grunted.

"Not in the least! She's possessed of large, pendulous breasts. Very intriguing. They floated on the watery surface and she obliged everyone's curiosity where those breasts were concerned. . . ."

Rumi's miming actions caused Masa to laugh heartily as she nodded, encouraging the young woman to continue.

"Well, yes," Rumi went on, speaking rapidly. "Her energy defies description. Each morning she arose at dawn with the birds, and was enthralled by the calls of cuckoos, whose calls she echoed skillfully. Then, before the torrid heat of the day began, we three stood naked, showering beneath the 'Waterfall of Brightness' which tumbled down into a great pool where shoals of *koi* glided at their leisure. . . ."

"How wondrous," Masa interjected dreamily.

"Yes! The entire experience was wondrous. My sister and I agreed that we saw anew through the eyes of the foreigner, who was charmed by things mundane to us. . . ." Rumi fell silent, lost in certain memories.

"Things, such as?" Again Masa encouraged with true interest.

"Umm? Oh, yes! Such as when, on one of our rambles, we came upon some moss-covered steps leading up to a neglected temple. The English lady took a white handkerchief from the sleeve of her *yukata* and tied it among the tattered prayer-slips dangling from branches of a holy tree. With tears in her eyes, she said, 'I'm sure that all prayers sent up from this world reach the One True God.' "

"She sounds revoltingly sentimental," Renzō commented.

"Not so. Renzō, you delighted in the graveyards and tombstones of Lady Marjorie's native England. She has a deep admiration for nature in all its forms. Now, did *you* ever weep at the glory of woodland trees and rocks?"

"Certainly not!"

"I thought as much! Our friend did. She spent hours of contemplation weeping at the beauty of towering cryptomeria trees. She became wild with delight on seeing our pink-cheeked monkeys scrambling through treetops. . . ."

"Is that so!" Masa said in a pleased voice.

"Yes. She loved the time-stained stone lanterns, thick moss-pads. On one occasion she threw herself down, laughing like a happy child, rolling over and over in the lush green grass. . . ."

"Are you sure the woman is not touched in the head?" Renzō interjected. "How did you and your sister react?"

"How? I'm not ashamed to admit that Aiko and I, throwing all dignity to the winds, followed suit. . . ." Rumi's laughter rang out gaily. "As males revert to childishness when they get together, so do we females if the chance arises. Is that not so, Mother?"

Masa, recalling the loneliness of her life following Sumiko's departure from the house on the hill in Yokohama, smiled fleetingly.

"So," Renzō said sourly, "a good time was had by all. Are you sure you're not exaggerating? For instance, I can't imagine your aloof sister behaving in such a naive manner."

"Little you know of Aiko . . ." Rumi smiled as though an illuminatingly wise thought had just slipped into her mind. "Little does anyone really know of those close to one. I find it ridiculous that we must always be on guard, seldom able to express true emotions."

Renzō, so deeply on guard where his own emotions were concerned, yawned, then declared irately, "Please order a bath for me. This humidity is most unpleasant."

"I agree. I shall join you." Rumi stood, saying, "While at the inn. Lady Marjorie insisted that we sleep with the windows wide open during the night. Naturally, I didn't object but scarcely slept a wink."

"It's the English way," Renzō muttered. "Was your sister also upset?"

"Aiko? I can't say. There was a full moon and she remained sitting up, staring at the sky for hours. She smoked cigarette after cigarette and ignored my suggestions that she lie down and catch some sleep. Finally, slightly annoyed by her behavior, I said to her, 'Aiko, sister, has the moon bewitched you? Have a care!' "

"And . . . ?" Renzō questioned casually.

"Her reply was quite frosty: 'Allow me my privacy,' she muttered. 'Quite often I remain sleepless, waging battles with myself.' " Rumi shrugged, then smiled, unwilling to betray her dislike of Aiko's haughty manners. "I just put my head beneath the covers and drifted into sleep. So, now I'll attend to my domestic duties. . . ."

The mother and son remaining in the room had no way of knowing that both their minds were thinking of one certain person.

Masa, conjuring up the memory of Aiko's visit to her, was certain that she was privy to the thoughts that had been in the young woman's mind as she sat bathed in cold moonlight, and her heart went out in sympathy.

Renzō, conjuring up the memory of his last meeting with Aiko, was certain that he understood the battle she had been waging against herself.

Rumi's voice filtered into their thoughts as she called out, "Nurse, bring Et-chan from her bed. I wish to take her to soak in the bath. It will ease her heat rash. . . ."

Renzō looked up, addressing his mother solemnly. "Truly, the child is suffering from this torrid heat. Shinichi, I notice, is lethargic. Mother, I raise a delicate question. Please answer frankly. Have you any objections to your grandchildren meeting with Rumi's mother in Kamakura?"

Masa hesitated before replying. She was undergoing a mighty struggle attempting to overthrow prejudices of class consciousness that had endured for so many centuries in her country.

"Times are changing," Renzō said encouragingly, at the same time trembling inwardly, yearning to free himself from domestic ties. "Both the children would benefit from several weeks beside the sea. Rumi would be delighted and would admire your generosity of spirit. Certainly, I realize that the geisha can never be accepted here. Please know that I respect your feelings on that score. I . . ."

Masa's voice was expressionless as she interjected, "Renzō, let it be as you wish. May I advise that you accompany your family to Kamakura. Recently, you appear overwrought at times, like one on thin ice."

"Thank you." He bowed slightly. "I admire your generous decision. But, as for myself . . ." Gesturing dramatically, he made it plain that the luxury of taking a vacation was out of the question for one burdened with the pressures of business. Then, re-energized, he got up to stride from the room, aglow with satisfaction.

Marjorie Coomber was seldom happier than when entertaining at her at-home afternoon tea parties. One never knew who would turn up apart from those regular, chosen friends and acquaintances who seldom let her down.

Today's reception was the final one of the season, for the summer's heat was emptying Tokyo of those who could afford the time and pleasure to move to cooler places. Lady Marjorie and Sir John were to travel to a mountain village recently discovered by American missionaries. She had invited Mr. Jonas Blunt today and was questioning the earnest shepherd of many Japanese converts. "Pastor, tell me how is it that you busy missionaries were the ones to so cleverly discover the village of Karuizawa?"

"May I say, Lady Coomber, by divine guidance?"

"Why not! Tell, is it really so delightful? I've heard that it nestles

at the foot of Mount Asama, an active volcano. Is that not dangerous?"

"It could be considered so." The frail man smiled whimsically.
"But no place could be more entrancing to end one's earthly life.
When do you take your leave from Tokyo?"

"Happily, sometime this week . . ." Marjorie, making her excuses,
moved forward as the Japanese butler, robed in black kimono and
wearing white gloves, approached carrying a silver salver on which
a visiting card rested.

Taking up the card, she moved farther forward toward the door,
her face creasing into a welcoming smile as she said cordially, "Renzō
Yamamoto—at last! So, Hilda Turton's 'handsome, dear samurai' has
deigned to call on me. . . ."

Renzō spent one long hour, carrying himself with confidence, but
his general air of self-assurance belied his inner despair. Feeling as
though he stood on a razor's edge, he had gazed about the crowded
room, not only hoping but fully expecting that Aiko Fukuda would
be present.

Punctiliously correct, he departed at the appropriate time, thanking his hostess with the exact measure of familiarity permissible because of their mutual friendship with Hilda Turton.

"So, you must leave!" Marjorie said cheerfully. "Please give my
regards to your charming wife."

"I shall indeed."

"Thank you, and when the autumn arrives, promise to call again.
We must not let Hilda down. She fully expects us to become
friends."

"I also hope so." He was tempted to mention Aiko, but hastily
corrected the thought by saying, "I was hoping to . . . yes, hoping
to view the Japanese house in your garden. My wife speaks of it
with tremendous admiration. Perhaps in the autumn."

"Oh, my 'Folly'! " As Marjorie smiled, he noticed that dimples
puckered her cheeks. "I'm ridiculously enamored of it. But why
wait until autumn?" After rapidly ticking appointments off on the
fingers of her left hand, she exclaimed animatedly, "Could you drop
in tomorrow afternoon? Around five? If so, I'll take you on a grand
tour. Yes, and serve *sake* to you. I would wear a kimono and then
write a tantalizing, teasing letter to Hilda about our tête-à-tête. No?"

Feeling as though he were being strangled and wanting escape,
Renzō bowed, saying lightly, "Nothing could give me more pleasure. Until tomorrow, then . . ."

Disappointed as he had been, Renzō was not one to suffer gladly, and after leaving the Coombers' residence he sought out Nakasone, exclaiming, "Let business matters rest for the time being. Join me in a drinking bout."

"Is that an order?" Nakasone quipped.

"A simple request from one friend to another. My spirit needs lifting."

"Then, I'm your man."

Many hours later and after an inordinate amount of whiskey, Renzō alighted from a ricksha and entered the Nihombashi house walking steadily, disappointingly sober.

Unable to sleep, he lay scorning himself, fully determined to put all thoughts of Aiko—such degenerate thoughts—out of his mind once and for all. Thinking coldly and clinically, he told himself that his wife's sister had, in fact, done him at least one good turn in having banished the courtesan Osen from his mind.

He had believed that an inherent sense of decency prevented him from visiting the Fukuda family home. But, he pondered, in truth, that was not really so. He had kept away because he wanted to meet Aiko away from her home ground.

Yes, and what was he hoping to attain? The answer was that he hoped to become caught up in a passionate affair with her. What quality of man was he? He concluded that he was despicable, also conceited in that he had led himself to believe that Aiko had been deeply attracted to him.

The young woman had in all probability thrown that hot glance his way intentionally to titillate him. Her reputation was that of a wayward, unconventional female. It could be that she took delight in arousing men's emotions, then moved off, amused and laughing to herself.

Frankly, he had never liked his cousin's wife. She was improper, altogether outrageously haughty, and yes, obviously *sadistic*. Certainly she had caused him to suffer, but no more. From now on he would consider those few moments alone with her as a trifling episode and get on with his life.

The carriage moved toward Kōjimachi at a spanking pace, carrying Renzō toward the British legation to keep his appointment with Marjorie Coomber.

He had awakened at noon and straightaway gone to a bathhouse and after a thorough steaming and an hour of relaxing massage he returned home to array himself in ceremonial Japanese garments, intent on presenting himself in the guise of a true samurai to please his hostess.

Feeling cleansed in body and spirit, and in a complacent mood, he gazed about, for the first time in weeks able to enjoy the world about him, even finding some charm in the city he had disliked ever since his first arrival there as a callow youth accompanied by Sudo.

Far, far away in the distance, he glimpsed the peerless beauty of Fuji San silhouetted against the hazy blue of the sky, and the sight of the mountain lifted his spirits to a further height of pleasure.

While awaiting at the entrance doors to be admitted into the Coombers' redbrick house, he admired the pair of carved *koma-inu* and *ama-inu*, so delightfully ferocious-looking with curled tails and manes, and he wondered which temple they had been purloined from. He thought of Victor Caswell, knowing how that man would appreciate the superbly wrought dogs which were said to ward off the attacks of evil spirits.

True to her word, Marjorie wore a flamboyant kimono. She was probably unaware that only a courtesan would have worn it, and that the sashed outfit made her full-bosomed figure quite ludicrous in his eyes. But, hiding his amusement, Renzō discovered that beneath the unsuitable costume lay a warmhearted, charming woman who soon caught him up into the net of her friendship.

The amber-colored sherry quaffed from crystal glasses enhanced the intimacy of their newfound relationship, so much so that the original idea that had prompted the visit faded completely from Renzō's mind. He would have gone on his way, but for Marjorie, who exclaimed, "But, no! Renzō, I insist, I *refuse* to have you leave before visiting the Folly."

She escorted him through the beautifully designed garden as though she were the native of the land and he the foreign visitor. Waving her arms widely, she exclaimed proudly, "I'm *so* sorry you were not here to view our cherry blossoms."

All at once she halted, obviously upset. "Renzō, unforgivable, I know, but would you mind viewing my little Folly on your lonesome? A neglected, a forgotten duty orders me urgently back to the house."

"Please, be easy. I understand completely. . . ."

She left him standing alone before a high wall made from freshly cut bamboo. Bereft of her sparkling company and with no interest in seeing the small house, he was sorely tempted to go on his way, but then, out of politeness, he slid open the wicket gate and at once his interest and his admiration grew.

He stood beneath a trelliswork from which white and purple wisteria blossoms trailed heavily down to the ground, their perfume so sweet that bumblebees floated in numbers, droning ecstatically as they loaded themselves with nectar.

In readiness for his visit, the entrance door was open. Removing his footwear, he entered the tiny house.

Once again Marjorie had been true to her word, for on a low table were two tiny bowls and close at hand was a *hibachi*, its coals glowing beneath an ancient iron pot, a trifle of true antiquity, which held a porcelain jar of rice wine.

"The dear woman." He murmured his amusement aloud. Determined to show his appreciation, he sat down and poured wine into one of the cups, then, about to raise the minute vessel to his lips, his gaze rested on one of the frescoed doors which was sliding silently open.

He remained as though frozen, acutely aware of muted sounds coming from the garden, of the rustle of leaves, the splash of a fish in the lily-strewn pond.

Dazed, he closed his eyes, then opened them as he rose to his feet, swaying slightly, intoxicated by the sight of Aiko, who stood there, so still, looking at him, her expression derisive.

Finally, scarcely recognizing his own voice, he said, "You expected to meet me here?"

"Yes." She spoke with no reserve. "Yes, I have been waiting. . . ."

During the heat-filled days of August and September, Renzō conducted both his domestic and public life behind a façade so skillfully constructed that no one could have suspected he was involved in an adulterous affair.

Ignoring for the most part the ethics of conventional moral sense, there were, however, moments when he shivered recalling how in former times his cousin Yuichi would have had the right to kill Aiko had he discovered her unfaithfulness. Also, there were of course elements of real peril which had to be dealt with.

Both he and Aiko were careful to depart from their meetings immaculately groomed. The threat of gossip perturbed him because of the presence of the devoted maid-servant, Yuki, but Aiko reassured him. "Rest easy, Yuki cares for no other life than mine. Rest easy. . . ."

He had never thought of women as timid, helpless creatures, but he was taken aback on finding them to be quite alarming, and so unashamedly inventive. Marjorie's awkward departure and Aiko's presence proved to him that a female sorority existed akin to the sodality of brotherly beneficence.

The many complexities of their situation were done away with by Aiko, who would say frankly, "Never have I been afraid of life in any respect!" And he admitted to himself, thereby quelling any feelings of guilt, that *she*, not he, had taken the decisive action arranging their first rendezvous.

Rumi and the two children returned from Kamakura glowing with health and so filled with chatter that all he was required to do was to respond with a series of monosyllabic replies, leaving his thoughts free to dwell on the delights of the mature relationship he had achieved with Aiko.

Renzō knew that his memories of those first sublimely passionate hours would never be erased from his mind. . . .

The soft rustle of Aiko's silken garments falling to the *tatami*. The scent of wisteria blossoms. The sweet modesty of the woman, her long scarlet petticoat tied about her waist, reclining on the *futon* which had been prepared in readiness before his arrival.

No word was spoken. They both knew why they were there.

Lying beside her at last, he was aware that she was trying to suppress her agitation, "Don't mind, don't mind . . ." she whispered pleadingly. "Don't mind. Later! Later, I'll explain later. . . ."

Soon he understood that she was alluding to her virginal state. His shock and consternation had been forgotten in his urgency.

Together, he and Aiko were swept along by their mutual passion.

Then, at peace they lay apart, stretched out on their backs in the sunlit brightness of the room.

After a while, he raised his head and gazed down at Aiko, who lay with her eyes closed, her hands clasped over her small, firm breasts and her lips curved in a mysteriously triumphant smile.

Later, at their third meeting, she said, her voice barely audible, her eyes averted, "I owe you an explanation."

He understood at once and curiosity kept him silent. She continued as though the matter was of no importance, "My husband, your cousin, has always behaved with me as though I were a male. Need I say more . . . ?"

Due to the intimacy that had been achieved so quickly in their relationship, Renzō felt free to murmur, "Disgraceful! Yes, and so cruel, so unfair to you!"

"So I have always felt. But it has been my duty to please him all these years."

"Enough is enough! You must try and convert him to more natural ways."

"You think so?"

"I do. You should insist."

Love was no part of their cleverly arranged meetings. Neither he nor Aiko had ever falsely uttered that word. He adored her honesty, her openly expressed ecstasy as they lay so close, and then her lack of guilt or reserve as they spoke together.

One afternoon as they relaxed talking and laughing, Aiko said, "I always found you to be pleasantly conceited."

"You did. What nonsense!"

"I agree. How did you once think of me? Be honest. . . ."

"Best not." He grinned. "But, *why not*! Frankly, I disliked you intensely. Also, I once told my mother that I suspected you of tribadism."

Aiko hesitated for an instant before murmuring, "And what was Aunt Masa's reply?"

"Hmmm . . . If I remember correctly, her reply was that I should more or less mind my own business."

"How *admirable* she is," Aiko laughed lightly. "Certainly, I care with deep affection for my few women friends, but sexual relationships with my own kind has never appealed. And with you?"

"Always, when without a woman, I've preferred to sleep alone."

The end of the month of September was bringing the first hint of cool breezes, and people were drifting back to the capital from vacation resorts. Although both Aiko and Renzō realized that their meetings at Marjorie's "Folly" were numbered, neither of them mentioned that fact.

They had unwittingly created an atmosphere of domesticity in the unique little abode. Renzō enjoyed it immensely and found special pleasure in talking with Aiko—never touching on family matters—about a variety of subjects. They often discussed music, and Aiko admitted that to her regret, she was unable to carry a tune.

She made the admission as they were enjoying a platter of *sushi*

which her maid-servant had brought in. They ate with the appetites
of healthy children after an energetic game and then washed the food
down with sherry from Marjorie's supply.

"You?" Renzō scoffed his disbelief. "Unable to carry a tune? I
don't believe that."

"It's true. Try me out."

After a moment's thought he hummed a melody from one of the
musicals which he had enjoyed so much in London—"I Dreamt I
Dwelt in Marble Halls." "Try that," he encouraged. "I challenge
you."

Aiko, frowning and concentrating deeply, gave voice. "Stop!
Hush! Absolutely horrible," he cried out pleadingly, and their
laughter rang out as Renzō replenished her glass, saying admiringly,
"You are able to quaff copious amounts of wine."

"Yes. I especially like this English sherry."

"Bittersweet! Like you."

"Is that how you think of me?"

"Yes."

"Hmmmm . . . I think of you as my—my perfect lover."

"But you don't love me!"

"I don't love you," she replied with careful deliberation, a
mocking grin spreading across her face. "I think of our association
thus:

> *"The sky is high*
> *The tips of tendrils*
> *Have nowhere to cling."*

Whenever they parted there were no lingering farewells, no mention of further meetings; both knew that arrangements made and
then broken by necessity caused damage.

Determined that those "tendrils" should reach even higher and
that no gossip be aroused, Renzō put his mind to finding another
hideaway after the Coombers returned to their home and the Folly
was no longer available.

No mention was made of his plan, but it was fully understood by
Aiko, who also realized that urgent business matters were causing
the delay. They went their own ways, occasionally meeting at social
events, at which they were more than careful to behave with the
right note of decorum.

Only on one occasion was Renzō's equilibrium shaken. Arriving home, he found Aiko sitting at her ease cuddling Etsu as she gossiped with Rumi and Lady Masa.

His small daughter ran to him, crying out, "Come, Puppa, come play with Et-chan."

Feeling as though he were walking on a tightrope, he cuddled the child close, then joined the group of women and tried to appear at his ease, careful not to let his eyes meet those of his wife's sister. He was nevertheless aware that his mother reacted, if but slightly, when he became momentarily off guard and exclaimed warmly, "Et-chan, Et-chan, you smell so sweetly of your Aunt Aiko's Parma Violet perfume. . . ."

The perilous moment was salvaged by Rumi, who declared to Aiko with humorous sarcasm, "My much-traveled husband is an expert on perfume used by the many ladies he has, may I say, *met with*."

Her comment caused some laughter, but his mother sat by in silence, her expression unreadable.

Following Aiko's visit, Lady Masa approached Renzō. "I would appreciate some time alone with you, to discuss a certain matter."

Much to his relief, the matter was of little concern to him. It was of Sudo the henchman that his mother spoke, her voice sad as she told how the man had paid a visit to the Nihombashi house.

"He arrived at the servants' entrance, requesting to speak with me."

"What impudence. I consider his visit highly insulting."

"I did not consider it so. I asked the servant to direct Sudo to the front entrance and I received him there."

"Altogether too kind. He betrayed his trust to our family."

"Renzō, usually . . ." Masa hesitated slightly. "I respect your ways and your comments but not so on this matter."

Slightly put out, Renzō prepared a cigar for smoking, carefully removing the paper brand-circle to keep for Estu, who fancied them as rings to wear on her fingers and toes. "What did the chap want?" he then inquired.

"He asked for naught. He came to pay his respects, and to say farewell."

"Farewell?"

"Yes. Truly my heart ached for him. You, Renzō, along with

many of your generation, have little feeling and understanding for the past. The childhood memories you do have are blurred and in many respects unreliable."

"Hmm . . . maybe so."

"Undoubtedly so. My memories of those times are clear, some beautiful, many sad and bitter. I understand Sudo's situation only too well. From early boyhood, he was exploited, treated only as a workhorse by your grandfather and by your father. . . ."

"Surely you exaggerate," Renzō interjected.

"Not at all. Kindly respect my opinions."

"Certainly. Please excuse me."

Masa bowed her acceptance of the apology, then said, "Sudo's entire life has consisted of insult after insult. Now, finally, he has been dismissed—no reason given—by your cousin Yuichi Fukuda."

"No better than he deserves. Sudo betrayed our trust in him. He must have betrayed Yuichi in some way."

Lady Masa gave Renzō one long look before saying, "Some years back, while living my lonely existence in Yokohama, I became acquainted with Germans named Dreyer. . . ."

"Is that so?" he interjected. "The owners of the famous Dreyer Eating House at Hommoku Bay? I had no idea you ever patronized the place."

Masa sighed before replying. "How little you know! Before fame fell upon them, they were simple, sincere missionaries. I sometimes visited and spoke with them. . . ." Lost in memories, Masa fell silent.

Renzō, becoming impatient, said briskly, "Yes, but what does all this have to do with the henchman Sudo?"

"Ah—yes! Your comment about Sudo's betrayal of us! My missionary acquaintance explained to me that part of the Christian creed is *'Judge not less you be also so judged.'* That impressed me greatly."

"Very commendable." Laughing, he murmured, "I bow low beneath your well-deserved reprimand. But what of Sudo?"

"Very little more. Just that he is to leave the land he has served so well with so little reward and no recognition."

"So, where is he to go?"

"He said maybe to Brazil. He appeared distracted. He has aged greatly."

"He *is* quite old."

"Old? He's but some seven years your senior." Masa glanced at her son; then, as though making a decision, she said cheerfully, "I felt it my duty to tell you of his visit. Renzō, when he mentioned your name, his eyes became suffused with tears. . . ."

Eager to be on his way, Renzō waited politely for his mother to complete her story.

Finally, he said, "So, that was all? Nothing else?"

"Nothing else," Masa said quietly. "Please be free to go your way. . . ." His attitude had chilled her spirit.

Renzō now had little time to spare as he prepared a choice collection of goods to be shipped to London.

Victor Caswell had written, enthusing about the bronze vases he had received. . . . *"Sold, all too soon. And for what a profit! The one so golden brown in color, the raised design of silver-tipped waves, I've kept for myself to gloat over. . . .*

"Those six-paneled folding screens, flower-designed on the matte gold backgrounds, each one so different and so fantastic. Nary a one left in my premises. Do your utmost to procure more of the same. . . .

"Contrary to our expectations, dear 'Prince Yamamoto,' the collection of parquetry boxes are proving to be popular here. So also are those peglike, ancient wooden dolls. Speaking of dolls, I'm green with jealousy, for one of my competitors, old Nathan Bennett in Savile Row, has a collection of exotically robed dolls, seated on a platform and representing the mikado, empress, so on and so on, down the noble scale. I'm told such collections are part of all samurai families. So, why are you holding out on me? Do get moving. The news that I'm to receive that immense Buddhist family altar, black-lacquered, gold-leafed, and bronzed-hinged, has me in such a state that Mrs. Caswell threatens to leave home unless I calm down. . . .

"By the way, that two foot-high wooden bear (you write that it was carved by the natives up north of your country, in Hokkaidō) I find quite repulsive, so, please stay with the exotic and the beautiful. . . ."

Renzō attended to Victor's requests, nevertheless his mind often dwelt on Aiko. His affair with her had enriched his life and, he believed, her life also. Plain decency and courtesy made it essential that Marjorie Coomber's "hospitality" was no longer taken advantage of, and he was annoyed at not having the leisure in which to find another place for their rendezvous.

Apart from enjoying the sensuality of their relationship, he had come to admire Aiko's sense of humor and her sharp analytical mind.

After several weeks of not so much as sighting her, he made up his mind to accompany Rumi to an evening concert. A group of visiting Russian musicians were to perform at the Imperial Academy of Music.

"Please, will you escort me?" Rumi requested. "Not only do I hope to enjoy the music, I also yearn to see my sister. Of late I've seen so little of Aiko."

"Aiko is to attend?" he asked casually.

"Yes. Also, without doubt, Yuichi. He has donated a large sum of money to the academy. What a diplomatic businessman he is."

He agreed, and attended the concert dressed in his Savile Row clothes, wearing his silk-lined evening cape.

Soon after entering the auditorium filled to capacity with people of many nationalities, he sought out the Fukuda couple, then settled back to enjoy a work composed by a young Russian named Peter Ilyich Tchaikovsky. Above all, he was eager to meet up with Aiko during the intermission.

During that all too short time while the foursome stood together chatting in a desultory fashion, he wondered if Aiko felt stabs of guilt as he did. If so, she gave no sign, concentrating on Rumi, saying, "Yes, as you say, Rumi, we Japanese have been easily converted to the charms of Western music. I, personally, have a passion for it in all its forms."

"I enjoy it," Rumi responded. "Nevertheless, I remain faithful to the music of our own land. It's shameful to take on the new, casting out the old. You agree?"

With extreme recklessness, Aiko looked directly at Renzō, a mischievous glint in her eye as she said, "Rumi, I refer your inquiry to my husband." Then, turning her gaze on Yuichi, she said, "Come, give Rumi your opinion. How do *you* feel about casting off certain customs and, yes, morals?"

Yuichi said derisively, "Well, Rumi, it depends on what one wishes to achieve. To get what I want from life, I'll go to any lengths."

"True?" Aiko quipped. "You want it. You get it?"

"Exactly!" Yuichi cast his gaze upward to the high, ornate ceiling. "On rare occasions, Aiko, you and I struggle together to achieve. Is that not so?"

Once again Aiko looked straight at Renzō as she said, "Yes, Yuichi, together, we struggle along." Even in the short space of a second Renzō felt certain that Aiko was letting him know that her husband was overcoming his unhealthy sexual fetish. Perhaps at last Yuichi was indulging in normal sexual activities so long overdue in his marriage bed.

He was unable to stifle a pang of hot jealousy. Taking a cue from Aiko, he exclaimed wearily, "Presently, I resemble an insect caught up in a spider's web. The toils of business are preventing me from following the desires of my heart. Next month I hope to be free to *relax*."

"Relaxation is death to a businessman." Yuichi gestured broadly, grinning as he said, "But, business and pleasure *can* be mixed. Renzō, join me in the fascinating journey I'm about to take."

"Where shall you go?"

"To Shanghai! First trip away from Japan."

"To be absent for how long?"

"Who can say? Business is business! Maybe one month, maybe two. I'm wanting my wife to accompany me. Only, of course, because she's able to gabble away in several languages . . ." Yuichi, speaking directly to Rumi, added most pathetically, "Will you not encourage your difficult sister to accompany me?"

Rumi, all seriousness, exclaimed, "Aiko, sister, will you not accompany your husband?"

"Why not!" Aiko replied in a mocking tone. "Always, I relish new experiences. . . ."

O*SHŌGATSU*, THE FIRST DAY OF the new year had arrived. As Nakasone strode through Tokyo's snow-covered streets, every step he took was deliberate and pleasurable. After Ono, his dog, this inveterate bachelor's affections went to his bamboo flute, and now as he walked he kept his hand clasped tenderly on the boxed instrument tucked in his sash.

Many men of his age and social status still staunchly opposed to Western ideas had retired into the twilight world of poverty, filled with resentments. From his point of view, however, Japanese society was being reconstructed sensibly and decently. The restored emperor was proving to be a man of classic stature. The country's leading men were determined to rally the entire population's loyal attention and devotion to the throne; at the same time they were working toward presenting the people with a cult of national ethics to be called State Shinto, which was not to replace or harm the gentle Shinto philosophy belonging to the shrines.

Nakasone arrived at a main thoroughfare, where he joined the milling crowds, all on their way to shrines, or to visit the homes of relatives, of superiors, to pay homage with gifts to mark the end of the old and the beginning of the new.

Smiling rather grimly, Nakasone's thoughts went to his aristo-cratic parents who would have considered that their son was de-meaning himself in considering Renzō Yamamoto to be his superior. A new-thinking man, he thought differently. In no hurry to reach the house in Nihombashi, he allowed himself to move with the mass of people who were entering one of Tokyo's main Buddhist tem-ples. Ignoring the priests' activities, he nevertheless obeyed the tra-ditional forms, bowing his head at the appointed times, and experienced a wave of deep pleasure at the pealing of the temple's bells. But he quickly repressed any sentimental inclinations and set off on his way again, taking pleasure instead in the sight of cheerful vendors selling bowls of steaming hot noodles, puffed rice, and black-sugared candies.

Passing along a residential street, he halted to observe a group of jubilant children all noisily at play. The boys flew gaily patterned kites and the girls hit feathered shuttlecocks with their brightly col-ored bats. Many of the children had small brothers and sisters strapped to their backs; rather than considering them a burden, they were clearly proud of their responsibility.

Nakasone had a fondness for children, and he dawdled to tease and laugh with the youngsters who called to him sweetly, "New Year's congratulations, Uncle en *Omedetō! Omedetō* . . ."

In front of every small house were the pine- and bamboo-branch traditional emblems, white-corded and decorated by the glow of orange fruit.

Snow was now drifting down heavily. Not wishing to arrive in a disheveled state, he strode on swiftly toward Nihombashi, glad that he was carrying the oiled-paper umbrella as well as the gift to be presented to the Yamamoto household.

Accustomed as he had become to the slipshod ways of the old servant who cared for his domestic needs, Nakasone enjoyed the elegance of the Yamamoto home and the refined manners of those partaking in the traditional New Year's food which had been so exquisitely prepared and presented.

Toso—the spiced rice wine, was held at forehead level before being quaffed during the formality of the cold fish and vegetable dishes, which were then followed by hot red-bean soup in which floated bite-size pieces of rice pounded into solid blocks.

Toward the end of the celebratory feast, all refinement and peace was shattered as Etsu, Renzō's small daughter, choked on a piece of the solid, sticky rice-cake. Nakasone had been through many times of danger together with Renzō in those early strife-torn years following the arrival of the American warships to Japan, but never had he seen his friend so unashamedly terrified.

Pandemonium broke out when the child's face turned dark as she struggled to breathe. Everyone screamed different instructions, but nothing relieved the distraught sufferer.

"She is dying . . ."

"Et-chan . . . Et-chan . . . Et-chan . . ."

"Not *that*! Like *this* . . . She is *dying* . . ."

Moved by the compelling urgency of the situation, Nakasone grabbed the child and stuck his forefinger deep into the narrow throat. Even though his fingernails cut into the tender flesh, he finally succeeded in clearing her throat, and passed the little girl to her father, saying gruffly, "No real danger existed! Come, come, Yamamoto, quiet down, just comfort her. . . ."

The panic faded and all present were filled with a wondrous sense of quiet exaltation. Nakasone realized that he was being accepted as an adoptive member of the Yamamoto household. Rather to his amusement, he was imbued by feelings of fatherly responsibility and became intent on comforting his "family's" shattered nerves.

He noticed that Renzō's son, Shinichi, was staring at him as if he were a holy savior. The unspoken sentiment of thankfulness was so overwhelming that Nakasone took on a jocular attitude which aroused no merriment, merely polite smiles. Finally, without notice, he brought out his bamboo flute and played it softly.

Soon after that comforting interlude, Nakasone made his formal farewell, feeling enriched but more than relieved to plunge back into a sphere where domesticity and women had no place.

Snow no longer fell, and the sting of the sharp wind was exhilarating as he hurried forward, eager to be at home with his young protégé, Kuboto, and to become happily, even uproariously drunk. . . .

. . .

Sumiko Fukuda had greeted in New Year alone but overtaken by surges of excitement, which she found almost impossible to deal with.

Confined to her bed, recovering from a severe chill, she desired no other company than that of the Australian bird with whom she had achieved a remarkable empathy. She found it satisfying to speak her most intimate thoughts to a feathered creature who gazed unblinkingly, head to one side, responding only with, "Hello Cocky!" Sumiko interpreted those two words to mean, "Now, is that so . . . ? You don't say . . . ? Tell me more!"

At times she felt that her husband's spirit had returned to reside in the body of the yellow-crested cockatoo, to comfort and tease the wife who still loved him above everything.

Quite often, when certain no eavesdroppers were present, she addressed his spirit directly. Now, as she reclined on her comfortable *futon* in the privacy of her quarters, she murmured passionately to the bird, "Ah, it is comforting to know that although unseen, the master still guards his home, directs the actions of the family in his own, inimitable way. . . ."

As though to please her, the bird fanned up his spectacular crest, reminding her most comically of Fukuda's devoted attention to her comments. Half laughing, half crying, she exclaimed, "Forgive—excuse me for doubting your wisdom in having chosen the girl, Aiko, for your son's wife. Listen, listen to Yuichi's letter. . . ."

Removing a much-read letter from the sash of her sleeping robe, she read aloud, *"Such splendid news! I am to return home from Shanghai in late January, not only glad but rejoicing wildly. Mother, before the New Year is halfway through, your grandchild will have arrived! . . ."*

With the festive season over, Tokyo's citizens voiced their discontent and spoke longingly about the coming of spring. Not so Sumiko. With the enjoyment of one returned recently to good health, she reveled in the splendid news which she was on her way to relay to the Nihombashi household. She had chosen to travel in an open ricksha, mainly to give citizens the pleasure of beholding the wondrous bird that perched on her shoulder.

"Almost as good as flying, eh, Cocky-chan?" she whispered, keeping a firm hand on the light chain fixed to his claw in case he should fly off to the mysterious land from whence he had come. . . .

Lady Masa responded to the news of Aiko's pregnancy with the exact measure of delight and congratulations warranted by the occasion, but her spirit was disturbed, and as the days went by, her mind was inundated with uninvited, outrageous thoughts.

Her son had received the news casually. From Masa's point of view, too casually, and her thoughts returned to the day he revealed that he knew which perfume his wife's sister used. His mother, of course, was aware of the mask of indifference he at once feigned in order to hide his having been caught off guard.

Startled, mindful of Yuichi's tragic complaint, then shamed by her thoughts that day, Masa spent the night holding her Buddhist rosary, praying to have her mind cleansed. Prayer, and faith in Renzō's integrity, had quelled her ugly suspicions, but now, like ghosts arisen from graves, they had returned to haunt her.

The house was all too quiet. For the past week Masa has been the only member of the family living in the place. Ever since that day of near tragedy, the child Et-chan had taken an aversion to solid food, refusing to be tempted by the delicacies offered her, thereby losing much weight, and Rumi, quite distraught, had taken her daughter to Kamakura, saying politely but determinedly, "My own sensible mother will bring Et-chan back to health."

Renzō had agreed, and after escorting his wife and daughter to Kamakura, he traveled to a distant southern township to purchase a collection of Satsuma ware, and cream-colored pottery, glazed to give a cracked effect and decorated with enamel colors and matte gold.

Shinichi, his brow furrowed and more determined than ever to excel in his studies, had received permission to board with the family of his American teacher of the English language. "It's imperative that I learn to use the language masterfully. I repeat, *imperative*, Father."

Renzō, gazing at his son thoughtfully, said, "So be it, then. But, Shin-chan, keep in mind that youth, so short a time in one's life, is irretrievable. . . ."

Irretrievable? Masa shivered as she thought of that ominous word and went to sit before her floor-desk. The drawers of the desk, and several chests, held the poems and short plays she had written over the years. Although saddened at the thought of destroying them, she felt it would be wise, for they held her most secret thoughts, and she preferred to have no one see them after her demise which, in all truth, could not be too far off. However, that task could wait. At present she had a more pressing affair to deal with.

Sitting erect, her hands moving with precision, she took up the special-delivery letter that had been brought to the house during the day. After perusing it for the third time, she set her face into stern lines and murmured, "I shall not reply to this strange epistle. I shall myself travel to Yokohama and deal with the matter in person. . . ."

Lady Masa sat crushed in a second-class compartment of the train speeding along the Tokaido line toward Yokohama.

Once in the port city, she noticed that ocean-going steamers at anchor in the harbor had taken precedence over the sailing vessels, and she was amazed at the huge navy yards, the newly arisen hotels, and the strange architectural styles of many private Western-style dwellings lining the streets.

Her ricksha runner deposited her at the Sacred Heart Church, the first Christian shrine built in Japan for over three centuries.

Exhausted by the strain of her journey, she sat down on one of the oaken pews, feeling agitated, but at the same time grimly determined to speak with the man who had written to her, one Father Joseph.

Disturbed by a touch on her shoulder, Masa was unable to think coherently as she gazed up into the face of one of her fellow countrymen, who wore the black robes of Christian priesthood.

"May I assist you?" the priest asked. "Excuse me, but are you not well, Lady?"

Gathering her thoughts together, she replied, saying, "Thank you. I have traveled from Edo—from Tokyo, to commune with one at this address. One by the name of Father Joseph. Would you kindly escort me to him?"

"I am he."

Father Joseph escorted her into an antechamber, patiently explaining his reason for writing to her. "Lady Masa, some months back a frail man named Sudo arrived here, offering his services as a cleaner, determined to receive no monetary reward for his labors. I urged him to reconsider the matter, but to no avail. He, Sudo, remained adamant and I, who am constantly amazed at people's behavior, spoke to my superior, who agreed to the man's unusual request. May I assume, Lady Masa, that you yourself are one of us?"

At that point Father Joseph glanced meaningfully at a framed picture on the wall depicting a beauteous blue-eyed, blond-haired man who held in his hand a bright red heart.

Not quite understanding, she gestured in the negative, and he bowed, saying, "Ah, then it will behoove me to explain to you that we, of the church, take every care never to violate rules laid down by the Holy Father in Rome. You understand?"

Once more she gestured in the negative and the priest spoke on, saying, "The man, Sudo, came here day after day, engaging himself in the most humble work and, without doubt, during those months he must have become deeply attracted to the faith. In no way do we underestimate his sincerity. He was intending to leave Japan. However, last week he fell prone to a sudden illness and, fearing that his days were numbered, he pleaded to be given the last rites. Unfortunately we were unable to honor his request. Now that he has gone, we find ourselves in a quandary."

Father Joseph leaned back, his hands clasped, gazing at Masa.

"So," she murmured. "So, he has gone? He recovered? Please assure me . . ."

Raising a hand to interrupt her, he said, "Excuse my clumsiness. Regretfully, Sudo is dead. The purpose of my letter to you is this. Among his meager belongings was a large sum of money, together with a written request that it be used to build a memorial here, in the church's precincts. A memorial inscribed to the memory of his parents.

"Once again, Lady Masa, I *stress*, the Church goes to great lengths not to violate rules. Just as we were unable to give the blessed sacraments to a dying man who could not substantiate the claim of being a Roman Catholic, we are, of course, unable to use his money as he requested. Among his belongings was your name and address. Therefore, we assumed that there was some connection. . . . A family relationship? Is that so?"

After a long pause, Masa murmured, "A family relationship? Not so."

"But, you knew him?"

"For many years I knew him."

"As . . . ?"

"As . . . ?" She hesitated, then said firmly, "As a good man. In all ways—a good man."

"Ah so!" Obviously dissatisfied, Father Joseph continued, his manner and tone gentle but persistent. "You know of his family background?"

"Yes. Sudo was the only child of good parents. They worked on a rice farm belonging to my husband's family."

"In Uraga?"

"In Uraga."

"So, you knew them, the parents, personally?"

"Unfortunately—no."

"Lady Masa, can you *substantiate* the deceased man's claim? Were his old parents Roman Catholics—*practicing* Roman Catholics?"

Filled with disdain, she glanced at the priest, saying scathingly, "*Practicing* Roman Catholics? If so, they would not have died peacefully. They would have been imprisoned, yes, or decapitated."

The priest flushed deeply before saying, "Of course, of course! One's apt to forget those old days."

"So it seems!" Masa was trembling with anger and sadness that the deceased henchman should have insults rained upon him even while in the spirit world. "Allow me to stake my honor!" she declared. "I believe implicitly that Sudo was sincere where his good parents were concerned."

"You—*believe*! Ah, yes. But, are you able to *substantiate* his claim?"

Pale and shaken by the insult, Masa rose to her feet, saying coldly, "Before taking my departure, may I say that your church's addiction to the laws of substantiation appear excessive to the extreme. Excuse me, but I'm forced into stating my opinions."

Gesturing for silence, she continued even more coldly. "Kindly inform me where Sudo San lies. I wish to pay tribute to him."

Father Joseph, now quite humbled, escorted her a short distance away from the church and there, in a spirit-chilling graveyard, he led her through graveled paths, past marbled tombstones, then farther beyond to a fenced portion where mounds of earth were dotted here and there.

Halting at one such mound, the priest said gently, "Sudo lies here. In unconsecrated ground. You understand?"

"I understand. Thank you for your trouble." Masa's bow to the priest was so slight it was scarcely discernible. It was a dismissal and he left.

She lingered on awhile, turning her gaze outward to the ocean, imagining that Sudo was alive, on the high seas making his way toward a happier clime than the one in which he had spent his downtrodden life. . . .

While traveling from Tokyo toward Yokohama, Masa had had it in mind to journey by carriage along the Marine Drive, away from the main city to Hommoku Bay, where she would gaze up again to the pine-clad hill upon which stood the old home she had lived in for the greatest part of her life.

However, the long trek on foot from the graveyard into the bustling city, combined with her sadness and her anger, had wearied not only her body but also her mind, and with every step she took she realized the futility of dwelling on the past.

While awaiting her return in the long queue at the railway's ticket office, she was unaware of the curious, admiring glances of bystanders attracted by her distinguished appearance. The train's compartment was overcrowded, and when an elderly foreign man insisted that she should take the seat he vacated for her, she accepted his courteous act gratefully.

Arriving back in the capital, Masa engaged a hired carriage to take her, not to the house in Nihombashi, but to the Fukuda home in Yoyogi. In dire need of comfort, she yearned to be with one who remembered not only Sudo, but life as it had been before the years had stolen her youth away.

Bathed and robed in one of Sumiko's soft cotton sleeping garments, Masa sat relaxing, enjoying being fussed over by her sister-in-law in the cozy little room. "Sumiko," she murmured, "your understanding and your kindness give me the feeling of being a child again. It's so comforting to be here with you."

"I'm more than honored! Masa, to *whom* else should you fly in times of stress? Plainly, your feathers have been cruelly ruffled. Now, here in this quiet nest, please be at peace. I've ordered us the *most* comforting of all repasts. Together now, let us sup these bland, steaming hot noodles. *Buckwheat*—my husband's favorite! Please, commence eating."

"I've little desire to eat. . . ."

"Masa, take up your chopsticks—eat!" Sumiko commanded with mock severity, and as Masa obeyed the order the two women broke into laughter. They felt perfectly at ease and saw each other, not as elderly, but simply as delightful, lifelong companions.

Invigorated after the nourishing noodles, Masa took the initiative and launched into a modified description of the day's events. Not wishing to distress Sumiko, she prudently left out certain details, and dwelt instead on the sadness of Sudo's lonely death and his failed career.

"Sumiko, do you by any chance know anything about his parents?"

"Certainly. They worked for my father for many years with absolute dedication."

"Yes. Yes, that I also know. But, do you, by any chance, know if they were of the Buddhist faith?"

"I think not. Masa, my hazy memory is that the Sudo family had the reputation of living secluded lives, of seldom leaving the confines of the farm."

"Is that so?"

"Yes. And, Masa, thinking back, even as a youth, Sudo kept himself apart from the other students at the school. No?"

"Yes." Masa sat examining the palms of her hands as she murmured, "Sumiko, could that humble family trio have belonged to the forbidden Christian sect?"

Sumiko sat pondering deeply, then said, her tone one of amazement, "Masa, that could be so! Your question gives me much food for thought. Certainly, there was more to the henchman than met the eye. . . ."

Breaking off in midstream, she gazed toward the dozing cockatoo, then murmured, "In a way, Sudo was a 'new-thought' man, was he not?"

As though having been prodded awake, the bird raised his crest and hopped about agitatedly on his perch. Masa laughed, then said tentatively, "Sumiko, what a diabolical chortle Cocky-chan has. In the most complimentary way, may I say that suddenly I'm reminded of your dear husband."

Sumiko smiled triumphantly and spread her arms wide as though to gather everything that was dear to her heart close into her embrace. "Masa," she whispered, "Masa, older sister, only *you* in all the world could have pleased me so much. . . ."

Relieved that her comment had been accepted without rancor, Masa sat by while Sumiko wept a little, then carefully folded and placed the tear-dampened tissue in the nearby wastebasket, saying, "Yes, well, now, where were we? Masa, of what were we speaking?"

"Of Sudo."

"Of course! So . . . well, yes, it could be that he and his old parents were of that minority who practiced the forbidden faith. But, Masa, there is no way to *substantiate* the matter. And, truthfully, I would prefer that we move on to more cheerful subjects. Do you mind?"

"Not at all." Masa, upset at having the priest's detestable word thrown at her by Sumiko, decided to put all thoughts of Sudo out of her mind for the time being.

Later, she would visit the Sacred Heart Church once again, and demand that the money Sudo had left be used as he had so desired.

Now, her face alight with joy, Sumiko spoke about her son's expected return to Japan and about Aiko, her "beloved" daughter-in-law, who was so soon to present her with that long-awaited grandchild. "Is it not wondrously happy news, Masa? At last, a grandchild—at last . . ."

Masa suppressed her ugly suspicions behind an unflinching smile and encouraged Sumiko to give full rein to thoughts of the bright future ahead.

She tried, as far as was possible, to keep her mind alert, but at times Sumiko's voice seemed incoherent, as though coming from a distant place. The voice was comforting and dear to her heart.

How could it be otherwise?

Sumiko, the little girl first met so many years back . . .

Kenichi's young sister . . .

Renzō's aunt Sumiko . . .

So many memories . . .

Ah, yes, all so long ago . . .

Renzō, a tiny boy perched high in the old oak tree, looking out toward the horizon as the red disc of the sun appeared. His treble voice, exultant, calling—"New day! A new day . . ."

But—now it was Sumiko's voice calling out to her loudly, urgently. "Masa . . . ? Masa . . . ?"

Hurried footsteps were heard in the corridors as servants came running. The room was filled with loud, anxious voices.

Masa felt as though she was being caught up into those swirling autumn mists in which she had always taken such melancholy joy.

Pressing one hand above her heart, she bowed her head low, so low that her forehead rested on the *tatami* floor. . . . Vaguely she felt that she was paying homage, homage not to those already departed from the world, but to those whom she had known and loved so dearly during her lifetime. . . .

WHEN THE ORNATE CLOCK IN Sir John Coomber's study struck ten silvery chimes, he had been working industriously for five hours.

Now he sat in an easy chair awaiting the arrival of his wife's maid to announce that the lady of the house had awakened and was partaking of her morning meal.

To all outward appearances he seemed to be half asleep, but he was, in fact, quite alert. His alertness was aided by the pinch of snuff he had just taken. Unlike many other men of his age, he had remained a "snuffer" instead of taking to the popular cigar or cigarette that had come into vogue early in the century.

Several of his colleagues had taken to sniffing cocaine. He had tried it but found it altogether too stimulating. Also, he feared that the substance could become addictive and produce a craving which could be injurious, and lessen the time he hopefully believed was still allotted to him.

Hidden beneath the affability of his nature, there was a steely edge that surfaced only when he was denied what he was determined to obtain. Now, aged sixty-four and due to retire from the diplomatic service, he had come to a crossroad and he knew the path he would tread. His mind was firmly made up, but so far he had refrained from mentioning those future plans to Marjorie. With all sincerity he hoped she would face the situation without too much dismay.

Sir John had never experienced fierce heats of passion, anger, or fear. His life had been pleasantly mild in all respects. But recently, he had been disturbingly and utterly seduced, not by a woman, but by a delightful substitute—a country.

He was in love with Japan and its myriad attractions which provided him with countless nerve-tingling surprises and emotions. He had gathered about himself a coterie of highly discerning Japanese scholars, each one entrenched in the arts, especially in the field of poetry.

In all cultures poets were respected and it was especially so in Japan. He, sadly no poet, was more than content translating their works into his native tongue. Sir John was determined to dedicate the remainder of his life to the preparation of a volume of poems for publication. It was no easy task. The poems were so concise and hit one with the force of arrows shot from tightly strung bows.

> *Glint of hoe*
> *Lifted high up:*
> *Fields of summer.*

Yes! Just nine words and there it all was!

Gradually, he was coming to understand the spirit of *wa*, the Japanese philosophy of "give and take," of placing top priority on harmony for the mutual welfare of all concerned.

Wa had begun long ago, in small rice-growing villages when oppressive farm rentals and land taxes had given farmers no choice other than to work closely together in order to exist. Now the philosophy continued on in many forms of enterprise.

Sir John believed that *wa* was unique to Japan. He found it admirable that if a worker fell ill his fellow workers, without any thought of remuneration, took over the job until the ailing man was fully recovered. In times of bereavement it was customary that a joint solatium be offered, thus everyone shared in both times of happiness and ill fortune. There were times when Sir John wondered if the spirit of *wa* would continue to exist into the future, especially in the large business concerns which were springing up in Japan. He thought it was unlikely.

He was also coming to understand many Japanese patterns of behavior. Personally, he disliked physical contact with strangers and he admired the aloofness of the Japanese bow, the custom of standing apart, showing recognition and respect by inclinations of one's head instead of the clutching of hands. He thought it quite charming too that one never made a call without taking along a simple gift-offering which was never alluded to and never opened until after the departure of the caller.

Gradually, he was learning. Still, he was so often at a loss, indeed quite irritated by the Japanese habit of giving a positive reply to any proposition put forward. That habit was causing havoc and distrust in business circles. His friend Renzō Yamamoto explained that a Japanese person quite often replied on a positive note *not* because he agreed, but because he was seeking to avoid disharmony. The habit was instinctive, since during the long years of feudalism an outright "refusal" would have meant the loss of one's head.

"Try to understand," Renzō said, "that yes in this country usually means yes, I *understand* your statement, your proposition, but . . . It does not mean yes, I shall go along with it."

Sir John was doing his utmost to understand the alien culture he had fallen in love with. However, he had no interest in the sexual freedoms. Secretly, he had always found the mechanics of sexual behavior comical to the extreme, and after the birth of his second son he had made up his mind that he was once and for all done with the extraordinary business. Although the matter had never been openly discussed between them, he believed that his wife was also pleased to be relieved of those occasional bedtime tussles they had gone through together. If Marjorie had ever indulged herself with other partners, she had done so with extraordinary style and finesse.

Moving to his desk, he took up a white envelope banded with black and white, containing a small sum of money. Weighing it in his hand, he was pleased that Marjorie had advised him of the fact that a family in mourning was by custom obliged to return a gift-tribute, that if donations were rich, return tokens would have to be in kind. Ah, yes, so many strict stylized customs to learn of.

Sir John frankly admitted that he had no desire to probe too deeply beneath the surface of Japanese culture, but he was becoming more and more attracted to the philosophies of Shintoism and Buddhism, particularly the latter. . . .

Ah, at last, Marjorie's maid, Toki San, was in the doorway, bowing and gesturing to him. . . .

On entering Marjorie's room, he blew several kisses her way, voicing his customary cheery morning salutation, "Heigh-ho, my dearest!"

"Heigh-ho, my dearest," she responded after swallowing down a mouthful of the oversweetened cocoa she favored. "How splendid you look all togged up formally so early in the day."

"And how charming you look. So cozy, eh."

"I'm much too fat."

"Not a bit of it and your complexion is as lovely as ever. I'm duty bound to pay a condolence call. Hence my dress."

"Who has taken off? Someone I know?"

"Not sure on that, my dearest . . ." Sir John grimaced, gesturing that he preferred not to join his wife in drinking cocoa from her cup, exclaiming firmly, "No, no. I only enjoy drinking Japanese tea. So sharp, so cleansing to the palate. Yes, but in reply to your query, Renzō Yamamoto's mother has passed away. Died suddenly, unexpectedly I've been told."

"The Lady Masa! Aiko Fukuda's aunt! How regrettable. I believe she was a most interesting woman. My dearest, did I ever mention to you that Renzō Yamamoto had an affair with Hilda Turton while he was in London?"

"Yes. I mean, yes, you've mentioned it many times. Can't say I admire his taste, but let's not dwell on the unspeakable. Little can be said with any certainty about the affairs and moralities of others. Tell me, what plans have you for the day?"

"Oh, my dearest, too many, but if you so wish I'll drop them without a pang. Should I accompany you to the Yamamoto house?"

"Not necessary, my dearest. But ..." Sir John hesitated as he experienced a sinking feeling, then, bearing up, he said, "I would appreciate it if we could spend an hour tête-à-tête later on in the day to discuss a matter of some importance to me."

"My dearest, but certainly." Marjorie's dimples deepened as she smiled. "But why not allow me to allay your fears and apprehensions now, at this moment?"

"Fears? Apprehensions? How well you know me. But, Marjorie, in your wildest imaginings you could not conjure up that which I wish to speak of."

"A wager of one pound that I can't guess?"

"Make that two."

"Two it is. Three guesses?"

"Three."

"Four pounds if my first guess is correct? Right on the nose."

"Five."

"Good! Now I shall be able to purchase a *divine* gold lacquer bowl I've been hankering after."

Sir John gazed at his good-natured wife some twenty years his junior, and as he gazed he felt that the time was not yet ripe to let her know that not only did he wish to stay on, live out the remainder of his life in Japan, but that he fully intended to do so.

Meanwhile, what could he possibly bring forth to replace the truth?

"What was that you said, my dearest?" he queried.

"I said—first guess! You would like us to stay on in Japan after retirement. Come, my dearest, pay up!"

Never before had Sir John Coomber been so shattered. There she was, so plump, complacent, and smiling at him as though he were as easy to see through as a child of tender years. And *we* she had said. "*We* should stay on in Japan." But ...?

"But ..." he stammered. "What of the boys, our sons ...?"

"What of them?" Marjorie waved a finger of toast as she cried airily. "Humphrey and Rupert will delight in visiting us. I speak for myself, of course, but I've become so enamored of Nippon that the very thought of bidding it *sayōnara* in the near future tears at my heart. My dearest, could we maybe lease a Japanese house? Live *tatami*-style."

As his wife burbled on in her warm, expressive manner, Sir John,

quite unconscious of his actions, went to her bedside and poured a
stream of dark, warm cocoa into her cup and drank it to the dregs,
relishing the cloying sweetness. After placing the cup back on the
tray, he took her hand, saying warmly, "I can think of no appropriate words with which to express my delight. . . ."

Driving through the streets of Tokyo toward Nihombashi, Sir
John wondered if anyone had ever traveled to pay a condolence call
upon a bereaved household with so merry a heart as his.

SPRING ARRIVED AND RUMI WAS acutely aware of Renzō's grief
over the Lady Masa's death and his withdrawal from everyday life,
but some inner voice warned her from attempting to alleviate the
tensions in the melancholy house.

On learning of Lady Masa's death, she had hastened back from
Kamakura to Tokyo, leaving Etsu in Keiko's care. While traveling
on the train, although saddened and shocked, she was unable to
prevent a surge of satisfaction on realizing that at long last she was
to be the mistress of her home.

Rumi sympathized and believed that she understood the trauma
Renzō had undergone on arriving home to discover that his mother
had died so suddenly, without any warning signals of ill health.

The circumstances had macabre overtones, for Lady Masa's body
had been carried through the night from the Fukuda mansion to lie
in the Nihombashi house, awaiting her son's return and her burial.

Sumiko's demeanor was admirable. She hid her grief and took
complete charge of the formal proceedings, choosing the correct
garments, the correct accessories, and allowing no hands other than
her own and Rumi's to robe the body of the woman so deeply loved
by her.

Telephone calls, telegrams, and urgent letters had been sent out
with the news of Masa's demise. All mirrors were covered, incense
was burning, and when Renzō finally entered the house, it was Sumiko who greeted him, on her knees, bowing deeply. Finally she
led him into the room where Lady Masa lay on a simple pallet,
covered with the crested cloak of black, the family sword beside
her. His mother was even more dignified in death than she had been
in life. . . .

Three months had now gone by since that bitter January day, and

Rumi was hoping that her husband might at least show some interest in his children. And perhaps some appreciation of his wife, who had dealt with the aftermath of the funeral, received callers, opened the condolence envelopes, written the names of the donors and the token amounts of money, then decided exactly on the appropriate gifts of thanks to be returned.

Certainly Renzō had followed all customary requirements with dignity, paying the many calls courtesy demanded to thank those who had paid homage to the passing of Lady Masa. "Such a variety of people," as Rumi had written to her mother, "from the Imperial Palace downward to the local fishmonger."

One donation brought to the house was anonymous and puzzling to the extreme. A large amount of money was delivered, so Rin had explained, by a Japanese priest of the Roman Catholic faith, without an enclosed note or an address. The matter was altogether too mysterious, but when she had mentioned it to Renzō he had merely shrugged and muttered, "Deal with the matter as you think fit."

Innately impatient and eager to enjoy the brighter side of life once more, Rumi donated the cash to a Buddhist shrine. She donated it as it had been received, anonymously, and then she put the matter out of her mind.

Now, having attended to all the formalities, she was feeling utterly at a loss. It was as though she sat in a splendid carriage, the reins in her hands, but there were no horses to drive. . . .

When his father, Kenichi, had died, Renzō had been physically overcome by the depth of his sorrow. He had wept uncontrollably and run out into the storm, to stand buffeted by the winds on a high cliff, as he shouted out, "Father . . . Father . . . Father . . ."

The death of his mother, however, had gripped him in a cold, iron vise. The warm glow he had dwelt in all his life had suddenly been doused. There was no consolation. He would awake with a start during the night, and painful memories would assail him.

How could he have been so callous, to have torn his mother away from the paradise she had made for herself in the old Yokohama house . . . ? She had never complained. How could he have so insulted her, by forcing her to live in Nihombashi? And how could he have placed the courtesan, Osen, in pride of place over his mother . . . ?

Distressed beyond measure, he would rise and trudge along silent, unlit streets, not troubling to shelter when rain fell, and return home

sodden, his heart heavy. At home, he was even more distressed once
he became aware of Rumi's true feelings. He understood them, but
disliked being in her company and shied away from any talk about
the past or the future.

He had instructed her to put seals on the chests and desks where
the Lady Masa's private papers were kept. He knew that Ohara's
wife had arrived at the house one morning with the honored obligation of going through his mother's store of personal belongings,
to decide which articles should be presented to family members and
close friends. He knew, but he had refused to recognize that the
time-honored ceremony had taken place.

For some time Shinichi had taken to addressing his parents as
Papa and Mama in place of *Otōsama* and *Okāsama*. He had no objections. It had become fashionable. One morning he overheard his son
saying "Mama, it seems as though Papa has forgotten how to smile."
His wife said disapprovingly, "I agree with you. I long to hear
laughter in this dear home once more. . . ."

Dear home? He found the place unendurable. He recalled how in
ancient days when a death took place a family would move out of
their small dwelling, often burning it to the ground or just leaving
it to fall down from neglect. Well, times had changed over the many
centuries, and if he set fire to this Tokyo house, he would be imprisoned and branded as an arsonist.

He resented Nakasone's attempts to coerce him into affairs of
business, and continued on his lonely mournful path. Even the
charms of his small daughter, Etsu, failed to cheer him. The sound
of casual chatter and laughter also filled him with resentment. When
dusk fell he would order the servants not to light the lamps, and
when his wife sensibly insisted they should be lit, he would leave
the house to roam about the city, compelling his mind into a state
of blankness.

He shied away from any contact with the Fukuda family, knowing only too well that the sight of his aunt Sumiko could cause him
the utmost despair. From Rumi he learned that Yuichi and Aiko had
returned from China. Then Yuichi arrived at the Nihombashi house
to make his obligatory condolence call. Renzō behaved impeccably,
nodding and bowing to his cousin's very sincere regrets at the sad
loss of Lady Masa.

He nodded and bowed also to his cousin's comments concerning
the delicate condition of his wife, Aiko. "My wife has been advised

to live most gently until the birth of our expected child. The doctor warns that the birth could be premature. . . ."

That mention of Aiko sent a throb of pain through his being, and he longed to be with her, not for any other reason but that he knew Aiko had had a true empathy with his mother.

One afternoon, exhausted from several months of suffering insomnia, he was horrified on seeing a funeral procession making its way toward him along the crowded road. Hastily, he entered the grounds of a Shinto shrine to wait until the depressing sight disappeared.

Once in the grounds of the shrine, there was no way that Renzō could have known that his father, Kenichi, had stood on the exact spot many, many years ago, filled with jealousy as he spied on Osen the courtesan, who had stolen his heart. Nevertheless, he was overcome with the strangest of feelings and sniffed at the air as animals sniff immediately before an earthquake occurs.

No such disruption took place, and from his vantage point, unseen, he watched as his wife, accompanied by his son and daughter, passed beneath the swaying branches of the willows. Bemused, he gazed about and realized that spring was well under way. He had not noticed.

As the familiar trio drew closer, he saw that Rumi's expression was joyless. He saw that she was not walking in her usual sprightly manner and that the children seemed to have lost the sparkle of untroubled childhood. In a flash, he was struck by how petulantly self-involved he had been over the last months.

Enough—enough!

Motivated by an upsurge of warm, protective feelings, he strode from his hiding place, calling out cheerfully, "Well met! How nice . . ."

The children greeted him with gladness, but Rumi was startled and gazed at him nervously. That night she wept a little, saying, "I'm not sad. Just so relieved. I feared you would never want to share my pillow again. It has been so long. . . ."

"What nonsense you talk," he replied, and went on to speak long and seriously, saying that not only did he appreciate all she had done over the past months but that he also needed her opinions and her advice on certain matters.

Rumi responded to his mood as wilting plants respond to a timely shower of rain, and was excited to learn that he had the idea of leasing out the house in Nihombashi. "I agree," she exclaimed. "It's filled with too many memories."

"Yes—too many memories. We, you and I, must begin anew."

"So, you intend moving back to the house on the hill in Yokohama, then?" she queried tentatively.

"No, no. Too many memories there also. Together we shall find a new home."

"Where, where?"

"We shall search and find a place pleasurable to us both."

To his slight irritation, Rumi began to weep again, murmuring, "If this be but a dream, *please* don't disturb it."

"It's no dream," Renzō replied with calm authority. "Now that my mother is no longer with us, I miss the atmosphere of having an elder in our home. I would be pleased if *your* mother would agree to join our family circle."

Both his mind and his body were wearied; nevertheless, he pleased his wife further by making love to her, not with passion but gently, then lying by her side, listening to her quiet breathing, he realized that one more of life's storms was almost over and done with.

Careful not to disturb Rumi's sleep, he made his way along the dark corridor to his mother's vacant room. Hesitating just for an instant, he then slid back the door and entered the chamber and after some fumbling he lit the *andon*.

Sitting alone in the flickering light, he buried his face in his hands and wept soundlessly. . . .

YUICHI FUKUDA WAS NO LONGER dependent on the chirping crickets he had once kept in the fragile bamboo cage. With remarkable self-assurance he was moving into areas of bureaucracy and international business dealings. He was greatly aided in social circles having been honored with the title of baron.

As a man who had no interest in gambling, easy women, or heavy bouts of drinking, he had gained the reputation for consistency, of being able to cope responsibly with countless problems.

The founding of the Bank of Japan made it possible for millions of citizens who were previously mere slaves working for the privileged class to become their own masters by opening bank accounts.

Many sons of farmers and artisans were being accepted as students into colleges and universities. They were youths who had no memory or knowledge of the conditions of the country before their birth. They had gained political status and were now all proud, free subjects of the emperor. In Yuichi's opinion, they were to be pitied, for he realized that in all probability many were doomed to be maimed or killed on battlefields when the country became caught up in wars in the future.

Yuichi believed that a shrine should be built and dedicated to the god "Hypocrisy." In the old days, Japan's fighting power had been restricted to the hereditary samurai caste. But now the soldiery came from all classes, forming an army with modern weapons whose evolution was progressing rapidly with the training and much-valued advice from countries in the Western world. Japan's citizens had little liking for their army, but as an island nation who had lived so long in terror of foreign invaders, they had pride and deep respect for their navy, the nucleus of which had been formed by the gift of two war vessels, one from Queen Victoria and the other from Holland.

The Fukuda Corporation had invested large amounts of money in the building of the country's first ironclad warship built in England in 1878. Following that dramatic investment, a naval force was being built up and trained by British officers under the command of Sir Archibald Douglas. The ramrod spit and polish of the British was so admired throughout Japan that there was nothing more elevating than to have a son gain a cadetship for an illustrious naval career.

Yuichi had no such ambitions. How could one have a son, nurture him, glory in him, then have him killed for no other reason than to further the finances of those involved in the manufacturing of armaments? Or, as fools would have it, for the glory of the emperor? No. Although he had no set pattern for *his* son's future, he would make sure that he would be protected from such a meaningless fate.

He had liked and had admired his aunt Masa and regretted her passing, but from his point of view her death had been timely. The woman's relatives and friends had been so grief-stricken that little interest had been given to Aiko's pregnancy and to the supposedly premature birth of the child she had carried.

"My joy is entwined with sadness," his mother cried out on the morning of Kentaro's arrival.

"I understand," he said. "Time will soothe your grief Mother, then you will take full joy in your grandson."

"Yes. Yes, certainly," she replied. However, and much to his disappointment, she appeared to find more delight in her ridiculous parrot than in the perfectly formed child.

"My mother's attitude is strange," he said to Aiko some months after the infant's birth. "Surely you agree with me?"

"The river of her life is drying up. Your mother grows old, she begins to live in the past." Aiko spoke absently, adding, "Her lack of intense interest in the child should please you."

"It evidently pleases you."

"It does."

"How about that other one, then?"

"Renzō? *His* lack of interest in the child must surely please both of us. No?"

"Naturally." Yuichi shrugged as though attempting to relieve an itch on his back. "He pays little enough attention to his own children."

"Not so. He has much delight in his daughter."

"True. But, when I'm in the vicinity, Et-chan always comes running to *my* side. Haven't you noticed?"

"I have. All children are attracted to you."

"I wonder why?"

"They recognize a certain element in your character."

"What, *which* element?"

"A childlike one."

"Is that so!" Yuichi, at first pleased, then aware of a slightly contemptuous tone in his wife's voice, gazed at her intently, and she gazed back at him steadily, her eyebrows raised. "Are you aware," he asked, "that for some time now you have developed a certain characteristic? One which I find positively nasty."

"Is that so?"

"Yes. I dislike it. Your tongue is so often in your cheek, your eyebrows are raised. Cynicism is unbecoming in a woman."

"Hmmm . . ." Aiko bowed in mock humility. "You must excuse me. I'm aware of this habit, but I prefer to have it described as quizzical rather than cynical."

"You must cure yourself of it. I insist."

"Is that so?" She spoke artlessly with a look of faint amusement. "How very direct you have become. Tell me, is it your title, so expensively purchased, that has wrought this change in you?"

"Change? Nonsense! My title was *not* purchased but well deserved. Come, let's cease this quibbling. It is disastrous to one's spirit. Of that I'm certain." Yuichi gestured dramatically. "Yes, enough of such chatter. Please cure yourself of your unpleasant facial contortions."

"Certainly I'll do my utmost. Yes, at all costs."

That quizzical expression, tongue in cheek, raised eyebrows, remained a characteristic in Aiko. Beneath her derisive façade she hid feelings of guilt and anguish which upset the balance of her existence.

Never once had she regretted having conceived Renzō Yamamoto's child, thereby supplying her husband with a son to bear his name. Never once had Yuichi mentioned the outrageous sacrifice which she, his wife, had made for his dignity.

"I am with child," she had said calmly, even casually one night as they lay on their *futon* in the dark chamber.

"I'm glad." He replied just as casually, just as calmly.

So it had been. He had accepted the travesty of his fatherhood with an ironic flair and from that moment on, and now, some three years later, he appeared to believe that he was indeed the man who had sired the child, Kentaro, who thrived and who was admired by one and all. Even strangers paused to exclaim, "Congratulations. Such a splendid boy!"

"This child shines like sunlight on a winter's day."

Kentaro's mother graciously denied those compliments as it befitted her. With every passing day she loved him more deeply, dreading the moment when Renzō Yamamoto would, without doubt, recognize the child as his son.

It was not in her nature to suffer too long in silence. One night as she lay by her sleeping husband, she made up her mind to share her burden. Prodding Yuichi awake, she said harshly, "We must speak together."

"What? What? Speak? Now? Speak of what?"

"Of the child. The matter is urgent."

Now Yuichi was wide-awake, all attention, his brow furrowed and his voice filled with concern. "Of Ken-chan? Is he ailing?"

"He is extremely well." As she spoke she lit a lamp.

Yuichi fixed his gaze disapprovingly on her. "I've no inclination to fritter the hours away chatting about inconsequential matters," he muttered. "How can you allow yourself to disturb my rest?"

"We must speak. I bore the child. I can no longer bear the dread I feel."

"Dread. Of what?" Yuichi stared closely into his wife's face, startled by her anguished expression then, reluctantly, he nodded his willingness to hear her.

Much to Aiko's own astonishment, she suddenly felt the need to torture the man of whom she had been so protective for so many years and in so many ways. She felt the need to have him bow low, to praise her, to thank her, and to admit the truth of their well-executed plans. They never spoke of them openly, but those plans had finally triumphed in the birth of the child who now lay breathing evenly on his small *futon* in the dimly lit room.

"Tell me," she drawled, "you do agree that our marriage is not exactly run of the mill?"

Mystified, he made no reply. "Please respond to my query," Aiko murmured.

"You insist?"

"Yes."

"Then, I agree that our marriage is unique. So . . . ?"

"So, excuse me, but I find it preposterous that you have shown no inclination to question me on certain matters these many years."

"You do?"

"I do."

Yuichi hesitated, then said gently, "My seeming disinterest implies no disrespect. Please know that I've always regarded those issues too delicate a matter for open discussion."

"Too delicate!" Aiko exclaimed scornfully. "Too *delicate*? You never cease to amaze me. *Indelicate* of me perhaps, but have you ever given thought to my feelings? To my emotions? Is it that you see me as a puppet made of cloth? Excuse *my* frankness, but you should know that I am of flesh. That blood runs through my veins. Does it not concern you that I, having experienced sexual intercourse, yes, with a virile, passionate man, may have not only the desire but also the intention of—"

"Enough!" Interrupting her, Yuichi spoke quietly. "Allow me to say directly—and I apologize for not having done so in the past—that I am far from being unfeeling and complacent. Where you are concerned, not only do I sympathize deeply but I suffer agonies of doubt and watch your every mood. Yes, I am gnawed by jealousy, imagining what took place between you and my cousin. . . ."

Yuichi's voice trailed off into silence, and the only sound in the room was the soft breathing of the sleeping child. Finally, Aiko murmured doubtfully, "Is what you say true?"

"It is true."

"I'm glad. I wish you had spoken like this before."

"I also." Yuichi paused, adding with a wry smile, "My fears prevented me from so doing. Tell me, must I remain always fearful?"

Aiko, cleansed of her anger but determined to clarify her true feelings, said, "I confess that at times I have been tempted to take up a dagger, cut off a lock of my hair, and send it to your cousin."

"Calling him back to you?"

"Calling him back to me."

"Poetical. Very. You have not done so."

"Of course not."

"But perhaps you will do so?"

Aiko smiled faintly. "It could be that Renzō might ignore my signal."

"You believe that?"

"No. I believe that he would be more than delighted."

"So? You believe that he relished his betrayal? That he would further betray me?"

"How very peculiar you are. Poor Renzō. We, you and I together, seduced and betrayed him. Come now, did we not?"

"We did. Yes. Frankly, there are times when in his company I have the impulse to touch my forehead to the ground in gratitude."

"Dangerous. He would wish to know your reason. Yes?"

"Exactly. I pity him."

"You do?"

"I do." Yuichi shook his head as though expressing deep regret. "How can it be otherwise. Compared to Shinichi and little Etsu, our boy stands out like a shining princeling. I never cease thanking the gods that Kentaro in no way bears any likeness to the Yamamoto clan."

"Ah! . . ." Aiko exclaimed. "Now—my reason for disturbing your sleep!" Rising up gracefully, she moved to the side of the sleeping child, then she beckoned Yuichi to join her and as they knelt together she whispered, "Look closely at him. Day by day he resembles her more. Day by day. Tell me, what are we to do? Tell me, how are we to deal with this undeniable likeness?"

"Likeness?" Yuichi stammered. "Likeness—to whom?"

Aiko made no reply. Covering her mouth with one hand, she gestured helplessly as Yuichi studied Kentaro's features intently. Then, ignoring her movement of intervention, he reached out to gather the boy into his arms, calling playfully, "Ken-chan, Ken-chan . . ."

Kentaro, all at once wide-awake, smiled, his eyes glinting mischievously, his lips stretched, closed. As though he had been knifed
in the back, Yuichi cried out, "How blind I have been." Crushing
the child close to his body, he added sternly, "Can it be that my
mother sees the resemblance?"

"All who knew Lady Masa must eventually become aware," Aiko
whispered fearfully.

"Yes. It's quite uncanny. Especially his strange smile . . ." Yuichi's
face darkened, then he turned to Aiko, saying briskly, "Only one
thing to do."

"Yes?" She breathed the words. "Tell me . . ."

"We can but brazen this out. Brazen it out. You understand?"

"Brazen it out? But . . ."

"Cease your agitation! Hush!" Yuichi now gave full attention to
the child, speaking playfully, promising him that wonderful things
were in store for obedient little boys who obeyed their father's orders. "So," he finished off, "Ken-chan now goes back to sleep. Yes?"

"Yes, Papa."

"So—you are asleep . . . ?"

The kneeling couple looked down at Kentaro, who lay still, his
eyes squeezed closed. "How lovely he is," Yuichi muttered. "Nothing must be allowed to discredit his life. *Nothing* . . ."

Yuichi and Aiko lay on their *futon*, Yuichi advising, Aiko listening
to the ideas he was putting forward. "In a way," Yuichi grunted,
"I find a rather pathetic charm in this situation. That is, where my
cousin is concerned. Unwittingly, he has gifted me with a child
whose veins run truly blue. One more noble than those other two
who carry *his* family name . . ."

"Please," Aiko interjected, "keep to the present. To the difficult
future . . ."

"Give me time. Let us view things not with foreboding but rather
with supreme confidence. Now, I see this as a rather impressive
drama."

"This talk is all so idiotic, so . . ."

"Not so. Obviously you hear gongs clashing and war cries. Empty
your mind of such things. Should we live in dread of Renzō finally
waking up to the fact that *he* has been abused? No. We must move
in, take command. Set the stage, so to speak. Yes, with subtlety you
shall draw his attention to Ken-chan's extraordinary resemblance to
Lady Masa. You shall have him know that *without doubt* you bore
not my child but his."

"This talk is not merely idiotic but disastrous. You underestimate your cousin."

"Ah!" Yuichi's chuckle held a slightly insulting tone. "Certainly you know him with an—" He hesitated, then added, "Shall I say— on a more *intimate* level than I."

"I object to that salacious remark."

"You do? So, then, I take it back. Now, to continue . . . Keep calm. Pay attention. This is the script we shall create. . . ."

"We are not about to present a drama on the Kabuki stage."

"Agreed. However, we are about to present a drama in real life and I'm determined that it be successful. Are you all attention?"

"Desperately so."

"Excellent. Now, put yourself in Renzō's place. He has violated the decency of family relationships, he has carried on an illicit affair with the wife of his cousin. There, he feels some guilt, or I must presume so. He discovers that a child has come from that dishonorable, adulterous affair. So, then . . ." Yuichi chuckled. "What is our samurai to do? Will he become enraged? Will he come out into the open? Announce to the world that he made a cuckold of his cousin? Will he come, brandishing his rusty sword, to our estate and lay claim to the child he sired so lustfully? Will he? Now, will he?"

Once again the only sound in the room was the soft breathing of the sleeping child. Finally, Yuichi said, "Your silence irritates me beyond patience. Never mind! To continue, let me say that whatever Renzō's emotions, he can follow no other course but to accept the situation. Not graciously, but in agonized silence, once and forever. He will always see *himself* as the sinner and *I* as the man sinned against. No? Yes?"

"Oh, maybe so."

"I dislike the dubious tone in your voice. Tell me, during that . . ." Yuichi searched for the correct words. "During that summer *incident*, of course you kept my unfortunate ailment secret from my cousin?"

"But—of course."

"But—of course! Excuse that needless query. So, then, let us take comfort that as time goes by, the memory of my aunt Masa's visage will fade. Those in our small, intimate circle will in all probability gossip among themselves. That is of little consequence."

"Of little consequence?" Aiko gasped. "Not so . . ."

"It must be so. Renzō *alone* is of any import. It is up to you. You will manage most skillfully."

"I am helpless."

"You? Helpless?" Yuichi broke out into unrestrained laughter. "Haughty, overbearing, yes. Helpless? Never! I turn the drama's script over to you from this moment on. Deal with it well. Excuse me, but I am exhausted. I must sleep."

"Then, sleep well, *Baron*."

"Baron! Baron Fukuda! Ah, if only my father were alive to delight in the honor bestowed on his name."

"Yes," Aiko responded rudely. "Yes, and also the crazy old ancestor. That one from the lower depths who . . ."

"Haughty, unpleasant as usual. Good night. I refuse to be provoked. . . ."

Sɪʀ ᴊᴏʜɴ ᴀɴᴅ ʟᴀᴅʏ ᴄᴏᴏᴍʙᴇʀ had been occupying the Yamamoto house at Nihombashi for several years, and the once pristine chamber, the sanctuary of Lady Masa, would have been unrecognizable to her had she been alive. Undoubtedly, her sensibilities would have been wounded on seeing how the heavy chairs dragged over its surface had damaged the floor. Large tables, covered with books, papers, and writing implements now dominated and were surrounded by tall, ungainly bookcases. Her horror would have known no bounds had she seen that the *tokonoma*, once the shrine for precious bowls arranged with season flowers, was now heaped high with books and scrolls, both ancient and modern.

Her sense of humor might have been aroused on viewing Lady Coomber's diversity of decors in the various apartments of the house. Masa might also have approved because, without disrupting the classical structure of certain rooms, the Englishwoman had achieved a harmonious atmosphere by furnishing them with treasures collected during her many visits to other lands.

Marjorie Coomber's energy and joie de vivre had increased with the passing of time. To Sir John's quiet amusement, his wife spoke Japanese atrociously. Her unintentional errors appeared to endear her even more to the usually touchy, easily insulted Japanese folk she mingled with.

She had become a self-appointed expert on all things pertaining to Japan. During her annual visits to England she was greatly in demand to lecture at gatherings, where she presented her "Beloved

Nippon—a paradise on earth." She encouraged people to pack their steamer trunks and visit the land of "smiles and cherry blossoms, sparkling cleanliness, politeness, and servants who would undoubtedly lay down their very lives for those they worked for . . ."

Quite a number of people had taken her advice only to have been somewhat dismayed on discovering that Lady Coomber had neglected to mention earthquake shocks, typhoons, freezing weather, lack of heating, the trying humidity in the heat of summer, and the vicious mosquitoes. She had never warned them that many Japanese citizens, rather than smile, stared at foreign tourists not merely with open curiosity but with actual dislike.

Marjorie's greatest desire was to bring harmony and peace to the world about her. She worked industriously to achieve her objectives, unwitting of the havoc she quite often left in her wake.

Her friendship with Aiko Fukuda flourished, each woman having confidence in the other's capability to listen and to keep the other's secrets. Their relationship was so close that after months of separation they would meet again and exclaim joyously, "Yes, well, yes! Now, as we were last saying . . ."

One afternoon in late spring the two women were among the motley throng crossing the Nihombashi bridge located in the center of Tokyo. The bridge was the starting point of the five highways that led to places which had been of strategic importance during the rule of the old Tokugawa shogun government.

The sky was cloudless and the silhouette of Fuji San rose in the distance. "Aiko, I feel strongly," Marjorie exclaimed, "that I'm a reincarnated person, that in a former existence I passed over this very bridge among sword-carrying warriors and their attendants. Yes, reincarnated without doubt. How else should I feel this way?"

"Best I make no comment. Best hold on to your imaginings," Aiko murmured, glancing obliquely at her companion.

"That quizzical expression again!" Marjorie cried out. "Aiko, come, be honest with me."

"Well, I dislike disillusioning you, but, Marjorie, only one hour ago you purchased a scroll depicting the very scene you have just described."

"Spoilsport!" Marjorie laughed. "Yes, that's true. Pity! You should have left me with my lovely, uncanny thoughts."

"So I told you," Aiko murmured. "Marjorie, stay with the reincarnation idea. It somehow becomes you."

"I shall. Much more fun and, who knows, maybe true . . ."

"*I* think not, but my husband would certainly agree with you."

"Really? I must confess that I see the baron as a more realistic, even a harsh man."

"Oh, Yuichi has many faces. One, of a man ready at all times to gain access to information likely to further his success in the business world. Another, of a man possessed of a crude sense of humor. Then, at times I'm confronted by a husband whose simplicity resembles that of a child."

"How inconsistent! I could not deal with such a husband. I admire your acceptance of him."

"We agree to disagree," Aiko murmured. "He allows me much freedom."

"*Allows* you? Come, come, dearest. As we say in my country, 'tis you that wears the pants. Oh, that reminds me, why is it that you no longer dress in male attire?"

"Motherhood has wrought changes in me."

"Pity! That garb became you well. How overrated motherhood is. It's forced upon us. We agonize, bring forth squalling little brats, have them shoved into our arms, and society insists that we have joined the holy society of maternal bliss. Personally, I admit to lacking deep maternal feelings. I have borne two very nice, dear boys, but, shame on me, I've not once felt the urge to sacrifice my own desires for their convenience. By the way, does your complex baron revel in his late-come fatherhood?"

"Yes. He quite enjoys the child."

"Does he not urge you to produce another?"

"On the contrary. Yuichi is *more* than content to have Kentaro."

"He is?"

"Definitely."

"Then, I must begin to admire him. Excuse my curiosity, Aiko. I care for your happiness. I'm not skilled in diplomacy. So, may I come directly to the point?"

"Please do."

"I shall. Some problem is weighing you down? Could I be of some assistance?"

"Have I been so apparent? I apologize. Yes, I need, I crave your help." Aiko hesitated, then added, "On a delicate matter."

"To do with . . . ?" Marjorie's manner was brisk as she slowed her steps. "I'm all attention."

"It concerns Renzō."

"Ah-hah! Ah-hah, say no more." Marjorie gazed admiringly at Aiko. "How unfortunate that I no longer have the lovely Folly to offer you. Now, let me think. What alternative hideaway can I provide you with? Just give me time, or, is the matter urgent? Certainly it's unwise to rush."

"You misunderstand," Aiko murmured. "I'm not about to indulge myself, to once again carry on a furtive affair with the man in question."

"No?"

"How disappointed you sound," Aiko murmured. "What a delightfully wicked lady you are."

"Delightfully wicked? Thank you for the compliment. Truly, I am a bit let down. Never mind. So, tell on."

"Simply put," Aiko said loftily, "*that* liaison died a swift death, on my side, that is. Renzō and I are members of the same family and our occasional meetings are becoming fraught with dangerous undercurrents!"

"Ah-hah! I begin to see the light. Our handsome samurai is not content to let the affair end?"

"Exactly! Yes. My desire—my need—is to rendezvous with him, tête-à-tête, away from home grounds. To explain my feelings and, I hope, have him be content to remain my friend."

"Leave it to me. Rest easy, dearest. What are friends for? No need for further discussion."

While the two women bade each other farewell, Marjorie Coomber, a true romantic, felt a pang of sympathy for Renzō Yamamoto. Then, against her will, she doubted Aiko's sincerity, wondering why beads of perspiration dewed her brow even though a chill wind had arisen. . . .

R ENZŌ HAD PURCHASED A SMALL estate situated midway between Tokyo and Yokohama which had been the property of a feudal lord. Once he had the family settled there he began to enjoy the life of sophisticated rusticity that had become available to him.

The house was surrounded by high whitewashed walls and, although portions of the dwelling had been restored and modernized, it retained a definite martial atmosphere.

Any feelings of austerity were balanced by the affability and so-
ciability of the family who dwelt there. The house was encircled by
a small wood that was the haunt of squirrels and foxes.

Over the years, and somewhat to his amusement, his new home
had come to resemble a stylish wayside inn, a place where acquaintances were apt to drop in casually, announcing, "Just passing by . . ."
They were all received cordially, as were the many invited guests,
who were entertained royally by Rumi. She had come to view herself as a hostess of some standing and prided herself on having
prominent members of Tokyo's international society accept her hospitality and revel in the rustic surroundings.

Rather to Renzō's embarrassment, his wife seldom failed to mention "My father, the Count Okura . . ." "My sister, the Baroness
Fukuda . . ."

He also realized that she took some pains to hide the fact that her
own mother had once been a geisha. Keiko, all understanding, graciously melded into the background when members of the samurai
class appeared. However Rumi presented her mother proudly to
foreign guests who, quite naturally, believed that the stout, motherly woman was the widow of a nobleman.

He had settled down, if not content, then quite prepared to live
out the remainder of his life as a family man. Nakasone was more
than ever his right-hand man. Their business was flourishing and
no thought was given to the fact that while the money flowed in
the country was being denuded of its art treasures and the heirlooms
of once wealthy aristocratic families.

On one occasion Victor Caswell had crossed the ocean to visit
Japan. The Englishman's mind was still as sharp as a whiplash, and
he had brought with him a truly sacrificial gift. Holding out a small
painting, he exclaimed, "I always *intended* to gift you with this Monet, but I was too despicably mean to do so. Now—ho-hum, Prince
Yamamoto, it is yours to more than treasure."

Renzō regretted that his mother was no longer present to see the
delicate yet powerful work that portrayed her most favored of all
flowers, the water lily.

Victor did not linger in Japan. "Short and sweet has always been
my policy," he had announced. "Bad taste to overstay when business has been completed . . ." He had then remarked testily, "What
a muddle, a mishmash of East and West, Nippon has become."

"You find my country displeasing?" Renzō had replied.

"No. More than fascinating, but I wish I had known the country when you all lived here in a state of delightful innocence. Pity that state has been disturbed."

A disturbing event of another kind, one of heartwrenching proportions, occurred when Marjorie Coomber advised Renzō that Aiko Fukuda was eager to meet with him. His first reaction was to send his apologies to the lady in question, and let the waters of his existence remain unruffled. Then, memories of those clamorously passionate hours spent with Aiko rose up, and, without guilt and secure in his conceit, he hurried to answer her tantalizing signal.

On his way to keep the rendezvous, ten years seemed to drop from his shoulders. He was flattered that Aiko had sent out a message signifying that those tendrils she had so poetically mentioned some four years ago had not withered, and that she was willing to have them grow higher.

He admired her. She was so positive, never coy. He liked the idea of meeting with her, not furtively, but out in the open, on the high parapet overlooking Ueno Park. The weather was perfect and he halted for several moments beside the park's great lake, admiring the way the sunshine made its surface gleam like pale blue satin.

Climbing the ancient stone steps leading to the parapet, he grinned in embarrassment, admonishing himself, for his heart had begun to beat erratically, not from exhaustion but from eagerness.

Knots of tourists and pleasure seekers stood about, but he immediately saw Aiko standing alone, leaning against the railing, seemingly lost in meditation of the view. Moving swiftly to her side, he said in teasing tones, "Baroness Fukuda! But, how amazing! How splendid to find you—of all people here!"

Facing him she responded in a colorless voice. "Thank you for coming." She looked him straight in the eye for some time then she returned her full attention to the view.

At once, his feelings of exhilaration vanished. Feeling awkward, he said derisively, "The view obviously fascinates you?"

"Not particularly," she replied flatly. "It has little to offer."

Suppressing feelings of irritation, he said, "Forgive me Aiko, but you *were* expecting me?"

"Yes."

"Then, it is perhaps presumptuous to ask but, why are we here?"

Receiving no reply he compelled himself to speak with an amused tolerance. "Aiko, from early boyhood I was trained to translate other languages into my native tongue. Unfortunately however, I am not skilled in reading the thoughts of others. Now I find myself in a ridiculous, even slightly bizarre situation."

"Bizarre . . ." Aiko's voice now crisp and aloof, echoed.

"Exactly. Frankly, I admit that your message aroused feelings of sanguine expectations in me. Why not? Aiko, our affair never ended. For some years I have likened it to a game."

"To a game? To a *game*?"

"Yes. To a game of chess interrupted by an earth tremor that scattered the pieces off the board. I've always wished to pick them up, start anew . . ." On a sudden impulse he reached out and lightly caressed her silk-clad shoulder, saying, "Please be at ease. Is it that you are embarrassed at having made the first move? Am I correct in my assumptions?"

"You are not correct. We are here for a discussion. One that is long overdue. I need to consult with you . . ." Her voice trailed off, then in an apparent effort to remain calm she continued on, her hands expressing a gesture of hopelessness as she said, "My husband, your cousin, is not the father of my child." Turning away she leaned against the rail of the parapet.

He stood stock-still, looking out from the balustrade. Mixed emotions warred within him as he attempted to grasp the implication of her statement.

"Yuichi? Not the child's father . . . ? Yuichi not the child's father?" he repeated. "Does *he* know that?"

She raised her head and looked at him, her eyes searching his face. Then, taking her time, she replied quietly, her manner all at once clandestine. "My husband does not know."

With a brusque nod he accepted the information, then said, "In all truth, I'm not sure how I should be reacting. Help me. Should I feel abhorrence? Guilt? Shame? Pleasure?"

"Whatever you will. We are not here to discuss *your* feelings."

"Then—why?"

"To advise me." Her manner, although still aloof, now became urgent. "Renzō, without your cooperation I am at a loss. Surely you are not unwilling to advise me?"

Despite his emotional turmoil he replied calmly, "I am more than willing. Be assured of that . . ."

"Thank you." Aiko bowed slightly. "Put plainly, knowing my husband so well, I am convinced that his pride might well prevent him from voicing suspicions."

"So! He does have suspicions?"

"He has not *voiced* them. But if by chance he should, then how am I, his wife, to deal with the appalling situation? I need your advice. Truly, I'm becoming so fearful. Renzō, day by day the resemblance grows . . ."

"Resemblance to whom?" Renzō ran a hand through his hair that was damp with sweat. "Certainly the child bears no resemblance to . . ."

His voice faltered, and speaking for him Aiko said, "To you? No. In no way does Kentaro resemble you."

He stood there, completely at a loss while Aiko gestured for him to follow her as she walked rapidly across the greensward to descend the steep flight of stone steps. Making no effort to overtake her, Renzō followed in a state of complete bewilderment.

Aiko halted at the edge of the lake he had admired such a short time before. Motionless, she waited there for him to join her.

Although mystified, he knew instinctively that he should bear with her behavior. To remain calm, he drew a cigar from his pocketcase, not wishing to smoke but needing a prop of some kind to hold. "What," he asked, more bluntly than he intended, "Aiko, what exactly are you requiring of me?"

She stayed motionless for a while longer, then stepped forward to Yuki, her elderly servant, instructing her to leave them alone. After the woman had moved off, he saw a child standing by the lake throwing pebbles of gravel into the water.

Aiko walked toward him, leading the little boy by the hand, saying, "Ken-chan, is this not nice! Do you remember this man?"

The child stared up at him unflinchingly as his mother continued cheerfully, "*This* man is Etsu's papa. I know how you love Et-chan."

Although he had seen the child on several occasions, Renzō had never given special heed to him. But now he studied Kentaro's appearance. His glossy black hair was cut in bangs above his dark eyes which gazed up as Aiko continued speaking. "Ken-chan, Ken-chan! Come, bow, be polite! Smile!"

The child, Kentaro, smiled. Renzō recognized the truth. The resemblance to his mother, Lady Masa, was startling. Yes, without doubt, this child was his.

For one brief moment he bared his feelings as a surge of love overpowered the shock he received. Reaching out a hand he placed it lightly on the boy's head, then he moved off to stand apart.

He would never know how long it had been before he heard Aiko's voice murmuring to him. "So . . . ?"

"So . . ." he responded. "He, our son, is beautiful!"

Their gazes met. A flood of desire coursed through his veins. Two feverish patches stained her pale cheeks as she whispered, "Yes, Renzō, I too recall those sweet stolen hours."

He realized that the servant had returned to attend to the child who was once again throwing pebbles into the shimmering water.

"Aiko, must it always just be memories between us?" he said quietly.

"Yes. Treasured. In secret for always."

"*Must* it be so?"

"It must be so. Surely I have your agreement?"

"Yes. Be consoled. Have no fears . . ."

"Ah, but I am filled with fears. Fears of discovery. Of scandal. Of gossip and—"

"Aiko, *have no fears*. Together, like two culprits, we will face the future."

Now she interjected in a whisper. "Help me. Tell me how we are to continue on?"

"How . . . ? We need time to—"

"To . . . ?"

Lost for words, he gazed about him as though in search of inspiration.

"Can we do anything else but brazen things out?" Aiko's tone was pathetically tentative. "Just—brazen things out?"

"Yes. Yes, how else? Yes, we shall brazen it out. Yes, so be it." He hesitated, then he said firmly, "I have two requests to make of you."

"Please name them."

"I wish to consider the child as a bond between us. A bond to be nurtured, to grow with the years. Are you in agreement?"

Aiko showed her agreement by bowing low. "So." He continued, little of his inner conflict showing, "I also request that you throw all fear away, refrain from worrying. Yes?"

Once again she bowed low. Without looking toward the child whom he yearned to snatch up and carry away, he returned her obeisance. She smiled openly at him.

Turning from her, he walked swiftly away.

. . .

When he returned home that evening Renzō felt a great need for solitude. So on the pretext of shooting game-birds on his woodland estate, hopefully to provide Rumi with the birds she needed for a banquet, he took up his English hunting gun and set off for the woods. As he walked over the soft springy turf, Renzō wondered if other men of his ilk had to deal with situations similar to that which he had been plummeted into that very day. Nevertheless, despite the shock, deep within himself he exulted in the fact that he had sired a child who bore a likeness to his mother.

Sadly he could not lay claim to the child but must go his way, scrupulously ignoring any elements of scandalous gossip which could, and in all probability would, arise.

He had no intention of relinquishing all paternal claims. Kentaro must become an integral part of his life. From this time on he would foster his relationship with the Fukuda family and renew the cousinly intimacy between himself and Yuichi.

Yuichi . . . ? That man who was outwardly so easygoing, trampled his way to heights of success in so many areas of life, announcing to all and sundry, "When I want something, I get it. The word *failure*. Well I refuse to recognize it . . ."

As he entered the small pine forest on his estate a falling object struck his hand sharply, and as he handled the pine cone which had fallen from one of the trees his brain began to race.

He, Aiko, and Yuichi standing beneath another pine tree . . .

Yuichi holding Etsu, his eyes abrim with amusement, saying "You could, you should give me one of your children . . ."

That jocular request had been complied with.

Proudly, and in all innocence, Yuichi had claimed that child.

In all innocence? By all the gods it had to be so. The alternative was too horrendous even to consider. He must put such thoughts from his mind. He would, once and for all. Yes, but where did the truth lie . . . ?

Had he been tricked? Used by that man? Yes, and by that woman, childless for so many years . . . ?

That preposterous thought caused him to shout out, "No. No, no . . ."

He raised his hunting gun, then aiming it skyward, he pulled the trigger. The gun's blast resounded loudly and against his will he grimaced, fully aware that for a moment he had been harboring a wild desire to mortally wound the man, yes, and the woman who might in fact have duped him so atrociously. Anger and suspicion caught at him again. Had there been an air of gentle mockery in Aiko's farewell smile as they parted in Ueno Park?

Shrugging, he immediately regretted suspecting her of being a ruthless, calculating female. In short, she was a woman apart. She had, with brave candor, made him her accomplice.

Yes, Yuichi alone was the victim, and his own duty now was to forget the ugly suspicions he had conjured up.

Renzō suddenly became aware that a strong wind had arisen. He decided to abandon any thought of shooting game and to return to the house at once. As he struggled his way homeward, buffeted by the wind, he realized that a typhoon of some strength was gathering its destructive forces.

Sumiko Fukuda stood gazing out from the open window, surveying the devastation of the garden she had nurtured and loved since those far-off days when she, a young wife, had fallen so deeply in love with her husband. Addressing her feathered pet, she murmured, "Ah, Cocky-chan, *Kami Kaze*—the god of wind, truly launched his fury upon us during the night. Just see that fallen oak tree! And the ruin of our iris garden! What havoc has been wrought . . ."

Breaking off in mid-speech, she gestured a greeting to her son as he entered the room. Then she said, "Come, mourn with me the ruin of my iris garden."

Obeying her request, Yuichi exclaimed, "Yes, yes, but never mind! The gardeners will restore it."

"You think so?" Tears welled from her eyes. "It means so much to me."

"I know. I know . . ." Yuichi spoke comfortingly, then added in a brisk tone, "Literally, I starve. May I eat with you here?"

"But, of course!"

"Good. Yes, and please have my wife and my son eat with us. I've not as yet greeted or spoken with them."

Hiding her disappointment, Sumiko cried out cheerfully, "A pleasing idea."

Kentaro was proud of his skill in managing the tiny chopsticks as he hungrily shoveled rice into his mouth. But his eyes were round in amazement as his elders gave their individual versions of the wild night hours. Having slept soundly, he was utterly bemused. He hoped that he would be allowed to escape so that he could ride the rocking horse that his mother's friend, Auntie Marjorie, had brought him from a faraway place called London.

Of whom should he request permission to leave the table? Eyeing the adult trio, he finally made his decision. Confident that he had made the right choice, he placed the chopsticks carefully upon their porcelain rest and crept up from the cushion to stand behind his father. Straightaway he pounded his fists against those hunched shoulders, crying out consolingly, "Puppa, Puppa, Ken-chan will fix the hurt in you. . . ."

"Thank you, thank you, thank you," his father exclaimed. "Hit a little higher! Yes, right *there*! Ah . . . good! Excellent! What a kind boy . . ."

How right he had been. Now his father pulled him close, smiling into his eyes. "May I ride my horse, Puppa? Right now?"

"Why not? Yes, off you go. Quick, run swiftly. Have a care! Perhaps Uma-chan has taken it into his mind to gallop off into the city."

As Kentaro ran from the room, Sumiko gazed at her parrot and murmured confidentially, "One wonders how parental laxity will affect the future of our nation in days to come."

Aiko, gazing at Sumiko, murmured casually, "Ken-chan behaved *very* nicely yesterday. I took him walking at Ueno Park. By the way, Mother, your nephew, Renzō, was there. We spoke with him. . . ."

"You did! How nice. I seldom see him. How did he appear? In good health and spirits?"

"He appeared as usual. Suave, very distinguished. He quite admired Ken-chan and expressed regret that over the past few years our two families, so closely related, have drifted apart."

"He did? Renzō said that?" Yuichi took up his gold-tipped ivory toothpick, speaking gutturally as he prodded his teeth with it. "Am I to gather that you had a pleasant, a meaningful discussion with him?"

Looking directly at him, Aiko shuddered disdainfully before replying, "Yes. Renzō was startled at certain of my opinions. But then he agreed with me."

"Good. Excellent. My cousin is an intelligent chap. . . ." He burst out laughing, then said, "So Renzō admired our son?" He laughed again, then stopped to look at his wife intently. "You parted on pleasant terms? He showed no animosity?"

"No animosity at all."

"Animosity . . . ?" Sumiko raised her voice in indignation, "Why should Renzō harbor animosity toward his one and only aunt's family?"

"Why?" Yuichi grinned. "Well Mother, to tell the truth, I've been feeling that Renzō sneers at certain honors bestowed upon me. Are you able to think of other reasons, Aiko?"

Aiko recalled the episode which had taken place beside the shimmering lake at Ueno Park. Vividly, she remembered the way in which Renzō had placed one hand lightly upon the child—his child, but lost to him.

Yuichi's triumphant attitude nauseated her. "I'm finding it difficult to express my thoughts," she murmured coldly. "I feel stifled. The air in this room is difficult to breathe." Speaking directly to her mother-in-law, she asked, "Excuse me, please?"

"I understand," Sumiko sympathized. "The atmosphere is always so humid after typhoons. Feel free to go your way. . . ."

Moving hurriedly through the labyrinth of highly polished corridors, Aiko finally slid open the door of Kentaro's nursery and stood there watching as he sat astride his huge dappled toy, shouting enthusiastically.

On sighting her mistress, the maid in attendance rose to her feet, saying, "What ails you, mistress?"

"Nothing," she replied untruthfully as she surveyed the room, disliking it intensely. It held far too many toys and had the mark of vulgarity.

She thought of Lady Masa and her exquisite tastes. The beautiful, imaginative child had inherited that noblewoman's features. She would do all that she could to insure that Kentaro's upbringing would foster an appreciation of aesthetic values, yes, and of scholarship.

The house and its surrounding grounds were noisy. Tradesmen of every ilk had invaded the premises to repair the storm damage.

Aiko entered the closely shuttered music salon. Her throat was aching, strangled by a confusion of emotions, and she hoped that in the dim privacy of the large chamber she might be able to gather her fragmented thoughts and regain her lost balance.

With trembling hands she lit one of the many red temple candles, and in its flickering light she stood before a gilt-framed mirror. The woman reflected there seemed to be a stranger, bitter and hard-faced, someone with no clear path to follow.

Snuffing out the light, relieved of that unpleasing female image, she cast her mind into a state of calm and began to tabulate her thoughts honestly.

Willingly, she had mortified her person adulterously. From that adulterous relationship a perfect and adored child had come. Under extreme duress from her husband she had overcome her scruples. Never had she acknowledged her own amorality.

What a fool she had been, tricking herself by pretending that no punishment lay in store for her actions. This late-come chastisement was excruciating.

There, in the park, close to the man to whom she had surrendered her virginity, she had yearned to say rashly and honestly, "Renzō, I hunger; I want so much to be with you again. Yes, again and again . . ."

Standing there beside him, the desire that had always been within her had suddenly become all too powerful. Would she be capable of containing this longing for him within the borders of her own being? Must she condemn herself to a life untouched by further passionate fulfillment?

All her life she had been decisive and acted without fear, regardless of what consequences might arise. For all Yuichi's bravado, she was the dominant partner in their charade of a marriage.

Yes, *"Aiko, you direct the drama from now on,"* he had insisted, his manner complacent.

She would do so. If he were to cry out, *"I disapprove! You go too far,"* she would laugh in his face and reply, *"Have no fear of gossip or scandal. Just know that whichever path I take I tread it with style, without harming you or my son. . . ."*

That night when Yuichi entered their sleeping chamber he at once expressed annoyance on finding that Kentaro's *futon* had been removed. Allowing him no time to voice further objections, Aiko exclaimed, "He is now too old to sleep here in this room with us."

"Nonsense, he's but an infant."

"Old enough to understand too much of what he might hear during our night chats . . ." While appearing to give full attention to tying the sash of her sleeping robe, she added casually, "I wish, rather, I *intend* to employ an English governess for him. English is the lingua franca of the world. Kentaro should understand and speak it faultlessly. You agree?"

"Wholeheartedly."

"I'm glad. I've many plans for Kentaro. And, Yuichi, please understand that it's very hard for me to say this, but I've no intention of living out my life suppressing certain emotions I feel. I shall, of course, always give more than considerate thought to my behavior. *Never* will there be even the suggestion of scandal.''

Glancing about the room with a heightened expression of amusement, Yuichi exclaimed, "This is not in any way a serious discourse?"

"In a broad sense—yes. Do you wish that I sum up my intentions more accurately?"

Yuichi, at once wary, said deliberately, "Aiko, just let me remind you that I was born with an extraordinary ability to distinguish between good and evil in people."

"Is that so?"

"It is so."

"Then, of course, you see only good in your wife, Baron?"

For several long moments Yuichi studied Aiko's face, his expression as blank as hers. Then he said quietly, "But, of course . . ."

Sleepless, Yuichi lay in the dark room giving deep consideration to all his wife had said, and, more important, to all she had not said. Against his will he could not help but admire her. He knew that he had become a blackmailed man. Yes, but he would pay any price to have the wayward woman remain his friend-wife. If only he had been there as an invisible presence in the park when his wife and his cousin had met!

In his everyday dealings he presented himself to the world as the most confident of men, while he saw himself as one who had been crippled and forever denied that which was taken for granted by the most humble of males the world over. He thought of his parents, and how they had loved each other. He wondered how his father would advise him, were he still alive. Merely thinking of that man caused him to smile with affection.

Aiko was brought back from the edge of sleep by a sudden cackle of laughter. "What amuses you?" she muttered suspiciously.

"I'm not amused."

"Not?"

"Not."

"Then, why the laughter?"

"You really wish to know?"

"Umm . . . not really."

"So, let the matter rest. Sleep well!"

"Tell me," Aiko muttered irritably, "how can I sleep? Confess. What are you thinking of?"

"Well . . ." Yuichi drawled. "At least I shall *not* be like the man in a loathsome poem I once read."

"A poem—loathsome? What poem?"

Yuichi recited:

> *In the whole village*
> *The husband alone*
> *Does not know of it.*

For a moment there was silence, then Aiko broke into a giggle. He also laughed, then said very quietly, "Losing you would be a great sorrow to me. You know that?"

"I know that." Aiko hesitated, then added, "Yuichi, shall we bring Ken-chan here to sleep? Just once more?"

"Yes. He might be feeling deserted." Yuichi left the room and returned with the child clasped in his arms. "He did not wake when I picked him up. Shall I have him beside me?"

"Yes. Have him sleep with you. He loves you so very much."

F OR SEVERAL YEARS RENZŌ HAD led a more or less lackadaisical life. He and Aiko between them had followed their scheme to brazen out the fact that Kentaro bore such a remarkable likeness to Lady Masa. During one family gathering, Aiko drew attention to her child, saying lightly, "Yes, and Ken-chan also strongly resembles *my* own mother, the Lady Akiko, a noble lady from Kyoto. In that city *so* many faces bear the same stamp. . . ."

"Yes," Yuichi exclaimed enthusiastically. "Yes, while visiting Kyoto, I was struck to find so many similar-looking people in the old capital. Personally, I put it down to too much intermarrying between closely related families. Good thing that *my* son has also been injected with blood from a healthy, humble ancestry!"

"I agree," Sumiko cried out. " 'Tis said that the intellect is likely to be weakened by generations of cousins marrying cousins. Personally, Kentaro's Kyoto-style smile delights my heart, keeping alive my memories of Masa. Renzō, it must also be pleasing to you. No?"

"Without doubt—yes, Aunt . . ."

"One thing is certain," Yuichi exclaimed jocularly. "There will be no joining in marriage between *our* progeny, Renzō. I would not agree to have *my* son wed *your* daughter, delightful as she undoubtedly is."

To Renzō's satisfaction, neither Yuichi nor Rumi had needed any persuasion to have the two families become closer. Kentaro was often in the midst of his family, pampered and loved, especially by Etsu.

Then, and much to Renzō's delight, he and Aiko had renewed their affair, neither one in love with the other but both reveling in their hours of passion. Of late, that passion was paling, but the clandestine meetings continued.

In short, he was content, asking no more of life than what he had. Then, late one night a police officer arrived at his home and to his bewilderment, he was handed a note signed by an American acquaintance, Thomas Trask, requesting that he should hasten without delay to a brothel in Yokohama, where a foreigner was causing a scandal of gigantic proportions.

Irritated beyond measure, he accompanied the officer on the short journey by train to the port city. There he climbed into the hired carriage ordered for his convenience and was driven at a breakneck pace out of the city's confines and along the Marine Drive toward Hommoku Bay. Once there, he gazed upward to see those familiar pine trees etched darkly against the night sky. But he subdued his nostalgia and made up his mind not to cast even one glance toward the old family home that was still occupied by his father's paramour, Osen.

A mob of shouting citizens rushed from the sidewalk onto the road, thus preventing further progress. "Drive on, drive on," he commanded, but the coachman dismounted, demanding his fare, and his official escort pointed, saying, "*That* house just along the road, that is your destination. *That house* is the brothel used by barbarian men we have taken into our land. . . ."

Dazed and disbelieving, Renzō saw that the wooden gate of his old home was no longer tastefully weather-worn but painted a garish red. Even more aghast, he entered the house and saw the overwhelming evidence to prove the escort's statement.

The house on the hill had been turned into a flourishing brothel.

Shocked, he nevertheless forced himself to behave in a rational way as a young police officer ushered him into an upstairs room, once Lady Masa's sleep chamber, but now furnished with atrocious vulgarity and dominated by a large bed on which lay the figure of a young girl.

A whore . . . His mother's room . . .

A paroxysm of anger coursed through him. He stumbled slightly, then attempted to evaluate his situation, readying himself to face up to the task ahead, whatever that might be.

As Renzō swept his gaze around and about, shrill-voiced, brazen-mouthed female onlookers fell silent as a besworded police officer strutted center stage, while simultaneously Thomas Trask grabbed at his arm, muttering, "God! You took your time getting here. Renzō, we've a demented chap to deal with. . . ."

Renzō now became aware of a broad-shouldered, somewhat disheveled foreigner who, moving away from the bed, came toward him, hand outstretched, exclaiming, "Mr. Yamamoto—Renzō! You, at last! Thank God . . ."

Into the vast turmoil filling his mind came a gradual recognition of the man. With an audible gasp of astonishment he rapped out, "Bixby? You—Arthur Bixby!" In the back of his mind he was thinking of days long past. Thinking, could this be the *gaijin* said to be causing mayhem, running amok?

The Englishman appeared to be fully in control of his reason, saying, "Thank you for coming! Let me make it abundantly clear. I ask only for your advice. Now. Tonight. Not tomorrow. Not later on—but now." Clenching both fists, he said, "Renzō, you must help me."

Renzō had the feeling of one having entered a theater halfway through the enactment of a melodrama. He needed time. Needed to regain his equilibrium. "Bixby," he exclaimed. "Allow me time. I'm confused. Finding you here, in this house like this. Meeting with you after such a lapse of time. You must understand. . . ."

"I understand," Bixby rejoined. "I offer you no apology. I'm hard-pressed. Yes, hard-pressed! Are you prepared to assist me?"

PART III

O N THOSE RARE OCCASIONS WHEN Arthur Bixby engaged in self-examination, he conjured up the illusion of a man rushing headlong toward a goal, distressed beyond measure because he had no knowledge of what or where that goal was.

Inheriting money had worked wonders in his life. He had thrown his cap over the windmill and set out planning to travel the world for an indefinite period before making wise investments with his small fortune and settling down.

The epitome of an English gentleman abroad, his good looks and cultivated voice made him a target for those of his countrywomen who, while traveling or dwelling in foreign lands, were known as the "Fishing Fleet," out to snare suitable husbands for their marriageable daughters.

Over the years, he had been tempted to marry and return home to England, but he always continued his journeys.

A strong sense of self-protection prevented him from traveling to places where he might find himself out of touch with people of his own kind, and although he despised his unadventurous spirit, he relished his independence, denying himself no luxuries as he went on his decadent way.

No matter the country he was in, there were always those bordellos where sexual favors were to be purchased by upper-class Englishmen whose preferences were for women of their own race. He had no liking for the exotic or the erotic, and seldom gave a second thought to any of those females whose services appeased his irregular surges of carnal desire.

His cautious approach to life was beyond his own understanding. As the years were frittered away, he would feel overwhelmed by loneliness, aware that he was moving again and again around the same circle, forming no meaningful friendships, attracted to various women of his own class up to a certain point, then moving on, lonelier than ever.

He had become accustomed to luxury, and it was an immense shock to learn that his inheritance had diminished. Forced to take stock of his situation, he had come to the conclusion that only two solutions were available. He could return to England and find employment, or follow in his brother Robert's footsteps and marry a woman whose dowry would allow him to live in comfort for the remainder of his days. Neither of the two solutions was attractive. Nevertheless, necessity demanded that he make a decision at once and without further delay.

Bixby would never forget the moment when that decision had been reached. There he had been, thousands of miles away from England, in Sydney, Australia, walking along Macquarie Street on his way to a luncheon, when, with the most uncharacteristic gesture, he had taken a silver half-crown from his pocket and tossed it in the air, muttering grimly, "Tails—a job! Heads—a rich wife!"

The sharp ting of that coin hitting the sidewalk pierced his ears, and the noonday sun glared down on the coin so brightly that he stooped low to see how it had landed. Heads up! The decision was made.

The idea of marrying and settling down in the colony never so much as entered his head. Australia was too huge, the sun too bright, and for all the hospitality of the people, he felt a stranger in their midst. Everything was so new and he was ill at ease in the company of men and women all aggressively proud of being Australians.

Three days later he was aboard the steamer *Northampton*, traveling on a most circuitous journey via the Orient back to the land of his birth.

When the vessel steamed toward the Japanese seaport of Nagasaki, Bixby, weary of seaboard life, decided to join a group of sight-seeing passengers and travel to Tokyo by train.

Trapped into traveling along mile after mile of iron rails through the golden glow of autumnal beauty, Bixby realized somewhat to his surprise that he was undergoing his first bout of homesickness. Travel had become irksome, and he knew with certainty that when he was once again in England he would be more than content to stay there for the remainder of his life.

The train seats were arranged lengthways, and many Japanese passengers sat with their feet tucked up, their discarded footwear on the floor. At every stopping place the stations were crowded with chattering folk either greeting or farewelling relatives and friends, one and all bowing and smiling. The meals were supplied in little wooden boxes, each one with a pair of chopsticks neatly fixed to the lid. Bixby could not stomach the Japanese food. Rice, in his opinion, was pudding material, not to be spiced with soya sauce or eaten with queer-smelling bits of fish and stinking radish pickles.

To his relief, sandwiches were obtainable, filled with ham, with cheese, neatly packaged and alluded to as *san-do-ichi*.

During the rail journey, several enthusiastic American tourists took to giving English lessons and to learning Japanese words and phrases. The stuffy, smoke-filled carriage resounded with much giggling and laughter as the exchange took place. "English—*one, two, three* . . ."

"Japanese! *Ichi, ni, san* . . ." came the Japanese chorus.

"English! *Thank you* . . ."

"Japanese! *Arigatō* . . ."

"English! *Beautiful* . . ."

"Japanese! *Kirei* . . ."

On and on it went, but the only word that took his fancy was, *sayōnara*—good-bye. He could scarcely wait to bid farewell to Japan once and for all. The thought of contacting Renzō Yamamoto entered his mind, but he dismissed the idea.

To his relief, the train finally pulled into Tokyo's main station. Unfortunately, there were no vacancies in any of the Western-style hotels in the great metropolis. The year was 1887 and Japan's first national fair had filled the city with businessmen and tourists. However, his entrée to a British club meant that he had accommodation.

Bixby arrived at the club, there to be welcomed by the club president, Sir John Coomber, who exclaimed, "Come, join me! Let's have a few drinks. A good chat!" His notion of a chat was a lengthy monologue about his admiration of things Japanese. "To my mind," he finally declared, "this country is one of nature's jewels. . . ."

At the mention of jewels, Bixby's business interests were aroused. Pearls! Bought cheaply in Japan! "Sir John," he exclaimed, "I'm interested in purchasing some jewels. Can you advise me?"

"No. My dear wife could, but Marjorie is out of town conducting a group of friends on a tour of Kyoto. Pity! Pity! When do you take leave of us?"

"Tomorrow afternoon. Sailing on the *Northampton*."

"So soon. Pity! Umm . . . are you free this evening? If so, Tom Trask, my American colleague, I'm sure, will come to your aid. Yes, Trask is your man."

"I would not impose on his time."

"Oh . . ." Sir John exclaimed, "Trask likes nothing more than having his conceits gratified. He has an extraordinary range of knowledge."

Bixby stood at the club bar awaiting the arrival of Thomas Trask, who, as Sir John had predicted, was more than agreeable to assist him, hurrying him from the club, grunting, "No need to thank me, Bixby. I was off to Yokohama, in any case."

"Yokohama? Is that necessary?"

"Yes. Ferdinando da Silva is the only man in Nippon to rely upon where jewels are concerned. Large community of Portuguese in Yokohama. Yes, take it from me, da Silva alone can be relied upon. No time to waste. Let's off to catch the train. . . ."

Arriving in the port city, he and Trask were driven from the Yokohama station in hired ricksha. As they passed through dark streets and narrow lanes, he involuntarily glanced backward, at times half believing that they were being followed.

The American, completely at ease, kept up a barrage of comments from the lead vehicle. "Won't be long now," he shouted. "Won't dismiss the runners. They can wait for us. . . .

"Won't be too long with da Silva. He is all for business. . . ." He paused. "Hope you won't mind traveling back to Tokyo on your own."

Bixby, taken aback, shouted, "Not at all. Not at all."

"Good! Excellent," Trask roared. "I pay occasional nocturnal visits to a certain brothel here. Purely a constitutional exercise . . . Glad to take you there. Just say the word. Place caters only to us foreigners . . ."

"Thanks," Bixby bellowed. "Thanks. Very decent of you . . ."

"Not at all . . ."

For the first time in ages, Bixby's sense of humor was tickled and he felt a kind of creeping excitement. He had been wondering vaguely if Trask could be approached for an introduction to a house that would cater to his needs.

Ferdinando da Silva's musty-smelling warehouse was crowded with crates, bales, and canvas-wrapped goods, and da Silva, with a flash of his white teeth, said, "Apart from precious stones, I also deal in fireworks, decorative tiles, food, and wines. . . ."

"Wines!" Trask held up an imaginary glass and at once the host brought forth three goblets and several bottles of wine.

"This wine comes from Portugal," da Silva murmured. "Red like liquid rubies . . ."

"Rubies!" Trask emptied his goblet, then said impatiently, "Yes, down to business. I'll leave you to it?" Taking up one of the lovely green bottles, he moved some distance off. Seating himself on a straw bale in a shadowy corner of the dimly lit chamber, he refilled his goblet.

Closeted with da Silva in a metal vault lit by a hanging oil lamp that shone brightly upon a tray of glittering rubies, emeralds, and diamonds, Bixby endured some embarrassment while he informed the merchant that he was desirous of buying bargain-priced pearls.

"Pearls? Just pearls?"

"Regretfully, yes."

"Well, this puts a new light on the matter. Just pearls, you say?"

"Yes. Preferably already strung."

"Pearls already strung?" Da Silva might never have heard of such an arrangement. "Señor, I deal only in precious stones."

"Then, I apologize for troubling you."

"Wait . . ." The man's expression changed from one of irritation to gentle curiosity. "Tell me, are the pearls for a señorita of extraordinary charm? Or, your wife maybe?"

"Er, er . . ." Bixby stammered. "Truthfully, no. I had in mind to resell them when I return to England."

"Most important! You are a businessman. So let me advise you. There is great business to be done in Japan."

"But I leave Japan tomorrow. . . ."

"Sailing on the *Northampton*?"

"Yes."

"Then, I am sorry. I can't oblige you. But at least please sample my excellent wine."

After having quaffed a goodly amount of the excellent wine Bixby and Trask realized that the man was becoming impatient, so they bade an effusive farewell to da Silva and went on their way.

The seaport city was now aglow with moonlight and the soft radiance and fitful shadows encouraged the sensual desires Bixby was suddenly eager to satisfy. Removing his hat, he leaned back in the ricksha which went on through the brightly lit city, along the Marine Drive, then upward to a high bluff that overlooked the ocean.

Slightly intoxicated and scarcely conscious of his surroundings, Bixby alighted from the vehicle and while Trask paid and dismissed the runners, he said uneasily, "Trask, I must return to the club in Tokyo tonight."

Trask spoke vacantly as though not clearly registering. "If you must, a train leaves at midnight."

Midnight . . . ? At least three hours were at his disposal. More than enough time in which to fulfill his needs. Shrugging, he paced up a graveled path that led to a spectacular Japanese house. Having gained entry to the place, Trask went off, leaving Bixby in the dimly lit entrance hall. Immediately a sharp-looking man came to his side, bowing and saying, "Please welcome! I am house master. Yuji Shiga. Ready to please you. You have special fetish?"

The man upset his nerves. "No fetish." He ground out the words. "Just—not a Japanese girl."

Shiga, disconcerted, replied, "All girls in my house are Japanese. No imported girls in my house."

Bixby realized that Trask had given him the wrong impression when saying that the brothel catered to foreigners. Could he leave? Make his getaway? But the ricksha had been dismissed. And where exactly was he?

"You will not use Japanese girl?" Shiga's tone was one of surprise and hurt. "You don't want that?"

"No. No. I don't want."

Shiga bowed, hesitated, then gestured to show his understanding, saying, "So! I can't please you. Japanese girl not good enough for you. Excuse me please."

Loathing the man's obsequious manner, Bixby said brusquely, "I mean no offense to your country's women." He hesitated, then blurted out, "Please name your price."

"So, you try! Turn off lights, all girls the same. No? I have certain prices. Most high is for unused girls. You have the good luck. Two new girls. I call them. Show you. You make choice."

"No. No," Bixby cut in hastily. "Either one will do. . . ." He followed Shiga along a dark corridor, up a flight of steep wooden stairs, along another corridor, then into a spacious lamp-lit room.

"Please to wait." Shiga slid the door shut, and as Bixby heard his steps hastening away, he shrugged and muttered, "I'll have the lamp doused out. Yes, in the dark all bought women are the same. . . ."

Shiga's nerves were stretched to breaking point. He knew that it would be unwise to send a rank amateur to service the pompous foreigner, but he had no other choice. As was usual, the full moon had netted in a crowd of customers. Every experienced harlot was fully occupied. He had come to loathe catering to the tastes of foreign men and dealing with recalcitrant country-bumpkin females, teaching them manners and training them in the art of man-pleasing.

He loathed every aspect of running the brothel, but he had been forced into adjusting himself to the work. The courtesan Osen's love of finery had not decreased over the years, and bills had to be met. He thought his sister to be the most selfish, the most difficult of women. Year after year, her one and only pleasure came from making purchases, never questioning the cost. Her days were spent before mirrors, posturing, posing, with no one but herself to admire the colorful picture she made.

When, in the early years, he had been desperate enough to criticize her extravagance, she had stared at him, her expression bewildered, then she had said firmly, "Yuji, adopted brother, but I am Osen! *Osen.* So respect and care for me."

"Gladly, sister. But my earnings are small. My reputation in the field of acupuncture grows slowly in the port city. . . ."

"Forget your piddling work. Use your head instead of your hands. Use this large house. Bring in harlots. Set them to work. . . ."

She had given him no rest, pleading, demanding, commanding, until he had finally given in.

The nefarious plan had been set in motion, aided by certain officials in the port city who took their cut of the profits while advising him to keep a low profile and to cater solely to high-ranking foreign men in the community. Many clients had become regulars who arrived and left unobtrusively.

Shiga pitied every aspect of his life. As a youth, he had been taken from his widowed mother's side and adopted out to live in a family of harlots. The Shiga women had been kindly, and it had been his unquestioned duty to accompany Osen when Renzō, that pampered son of Kenichi Yamamoto, had cast her out of the cozy nest at Nihombashi, forcing her to live in the Yokohama house overlooking the ocean.

Osen had a horror of the sea. She never ventured outdoors. On nights when the wind raged and the waves crashed against the shore, she cringed, moaning and crying out that the calls of gulls were the souls of dead people, haunting her, shrieking out for help.

Shiga thought of Osen as one who lived in a world where time had stopped. The Buddhist proverb described her well: *"The fallen flower returns not to its branch."* She had nowhere to go, nothing to do but pamper herself and delight in her own person, unaware of the havoc the years had wrought.

An ironic twist of fate had sent him to dwell on the hill overlooking Hommoku Bay. Some weeks after his arrival, he had gone down to the beach and, like a ghost, he had entered his childhood home, unrecognized by his mother, who had grown wizened and bent. Then how she had wept! Yes, and how he had wept. Such anguish and such bitter pain.

The old woman had passed on into the spirit world soon after that reunion. She had died quietly, pleading in a whisper, "Yuji, Yuji, my good son, you will care for Taro . . . ?"

"I shall," he had promised, and that legacy had become a heavy burden. His brother, Taro, had an insane streak, and there was always the threat that he might go berserk if not given his own way. The good-natured fisherfolk of Hommoku Bay had been relieved when Taro had snarled, "From now on I, Taro, shall live in the grand house of the Yamamoto clan."

He had moved in, to the despair of Osen, who despised his rough manners. Nevertheless, she agreed that he had his uses, for it was Taro whose brawny frame, tattooed torso, and threats frightened most recalcitrant girls into submission.

Shiga considered Taro's job less odious than the task he was forced to carry out, traveling to country regions, nosing his way into small villages, listening to local gossip, dealing with share-farmers who were so poverty-stricken that after some coercion, distressed parents agreed to hire out their daughters for a price.

He was not altogether a callous man. There were times when his heart ached in those hovels when young daughters cried out proudly, "Mumma, Mumma, please agree. Mumma, I'm strong. Take the cash. Please let me help. . . ."

Skillfully, he would dangle the prospect of the girl living in a fine house. Doing light work. What kind of work? "Many kinds. Useful work. She would learn much, then return home with fine clothes, ready to make a good marriage. Why not accept the cash? Why not? Why not . . . ?"

His method seldom failed. Those simple country girls were terrified on discovering what was expected of them, but having accepted payment in advance, and realizing they had been caught in their own web, they were helpless.

Some proved to be difficult and sullen, but they soon fell into line, especially after a roughing-up from Taro. Of late, however, Shiga had the feeling that everything was getting out of hand. He longed to be free of Osen. Her demise alone would allow him to leave Japan and migrate to a place in America called California, where it was said gold could be dug out of the ground.

Now he entered the lavish boudoir of the old courtesan. The once-beautiful woman had grown into a monstrous hulk who babbled endless complaints and orders, believing that Kenichi Yamamoto, her patron, was due to arrive and that she must have help to present herself to him groomed and gowned to perfection. She addressed her nonsense to his wife, Fuji, whose time was spent patiently catering to the demands of her mistress. Fuji carefully followed the edicts of the Roman Catholic religion she had been converted to, so her own devotion and kindness to Osen did not seem at all extraordinary to her. She was determined that when the time came, Osen, like it or not, would leave this world not as a heathen, but as a respectable Roman Catholic.

Shiga was relieved when he saw that Osen had fallen into a light doze. He wondered what Kenichi Yamamoto would have thought had he been able to see the ludicrous figure his paramour now made, robed grandly, her face painted white and heavily rouged beneath the exotically dressed wig, and her mouth hanging open.

Exhausted after the lengthy tussle of preparing Osen, Fuji smiled at him as she made the sign of the cross and said under her breath, "Praise to the saints, Osen sleeps! Husband, may we go outdoors for a spell? The moon is full."

He waved her request away, saying urgently, "A difficult client awaits. All our experienced workers are hard at it. What of those two newcomers? Which one do you suggest?"

Fuji pondered a moment before whispering, "A difficult decision! Neither girl is attractive. You threw good cash away on them. . . ."

"Maybe so! But the client awaits! So which one?"

"*Komatta ni*—so difficult! Hiroko, the best of the two, lies bruised and red-eyed from weeping. Taro has been working her over."

"What of the other? Tomiko?"

Fuji grimaced worriedly, "Excuse me, but it will be best not to use the girl Tomiko tonight."

"Why not?"

"Taro, your brother, fancies her. You know how he delights in virgins. Yes, and as *you* so wisely say, foreign men take no special pleasure in that area. . . ."

"All that I know. *But the client awaits. . . .*" Shiga's nerves were at breaking point as he whispered in a conspiratorial tone, "Tell me, where is Taro?"

"Well you may ask! Taro is lying beneath the old persimmon tree out in the moonlight. Drunk, and still drinking . . ."

"That's at least a tiny measure of consolation. Fortunately, the client requests but a short time. Hasten! Prepare the girl. . . ."

The rules of the house were unwritten, but Fuji knew them well.

The key factors were to satisfy clients and to have untried young girls fully prepared before giving their bodies over to the whims of foreign men. Quite often she went out of her way to lecture newcomers in a motherly fashion, coaxing gently, "No need to fear. Be comforted knowing that you are able to help your dear family. Foreigners are very little different from our own people. The emperor himself admires their ways. . . ."

Usually, after a few weeks, a girl would accept her lot and would accustom herself to satisfying the foreign customers, who were easy to please. After some months it was not unusual to hear the girls gossiping together in the dormitory, even laughing hilariously at *gaijin* antics.

However certain clients' fetishes were not considered so amusing, and Fuji hoped that the new girl, Tomiko, would not have to undergo anything more unbearable than a straight-out rape. In every respect that would be preferable to letting the drunken Taro have his savage way with her.

Tapping Tomiko awake, Fuji said cheerfully, "Wake up! Wake up! No need to fear! Be comforted knowing that you're able to help your dear family. Tomiko, it's time to begin your duties. No need to fear . . ." Unfortunately her husband's voice ordering her to hasten prevented her from continuing on, and she quickly peeled the girl's shabby sleep robe off, replacing it with a freshly laundered cotton kimono patterned with bright flowers. She sashed the garment and even more speedily brushed Tomiko's hair into a semblance of order. Feeling that she was dealing with a puppet, she led the girl from the room, repeating over and over, "No need to fear! No need to fear . . ."

"Mumma . . ." the girl called out hopelessly. "Mumma . . ."

It seemed to Bixby that he had traveled a long way to reach the remote Japanese brothel, and all to no avail. For some ten minutes he waited alone, on edge. At first he was indignant, then gradually he became interested in the surroundings.

A plump old cat lay asleep on a bed with a gaudy coverlet that offended his aesthetic senses. It was freakishly out of place, as was the washstand with its cheap china bowl and water jug.

His nostrils were assailed by a stale odor. He realized that the stench came from a water-filled ashtray in which a half-smoked cigar had been recently stubbed out. Repulsed, he slid open the tattered rice-paper door-screens and stepped out onto a roofed veranda, where he filled his lungs with unpolluted air.

The moon was now high on the horizon and sent its glow over the wide terrain. Dazzled, he gazed out to where hundreds of glittering lantern-lit craft drifted on the calm surface of the bay.

From somewhere nearby came sounds of festivity. A gong was being beaten rhythmically and voices were raised in song. Such carefree camaraderie always made him feel dejected, because all his life he had found it difficult to make friends; it was as though he could give out only the limited amount of affection he had received in his formative years. He felt utterly alone, isolated in an alien land. During his years of travel it had often been so, but this was different from the loneliness of earlier times. He decided to leave the brothel and hasten back to the English club in Tokyo.

About to re-enter the room, he hesitated on the threshold as the door slid open. A shadowy figure pushed a girl in. The door was slid shut and the girl remained motionless, her back pressed to the door, thereby blocking his exit.

Try as he might, he could not move or drag his gaze from her even for an instant as she stood beneath the glare of the hanging oil lamp. Bereft of all sensual desire, he saw her not as a living person but more as a painting of a tall child. But paradoxically, the simple gown hugged her figure seductively, both concealing and revealing it. Her complexion brought to his mind sunlight and ripe apricots. She had full lips and a rather wide mouth, and beads of sweat stuck wisps of hair to her forehead. The only sound in the room was that of her short, sharp breathing. She resembled a young doe, snared and defenseless, awaiting a huntsman's savage attack.

He searched desperately for a way to communicate, to put her fears at rest and let her know that he had no intention of harming her. Have her know . . .

Have her know . . . what?

He could not decipher his emotions clearly. They were too numerous, too strong and unfamiliar to him. Had he become moonstruck? His mind unbalanced? Never before had he felt such compassion for a fellow being.

He despised sentimentality. Common sense took over and straightaway he decided to take his leave.

The girl, as though responding to his thoughts, moved aside, her attention no longer on him but concentrating on a sudden outbreak of strident, raised voices and the sounds of heavy footsteps pounding along the corridor.

The cat on the bed stood, stretched, yawned, then curled up again, impervious to the tension in the room. But the girl's darting eyes were filled with terror and as she fled, panic-stricken, toward the open *shōji*, he knew intuitively that she intended to throw herself from the high veranda.

Instinctively, he caught at her, and while she struggled against his hold, the room's fragile door stove in and a man in a loincloth plunged forward to wrest the girl from his grasp, then crushed her close against his sweating torso, gesturing and snarling that the foreigner should get out of the way.

Bixby's policy had always been to avoid trouble, but during the ensuing moments, although his mind seemed to be coming apart, he felt amazingly refreshed, more self-possessed than he had ever been. It was perfectly clear to him that come what may, he would vanquish the man whose beastliness was arousing a storm of hatred in the depths of his being. Unaware of the flurry of a gathering audience, all in various stages of undress, Bixby sucked air through his clenched teeth and went into the attack. . . .

To those assembled observers the excitement grew as it became obvious that the unlikely combatants were out to draw blood. They fought on, wrestling and hitting brutally, while no notice was taken of the crumpled figure that had been slung into the alcove. Shiga deeply regretted not having taken his wife's advice. *"I told you so!"* she screamed out fearfully when Taro first lurched in from the garden calling slurringly that he was ready to take on the second new girl, Tomiko.

This was a troublesome night. "Take a low profile," Shiga had been advised, and so he always had. The foreign clients had come and gone most circumspectly over the years, all appreciating the service he gave.

Now, in one fell swoop, his reputation had been ruined. "Only yourself to blame," Fuji was crying out, and he fully agreed with her.

He had followed in Taro's wake as he ran berserk along the corridors, bursting into occupied rooms, interrupting the private goings-on in his determination to find the girl he was determined to ravish.

Early on during the tumult Shiga was aware that his foreign clients, all except for Trask San, had made a hasty getaway. For a while he had been puzzled, wondering why the house was so crowded, so noisy, then he realized that a group of *sake*-laden moon-viewers had come barging into his premises, drawn there by the shouts of the fighting men and by the shrieking catcalls of the excited whores.

He was aghast at the confusion around him. Unable to comprehend why his drunken brother was locked in battle with the foreigner who at first had appeared to be not only sober, but a sober-minded man.

It was all so terrifying. Even as he watched the brutal scene, his brother snatched up the girl, and roaring with crazed laughter, was using her body as a shield. Now, uppermost in Shiga's mind was the thought that the girl might be seriously harmed, even killed.

Hating official intervention he nevertheless was deeply relieved when the senior police official, Captain Suzuki, who had been called in by his juniors, strode into the room. The police officer was a short, slight man but his commands took immediate effects. As Taro let his human burden fall to the floor a combined sigh of relief filtered through the crowd of onlookers. But Bixby, caught off guard by the turn of events, was unable to rationalize his emotions. He stood for a few moments trying to recall why he and the Japanese man had been engaged in the fierce brawl.

He had been out to defend himself—but why? *Had* he been defending himself? No. It was he who had been the attacker. Yes—but why . . . ?

He was exhausted but also exhilarated, as though purged of insidious poisons. The smoldering hatred he had felt toward the hulking Japanese male had turned to feelings of contempt, for the fellow was now humble, his head bowed, a ludicrous, blood-streaked figure, but Bixby could not understand what had brought the sudden change.

A hand grasped at his shoulder firmly. He resented that commanding hand. "Trask, unhand me," he ordered.

"Pull yourself together, Bixby," Trask shouted, his voice outraged and exasperated. "This is *Japan*! *Not* a British colony! Pull yourself together. Say nothing. Leave me to deal with the police. It's wise that you be *assiduously docile and polite*. Understand?"

All Bixby understood was the distressing sight of a young girl, her garments torn and her long hair flowing in a dark stream on the floor at his feet.

Yes. Now he remembered. Kneeling, he gazed upon the girl, feeling that she and he were alone, not only in the room, but in the world. He was overcome by a flood of tenderness, by feelings of obligations to her; it was all so puzzling, so illogical.

Logic? Logic had little to do with these feelings of compassion, and of strong, jealous protectiveness. All his life he had failed to achieve a sense of his true place in the universe. Now it was as though self-interest had been transferred to this pathetic slip of a girl.

But . . . ? Useless to question! It was as though the girl were a drug to which he had succumbed and without her he would lose his own identity. It was the girl's welfare which was all-important. He would not leave her here, in this foul brothel.

The past no longer existed and the future lay mysteriously hidden. That was all he knew. Never had he been so sure of himself. Never before had he felt more balanced and capable of taking the right path. He knew that this was the turning point of his life.

Trask looked on as the Englishman gathered up the unconscious girl and carried her to the bed, then arranged her garments, modestly covering her bared thighs.

He believed that Bixby was not right in his mind. Well, that was how the world went. He had his own peculiarities and dealt with them in his own way. He hoped to God that no powder or rouge had been left on his smoothly shaved cheeks. He cursed Bixby for having interrupted his private enjoyment. He thanked God that he spoke the Japanese language fluently, but he knew that he was in for a long, grueling time.

He looked about uneasily, fidgeting and fastening his waistcoat buttons, relieved to see that Bixby had taken his advice. The man was standing aloof, his back to the girl, gaze fixed on the ceiling, seemingly unaware of the havoc he had created.

Trask went into action with aplomb. His initial bow to Captain Suzuki was beyond reproach, and Suzuki's return bow reflected his own. Trask's knowledge of Japan stood him in good stead, for he understood that the ancient Rule of the Sword had not gone completely and was still represented by those strutting men in the modern police force.

He bowed again, saying with an air of puzzlement, "Captain, surely this upset is but the result of men struck by moonlight and too much *sake*? Do you agree?"

"Hmmm . . ." Captain Suzuki glanced about, his expression both thoughtful and contemptuous. "That could be so. Yes, that could be so."

"Captain, as you wisely say, that could be so. Yes, it's fortunate that no real harm has been done."

"You think so?"

"I know so, Captain." Trask gestured toward Bixby. "Captain, my friend has suffered much indignity here in this house this evening. Would you agree that publicity should be avoided at all costs?"

"The main thing as far as I'm concerned is to ascertain that no bodily harm has been done to the young woman. I shall telephone, have a doctor called in." Captain Suzuki left the room with a swaggering air and short, quick steps.

Moving to Bixby's side, Trask said harshly, "What the hell has been going on? What took place? Fill me in on details. While doing so, clean, tidy yourself up. Use the water, the soap, the towels. Hurry yourself. Get on with it. Was it you who knocked the girl around? For Christ's sake, what kind of man are you?"

Bixby obeyed his instructions so calmly that he might not have had a worry in the world, his every action restrained, slow, and strangely remote. As he completed his ablutions and attempted to repair the dishevelment of his garments, he glanced at Trask and said almost inaudibly, "Now that the storm is over, can we leave this moon-drenched old house?"

Trask remained silent as a wave of nausea swept through him. His own secret torments had not been allayed. This man Bixby, this stranger, had broken into the magic spell he had so painstakingly woven over the years. It was unwitting on Bixby's part, but still, he longed to injure the fellow. All he had to do was walk out of the situation, but an unwritten law decreed that in Japan foreigners stood by one another no matter the circumstances. There was no point in being unpleasant. *Moon-drenched old house* the chap had said. He liked the description. It had a mysterious depth to it.

In truth the entire situation seemed to be part of a larger mystery. An old Japanese house high on a bluff overlooking the ocean, probably once occupied by proud samurai then taken over and defamed by folk from the "lower depths." An amoral place housing harlots, and yet a sanctuary for men such as he, for men of many nationalities cast ashore, away from their homes and things familiar.

There was something appealing about the young whore who lay on the gaudily covered bed, her kimono torn, her eyes gazing vacantly at the ceiling. He hoped to heaven she had not been injured. That could cause complications and scandal. There was even something appealing about the Englishman who was once again standing, his back to the bed, arms folded, his lips pressed in a firm line, his eyes also gazing at the ceiling.

Trask wondered if the legendary Osen, the Edo courtesan, still lived in the house. Many poems had been written about her and many portraits painted. He owned one of them and admired it greatly. His thoughts were interrupted by Bixby's urgent voice. "Trask, she must have a decent garment to wear. Is it possible to order a carriage? She's not fit to travel in one of those confounded ricksha."

"Good God, are you suggesting that the girl come with us?"

"Are *you* suggesting that she be deserted? Left here?"

"Deserted? What utter rot! Again I stress, this is *Japan*! The girl, in all probability, willingly contracted to work here. Shiga will have paid in advance for her services. Understand?"

"Explain more fully?"

"It's an acceptable custom. Girls are purchased to work for extended periods. No girl is free to leave until her time is up."

"Then, as I see it, no problem stands in the way. I shall reimburse the brothel keeper. Free her from her obligations."

"My God, you're more fool than I thought you to be. Now, get this straight. You are a stranger here. You've not the slightest chance of taking a harlot from this house to do with her as you please."

For an instant the muscles around Bixby's mouth twitched, then he said quietly, "I'm not leaving without this girl. Do me the favor of calling the British consul here. He will vouch for my character. He will—"

"No," Trask interjected, lowering his voice. "All this, if managed correctly, could turn out to be no more than a storm in a teacup. Bring in a foreign official and it could become a scandal of international magnitude. Also, it would be considered an enormous insult to the Japanese. . . ." Trask, baffled, drummed his fingers against his head, then continued, speaking calmly as though to an unmanageable child. "My dear fellow, I shudder to think what repercussions any reckless behavior could arouse in the foreign community. We who live here tread very carefully and avoid all unnecessary confrontations between consular and Japanese officialdom."

"How then do you manage?"

"Manage?"

"Yes. Manage! When problems arise, or are you saying that all foreigners dwelling here face no problems?"

"We face many problems. . . ."

"So . . ." Bixby interjected, "who performs the smoothing-out process? Come, tell me that."

"Useless information to you, a mere tourist."

"Allow me to decide that. Who . . ."

"No point in continuing this senseless diatribe . . ."

"Once more, allow me to decide that."

"God damn your stupidity. You are out to make trouble," Trask continued in an exasperated voice. "We who live here fortunately have influential Japanese friends who willingly step in to vouch for us. They seldom fail to smooth matters. Now, enough of this. Take my advice."

Bixby looked at Trask with strangely cold eyes and said, "Don't underestimate *me*. It so happens that I have a friend who, I have reason to believe, is a man of some substance. His name is Yamamoto. Renzō Yamamoto. He deals in antiques. I believe he lives in—"

Trask, taken aback, blurted out, "Extraordinary! Renzō happens to be a friend of mine. He—"

Gesturing for silence, Bixby said sharply, "Then—get him here. . . ."

"I'll be glad to oblige. But, understand I must make no move until the doctor gives the girl a clean bill of health. Do nothing to upstage the police captain. I implore you to cooperate. Remember what I've been saying. . . ." Trask fell silent as the policeman accompanied the frail, silver-haired doctor into the room, who said quaveringly, "Her name? What is her name? I like to know my patient's name. . . ."

"Tomiko. She is named Tomiko," Shiga whispered. . . .

T HUS IT WAS THAT RENZŌ Yamamoto found himself face-to-face again with the Englishman Arthur Bixby. All he understood was that Bixby insisted on having the injured young girl taken from the brothel.

Captain Suzuki was extremely officious, asking question after question. Unsatisfied with the answers, he raised his voice threateningly and insisted that Shiga was lying, that he must have made certain monetary arrangements with the Englishman Bixby in order for him to take the harlot Tomiko away from the house with him.

At weeping point, Shiga repeated, "No. *No*. The client paid merely for a short time. Only for a short time . . ."

Trask, at his wit's end, kept muttering angrily, "Hurry things up, Renzō! Hurry things along. For God's sake, put an end to this lunatic business."

Bixby stood by, calm and silent, but finally said, "Trask, ranting and arguments will do no good." Then he murmured, "Renzō, just find out what the stumbling block is and get it out of the way."

As he gestured that Bixby should give him time, a cynical smile flickered across Renzō's face. He knew that for all the new ways of the Age of Enlightenment, time-honored class distinctions still held sway. Rightly or wrongly, he decided to bide his time, for he knew that when he so wished he could cut the policeman down to size, but he had no intention of denigrating the officialdom of his country in the presence of outsiders. For all their differences, he and Captain Suzuki had their nationality in common.

He stood for some time, his gaze fixed on something in the middle distance. Voices from the past came to him in ghostly echoes. Then he stepped in to negotiate.

He and Suzuki played the game they understood so well. Renzō knew that officialdom must not be seen to be crushed too easily. He bolstered up Suzuki's self-confidence. Suzuki knew the outcome already but faced the situation with expertise and dignity. Both men were adept in the art of long silences to fill the gaps in their lengthy dialogues.

Renzō stressed the importance of closing down the illegal brothel "used so shamefully for the convenience of lustful foreigners." He also pointed out that someone high up in the police force—naturally, no name mentioned—must be accepting a cut from Shiga's profits. Surely, they were treading on dangerous ground where *that* was concerned? "That the brothel system encouraged corruption could not be denied?"

Suzuki's bombastic attitude disappeared. Renzō took out his English cigar case and offered a cigar to the police officer. Taking their time, each one puffed away thoughtfully, all of a sudden friends of a kind.

Suzuki said adamantly, "Yamamoto Sama, I wish to manage this unsavory business without attracting *any unnecessary* publicity."

"I agree fully with you, Captain Suzuki."

"You do?"

"I do."

"Naturally, I'll confer with my superiors first, before acting."

"First?"

"Yes. I allude to the closing down of this brothel."

"But, of course! Yes, best to tread softly in such unsavory matters."

"Yes. Now, about the girl?"

"Ah, that unfortunate young person! Yes, what of her? Fortunately she suffered no physical injury. Just shock."

"She presents a problem. But at least the girl has been saved from falling into the hands of the Englishman. The American, Trask, insists that his friend is soon to leave our country. I suspect he lies."

"No. Trask spoke the truth. Be assured the Englishman sails off tomorrow, on board the vessel *Northampton*."

"That's good! He, the Englishman, is well known to you? Personally, I find him extraordinary. So much fuss and bother all for a harlot with whom he spent but a moment."

"Never mind about him. Now, Captain, what exactly do you intend to do for the girl?"

Suzuki grinned widely. "How you joke! What exactly do *you* have in mind?"

In the same light vein, Renzō replied, "I have a natural sympathy for all young females. Between us, shall we give the girl a chance to live a decent life?"

"Hmm . . . The idea appeals. But, exactly how?"

Struck by an inspirational thought, Renzō replied firmly, "By allowing Keiko Sama, my wife's mother, to take the girl into her small Kamakura cottage. Train her there as a housemaid. How about it? Naturally the decision is yours."

"Yamamoto Sama." Once again Suzuki grinned. "Shall we agree that the decision is—ours."

That matter settled, more important to Renzō was the overwhelming shadow of Kenichi Yamamoto's spirit, and he made it clear to the police officer that the aged courtesan, Osen, should stay on in the Yokohama house until her demise. He spoke candidly, saying, "I was unprepared to find my family's home so defamed."

"A grueling experience," Suzuki sympathized. "Trust me. The man, Shiga, will get more than he bargained for."

"Umm . . . Captain, Shiga is the old courtesan's adopted brother. Perhaps it would be wise not to overreact? May I leave the complicated matter in your hands?"

"You may! Yes, thank you for confiding in me. I shall respect your wishes and try to cause as few waves as possible. . . ." Suzuki sighed deeply, then added, "A police officer's life is hard. So many unpleasant issues to deal with . . . Ah, Shiga's good wife is bringing us tea. Good. Good . . ."

Having assured Captain Suzuki that he would take charge of To-miko, Renzō telephoned his home and arranged to rendezvous with the only person whom he believed would be bold and kindly enough to come to his assistance.

Keiko, unperturbed by the lateness of the hour did not question him unduly. "I'm in need of your help," he said. "Greatly in need. Can you come to Yokohama? Now, at once?"

"But of course! Thank you for asking me," she replied quietly. "Should I be concerned about your well-being, Renzō?"

"No, rest easy on that point. Briefly, I've become embroiled in a distasteful situation."

After arranging to meet Keiko at the station, he strode back to the shambles in the room, where he patiently explained the arrangements to Bixby, and strongly advised him not to create further trouble while he was away meeting Keiko. Bixby nodded his assent but did not move from his stance in front of the bed. Leaving a disgruntled Trask in charge, Renzō walked briskly from the house. He ignored the crowd still gathered outside. With a brusque gesture he dismissed the approach of a news reporter eager to question him. He hailed a ricksha hovering outside and ordered the runner, "Take me to the station."

Some thirty minutes later, the sight of Keiko's well-known figure alighting from the train filled him with warmth, and a sense of gratitude for her immediate response to his request. As they were driven toward the house on the hill, he was relieved to find that Keiko's presence had a calming effect. "Just tell me," she said, "exactly why you have need of me?"

After he had explained his understanding of the complex situation, she finally said, "Renzō, clarify certain details if you please. The man Bixby, is, I gather, of English samurai class?"

"Correct."

"What manner of man is he?"

"He *was* the acme of British pomposity, but he is greatly changed. I scarcely recognized the chap."

"Excuse me, please, but what can I do?"

"Take the unfortunate girl to the cottage in Kamakura. My plan, which you alone can assist, is to prevent Bixby from involving any consular interference and to have his whim satisfied. A rude imposition upon you, I know, but will you help?"

"Need you ask! My pity goes out to the girl. What a *remarkable* business this is. Could it be that the man Bixby is of the missionary ilk? Those missionaries, so I hear from Rumi, see our society as decadent. Rumi-chan tells me that they frown upon all open show of sensuality."

"Umm . . . true," he murmured vacantly.

"Shinichi tells me that to placate foreigners, our government seems determined to teach the nation lessons in prudery. True?"

"True, yes. Believe it or not . . ." Miserable as he was, Renzō smiled at the plump woman. He understood her chatter was to take his mind off his problems. No one was more charitable than Keiko, and he knew she was flattered by his need for her assistance.

Alighting from the carriage after it pulled up at the garish red gate, Keiko pushed her way through the curious crowd and quickly entered the house.

Once inside the upstairs room, she disregarded the chaos and the vulgarity of harlots in a holiday mood shouting down to the bystanders. After bowing to the police officer, Keiko gave her attention to the figure on the bed. The girl lay as though hypnotized, her eyes wide open, staring at the ceiling.

All those present stood by watching as the elderly woman took on the stance of a militant organizer.

A paneled screen was brought in and placed about the bed. Sternly, Keiko gestured to Bixby that she demanded privacy for her charge. At once, he moved away from his post, as, with no compunction, Keiko chased out the gossiping harlots, sliding shut the damaged door to the corridor which opened only when the nerve-racked Fuji came in and out bringing fresh water, towels, fresh garments.

The female activity going on behind the screen had a strong effect on the four males in the room. One and all they appeared to be at a loss, preferring not to meet each others' eyes.

Finally, Renzō spoke to Suzuki, explaining what he intended to say to the foreign troublemaker Bixby. Then, having the officer's agreement, he drew Trask and the Englishman out to the veranda-platform, saying, "Surely now we must discuss the girl's future welfare, calmly and with honesty. Bixby—you agree?"

"I have no other choice," Bixby replied harshy. "Renzō, I rely on you. Trust you. Yes, trust you completely . . ."

"How long," Trask put in irefully, "is this powwow to continue? I can't take much more. I've a busy day ahead. I . . ."

"My apologies," Bixby said courteously. "Trask, let me delay
you no longer. . . ."

Having been assured by Bixby that he could make his own way
back to the club in Tokyo, Thomas Trask, resembling one escaping
from a burning house, made his departure, much to the envy of
Renzō, who, with extraordinary fortitude spent the next hour explaining detail upon detail of the plans which were to be carried out
for the welfare of the girl Tomiko. With every passing minute Bixby
became more relaxed. There was a softening of the tension around
his mouth, a something akin to humor tugging at it as he said,
"Renzō, many years ago, in London, you advised me to visit your
country. You remember?"

"I do."

"You recommended Japanese brothels. You remember?"

"Only too well." Renzō, unable to prevent a grin, added, "I certainly lacked the ability to foresee the consequences."

Exhausted, sorely tried by the unpleasant experience he had lived
through, he wasted no time in ordering a carriage for Bixby's trip
to the station. After the man had gone on his way, Renzō turned to
Captain Suzuki, declaring, "My feelings are of the most sincere
gratitude to you."

"Ah! Don't mention it!" Suzuki frowned, then murmured, "I can't
help feeling that something is strangely amiss with the Englishman."

"Amiss?"

"Yes. His intelligence is limited. How else after taking such a
frantic interest in the girl could he march off without so much as
casting a glance in her direction? Did you not find that peculiar?"
He shrugged contemptuously.

"A peculiar business all around." Renzō also shrugged. "So, Captain, shall we just wish Bixby San a rough sea trip back to England.
Agreed?"

"Agreed!" The police officer laughed heartily. . . .

Instead of returning to his home, Renzō went straightaway to visit
his aunt Sumiko. Although she was now very much out of life's
stream, leading a quiet life in her twilight years, he knew that she
alone would be able to fully comprehend his feelings, and sympathize with him.

Throughout the interlude spent in Sumiko's cozy sitting room, he
felt secure and free to blurt out his anger. From time to time she

interjected with comments like "There's no limit to the wickedness of human behavior.

"Hold nothing back! Renzō, you and I are the only ones left who are familiar with the past concerning the old home. Family affairs, like morning-glory blossoms, must not be roughly handled by outsiders.

"Renzō, I'm forced to admit that I'm not particularly shocked or surprised to learn of the courtesan Osen's betrayal in having made our beloved home into a brothel. My dear husband always declared that Kenichi's obsession for the woman was the height of tastelessness. Yes, and let me add that your father, *my brother*, was a *grossly* insensitive man in many respects." Gazing at him tenderly, she murmured, "My advice may not seem profound, however, allow me to say that to be fair, you should continue to regard your father's spirit with kindliness. He was but a typical man of his times. Different indeed from *my* dear husband. He, your uncle, was a man apart. . . ." Tears fell freely from her eyes as she cried out, her voice tinged with sorrow. "Dear, wonderful man." Then she added firmly, "Renzō, I hope that you often give thought to him?"

"I do. Indeed, I do, Aunt," he said, now eager to soothe the one who had soothed him. "Also, I agree with you that we alone should be the ones to know details of what happened in that once-honored house on the hill overlooking Hommoku Bay."

"I agree absolutely. Yes . . ."

Sumiko broke off when Kentaro slid open the door and thrust his head in. "Ken-chan!" she admonished her grandson sternly, "apologize at once, then away with you. . . ."

"Please," Renzō interceded, "let him come in, Aunt. Soon I must be on my way. Come, Ken-chan, sit by me for a moment."

The little boy ran to his side, and Renzō played a childish game with the son whom he could not acknowledge as his own. He loved him dearly but could show only a modicum of his true feelings.

After making his farewell, he felt cheered by his aunt's company. He admired Sumiko for not having alluded to the young harlot Tomiko. He understood that it would be unseemly to mention such a person in her hallowed sanctum. The young girl's future was of little concern to him, but together with Keiko, he would see to it that she was set free and sent back to her family if that was what she desired. . . .

. . .

Early the following day Thomas Trask arrived at the Yamamoto home, carrying several worn suitcases which he dumped on the floor, saying irately, "I want no more to do with the ludicrous affair. Renzō, may I call upon you to have this luggage delivered?"

"Naturally—gladly! But deliver it to *whom* and exactly *where*?"

"Allow me to enlighten you." Trask spoke with weary indignation. "That troublesome chap Bixby, the devil take him, left a message at my club. He is staying at the hotel in Kamakura, minus luggage, and requests it be brought to him without delay."

Seldom had Renzō been so taken aback. "By all the gods!" he exclaimed. "I thought him to be on the high seas!"

"Well, you are sadly in error. He is still with us. The *Northampton* has left and he was *not* on board."

"Intentionally?"

"How should I know?"

"Hmmm . . . yes, why *should* you know!"

Following Trask's departure, Renzō wondered whether Bixby might not in fact be mentally disturbed. He thought not. Did he really have the welfare of the prostitute at heart? That idea was too nonsensical altogether. So . . . ?

He sent his manservant, Rin, off to Kamakura with Bixby's luggage, together with a note saying that he would call on him at Kamakura as soon as he could. Soon after, a hastily brushed letter arrived from Keiko, explaining how Bixby had brashly accompanied her and the girl Tomiko on the train trip to Kamakura. She was in need of his advice.

Renzō replied by courier service and then relaxed, for now he could attend to Bixby's and Keiko's affairs without causing much inconvenience to himself.

He was pleased to receive the information that Captain Suzuki had, in his own way, dealt with certain unpleasant issues. Quite miraculously, all malicious gossip and rumors had been silenced. The residence, no longer a brothel, housed only the courtesan who was cared for by her adopted brother and his wraithlike wife, Fuji. The news was like a breath of fresh air for Renzō; nevertheless, it did not compensate for the fact that the dignity of his old home had been irretrievably desecrated.

In the meantime, he had more pleasant things to do. With a light heart he bade a fond farewell to his family and traveled by train to Tokyo.

Renzō had come to a point in life when he refused to magnify problems. He was apt to declare, " 'Twas *I* who began the popular pastime of *ginbura*—killing time on the Ginza. It never fails to intrigue me. . . ." And certainly he was often to be seen on the famous street. But he was not interested in the dazzling surroundings now, for he was more intent on reaching a narrow side lane that ran off the main thoroughfare.

The lane itself had a dilapidated air. The ancient shops and dwellings were occupied by people who scratched out a living telling fortunes, training dogs to dance or bears to wrestle, or by selling cheap, third-hand clothing.

Renzō had purchased a rundown curio shop in the lane, his only interest in the place being the two-room apartment upstairs which both he and Aiko Fukuda alluded to as "Our Second Folly." He kept the bleary-eyed caretaker on to do necessary chores, and the old man was always on hand to unlatch the entry door.

As usual when entering that apartment, Renzō was overcome by feelings of contentment in the intimate atmosphere which he and Aiko had created.

In a leisurely manner he exchanged his Western garments for a cotton *yukata*. Tying its wide black sash loosely, he gazed around the room, pacified by the assortments of books, magazines, his English pipe rack and Aiko's lacquered sewing box filled with unfinished embroideries.

The tangible intimacy of the room had a sensuous yet tranquilizing effect on him.

The complexities of the outside world were forgotten as he fired charcoal in the bath-stove, hoping that the water would be heated by the time Aiko arrived. Bathing together dispelled any feelings of guilt they might have brought with them, and the relaxing effect of water influenced their lovemaking. They both agreed that there was something wondrously exciting about freshly bathed bodies. If so inclined, they would remain in the bath for quite a while, at times silent, at times talking animatedly of events that had taken place since their last rendezvous.

He always felt better about himself after stolen hours in Aiko's company. Situations that had seemed to be untenable became less important. She was someone with whom he could be almost completely honest, and he hoped that she felt as he did. Indeed the very thought of Aiko holding back from total honesty caused him pain.

Aiko arrived exactly at the appointed time, rather more stilted in manner than usual. There were dark smudges beneath her eyes, and although eager to air certain of his problems, he said sympathetically, "The bath is ready, but perhaps a tot of cognac first?"

"You know me too well. As the English say, I've been burning my candle at both ends. A little too much revelry."

Accepting the tiny bowl of brandy, Aiko took one delicate sip, then sighed. "Ah, Renzō, already I feel more at ease. You and I, like our country, lead a double life. Japan, a mixture of the domestic and the imported! We . . . ? How to describe us?"

"Why bother!"

"Yes. Why bother. I'm more interested to learn how and why *you* were drawn into that scandalous Yokohama affair while I was in Kyoto with Marjorie."

Renzō frowned, then said lightly, "The entire affair was blown out of proportion. Come, entertain me. I revel in hearing of Marjorie's glorious gaffes."

"Well," Aiko replied, laughing, "have you days to spare?"

"Unfortunately, no. Exactly three hours. I've an appointment to keep. A train to catch."

"Off to . . . ?"

"To Kamakura. That place you know so very well from your early days."

"Too well! It holds few charms for me. So, will you be calling on old Ohara Sama?"

"Not this time." Renzō caressed his pipe. "Aiko, I'm concerned about the way you punish yourself, gallivanting about, endlessly on the go."

"Thank you for caring, but in the current social climate, parties are in vogue. I, being the 'perfect wife,' follow humbly in my husband's footsteps." She looked at him defiantly and added, "You don't consider me to be a perfect wife? Perfect—anything?"

"To my mind," he said, "you are *almost* perfect in every way. How dreary to be quite perfect. No?"

"True. I hope I'm never dreary."

"Never!"

"Foolish of me, I know, but at times I need to have you compliment me. It's pathetic how one longs to be praised. Enough of my ennui! Only with you, Renzō, can I be blatantly frank—I've no desire to share the pillow with you today. Do you mind?"

"Mind? I'm devastated!"

"Sweet liar! Light me a cigarette. Come tell me about the crazy Englishman Bixby. About the young harlot who now dwells in the cottage at Kamakura. Tell me the whole truth. My sister, Rumi, told me such a muddled tale. . . ."

"Rumi?" Renzō said disapprovingly, "I told her but little."

"Maybe so! But *her* mother, the old geisha, naturally confides in her daughter. Rumi, naturally, has spoken to my mother-in-law. She, your aunt Sumiko, naturally, has spoken to *me*. I, naturally, have gossiped with *Marjorie*. So . . . ?"

"How women love to gossip on the telephone!"

Waving her arms airily, Aiko replied, "Yes, and how you men supply us with titillating material."

"Touché! Hmmm, yes . . ." Renzō grinned disarmingly.

"So," Aiko commanded, "tell on! Sir John Coomber insists that no nation more than ours revels in scandals, in any *affaire d'amour*."

"*Love* affairs?"

"According to Rumi, a torrid love affair goes on in Kamakura. No?"

"Not from my point of view."

"What then? A mere dalliance?"

"I think not even that. It's possible that Bixby's interest in the girl is purely humanistic."

Aiko, eyebrows raised, inhaled smoke from the cigarette she had placed in a slender jade holder. Exhaling, she exclaimed provokingly, "You disappoint me. So close-lipped. Never mind. So, it's purely a man-to-man business? Excuse my female interference."

"You misunderstand."

"Obviously. Again, never mind."

Renzō refilled his bowl from the brandy bottle, then said thoughtfully, "Aiko, there are so many threads to unravel. I fully expected that Bixby would return to England on board the *Northampton*. Imagine my astonishment when—" His voice ceased and he frowned at her.

"When what?" Aiko queried impatiently.

"Well, he has stayed on, allowing the ship to steam away with his main luggage on board. He accompanied Keiko and the girl on the train trip to Kamakura, and actually went into the cottage."

"Yes? And . . . ?"

"And stayed on throughout the night. Keiko says that to the man's credit, he did not so much as lay a hand on the girl. Keiko, at a loss, offered him the meager meal of rice and pickles that she had prepared, which Bixby apparently ate with relish."

"Does the man still remain in the old geisha's cottage?"

"No. Evidently Keiko has been able to convince Bixby that the girl is in no danger of being taken from her care. She persuaded him to book himself into the hotel nearby. An extraordinary business, is it not?"

"Yes. All the elements of a crazy melodrama! Lady Marjorie tells me that the Englishman is of good stock. *You* tell me that his interest in a Japanese harlot is pure, humanistic. Truly, I must meet with this rare bird—as your aunt Sumiko would say."

Aiko's actions made it apparent that she was intending to take her leave. Renzō reached out to catch at her flowing sleeve. "Please— don't leave!"

"Excuse me!" She spoke without moving her lips, reminding him with a bitter sweetness of his mother.

"How have I annoyed you?" he asked.

"You flatter yourself. I'm just plainly bored. I must leave."

"I want you to stay."

"I must go."

"Why? Be honest. Tell me why?"

"I'm not exactly sure. There are times when I'm not certain of anything." Aiko shrugged her shoulders hopelessly, then suddenly she laughed, all irritation gone, and gestured that she might disrobe.

Relieved that she was not about to run off, Renzō said admiringly, "You don't mind in the least that I shall miss that four o'clock train, do you?"

"I mind not in the least," she replied. "Not in the least." She shook her head sadly, but there was a gleam of satisfaction in her eyes.

Renzō knew that their relationship thrived on their mutual needs, but there were times when he wondered how much pressure it could withstand. Then he thought only of the woman as he watched with delight while she shed her garments.

Aiko, so warm, so eager, lying entwined with him . . . Everything else disappeared from his mind. Bixby, awaiting his arrival in Kamakura, might not have existed.

Rumi Yamamoto awakened slowly and with some regret. She had been dreaming of childhood days spent in the cottage at Kamakura.

She and her mother had wandered to the seashore to picnic beneath the shade of the rugged pine trees so famous in the district. Miraculously, an old fisherman appeared at their side, bowing and offering them a wicker basket brimming with silver sardines. "How kind!" Keiko had murmured. "Ah, Rumi-chan, what a delicious feast awaits us . . ." A dream-bird sang, and continued to sing even though the dream was over.

"How peculiar," Rumi mused, then realized that the sweet trilling was coming from the throat of Etsu's pet canary.

She lay very still in the darkness of the shuttered room, but her full lips twitched slightly. She smiled, sanguine and content. Feigning sleep, she remained still as Renzō yawned, stretched, then rose from his *futon* and left the room. For some years he had enjoyed the exercise of early morning sex with her, but, much to her amusement, never when the odor of violet-scented perfume clung to his person.

There were certain times when she had been tempted to inquire lightly, "Renzō, husband, tell me, how was my sister, Aiko, yesterday?" How aghast Renzō would be!

Lost in a maze of inward contemplation, Rumi wondered a little about her own sense of morality. Her husband was a handsome, considerate man, and a good father. If he, like most men, indulged in an extramarital affair, she considered it pleasing rather than disgraceful that it should be with her half sister. If her husband engaged with unknown females, she would be worried. Also, in a way, knowing the truth gave her a feeling of power. She found it fascinating to watch the interplay between the man and the woman during family gatherings. Both were so confident that they were managing to hoodwink society! She knew that they were both possessed of unswerving devotion to their individual families. So it was best to accept the situation and maintain harmony. Let her husband and sister keep their sexual behavior a secret. Why cause them shame and guilt?

They mistakenly believed that they had a shared secret. She was sharing hers with the mother to whom she was so close and, as Keiko had said so wisely, "We all carry secrets. They are an important part of our uniqueness. They may be trivial. This one of yours is not, but, daughter, you show wisdom by not allowing yourself the luxury of belittling your husband and your sister. Poor Aiko! Neither of her parents loved her. You, as you know, were adored from the moment of your birth by your noble father."

Rumi now yawned, stretched her limbs, and snuggled down to listen to the familiar sounds of the awakening household. Servants were clattering about, opening shutters to welcome autumn's sunshine into the house. Etsu was feeding her canary and Renzō was calling loudly, "Move yourself, Shinichi! Rin's saddling the horses."

So Renzō had persuaded his son to join him on his daily gallop through the countryside. The youth would not be too enthusiastic about that. How handsome her son was. Folk were apt to liken Shinichi to his father, but in her opinion Renzō had been in no way as good-looking in his youth.

A servant slid open the door, saying, "May I open the shutters, mistress?"

"*Dōzo*—please," she replied briskly. The day ahead stretched out before her. So much, so many enjoyable things to do. She was especially eager to receive another gossipy telephone call from Keiko, to hear in detail all that was happening in Kamakura. Renzō was being extremely secretive about that peculiar situation. He was at times provoking in the extreme.

T HE THREE PEOPLE SAT TOGETHER in the main room of the cottage that was hidden away on Ohara's large Kamakura estate. The girl Tomiko was unable to comprehend why she had been brought from Yokohama. She sat immobile, hiding her fears. The woman Keiko had tricked her, she was sure. If not, why should the barbarian man come to the house every day? Having decided to accept her fate, she was finding the waiting game now being played out in the isolated house just as terrifying as the horror and commotion of the brothel scene. Each night she would lie awake, disturbed by the slightest sounds. Every morning the bird song announced for her a new day of fear.

Bixby sat engrossed in his thoughts, frequently filled with anger, for he believed that Renzō Yamamoto was out to insult him. Why else should he not have kept his word and come to discuss matters? His position was intolerable. He was powerless, unable to communicate adequately with the elderly woman who bustled about preparing unpalatable meals, and who was now sitting on a floor-cushion, obviously guarding the girl, while she stitched narrow lengths of material, smiling sometimes, speaking to him in her sparse English.

Keiko herself had seldom been at such a loss. She trembled with anger toward Renzō, who had placed her in so insidious a situation. With all the goodwill in the world she had obeyed his every instruction, but he had not told her that the foreign man was to be part of the deal. His instructions had been disarmingly simple: "Take the girl under your care. Keep close watch over her. Soon, I'll take charge of the matter."

Never before had she been so flagrantly insulted. As a geisha, skilled entertainer, and as a woman, she despised those who were involved in the trafficking of prostitutes. She, who had loved and been loved, believed that no female had ever freely chosen to work in the realm of harlotry. Now she felt that she had been placed in the role of a brothel madam, that unwittingly she had become a tool of male brotherhood, utilized to transport Tomiko to this secret place, not for the girl's benefit, as Renzō had intimated.

The girl's passivity was distressing. Showing no signs of anguish, she accepted all Keiko's attentions, bowing, saying monotonously, "*Gomen nasai*—excuse me, please! Excuse me, please . . ."

Three days earlier a special-delivery letter had come from Renzō in reply to the one she had sent him explaining their dilemma and asking for assistance. Renzō's reply had been all too casual. "*Be easy . . .*" he wrote. "*The man Bixby poses no threat. Of that I'm convinced. Ignore his bluff, his bad manners. Understand that I'm presently caught up, dealing with the unpleasant business of ridding my ancestral home of the disgrace which has befouled it. Without fail I shall be with you soon. To be exact, on Friday. Arriving on the four o'clock train . . .*"

He had not kept his word. He had not arrived.

How the time dragged! Fits of drowsiness overcame Keiko, and her head began to droop. She glanced at the man who was obviously lost in his thoughts, and then at Tomiko, whose eyelids were closed as though in sleep. Surely neither of the pair would notice if she dozed off for a minute or two . . . ?

Aware that the elderly woman had fallen asleep, Bixby remained still. An exquisite sense of happiness swept through him. For the first time since his initial glimpse of Tomiko in the brothel, he and she were together without being watched. He had given up all thoughts of attempting to understand his emotions. His feelings toward Tomiko grew stronger. Unknowingly, he had been searching, *longing* for one special girl, and here, in the small room, she sat close by.

But she was terrified of him. How that knowledge hurt! He loved

her and knew that he was to love her all the days of his life. But he
was terrified that she would never care for him and that he would
lose her.

He gave no thought to what people might think of him. As far
as he was concerned, the entire world could blunder on as it would.
Never had he believed or even imagined that love could strike so
suddenly, so powerfully.

The arrival of Renzō's manservant, Rin, bringing his belongings
from the Tokyo club had relieved him greatly, but not as much as
the letter stating that Renzō himself would be arriving to help sort
things out. The Japanese man owed him nothing; nevertheless, it
was reprehensible of him not to keep his word.

Daylight was gradually fading, and from the giant oak tree near
the open door came the sound of creatures preparing for the night
ahead. A bushy-tailed squirrel clutching an acorn scampered down
from the tree and dropped his booty which rolled into the room.
The bright-eyed little animal peered around quizzically, obviously
not daring to venture farther forward. Tomiko, fascinated, was leaning slightly forward, her gaze darting from the acorn to the squirrel.
Bixby flicked the shiny nut toward the door and the perky forager
grabbed it before making a hasty retreat back up the tree.

Tomiko looked him straight in the eye for a brief half second and
a shadowy smile crossed her face before she lowered her head.

Unaware of the magic moment that had occurred for Bixby, Keiko
dozed on. Bixby took his leave. He did not return to the hotel but
went instead to the seashore, where the last of the sunlight glittered
on granite boulders.

Memories of people and incidents from his past came back to him,
and he relinquished them all. His family home in Brunton Street
belonged to another world and time. His future was now completely
dependent on the welfare of Tomiko. It was as if he were struggling
up a mountain that was shrouded in mist. Night fell and the sea
became ink black.

SHINICHI YAMAMOTO HAD A DEEP affection for every member of
his family. He admired his uncle Yuichi, the intrepid entrepreneur
and trailblazer in the forces of bureaucracy and big business. And
he loved his father, that ingenious man who lived stylishly without

expending too much energy. Shinichi genuinely looked forward to his frequent morning horseback rides with his father, though he felt most alive in the company of his peers.

Together with Gen Ohara and Hans Dreyer, his close friends since childhood days, he despised aggressiveness. All three had decided to embark on a crusade to discover a formula that would allow them to remain perennial students and to devote their lives to the study of the human animal.

"We shall move forward into the future with an unflagging confidence," Shinichi expounded.

"Exactly," Gen agreed with gusto. "The past is unchangeable. The future is ours to form. As far as I'm concerned, I've a degree of loyalty to my country and, to a smaller extent, to the person of the emperor. For the rest, well, I'm determined to follow my own desires."

The Ohara mansion in Kamakura was open to Gen's friends at all times, and Shinichi and Hans seldom missed an opportunity to spend time on the seaside estate, especially during the summer months, when they bathed in the ocean during the day and at night often fished for monster crabs.

The aristocratic Ohara clan had an ongoing love affair with France and everything French, a fact that aroused scorn in Hans Dreyer, the only child of the rich Dreyer family of German descent. Born and raised in Japan, he felt himself to be more Japanese than either of his two friends. He had no desire to travel abroad and often declared, "Yamamoto, you go off to the United States and study your head off as you will. Ohara, off to the Sorbonne as you will! Tokyo's Waseda University more than suits *my* needs."

Renzō, friendless in his own youthful days, took pleasure in the male trio, while, at the same time, he considered them to be much too pampered and was often irritated by their naive self-assurance. As he and Shinichi set out on their morning gallop, Renzō was glad to have his son to himself. They rode their horses hard and in silence, relishing the invigorating morning air and the power and strength of their mounts.

Dismounting as they returned to the stables, Renzō said casually, "Shinichi, have you plans for the day? I've an overdue appointment in Kamakura. I'd be obliged if you would come with me."

Although dismayed, Shinichi discarded his own plans without hesitation, and said, "I'm complimented, Father," and Renzō hurried him along enthusiastically.

Against his own will, Shinichi followed his father's instructions that he should dress in classic Japanese garments. While examining his stylish reflection in a long mirror, he grinned and muttered, "I'm fittingly clothed to attend a royal garden party." Nonetheless, he liked the dignified outfit, especially the stiffly pleated divided skirt made of tough black silk that was exquisite to touch.

His sister, Etsu, gazed at him adoringly, crying out, "I've the *most* handsome brother!"

"I? Handsome?" he replied sincerely. "Nonsense, Et-chan."

Truthfully, he was not aware of his good looks, and when he and his father finally entered the crowded lobby of the hotel in Kamakura, he believed that the many admiring glances from the women present were for Renzō alone.

After his introduction to the gaunt-faced Englishman, Shinichi realized that he alone was relishing the lunch of lobster broiled in butter and prepared over a charcoal fire. The two older men were ill at ease, treating each other warily as they recalled times they had experienced in London so many years earlier.

Renzō for his part was startled by the changes in Bixby's appearance in such a short space of time. He was the epitome of a man under stress who is determined to bear up under the strain.

He realized that Bixby understood why he had brought Shinichi along, his way of saying that he had no intention of becoming further entangled in Bixby's affairs.

After Renzō commiserated with the foreigner about the fact that the ship steamed off without him on board, Bixby had retorted harshly, "It was no accident. I acted deliberately." His wan appearance and his impatience clearly showed that he was in need of assistance. But when Renzō indicated that he had no intention of giving further aid, Bixby spoke courteously to Shinichi and then thanked his host for the pleasant meal. He got up, nodded abruptly, and moved off without saying good-bye.

"Now, that hasty exit strikes me as being rather odd, Father!" Shinichi exclaimed. "As Aunt Sumiko would say, 'That man was on the very *brink* of tears!' What ails him? I quite like the sad fellow. Take *my* advice, go after him."

Casting a sharp glance at his son, Renzō said reprovingly, "Kindly don't interfere with things beyond your understanding. I've no need of your advice."

"Thank you for being frank, Father. It's so refreshing. People in general seldom speak their minds."

Renzō, intent on keeping his dignity, said stiffly, "Regardless of your unasked-for advice, I am going after him. Stay here and finish your meal." As he rose to his feet, Renzō added, "Entertain yourself for several hours. Understood?"

"Certainly. Anything to oblige," Shinichi replied. "Out of common politeness, I'll visit my grandmother. I'll look into the so-called sordid little affair which goes on in her cottage."

"Keep away from the cottage," Renzō interjected. "Apart from that, do as you please, call on your friend Gen. Then meet me back here."

"Certainly! At what time?"

"When it suits my convenience to be here." Renzō nodded abruptly and moved off, half ashamed, half amused at his churlishness. Could it be that he was jealous of his son's athletic youthfulness? No, but just a little nostalgic for his own lost youth.

He regretted that the Englishman had seen through his thinly disguised lack of interest in his affairs. Memories of Bixby's prejudices about *him*, in London, had been souring him. He must kill those niggling feelings and become open-minded. Yes, redeem himself, act with style. Go all-out to help the fellow. If—preposterous as it was—Bixby was obsessed by Tomiko, who was he to stand in judgment? Or stand in the way of a man desirous of indulging in sensual experience?

All churlishness gone, he hastened to reach Bixby. Gesturing with his walking stick toward a rustic tea house, he said, "Come, my friend. Let's talk."

The tea house was fitted out with wicker chairs and tables to suit the convenience of foreign tourists. Fortunately only a group of country people on vacation occupied the place. They ignored the two gentlemen, carrying on with their medley of loud talk, laughter, and bawdy songs.

It seemed to Renzō that he and Bixby stood at opposite ends of a long bridge. Perhaps they would be able to meet in the middle with accord? "Man to man," he exclaimed with warmth. "Bixby, what exactly can I do for you?"

"I have no wish to exploit our friendship. Please understand that."

"I understand. My mind is open."

Bixby hesitated, then as if with no time to spare, blurted out, "Is there a law in Japan forbidding foreigners and Japanese to live beneath the same roof. Intimately?"

"Certainly none, so far as I am aware. On the contrary, many foreign men live most pleasantly with Japanese women. Also," he added, half smiling, "with charming youths. Whatever they prefer." Renzō, relieved to have come so quickly to the crux of the matter, continued. "Bixby, such matters are in no way considered to be improper here."

The Englishman looked at him for several moments, then, leaning forward, he said with a disarming simplicity, "I speak of Tomiko. She has reshaped my life."

"I understand," Renzō, not understanding, murmured. "Yes, there are many chance happenings in our lives. Allow me, at least, to put you at ease in one respect." He dismissed a momentary surge of anger and said calmly, "*That* brothel has been closed down. Now, am I correct in assuming that you want to become the girl's patron? If so—please excuse my curiosity—how long are you intending to stay on in my country? For several weeks? Maybe several months?"

He fell silent, aware that Bixby was listening to him impatiently, if politely. In a cool manner he said, "Although many of our old ways and laws are now disappearing, our women are not to be shanghaied."

"Shanghaied?" Bixby queried hotly. "What of your brothel system?"

"Yes, that's a subject for lively debate. The world of international brotherhood has much to be ashamed of. However, the law is the law."

"Is there," Bixby queried, "a law preventing marriage between Japanese women and foreign men?"

Renzō, in some surprise, sat silent as if pondering the question.

"Is there?" Bixby insisted.

"No. Not so far as I know. But without doubt it is frowned upon."

"By whom?"

"By . . . ?" Renzō dug into his mind. "A moot point! Yes, quite so!" Rather to his amusement, he found he was getting caught up in Bixby's predicament. "In fact, one such marriage I know of *has* taken place. Between a Russian diplomat and a lady from a fine Japanese family."

"Diplomats and fine ladies!" Bixby stared down at his clenched hands. "Renzō, I can't expect you to understand. In all truth I don't

understand. Plainly put, I intend to spend the remainder of my life
with Tomiko. I appeal for your assistance. For the love of God—
help me."

"I shall do my best," Renzō said gently. "Thank you for confiding
in me. Now," he added briskly, "I've most respect for common
sense among all the virtues. So, my friend, how are we to proceed?"

Three days later, the humble cottage on the Ohara estate lay empty.
Keiko, much to her relief, was back among the family. The English-
man Bixby was now established in Tokyo in a small house of
Japanese structure fitted out with the comforts necessary for
Western-style living.

Wang, a young Chinese man skilled in the culinary arts, was in
charge of the kitchen, and Tanaka, a youth of fourteen, who lived
in terror of Wang's temperamental outbursts, was employed to carry
out household tasks.

Grudgingly, Bixby had agreed to have Tomiko believe that she
had been brought to the house in Tokyo to work out her indentured
time. He was deeply grateful to Renzō Yamamoto for having come
to his aid, and he scrupulously followed the Japanese man's instructions, aware that he could not manage without his help.

Bixby realized that he would never understand certain Japanese
customs, but did his utmost not to offend those persons who, full
of curiosity, came to the house. He especially welcomed Renzō's
son, Shinichi, and his two friends, Gen and Hans, who, with dedicated enthusiasm, acted as his tutors. With grim determination he
began to learn their language, not minding when the youths burst
out in hilarious laughter.

Thomas Trask would call, accompanied by Sir John Coomber,
who went out of his way to make whimsical comments, insisting
that he had every intention of stealing Wang, the Chinese cook.
"For years, as a moth seeks a flame, I've sought out such a chef."

Bixby was constantly delighted by the miracles that came to the
table from Wang's kitchen. The bad-tempered pigtailed man was
truly a genius, and Bixby never failed to compliment his chef. Wang,
Bixby surmised, would not easily be lured into the Coombers'
kitchen. "No likee make food for women," he would sneer. "Mu-
chee chow for the young woman here comes in from the eating
house down the street."

"She eats well?" he asked.

"She does. Eating well. Liking the flowers. Liking everything."

Wang had dismissed Tomiko's welfare with a savage gesture, slashing his chopping knife in the direction of his assistant, Tanaka, whose face grew pale and whose hands trembled.

Bixby knew that he had become a controversial figure, not only in the foreign community, but also in the eyes of his Japanese friends. He was not thought to be acceptable as a guest in their homes, to meet their wives and daughters.

F ROM TOMIKO'S POINT OF VIEW no room could be more luxurious than the one in which she had been living for many months. She hoped to describe it in detail when she returned home, but doubted her ability to do so.

Although summer could not come quickly enough, her pangs of homesickness were no longer so terrible. At times she could not help smiling a little, taking pleasure in the new identity she had assumed. Living in isolation, she had learned to create a world of her own. She had never been so well nourished, clear-minded, or energetic. She was experiencing feelings of freedom she had never dreamed of. She had not considered leaving the foreigner's house until her period of indenture came to an end, but she had made her preparations.

Quite often, through the long winter months, she had sat quietly in the warm comfort of her room, thinking back to that brothel, then to the small house in Kamakura and of her hasty exodus to this residence in Tokyo.

Several days after she was brought to the house, Yamamoto Sama had spoken to her, coldly explaining that she was to work out her time under the patronage of a foreigner. "Better by far," he said, "to oblige one man instead of many. Do you not agree?"

She bowed her agreement.

"Bixby San hopes that you will spend time beneath his roof pleasantly. He has requested me to give you this."

She took the brocaded money bag and placed it down upon the *tatami*. "Bixby San," he continued, "wishes you to feel free to move about his house and in the marketplace. Indulge yourself. Buy things you might fancy. Hire ricksha if you so wish and see the city. Do you understand me?"

Again she had bowed. Then she had looked at him directly and said, "Shall I be free to return to my village when the summer season finally arrives?"

"If you wish." He spoke wryly. "Meanwhile, keep your integrity. Remember that no true Japanese ever fails to repay debts."

For a long time after that interview with the haughty samurai, she remained in the quarters allotted to her, waiting to fulfill her duties. She scarcely touched the meals brought to her by the nervous houseboy, Tanaka. Night after night she lay awake, her eyes fixed on the doors, dreading the moment they would slide open.

Every daybreak a bell from the nearby temple would toll and she would arise, feeling that in some horrible way she was becoming like a figure made of hard, cold clay, who no longer cared about what lay in store for her. Foolish thoughts filled her mind. She wondered if she had, in fact, died and entered the eternal land to remain there, with nothing ever changing.

Could it be that the door of her room would never slide open for him to enter and take and use her body? He had never so much as looked on her in a lustful way. He had never put one foot into the quarters she dwelt in. Many men called at the house. She would hear their voices, loud male laughter. Back home in the village she had heard of men who preferred the love of other men to that of women. Gradually, she became convinced that Bixby San was such a person. That for social reasons she was being used as a "token" female. All at once she felt overcome by relief. She was unscathed, unmolested. Feeling as light as air, she got up and examined the articles of clothing that had been provided for her use.

She would wear those garments. She would leave the house and go into the city, taking a small sum of cash from the brocaded bag— just enough to purchase needles, threads, and lengths of strong, cheap material, from which she would fashion the kimono for her return home. . . .

That kimono now lay neatly folded on a special shelf. One morning she tried on the garment. Examining her reflection, she beheld in the mirror not the girl Tomiko who had dwelt in the village, but a comparative stranger, her complexion light, her hair glossy. Her hands were no longer work-worn, with broken nails.

A current of calm passed through her body and that day she went out into the street to wander along, breathing in the cold air, happy without knowing why. Now she would leave the house daily, oblivious of the weather, smiling at those who smiled at her, be-

coming accustomed to the extraordinary sight of horse-drawn om-
nibuses driven by men in bright Western livery, cocked hats upon
their heads.

No longer did she scuttle away from sword-carrying policemen.
No longer did she see foreigners as strange creatures. Some, without
doubt, were nice to look at, especially the children. That was only
natural; even in the animal world small creatures were always
charming.

When she inadvertently came face-to-face with the master of the
house, her heart froze. Most of those unexpected meetings took
place in the narrow, dim corridor they each had to use in order to
reach the bathroom.

When she discovered a public bathhouse in the vicinity, she visited it daily, leaving the house with her toiletries in a cheap basket.
The cash she was spending, small as it was, lay heavily on her conscience. So she purchased some bundles of bamboo sticks and several sharp knives. Just as her father had once done, she turned the
sticks into flute-whistles, working industriously for hours during
the night.

Finally, she took her wares into the grounds of a shrine and sold
them; she used the cash to buy more bamboo, always keeping a
strict record of her expenditures. After several weeks she was able
to pay for her own bath time, and, even better, to replace the cash
she had taken from the brocade bag.

She began to regard Bixby with some curiosity. She no longer
cringed back when they came face-to-face, but stood aside, allowing
him the right of way which, most politely, he took with no hesitation.

He was, she realized, of samurai stock. His politeness proved that
as well as his indisputable wealth. One day she asked Tanaka what
kind of master Bixby was.

"I'd say he's some kind of fool," the youth replied.

"Then, brother, why do you stay on in this place?" Her country
manner in addressing the servant in so familiar a way unnerved the
callow youth. Somewhat rudely he blurted out, "Sister, as *you* know,
not everyone is free to pick and choose."

Following his departure, she attempted to untangle his statement,
flushing deeply at the innuendo that she was a bought female, not
free to follow her own will.

. . .

Tomiko sat in a huddle, her shoulders slumped, suddenly aware that for some time she had not given a thought to her return-home kimono.

Her heart smoldered with shame. Could it be that she had come to like the way of life she was leading? Surely not. But why deceive herself? Back in the village, life had been hard. Death had been her father's reward for years of backbreaking labor with so little return. If the goddess of mercy had not stepped in, providing Shiga's money, it was more than possible that her entire family would now be gone from the world. Bad seasons would come again. What then?

Once again she recalled the voices of her small brothers calling, *"Elder sister, we are so hungry."*

Those plaintive memories saddened her. She sat very still, unaware that night's shadows were darkening the room, not hearing the drums and gongs coming from the nearby temple. Like a young soldier thrust into a battlefield, she had endured times of terror. Somehow she had survived. She suddenly cried out, "No longer will I fear life in any way."

Tomiko gave up going to the public bathhouse. She spent all her money buying load after load of bamboo sticks. Every night until the small hours she worked away, her fingers flying as she produced flute-whistle upon flute-whistle. Each one she decorated with the insignia of a dragonfly. As she worked on, her determination grew stronger. The longer she stayed on in the city, the more cash she would accrue to take home to the family.

As she worked she imagined lovely scenes . . . *Herself robed in the kimono she had made. She was laden down with small gifts, and tramping across the swaying bridge, beneath a cloudless blue sky. Then, swift as a bird, she went along paths edged by rank summer grasses and her family caught sight of her. "Our sister is returning to us. . . ."*

At regular intervals Yamamoto Sama had interviewed her in the entrance hall of the house, his voice distant but polite as he inquired about her welfare. "Have you any problems? Are you content?" She replied in a whisper, "No problems. I am content." On one occasion he was accompanied by a frail, very old gentleman by the name of Ohara, who had examined her from head to toe, the way her father would examine a pig he wanted to purchase. Ohara's expression had clearly shown that in his opinion she was not a bargain at any price. That had been a humbling experience. She had not seen the old man again, and now Yamamoto Sama appeared to have forgotten that she existed.

Tomiko now saw herself as a woman of business. She ignored snowstorms and howling winds to take her wares to the shrines on days when only the hardiest of souls would dare venture out. If one flute was sold, that was better than nothing.

Arriving home one blustery afternoon, she slipped and fell upon a mound of hard snow. Strong hands lifted her up as she cried out. She felt a sharp pain in her right arm and knew that the injury would prevent her from working. The precious flutes lay scattered about her.

That night, unable to sleep with the pain, she lay staring into the darkness, thinking of Bixby San. He was the one who had come so quickly to her aid and helped her up, saying solicitously, "Are you all right? Are you all right?" He had gathered up the flutes and carried them into the entrance hall, leaving her to make her own way back to her quarters.

Shortly afterward, and much to her amazement, a foreign woman had come to her room. Speaking in fluent Japanese, she explained that she was a doctor from the American hospital. "Bixby San wishes me to examine your arm. He fears you've an injury."

Now her arm was bandaged and in a sling. How gentle the woman's touch had been. How remarkable for a woman to have become a doctor of medicine. Puzzled, she wondered if Bixby San had spoken to her in her own language? How else could she have understood him? Had she thanked him? She could not remember doing so. How could she thank him? He had by this time probably forgotten the entire incident. It was best to leave things as they were. When her time was up, she would present him with a flute-whistle as a farewell gift.

T HE COLD GRAY MONTHS OF winter were over, and the people's spirits were renewed. In March, the wild geese had migrated northward. The nostalgic loveliness of blossom time was over, and during the month of May, during the Boys' Festival, pennants in the shape of carp had been flown at the head of bamboo poles by houses in which there were sons. Now, in June, elegant old Ohara, feeling especially spry, had invited Renzō to join and to partake of the midday meal with him.

He had inveigled his friend into traveling through the streets of Tokyo by ricksha in place of a hired carriage.

"This metropolis," he called out, "grows like a well-nourished child. Renzō, your father, and Aiko's father, Count Okura, would have gloried to be alive today. Everything so handy, so modern. 'Tis said that some ninety thousand ricksha now have the run of Tokyo's streets. Do you recall those lewd paintings which decorated all the first ricksha?"

"I do." Renzō grinned widely. "I remember them clearly."

"Ah! They were such *fun*. Banned now. Ah, among so many other things, the West is teaching us modesty."

Ohara clutched at his chest as their vehicles jolted to a sudden stop in a traffic jam. Their runners exchanged bawdy insults with other runners and the drivers of carriages and trolley cars.

"Ohara Sama, shall we continue on foot?"

"*Certainement, mon ami!* It's only a five-minute walk to the Kojunsha. I was a founding member back in 1880 of the gentlemen's social club."

Renzō was not a member of the club, but was well known to many of the men who met together in the luxuriously furnished Western-style building. The atmosphere was convivial and white-gloved waiters glided from table to table, bearing black-lacquered trays laden with imported crystal glasses filled with drinks in which ice cubes clinked delicately.

Halfway through his second sweet sherry, Ohara said, "Renzō, I'm a little muddled about that chap Bixby and his paddyfield lass. She could not have come up to his expectations. To my eyes, he looks to be more gloomy than ever every time I visit his love nest. Am I mistaken?"

"Hmmm . . . not altogether. Bixby is certainly downcast. But, believe it or not, the pathetic chap has so far not shared the pillow with the girl. He is still courting her."

"Still courting her? I'm astonished!" Ohara set his glass carefully on the table, then clapped his hands sharply for service. "I'm in need of a strong whiskey," he said. "You too, Renzō?"

"Yes. Make it a double." Renzō, frowning slightly, took out a cigar, hesitating for an instant before discarding its paper ring. "I'll be more than pleased when Bixby finally comes to his senses. Comes to realize the sheer stupidity of the exercise."

"Pity! Pity, but I'm forced to agree with you. There's not much more he can do. He's shaved off his handsome mustache. Persists most valiantly in learning to speak our complicated language. Oh." Ohara lowered his voice to a whisper, saying, "Renzō, my difficult daughter-in-law insists that Gen should stay away from Bixby's place. . . ."

"My wife has been against Shinichi going there from the beginning. She complains quite bitterly."

"Ah, mothers! So protective of their sons. Foolish of them." Ohara dumped his emptied glass down, then said, "However, shall we put that house off limits to that curious young trio who descend on it resembling pigeons hungry for crumbs. No?"

"Yes. At once! Frankly, I believe that we should all cease calling on Bixby. Stop encouraging him with his foolish obsession."

Ohara, slightly put out, murmured, "You think so? Pity! At my age most things are rather boring. I've relished my involvement in the sad little romance. But—yes, I agree! So—we leave him to his own devices!"

"Exactly."

Ohara rubbed his palms together thoughtfully, then he said, "Soon, after the rainy season, when summer arrives, the girl will feel free to go back to her village. Does Bixby understand that?"

"He does."

"What then do you think he will do? After she departs?"

Renzō replied somewhat uneasily. "I really don't know." With extreme delicacy he tapped the ash from his cigar into the ornate ashtray.

At that moment Nakasone appeared and joined his friends. His arrival was no surprise to the older man, and when the formalities were concluded, Renzō realized that his business partner had come to the club in order to keep an appointment.

Knowing that Ohara had been close friends from early days with Nakasone's father, Renzō sought to excuse himself but settled back when the elderly samurai exclaimed, "Please stay, Renzō! Here we are, the three of us together—at last. Excellent! Renzō, I beg to have your attention for a delicate matter."

Renzō looked from one man to the other as Nakasone murmured, "Ohara Sama has requested me to bring up the matter of his grandson, Gen, and his future marriage. Certainly, there is no need for a hasty decision."

"No need at all," Ohara murmured. "My grandson intends to take up his studies at the Sorbonne."

"True," Nakasone agreed. His tone was ponderous. "Renzō, may I ask your opinion of the youth?"

Renzō, his mind stumbling, realized that he was being approached about his daughter Etsu's future marriage. He bowed to each of his companions, then responded with gravity. "Gen? He is an interesting character. Like my own son, he's apt to pontificate about life, though he is still woefully ignorant. That's not surprising. Both youths have led sheltered lives."

"True," Nakasone agreed. "One envies their impetuous ways. Youth is all too short. Ohara Sama is desirous of preventing his grandson from leaving his homeland without firm plans for his future."

In a perverse way Renzō disliked the thought of Etsu's future being arranged for her, even though no marriage would take place for many years to come. "I have no desire," he said, "to tell my children what to do."

"Admirable." Nakasone, with some difficulty, smothered a grin and looked his friend straight in the eye. "Renzō, do you wish to abandon this subject?"

Without a doubt, Renzō thought, Nakasone knew how to operate in the business world, but he was not much of a marriage broker. "Indeed, I shall be honored to continue this discussion," he replied.

Renzō wanted to restore matrimonial harmony with no loss to his dignity, and so on returning home from the Kojunsha club he sought out his wife and announced bluntly, "An important matter has arisen. We must discuss it."

"Trouble?" Rumi's smooth brow became slightly creased.

"On the contrary."

"Then, let us talk." She listened without comment while he told her that the Ohara family were making approaches to have Etsu enter into their clan when she was of marriageable age.

Finally Rumi murmured, "And what are your feelings?"

"I prefer to bide my time before expressing my thoughts. I want to hear what you and other members of our family think. Should we bring Shinichi into our confidence?"

"I don't think it would be wise, at the moment, to encourage our son's overconfidence."

"My thoughts exactly. I've noticed lately that Shinichi goes about like an army captain in battle."

"Yes." Rumi laughed admiringly. "His mind is so agile." She frowned, smiled, then frowned again. "Excuse me, but I must say that I'm still filled with anger about my son's visits to the Englishman's house."

"Then allow me to console you. I'm placing that house off limits to him."

"May I ask why?"

"Why else but to console you?" Renzō, unashamed of his blatant lie, went on. "Gossip presents things in twisted forms. Bixby was helpful to me while I dwelt in his country. Helping him out here is my duty."

With a dismissive gesture he waved the subject from their midst, speaking in a conspiratorial way, saying, "As you wisely remarked, Shinichi's mind is so agile, it will be difficult to keep our thoughts from him."

Rumi gazed around as if she expected her son to appear out of thin air. "No one would know better than Shinichi the shortcomings in Gen Ohara's character. And no brother admires a sister more than our son admires Etsu. Let us bring him into the picture right now."

"I agree. For Et-chan's sake."

"When shall we speak with him?"

"Not today." Renzō, feeling that his senses had been assaulted more than enough for the time being, rubbed a hand across his eyes. "But before too long. Ohara is eager to have our answer before his grandson leaves to study at the Sorbonne."

"In Paris." Rumi paused then commented tartly, "What freedom men have. Even in these days of enlightenment, women have to endure so much. Men just spin about, unable to control their emotions, to grasp how their wives ache and suffer."

For one mad instant Renzō was tempted to blurt out, "So you know about my affair with your sister?" Instead, he said casually, "It's a male characteristic to pretend to have affair after affair."

Husband and wife gazed into each other's eyes, both relieved that family responsibilities had brought harmony back into their relationship.

The family conference took place on the following Sunday, at noon, in an exclusive restaurant. The private room held a sixteen-paneled folding screen, more precious than had it been made of gold because of its antiquity. Depicting storks in flight, it was auspicious for the occasion, as a stork was the symbol of good fortune.

Assuring the restaurant's manager that all was to his liking, Renzō went to the entrance doors to await the arrival of his guests. He felt depressed but could not work out why. Perhaps the six floor-cushions were responsible? Only six? How pathetically small a family group. He should have insisted that Keiko come along. That would have pleased Rumi. Yes, but how would Sumiko and Aiko have reacted? Best not to step out of line on such an important occasion.

He moved forward to greet the Fukuda trio as they descended from their carriage, his sadness turning to irritation that his wife and son had not as yet put in their appearance.

Finally they arrived, and when all were assembled, the meal began. Unknown to Renzō, the full significance of the gathering was already known to everyone present. Rumi had spoken in confidence to Aiko, who had told Yuichi, who had wisely informed his mother, saying to Aiko before he did so, "It's best to prepare Mother. One never knows how she will react these days."

Shinichi was not only privy to the matter, but, because he and Gen Ohara had set the plan in motion, he was viewing the proceedings as though from a lofty peak. As the lavish meal proceeded, he quite admired his own understated attitude, and the pleasure others took in his modest behavior.

"Shinichi, you grow more like my brother, Kenichi, with every passing month," Sumiko murmured.

Yuichi chuckled. "What a colorful character my uncle was."

"Surely," Aiko commented coldly. "He departed to the spirit world shortly after you were born. You would remember little of him."

"Not so," Sumiko cried out indignantly. "My son never exaggerates. It would be beneath his dignity. He resembles his *father*."

Yuichi grinned. "What would I do without a mother to defend me?"

Rumi thought with bitterness of her own mother, who was not considered fine enough to be present. Renzō's heart ached as he recalled the one who had given him life. Shinichi gazed at Rumi thinking that no one could be prettier than *his* mother. She had on a jet-black kimono of fine silk. He noticed that everyone present, including himself, wore wristwatches, now one of the symbols of True Enlightenment. Beer, another such symbol, was being served.

Renzō thought the whole event was moving along rather too slowly. But etiquette made it impossible for him to bring the reason for the meeting out into the open until the meal was over.

Scarcely had the doors slid shut and the waiters departed than the tone of the gathering changed. All eyes turned to Shinichi. Never before had he been so quizzed by so many. Without too much enthusiasm, he pointed out Gen Ohara's admirable characteristics, but his aunt Sumiko was skeptical.

"*Impossible* for a youth to have quite so many merits. What of his *faults?*" she intoned sternly.

"Gen's faults?" Shinichi took his time, wondering which faults could be considered virtues. "Gen is, unfortunately, overly generous. . . ."

"Scarcely a blemish," Sumiko cried out. "I consider that a *plus.*"

"Certainly Gen is not *handsome.*"

"It's important," Yuichi rasped, "to consider much more than character and appearance. From my point of view, it's too premature to consider Etsu's future. Why tie her down? I'm against the suppression of individual freedom."

"That," Aiko commented scathingly, "is a bit rich, especially coming from you."

Sumiko, protective as always, cried out, "Yuichi *must* be heard, Aiko."

For the first time Shinichi became aware of conflicts in the Fukuda family. He had thought the couple were easygoing, much happier than his own parents. Perhaps, he pondered, no marriage could be completely perfect. Folding his arms, he gazed upon his elders, his expression kindly. At times he nodded his head in silent assent.

During the lengthy discussion taking place, Shinichi was shocked to discover that the Yamamoto family had become relatively obscure and was not in the mainstream of high society as he had imagined.

Finally, Yuichi Fukuda announced, "I admit that the idea has some merit. *My* main objection is that young Gen Ohara is such an ordinary fellow. But then"—he shrugged—"my father once said that there is no such thing as an ordinary person."

Aiko remained silent. A frown crossed her face. Then she addressed Shinichi directly, saying sharply, "What are *your* feelings on the matter?"

Allowing a frown to furrow *his* brow, he muttered, "That's a tricky question, Aunt."

"Tricky?"

"Yes. Naturally my sister's well-being rests heavily on my mind."

"Naturally so? You've always been *overly* devoted to Et-chan."

"*Overly* devoted?" Rumi, flushing deeply, stared at Aiko. "What, exactly, are you insinuating?"

"Nothing!" Aiko laughed outright. "I find nothing sinister in Shinichi's brotherly love for his sister. I find it admirable. . . ."

"Am I to gather," Sumiko interrupted, "that the prevailing opinion is that we should enter into negotiations with the Ohara clan?" Waving off any interruptions, she continued. "Few agreements suit everyone. But this arrangement, when finalized, will circumvent other, less satisfactory young men from being considered as husbands for Masa's granddaughter. I give my *full* support."

"Nothing is final," Renzō muttered with some abruptness. Then he bowed. "Thank you, Aunt, for giving such thought to my daughter's future."

"Don't mention it, Renzō. Call upon me at any time when crucial steps are to be taken." Sumiko turned her gaze upon Shinichi and said, "I hope you have not given us false impressions about the worthiness of Gen Ohara?"

"I sincerely hope not, Aunt," he replied. "Did I mention that Gen's high-pitched laugh can, at times, grate on one's ears?"

"You did not. What a courageous disclosure to make about your close friend." Sumiko pursed her lips before saying, "It will behoove *us* to hide the fact that Etsu has a hasty temper."

"Impossible." Yuichi chuckled. "Nothing can be hidden. How smart of the Oharas to choose Nakasone as their intermediary. He's known Et-chan since she was a babe."

"True," Rumi cried out. "He once saved her life."

"Et-chan is temperamental, but her outbursts add to her charm." Yuichi grinned. "No real man admires a wife who can't burst out into flames now and then."

Noticing the amused glances exchanged between the Fukuda couple, Shinichi thought that in a peculiar way they cared for each other. More deeply than his own parents? He thought so. There was his father, square-jawed, handsome. There was his mother, her face luminous in its beauty. In no way was their marriage a sorry mess, but neither was it glowingly warm. Nevertheless, they were good parents.

Closing his ears to the various exchanges taking place, Shinichi reached into a pocket, fondling the bowl of one of his father's pipes. He had not as yet attempted to smoke it, but merely caressing the article assisted his thinking process.

The hot exchange between his mother and Aunt Aiko about his devotion to Etsu excited his curiosity. He was not sure why he had always felt that her well-being rested on his shoulders. Above everyone, he cared most for her. He loved her. Had there been a tinge of suspicion in his aunt's voice? Did she suspect that he harbored lustful thoughts toward Etsu?

Aiko's comment was disturbing him. He had always failed to understand, even in a vague sort of way, why he felt as he did—so protective, so angry when he imagined Etsu as a young woman, taken to wed, and to bed, by a man who might not treat her with true devotion and delicacy. Gen, he was certain, could be trusted, and he himself would always be near to watch over her.

Lost in troublesome musings, he took the pipe from his pocket, to hear Renzō exclaim, "That pipe! My favorite! You rascal! When I recall the hours I wasted searching for it, my blood runs hot. Hand it over. What punishment can I give you?" Laughing heartily, Renzō rose from his floor-cushion and gave the sign that the gathering should break up.

During the flurry of bowings and farewells, Shinichi, the youngest of those present and the last to leave the room, noticed Renzō's pipe lying on the table. He retrieved it and put it back in his pocket.

Gen Ohara, although exhausted after several hours of strenuous judo practice in one of the many schools in the sleazy Asakusa district, strode along, intent on keeping an appointment with Shinichi Yamamoto. He could scarcely contain his excitement, and viewed his surroundings with detachment, even the bawdy woman wearing tights and huge gloves who shouted out, "Pay your money! See a remarkable sight! Come into the tent! See me compete in the ring, box against a giant kangaroo, brought here to Nippon all the way from the shores of Australia. . . ."

He had no time to spare for that, but his attention was caught as he drew near to a shoe repair booth. Halting, he noticed that the repair man, an Eta—a social outcast—wore an inscrutable expression as folk handed their footwear to him at the end of a pole. Gen grimaced, wondering how it would feel to be treated as an untouchable. As he pondered this, he caught sight of Shinichi cutting through the crowd, hurrying toward him.

Gen's chubby cheeks flushed as he shouted, hailing his friend, "So? How did things go?"

Throwing dignity to the winds, Shinichi took on a warrior's stance and yelled out triumphantly, "Waaah!"

A flock of pigeons rose up from the road in flight while the youths pummeled each other and then went into a long pleasure gallery where the small tables were all presided over by girls with heavily painted faces, each one an expert in treating callow youths as mature men, coaxing them bawdily to buy some fun in a room upstairs.

They waved the sirens away. "Hardly fitting under the circumstances," Shinichi muttered pompously. "Agreed?"

"Absolutely. Besides, I'm worn out from judo practice." Gen clapped his hands twice. "Bring beer," he ordered the girl.

"*Hai, hai.* At once!" Two huge pottery steins were placed on the table, and quickly emptied.

"Now." Gen grinned. "Get to the core. Our plan was approved by one and all?"

"Yes. All approved. Shall we order more beer?"

"No." Gen gazed about the seedy surroundings. "This is no place to speak of your sister."

The guilt Shinichi had felt in having preempted his father in plans for Etsu's future faded. With certainty he felt that he had acted not wrongly but wisely. True, Gen was no genius, but he was good.

The youths were walking beside the Sumida River in the clear, cool air, with branches swaying in the breeze. "This place is better by far," Gen said pensively. "I feel so complimented. I'm such an ordinary fellow. But my future no longer looms as vague and uncertain."

"*Your* future?"

"*Our* futures," Gen corrected himself hastily. "Yours, Etsu's, and mine . . ."

"Certainly the chosen intermediaries will dig deeply into the genealogy of our respective clans. But, I believe that all the skeletons hidden away in the Yamamoto closet are already known to your grandfather."

"Probably so." Gen laughed. "I don't think we have any. We Oharas are rather a dull lot. Let's have no negative thoughts."

"Yes. Forward march. When are you leaving for France?"

"Next year. As you know, due to my father's diplomatic posting, my parents will be staying in Paris."

"Their presence won't hinder you from enjoying yourself?"

"On the contrary. Never would they attempt to deprive me of relishing life. They will be interested and exhilarated if I'm fortunate enough to have a romantic affair while in Paris."

"I hope you will. But . . ." Shinichi said uneasily, "just as long as you keep it as a minor event."

"Could it be any other way?" Gen replied sincerely. "With Etsu growing up, awaiting my return?"

Halting in their walk, each knew the other's thoughts. Both longed to say, "I'm going to miss your companionship so much."

Gen said with a wide grin, "Don't you take a wife for many years."

"No intention of so doing. But why the admonition?"

"Can't you see us—you, Etsu, and I, living together. Young, free, a ménage-à-trois arrangement? A household of three?" Gen's eyes expressed nothing but innocence. "Selfish, I know, but to dwell with Etsu as my wife and with you as my brother under one roof is—as the English say—my idea of heaven. Not yours, eh?"

"I like the idea." Shinichi slapped Gen's shoulder and added, "But, let me tell you that you'll need all your wits to deal with Et-chan. Even now, although but a child, she can make our home rock when things don't please her."

"Thanks for telling me. Being so even-natured, I like being jolted out of phlegmatic states."

"I know. Your natures will complement each other." Shinichi, eager to change the subject, frowned and asked, "By the way, how about your *mother*?"

"My mother?"

"As a mother-in-law?"

"Incapable of unkindness. Have no doubts on that score. She always wished for a daughter. She often says—and I quote, 'I shall be the *perfect* mother-in-law.' "

"Sounds too good to be true."

"Oh, it's true. Early in her marriage she went through a hard time. My grandmother disliked her *intensely*."

"What about now?"

"The farther they are apart, the better. Need I say more? How was it with your mother and Lady Masa?"

Shinichi recalled certain occasions when Lady Masa's fan had pointed directly at his mother and he grinned. "My grandmother controlled the family home until the day she died. But always with grace and style. I'm quite certain that her spirit still holds sway over us all."

"Would she approve of the way in which we are out to arrange our own marriages?"

Taking the pipe from his pocket, Shinichi gazed at it thoughtfully.

"Impossible to know with certainty. But, yes, I think she would. She married 'blind' when very young. Maybe she suffered."

"Mother-in-law problems?"

"There was no mother-in-law in the old Yokohama house. From family talk it's said that her husband, my grandfather, Kenichi, had no time for her. He kept a courtesan."

"So I've heard. You know how women delight in gossip."

"Yes, it's a female trait." Sticking the empty pipe between his teeth, Shinichi muttered, "I wonder how things go with Bixby and the girl Tomiko? Bad luck we never set eyes on the girl, and now we never will. Have you any news of them?"

"Not a scrap. I resent my grandfather ordering me to keep away from that house. No explanations given."

"Yes, I find it ludicrous at my age to have my father tell me, 'You have freedom of choice,' then he tells me what to choose." Shinichi placed the pipe between his teeth again, speaking with some difficulty. "I actually overheard Mother telling my grandmother that the girl Tomiko had thoughts of coaxing *me* to share her pillow."

Aghast, Gen muttered, "From whom could your mother have heard that bit of nonsense?"

"Nonsense is right. I'm furious. I enjoyed tutoring Bix San. According to Nakasone, Tomiko will return to her native village when summer comes."

"Then what about Bix San?"

"Nakasone says the Englishman will return to his homeland. It's said that his financial future is grim, that he cannot linger on here."

"Ah, well, although Bix San is not enthusiastic about our country, he's having a good time here."

"He is, yes. A *minor* romance."

Gen's high-pitched laugh rang out. "Yes. Better by far than having a love affair powerful enough to turn a fellow's life upside down!"

"Let no such curse fall on either you or me." Shinichi grabbed at Gen's arm and said, "The fangs of hunger gnaw at my belly!"

"Then on to the Ginza! A new *sukiyaki* restaurant has recently opened."

Tomiko was unable to fathom why she felt glad just to be alive. As she worked on her flutes and dreamed of the future, a newfound happiness heightened her appreciation of the world around her.

No longer was she intimidated by Bixby. She would always remember his aloof kindness during those weeks when her injured arm had been supported by a sling. He had taken to visiting the garden fronting her quarters, intent on examining the welfare of the lilac tree there.

One blustery morning she had opened the window and with some temerity had called out, "Bixby San—your kindness to me has no end."

How startled he had been by her boldness, but then he called out, "*Tenki samui desu*—cold weather!"

"*Hai, samui desu*—yes, cold weather . . ." she replied. He continued to examine the leafless tree. Evidently he cared for trees. Later, in early spring, several gardeners arrived carrying large wooden tubs holding cherry trees, and one morning she had awakened to behold the garden blessed by a flowering of pink blossoms.

Bixby had been in the garden obviously admiring the display, and forgetting that her hair fell carelessly about her shoulders she had opened the window, calling ecstatically, "*Kirei na*—so beautiful . . ."

Once again, her boldness had startled him. He had stared as though seeing her for the first time.

From that time on, they quite often came face-to-face in the house and sometimes out in the city streets. He was more polite to her than certain other people were. Only today, while in the grounds of a grand shrine, a distinguished couple accompanied by a small boy walked by. The child, glancing at her stall, paused, then dashed to her booth, calling, "Mumma, come see the nice flute-whistles. . . ."

Late that night, lying in bed, Tomiko was assailed by conflicting emotions. The child had inveigled his parents into purchasing three flutes. "One for me, *Kentaro.* One for *Et-chan.* One for my old *grand-mother* . . ."

Then they had moved on. That man, the samurai Yamamoto, standing so close to her, placing cash in her hand, had not so much as recognized her.

Feelings of anger now awakened within her, for could there be anything more insulting than not to be remembered after so many meetings? Not to be seen. To be treated not as a person but merely as an object . . .

In her agitation, sleep would not come. Tomiko got up, dressed hastily, and crept from the house.

It was dark. Rain fell and the streets were empty. As she walked she failed to understand why she was allowing Yamamoto's non-recognition of her to hurt her pride so much. Close to tears, she stood motionless in the darkness which was now sinister, alive with imagined threats. Suddenly aware of heavy footsteps approaching, she gathered up her constricting robe and fled back toward the house.

Back, safe in the sanctuary of her room, she wondered what Bixby San had thought of her midnight wandering. But he had concealed his astonishment and greeted her calmly, saying, "Nasty weather tonight!"

Conscious of her dripping wet clothes, her hair plastered to her cheeks, she had bowed and then hastened inside the house.

Now naked, she toweled her long hair dry and while brushing it she decided to go early to the neighboring shrine and there thank the gods that no menacing stranger had caught up with her. Just Bixby San, probably returning from one of his evening's revels.

Unable to suppress a smile, she could hear in memory his voice saying, "*Oyasumī nasai*—good night!" in his funny foreign way.

How strange life was. Just a short while ago the very thought of him had been more than terrifying, but on this rainy night she felt protected by his presence in the house.

Recalling her mother's instructions, she arranged her limbs modestly as she prepared to sleep. But still sleep refused to arrive. She lay wondering why. Her thoughts were not unhappy but confused.

If life had not been so cruel, if her father had not died, in all probability her parents would have been negotiating with the marriage broker on her behalf.

The days of her childhood were long over. Turning to lie facedown, she pressed her body to the mattress, fully aware for the first time that she was a woman with womanly yearnings and desires.

Bixby sat at the desk in his upstairs study. Rain was falling in mean drizzles, and he noticed that the damp air had cast layers of mold on surfaces, causing unpleasant odors. How he hated this rainy season. Tokyo's humidity was unendurable.

Of late he had the feeling of one who stood on the edge of a yawning chasm. For months on end he had been lulling himself with false hopes, ignoring the relentless passing of time. In the not too distant future he would be sorely in need of lucrative employment. He was not worried about that, nor was he upset about his lack of acceptance in certain social quarters. His life had changed its course and those wasted, restless years of travel seemed to be part of some other man's life.

The Orient held no charms for him. He disliked Japanese food and most of the country's customs, finding them eccentric, altogether too different from English ways.

By absenting themselves, Renzō Yamamoto and his coterie had left him marooned. He was living under stress, without support of any kind.

Bixby gave a gruff, cynical laugh and riffled through the pile of letters lying on his desk. He had read but not replied to any of them. His brother Robert had sent him two insulting letters, demanding that he must return to England without delay. Cease desecrating the family name. *"Your disgraceful affair with a Jap prostitute is being gossiped about in the clubs."* He then skimmed through a note from Renzō Yamamoto. *"Presently so caught up by business and family concerns . . ."*

A letter from elegant old Ohara . . . *"Presently caught up by family matters . . . Gen, my grandson, is soon to depart for France . . . Accept our good wishes . . ."*

On receiving these epistles along with those from Nakasone and Sir John Coomber, he realized that a unanimous unspoken decision had, for some reason, put his dwelling off limits. For a while he had been upset, but no longer.

The girl who dominated his life was still under his protection. He worried and wondered constantly how she perceived him. Like that wolf in the Red Riding Hood fable? God, he hoped not. How perturbed he had been, watching, then following her on that night she had fled from the house out into the dark streets. What had caused her to act so rashly?

With a despairing gesture, Bixby cast the pile of unanswered letters to the floor. They lay there limply while he muttered with self-contempt, "Incompetent fool! What the hell *should* I do?"

A miracle was needed. He, an agnostic, had no faith in miracles of any kind. But he shouted, "God help me," only to have that demand answered by footsteps pounding up the stairs. Tanaka blundered into the room and stammered, "You call? You want?"

"Bring whiskey."

"*Hai*—yes."

Slightly cheered by the whiskey, Bixby recalled to mind, as he had countless times before, that first glimpse of Tomiko on that moonlit night in Yokohama. . . .

Tomiko, hurt, disheveled, lying on that bed in the brothel . . . Tomiko in the cottage of Kamakura. That faint smile flickering across her face. Her eyes meeting his for the first time ever . . .

Tomiko in this Tokyo house. Terrified of him, crouching against the wall in the corridor . . .

Tomiko facedown in the street that blustery day. He, all concern, helping her up. She, creeping back into the house which she must think of as a prison. He, her jailer . . .

In the garden, having Tomiko's voice trembling, mentioning his name for the first time, calling, thanking him for having sent the doctor to attend to her injured arm . . .

The sight of her standing at the open window, her hair falling about her shoulders, exclaiming ecstatically, "Beautiful! How beautiful . . ."

"Yes—beautiful . . ." he had replied, not alluding to the cherry trees he had brought in the hope of making her happy.

At the sound of a far-off boom, Bixby's reveries came to an abrupt end. Like all Tokyo citizens, he had taken to setting his watch exactly at noon, when the cannon on the plaza in front of the Imperial Palace fired out a resounding shot.

Bixby shoved the window open. He needed fresh air, but a stomach-churning stench floated upward from a bullock-drawn lavatory cart in the street below. Disgusted and about to close the window, he saw Tomiko approaching, a cloth bundle slung on her back and a garishly colored paper umbrella angled over her slender body. She stopped in order to greet the cleaner, who had emerged, lugging two wooden buckets of human waste.

For a moment Bixby's attention was caught by a gleaming carriage that swept by. Then he looked back to the couple who stood by the cart, both at their ease, bowing and speaking cheerfully.

The sight devastated him. Memories of his fastidious mother, Lady Honoria, crowded in and sweat poured from his forehead. He felt that his world was cracking up into icy splinters. He remembered himself as a lonely child, imprisoned in the upstairs nursery in the

Brunton Street mansion, waiting for his sweetly perfumed mother to come upstairs to kiss her son good night.

Always he had waited in vain. His mother had him learn that love does not come when you wait for it.

It now seemed that he had traveled a long journey only to understand once and for all how true that was. He, it seemed, was not meant to be loved. It was up to him to accept his fate. Yes, but he *knew what it was to love.*

A new deluge of rain poured down and he saw that Tomiko, catching up the hem of her kimono, ran to shelter in the house. The cologne on the handkerchief pressed to his nostrils blended with the pervading stench from the cart's foul harvest.

He had no detailed knowledge of Tomiko's life. From the very beginning everything about her had filled him with poignancy. Her appearance, her bravery, and her innocence.

When Renzō Yamamoto had advised him, "Don't take that rascal Shiga's recommendation on the girl being a virgin seriously," he had growled, "Can't you understand, Renzō, as she is, so I love her. . . ."

As she was? In every aspect? Even her humble background? Was that true? Yes. His love for her was a strange mixture of passion, desire, and of wanting above all to have her unburdened and light-hearted. In his clumsy way he had gone about courting her, keeping his distance, living beneath the same roof, not only hoping but determined that it must be she and not he who would direct the action. He had been resolute on that score.

Simply by providing comforts for her ordinary existence, had he expected her to comprehend the significance of his actions? What conflicting emotions she must have suffered, must still be suffering, living in the belief that she was under contract and not free to leave his house. The answers to those questions filled him with shame but not with remorse. Terms of endearment—my dearest, heart of my heart—were all implicit in her name! He had kept to his plan, never forcing her, but neither had he set out to persuade her, fool, fool that he was. *There was so little time left.*

He made his way down the steep stairs, then along the corridor. The house was hushed except for the drumbeats thrumming in from the neighboring shrine. The door to Tomiko's room was not yet closed. Furnished sparsely with a low table and several floor-cushions, her quarters appeared to Bixby as an oasis.

She knelt by the *hibachi*, blowing on the charcoal, ready to heat water in the iron kettle on the tripod. She looked up, startled at his unexpected visit, then she smiled tentatively and said, "*Ame ga furu*— How it rains."

"*Hai*—yes," he said. Then, carefully, slowly, he tried out his newly acquired language to inquire if she was boiling the water in preparation to make tea.

"*Hai*—yes." She bowed slightly.

He asked if he could join her. Again she bowed and, removing his footwear, he stepped into the room to seat himself on the cushion she hastily placed beside the low cherrywood table.

L IFE HAD TAKEN AN EXTRAORDINARY turn. Tomiko had become a teacher and tour guide. A long time seemed to have gone by since Bixby San had first entered her room and, while sipping the tea she had prepared, announced that he was eager to improve his knowledge of her language.

Would she, he had requested, come to his aid? How could she have refused? Never had she been so honored.

The next day he arrived carrying a notebook and a red lead pencil.

In the beginning, every morning, long before he was due, she had things prepared for lessons. Her *futon* was rolled up and put away in its cupboard. The tabletop was bare, ready for his notebook. His cushion was ready. Everything in order. Her hair pulled back from her forehead, unadorned, as befitted a teacher.

At first the rank odor of his cigars almost stupefied her, but she had grown to like the smell. When unable to pronounce certain sounds such as *tsu*, he would break out in laughter while she waited, looking serious as a teacher should.

He had taken to bringing foreign books along filled with drawings and paintings strange to her eyes. Buildings of never-imagined grandeur. Pictures of maps, people from many lands and of strange animals. At times she felt *he* had become the teacher. . . .

The lessons often lasted until dusk fell and Tanaka arrived to light the lamps. How relaxed Tanaka had become. Wang, the fearsome Chinese cook, had been sent on vacation. With no chef in the kitchen, peace reigned in the house and meals were brought in from a nearby eating house. Naturally, Bixby San's meals had been set up for him in the upstairs dining room and hers in her room. On the third day of Wang's absence Tanaka brought in her tray and hesitated, not knowing where to place it. Bixby San, engrossed in his lesson, grunted out, "*Mendō na*—What a nuisance!" Then he asked if she minded having his meal brought to the "schoolroom," in order to save time.

Sitting directly opposite him, eating, had made her feel very shy. Then she saw how clumsily he managed the chopsticks and her eyes glinted with amusement.

He did not mind, but said, "Tomiko, maybe you can teach me!"

That lesson went on and on. The rice turned cold. "No longer good to eat," he declared. He summoned Tanaka and ordered him to have ricksha brought to the house.

She would never be absolutely certain how it had come about that she, traveling ricksha-style, with a man whom her parents would have called a barbarian, found herself being twirled through busy streets in the capital city, seeing for the first time the famous Ginza. They stepped from their vehicles and entered an eating house peopled by folk of different nationalities, all seated at white-clothed tables decorated by flowers. Flowers? On *eating* tables!

No one paid undue attention to her. The buzz of talk continued while she sat at one of the tables and looked with dismay at the array of eating utensils. She put her hands in her lap and stared straight ahead, her back held so straight that she feared it would never bend. How fortunate it was when her companion suddenly declared that in truth, all he fancied was a bowl of ice cream and how about her?

Her relief had known no bounds on discovering that ice cream was eaten by spoon. That food—ice cream—was surely meant only for the emperor and the empress. Then she agreed with Bixby San that two servings of the delicacy would not be excessive.

Several days after that sortie, two ricksha twirled her and Bixby San along narrow alleys to a tree-lined avenue. Together she and the foreigner had run for shelter from the rain into the pebbled entrance of a restaurant.

An atmosphere of dedicated pleasure-taking had prevailed. She knew that never again would she partake of such a delicate meal, accompanied by hot *sake*. The serving girl, almost too pretty to be real, gave full attention to Bixby San, and the handsomely robed geisha who entered the room sat close to him, twanging her *shamisen* and fluttering her eyelids, intent on gaining his admiration. "Foolish girl," Tomiko thought with a newfound cynicism. "Lady, you waste your time. *This* foreign samurai cares not at all for females."

She often wondered if in the future her grandchildren would believe her tales. "Once," she would say, "a long time ago, I was teacher of a foreign man. . . ."

The imaginary grandchildren vanished but her smile lingered on as she recalled how Bixby San had expressed a wish to wander about the city visiting shrines and temples, and that she should explain things puzzling to him. Oblivious of the chill and the drizzling continual rain, he would trudge along graveled courtyards while, as best she could, she explained Japanese culture to him. He, ever eager to improve his knowledge, paid strict attention to her every word and gesture, gazing at her against the background sounds of gongs, bells, and of priestly chantings.

Nothing had prepared her for the day's long walk through the confusion of streets, on and on, crossing footbridges, coming at last to the Sumida River, where they went aboard a banner-clad pleasure craft. For the first time ever, she had been afloat on water. She held her breath as the vessel cut loose from the pier, then lost herself in the sights and sounds as the boat, crowded with passengers all out for enjoyment, made its way along the river.

Her pleasure and excitement had not lasted for long. A group of wine-laden young rustics had spoken bawdy words, openly directing them toward her and her *gaijin* companion.

She hoped that Bixby San had not understood any of those coarse comments. She thought he had not, for his expression had remained calm, dignified, as was usual. To the best of her ability she had copied his demeanor, and with the trip over, it had been more than wonderful to be back home, with Tanaka all smiles, sliding open the entrance door, Bixby San announcing, "Time to eat! Time to eat!"

Those steaming hot noodles supped in the glow of lamplight in her room seemed to have given more pleasure to the Englishman than any grand banquet.

Following Bixby's departure from the room, Tomiko felt edgy and at a loss. Unable to forget the unpleasant experience on the riverboat, she could not remain still. The master of the house, she knew, had gone out again. She bathed and donned her cotton sleep-kimono. Never had she felt so lonely. Everything was altogether too quiet, then from the servants' quarters came a discordant sound. Tanaka was playing the flute she had presented to him some months ago.

Tomiko slid open the wall cupboard, frowning as she beheld the pile of bamboo sticks. Her recent spate of teaching and traveling about the metropolis had left no time for fashioning them into musical instruments. Soon, in a few weeks, summer would arrive, and she would be returning home. So little time left, and the flute intended as a farewell gift for Bixby San had not yet been made. Examining the sticks carefully, she selected one and set to work.

She seemed to have lost her skill. Three flutes were completed and tested for sound. The nicest one she put aside. It was not good enough, but she was numb from weariness. Many hours fled by. The tea in her bowl was cold and bitter. She brewed a fresh pot, but it too had a bitter taste, or, maybe the bitterness was in her heart . . . ?

Bitterness? No! Then—what? Thoughts resembling the branches of trees in a storm tossed and swayed, filling her mind, and she was afraid of the emotions that were crowding, burning into her heart.

With a tremendous effort Tomiko sent her memory back to times spent gossiping and giggling with girls in the village, when they had whispered among themselves of amorous things, of how one day a handsome samurai would pass through the rice lands, only to fall head over heels in love with one of them. They had given no thought to having the girl fall hopelessly in love with the nobleman.

Tomiko straightened her back, sat with her head held high, determined to quench her feelings. Unwise in the ways of love, she was certain that before too long the turmoil, so unexpected, so cruel and painful, would be forgotten. This, she told herself, was but another bridge that she must, perforce, cross.

The Englishman's notebook was on the table. For one instant she allowed a hand to lie upon it lightly, caressingly. Then she crawled across the *tatami* and lay motionless, stretched full-length on the *futon*, staring at the closed door that on so many nights in the past she had dreaded would slide open. But now?

How cruel, how mischievous was love! How strange it was that she loved one who had no desire for women. How strange it was that she now loved such a man. That man who had found his way to a brothel. To . . . To . . . ?

What else but to purchase the favor of a female's body? A *female* body? *Yes, that was so* and the man Shiga had intended that she, Tomiko, should be that person.

"Above all," her father had taught her, "be honest in all things. The gods know your innermost thoughts." Was she to disobey not only her father, but also the gods? Was she to spend the rest of her life, always unhappy, recollecting this cruel, hot longing? She who knew of no artful tricks, had no talent for subterfuge. To ignore her emotions—so strong, so pure—would be cowardly. Should she do what her heart was set upon doing?

There came the sounds of the entrance door opening, of Bixby San's slow footsteps treading the wooden steps leading up to his quarters. It was not for her to wonder from where he was returning.

She stood upright, neatening the sash of her *yukata*, then shoving the heavy wooden shutters aside, she saw that morning had broken. No rain fell, and the sky was blue with just a ridge of cloud here and there.

Never before had Tomiko ventured up the flight of steps leading to the top floor, but she moved forward with determination, willing to take the responsibility for her actions. . . .

Bixby had come to dread the night hours spent either sleepless or in dreams from which he would awake feeling increasingly hopeless and depressed, dreams so untenable that he would leave the house to wander through deserted streets.

On this night he had walked himself into a state of near exhaustion and, once more back in his room, he divested himself of the raincoat he wore, letting it fall where it would. He grimaced on hearing bells from the nearby temple. Those bells always reminded him how time was passing. Time, he felt, was a deadly weapon being pointed at him.

Intending to turn the lamp's wick up, he hesitated. The light of dawn grew brighter moment by moment. All at once, as when one is suddenly conscious of another in a place where one thinks one is alone, he swung around. Tomiko stood in the open doorway.

Startled, he looked at her intently, lost in a morass of uncertainties, wondering why she had come upstairs, wondering how he should react. Words died on his lips as she reached out a hand to him. Baffled, he wondered if she was expecting him to approach her and accept the bamboo toy she was holding.

As if it were an object of no consequence, she let the flute fall to the floor. Then she smiled, not shyly, but with a challenge, as her eyes sought for his answer.

His heart was beating too fast. As though in a trance he reached out his arms, and without hesitation she ran forward into his embrace. He held her close, gently, as though she were a beloved child, lost, desperately sought for and found at last.

Overwhelmed by his feelings, Bixby knew that no matter what the future held in store, nothing would outshine the wonder of having Tomiko, of her own accord, in his arms.

She raised one hand and, with her fingers trembling, delicately outlined the contours of his lips.

There was no need for words. . . .

T HE SEPTEMBER DAY WAS BRIGHT and beautiful, its cloying heat softened by gusts of air blowing from the ocean; but Renzō Yamamoto walked with dragging steps toward the Church of the Sacred Heart.

For several weeks he had been luxuriating in the alpine village of Karuizawa, staying with his wife and daughter in the Fukuda family's villa, and in the company of Aiko and her son, Kentaro.

When the courier letter from the Japanese priest in Yokohama had come to hand, he was first inclined to ignore its contents, but duty got the better of him.

Osen, the letter informed him, was dead. The news had in no way shocked him, but he was astonished to learn that the woman had been converted to the Roman Catholic faith.

Acting as a substitute for his deceased father, Renzō presented himself to the priet with politeness.

"Yamamoto Sama," Father Joseph said gently, "please bear with me while I explain. . . ."

Some thirty minutes later, seated in the main body of the church, Renzō wondered what Lady Masa would have thought of this final farewell for the courtesan. To his own mind nothing could be odder than the ceremony that was about to take place in the church with its ivory crucifix and marble angels.

Listening to Father Joseph's simple tale, he had with some difficulty restrained his disbelief when told that during the latter days of her life, Osen had become a convert. Through the good offices of her nurse, Fuji Shiga, she had bequeathed all her worldly possessions to the church.

"Fuji is of your faith, then?" he had asked the priest.

"A true convert. In her own small way, she is a missionary determined to save the souls of her heathen brothers and sisters. May I ask you, Yamamoto Sama, was Osen a member of your family?"

"Not . . ." Renzō hesitated, then muttered, grimly, "More a family responsibility."

"Ah! And you have no objections concerning her gift to the church? Her rich garments. Brocades. A collection of jewels . . . ?"

"No objections."

"No objections to her desire for Catholic ceremonial burial rites?"

"No objections." His one desire was to have the matter over and done with, but now, confronted with the highly polished coffin resting by the altar, his line of thought became fragmented as his eyes scanned those who had congregated to pay homage to the woman whom he believed had held his father's heart in her grasp up until the last day of his existence.

In the theatrical lighting he noticed a group of garishly robed old harlots, their painted faces bizarrely offset by the gloom of the church's palatial interior. Glimmers of blue, gold, and purple from the stained glass windows fell on the coffin. He wondered how word had gotten around about the demise of the old courtesan. Obviously the news had spread far and wide, acting as a clarion call to various men and women from different strata of society, who had in the dim past known Osen, and, in all probability, known Kenichi Yamamoto.

Directly in front of him sat the ex-geisha Keiko and the noble Ohara. Their shoulders were touching, and they murmured one to the other. Straining his ears, he caught the mention of his father's name as well as that of Shiro. "Shiro, so valiant!" Keiko was murmuring. "So *cruelly* decapitated."

"So. So, so," Ohara, his voice slightly raised, replied. "Tragic indeed. Kenichi was *devastated*. Count Okura, Shiro's half brother, went quite *berserk*."

"I know, Ohara Sama. I remember."

"All so long ago, Keiko. How young we were . . ."

"Yes, and how happy. Those days in Edo . . ."

"How clearly I recall the extraordinary beauty of Osen. How her name echoed through those times. We men envied Kenichi's possession of her."

"Not all men were jealous of Kenichi, Ohara Sama!" Keiko's voice was tinged with hurt pride. "Not *all* men."

"I stand corrected. I recall Count Okura's dedication to you who dwelt in his second home."

"Thank you, Ohara Sama." The old people, seemingly unaware of onlookers, turned to bow to each other. Renzō saw that they were smiling.

He made his way from the oaken pew. For a while he remained by the heavily padded entrance doors, disturbed by the feeling that he was in the presence of folk drawn together by the breaking of one more link in the chain of their lives. They were there to remember but also to relish the fact that they still trod the earth. There they were—the elegant old Ohara; Keiko, the geisha mistress of a nobleman; and a troupe of cronelike prostitutes under the spired roof of a barbarian temple.

The decrepit group saddened his spirit and, shutting his eyes, Renzō envisioned the handsome figure of his father accompanied by Count Okura, Fukuda, Shiro, Ohara, all young and sprightly, each one two-sworded, bursting into the pagan shrine, laughing loudly, threatening to capture and carry Osen's coffin off and away to a more fitting place.

The vision faded, replaced by one of himself as a callow youth standing outside the house at Nihombashi and of Osen, in all her exotic beauty, stepping past him to enter her awaiting palanquin.

For one moment he held on to the vision of Osen as a flamelike apparition suspended in fathomless darkness. Then that light was extinguished, gone forever.

Casting one last glance at the coffin, Renzō felt that he had had more than enough. In respect to his father, he bowed low, then he hastened from the church.

Coming out into the glare of the noonday sun, Renzō felt disoriented. Quickly regaining his composure, he hailed a passing ricksha, and with no plan in mind ordered the brawny-shouldered young man to run him along the recently completed Marine Drive, which skirted the ocean.

The cosmopolitan city, so rambunctious, bore no resemblance to the tiny fishing hamlet once so familiar to him. A surge of nostalgia sent his mind spinning back, and those times spent before the enforced opening of Japan's doors to the rest of the world appeared to him as a series of happy events, of kindly people, music, and laughter.

On the spur of the moment he decided to make his way to Hommoku Bay and, once there, he walked up the twisting path which he, his mother, and Aunt Sumiko had trodden so many times before. A path no longer edged by sweet-smelling field grasses but now neatly paved.

For the first time in many years Renzō stood before the high wooden gates of the school where he, his father, and grandfather had endured those long periods of enforced studies. The massive iron hinges had rusted and one gate sagged open. On entering the forecourt his boots sank into the layers of debris and rotting leaves that covered the gravel once so meticulously kept by daily rakings.

From out of the mists of his childhood there came a vague memory of a small boy wishing to punish the faithful keeper of the door for having refused him entry. There was no one to keep him out now.

As he passed through the dark, deserted rooms, he felt as though he were a ghost returning to old haunts, half expecting to meet with the wraiths of Dr. Yamamoto and those other dedicated, long-gone scholars.

Shafts of sunlight filtered in from holes in the roof. Rats, undismayed by his presence, scurried about in the high rafters and over the threadbare *tatami*, squealing, squabbling as they gnawed at scattered parchments and the remains of invaluable books.

This sabotage by neglect appeared to Renzō to be an insult aimed at his grandfather, and his father too. In a peculiar way he felt as though he had been directed to the school. That it was his *giri*— duty to give surcease to the troubled spirits of his ancestors. Perhaps take the matter in hand? Have the classic building restored to be enjoyed as a museum?

Duty! Obligations! A pall of depression settled over him, and as though to accentuate this feeling, from outside came the sounds of a ship's siren hooting a drawn-out melancholy signal as it departed from the docks.

Renzō shrugged. The notion of disrupting the indolent tempo of his life was in no way pleasing. Galvanized into action, he left the derelict schoolhouse. Bypassing the now-vacant family residence, he hurried away, eager to find refreshment of spirit in the company of his tried and true business partner.

Nakasone's cool, arrogant manner was like a benison for Renzō, who announced with a sardonic grin, "I'm in need of stimulation. Any suggestions?"

"None. My powers of imagination are limited," Nakasone said

derisively. "Nevertheless, when hard-pressed, I'm prepared to sympathize. My thoughts dwell on the logical, and it strikes me that you are missing your son Shinichi. Yes?"

"Up to a point. But in truth, the funeral service I've just come from has disturbed the rhythm of my life."

"Hmmm . . . You and your overly emotional reactions. Best shrug the matter off. Why did you attend the courtesan's burial ceremony?"

Renzō was silent for a few moments before muttering, "Ceremonies are important. They mark, or, more importantly, help us dodge turning points in our lives."

"I refuse to have my senses assaulted by final ceremonies of any ilk," Nakasone said flatly. "Life goes on. We must be continuously on the search for new challenges."

The two men were in the Yokohama warehouse used to store goods before putting them aboard steamers bound for England. The place was a vast cavern, but they found it convenient and quite liked the dockside neighborhood peopled by Chinese, Portuguese, and Indian merchants, all involved in the import-export trade.

Renzō had a casual attitude toward the now-well-established export company, but Nakasone, in charge of accounts, knew only too well that the time had arrived to make adjustments. Japan was being denuded of artifacts. Not only were Japanese merchants out on buying sprees, but many foreigners living in the country had become avid collectors.

"It strikes me," Nakasone said briskly, "that to understand today's business world demands an examination of the past. Our people always go for things fashionable. Now, believe me, Renzō, to keep afloat we can't just export. We must enter the realm of importing."

Many people were put off by Nakasone's brusqueness, but not Renzō. "If you say so," he replied calmly. "Do things go so badly?"

"Nothing to be alarmed about—yet." With a sardonic smile, he muttered, "My powers of imagination are limited. You know that. *Your* interest in free trade is nil. *I* know that."

"It's true. A developing society such as ours requires change. It's difficult to break inherited patterns of behavior. I want nothing to do with the import business. So will you organize things? I'm open to any ideas you might have."

"Such as bringing in a new man, preferably an enthusiastic man, desperate to succeed in business?" Nakasone asked tentatively. "But there is no such fellow, eh?"

Struck by a sudden thought, Renzō said, "In fact, there is such a fellow. The Englishman Bixby!"

"Bixby? He's still in Japan?" Nakasone expressed surprise.

"Very much so. Now a married man."

"So, he finished with the young harlot. Regained his senses. That's good to know."

"Not so! He *married* the girl. Some months back. Here, in Yokohama at the British consulate. I stood by him. Frankly, I find them a pathetic couple. The marriage can't last, but meanwhile they have to eat and he must find employment."

"Ah, well." Nakasone grinned. "What is life but a brief space between birth and death! Excuse *that* trivial comment and enlarge on Bixby's qualifications."

Several hours later Renzō, sweetly tipsy, was convinced that Nakasone's bachelor way of life was one to be envied. What more could a man ask for than to be free of family affairs? Battleworn, Nakasone was hard-fisted and hard-headed but not entirely hard-hearted. He had become a celibate, a man whose affection was now concentrated on his old dog, Ono, and on the peony plants of which he was undoubtedly a connoisseur.

This was Renzō's first visit to the house Nakasone had moved into a year earlier, and he was greatly taken with it. The house was in the Chinese quarter of the port city, and boasted four pavilions united by stone-paved corridors protected by roofs resting on crimson-lacquered columns. The pavilions were divided by courtyards, the first of pink tiles with huge glazed pots holding orange and lemon trees, their leaves glossy, the fruit bright baubles of nature's art.

"Enchanting," Renzō exclaimed. "Absolutely enchanting."

"I like it," Nakasone replied. "Come, let's move on."

The second courtyard, with its earthen floor, held a pond on which mandarin ducks floated in the shade of one spreading pine tree.

"Peaceful beyond description," Renzō said.

"I like it," his host replied. "Come, let's move on."

Ensconced in an easy chair, pipe in hand, whiskey glass beside him, Renzō sat gazing out on the third courtyard that was his friend's pride and joy. Nakasone appeared to have taken on a new identity as he raved on like a man crazed by love, striding about, arms going

all ways, pointing out, describing the attributes of his great bold
peony blossoms. "See this. Come closer. Bend down, look deeply
into this, my 'Blessed Heaven's Fragrance.' Apart from their glorious hues, these flowers contain more subtlety and elaborate detail
than any other blooms. I intend to spend my remaining years cul-
tivating them. Renzō, come closer, bend over, gaze into the center
of this dark red beauty. . . ."

"You should write a book on peonies."

"Not so," Nakasone interrupted. "Enough of my blathering."

The two men relaxed, enjoying the inexpressible comfort of being
at ease in each other's company with no need to weigh thoughts, or
to measure words.

"So," Nakasone, speaking in English, exclaimed. "You like my
new home?"

"Very much. How did you come upon it?"

"Ono found it for me."

"Smart dog."

"Yes. He got himself lost and a girl who lives here found him
and returned him to me. I'm more than relieved to have him safe."
A smile etched the harsh outlines of Nakasone's lips as he scratched
his pet behind the ear.

Renzō, enjoying his friend's contentment, waited a moment before saying, "By the way, I'm in need of advice."

"Concerning?"

"My family home."

"The house on the hill at Hommoku Bay?"

"Yes. That one."

"A fine house in a prime position."

"You think so?"

"I do. Of course with the old courtesan gone, it now stands un-
occupied."

"Exactly."

"So where is your need of advice? Ah, now I remember. Rumi
had no liking for it, and now you want to move back there. I understand. My advice is be strong. Move back. . . ."

"You're speaking without thinking," Renzō exclaimed harshly.
"The place has been defiled. I intend to have it razed to the ground."

"What nonsense. What a waste!"

"I've a wild anger in me. I loved that house. My childhood home."

"I find your attitude ludicrous. At least *your* family home *stands*,
unscathed."

"Defiled! Befouled!"

"Others would consider it fortunate to have it standing unharmed. Especially compared with other estates that have been destroyed."

"Your family home, for instance?"

"*This* is now my home."

"I envy you."

"Yes, I'm a fortunate fellow," he said derisively. "No wife. No sons or daughters. No future responsibilities, but, if I had children, I would not casually denude them of their inheritance. Don't be a fool, Renzō. Rein in the wild horses trampling through your mind. We no longer wear two swords, my friend. We are but men of business who might be in for hard times before too long."

Suddenly Renzō felt despondent. "What then," he asked, "do you advise?"

Before replying, Nakasone examined his nails. They were in need of attention. He recalled his grandfather, a famous dandy, who, when aged seventy, employed several valets to care for his person. The old man's nails had been polished daily with scented wood, his hair had been oiled with the oil of plum-tree flowers. Nakasone said sharply, "Lease the house out."

"To whom?"

"That's up to you."

"Difficult! Its reputation is scarcely edifying."

"Why not lease the place to a foreign family?"

"It's a thought." Renzō stared at Nakasone, who had broken into a gale of raucous laughter.

"Crude of me, I admit, but why not offer the house to your protégé, Bixby?"

"Of all persons, not him! Such an insult."

"Just a thought. Just a thought. The idea pleases me. Let me take the matter in hand. Yes?"

Renzō took up his empty glass, then nodded assent.

"Excellent!" Nakasone sprang to his feet, and as he refilled his friend's glass he boomed out, "Come, let's drink to the love-crazed fellow and his unseemly marriage."

As the hours went by, both Nakasone and Renzō were content to stay put, aware that they were increasingly less interested in pleasure seeking. "Lately," Nakasone said, "I find it best to sit silent and look wise in company."

"You've always had a tendency to do just that. . . . Frankly, I'm not certain if I'm drunk or sober. It's a marvelous feeling. My mind keeps going off in two directions. Do you find it best not to look in the mirror these days?"

"Yes. You have a talent for expressing the greatest truths in the simplest language. How good it is to be with you like this. Fill my glass, please. Do you mind? Ono's so comfortable here on my knees."

"My pleasure . . ." Swaying, Renzō attended to his host's needs, then without asking permission attended to his own, saying, "Had you perchance died on your recent trip, I would be filled with regret."

"An innocuous statement. Explanation is required. Are you somehow guilt-ridden?"

"In a way—yes. My regret would come from the fact I've never openly stated how I appreciate your friendship."

Renzō reached out a hand to pull at Ono's drooping ears with a kind of exasperated tenderness, then, satisfied that Nakasone understood once and for all how valued he was, sat back. He knew he was speaking like this because of the funeral. Death, one's final link with the world. The thought of his own demise filled him with anguish, and he was all of a sudden overcome by hunger. "Have you no kitchen here?" he grunted. "Truly, Nakasone, I'm in need of food."

On hearing that magic word, Ono scrambled to the floor and his master rose up, saying, "Come then, let's off to the Fourth Pavilion. . . ."

With Ono leading the way, he and Nakasone halted before a gate decorated with grimacing gargoyles. " 'Tis said they scare away evil spirits." Nakasone spoke slurringly. Pushing the gate open, he shouted dramatically, "Humble visitors! Begging permission to enter."

No answer was given to that ridiculous announcement, and for quite some time they stood waiting in the square courtyard where three giant gilded bowls were filled with perfumed oil, floating with wicks that lit up the surroundings beneath the violet-dark of the night sky.

Without more ado, Nakasone led Renzō into a room which resembled a makeshift setting for an ancient drama. "Don't be abashed," Nakasone said, "subdue your hunger, enjoy a unique entertainment."

Taken aback, Renzō stared at the exquisitely robed individual who sat in a rickety sedan chair. Under a wide hat of silk held in place by bright yellow ribbons, the figure wore a sumptuous seventeenth-century brocade robe adorned with gossamer floats. A Nō mask expressing anger hid the person's face, and Renzō started back as a high, frail voice shrieked out: *"Light-fingered persons are not welcome here! Honest persons will be treated with respect and consideration."*

"Honest we are, Lady," Nakasone cried out sonorously. "Here to pay tribute!"

"Then let us all to mad chases through the gardens. Nights and days must be given over to pleasure. Bring on the flutes and drums."

Somewhere close by came drum taps accompanied by flute music, discordant and amateurish. Renzō grimaced. "Too weird for me," he said.

"Bear with it! Bear with it!" Nakasone laughingly insisted. "Sit yourself down."

The floor was of brick. There were no cushions, no chairs. There he sat, his mind whirling, feeling more than foolish, his gaze fixed on the masked creature whose pathetic warbling narratives had a blood-chilling effect.

"How can I emphasize the extent of my displeasure . . . ?" The voice ceased abruptly. Renzō, about to emphasize his own displeasure by taking his leave, stayed put as an elderly woman entered the room carrying a food-laden tray. She placed the tray before the men, saying, "Please, partake of this poor fare."

Nakasone, completely at ease, attacked the delicious food, but Renzō's own appetite had disappeared. He was overcome by curiosity, then he recalled having heard that Nakasone had given lodging to an ancient Nō actor, pandering with extreme kindness to the old man's dreams of past glories when his roles portraying women had been applauded throughout Edo. The elderly servant came close to Renzō. "Always," she whispered. "We treat the old artist like a queen graciously receiving envoys into her presence."

"He is asleep. He needs propping up," Nakasone interjected, aiming his chopsticks toward the decrepit, betassled sedan-chair. "Best let the curtain fall."

The gorgeously attired old creature had slipped sideways and the woman straightened him, adjusting the beribboned headdress, then coaxed him into sipping tea.

Renzō decided it was all too much. "Nakasone," he declared, "I must away now."

"By all means," his friend replied blithely. "But first, better take food. You are very drunk."

"Not very."

"Nicely so." Raising his voice, Nakasone shouted, "Bring hot tea for Yamamoto Sama."

"Page!" Again the old actor's falsetto voice quavered out querulously, *"Page! Come forth! Bring sustenance for the honorable guest."*

Tall, slender, robed in the manner of an executioner from ancient times, head hooded in black, wearing black trousers, a short black-belted coat, and sheathed dagger, a figure strode across the bricked floor, and knelt close, proffering Renzō not a bowl of tea, but a branch of purple silk flowers. An appealing musky fragrance arose from the dark, cocooned figure whose eyes, glimmering with gaiety and impudence, gazed challengingly into Renzō's eyes. Startled, convinced that a youth was seducing him, he experienced moments of physical turmoil, of orgiastic abandonment. Lost to reality, he reached out toward the figure with an anguished groan.

At that juncture, coming as though from another realm, Naka-sone's voice, teasingly hilarious, cried out, "A fine performance. Now then, Tama Yano, put an end to the playacting."

Immediately, the black hood was tossed back and a mane of glossy hair fell down over Tama Yano's shoulders, her voice revealing her sex as she cried out impishly, "Please excuse my teasing, my lack of theatrical skill. Here, in the Fourth Pavilion, hoping to comfort the honorable old actor, we do the best we can."

All at once Renzō was brought down to earth, as though falling from a great height. He felt that he had been ruthlessly tricked and was overcome by hostility for having been hoodwinked. He vowed to himself that he would keep well away from Nakasone's exotic Chinese-style house. He wanted no new emotional entanglements of any kind—ever.

B IXBY, AWAKENED BY THE TEMPLE'S dawn bell, thought it the sweetest of sounds. Although plagued by monetary and various other problems, he now viewed the world around him with a new freshness. Never had he imagined such a sense of spiritual and physical well-being as that which he was now experiencing.

The girl for whom he had hungered so desperately was lying close at his side. As he had attempted to rise from their *futon*, she had caught at his arm and murmured dreamily, "Has day come already?"

"It has." He turned to her and there no longer existed in the entire world any other person or thing than Tomiko, his wife. . . .

Awakening, surprised to find that he had once again been asleep, he saw that the *shōji* were opened wide to the autumn morning. Tomiko, bathed and dressed, sat close by on the *tatami*, hands clasped in the hollow of her lap, her gaze fixed on him, her expression expectant, like a young girl waiting for the theater curtain to rise.

He smiled, and although her smile in return was spontaneous, they both knew that disagreeable aspects of life had to be dealt with. There were no barriers between them. Both were imbued with a fierce stubbornness to win out in the face of every obstacle raised up before them.

He understood that Tomiko suffered deeply because her family clan—in fact the entire village—shocked by her rebellious behavior, wanted nothing evermore to do with her. "Maybe," he had said to comfort her, "time will change their attitude." Her full lips were pulled into a straight line and expressed her disbelief.

She understood that he was without money or property, and that, most urgently, he had to find employment. She understood that life in Japan had no attractions for him, that he intended to leave the country and find a new land where they could live together.

"Will you mind very much?" he had asked.

"Very much" was her reply. "I love my country. Don't you know that?"

"I know that."

"Then there is no need to question me. But, let me question you. May I?"

"Please do."

"To which land shall we travel? To your land, England?" That discussion had ended with laughter, for Tomiko fully understood that his family wanted no part of him.

"You and I," he had said with some cynicism, "are outcasts."

"Yes, but by our own choice," Tomiko declared with calm common sense.

During the morning a special delivery letter came from Renzō Yamamoto inviting Bixby to join him at the Dreyer's restaurant for lunch. "There is a matter I wish to discuss with you," the letter ended.

The sun was beating down on Yokohama but as always the morale of her citizens was high. The port city had grown up defiantly with a sort of impertinent bravado and it was still growing.

Having arrived with time to spare before keeping his appointment with Renzō, Bixby took a walk around the place, finding it exhilarating. Ships from many nations were at anchor in the great harbor and people of many nationalities filled the wide, paved streets.

This young, cosmopolitan city was entirely different from ancient, claustrophobic Tokyo. For the first time since his arrival in Japan, he felt at ease in his surroundings. Surely, here, in Yokohama he might find employment of a kind?

Recalling his appointment with Renzō, Bixby hailed a ricksha and was bowled along the waterfront. When he arrived at his destination, he felt that young Hans Dreyer had underestimated the charms of his family's famous old restaurant, so unpretentious, nestling in the midst of thatch-roofed huts scattered along the crescent-shaped beach at Hommoku Bay.

Renzō Yamamoto's friend, Nakasone, came forward to greet him, exclaiming, "Kind of you to come here at such short notice. Unfortunately, Mr. Yamamoto is unable to keep his appointment with you."

Bixby, depressed, found himself wondering why he had been invited to lunch. Nakasone was a jocular fellow, but certainly not one to waste his time with a comparative stranger. Even before consulting the menu, he cast an impatient glance at his timepiece, then said brusquely, "Our export firm is but a modest concern. Would you by any chance have an interest in joining forces with Yamamoto and me?"

Minutes seemed to pass before Bixby was capable of answering. "To admit interest would be an understatement."

Nakasone, not one to beat about the bush, exclaimed briskly, "Part and parcel of the arrangement is that you should live here in the port city. Our headquarters are situated close to the dock area. Of course, you are not bound to agree."

"I agree wholeheartedly," Bixby said. "I'll find a small, suitable house and . . ."

Nakasone massaged his chin. "Speaking of houses. I hesitate to bring up a delicate matter. One which could prove to be distasteful to you and perhaps even more so to Mrs. Bixby."

For an instant Bixby's mind stumbled at the reference to "Mrs. Bixby." Then he said in an arrogant tone, "My wife and I think alike. Please understand that regardless of public opinion, neither of us will yield even one inch, make any concessions injurious to our life together."

"So! Just as I thought. Frankly, I'd be appalled if that were not so. I like to think of myself as a man of some perception. May I continue . . . ?"

The house in Tokyo had served its purpose. Both Bixby and To-miko, feeling the need to celebrate their good fortune, stayed up all night, wandering through the city toward the Sumida River, where they stood listening to the sounds of oars splashing and voices call-ing, where the flames of lanterns were reflected in the water.

Tomiko thought only of the man she loved, but Bixby's mind concentrated on his relationship with Renzō Yamamoto. Did fate actually direct one's pathway? He found the idea altogether too ab-stract, even nonsensical, but how strange it was that the Japanese man who had casually entered Victor Caswell's Bond Street shop many years before owned that house on that hill in Yokohama.

There he had met the girl who was his wife.

There, in that house, now cleansed and vacant, he and Tomiko were to live. . . .

Renzō had come to envy those young enough to climb stairs three steps at a time.

The summer day of 1906 spent among shuffling crowds paying homage in the shrines and temples to all those who died in the Russo-Japanese War had left him exhausted. He was now relieved to be sitting at ease in Aiko's company, smoking his pipe in the apartment above the old curio shop.

Since the turn of the century their meetings had become infrequent. Passion no longer played a part, but they received immense comfort from each other's company and enjoyed sharing their intimate thoughts openly.

Kentaro, born of their union, was now a junior member of Japan's diplomatic corps. Recently he had been posted to Washington, D.C., and Renzō listened as Aiko read aloud his latest letter. It was a frivolous, amusing epistle, but the smile on Renzō's lips came from the sight of Aiko, so intent, unconscious of the tender expression in her voice. As she read on, repeating certain portions, his thoughts traveled back some three years to the time of Nakasone's death.

For the past sixteen years, it had seemed to Renzō that he was always saying good-bye to someone. To those leaving on short trips, journeying to other lands, and then those sad, final deathbed farewells to family members and good friends.

All the wonders of Western medical science had not been able to prevent his wife from dying of the scourge of tuberculosis.

Rumi's death had affected her husband and her half sister's relationship in many ways, causing them to avoid each other, until Aiko, with good sense, made the first approach, saying, "Renzō, I insist that we talk about Rumi. We were very close. No one can take her place in my heart, nor in yours. The rest is unimportant."

"Unimportant? I'm filled with guilt."

"What hypocrisy! Frankly, I find it distasteful that while Rumi lived, you never once felt troubled about our illicit relationship. You disappoint me."

"I understand your poor opinion of me. But Rumi was so loyal a wife, I can't help but agonize when wondering if she knew about us."

For several long moments Aiko had stared at him, her face pale
with tension, then she had said, "If Rumi knew, or suspected us, we
shall never know. She was my father's daughter, out to grasp the
good things in life. I believe that if she had doubts about us, she
preferred to ignore them. Yes, and she would even have taken some
delight in that knowledge. Rumi viewed life so objectively. And she
loathed being made to look inconsequential. Above all, she loathed
unpleasantness."

"Maybe so, but I keep asking myself why I was never able to
love her as she deserved to be loved."

"Be careful, Renzō. Don't reduce me to tears of boredom."

"Are you threatening me, Baroness?" he retorted with a wry grin.

"In a way, yes. I feel confused, even panic-stricken to see you
moving away from me." Their friendship had remained firm.

Now, starting guiltily, Renzō returned to the present, saying,
"Kentaro does write colorful screeds."

"He does." Aiko folded the letter with loving care, tucking it
beneath her *obi*-sash, patting it complacently before adding, "Have
we time for further dalliance? I hope so. Yuichi has told me that he
is in full agreement with Etsu's plans to live in the Nihombashi
house. What a *peculiar* history that little building has."

"True! Good thing it can't talk. So Etsu has gone running to her
uncle Yuichi for advice?"

"Why should she not? Many people run to Yuichi when things
don't go smoothly."

"Even you?"

"*He* comes running to *me*." Aiko gazed up, tongue in cheek,
eyebrows raised. "It's you, Yamamoto Sama, that I go running
to. Haven't you noticed? Renzō," she murmured pleadingly, "have
you completely forgotten the sweetness, the gaiety of days gone
by?"

For one bittersweet moment the years fell away. "I've not forgotten one moment of the times spent with you," Renzō exclaimed.
"Ah, that summer day when we stood together under the pine tree
in Fukuda's garden. Aiko, you threw me into a state of such utter
turmoil. . . ."

"Enough, enough!" Aiko took up her fan and fluttered it close to
her face, then said, "Never having lived in a house for which I had
any pride or affection, I find it difficult to understand other people's
feelings. Now that Rumi has gone, you have obviously taken a dislike to the house she took such pride in."

"It's too large for my needs."

"So sell it. Ignore Etsu's plans. Move back to Nihombashi!"

"Never! Too many ghostly memories there."

"How sensitive you are. So, then, why not return to the Yokohama house? It's close to your place of business. At your age, you should conserve your strength."

"Unkind of you to remind me of my decrepit condition." Renzō shook his fist playfully. "The truth is that since Nakasone's death, Bixby runs everything. We've almost given up exporting. I've become—to use a modern expression—a sleeping partner."

"*Scarcely* a tasteful expression coming from you to me," Aiko interrupted, her tone only half playful. "But, no offense taken. So, once again I put forward the idea that you move back to Yokohama. Don't exasperate me further with talk of ghostly echoes."

"If you excuse my shortcomings, I'll excuse your lack of understanding. Agreed?"

"Agreed."

"Good." Renzō said lightly, "I've done away with ghosts. When I visit my old home in Yokohama—which I quite often do—I quite like the atmosphere in the Bixby household."

"Really? Are you saying that the Englishman's marriage to *that person* has not as yet broken down? After all these years?"

"It flourishes."

Aiko, somewhat taken aback, spoke thoughtfully. "I've no understanding of such a love."

"Nor have I. The Bixby couple seem to be unafraid of anybody or of anything. It's impossible to doubt their dedication to each other. And to young Archie, their son."

"You paint a picture too quaint for my taste. All your sentimental burblings will not alter society's attitude toward that ill-matched pair."

Some five minutes later the friends departed from their secret meeting place. Aiko, laughing, said, "Please note that I brought no escort-maid. I'm a woman of today. Believe it or not, at times I actually carry my own *furoshiki* through the streets. . . ."

They made no mention of any future assignation, and as Renzō strolled along the crowded Ginza his feelings of refreshment faded. He had several problems. His main concern, though, was for his son, Shinichi—that son, so vital, so splendid in his youth but now, at thirty-five, a dispirited man seemingly with no interests, no ambitions.

Year after year he had ignored his parent's requests that he should sacrifice the busy, the intellectual life he was relishing so much in America and return to his family.

Making excuses, always promising that he would be returning home in the near future, sixteen long years had gone by before he had kept his word. During his absence, Rumi, the mother who had loved him so dearly had passed away into the spirit world without the comfort of her only son's presence.

His once handsome face carried several deep scars. Scars that no one mentioned, surmising that he had been wounded during his time as a war-correspondent, and that he would resent both sympathy and praise.

Glad as he was to have Shinichi home, it hurt deeply to have him so bruised both in his body and spirit.

Renzō sighed deeply. He felt helpless, quite at a loss, longing to help his son but not knowing what action to take.

Shinichi Yamamoto often wondered if he had made a mistake in returning to Japan. So many changes had taken place. He felt there was nowhere for him in all of it. The family home without the presence of his gregarious, beautiful mother held no warmth. He was painfully aware that, try as he might, his father could not hide the distress he felt at his son's mutilated visage. They now went out of their way to avoid being together. Old Sumiko and his grand-mother, Keiko, had gone from the world and he had lost touch with old friends and classmates. And, there was Etsu. So innocent.

Etsu! His sister! She must never know that he loved her. Bitterly, he realized that by coming home he had made the fatal mistake of believing that his unnatural feelings towards her would have paled. But immediately on seeing the alluring, beautiful woman he realized how mistaken he had been.

That all-consuming, more than brotherly love for his sister was the reason he had stayed away from Japan for those first six years of his self-banishment. He had had no intention of being present and witnessing her marriage to Gen Ohara.

After the finality of that event, in a macabre way a part of him was relieved when during a laboratory experiment he had been burnt by acid and his face had been disfigured. Overly sensitive, ashamed of his appearance, he had been unable to face the ordeal of returning home, knowing how his adored mother would suffer on beholding his impairment. He had dreaded having to deal with the sympathy which would have flowed about him from relatives and friends. Making false promises to his parents, he had stayed on in America, growing to love the country, making friends, feeling at ease with his colleagues, and although devastated on learning of his mother's death he had not returned home to honor her spirit.

During the following ten years, he had been grateful for the stream of letters from the hand of his uncle Yuichi. Letters aglow with family gossip, with snippets of advice, and of commendation, saying that he approved of him staying abroad while the war between Japan and China went on. *"Better a living nephew than a dead one"* he had written. *"Shinichi, this war with China has set us on a dangerous pathway where we shall be exploited as a mere tool by Western powers. Meantime, flag-waving and victory banquets cover up the fact, for the time being at least, that our country is economically crippled. . . ."*

He had paid little heed to Yuichi's dire predictions but time had proved him right on several counts, for over the following five years Japan had been coerced into giving up a number of the fruits of previous victories. Port Arthur had been handed over to Russia. The Russians built the Siberian railway through Chinese territory, to Vladivostok, thereby taking control of all northern Manchuria.

Not only Russia and Japan had designs on gaining new territory, and the ancient realm of China was being sliced up like a melon by Western powers as well.

As the game of international politics continued, it seemed to Shinichi that nothing was clearly good or evil. That no country ever had absolute right on their side.

When tiny Japan, now a full ally of Britain, boldly went to war with mighty Russia, Yuichi's letters voiced feelings which would have brought him embarrassment, and have caused trouble to his family had he spoken of them publicly in his own country.

Shinichi had always had a deep affection for his uncle, admiring the man's rather flamboyant attitudes and when diplomatic negotiations between Tokyo and St. Petersburg were broken and the fully fledged warfare broke out he received the first wartime letter.

"Presently, in Japan," Yuichi wrote, *"all political in-fighting has ceased and a great wave of patriotism has risen up, which to my mind is altogether too melodramatic. But, naturally, not wishing to blot my reputation I have joined in with the banking community and important business houses and I have donated huge sums of money to the war effort. I am lending my name to various organizations and fund-raising rallies, but I think of myself as a man set apart, forced to act in hypocritical ways instead of speaking out,*

bravely, expressing my deep disgust about the subtle ways in which the government is going all-out to romanticize the horrors of warfare to the common people.

"As military bands play, as banners and flags fly high, already bereaved and grieving folk of every class pay obeisance, their heads bowed before temple altars.

"I find it ludicrous that hymns of praise are given to nobles and aristocrats said to be economizing on food. I find it sanctimonious of my colleagues, men of great wealth, who announce piously that they are denying themselves the pleasure of sport, and the luxury of supporting a mistress. Ladies, even the empress, it is rumored, are selling some of their personal treasures as a token sacrifice. On the quiet, I have purchased my wife's jewels, donating the cash, intending to restore her the trinkets when the time comes. I find it hard to write this but I have given my six splendid horses, to be sent into battle. This I have done solely for superstitious reasons, one might say, to propitiate the gods, for to avoid having dire complications interfere with Kentaro's wellbeing, I've taken the precaution of shipping him off to join you in New York. He will attend a university there. You must watch over him. You must treat him as you would treat a beloved brother. Remember, he is my only son.

"My heart pounds with rage knowing that youths, subtly indoctrinated, are actually searching for ways to die just for the glory of it. It is being widely reported that soldiers in their death throes are shouting out praise of their emperor. During my own youth, I heard on good authority from a hardy old warrior that agonized men dying on the battlefields call out—not patriotic slogans—but call out in fear and in despair for their mothers. Absolutely, without a shadow of doubt, I believe the old warrior's version. . . ."

On his arrival in New York, Kentaro, with great tact, had disguised the shock he had undergone on seeing his cousin's changed appearance. Smiling, he had said lightly, while gesturing to Shinichi's scarred face, "Now, *that's* a well-kept secret!"

Kentaro, too handsome for his own good, and with no ambition to spend all his time abroad furthering his academic studies, immediately took to the pleasures of the colorful, exciting city.

Following the young man's arrival, a barrage of letters had come from members of the Fukuda clan; one from his great-aunt Sumiko, in characters brushed by her trembling hand saying, *"Shinichi, it is now your bounden duty to watch over my grandson, Kentaro, so innocent, so immature . . ."*

Kentaro had laughed hilariously on reading that stern letter from

Sumiko, then he had said, "Truly, it's I who should watch over *you*. Shinichi, as your junior, I've no right to advise you . . ."

"Exactly!" he had snapped back. "So don't!" A hot debate had ensued with the cousins finally making a pact to mind their own business on all scores.

However, Shinichi had been relieved when Kentaro, with a show of common sense, threw himself into a spate of study, not from choice but solely to have it known that he was not frittering his time away in an exotic, foreign land instead of returning home to fight the good fight as a soldier of Nippon.

Being with a family member, and enjoying the ebullient young man's company, and conversing in his native language, had made him desperately homesick for Japan and for things Japanese.

But eager as he was to return home he could scarcely turn up like a man from nowhere, a *rōnin*, with unexplained scars on his face.

From his point of view the outbreak of the Russo-Japanese war had come as a blessing in disguise.

An unexpected meeting with an American colleague who had become a news reporter of some repute inspired him with an idea, and with some guile he obtained permission from a leading Tokyo newspaper to act as a free-lance war-correspondent for their publication.

Seeking out Kentaro he had spoken with enthusiasm, pouring out his plans, saying, with pseudo-humor, "Once back home, these old scars of mine could be seen as the war wounds of a hero?"

Seeing his cousin's blank expression, he said, "Don't you get my meaning?"

"Not really. No."

"Can't you see that my disfigurement, if seen as a war wound would not be looked upon as an unacceptable blemish? Can't you see that?"

"No." Kentaro had cried out, "But do as you wish. I'm not qualified in dealing with subterfuges. Do as you wish."

So, he had carried out his plans. Leaving America he spent the following nine months close to the war zones, often under fire. He was never harmed. The articles he wrote were accepted and the colorful, skilled dispatches earned him admiration and praise from various quarters.

Finally, Japan astounded the world by gaining victory over mighty Russia. The tiny feudal country whose doors had been forced open

by American gunboats just half a century before had achieved a
firm foothold in Asia which made her not only a force to be reck-
oned with, but undoubtedly the East's most dominant power.

Standing on the hill at Port Arthur the day after Russia's surren-
der, Shinichi had gazed out over the shell-torn slopes. Farther out,
as far as the eye could see, the land was scarred, defaced by the
smashed tools of war. All about him were countless trenches filled
with the nauseating stench of barely covered Russian and Japanese
corpses.

"Madness! Madness," he had cried out explosively. "What utter
madness . . ."

Now, back in Japan, there were times when he wished that he
had died on that battleground.

In every way his life had become a third-rate affair, and he lacked
the initiative to make something more of it. In all truth he would
have to find a refuge to hide in. But where? Soon he would move
on, go somewhere far off. In the meantime it was up to him to
straighten up. Show a cheerful face to the world . . .

ETSU HAD EMERGED AS A woman who had captured the new spirit
of feminine independence. Chic and intelligent, she faced life with a
sense of humor and replied to criticism by saying with a smile,
"Maybe I'm conceited, but I do set some value on myself."

She and Shinichi were meandering from room to room in the
now-vacant house at Nihombashi.

Etsu, dressed in a uniform proudly worn by women who had
become working members of the International Red Cross during
the Russo-Japanese War, was saying, "It's nice to remember that as
children we once lived in this old house. You would remember
better than I—has it changed very much?"

"It has. But I'm more interested to discover where my pampered,
fiery-tempered little sister now dwells?"

"Oh! That one? She grew up."

"Married, became a wife."

"She did."

"Is now a divorced woman."

"Thankfully so. Yes."

"Was the marriage so bad, then?"

"Have no guilt." She grinned at him. "Gen quite often regaled me—in detail—about how you two rascals engineered that marriage. In no way was it *bad*. We had a great deal of fun together."

"Fun?"

"So! Yes. Nothing in common, but a great deal of *fun*. Gen and I will always be on pleasant terms."

"Then, why the divorce?"

"For one thing, Gen's mother loathed me." Etsu smiled grimly. "I loathed her even more. I found her pretentious. She found me— and I quote—'conceited, undereducated in the arts, and unable to converse in the French language.' Poor Gen was caught up in the middle. We were both overjoyed when the dread subject of divorce was brought up."

"Gen's mother was responsible, then?"

"Not entirely." Etsu pulled a wry face, then said brightly, "Gen has remarried. Most happily, so he told me in a letter. That's nice, isn't it?"

"What's nice?"

"To be happy."

"Are you?"

"Am I what?"

"Happy."

"Why not? I enjoy the challenges life keeps throwing before me. I never look back. I've got you back home at last. I've many women friends. Who knows, maybe among them there's a wife for you."

"Thank you, but no thank you!" Shinichi, as though suddenly conscious of his disfigurement, turned away from his sister. "Be honest," he exclaimed lightly. "Who could agree to marry this scarred-faced chap?"

Etsu hesitated, then began speaking rapidly, "Shin-chan, it's *you* who should be honest. Father and I—we are not simpletons. Won't you—out of respect for our mother's spirit—tell us of your own accord exactly how you were afflicted with the scars you bear? Why be so close-mouthed?"

"Why indeed! You've quite a skill for making speeches." Shinichi continued in a light tone, "So I'm being gossiped about behind my back, eh? I find that deplorable."

"Not so! But we *care* for you. You should know that! Naturally, I have my own thoughts."

"You do?"

"I do."

"Well?"

"Well, my intuition tells me that you were injured *before* our mother died. Please tell me? Is that so?"

"Yes. That is so."

"Shinichi, I clearly understand your motive for staying away, protecting Mumma's feelings. I consider you heroic. Our mother died happy believing you still whole and handsome. Her illness was short, she faded so rapidly. Yours was the last name she mentioned. So! Please bring everything out into the open. Put an end to the farce. Father will be so relieved . . ."

A sharp gesture from Shinichi halted Etsu's speech. Being alone with her was almost too much happiness to bear. "So," he queried, vaguely, "you think it's not too late to remedy my grossness?"

"I'm certain of it. You will speak with Father? Tell him everything?"

Hesitating for an instant, knowing that the whole truth could never be told, Shinichi said, "Yes, Etsu. I will speak with him."

Etsu bowed her thanks, then exclaimed brightly, "Now to *my* affairs. What do you think of this old building?"

"Very ramshackle. By the by, what became of that jolly English couple who were living here before I left for New York?"

"The Coombers! Don't you know? Dear old Sir John died most joyously, pen in hand, while sitting at his desk in this very room."

"Lady Marjorie?"

"Much to Aunt Aiko's disappointment, that lady became so enamored of her grandchildren while paying 'just a flying visit back to England, my dearests' that she has never returned to Japan."

"Huh! What of old Thomas Trask? I liked him immensely."

"Trask San lives on. He has become famous. His English translations of *haiku* are on everybody's lips. You should know *that*."

"Am I in for another lecture?"

"Sorry!" Etsu bowed with mock humility. "No lectures ever again. Brother, will you put my heart completely at rest?"

"If possible."

"Don't go away again. Take a teaching post here at Waseda University."

"At present I've no wish to go away. Leave it at that."

"For the present I'll be satisfied." Etsu cast a cheeky glance in his direction. "Tell me, aren't you surprised that Father has given in. Let me have this old house?"

"I am. I'm amazed that you should want it."

"Well, I'm not eager to live on into old age beneath the family roof. I intend to set up my own home. Are you shocked?"

"No."

"Good. We women of today embrace independence. We're out to pursue careers."

"May I," Shinichi inquired teasingly, "know of the career which *you* intend to pursue?"

"Nothing in mind at present. Don't *push* me."

Etsu, conscious of her brother's suppressed amusement and on the point of losing her temper, broke into laughter. "Uncle Yuichi has encouraged me every step along the way. Now I'd value your seal of approval."

Shinichi gazed at his sister, taking in her flawless beauty, then he gave her a nod of assent.

There were times when Etsu wondered about her calm in the face of various aspects of her life. She could not help but realize that she was exceptionally beautiful. She took her appearance for granted, knowing that in no way was she responsible for it. The only event clouding her girlhood had been the loss of her brother's companionship, but she had decided, "Why cry when tears will not bring Shinichi back?"

At the age of twelve she would practice her piano lessons with abandon, pressing down on the loud pedal while shouting out in answer to her father's complaints, "It doesn't *matter* that I'm hitting the wrong notes, Papa. It's the *spirit* of my music that counts."

At Tsuda College, the exclusive school for girls where top priority was given to the study of English, Etsu outstripped many of her classmates in knowledge and fluency, but admitted frankly, "It's no real credit to me. For years I've shared my cousin's English tutor. And my father has always corrected my pronunciation and read to me in English."

When she realized that her marriage was a passionless, flaccid affair, she behaved pleasantly throughout it, making no complaints to her parents, and when she was cast out, divorced, she refused to be embarrassed but exclaimed, "So, it didn't work out. Better luck next time."

"Such indelicacy!" her ancient aunt Sumiko gasped.

When that treasured old lady died, the family wept floods of tears, but Etsu stated calmly, "She lived long and happily."

During her mother's illness Etsu had taken command. Paying no heed to the dangers of infection, she tended to the dying woman's most intimate needs, staying close to her side both night and day, her heart aching, keeping a cheerful manner while saying to herself, "I love her. I know that she will soon die. It's no use grasping at straws."

There was a pact between mother and daughter that they would give comfort to members of the family who refused to accept the inevitable, and would bring in not only rafts of skilled physicians but also experts in the field of acupuncture, moxa, and herbal remedies.

"Why not pretend to believe in miracles?" Rumi had murmured.

"Yes," she had agreed. "Why not, Mumma. At least it will raise the spirits of those who love you so dearly."

"*Your* attitude, Et-chan, consoles me above all else. We are so alike."

After Rumi's death, Keiko had wept unconsolably and Renzō had withdrawn into himself. He neglected his appearance and refused to eat, to meet with his friends.

Etsu, distressed, went to her aunt Aiko and said quietly, "Aunt, a darkness is falling over my father. My mother's spirit suffers. For *her* sake will you attempt to comfort your sister's bereft husband?"

Aiko had smiled faintly, then murmured, "Thank you for confiding in me. I shall act immediately."

Her aunt had then said, "Your uncle Yuichi frets about *you*, Etsu."

"Please tell him not to fret."

"But I believe he has cause. What have you to say about that?"

"I'm at a loss."

"Exactly! We feel that you *are* at a loss. As a divorced woman, you suffer a lack of self-esteem."

"Not so. I'm enjoying my independence."

Aiko waved her hands in the manner of two butterflies fluttering to and fro. "But one needs discipline. Too much freedom can be dangerous."

"And maybe boring?"

"Yes, Et-chan, why don't you offer your services to the Red Cross?"

Etsu pulled a face and Aiko shrugged. "Just think it over!"

How quickly and how cruelly she had learned the true meaning of the word *discipline*. How proudly she had worn the nursing-aide uniform, emblazoned with its red cross, the colors of the Swiss flag reversed, together with the badge of its motto *Inter Arma Caritas*.

Those last five months of the Russo-Japanese War had taken her into a completely new world. She had been posted to Kure, the most important of all Japan's naval harbors, which had been amassed with battleships, torpedo craft, and gunboats.

Japan's entire navy was keeping its ceaseless vigil in the surrounding sea. Thousands of military troops were pouring into the port to be rapidly sent out again into the troopships that went off to the war zones.

Those white-hulled vessels, protected by the great red crosses on their funnels, had been dazzlingly beautiful to behold, but not so the lines of stretchers brought ashore carrying the shattered bodies of young men, among them numbers of wounded Russians, no longer considered as the enemy, but as patients to be nurtured and cared for.

Quite a number of the nurses had broken down under the stress and strain, but Etsu had closed her mind to everything except her duties. She came to understand how women could work together as a sisterhood, where there was trust and idealism. . . .

Yuichi and Aiko Fukuda stood side by side on the front steps of the family mansion discussing the rehabilitation of the garden. The August afternoon was stiflingly hot, and as they spoke they kept their fans at a continuous flutter. "I," Yuichi was saying, "am immensely pleased. The gardeners have followed my every instruction."

"They most certainly have," Aiko replied.

He gave her a sharp look, not sure whether to be insulted or flattered. "Don't you agree that the garden was altogether too spartan?"

"I fully agree." A fleeting expression of impatience rippled across her face and a tinge of asperity livened the flat tone of her voice. "Excuse me, please, I've no time to linger. I'm to attend the performance of the noted German violinist this afternoon."

"Is that so? Well, I suggest you take a long, cool bath. It will refresh your mind as well as your body."

"Such husbandly concern!" As she headed for the door he called out, "I'll join you in the bathroom shortly. . . ." A slight bow was her reply. Preferable, he thought, to one of her sharp comments.

He gazed up at the azure sky, then at the expanse of velvety lawn backed by clipped shrubbery. In the center of the lawn was an Italianate marble fountain complete with water-spouting dolphins and cherubs. To his delight, the sun sparkled on the flying drops of water, creating the additional pleasure of effervescent rainbows.

Yuichi moved close to the fountain to gaze admiringly at one of the cherubic figures. It brought back to him memories of Kentaro as a babe. How perfect, how lovely he had been. What a charming man he had become. He accepted the fact that the insouciant young chap had no talent for the business responsibilities which he himself had taken on and fulfilled so successfully.

He thought of his own father. Few men had known more about clandestine transactions, and he had done his utmost to emulate him, but unlike his father, he was not popular in corporate circles and attended geisha parties only under duress. "I'm thought of by my colleagues," he once confessed to Aiko, "as a chap too domesticated."

"Ah, well, I suppose it's natural that they consider you to be rather a lame duck," she replied not unkindly, adding, "Never mind."

He had stared at her aggressively and said, "Will you never cease rubbing salt in my wound?"

"How touchy you are becoming," she responded. "I intended no insult. Surely after all these years you can't think that I would allude to your physical lack? You should offer me an apology."

"Well"—he grinned at her—"maybe I'm altogether too sensitive. I miss my mother's praise and encouragement."

"A unique apology." She returned his grin. "But I accept it."

Suddenly the chirp of a cricket triggered off Yuichi's memories of childhood days when he felt that all he had to do when thwarted was fly into a tantrum. That child in him had never gone.

The sun was making him hot and fatigued. He felt like a whale stranded on a beach. Why, he pondered, was he now feeling so thwarted; why was his spirit so sour? Seating himself on the marble edge of the pond, he bit at his lip.

Was it because of his age? Because life was rushing along like an express train toward its journey's end? Suddenly he knew that he should find a new challenge. He required fresh fields to conquer. Many of his elderly, retired colleagues found relief in relationships with attractive, younger women. What a disaster his malady was. He loved the company of women. His was a warm, hospitable nature. Yes, he was bright and witty too, in spite of Aiko's opinion of him.

Aiko? How blatantly she reveled in her long-standing affair with his cousin. And Renzō was so suave, so samurai confident. Yet he loved that man and that woman dearly. He owed them both so much.

Smiling ruefully, he went into the house. The rooms he meandered through glistened with costly ornaments, many of them gifts from those who had received favors from him, Baron Fukuda.

His wife described their home as "the epitome of bad taste." She also complained that it was vulgar to have so many servants. He agreed with her on that point but found it quite impossible to discard old family retainers.

He glanced into the handsomely furnished Western-style dining room, where the ancient butler and three aged housemaids were chatting and laughing as they polished the furniture. "Hard at it!" he called to them cheerfully, and although he had cigarettes in his pocket, he requested one. A flurry of bows and scampers ensued, and in a trice he was seated at the table with a silver box filled with cigarettes, together with an alabaster ashtray and a tube of waxed matches.

He thought of Kentaro and recalled how they had spoken together prior to the younger man's departure to Washington.

"Without any wish to influence you, Kentaro," he had said in a fatherly manner, "may I put into your mind an idea I've discussed with your mother?"

Kentaro had shifted uneasily on his chair, muttering, "This could develop into an absorbing discussion, Father. I intend to go far in the diplomatic service and, by the way, I *already* know that Count Ota's daughter, Maya, is attending college in Washington."

"Is that so!" Yuichi said approvingly. "Your mother agrees that the girl Maya would be an excellent choice." Yuichi studied the handsome young face, then added, "I've heard that the count's daughter is intelligent but not noted for her comeliness. How does that affect you?"

"Not unduly," Kentaro said seriously. "I much prefer an intelligent wife to a mere beauty."

"That's the truth?"

"It is." Kentaro had smiled and Yuichi, recalling the smile of Renzō Yamamoto's mother, Lady Masa, had pressed a hand over his heart to suppress its sudden upsurge of beating.

"Are you all right, Father?" Kentaro's voice was anxious.

"Yes, yes," he replied. "Just at times I feel tired. Especially when I allow my emotions to get the better of me . . ."

Yuichi came back to the present with a jolt when he remembered telling Aiko that he would join her in the bathroom. He crushed out the stub of his cigarette and made his way along the corridors, his spirit once again sour.

He still talked to himself like a child, especially when he was unhappy. Now, he murmured, "Yuichi, *exactly* what is troubling you?"

"I'm not clear on the matter."

"How is your health?"

"Excellent."

"Have you business worries?"

"No."

"Scared of growing old, of dying?"

"No more so than usual."

"Then, maybe a little scared of your life as it is?"

"Not scared. Simply discontented."

"Why should you be?"

"Well, lately I've been *extremely* jealous of my wife's continuing relationship with my cousin."

There it was! Out in the open at last! What to do?

"So, Yuichi, fix it! Control your emotions. You've always been expert at solving your problems and those of others."

So, of course! Renzō must be inveigled into taking a new wife.

He would go about the matter with extreme subtlety. First he would approach Etsu and Shinichi, bringing up the subject of their father's lonely plight, saying, "Now, I've no desire to influence anybody unduly. But . . ."

How would Aiko react? He was not at all sure. It was foolish to take her attitude for granted. It would behoove him to keep her in the dark until it was too late for her to interfere.

The sweetly smelling bathroom was empty. Aiko had completed her ablutions. He had tarried too long. He was sorry, for he always enjoyed bathing with her. He found her the most feminine of creatures, with a passion for Western-style lingerie—she possessed countless chemises, camisoles, petticoats, and corset covers, all hand sewn and imported from France.

She was in her dressing room, preparing for her outing, wearing a black kimono patterned with white flower petals. Her maid was unfolding the silver-gray brocaded *obi*-sash and it trailed across the *tatami* like a stream of water in moonlight.

Aware of his figure in the doorway, Aiko smiled. "I was hoping for your company while I bathed. What were you doing?"

He could not repress a sharp intake of breath; he loved it so much when she showed her affection for him. "Doing?" he replied blankly. "Nothing of any importance."

"An unusually modest statement," she murmured.

"Not so," Yuichi retaliated. "Few men are more modest than I, or more thoughtful for the welfare of others."

"Ah, now the *true man* speaks." Aiko laughed scathingly. "So, Yuichi, then maybe it's time to give some attention to your cousin Renzō's plight?"

Amazed, he showed no emotion while she stared at him coldly and took up a fan. Waving it in circles, she said, "Recently, the thought came to me that Renzō should marry again. It's pathetic for him to slide into old age alone."

Dumbfounded, Yuichi burst out laughing, and then said, "You and I! We often each cherish the same ideas, but that Renzō should take a *wife* had not occurred to *me*."

"Is that so? 'Tis said that most elderly men, after losing a wife, are apt to fall by the wayside. Tell me, what do you think of my suggestion?"

"Well, the very thought of putting the idea to Renzō chills me."

"I agree. He never takes kindly to advice of any kind. So—he must be gently coerced."

"Can it be that you have a suitable woman in mind?"

"Believe it or not, I have." Gesturing that the maid should make herself scarce, Aiko continued on in a conspiratorial manner. "Tell me, Yuichi, what is your opinion of the widow Kawabata?"

"Ummm . . . so entirely different from Rumi."

"Yes. I consider that most important."

"How *sensible* you are. Have you already approached the widow?"

"I have. She is in no way opposed to the idea."

"How *remarkable* you are. But I never underrate your aptitude for stepping in where others fear to tread."

Aiko smiled disarmingly. "In you I've had a brilliant instructor. But never mind about all that. Let's to the future. Agreed?"

"Not as yet. Not fully." Yuichi allowed his forehead to furrow deeply. "Shinichi and Etsu must be taken into consideration. They might resent our interference. Rumi was most dear to them."

Aiko was silent, then she clapped her hands sharply, and as her maid re-entered the room, she said briskly, "Yuichi, I've no wish to be late for the concert. Excuse me please. Just tell me if I'm on the right track? My thought is to take the young ones into our confidence. Win their approval. Yes?"

"Yes, yes, I find your plans admirable."

"Thank you!" Aiko gave her full attention to the intricate task of having the *obi*-sash arranged to her liking.

Taking up her discarded fan, Yuichi wielded it back and forth. His inner feelings were those of satisfaction and rib-tickling amusement. He doubted that from Aiko's point of view there was any other available woman in Japan who could have more prerequisites than the widow Kawabata as a wife for Renzō. She was childless, wealthy, of fine samurai stock. She was well-traveled, stout-figured, and, *she was five years Aiko's senior.*

Tucking the fan beneath his arm, he left the room with a wide grin and with his mind aglow with admiration for his wife.

T HE ERA OF THE HORSELESS carriage had arrived and the public's confidence in the reliability of the motorcar was increasing. Renzō, eager to bolster up Shinichi's confidence, had imported a Daimler Phaeton.

He disliked the smell of petroleum, but Shinichi reveled in it, exclaiming, "Have no fears, Father. No. No, it won't explode. Have no fears. See how I'm steering her with one hand?"

"I see."

"Would you care to take a turn at the wheel?"

"Maybe some time later," he answered, knowing that he never would. As the machine racketed along rough roads, Renzō was filled again with indignation as he thought of Rin, that faithful family retainer, who had left Japan with his family to begin a new life in California. Rin's son would have made an excellent chauffeur.

As far as he knew, there were but forty or so of the mechanical monsters in Tokyo, each one causing a sensation. Men, women, and children were apt to run alongside as they traveled bumpy roads, cheering derisively when a breakdown occurred. In his opinion, there was an enmity between motorcar drivers and the drivers of other vehicles. If cars took precedence on the roads of the future, it would be a nightmare; he hoped that the motorcar would remain a rich man's toy.

"Father," Etsu had insisted, "please don't be so old-fashioned. The automobile is a symbol of progress."

Well, he preferred not to think along those lines. His mind was occupied by other and more interesting things by far. For some time he had resented the cloying efforts of his children, so intent on cheering him out of his dour moods, and tempting him to widen his interests. "Learn to play golf, Father."

"Maybe take an interest in gardening, Father."

"Father, please stop refusing all the invitations that come your way."

Now he was grateful for their encouragement and grateful to the Fukuda couple who had gone to so much trouble on his behalf, inviting him to dinner, to the theater, making certain that the company was always amusing.

For the remainder of his life—however long or short it was to be—he would not forget the kindness shown him, and he hoped that his plan to remarry would not be received too unhappily.

Here he was, already in his sixties, ready to take life on with new vigor.

What a remarkable influence Victor Caswell had over his well-being! Recently he had been saddened to learn of the old man's death, and he had gone to Yokohama, eager to meet with Bixby to honor their mutual friend's departure from life by drinking a toast to his memory.

Bixby had developed into a man highly respected in the business and social life of the port city. His son, Archie, now a youth of nearly sixteen, had a happy-go-lucky approach to life. He had inherited his father's tall, stalwart figure and his mother's dark hair. His oblique eyes were long-lashed and smoky in color, giving him an exotic appearance.

After a lengthy and nostalgic lunch, Bixby brought up problems concerning stock he was unable to unload. "The warehouse should have a clearance sale, Renzō," he declared firmly. "I need your advice. Have you time to spare?"

Having too much time to spare, he agreed with alacrity. In the large, dusky warehouse his spirits dropped and he exclaimed, "Frankly, Bixby, I've no idea how to rid ourselves of these outmoded chests. Who lumbered us with them?"

"You did." Bixby grinned with some relish. "Some ten years ago. Don't you remember?"

"Touché, touché." He smiled wryly, muttering, "Everyone makes mistakes. . . ."

At that moment Tomiko Bixby, accompanied by a woman friend, arrived, and in the flurry of greetings, business matters were shelved.

Tomiko Bixby had become a self-confident person. As she introduced him to her companion, Renzō became conscious that the young woman was looking at him as though she were peering into a mirror.

"*Shibaraku desu*—It has been many years since we met," she exclaimed in a forthright manner. "Time has been kind to you, Yamamoto Sama."

He studied her, a frown furrowing his brow, while she smiled, waiting for the moment of recognition.

Her voice had a peculiar grittiness, distinctive and compelling. Raising her penciled brows, she ended his discomfort, murmuring wryly, "Evidently time has not been quite so kind to me." Then addressing Bixby in English she added, "Or is my memory at fault? Am I mistaken? Is not Yamamoto Sama the one and same man so dear to Nakasone?"

"One and the same," Bixby replied. "Have no fears about your memory, Tama."

Tama? Tama Yano! Nakasone's Chinese-style house? That garden of magnificent peonies? That macabre interlude where the old Nō actor had warbled so dramatically from the sedan chair. Tama? The young girl cocooned in black? His sudden, overwhelming surge of passionate arousal?

Tama Yano's voice broke into his confused mind. "So, Yamamoto Sama, you do remember." Once more she addressed herself to Bixby. "Your friend once visited the House of Four Pavilions. The atmosphere there was not to his liking." Flashing a glance his way, she asked, "Is that not so?"

"Not so." He floundered about. "Not so . . ."

Dust motes danced in a shaft of sunlight filtering through the barred windows, and through the haze he studied Tama, wondering with some amusement how she would react if he declared, "Young woman. You once sent me into an explosive, a passionate climax, startling me like a clap of thunder from a blue sky."

Instead, he said, "My visit to that house left an indelible impression on me. You still live there?"

"No. Not for some years. It did not suit my personality."

"How true," Tomiko exclaimed. "The beach house allows you more freedom, Tama."

"Yes, perhaps in a former existence I was a dolphin?"

"Or," Bixby interjected, "a petrel flying against the wind?"

"Who knows?" She smiled, revealing strong white teeth and then, making an impatient gesture, exclaimed, "Bix, Tomiko and I are here to drag you from this dank-smelling place, to my house. Please say yes."

Bixby glanced at his wife. With no hesitation she bowed slightly and said, "Excuse our unannounced arrival. We are interrupting your time with Yamamoto Sama?"

Renzō, with no compunction, answered for Bixby. "Not at all! Not at all! Our business discussion has been completed."

Unconcerned about the impropriety of foisting himself on them, a self-invited guest, he turned the trio into a foursome, and seated himself in the shabby hired carriage. The driver snapped a whip and the vehicle moved off swiftly. Heedless of his own person, he was conscious only of the carefree atmosphere, of the affection so openly displayed by Bixby toward his wife.

Suddenly he thought of Aiko's friend and confidante, the widow Kawabata, and it came to him with enormous impact that *he* was dangerously on the way to becoming trapped into an unwanted marriage. He would do well to be on his guard. Not only for his own sake but to prevent the widow Kawabata from needless embarrassment. He held her in some esteem. Yes, even though he was now certain that she was in cahoots with his son, his daughter, and the Fukuda couple.

Without delay he wanted it widely known that he was determined to take full responsibility for his own life. He would use the excuse of the pressures of business affairs and absent himself from Tokyo to spend a few weeks at the Bund Hotel in Yokohama.

Innocently he had nibbled at the matrimonial bait that had been prepared for him but thanks to all the gods he had not swallowed it.

Tama Yano's beachside house had been built some years before, designed by Hans Dreyer for Western-style living. He and his young wife, Jutta, had been the first tenants.

Jutta, blonde, with eyes of gentian blue had come to Yokohama from her home in Bavaria to act as a governess in the home of a Japanese professor. Hans, a frequent visitor to the house had met and fallen passionately in love with the German girl. His feelings had been reciprocated and they had married to live in a state of bliss for ten years. Then tragedy struck. Jutta, proud and happy to have become pregnant after so many years had died in great agony as she labored to give birth.

All kinds of emotions had welled up in Hans Dreyer's heart. Mad with sorrow, wild with anger at the world, the very sight of the fragile female infant repulsed him. Out of respect for his long deceased missionary grandparents he had had the child christened, naming her, Anna. Having gone through that time-honored ceremony he had placed his daughter in the old Dreyer cottage beneath the care of servants.

Wanting no more to do with past memories he sold the beachside house to his friend, Tama Yano, then convinced that he must escape from reality he traveled to Japan's far North and into the sanctity of a Buddhist retreat.

Renzō had often been a guest in the charming house and had quaffed down many a stein of foamy German beer beneath its roof. Now, to his consternation, the only beverage offered was hot, fragrant tea.

Yearning for something stronger, he sat, tea bowl in hand, exchanging small talk with his hostess and the Bixby couple.

He then told them of his mother and his aunt, of how they had gone paddling along the water's edge with their gowns tucked up. He told them how he, aged twelve, had once galloped a great black stallion along the sandy shore of the crescent-shaped beach.

Bixby and Tomiko, as if impelled by identical thoughts, got up and wandered to the water's edge.

"How nice your family must have been," Tama commented. "My family history is in no way as nice. I'm not conventional. But then, writers of fiction seldom are."

"So," he said, "a writer! Congratulations!"

"Not yet in order," she quipped. "My works have not yet been published."

"Too bad."

"Yes. But I struggle on. I'm attempting to translate one of my short stories into English." A frown of irritation shadowed her face. "It goes badly and too slowly."

"Maybe I could assist you. I'm a skilled translator. I've got time at my disposal. . . ." The words escaped his lips as though of their own volition. He regretted his offer, which was immediately accepted, and Tama, eyes glittering, sent him on his way with a manuscript tucked beneath his arm.

Even at that early stage of their relationship, conventional barriers had been swept aside, and as the days went by, they hid little one from the other. Tama would exclaim, "Renzō, do you find me altogether too outspoken? Of course, I refer to my writing."

"I cherish your attitudes," he responded, "both written and otherwise."

"Go on, go on. Compliment me but don't be *too* excessive."

That exchange had taken place in her study, a miniature Japanese house originally built in the garden for the servants. He would arrive there every morning, and with the air of conspirators they would sit close, reading through and discussing his translations. Her spoken English was excellent, her written attempts clumsy in the extreme, and although her story was not to his taste, he found it amusing and said so.

Grimacing, she said, "I'm open to your criticism."

Lighting up a mild Dutch cigar, he gazed at her thoughtfully, saying, "What a curious mind you have."

"You think so?"

"Yes. Why else should you spend time writing a story all to do with erotic encounters between dolphins?"

"Why should I not?"

"Why *should* you was my question."

They sat perfectly still for a few moments, then Tama reached out and took the pen from his hand and placed it on the table, saying, "Renzō, my sole aim in giving you my silly script was to have you visit me again." She laughed rather hysterically. "But of course you knew that, didn't you?"

Tama sat, chin in hand, frowning, staring at him intently. "I see by your expression that I'm upsetting you. Never mind! Truth telling is a magic game that few people dare to play. So, let's change the subject. Perhaps you could tell me more of your years in the school of Dutch learning, or you could tell me whether you believe that our nation is becoming more and more influenced by 'imported puritanism.'"

"Believe me," he had said. "I prefer the truth."

"So. Then I'll continue. If you become bored, just say the word. It's widely said that men spend lonely nights without female company. Never have I heard it said that it's the same for women without males. We are said to be content to sit alone in the lamplight and read mind-improving books. . . ." She broke into cynical laughter. "Excuse me, but I speak with some knowledge, of myself, and of other women. None of us is content to be so passive. Do you find that disgraceful?"

"Just interesting. But I'm not yet able to see where this all leads."

"Well, to get to the point, you *implied* that I've written an erotic tale about dolphins because I shy away from human involvement. Do you really believe that?"

In a state of befuddlement, he was suddenly conscious of his breathing. He was by nature one who needed the comfort of a close relationship. Could it be that Tama Yano might supply his needs?

Was she beautiful? He could not decide. Who exactly was she? Was her family background of any importance? There was an air of mystery about her. But he was old and she was so young.

As though in reply to his thoughts, she said, "I've passed my thirtieth year." Her words were scarcely audible. "Always I've fought against giving up my independence. But now my resistance is in a shambles."

She took up the pages of her manuscript and tossed them into the air. "Please feel free to leave. We are both in a state of confusion. Correct?"

"Correct."

"Should I apologize?"

"For what?"

"I'm not sure."

Both her face and voice were expressionless and, as she rose to her feet and moved toward the open *shōji*, he was filled with sheer amazement and amusement at the thought that filtered into his mind. For the first time in a long while he burst out laughing. She stared at him coldly. Finally, he said, "Too difficult to explain fully just now. In a word, I was imagining the reactions of certain persons when I announce to them that I'm to marry again."

"You are proposing? We are to marry?" she queried tentatively.

"Are we not?"

Her response was immediate. "Yes," she said warmly and with confidence. "Renzō, let's not wait too long. And—excuse me for chasing after you so boldly."

A slight chill ran down his spine. Was he doing the right thing? Looking again at Tama, he believed that he was.

They went walking along the beach, and, as waves crashed against the rocks tossing up spray like pear blossoms, he felt that supernatural powers were directing his life.

The fisherfolk were preparing their boats for the night's work. Tama walked ahead of him over the sand sprinkled, as if by design, with delicate shells.

Renzō, looking up, glimpsed the house on the hill and remembered the years of strenuous study spent beneath the stern old scholars' tutelage.

Ah, so long ago! How little he had achieved. Could he, with Tama beside him, make use of his scholarly prowess?

He breathed the sea air deeply, sending the blood faster through his veins. He felt hopeful and energetic. When Tama, her hair tousled by the wind, came running to his side, they exchanged smiles, then walked back toward the house.

IT WAS WITH SOME TREPIDATION that Etsu and Shinichi Yamamoto broke the news of their father and Tama Yano's marriage to the Fukuda couple. Sumiko's small citadel, now seldom occupied, was the scene for the disclosure, and all four sat about the low cherry-wood table avoiding one another's eyes, giving full attention to the tiny cups that they held as though afraid the liquid were deadly poison instead of mild rice-wine.

Yuichi raised his cup and said, "So—your father confided in no one?"

"In no one! And like a politician, he has no desire to be cross-examined," Etsu murmured.

"I have no wish to question Father." Shinichi's lopsided smile flashed out briefly. "Frankly, I'm glad to see him more like his old self again."

Yuichi shrugged his lean, fidgety shoulders. "Renzō was not at all embarrassed?" he asked. "No chance that he has been bewitched by the young woman?"

"No." Shinichi grinned. "Uncle, may I suggest that we keep any ill feelings hidden?"

"I," Yuichi exclaimed firmly, "have *no* ill feelings to hide. The odds that a man of his age might find a mate with whom he can share the rest of his life happily are extremely long. What a *fortunate* fellow he is, but then"—Yuichi shook his head as though in wonder—"Renzō has always been drooled over by women."

"I've never seen evidence of that," Aiko, speaking for the first time, said coldly. "Personally, I'm filled with extreme displeasure. Renzō's behavior is intolerable."

Yuichi bowed slightly. "Maybe so, but the dominant element in this intriguing discussion has nothing to do with your feelings, Aiko."

"I scarcely need have you remind me of that, Baron." Aiko, flushing deeply, spoke ironically. "I am concerned for the widow. For Kawabata. My treasured friend. What of *her* wounded pride?"

Shinichi, with an air of bravado, cut in, exclaiming, "Aunt, you should have warned Matsu Kawabata of the danger of being overconfident. I quite like the woman. There *must* be a way to save her from loss of face."

"How?" Aiko interjected. "Answer me that, if you please."

"It's all a bit too complex for me." Shinichi punctuated his speech with abrupt gestures. "Maybe we could find a compromise of some sort."

Aiko shrugged her shoulders in disgust, but there was a sudden shift in Yuichi's attitude. He gazed about the room, his manner dreamy, his eyes narrowed. "Do you suppose," he said absently, "do you *suppose*?" Laughing lightly, he shook his head, saying with the air of a shy adolescent, "No, no, *no*! Altogether too outrageous a thought. Never mind! Etsu, fill your old uncle's wine cup, please."

"With pleasure."

"Thank you," Yuichi said. "Please, all of you, forget my outrageous suggestion. Age is certainly catching up with me."

"Oh," Aiko cried out exasperatedly. "How I *dislike* your pretentiousness. How *can* we forget what we have not heard?"

"Very well." Yuichi raised his arms in a helpless gesture. He now spoke, his voice barely audible, and from time to time a puzzled frown creased his forehead. "We Japanese, when faced with the unexpected, act with courage. From my observance of her, the lady in question certainly enjoys intrigues. By following in Renzō's footsteps—in reverse fashion—Kawabata would gain admiration and no little acclaim. So what do you all think?"

"Yuichi, can you *never* come out in the open?"

"Yes," Etsu said imploringly. "Must you be so obtuse?"

Quite undismayed, Yuichi said firmly, his gaze fixed on Shinichi, "Did you not say that you quite like the widow Kawabata?"

"I did say that," Shinichi replied lamely.

"And was it not *you* who suggested a compromise of sorts?"

"Did I?"

"You did! Yes, and during your father's absence from the Tokyo scene, did you not escort the widow to Kamakura?"

"Out of sheer politeness. Matsu had expected my father to escort her to the fireworks display there."

"I can't believe it," Aiko interrupted grimly. "I was not confided in. My friend never mentioned—"

"Aiko," Yuichi interrupted. "Clever as you are at times, you've never learned to think backward, inside out, or upside down."

"Correct," she said explosively. "Only peculiar people do that."

"I'll take that as a compliment." Yuichi kept his eyes on Shinichi as he said, "It intrigues me that you call the widow by her familiar name, Matsu."

"Oh," Etsu interjected, "it's just the modern way, Uncle."

"Maybe so, Et-chan, maybe so," Yuichi replied kindly. "Now, can it be that I've supped too deeply of this wine? Am being too imaginative? If so, excuse me." Suddenly he seized Shinichi by the arm, pulling him close, saying with affection, "I want you to stay on in Japan."

"But," Aiko cried out, "you recently said that Shinichi would be better off in America. That our country is not a comfortable one to live in when one's face is disfigured, and—"

"I've changed my mind." Yuichi pulled Shinichi even closer. "Excuse your aunt's tactlessness. Listen to me. Did I not detect a tone of warmth in your voice when you said the name—Matsu? Don't answer that. Is the idea of marrying a rich old woman unpalatable to you? Don't answer that. If, with all propriety, the widow was approached and then agreed to the proposition—would you marry with her?"

Both men remained perfectly still, showing no emotion as they sat eye to eye.

"Enough of this nonsense," cried Aiko. "My friend would *never agree*."

"How can you know that, Aunt?" Etsu began to weep and said brokenly, "Any worthwhile woman, regardless of her age, could not help but admire my brother's character. His stoicism . . ."

Gazing at Etsu, Shinichi's heart ached unendurably. By all the gods, he thought, I must get away from her. The way had been made clear. Turning to Yuichi, he said coldly, "If Matsu agrees—I'll marry her."

Yuichi also began to weep. Aiko sat stiffly, dry-eyed. "It's my conviction," Aiko announced coldly, "that all three of you are most distastefully intoxicated."

His fit of weeping ended, Yuichi declared triumphantly, "Drunk we may be. But with relief and happiness. Leave all the negotiations to me, nephew. Let anyone who wishes to now voice their objections."

When no voice was raised, Yuichi thumped Shinichi's shoulders, hastily saying, "Now let's all relax."

Later on in the afternoon, following the departure of the brother and sister, Aiko sought out her husband, finally discovering him in the garden, standing before the marble fountain and gazing skyward. "Come, join me," he said coaxingly. "Look! See those wild birds up there flying through the autumn mist. See how they beat their wings against the sky."

"I see them," she replied flatly. "Yuichi, will you never cease interfering with people's lives?"

"Never mind about all that!" Casting a glance her way, he noticed that age was blunting the sharp outline of her jaw and a note of compassion entered his voice as he said, "Aiko, surely you are not jealous that Renzō has married such a young woman?"

"How you revel in insulting me." Aiko spoke with bitter sarcasm. "It's just that my comprehension of his deceitfulness might be helped by some knowledge of Tama Yano's origins."

"Ah? Ah-ah! Then allow me to enlighten you, if only briefly. The lady is of noble origin. I was once entertained in her grandfather's mansion. So grand, it makes our dwelling melt into insignificance."

"That says little for it."

"How unkind you are. Never mind. At the Yano mansion, conceited as I am, I admit to having felt that I was but a weed in a garden of exotic plants. A member of the imperial family was present. My host, Tama's grandfather, was like a prince who has stepped out of an ancient print. His wife—"

"Really," Aiko exclaimed impatiently. "No need to go over *every* detail."

"All right. Calm down. Understand my chief aim is to keep Renzō close to us!" Again he hesitated before saying, "Shall I continue?"

"Yes." Aiko began to laugh. "But best I throw questions your way. Time passes and we—humble though we are—give a musical soiree here this evening. Was *Renzō's* woman present at that dinner?"

"She was not. Excuse me, but may I refer to her by her name?"

"Don't be foolish."

"I'll try not. Tama, Renzō's wife, so happens to be born of an illicit relationship between a daughter of the family and a man whose background was not acceptable. Disgraced, the daughter took her life after Tama's birth. Rightly or wrongly, sadly or happily, it depends how one looks at it."

"How do you know all this?"

"From Nakasone. He was a distant family connection. The keynote to this story is that although Tama is accepted as a family member, from early years she was closeted in a Catholic convent in Yokohama. The family clan in all probability hoped that eventually she would become a nun and be heard of no more." Yuichi grinned widely. "Obviously, all their hopes were crushed. Next question?"

"No time for more. I've much to attend to." Aiko called to him over her shoulder as she hurried toward the house. "Hasten, Yuichi. We must dress."

Later on that evening, Yuichi's spirits were so high that he willingly applauded the piano music which in fact set his nerves on edge.

He hoped that Tama Yano was a strong-minded woman who would put an end once and for all to the long-standing affair between Renzō and Aiko.

He raised his champagne goblet in a toast to himself. A man who always got what he wanted.

THE GARDEN SURROUNDING YOUNG ARCHIE Bixby's home on the hill had become a harmonious blending of Western and Japanese landscaping. The garden was the pride and joy of his parents, who spent interminable hours working in it, loving its many moods brought about by seasonal changes.

Over the passage of time Archie had been told how his parents had first met. How they had fallen in love and had overcome all barriers, determined to have their way and letting the world think what and how it would. They had not tried to gloss over the fact that Tomiko had been recruited to a house of prostitution.

Among Archie's childhood memories was the sound of unrestrained laughter floating from his parents' sitting room when they were there tête-à-tête.

Without doubt the Bixbys were happy and so was he, their son, who led a simple but charmed life. He loved to cycle about the city, quite often calling in at his father's place of business to roam about the huge warehouse helping to uncrate goods which were brought in from various countries.

As his sixteenth birthday approached, Archie wanted to invite a group of young friends to his home. His parents agreed and a garden party was decided upon. "Why not?" Bixby exclaimed enthusiastically. "The garden's at its best."

Invitations had gone out far and wide and, somewhat to Archie's consternation, some eighty guests, mostly friends and acquaintances of his father, turned up on the afternoon of August the thirty-first. The affair had been so enjoyable that Bixby decreed that it should be repeated every year, on the same day. Then turning to his son, he asked, "Did *you* enjoy yourself, Arch?"

"Yes, Father. *Actually*, I *more* than enjoyed myself."

Later that night he crept out into the deep stillness of the shadowy bamboo grove and stood motionless, recalling in every detail those moments that had plunged him into an entirely new world.

"Natasha," he murmured. "Did you feel as I felt? Natasha?"

The sound of her name set his mind spinning. How terrible if Natasha felt different after having made him her captive. There had been *something* between them. Something *deep*. How steadfast her expression had been. How pretty she was. There was a sadness about her. Not for one instant would he dare imagine himself kissing her. But just to be able to see her again, to brush her cheek ever so lightly with his hand.

During breakfast Tomiko remarked solicitously, "Archie, how tired you seem. Is your stomach upset?"

"I'm perfectly well, Mother." Clearing his throat nervously, he continued on. "I was glad Natasha Shifa came to the party."

"Who?" Bixby inquired. "To whom are you referring?"

"To Natasha. Daughter of that Russian violinist. Yes, I thought that she sang rather nicely. . . ."

"You did? Well, frankly, I took an instant dislike to that Russian fiddler. And, to his fat Irish wife. We'll have no more of employing *them*. The name is Shifa, is it? *Shifty* suits them better. Did the daughter sing? I don't recall."

"She sang," Tomiko murmured, "but her voice was scarcely audible above all the talk and laughter. Ah, what a happy time was had by all."

Archie, his fists clenched, his eyes misty, sat listening to his parents. How selfish they were in their own happiness, not caring that their son was suffering so acutely. He made his escape, his heart thudding with the confusion of his emotions.

How was he to find the girl Natasha, hidden away somewhere in Yokohama? He tried to imagine every detail of Natasha's apparel. She had worn a flounced white muslin dress. But those flounces had had a sleazy look about them. She had worn black pumps with pointed toes and low Louis heels. But those heels had been chipped and shabby.

For hours he wandered about aimlessly until, his body and mind dulled from exhaustion, he realized that night had fallen. Hunger clawed at his belly and a tantalizing odor led him into a small city park, where he bought and relished a bowl of spiced noodles. The park was crowded with men, women, and children from the poorer class, all gathered there to relax. It cost little to patronize vendors of strange concoctions, fake medicinal cure-alls, and flowers, or to be entertained by fortune-tellers, magicians, and by itinerant musicians. Musicians . . . ?

Five months after that September evening, Archie and Natasha ambled along a narrow country road between wheat fields whose neatly arranged stalks resembled immense lengths of ribbed white corduroy. Snow was falling and Archie was sighing in a voice of wonderment. "Tashie, that night! When I came upon you in the park I actually *reeled in shock* at the sight of you."

"You did? Archie, tell me again how you searched and searched for me that day."

"I will, but after *you* tell *me* again how *you* felt at the garden party. Is it really true you *knew* we would meet again?"

"It's true. I knew it in my bones."

Every episode of their lives, no matter how often repeated, was of passionate interest to them. "Tashie, tell me again about the time when you lived in Shanghai."

"Have I told you that I went to school there for a while? A convent. It was nice but, as usual, we moved on, finding work in small Chinese cities. Archie, did I ever tell you about Volga?"

"Your pet finch? Yes, and how it would sit on your shoulder when you sang in the music halls . . ."

"And have I told you how Mummy was a famous actress on the London stage? That Puppa was a virtuoso, a famous violinist?"

As usual, Archie had his doubts at this point, but said, "Tashie, how awful it must have been for your father to flee Russia . . ."

"Yes. Terrible. Just Puppa with no belongings except for his precious fiddle. Long before I was born. Then he met Mumma."

"And they fell in love!"

"At first sight!"

"As with my parents! And now with us!"

Natasha smiled; then, much to her companion's astonishment, she burst into tears and said hastily, "Archie, don't mind my Russian tears. It's been so very lovely being with you. I've never, never been so happy. Maybe I'll never be so happy ever again. . . ." Hesitating, she continued casually. "We are leaving Japan, going back to live in Shanghai."

Archie's mind went blank. He had no idea that he had stopped still in the middle of the road. He focused his gaze on Natasha's shabby mink cap and the clumsy padded-cotton coat she wore.

From the very beginning she had told him, and now she was telling him again, that her parents disliked Japan. The food was unpalatable to them and the people were rude, with no sense of humor. It was demeaning, living in a lodging house, sleeping on floor-mats. The ignorant Japanese had no liking for foreigners. It was different in China. In China foreigners were given respect. . . .

Something was stirring deep within Archie's spirit. He was Tomiko's son, possessed of a great love for Japan and things Japanese. Taking a crumpled pack from the silk-lined pocket of his English topcoat, he lit, then took two puffs from a cigarette before handing it to Natasha, who took several puffs. Back and forward the cigarette went before it was cast down in the snow.

"When do you leave?" he asked Natasha flatly.

"Tomorrow. We leave tomorrow."

"How long have you known?"

"A few days."

"Well, that's that! I suppose people have different feelings. Obviously it's so with *us*." He added in a dull tone, "Now, unless we want to end up frozen, we'd best move on."

"If that's your attitude—yes." Natasha, head held high, moved toward the suburban railway station. Archie followed in her wake, his mood bitter and brooding. He was ashamed that he had been beguiled into believing that Natasha loved him.

There had been that wondrously sweet night together. He was trembling, nervous and unsure. She was so shy and cried out softly, "Feel no guilt. I want this as much as you do. . . ."

Three long months had gone by since that cool, dark night when their bodies had been afire, cushioned by the soft sand of Hommoku Beach.

Never once had he made a mention of the future. With arrogant casualness he had given no thought of it. Now, no future existed for them.

They were already close to the toylike station. Soon, a train would arrive. How extraordinary it was that the girl trudging along the snow had become a complete stranger to him.

The fifteen-minute train journey was spent in silence. He refrained from casting even one glance Natasha's way. He decided to behave toward her with a coolness to match hers. One thing was certain. She had made a complete fool of him.

Yokohama Station was scarcely a suitable place for the dramatic scene he had been rehearsing, but it was Natasha who directed the action. Oblivious to the crowds, she cried out, "Archie, keep me in your memory. I must go now. Ships don't wait for people. Good luck—always. Good-bye."

At almost the same moment a hand rested upon his shoulder and he heard his father's voice exclaiming, "Arch! Who was that girl? Was she propositioning you? What a tart!" Bixby was amused, but his son looked wild-eyed and his teeth were chattering as though with intense cold.

Tomiko, shocked, had called a doctor to the house. He spoke in grave tones. Inflammation of the lungs should never be treated casually.

After several weeks in bed, Archie stood on weakened legs, looking into the mirror. How gaunt his face was. He seemed to have aged. Natasha had once said something about life being a festival. Just thinking of her made him feel smaller than a flea.

He groaned aloud, more loudly than he meant to, which brought

Tomiko into his room, exclaiming, "What now, Archie? Where do you hurt?"

Archie wanted to scream out, "Everywhere. *Everywhere.* Go away. *Leave me alone* . . ." but said instead, "I feel restless, Mother. I'd like to go away for a while. Maybe take a trip somewhere . . ." adding hastily, "I mean on my own."

The room was hushed for several moments, then Tomiko said briskly, "A wise idea. Perhaps Kyoto? It is said that the old capital is so interesting and . . ."

"No. I want a challenge. To toughen myself. I want . . ."

Two months later Archie sat immersed in the water of a public bathhouse, the meeting place for residents in a village some hundreds of miles away from Yokohama. Men, women, and children were mingling together in the steamy atmosphere, yelling, gossiping, and laughing.

His once-tender skin now bore several rather dramatic scars of which he was immensely proud. His leg and arm muscles had developed, and he had taken to the barber's razor. He felt that he had proved himself and had become a man.

All alone, he had traveled through unchartered northern regions. He had stood on the top of the inflamed walls of volcanic craters, gazing in horrified fascination down upon a lake of boiling, sulphurous water. Just one careless step forward would have ended his life.

Farther north, he had braved the filthy conditions of miserable inns, had slept on ragged pallets, and awoken to find fleas feasting on his blood.

Farther north still, he had ventured into an Ainu village and was amazed at the poverty of the people whom he could not recognize as Japanese. They wore extremely long beards and their locks were shaggy. The sight of Ainu women, disfigured by the broad black mustaches tattooed on their upper lips, had, as his English father would put it, "knocked him for six." Many of the women had thick patterns and designs tattooed across their foreheads, their arms, even on their hands.

But after several days he no longer felt fear and disgust at these people. His nostrils were no longer offended by the omnipresent stench. He sat in a humble abode, quite at ease, sipping carefully at the roughly brewed *sake* which his dour host gulped down as though it were water until he keeled over, quite insensible.

The following day that same aborigine, Konō, had escorted Archie into virgin forest, the haunt of savage bears. He wanted to return home with a bearskin, head and all, to fling it down, announcing casually, "Just a memento of my trip. Captured single-handed."

After several days of treading stealthily through dense forest, Konō, the Ainu, had stripped naked and tied a musty animal skin about himself. Gesturing to his companion to remain silent, Konō had played bear, giving out a series of cries and grunts that immediately brought a great snarling brute from its lair, out into the open to grapple with its enemy, who dodged the creature's thrashing paws and attacked it from the rear with a hunting knife. Then he leapt backward and with his bow discharged several arrows into the prey. The bear had fallen. Archie ran forward, shouting out victoriously. The bear, still very much alive, rose to its full height and grappled Archie Bixby into a death hug.

He had not understood that the tip of Konō's arrow bore a poison that knocked the bear out but did not cause immediate death. He had no memory of how he had been rescued. All he recalled was coming back to consciousness, lying on the ground beside a dead bear, conscious of pain in his arm such as he never before experienced.

Before he left the village he felt he should make an offering, and he wandered about in search of a shrine. Finding none, he discovered that there was no temple, no priest in the vicinity. And he learned from one of the mustached women that the gods were many, and that in every dwelling hut hung clusters of willow sticks to which prayers were directed.

He had gone on his way, his left arm supported by a sling made of his last clean shirt. He left behind him a race of despised and neglected people. He was sorry for them but rejoiced that his own life was intact.

Now Archie climbed out of the bathwater. In a few days he would be back home. With a grin he foresaw the welcome he would receive. He had no intention of admitting that his magnificent bearskin had been purchased at a fur trader's shop. If any questions arose, all he had to do was bare his arm, expose the wound which was healing over into a quite spectacular scar.

But on his return home, at first sight of him Tomiko had cried out, "Archie, you at last. Please hasten at once to your father's warehouse. An urgent matter."

"You mean *now*? Right *now*? Mother, tell me?"

"Archie, just be obedient."

Quite disoriented, he ran through the streets to the warehouse, wondering at the reproach in his mother's voice and expression.

"Ah! Ah! So here you are, at last." Bixby glared at his son with anger and suspicion. "Come into my office. I've words to have with you."

The discourse in that richly furnished sanctum had been sharp and to the point. "Just answer me yes or no, Arch. Is it true that you got to know the daughter of that Russian fiddler Shifa?"

"Yes."

"My God! That girl's parents are insisting that you violated their daughter's chastity. Is that true?"

"Yes."

"You young fool! Did you know the girl was pregnant when she left for China?"

"I did not know."

"You swear to that?"

"I swear to that."

"Is there a possibility that the girl was sleeping with another chap?"

"Absolutely not."

"Arch, the girl's with child. Your child. Some weeks ago our home was thrown into a state of confusion. That disreputable Shifa family landed on the doorstep. No amount of money interests them. The peace of our home has been destroyed. Day after day the girl's mother screeches out, 'Marriage alone can restore our sense of right and dignity.' "

"I agree with that, Father."

"You fool! You young fool."

Some three months after the marriage took place Bixby and Tomiko became grandparents of twins. As if by magic they became a doting couple, never tired of cosseting the tiny boy and the tiny girl who had enlarged their family. "I want them named Victor and Madeline," Bixby announced firmly. "I'll brook no arguments."

No arguments arose. Archie and Natasha once again endlessly discussed the miraculous workings of fate, which obviously had intended that they should be married—to live happily ever after.

O<small>N A DARK NIGHT IN</small> September 1912, Renzō Yamamoto was but one person among the millions gathered in Tokyo to mourn the death of their emperor. Forty-five years had gone by since that chilly but sunlit day in November which had begun the "Enlightenment of Brilliant Rule." On that day, Mutsuhito, the royal youth, had entered Japan's capital, heading a spectacular procession, streaming along a river of glowing gold, silver, and all the colors of the rainbow, so different from the somber assembly now gathered.

According to sacred rites, the funeral ceremony was taking place at night. Renzō had stationed himself close to the pavilion at the Akasaka military parade ground. The entire city was hushed. Houses and buildings were shuttered and the street lights had been doused. The air smelled of the sesame smoke that drifted in great clouds from shrines and temples.

Renzō's emotions were clutching at his mind and heart, mustering up things unseen but felt. He allowed his thoughts more or less to float along gently, coming and going as they would. . . .

For the first time since their marriage, he was relieved to be apart from Tama and from their four-year-old son, Haru. This solemn occasion was better gone through alone.

Suddenly, a gun salute shattered the silence. An answer came from naval vessels anchored off the Shinagawa River. Then the temple bells throughout the city started tolling, and like the blade of a slashing sword came a bugle call announcing that the cortege was leaving for the funeral pavilion.

What could be more heartrending? Five oxen, humble working beasts, in single line drawing the hearse of a noble emperor. Attendants garbed in ancient regalia, others wearing modern service uniforms, slow-marched to dirges played by the Guards band. Pine torches, their flames licking through the darkness, illuminated curious and impassioned faces.

The mikado, Mutsuhito, was being taken to his final resting place. Shudders ran through the crowds accompanied by drawn-out moaning sounds. Renzō, unable to move in the crush, closed his mind to the knowledge that even the greatest of persons was not indispensable.

The Meiji Era had run its full course. It had taken the country from feudalism into the world, winning recognition there.

Taishō, a new era, was about to begin. . . .

E TSU YAMAMOTO MOVED EFFORTLESSLY AMONG a circle of educated women courageously working against heavy odds to change the brutal conditions in Japan's industrial plants and factories, where children were employed under contract for a pittance. Overworked and undernourished, they were doomed to early death from mal-nutrition and lung complaints.

It was with a sense of outrage that Etsu viewed the lot of those children. She had spoken to her family about them, only to be told, "Perhaps there *is* a lack of social justice in our society but, Etsu, please don't become a boring do-gooder."

Blessed with the ability to control her inner emotions, she smiled politely while continuing to beat her own drum. She had also be-come skilled at fending off the efforts of matchmakers. She would never marry again. Her own future? Best not think forward! Keep tight closed the door on her guilt-ridden emotions. Shinichi's mar-riage to the gregarious widow Kawabata had aroused a raging storm of jealousy in her being. Shocked beyond measure, she had realized that she loved her brother, and not just in a sisterly fashion. Her one solace was that he was unaware, and always would be, of her un-natural desires. Fortunately, the unlikely couple were fond of trav-eling abroad. Their trips home were infrequent and brief. And there was much for her to do. Much to distract her, divert her and keep her busy.

Tokyo's population had increased greatly. Modern buildings were being erected, and most businessmen were wearing Western-style garments.

For women, the kimono still held pride of place, but those who favored Western garments, following fashion, did away with bustles and tight corsets, changing over to the comfort of loose sleeves and high-waisted gowns with V necklines.

Kabuki and Nō dramas were now thought of as old-fashioned entertainments. In contrast, a Free Theatre was presenting plays by Shakespeare, Maeterlinck, and Ibsen. Etsu had attended many such performances with her aunt Aiko, whose passion for fashion and the arts in all forms still prevailed.

True to women of her class, Aiko gave no thought to the great mass of Japanese citizens who went their ways almost untouched by Western culture, with no wish to replace time-honored customs with new. But like those people, when the thirteenth day of July would arrive, Aiko, without fail, observed *Obon*, the Festival of the Dead. Her spirit, like those of so many, would be moved at the thought of those returning spirits paying their visits to household shrines. She, truly at one with the nation, rejoiced at the bittersweet emotions felt while lighting a lantern, just one among the millions lit throughout the land to guide the beloved spirits to their homes.

One summer afternoon, shortly after the *Obon* festival of 1914, Aiko sat in a wicker chair in the garden beneath an oak tree, its branches mirrored in the placid depths of a pond. Lost to the world about her, she was reading the final paragraph of Renzō Yamamoto's latest novel, entitled *Moto San—The Silk Merchant*. Renzō's work was winning acclaim from the critics. Although influenced by contemporary English authors, it was distinctly his own creation, and quite impersonal, describing the life of merchant-class people, who, freed from feudalism, had taken on a new and brash outlook.

As Aiko closed the book, it occurred to her that never once had she been alone with Renzō since his marriage to Tama, the young woman who spent her time hovering protectively around her elderly husband.

At times Aiko wondered if Tama had knowledge of Renzō's affair with his first wife's sister. The thought was insufferable and now she passed a hand across her face as though to wipe it away.

Rather to her annoyance, Yuichi, never to be found when needed, now joined her. He glanced at the book lying on her silken lap and said dolefully, "Reading that story again, eh? I must skim through it before too long. Renzō seems to take little enjoyment in his late-gained literary reputation. Have you noticed?"

"I've not noticed."

"I thought you might have. There's a pathetic air about him. *I* understand how he feels. What use is fame when it comes so late?"

"Better than never having achieved it."

"I think not. One always yearns to be praised by those who knew one throughout one's life. Praise from strangers and young people

means little. Renzō, with little time left, now seeks my companionship. Naturally I'm pleased to make myself available. Our friendship
has ebbed and flowed over these many years."

Aiko said coolly, "Yuichi, why exactly have you joined me here?
What's on your mind?"

Giving her a reproachful look, Yuichi sighed deeply, then said,
"The death of our great emperor has had an adverse effect on
me. The present government lacks the purpose of our former leaders.
The younger generation all scramble about with nothing in their
hands and little in their minds. Isn't it so?"

Aiko hesitated. "Maybe so. At times I'm overcome by feelings of
loneliness, especially when in the midst of a happy gathering." Giving a cynical laugh, she added, "We all grow old unwillingly."

"Old age!" Yuichi scoffed. "Frankly, you've seldom looked more
attractive."

Aiko, not displeased, murmured, "I've taken on the *Taishō* look.
I'm merely following the new trends. Surely you have noticed how
we women now dress our hair, covering our ears and the napes of
our necks. We wear makeup about the eyes and just a touch of lip
rouge."

"I like it. It produces a wan, lethargic look. Quite consumptive
in a way."

"It no longer bothers me that any compliment you pay holds a
ferocious twist in the tail. Ah, how I envy the young women of
today. To think that in my youth, females were banned from acting
in the theater. Tell me, were you not at the Free Theatre's performance of *A Doll's House* yesterday afternoon?"

"I was. I attended with Renzō."

"And your opinion?"

"Well, from all accounts, Ibsen's Nora is said to be a strong-
charactered woman. What did I find? Nothing but a fluffy pussycat
when compared with the women under whose rule *I've* lived
throughout my life."

Aiko, whose composure seldom deserted her, rose and walked
about the lawn, calling out, "You are a typical Japanese male. Terrified of womanhood! But tell me, what was Renzō's feeling about
Ibsen's play?"

"He thought it the work of a genius."

"Rightly so."

"But of course. In *your* opinion, *his* opinions are never at fault."

"Not so. Neither Etsu nor I can forgive the praise he hands out to Puccini's *Madama Butterfly*. We Japanese women are *distraught* at being presented to the world as a simpering victim of misplaced love. We shall never lose the reputation which that ridiculous Puccini has bestowed upon us."

"Ho, ho!" Yuichi waved both hands skyward in a victory salute. "*Exactly!* He should have portrayed his heroine as a bee with a sting that sometimes even kills."

Aiko, unable to conceal her amusement, grinned. "*Hachi*—a bee? *Madama Hachi?* Yes. I much prefer that."

"Pity Puccini never visited Japan. He might have met the Englishman Bixby and his hardy Tomiko. Have you ever met the Bixbys?"

"I have not, nor do I wish to." Aiko fell silent, concentrating on the rattle of a train passing close by. "To think," she muttered, "that when I came here as a bride of tender years, this house was surrounded by acres of woodland. How things have changed." Shrugging her shoulders, she said briskly, "But mostly for the better."

"You think so?"

"I do. For one thing, friendships I've formed with foreigners have greatly enriched my life."

"Not mine. Foreign influences now wax too strongly throughout our society. Our lives have become unwieldly. Recently I put forward an idea to Renzō. *He* was most enthusiastic, but Tama wasn't."

Aiko, all attention, but determined to cover her interest, remarked casually, "What, exactly, did you have in mind?"

"I put forward the idea to Renzō that family members should gather together to enjoy a nostalgic time away from Western influences in an isolated rustic place."

"Tama is against the plan?"

"Sadly, yes."

Aiko was firm. "It's a *splendid* idea. Leave it to me to arrange."

"Thank you," Yuichi replied meekly. "I was hoping you might. . . ."

Determined to have no family member left out of the journey back into the past, Yuichi summoned Shinichi and his wife—affectionately alluded to as Kawabata—from Kyoto. In the first week of August, nine adults and three children accompanied by four servants, all heavily laden, straggled along a narrow woodland track shaded by tall trees.

For Tama, the travelers resembled a circus troupe on their way to stage a performance. She finally agreed in every way with Yuichi

Fukuda's edict that no touch of Westernization should stain the purity of the vacation.

Apparently, the one recalcitrant member of the group was her own son, Haru, who was not as yet aware that his mother knew about the baseball and catcher's mitt hidden in the cloth bundle slung over his shoulder. Glancing backward, she noticed that he had picked up a strong batlike stick. She waited for him to catch up with her, then took his arm. "You know the rules," she murmured. "Haru, put the stick down and throw away the ball and mitt. Right now."

He smiled, revealing the new gap in his white teeth. "No," he answered firmly. "Brother Shinichi gave me them. They must never be thrown away."

"Then," she suggested, "I'll look after them for the time being."

To her embarrassment, the child sat on his heels in the grass at the side of the road, unable to stop laughing.

"Halt!" Yuichi brought the procession to a sudden stop. "Now what goes on?"

"Please ignore him, Yuichi," Renzō shouted. "He gets fits of laughing-sickness at times. Tama, let Haru be. Leave him to the servants. Come, walk with me. Ah, this is nature at its best."

As Tama went to join Renzō, she murmured to Yuichi, "I yearn for Haru to become more mature. Please excuse him."

Paying no heed to her apology, Yuichi rushed to Aiko's side as she cried out, "Oh, my weary legs. Oh, for a ricksha."

"Never mind, never mind," he cried encouragingly, "Kentaro will carry you pick-a-back."

Aiko glared at her husband. "Thank you, but no. I'd rather die of exhaustion than seem so undignified. How much farther to your promise of paradise?"

"Not much farther." Yuichi raised his voice to a shout. "We now tread in our ancestors' footsteps. More than half a century ago, my father, Fukuda, Renzō's father, Kenichi, Aiko's father, Count Okura, along with their samurai friends, spent halcyon times in this area."

"Your father is completely happy," Kawabata murmured to Kentaro. "Look at his face."

"Yes. Let's hope he gets less long-winded," Kentaro said, then walked on, whistling through his teeth as though out to cheer himself up, heedless of his wife, Maya, who trod behind him, with a small daughter on either side and with an expected child in her protruding belly.

Thirty minutes later the entire group stood transfixed, their faces upturned, all gazing together at snow-topped Fuji San towering grandly before them.

Etsu's voice rang out. "Too beautiful! Almost too perfect to bear."

Tama, nodding in agreement, gazed at the green tree-clad skirts of land sweeping in magnificent curves into the liquid blue of the lake around which the woods and grassy fields were tinted with every hue known to nature. Birds swooped overhead, and there were skylarks in such numbers that she cried out, "The fields here are a sea of music."

They lingered there for some time, unwilling to move on. Yuichi saw that tears were sparkling in Aiko's eyes. "Thank you," he said, "for all your help." She wiped her tears away and bowed slightly before walking on.

Three days later, Tama, her hair plaited into a thick black braid coiled on top of her head, the lower portion of her body clad in a crimson waist-high underslip, lay barebreasted, luxuriating in one of the moss-surrounded hot-spring pools.

Smiling, she thought that if Yuichi Fukuda had been less of a man, he would have been upset in asking his arrogant relatives to take up residence in the house of pleasure that had been built so long ago but was now dilapidated, with shingles missing from its roof and with birds brazenly nesting in the rooms.

On their arrival, an old caretaker, amazed and very put out, had announced, "For the past thirty years this place has not catered to guests."

The whole front of the building was festooned with heavily flowering vines, the perfume attracting bees and clouds of tiny white butterflies. Yuichi grinned proudly as various voices gave opinions. Etsu called out yearningly, "How I would *love* this place for a children's refuge."

"The old caretaker might have stepped from an ancient print," Aiko declared. "Don't you agree, Kentaro?"

"I do, Mother," he declared lazily. "But we'll get no service here."

"Service!" Kawabata exclaimed enthusiastically. "We've brought with us a positive army of servants. What they can't manage we shall tend ourselves. What a challenge! Is it not, husband?"

Shinichi, standing erect like a stone figure, gestured at a finch that flew down onto a delicate twig. The bird lifted its head, expanded its feathered chest, and trilled so sweetly that those watching clapped their hands in applause but made no sound.

For two days Yuichi had taken complete charge, greatly aided by Kawabata, who had become his second in command, both of them rising at dawn, insisting that their troupe join them, bowing low to Fuji San, and then singing a well-known song of praise to the mountain.

"Why must we do this?" Kentaro complained. "It's ludicrous!"

"It's a time-honored custom," his father shouted. "Now, all together! Sing!"

"Do you expect us to sing from dawn to dusk?" Aiko cried out irately.

"Oh, go along with him, Aiko," Renzō said, knocking his pipe out with a great clatter against a branch of bamboo. "Don't dampen his spirits. He'll soon become more reasonable."

Tama now sat on one of the high mossy pads, hugging her knees. A soft breeze was playing with the reeds and the sky was covered with tattered wisps of cloud. The sun dappled her body with light, and she laughed aloud, glad to be alive and on her own for a while.

She had noticed how members of the party had paired off: Yuichi and Kawabata, Kentaro and Etsu, Renzō and Aiko; Maya made a trio with her two little daughters. Much to her relief, Haru had become enamored of his half brother, Shinichi, which left her free from worrying about the safety of her unruly little son. She thought of Haru as a precious gift that she had presented to Renzō, whose faithful disciple she had become. Close as they were, and for all the warmth in their relationship, neither had ever attempted to delve into the other's past. Renzō once said, "It's not possible to clarify relationships. Tama, let's you and I not make any attempt to do so." She had agreed, but as time went by she had no doubt that Renzō and Aiko had been lovers. No doubt that Aiko's feelings toward him were still possessive and that he was still bound to her by an invisible thread.

After Haru's birth, Tama had sought advice from the retired madam of a prestigious brothel in Yokohama. "Over the years, many caring wives have sought my advice," the woman confided. "Who else could better assist them in managing their aged husbands' welfare? What, exactly, is your problem? Does he demand too much of you? Please be frank."

"Never," she replied, "is my husband too demanding. Our intimate life up until now has been wondrously active, but I worry about his age. Using up so much energy must surely be injurious. I'm out to protect his dignity. But he must never be aware of that. He is not easily fooled."

"Then, do not fool him. Gradually introduce new techniques into your lovemaking. Be the instigator. Allow me to explain the ways in which we help aged clients in my establishments. . . ."

Tama never neglected to send a flowering plant to the wise old woman during festival seasons. Her only regret was that she could not share the story with Renzō.

Now she heard Renzō's laughter boom out, and from her vantage point saw that he and Aiko stood close together, watching as Kentaro, Shinichi, and Haru put on a makeshift display of baseball. "Be careful, you rascals," Renzō called. "Don't use that wretched ball as a weapon. . . ."

Tama admired the way Yuichi was accepting his defeat. All his scheming and planning for a return to the past had turned into a complete fiasco as, one by one, members of the party brought out forbidden loot from personal bundles. First Renzō produced his Dunhill pipe, his English tobacco, his bottle of Johnnie Walker Black Label whiskey.

Kentaro's wife, discarding the bamboo horse-sticks supplied to her daughters, boldly presented them with their beloved English dolls. Maya herself, wearing her American horn-rimmed spectacles, sat lost to the world reading the Japanese translation of Ralph Waldo Emerson's *Essays on Representative Man*.

Etsu and Aiko had begun the day wearing short-sleeved blouses and long cotton skirts, while Renzō, Kentaro, and Shinichi wore white flannels and soft-collared shirts, each man with a watch strapped to his wrist.

Kawabata, after some hesitation, produced a box of French bonbons, offering them around. "Just to give a fillip to the rather monotonous diet we've been on."

Yuichi, making no comment, reached out and took one of the sweet morsels.

Only she, Tama, had been prepared to play the game fair and square. Of theatrical bent, she had wanted to go back into the past, as if she were an actress playing a role. But it comforted her to know that her son had not been alone in his cheating. Although she never felt part and parcel of the family group, she rejoiced that her child slotted in so smoothly.

She felt uneasy in Shinichi's company. He seemed bitter, and she believed that he resented her for taking his own mother's place in his father's life. Certainly, both Etsu and Aiko, for all their kindness to her, seldom failed to bring up Rumi's name. She did not mind. Their behavior was natural and human. Renzō himself quite often spoke of Rumi, always in a complimentary way but without the yearning he was unable to disguise when he mentioned his mother, Lady Masa.

There had been moments during the past few days when Tama had felt surrounded by the ghosts of departed Yamamoto and Fukuda family members, unable to understand certain allusions to half-forgotten episodes and adventures.

During the family reunion, Shinichi had given Etsu the impression that he now faced life with self-confidence. But she felt that he was constantly wary of any intimate discussions which she might spring upon him, and was careful never to be alone with her.

For several days she anguished, wondering if her brother had become aware of the feelings she harbored toward him. Then, to her consternation, she discovered that Shinichi had become addicted to opium. She recognized the narcotic odor that emanated from his breath and the way his pupils contracted after he had taken a dose of the "medicine" which, he declared, had been prescribed for him by a physician in America to alleviate a "hacking cough."

Aiko was suspicious. "Shinichi, not once have I heard you coughing."

But Yuichi exclaimed, "Aiko, Aiko, how illogical you are. The *medicine* is preventing my nephew's ailment."

The holiday group was sitting around a fire of pine chips. Aiko, blaming the smoke, had a bout of coughing, making her husband exclaim, "Bring on your medicine, Shinichi. Have your aunt test its miraculous power."

"No, no," Shinichi replied hastily. "It's not meant to be taken unless prescribed."

"How well do I know that," Kawabata cried out, waving one hand dramatically over her loosely tied sash. "Some time ago, while on a sea voyage, I was struck down by a chest complaint. Naturally, wishing to attend the captain's party, I helped myself to a mouthful of my dear husband's medication. The result . . . !" She shuddered and grimaced.

"Tell on," Yuichi implored. "What happened?"

"Well may you ask, Baron. I broke out in a cold sweat. My breathing became slow and noisy. . . ."

"Say no more," Yuichi interjected. "Our time here goes by so swiftly. Haru, look about you. Describe what you see. Fuji San's snowy top is tinged with violet hues. The sacred mountain is reflected in the still lake. What does it remind you of?"

"Of a mountain reflected in a lake, Uncle."

"Too mundane altogether! I won't have it! Can't you see that the reflected mountain resembles a great inverted fan?"

Haru produced a foolish, fixed grin, then fell to the ground laughing. Yuichi caught at the child, saying, "Now, now! Enough of this silly behavior. How unfortunate it is that Haru is too babyish to join in the night's revelries. Sad, sad, that he must stay with the old landlord while we others, servants and all, go off to enjoy a delightful frolic."

Haru, instantly silent and serious, fell upon Yuichi, who hugged him close, saying warmly, "Good! You must become more civilized."

"I'm very civilized, Uncle. Tell me what happens tonight?"

"Are you scared of the dark?"

"I *love* the dark," Haru lied valiantly. "Why do you ask?"

"I ask because tonight there will be no moon. Like warriors, we are to brave the darkness and march through the fox-infested woods, then onto a lakeside field to witness a wondrous sight. . . ."

The moonless night was a black velvet backdrop for swarms of fireflies that floated in brilliant drifts, lighting up the surrounding dew-dampened fields, then gleaming away toward the woods. On they came, swarm after swarm, gliding out far and wide over the surface of the lake, sweeping across the fields, lighting up the faces of those on the firefly hunt in a luminous, theatrical way.

The women, their light muslin kimono tucked up, called out, and their laughter blended in with the deeper tones of male voices so harmoniously that Tama cried out, "This sweet orchestra will remain forever in my memory."

"I agree, Tama." Kawabata, eager to enhance the atmosphere, raised her flute to her lips, and the plaintive melody tore at Etsu's heart. Unable to subdue her emotions, she left the group, running through the darkness, at times stumbling, then rising to run on toward the dilapidated old house of pleasure.

Her muslin kimono, damp with sweat, stained by grass, clung to her body, and as she ran she untied the sash, taking the garment off and casting it away, running on barebreasted, clad only in her waist-high crimson slip.

On reaching the old building, she threw herself down on the stone steps and broke into a deluge of weeping that ceased abruptly as Shinichi's voice, puzzled and concerned, broke into her wounded mind. "What's happened? Etsu! Are you hurt?"

Receiving no reply, he reached out as though to pull her to her feet, but drew back as she recoiled from his touch, whispering, "Don't *touch* me! You! Out to make my life untenable . . ."

"Untenable! Your life?" Perplexed, he felt that it would behoove him to be on guard. Picking his words carefully, he spoke lightly, teasingly. "It's more to the point that you are making my time here untenable. Prying into my personal habits. Isn't that so?"

His casual manner set Etsu's mind aflame. "You!" she cried out. "Always you! Your colossal egotism! Fobbing me off in marriage to your stupid classmate Gen Ohara. I *despise*, I hate you. You! Going away, staying away from all responsibilities. Leaving me to care for our dying mother. Throwing away all your skills. Marrying a rich old woman. A *stupid* old woman who plies you with—"

"Shut up, Etsu," Shinichi interrupted her uncontrolled outburst. "You understand nothing of my life. Never mind!" He hesitated, feeling that he had reached the most difficult, unbearable moment in his life. After a long pause, and against his own will, he said very gently, "I could never bear to see you weep and suffer. I know that you neither despise nor hate me. Etsu, why not say how you really feel?"

It seemed to Etsu that a curtain had been pulled aside, allowing her to see into the depths of Shinichi's mind. A great flood of joy and of relief salved her guilts and her grief. "So . . ." she whispered. "You know? Know of the cruel, hungry longings in my heart?"

"In my heart also. Always it has been so!"

"So—you went—you stayed away?"

"Yes. What else? There are barriers that must never be crossed. You know that."

"So—we are trapped? Forever?"

"Yes. Trapped. Forever."

"No. No. This love can't be wrong."

"It is wrong, Etsu."

"I don't care! I don't care! We love. It's simple. We make love. If only tonight. Just this once. Just once. Life owes us that. . . ."

"No. Impossible."

"Possible! Shinichi. Brother. Give me some hope. Be *kind* to me. . . ."

"Kind?" Shinichi knelt by her side, taking her hands in his. "Kind?" he repeated. "Don't use that pitiable word. Etsu, for years I've hidden my inglorious passion."

"Assisted by opium . . ."

"Never mind about that. Listen! You are dearer than life to me. Knowing how you feel is more than enough. . . ."

"No. No . . ."

"Etsu. It *must* be so. . . ." He ceased speaking as voices, laughing, calling, drew close to the building. Standing, he pulled Etsu to her feet, holding her at arm's length, but Etsu pressed close against his body, whispering pleadingly, "At least tell me. *Tell* me once and for all time. . . ."

Holding her even closer, Shinichi spoke, in anguish, those words of passionate love so long denied. Pushing her from him he said "Enough! Enough! Etsu—sister . . ." Taking her hand, he pressed it against his lips for an instant. Then he moved abruptly away.

Etsu reached her empty hands into the darkness, crying out, "*Nigai, nigai*—so bitter, so bitter . . ."

Later that night Tama lay awake on her thin sleeping pallet, disturbed by the thoughts filling her mind. Haru had captured a number of fireflies and bottled them up in a glass jar that stood on the *tatami* beside the sleeping child's pillow. They gave out a mysterious glow, one which excited her, and she recalled having been told that the insects' glow was their love-signal lighting their way to one another.

While returning from the firefly hunt, she had discovered Etsu's discarded kimono. She made no mention of the find to the group as they gathered in the open, about a pine-chip fire, slapping away the mosquitoes. While noodles and other delicacies were served, along with hot tea, Tama, always the observer, sat by.

Shinichi, with Haru sleeping in his arms, was seemingly lost in his silence, while Kawabata and Yuichi discussed the state of the country, the world, and their thoughts on life in the hereafter. To everyone's amazement, Etsu, usually abstemious, purloined Yuichi's glass of neat brandy and quaffed it down, throwing the empty vessel into the crackling flames. Then, feeling the effects of the strong liquor, she fell sideways against Kawabata, who graciously provided the young woman with a comfortable nest on her lap, saying, "Be easy, Etsu. Best you have a little nap."

Now Tama yearned to be in her husband's comforting embrace, but even as she moved close, he, already asleep, called out ecstatically, "Osen, Osen."

She thought it wise not to disturb his dreaming, and felt that it was better to have him dreaming of the deceased courtesan than of Aiko, alive, and still attracted to him.

Dawn brought not only daylight and perfect weather but also an exuberant group of rustic men and women, the members of a bird-catching guild, all laden with luggage, including their long poles, buckets of lime, and various types of traps. These were brawny folk who, without so much as asking permission, entered the old house and took over. Yuichi, greatly annoyed, faced up to the leader of the guild, who said, "We want no shouting, sir. For twenty years our honorable guild members have come here. 'Tis our duty to provide Tokyo's bird vendors with finches found in this district."

Renzō stepped into the breach, saying calmly, "Enough is enough. We must have respect for these working folk. Let's up and away."

Packing up was quickly completed, and by midmorning the bird-catchers stood by triumphantly, watching Yuichi lead his bedraggled followers away.

By midafternoon they were on the train rattling back to Tokyo where, to everyone's consternation, the capital city was in a turmoil.

It was August 1914. The Great War had broken out.

ARTHUR BIXBY HAD A PROFOUND interest in the war in Europe and its likely outcome. He realized that while Japan's navy was protecting British ships from German submarine attacks, the country was, at the same time, gaining valuable economic considerations. With England's cotton mills cut off from Asian markets, Japan's business concerns made inroads in places so long monopolized by Europe.

One subject continuously under discussion was the airplane. Ever since Blériot's flight across the English Channel in 1909, the world's governments had focused attention on the military prospects of the machine. The war had the effect of accelerating every department of flying with specially designed machines being produced for various war purposes. "Unless governments form an alliance to ban the use of the terrifying invention," Bixby declared, "it would bring about the end of civilization as we know it. . . ."

For young Anna Dreyer the outbreak of the war had come as a blessing, preventing her from being shipped away from Japan, from everything familiar, to live with a distant relative in Germany.

Her father, Hans, still grieving over the death of his wife, paid little attention to his daughter, whose fragile beauty so resembled her mother's. Neglectful of Anna's welfare, he went further and further into the realms of Zen meditation, unaware, or not caring, that his child had become scavenger, searching for recognition of any kind, visiting various homes in the vicinity to ingratiate herself and find niches into which she could fit comfortably.

Several months before the war had begun, Hans had told Anna of his plans for her future in Germany. He then returned to the Buddhist monastery up north in Hokkaidō, leaving her under the care of servants. At the outbreak of hostilities his one and only fatherly action had been to write two brief letters: one to Renzō Yamamoto, the other to Arthur Bixby, requesting that they might give some kindly attention to Anna while he was away.

Those two gentlemen, together with their wives, had agreed that the child would gain from living with a large family, and to Anna's joy she had moved into the Bixby household. She began to pray daily, whispering passionately, "Thank you, God. Let the war go on and on until I'm an old woman." And to strengthen those pleas she bought Buddhist prayer-slips and tied them to a tree in the old monastery which stood on the edge of the high cliff overlooking Hommoku Bay.

Anna loved the rambling old house on the hill that was filled with both luxurious and shabby odds and ends of furniture, with precious artifacts, and with people.

Grandpa Bixby had a passion for beautiful carpets, and the downstairs rooms were aglow with their colors. The carpet in the main sitting room was huge, silken, and silver-blue, and when Anna was very young, she, along with the Bixby twins, Victor and Maddy-chan, had sailed cushion-boats over its surface, beneath the grand piano, past the striped satin-covered sofas and crimson leather club chairs. Like all the carpets, it was laid on top of springy *tatami* matting and one bounced a little when walking.

For all the scathing remarks made about a wicked old woman, Osen, and an even more evil person called Shiga, Anna believed that they should at least be given praise for having constructed within this wondrous house the immense, erotically decorated bathroom. The floor was tiled, and the painted walls resembled a deep blue lake in which naked ladies and gentlemen floated at leisure amid shoals of fish with popping eyes and fantastic tails, all swimming provocatively around the floating figures. In the middle of the floor was an immense sunken metal tub large enough to hold at least five bathers. The bathroom doors were seldom shut and maid-servants, stripped to their underwear, were often in attendance, joining in when Anna, Haru Yamamoto, and the twins had glorious water-battles.

There was a room where two men fought and yelled at each other from dawn until all hours of the night, and from that room of bangs, crashes, and bad language came some of the most delicious food ever eaten. Wang, the Chinese cook, and Tanaka San, his assistant, for all the hostility between them, managed to prepare perfect meals, served exactly on time, year in and year out.

At the table, the two Bixby couples sat side by side, as did Victor and Maddy-chan; each pair was quite separate from the others, chatting together without embarrassment. When an occasional argument broke out, Anna would sit silently as family members defended their ideas and principles. Never once did she hear a husband or wife side against each other.

When, as he sometimes did, Grandpa Bixby accused his daughter-in-law, Natasha, of having no character, "No character worth mentioning, by Gad!" his wife, Tomiko, would softly agree with him.

All eyes would be on Natasha, and if things went too far, her husband, Archie, would announce firmly, "There's nothing wrong with Tashie. She is *perfect!*" and his wife would rest her head on his shoulder, smiling triumphantly.

On humid summer evenings, the sliding doors were opened wide to the garden and the family would sing songs from many lands. Anna's eyes would mist over as Natasha's piercingly sweet voice sang Russian songs and the haunting Scottish lament, *"But ah—he left the thorn with me. . . ."*

Anna was not aware that outside the safe walls of the Bixby

household, Japan itself was a world in turmoil. Waves of radicalism and rioting were engulfing the country as factory workers and poverty-stricken share-farmers, influenced by infiltrating Bolshevik philosophies, demonstrated against the high-powered ruling cliques, who had the law on their side. The police arrested thousands and killed many of the unruly demonstrators. But these events did not affect the lives of those in the Bixby household.

The children paid little attention to the lengthy diatribes that took place at the table between the Bixby men, Renzō Yamamoto, and other gentlemen guests, all of whom concluded that "Things will never be the same again after this savagely destructive war. . . . There'll never be another war. . . ."

When in 1918 the "war to end all wars" did finally end, the shock to Anna Dreyer left her disillusioned. From then on she no longer gave credence to prayers of any description.

ONE NOVEMBER MORNING IN 1922, Haru Yamamoto watched his mother, who, with pursed lips, was studying five russet-colored chrysanthemums arranged in the tall blue and white pear-shaped vase that stood on the old rosewood table. Both vase and flowers were reflected in the table's highly polished surface, and he exclaimed, "Hah! Now we have *ten* chrysanthemums for the price of five."

"What a thing to say!" Tama replied. "Haru, go at once and put on your new knickerbocker suit and *do not wear* those toy Harold Lloyd glasses when the guests arrive. Promise?"

"If you say so." He spoke petulantly. "Mother, why do we have so many visitors?"

"Why? Well . . ." Tama, her attention once again on her flower arrangement, continued absently, "well, because we like it and, of course, because your father has many admirers."

"Because of his books?"

"That's one reason."

"Have *you* read the new one?"

"Don't be silly. You know I am his scribe."

"Is it a true story?"

"True to life."

"Then is *Father* the young chap who did all those queer things with girls that he wrote about in *Yoshiwara Frolics*?"

"You were told not to read the novel until you were older."

"I grew a whole month older before I read it. *Was* Father the man?"

Tama, her eyes glimmering mischievously, said, "Ask him yourself, if you dare. Now go and get ready. But first take Pandi out for a run along the beach."

"Must it be a long run? And is it true that *all* the family are coming to take lunch with us?"

"A short run will do, and yes, *all* the family are expected."

"Not those Fukuda girl cousins. Not *all* of them."

"I sincerely hope so. Haru, give me your true opinion of my flower arrangement."

"It looks nice."

"Nice!" Tama grimaced. "I wish I hadn't asked."

"Well, it looks *very* nice."

With Haru out of the way, Tama lit a cigarette and looked about the room, feeling pleased that everything was in order. Renzō had a fondness for entertaining, and it had been some time since members of the family had gathered together beneath his roof. She was not cut out to shine in company; however, she enjoyed hearing about the antics of society. The high point of Japan's social calendar had been the visit to Japan by His Royal Highness, Edward, the Prince of Wales. There had been flurries of excitement, a brushing up of Western manners, and she had found this rather amusing. Protocol had been disrupted most indecorously by a radical chap who had blown himself to bits directly in front of the Imperial Palace, so strongly had he objected to the attention being paid to a visiting barbarian. The man's foolish, outdated actions had in no way dampened the people's enthusiasm.

Eager crowds had gathered to catch even one glimpse of "England's Prince Charming." Never before had the press lauded a visiting dignitary in such cloying terms. *"His Royal Highness,"* it was stated, *"for all the grandeur of his position, has deep understanding—and sympathy—for those belonging to the low orders in society."*

Great pains had been taken by the foreign ministry in choosing those who would attend the many soirees and banquets. Tama was visiting Aiko when Baron Fukuda, *not* included among those privileged to meet the English prince, declared, "Let me make it quite clear that in my opinion, government money should not be spent entertaining that pretty fellow. They should concentrate on more important matters."

"Such as?" Aiko haughtily inquired.

"Hmmm. Yes, well, such as improving transport for the general populace. Streetcar after streetcar comes along, moves off, overcrowded, leaving weary, work-worn folk abandoned. Mannerliness is forgotten as people shove and shout quite ferociously. And it's no wonder."

"So! Yes, and . . . ?" Aiko had prodded. "In addition to that?"

Baron Fukuda spoke hotly about the problems of sewage disposal and night-soil carts that still operated in many quarters. "In days gone by, farmers preferred to fertilize their fields with waste from the latrines of aristocratic mansions. Perhaps the guests chosen to honor the heir to the British throne were decided on in such a way."

"I think not, Yuichi," Aiko exclaimed with false modesty. "If so,

Tama and I, as daughters of noble families, would undoubtedly have been included." Then out to cheer her husband, she had added, "Yuichi, put away your injured dignity. Take pleasure that Kentaro and Maya are able to relate, at first hand, how they dined at the same table with the prince who is destined to rule over Britain's mighty empire. . . ."

Tama had ceased to feel embarrassed at the Fukuda couple's bickerings. Somehow she managed to keep on pleasant terms with every member of Renzō's extended family. She resolved never to interfere in family matters, but there were times when her sense of fair play tempted her to mention Renzō's lack of interest in his financial situation.

Money was not exactly short, but if the old house in Nihombashi were sold, she would not have to cut corners as a result of Renzō's delight in financing promising young writers' trips abroad. "It's my bounden duty," he would announce blandly, "to act as patron to those who would otherwise be forced to starve in their hovels."

Stubbing out her cigarette, Tama took up and lit another, murmuring guiltily, "How addicted I am to this habit. Ah, well, it calms my nerves and stimulates my thinking."

Now that everything was in order for the onslaught of guests, she sat back, relaxed in the cozy atmosphere of her home, and thought how very different it was from the atmosphere Etsu had created in the Nihombashi house.

She found it depressing beyond measure to visit her stepdaughter, who, in her opinion, was living a mere imitation of life. She thought Etsu's present style of living was vulgar and was at a loss to understand why the young woman had changed so much. It would have been better, Tama mused, for Etsu to have kept up her charitable interests than to have become enraptured by her own undeniable beauty, flaunting it in a never-ceasing round of entertainments in a somewhat questionable circle of Tokyo society.

Tama's train of thought was interrupted as Renzō entered the room, looking spick-and-span, saying, "Time ticks on. Tama, a tot of cognac before our guests arrive?"

"A good idea," she replied. "But first, give me your true opinion on my arrangement of those chrysanthemums."

"Very nice," Renzō declared casually. "Yes, quite nice . . ."

Later on in the day, Kentaro Fukuda, who had spent the war years in the United States, stood in the Yamamotos' long, narrow living room gazing out to where the ocean was a calm, gunmetal gray. Not wanting serious, drawn-out discussions, he half jokingly interrupted the talk between his elders, taking the words from their mouths and speaking in a rapid-fire manner. "Why should we mind that our country is unpopular in the West because of political unrest? Even though many of our leftist hotheads are still out to assassinate those on the right, bear in mind that 'government-by-assassination' is in no way a Japanese monopoly. In my opinion, *our* nationalists are rather restrained in their search for Utopia. . . ." Raising one hand, he gestured dramatically. "At this time most of Europe is being savagely split. Some out for democracy. Others determined to hold on to their privileges. Things will settle down. Take my word for it."

"Good advice." Yuichi rose to stand beside Kentaro. "You've inherited my dear father's political awareness."

"Not so. Not so." Aiko's voice was explosive. "How *could* he? Kentaro, ignore that foolish remark. . . ."

All eyes rested on Aiko as her husband broke into her speech, crying out, "Aiko, Aiko, it's unwise to upset yourself with rushes of wild emotion."

"Yes, Aunt," Etsu murmured. "Tell me, what do you think of my new hairstyle?" Etsu waited calmly for the verdict of the room, a perfect example of the emancipated woman who took her cue from postwar fashion and the Hollywood cinema.

"The new styles *do* become you," Aiko said. "That turban over your bobbed hair. Eyelashes, heavy with mascara—you remind me of Pola Negri in the film *One Arabian Night*."

"No," Renzō rumbled out, "more like Gloria Swanson in *The Affairs of Anatol*."

"You can keep those Hollywood vamps," Yuichi broke in adamantly. "Just give me Charlie Chaplin."

"No, no . . ." Haru shouted. "Harold *Lloyd* wins *my* vote. . . ."

Kentaro's wife, Maya, due to give birth to her fourth child and desperately hoping for a boy, surprised everyone by saying with a coquettish shrug, "Do you know I've gone to see *The Shiek* seven times."

"What's this?" Kentaro cried out in mock anger. "Shame on you, Maya, delighting in that extravaganza of rape and romantic posturing. Delighting in that vagabond Valentino . . . so sleek and oily."

Tama, ever-observant, remarked, "Has anyone noticed that Kentaro now wears *his* hair Valentino-style?"

"Do I? Is that what it's called?" Kentaro, not at all put out, ran a hand carefully over his pomaded hair, which, unparted, was brushed back from his forehead. Gazing at him, Renzō's heart missed a beat or two. Removing Pandi, his adored Pekingese, from the cushion on his knees, he got up and walked into the garden to stand in the still, cold air, gazing at the horizon, his spirit saddened almost beyond endurance by the thought of his son, Shinichi, now lost to him forever. The worldwide influenza epidemic had caught Shinichi in its deadly grip, and ended his life. Just one victim among millions of others, but that fact gave his father no comfort. Strangely, he could now remember Shinichi only as the handsome youth he had so loved.

He could scarcely endure the sight of Kawabata, that elderly, twice-widowed woman. He found it distasteful, even bizarre, that Etsu had invited Shinichi's widow to dwell with her at the Nihombashi house. They could have nothing in common. The older he became, the less he could understand the ways of women.

Tama, her voice anxious, called, "Renzō, don't catch a chill. Best come inside."

"Thank you—no," he replied with false heartiness. "Please have Haru bring me my old English hunting jacket."

It was Kentaro who arrived with the requested article, helping Renzō into it with skill, saying, "Uncle, shall we saunter along the beach away from the chattering crowd. . . ."

Lying in his bed that night, Renzō went, step by step, over the time spent with Kentaro, his unclaimable son. Sometimes the gods were kind to him. Yes, maybe more often than was his due. He loved Haru, son of his second marriage, but the boy was too young to be a boon companion to an aged father.

With Kentaro he had discussed matters of grave importance. Together the two men, in whose veins flowed the blood of Kenichi Yamamoto and Lady Masa, had spoken with regret, and with complete openness, of problems existing in royal circles.

"Of course," Kentaro had confided quietly, "in certain circles it's widely acknowledged that the emperor Yoshihito is mentally deficient; that for the last few years he has been incapable of dealing with government duties, even having to relinquish attending ceremonial functions. Uncle, were you privy to that?"

"I've been aware of rumors. So it's now a certainty that young Hirohito is to be appointed as prince regent?"

"Yes."

Renzō caught at Kentaro's arm for support. "It's a sad business. What now, politically?"

"I'm no prophet, Uncle," Kentaro said briskly, "but I don't mind wagering that a prosperous time looms up ahead; ruled over, not by a youthful prince, but by our country's all-powerful, military-flavored bureaucracy."

"Shades of the shogun, eh . . . ?"

As the men made their return journey to the house, rain began to pelt down and Haru came running with an oiled-paper umbrella held aloft, crying out hilariously, "Mother is scared you might drown."

There he was, a son on each side, and he called out, unthinkingly, "Ah, if only your brother Shinichi were here with us. . . ."

Now, about to fall asleep, he was struck by the memory of Kentaro's voice saying, "Yes. Yes, if only he were."

At once wide-awake, Renzō wondered if Aiko had in some way enlightened Kentaro about his true parentage.

He thought not. He hoped not. Just let time flow on undisturbed by emotional upsets. The rainstorm raging outside was quite enough.

He hoped that Bixby had taken his advice and propped up the old oak tree. He had the nonsensical notion that his own life depended on the welfare of that ancient tree, so important to him in childhood days.

Prodding Tama awake, he said, "Remind me to go up to the house on the hill tomorrow. I must see how my old oak tree is faring."

"I'll go for you," she replied. "Tomorrow, the Writers Guild is expecting a lecture from you in Tokyo. Had you forgotten?"

He had forgotten, but he said very sweetly, "Now, Tama, don't you think I can manage those two little jobs?"

"I know you will, and both of them with your usual expertise. Renzō, I would like a bowl of tea. Would you?"

"I would," he replied. "What we Japanese would do without tea I dread to think. . . ."

Upon awakening, Renzō's first thought was how good it is to be alive! In the dim light of dawn his gaze went to the alcove in which hung the plover bird scroll-painting presented to him more than half a century earlier by his father, Kenichi. Against one wall stood Kenichi's lacquered chest, still in pristine condition. Only he knew that in one of those drawers was a toy sword wrapped in a bit of bright blue velvet.

Beside that chest were three others, and the low floor-desk, which held the private papers and diaries of Lady Masa. One day he hoped to unseal those locked compartments, to discover the thoughts, dreams, and problems his mother must surely have chronicled. They could have great value in a published work.

He must remember to mention that plan to Tama. He was so busy, so involved. His life was so fascinating. He was holding up very well, was in no way ready to make his exit into the unknown.

From a Japanese standpoint, Tama would not be considered a dutiful wife, but her habit of staying up late, of sleeping in late, pleased him. He deeply appreciated his early morning hours of privacy.

Careful not to disturb her, he stretched his limbs, then, with some effort, rose up and padded on slippered feet into the living room, where, after a rapturous Pekingese greeting, he opened the wide French doors and breathed in the air.

The rainstorm was over. The clouds were high and the gray sky was reflected so clearly in the still bay that it was difficult to tell which was sky and which was water.

A lone junk, its sails rippling softly, was visible in the mist as it slid toward the shore.

"Lovely," he thought, "everything so peaceful."

Sometime later, dressed for the day, he made obeisance before the household shrine, suffering a stab of pain as his gaze took in the tablet inscribed with Shinichi's name. Wafting odors of frying bacon coming from the kitchen cheered him up, and his heart grew ever lighter as he sat with Tama and Haru, chatting and laughing with them as they relished the delights of the "English breakfast" which he still declared he simply could not do without.

Replenished, Renzō sat back to relish that all-important first smoke of the day, meanwhile advising his son, "Haru, recently there's been a rumor that inhaling tobacco smoke is injurious to one's lungs. Probably just a lot of nonsense. However, maybe best for you never to take up the habit."

"Thanks for the advice, Puppa," Haru murmured, his tone angelic and insincere.

G RADUALLY TOMIKO BIXBY HAD BECOME attuned to the ways of foreigners. But members of her household had taken on many Japanese ways through her own surreptitious tutelage.

Although she understood the English language, having studied it diligently for many years, she usually spoke in Japanese, thus forcing others to converse in *her* language, no matter how difficult it became at times.

Busily at work repairing storm damage in her much loved garden, suddenly Tomiko's mind harked back to the past, not in a sad way but gladly as she gazed at the grand old house, recalling how Renzō Yamamoto, its owner, had so generously assisted two desperate people to stay on in Japan.

The sight of the rain-drenched chrysanthemum blooms reminded her of why she was holding the cutting shears. But then a shiver tingled through her veins as she stared nervously at the man who was being hauled by ricksha through the gate. Yamamoto Sama! Of whom she had just been thinking! How unfortunate that she, alone, was there to greet him. She knew that for the samurai she would never be anything but a person of low extraction. Laying down the gardening tool, she went to greet him.

"Ah, how nice to see you," he exclaimed. "I and my little dog have come to pay our respects to the ancient oak tree. Not much time to spare. I've a lecture to give in Tokyo later today. How beautifully you care for the gardens. By the way, are there any *cats* in the vicinity?"

"No cats, Yamamoto Sama."

"Good—good!" Placing the Pekingese on the ground, he added, "Cats! Wretched clawed creatures, could harm his eyes. Just look at him! Is he not enchanting?"

"*Hai*—yes!" Tomiko laughed as she watched the small dog, its tail plume furled high as it snuffled around the garden. Suddenly she felt purged of her nervousness. "Come, Yamamoto Sama," she exclaimed, "the oak tree, as always, awaits your visit."

Renzō's literary lecture on how the West views Japan had been on a light note. "It's of interest to note," he had quipped, "that in the West they see a *man* in the moon. We, in Japan, see a *hare*. . . ."

This had aroused some laughter and applause. By the time the lecture was over, his legs felt a bit weak and he was glad to sit down, delighted to discover that Baron and Baroness Fukuda, unbeknownst to him, had been present in the auditorium.

They drove afterward to a restaurant known only to a special clientele. It was so cozy, like a journey back to the past, but during that lengthy dinner in the private chamber, listening to Aiko's warm, familiar voice, there were moments when he wished that Yuichi were not present.

Old, yes, old as he was, delicate whiffs of violet scent, together with subtle comments made by Aiko, touching on their long-lived relationship, had made him feel quite spry.

Aiko had not lost her aristocratic panache: Her biting wit and her gamin grin still had the power to enchant him.

Not once during that meal did he give thought to Tama, and he parted from the couple with regret, exclaiming, "So *good* to be together! We, who have so much in common."

"Ah—yes," Aiko murmured mischievously. "So *very* much in common."

Alone, traveling toward Tokyo Station by hired motorcab, he was overtaken by extreme weariness, and on the spur of the moment ordered the driver to take him to his daughter's home at Nihombashi.

Always, when entering the house which had given shelter to four generations of his family, also to various other persons, including a covey of harlots and an English diplomat and his wife, Renzō's senses were apt to be evoked in many peculiar ways. The place was now occupied by Etsu and his son's widow, Kawabata, who welcomed him with a show of cordiality that set his nerves on edge. Without a doubt, he mused, the old house was a breeding ground for strange relationships!

Ensconced in an armchair, he surveyed the room, slightly puzzled, taking in the recent changes that had been wrought. From his viewpoint the changes were distasteful. The *tatami* had been taken up and replaced by a parquet floor which quarreled with the room's low wooden ceiling. Too many paintings were hanging on the walls. He examined one intently. "Can it be," he inquired enviously, "that I'm seeing an original Degas?"

"No fakes on these walls, Father," Etsu murmured. "Kawabata generously gave that little painting to me."

His eyes went on swooping about and took in the grand piano and the American gramophone. "Do you always have so many flowers in the house?" he asked.

"Always," Etsu murmured. "Kawabata has them delivered every day. Father, have you ever seen more gorgeous roses?"

"I have, but never before in one small room."

Small? The room was not small any longer! All at once Renzō understood. He had not been told that most of the garden had been swallowed up in order to enlarge the living room. Controlling his anger, he exclaimed, "Etsu, what have you done with my mother's snow-viewing garden lantern?"

"Oh, that!" Etsu assumed an air of disarming candor. "It's stored away, Father. I entertain a lot. I seldom use the garden. We like to dance hence the polished wooden floor. I hope you approve of the changes."

Renzō stared at his daughter thoughtfully, and wondered what would happen if he didn't approve. But then he said, "I've had quite a day of it. Etsu, I want to speak with you before I return to Yokohama."

"Excuse me," Kawabata murmured, "I shall at once make myself scarce."

"No, no, no," Etsu murmured laconically. "Not at all, Kawabata."

"Not at all." Renzō bowed most politely. "My daughter and I shall have a chat in the morning."

Lying on a *futon* in the only room that still had its *tatami* floor intact, Renzō was convinced that he was in for a sleepless night. Something had gone badly amiss with his daughter's life. It was unnatural for her to be living with the garrulous old woman. Twice during the evening Etsu had spoken rather insultingly to Kawabata. He had been shocked by her sharp manner. He disapproved of everything about her, and especially her overrouged mouth which stood out like a wound on her face.

For the first time in ages, Renzō's spirit went out to his first wife. "Rumi, Rumi . . ." he whispered. For all her exquisite beauty, she had never touched the spring of passion within him, and yet there had been great understanding between them. Rumi, so complacent, her feet always planted firmly on the ground, had possessed something strong and radiant in her character. No man could have had a more reliable wife, and she had been a perfect mother to his children. They had adored her. He was convinced that had Rumi lived on,

Shinichi would still be alive and Etsu's mode of life would be less reprehensible.

Reprehensible? Surely too strong a word! But some twist of fate had turned his daughter into a disconsolate, embittered woman. He longed to have her confide in him. How could she accept expensive gifts from wealthy Kawabata, whom she then stared at in provocative, or sadistic ways? Completely at a loss, he all at once felt that Rumi was instructing him, saying, "Don't put our daughter in an awkward position. Approach her as a friend. . . ."

On that note, Renzō drifted off to sleep. . . .

K AWABATA HAD RETIRED TO BED, but Etsu remained downstairs, curled up in the chair her father had recently vacated. Now aged thirty-four, she was greatly admired in the social circles she moved in, but there was no safe harbor where her spirit could come to rest.

Aware of her father's displeasure, she felt contemptuous of herself. While Shinichi had been alive, her love for him had been all-powerful. Always there had been hope in her heart. His sudden death had left her broken, with no objective in life. At times she dreamed that her brother was rowing a boat toward a sunlit shore where she was waiting for him, her arms outstretched, her face radiant with joy. Then she would wake to cold reality.

Her mind would cloud over, she would become obsessed by the idea of ending her grief. She had read so many poems extolling the virtues of a self-taken life that the idea of suicide brought feelings of immeasurable calm. After much contemplation, though, she decided that death by apparent misadventure would be more acceptable in the family circle.

Etsu had never lived in the old family house on the hill above Hommoku Bay, but Shinichi had always told her to take great care when standing on the high cliff. Now, wakeful, she remembered standing on that cliff, and the events that followed. . . .

Impeccably dressed, with makeup cleverly disguising her ravaged beauty, she had paid a visit to the Bixby family, her manner befitting a sister who had recently suffered the loss of an elder brother. Tomiko Bixby murmured gently, "There can be no recompense for your loss," and she bowed her head in agreement. Then, in need of a witness, Etsu requested that Tomiko accompany her on a ramble to the wooded headland.

The two women walked along through the lush, fox-infested terrain, saying few words to each other. When they finally reached their destination, Tomiko halted, saying, "Here, my grandchildren and their friends often come to fly their kites. . . ." She kept speaking, but Etsu, her mind in a daze, walked on and stood motionless, perilously close to the cliff's edge.

"Etsu, be careful." Tomiko moved forward, calling out anxiously. "The cliff is high enough to make anyone dizzy." She caught her companion's arm and Etsu, staring down at the giant waves of the ocean thundering and breaking upon the jagged granite rocks, allowed herself to be led away, her head bowed in defeat.

For several weeks she suffered moods of hopelessness and melancholy, knowing full well that she was incapable of taking her own life. But her determination to die grew stronger. The solution was not to kill herself, but to *be* killed.

One hot, humid night when fierce rioting broke out in the city, she left her home to run panting along street after street, to finally force her body into the human whirlpool. Caught into the mass of mutinous protesters, she gave herself up to be jostled amongst the angered, desperate men and women all out to demand their rights, chanting, shouting, "Rice . . . Rice . . . Rice . . . Give us rice . . ."

Her own voice, wild, uninhibited, shrilling out her personal demand to finish with herself, "Now . . . now . . . now . . ."

Struggling, struggling not to remain upright . . .

Struggling, determined to fall, to be crushed into oblivion by trampling feet . . .

But there was no room to fall as the angered crowd swept onward like a torrent released from an opened sluice gate. Etsu, blood from strangers on her delicate gown, was carried along with it. Her feet were off the ground, her eyes were protruding as if about to burst from their sockets, her mind was aflame and confused, and then, as the rioters, packed so close, ran amok in the roaring din, she suddenly became terrified of falling, joining those who were being trampled underfoot. She wanted to survive. She wanted to *live.*

Her world misted over—all was dark. Then, shame and ignominy. She was being dragged along by a military cadet who believed he was dealing with a rioter out to better the economic status of the underprivileged.

She struggled wildly but futilely against her captor, whose baton struck her about her head and shoulders, battering her into submission.

A few days later, feeling that her spirit had been wounded beyond repair, Etsu sat before the bedroom mirror gazing at her bruised and swollen face. Suddenly she said out loud, "If life *has* to be lived, best spend it laughing rather than crying. Why make it an uphill struggle? Beware of self-pity, Etsu. It puts an ugly rash on the soul."

Hiding her face behind the shelter of her hands, she gave out one sob and from that moment on took a grip on herself. She wore a mask of smiling calm. No longer interested in welfare work, with no political interests, she deliberately expanded her circle of acquaintances, becoming popular with Tokyo's cosmopolitan nonconformists, that virile society that considered nothing to be against the rules, where it was fashionable to admire the bizarre and the odd, and where such words as *sadism, masochism,* and *deviate* tripped easily from one's lips.

Staying up until all hours of the night became the accepted pattern of her life. She smoked cigarettes and drank straight bourbon. She gambled and, finding herself out of pocket, unashamedly turned to Kawabata, who gladly came to her aid and paid off her debts. "Etsu, sister of my departed husband." Tears sprang into the woman's eyes as she said mournfully, "Without his needs to cater to, there's no longer any point to my life. I am so lonely. At my age, would it be shameful to seek a new husband?"

"Oh, how you must have bored my brother," Etsu thought, but said, "My brother's spirit surely wishes only to have you happy, Kawabata."

"Then, tell me, Etsu, what should I do?"

Staring into the woman's innocent, puffy face, Etsu said, "Why don't you come and live with me?" No sooner had the words left her mouth than she regretted speaking them.

She had become the self-appointed dictator of Kawabata's life. Apart from the strain of having too much of the woman's humdrum company, the new living arrangements were advantageous in more ways than one. Etsu's family allowance in no way sufficed for her newly acquired luxurious tastes. Kawabata's generosity knew no bounds, and with careless shrugs the younger woman accepted money and gifts as though merely taking her due. To her mind it was all tit for tat.

Shamed, her heart aflame with jealousy, but unable to prevent herself, Etsu would tempt the woman to speak of her intimate life with Shinichi. One night, speaking with cool detachment, she exclaimed, "Kawabata, my brother must surely have been pleased to have married a woman of experience and knowledge of things sensual. No?"

Smiling complacently, Kawabata murmured, "In all truth, Etsu, it was I who followed my husband's ways. From him I learnt the pleasures of voyeurism."

"I find it distasteful to think of Shinichi as a salacious man."

"*Quel horreur!* Salacious? Not so! My husband had no liking for the physical side of things sensual. Ah, it was a pleasure to me whose first husband was apt to use me too often and with insensitivity. Certainly, Etsu, at first I was suspicious and uneasy, fearing my young husband to be unfaithful . . ."

Kawabata broke into laughter, then said, "Ah, Etsu, how joyous it was to learn that my young husband wished to educate me into undestanding his fetish. Together we enjoyed attending clubs—prestigious ones, naturally, where tasteful exhibitions of erotic sexual intercourse are the mode of entertainment . . ."

Again, recalling those times, Kawabata's laughter rang out, "Ah—it was all so vastly entertaining and more than satisfied our needs for sex and love. Yes. Yes, there are so many kinds of love. Etsu don't you agree?"

For a long moment Etsu remained silent, then breaking out into an impassioned fit of weeping she cried out, "Yes. Yes, there are so many kinds of love. *So many kinds of love . . .*"

Kawabata attributed Etsu's odd behavior to the amounts of bourbon she had drunk, but Etsu, purged of all jealousy and knowing that it had been she alone whom Shinichi had loved and desired, wanted to ring bells, lay out flower mats to express her feelings of joy. They—he and she—in their own ways had been faithful to each other.

From that time on, Etsu's spirit was salved, even though there were periods when the idea of going shaven-headed into a Buddhist convent seemed attractive. Little by little she realized that her character was hardening, that worldly affairs could be enjoyed, especially when money was plentiful.

With amused politeness she listened to proposals of marriage put to her by her family and friends before graciously refusing them.

She truly loved every member of her clan, had affection for

women friends, also platonic friendships with males, especially those who favored "manly love" rather than a love for women. Such men, making no demands, no embarrassing sexual approaches, were so easy to get along with.

Her sole regret was that she would never mother a child. Knowing that such fulfillment would not come to her, she directed her maternal yearnings at Haru and his friends. She was considered the most delightful of aunts for Kentaro's little daughters, never failing to visit them on the third of March, the day of the "Girls' Festival," when dolls depicting the emperor, empress, and their attendants in the ancient imperial court were placed on display and presented with special pink and white rice biscuits.

Her intention now was to live one day at a time. Her life, while not joyous, was seldom distasteful. She had an appreciation of fine food, beautiful clothes, and after having struggled against times of despair, she felt that she had regained a rational outlook on life. . . .

Etsu's musings were broken into by a sleepy servant who entered the room exclaiming, "May I bring you tea? Perhaps some other refreshment?"

For one instant Etsu stared at the girl truculently, then she smiled, saying, "Thank you, but no. I'm about to retire."

She went up the stairs and, about to pass by the room Renzō was occupying, she hesitated, then sliding open the door she gazed down at his sleeping figure. Renzō, opening his eyes, looked dreamily into hers and murmured, "Rumi . . . ? Rumi . . . ?"

"*Hai*—yes," she whispered. "All is well."

At once he went back to sleep and she crept away, her eyes misty. It was so lovely to hear her father mention her beloved mother's name. . . .

T HE JANUARY MORNING FOLLOWING THE birth of Kentaro Fukuda's fourth daughter, he hastened to his parents' home to relay the news in person, driving through the snow which had been falling all night and was still coming down, covering the ground like a dazzling white quilt.

After his announcement, all was silent in the small cozy room which the Fukuda couple had recently taken a liking to.

Aiko, wearing a gray kimono, her hair done up in a glossy bun, was gazing disdainfully at her husband, who sat as though under a spell, holding a rice bowl in his right hand, chopsticks in his left, then a sudden squawk from the disreputable old bird, Cocky-chan, stirred Yuichi from his reverie. "So . . ." he grunted disconsolately, "another *girl*! Since we are all so miserable, let's have a strong drink."

"Speak for yourself," Aiko said sharply. "I am far from feeling miserable. On the contrary, I'm overjoyed and shall go to congratulate Maya." She walked from the room gracefully, her head held high.

"At times your mother," Yuichi muttered, "reminds me of a conceited swan." Putting his head to one side, he looked at Kentaro. "Why didn't your wife produce a son this time?"

"You might as well put that question to the moon, Father. Don't feel so bad about it."

"Feel bad! That's only part of it. Time goes by so swiftly. Soon she will be beyond childbearing age. I must have a grandson. Kentaro, you must get a divorce. Marry a young girl."

"Father! Let's not start having foolish notions. My father-in-law has much influence in the foreign affairs department. Frankly, any insult paid his daughter would put an end to my career."

"Forget about your career." Yuichi spoke impatiently. "You have plenty to fall back on. Property, wealth, good looks, and health. Now, tell me, hold nothing back. Is it only your career that stands in the way?"

"My character is easygoing. I dislike complex situations. . . ." He stopped and fumbled in his pocket, taking out a gold cigarette case. "My wife is a very nice person. I have a deep affection for Maya. For all my wicked ways, I've yet to hurt anyone intentionally. I hope never to do so. Now, how about the drink you mentioned."

At that instant, Aiko appeared in the doorway wearing a *haori* coat and with one hand already gloved. "Well, Yuichi, have you poured out all your woes?" she asked.

"Not quite all," he replied calmly. "Aiko, for an intelligent woman, you sometimes speak very foolishly. It so happens that I've been advising my son about his marriage. Is that not so, Kentaro?"

As Kentaro threw a long quizzical glance at his father, Aiko, impatient, gestured at the bird who was busily scattering seed on the *tatami*. "Yuichi, your mother's pet needs attention. Kindly look after him. I'm off to visit the new arrival. Kentaro, does your chauffeur await?"

"He does, Mother. Father, I must be on my way."

Alone in the room that held so many memories, Yuichi gave no thought to the old bird's hunger. All his attention was concentrated on his own stomach which he began to massage strenuously, pressing and prodding until finally he gave vent to a resounding belch. "Ah—that's better," he grunted.

Getting up with some effort, he approached the ancient cockatoo, murmuring, "So—you want a bit of attention, eh?" With a forefinger he scratched delicately on the bird's thinly plumaged breast. "Now, will that seed I planted in my son's mind grow and bear fruit? Despite his protestations, he'll keep it in mind. Yes, he'll keep it in mind."

Aiko, taken aback on discovering that the chauffeur alluded to was Kentaro himself, exclaimed, "Should you be risking your life driving in the snow over slippery roads?"

"Do you think that I'd risk *your* life, Mother?" he replied, and for the duration of the fifteen-minute journey the mother and son chatted companionably, as they discussed the plethora of French novels recently translated into Japanese, including de Maupassant's intriguing novel *Clair de Lune*, she, preferring it to *Bel-Ami*, he, charmingly disagreeing. Just as charmingly Aiko pretended interest in his new automobile, a Winton, equipped with roll-up door-glass and a division window. Kentaro threw a thoughtful glance her way, then said, "Mother, it's so seldom we are alone together. Shall we drop into a coffee house?"

"A lovely idea! Kentaro, take me to one of the popular haunts you favor."

Alighting from the car, and as they walked along the Ginza, Aiko was shocked to see how many buildings belonging to the Meiji Era were being demolished.

"Such changes, such dramatic changes!" she murmured. "All to the good . . . I suppose."

"Only *suppose*?" Kentaro teased. "You have reservations?"

"Naturally so. But let's not waste time prodding my old-fashioned attitudes."

They went past countless bars, cafés, beer halls, shops selling traditional Japanese sweets, and others that offered candies and cakes of Western varieties. On the spur of the moment Aiko halted, exclaiming, "Kentaro, I must purchase candy from this innovative shop."

The *fuugetsudo* was crowded with sweet-toothed customers, and while waiting for service, Aiko murmured, "Personally, I dislike sweets of these kinds, but my husband eats candies with childlike greed. Now he has a craving for Charlie Chaplin caramels."

Finally they were seated in the Plantain, one of the first coffee shops that had opened during the early days of the Meiji. Kentaro longed to bring up a subject that had been germinating in his mind, and after some light parley he said, "Mother, I regret bringing this subject up, but I'm concerned about my father."

The raising of her eyebrows gave him permission to continue, and he spoke quietly saying, "Of late he comes up with deeply embarrassing comments. This morning he practically *ordered* me to divorce Maya. At times he goes too far. So peculiar. Don't you agree?"

Aiko nodded her thanks to the girl who was setting a cup of coffee before her, then, with a shrug she said, "My husband has *always* been very peculiar. So, why cite that one example?"

"Mother . . ." Kentaro responded lightly, "why do you always refer to him as 'my husband' and never as 'your father'?"

Aiko's hands lay in her lap, unseen by her son, and now they clenched, opened, and clenched again. She feared that she was about to sail into stormy waters. Gathering her confused thoughts, she exclaimed bluntly, "Kentaro, what exactly are you driving at?"

"It's difficult, but I need to know. I've no obsessive interest in family matters, but is it true that old Fukuda, my grandfather, was struck down by mental illness in his latter years?"

A wave of relief flowed into Aiko's mind, and she lied, saying, "It's not true. Why this inquisition? Why should you care?"

"Why? Because sometimes I believe my father is going the same way. I can't help but fear that it's an inherited curse. Need I say more?"

Over the years Aiko had been driven into many a tight corner, but never before had she felt so anguished. Attempting to gain time, she sipped the sweetened coffee, but it turned sour to her taste. As though from afar she heard her son's voice saying, "So—you share my fears! I know you do by the look in your eyes." He laughed unpleasantly. "I'm glad about not having a son."

Unable to speak, Aiko stared straight ahead, knowing that if she looked into the face of the young man whom she loved more than anything else in her life, she would confess the truth.

There he sat. Not one drop of Fukuda blood in his veins. The

great-grandson of an illustrious scholar, grandson of Kenichi Yamamoto, Renzō's son.

There he sat, waiting for her to speak. She knew he loved and
admired her. But there was a slender margin between love and hatred. The mere thought of him hating her was too terrible to contemplate.

Aiko laughed. Her acting abilities were so superb that the laughter
sounded genuine. "Kentaro," she said in a leisurely tone, stressing
the words, "your *father*, my *husband*, has, without doubt, many odd
ways. No one can deny that. But the older he grows the more lucid
he becomes. Let's have no more talk of senility, inherited or otherwise." With an imperious movement she arched her neck, saying,
"Kindly remember that you are also *my son*. Your *maternal* ancestors
were brilliant, noble men."

He looked at her for a long moment without replying, then bowed
his head and said, "Thank you for removing the cloud from my
mind."

That evening, Kentaro drove away from his opulent Western-
style house, eager to escape its atmosphere of cloying domesticity.
At times he enjoyed having his family clustered about him, but
enough was enough.

As he drove along, his mind was filled with random thoughts. He
had an urge to spend the evening enjoying a few hours of entertainment. Several of his colleagues patronized the Yoshiwara, but his
tastes had matured beyond finding satisfaction in easily purchased
sexual favors. Never would he follow his father's outrageous suggestion about divorce. Nevertheless, the thought of having a mistress became rather intriguing. If the old Yamamoto house at
Nihombashi was to be sold, he could purchase it. Have a girl installed, have it as a home away from home. According to family
gossip, a legendary courtesan had once lived there. He was sure that
many a romance must have blossomed within the walls.

He might put the idea of finding a mistress to his cousin Etsu.
She had a wide circle of acquaintances and a liking for intrigue. Not
at all like his straightlaced mother. Naturally he would have her no
other way. His mother, wife, and daughters were sacrosanct. Did
he feel that all other women were fair game? The answer was in the
affirmative.

Now he was driving through Shimbashi. Beneath the glow of
street lights businessmen were coming out of the portals of their

office buildings. Kentaro surmised that many of those men would not be making their way home but would patronize one of the many geisha houses in the vicinity.

He recalled the times he had been questioned by men, and even more curiously by women, while dining at their tables in America. "No, no," he would explain. "Geisha are not women of easy virtue. They are highly revered, skilled entertainers." He had never been believed and had given up trying to explain. For many of those foreigners who had never set foot in Japan, their image of his country would remain one of a Gilbert and Sullivan land, with whirling paper umbrellas and firmaments of fluttering fans. The land of Yum-Yum and Pitty-sing.

New laws prohibited poverty-stricken parents from hiring out their daughters as prostitutes, but country-bred girls were crowding into the metropolis eager to become "taxi dancers" in common dance halls. Without doubt, parental control was under siege as boys and girls became assimilated into the widening stream of Western life. Their new gods were American film stars. Baseball was the sport of all sports.

Baseball! Ah, how he longed to have a son. Suddenly feeling depressed, Kentaro finally entered the portals of the exclusive Kojunsha club. Once inside he settled down to spend several convivial hours with men of his own ilk.

IT HAD BEEN WITH SOME trepidation that Tama Yamamoto approached Etsu to speak about the precarious condition of Renzō's financial affairs. Finally she pleaded, "Etsu, above all, please don't betray this confidence. Your father is so proud. But, of course, *you*, even more than I, know that."

"I won't dispute that point, Tama." Etsu waved one hand impatiently, saying ironically, "Unfortunately, I'm in no position to give any assistance."

"I believe you could."

"You have me at a loss. Raise the curtain a bit higher, Tama. Be more explicit."

The talk between the two women was conducted in low voices and Tama's fell even lower as she said, "Renzō would be on easy street for the remainder of his days if this valuable Nihombashi property were to be sold. There's not a shadow of a doubt on that score. But he refuses to inconvenience, or cause you unhappiness of any kind."

Uppermost in Etsu's mind were her stepmother's words—for the remainder of his days. She had never thought of her father as a mere man, but more as a landscape, one larger than life. Suddenly she lifted her hands, as if to push away the thought of his eventual death, then exclaimed brusquely, "Tama, please, in your own diplomatic way, let Father know that his monetary problems are over. Encourage him to sell."

Tama bowed her gratitude. "He will be more than relieved. Especially if his daughter would consider living beneath his roof once again."

"Tama, never would I impose on *your* good nature. Also, I've become set in my ways. Certainly sell the old house with my blessing. I shall find another dwelling, here in Tokyo. My friends all live in the capital."

Prudently, Tama put no argument forward, but after a prolonged silence murmured, "Etsu, your father's *final* ambition is to study Lady Masa's diaries."

Etsu fidgeted, showing her irritation. "So—what prevents him?"

With a degree of self-sacrifice, but willing to belittle herself, Tama said, "In the past your father has gladly accepted my assistance. But where the personal papers of his mother are concerned . . ." Glancing everywhere but into Etsu's eyes, she added, "It's clear to me that Renzō does not want an outsider to view those intimate documents. I'm *deeply* conscious of that."

Unaware of the lilt in her voice, Etsu exclaimed, "Father's attitude is natural. Tama, do you suppose he would care to have my assistance?"

Tama, her mind flashing forward to when she would next make her confession to Father Joseph, lied once more. "How can I know? If you are willing to serve your father, then why not ask that question of him?"

Etsu had expressed her enthusiasm for that suggestion in a fashion more suitable to an empress than to a dutiful daughter. With a single-minded devotion she had gone into the complex business of organizing her move from Tokyo, to Yokohama, and it had become vividly apparent to Tama that her stepdaughter, in the manner of a warrior, had in one fell swoop cleaned the rust from a long-neglected sword, wielding it with rekindled skill and energy.

Before the month of February was over, the Nihombashi house was made vacant. Furniture was stored in Yuichi's warehouse, and Kawabata, after weeping copious tears, had agreed to "stay just for the time being" as a guest in the Fukuda mansion at Yoyogi.

Etsu, displaying a complete lack of concern for the feelings of her benefactor, declared firmly, "Kawabata, I shall always appreciate your kindness, but my father has needs that I alone can fulfill. To refuse his request would be beyond the pale. Surely you agree?"

Holding back her hurt feelings, Kawabata halfheartedly agreed but wondered why she had not been aware of the hard streak in the younger woman's character.

Renzō welcomed Etsu's presence in his home with open delight. For the first few weeks he could scarcely bear to take his eyes off her. He took her riding along the Marine Drive, introduced her proudly to acquaintances, shepherded her to various shops on Mo-tomachi, insisting that she should give him the pleasure of buying her gifts—a handbag, a string of pearls, delicate silken scarves, and he pretended to feel hurt when she cried out softly, "Please, Father, don't pamper me like this."

"Who else should I pamper?" he exclaimed heartily.

Etsu, enjoying his euphoria, fretted, wondering how Tama viewed her husband's spending spree. She also wondered when Renzō would bring up the subject of Lady Masa's diaries.

Always slightly ill at ease with her father's second wife, Etsu traveled to Tokyo, intent on drawing Aiko into the picture. "Aunt, my position is becoming untenable. Father's attachment to me must be hurtful to Tama. She's exceedingly pleasant. But . . ."

Aiko replied nonchalantly, "Renzō is probably not conscious of neglecting his wife. Now, as to those *diaries*? Etsu, allow Renzō to move at his own pace. Be patient. But, in all truth I think it indelicate to unlock the secrets of one gone from the world."

"You do?"

Aiko did not reply at once. Her thoughts swept back to the day, so long ago, when she had told Lady Masa of Yuichi's incapacity to father a child. Had *that* information been chronicled? Then, with lowered lids she said, "Etsu, if *you* had documented certain events in your own life, along with your opinions of other people, would you care to have all that seen by others after your death?"

"I would not. My spirit would resent it."

She had spoken so strongly that a ripple of laughter came from Aiko. "So," she said, "we are in agreement. Now, you should put that thought to your father. As to Tama, be *especially* thoughtful of her."

"Difficult with the two of us together under the same roof."

"So, why not move into the little garden house? Play a sweet game."

"I'm too old for games," Etsu muttered.

As Etsu checked the condition of her fingernails intently, Aiko gazed at her thoughtfully, then said, "Would it help if I took the reins into my own hands?"

"They would need to be very long reins, Aunt."

"Not so. I might be spending some time in Yokohama this summer. Etsu, leave everything to me."

Aiko, examining her own fingernails intently, murmured, "I look forward to the summer months with enthusiasm."

Etsu's observations had been correct, for Tama had been feeling twinges of jealousy observing the closeness of the father-daughter relationship. She wondered if Etsu, so self-opinionated and spoiled, would agree to move into the tiny garden house. But not wishing to cause even a slight ripple, she put the idea aside. Instead, she would make efforts to show more warmth to Etsu.

Thinking along those lines, Tama went to a fish market at the end of a long afternoon of shopping and ordered a freshly caught lobster. "Have it delivered immediately," she requested. Lobster, she knew, was a delicacy much favored by Etsu.

Arriving home, she was startled to discover that Etsu had moved from the main house into the garden cottage. "Excuse me not having first asked your permission, Tama," she declared casually. "At times I need to be on my own."

"I understand. But, Etsu, you're so accustomed to luxury. I fear you'll soon tire of the humble little abode."

"Tama, how little you know me. Not everything in my life has been the ringing of bells, dancing, and quaffing champagne. Far from it. My hands have been bloodied when caring for dying soldiers. When quite young I tended my mother as she went, painfully, slowly from this life. I endured the ignominy of divorce. Please, know that I'm more than gratified just to be here, close to my father and close to my brother, Haru." Hesitating, she murmured, not quite jokingly, "We both know that the classical character of strife depicts two grown women living beneath one roof." She bowed with exaggerated respect. "Tama, believe me, the simplicity of the little house will soothe my spirit."

"Thank you for being so frank," Tama murmured. "I'm so glad having you here." From that day on she saw Renzō's daughter in a different light—as an unfulfilled, unhappy woman—and she pitied her greatly.

Lenia, THE RUSSIAN EMIGRE DRESSMAKER, was the only one of Etsu's new acquaintances who had appealed to Aiko. After having been introduced, a firm friendship had been formed, and seldom a week went by without the two women meeting, sometimes just to stroll about in the woodland atmosphere of Ueno Park. Lenia would arrive, smiling, saying cheerfully, "Here I am! Stateless! No passport. With a difficult invalid husband to support. Never mind! Never shall I give up!"

Aiko, reminded of the companionship she once shared with Marjorie Coomber, enjoyed every aspect of the friendship. Her own social life had diminished, and being with Lenia provided her with new zest. She admired her friend's brave acceptance of her plight and her inborn sense of style. She yearned to assist Lenia financially, but had too much taste even to suggest doing so. Therefore, it came as a relief when the Russian, all enthusiasm, told her, "Baroness, I have struck gold. From now on I shall be swimming among the lilies. . . ."

Curious, but refraining from questioning Lenia, Aiko had approached Etsu, who replied casually, "Oh, yes! Fortunately, I was able to dig up some high-paying clients for Lenia . . ."

"Dig up?" Aiko interjected curiously. "What strange expressions you use."

"Well"—Etsu grinned—"they are strange clients. All *gaijin*. All males. Who, to indulge their decadent fancies, dress up in female attire. Of course, they pay highly in return for complete secrecy. Quite a few are married men in high positions here. You understand?"

Aiko stared at Etsu disdainfully, suppressing her longing to say,

"At times human behavior fills me with despair." Instead, she murmured quietly, "I'm pleased for Lenia's sake."

Etsu's popularity had been proven by the steady stream of acquaintances who came from Tokyo to visit her as summer advanced. Quite a few, enraptured by the port city's easygoing tempo, resented having to return to the stifling humidity and heat of the capital.

Lenia Marakov, on her initial visit, made a bold decision, exclaiming, "Etsu, my Russian soul is *intoxicated*. Here—until sanity is regained in my motherland—I shall set up my tent."

Before a month had gone by, Lenia had opened a new establishment tucked away in a side street.

Aiko, to everyone's surprise, reserved a suite at the Grand Hotel for the duration of the summer. She paid dutiful visits to Yuichi, who, with Kawabata at his side, declared, "Aiko, *frankly*, we don't miss you. Your arrogant attitude distresses the spirits we wish to conjure, as we use this marvelous ouija board, so popular the world over these days."

"Conjure away, enjoy your games," she replied kindly. "*Frankly*, I'm more interested in the living."

Rather to Aiko's annoyance, Kentaro installed his wife and children in an adjoining suite. "Mother," he explained brightly, "what better way for the girls to spend the summer vacation than here, by the ocean. Close by you. Sadly, I'll suffer Tokyo's vile climate on my own."

Aiko studied him fondly for a moment before murmuring, "So, you are up to some mischief?"

"Well, let's just say that I find the idea of a few weeks of bachelor life attractive."

"Say no more. I fully understand. How fortunate that your wife is such an accommodating person."

"Maya," Kentaro sighed out thankfully, "can be described only as the perfect mother and wife. But," he teased, "are *you* up to some mischief? Come, Mother. Tell me."

"Mischief? Indeed no. There is little to tell. My valued friend, the widow Nomura, is also staying here at the hotel. We've much in common. She has with her a promising young pianist—one of her protégées—Mitsu Ogata. Her only son, Fumio, a widower, is presently visiting with his mother."

"Is that so! She has matrimony for him in mind?"

"She has." Aiko frowned slightly. "He, the son, is stationed in London. A journalist, he makes only fleeting visits to Japan. . . ." A smile chased the frown from her face. "But enough of such small talk! Shall we now pay a visit to Renzō's beachside home? Have you time before the train to Tokyo?"

"Yes, several hours are at my disposal. Shall I bring Maya and the children along?"

Aiko, thinking solely of Kentaro's marital welfare, said regretfully, "What a nice idea. Yes. Bring them all along."

Somewhat to Tama's despair, the seaside home had taken on the atmosphere of a holiday inn. But gradually the flamboyant streak in her nature came alive and she threw herself into the round of holiday festivities, orchestrating daily bathing parties and picnics on the shimmering beach in front of the house.

Servants, out to enjoy themselves, joined in the merriment while working diligently. Barefooted, their kimono sleeves tucked up, they carried food and drink to those who lounged about laughing and gossiping while the sun turned their skins the shade of brown eggshells.

Haru and his friends, the Bixby twins, and Anna Dreyer had never been so amenable. Polite to their elders, they happily took charge of Maya's daughters, teaching them to swim and taking them for short sails.

On one such blue-skied morning, Maya and Tama threw glances toward Aiko, who, wearing a cotton robe, her hair immaculate, sat upright on a violet-colored cushion beneath an immense paper umbrella. She was smiling, murmuring endearments to the baby Masa, her new granddaughter. Renzō came meandering from the house and stood shading his eyes from the sun's glare; then, straightaway he moved to Aiko's side.

"Yamamoto Sama," Maya exclaimed, "obviously loves children. Pity that he has no grandchild."

"You think so?" Etsu said, her voice acid. Maya's face flushed and Tama heaved a sigh of relief as Lenia Marakov arrived on the scene. After greeting her effervescent friend, Etsu, making no excuses, walked from the beach to her cottage, nodding abruptly at a group of new arrivals—Aiko's friend, the widow Nomura, accompanied by her journalist son and her protégée, the young, effervescent, Mitsu Ogata.

. . .

The young pianist Mitsu Ogata's air of self-confidence and her bright spirit were infectious. She joined in the swimming and boating, chatting happily with everyone during the sun-filled hours spent on the beach at Hommoku Bay. "I intend," she declared one morning, "to live to the full—always. That means not only a musical career, but studying abroad, marrying a kindly, understanding husband. Yes, and I intend having two children. Preferably—boys."

"Mitsu," Anna Dreyer had cried out admiringly, "I feel sure nothing will stand in your way. I find you quite intimidating. Personally, *my* ambitions change daily. I *long* to grow up and have a romance."

"Romance *is* in the air," Maya stated firmly. "What a delightful summer this is turning out to be. So many hearts are turning to love, due perhaps to young Prince Hirohito's betrothal to the Princess Nagako." Looking directly at Fumio Nomura, she asked with deep interest, "Tell us, Nomura San, in London, are there rumors of marriage where the young Prince of Wales is concerned?"

"Rumors in abundance," he replied in his lazy drawl. "However, I've no interest in royal activities. Best"—he grinned—"not to delve deeply into their lives. The veneer, so smooth, could be easily rubbed off." With a casual general bow, he strolled off to join his mother and Aiko.

Late that same night Etsu sat on a floor-cushion by the open *shōji* of the garden cottage. The beach now was empty of people but the moon continued to light the surroundings as though with a haughty indifference to anyone who would prefer the darkness.

Taking up a pack of cigarettes, Etsu grimaced on discovering that it was empty. "So," she muttered, "control the desire. I for one will be glad when this summer is over."

The life she was living had turned out to be a sham in more ways than one. Renzō, now accustomed to her presence, treated her with quiet affection, but at Aiko's suggestion he had decided to discontinue the readings of his mother's diaries, saying to Etsu, "Somehow, I find it unseemly now to delve into my mother's writings. Do you agree?"

"As you wish, Father."

Renzō closed and locked the chest holding brushed comments, drawings, and trinkets that had been placed there by a ten-year-old girl many, many years ago in the ancient capital, Kyoto.

Etsu had been deeply moved by the things pertaining to her

scarcely remembered grandmother. The old chest held an antiquated type of sleep-pillow, a little lacquered stand with a soft pad on top which would have fitted the neck of the noble child without disarranging her elaborate coiffure, and in the base of the stand there was a tiny drawer meant to hold a comb and pins but which held instead a tightly rolled scroll. When unfurled it read, *"Today I was scolded by my tutor. From now on I shall assiduously work to improve my calligraphy. Yes, but solely to please myself. Not him, who creeps about the place like a spider, paying no respect to me."*

With some adroitness, the little girl had drawn a net, hovered over by a spider, grimacing hideously. *"I,"* Masa had written, *"have little respect for him. And absolutely no fear."*

Other scrolls found in the chest showed that the girl had kept her word. The brushed words and drawn vignettes had been quite ironical for one of tender years.

"Today, I have decided to follow edicts of superior wisdom." Attached to the scroll was a cheeky drawing depicting the three wise monkeys.

Another example showed an eagle, its feathers bristling while a small bird hid from it. *"Today Father told of heavy gambling losses. He spoke loudly to Mother about a rich husband for his daughter. Father has never understood that walls have ears. My mother prays for his good fortune. May her prayers be answered. I would rather die than be forced to leave Kyoto and Mother.*

"Masa—myself—has trod the earth eleven years. Walked with Mother (how I love her). Wysteria vines have burst into blossom. Blue sky above. Fearing no rebuff, deer nibbled at the moss. Mother, eyes bright with happiness. Father must have recouped his recent losses. There is no need for words. Such relief in my heart."

The final scroll read then put carefully back into the chest had been brushed by a trembling hand. *"I am now fourteen. The family waters are troubled. Mother avoids my eyes. The marriage broker now haunts our lovely home."*

"Enough for now," Renzō had said somewhat hazily. "When autumn arrives, maybe we shall continue. Etsu, can you picture my mother's girlhood life?"

"Clearly, Father. I'm beginning to love her."

Lifting Pandi into his arms, Renzō walked out into the sunshine, back to the world of the living, leaving Etsu feeling strangely bereft as she hovered over her grandmother's locked chests.

However, she felt that Aiko was correct in her ideas, for what right did anyone have to spy into the secrets of those dead and gone?

Better by far that those flames which had glowed when one was alive should be allowed to drift away like smoke from an incense burner.

Lost in thoughts of her heritage Etsu suddenly became aware that fishing boats were approaching the shore, and some ten minutes later she stood on the damp sand at the water's edge, puffing at a cigarette given her by an obliging old fisherman. The rank tobacco tore at her throat.

Restless, she drifted back to the cottage. Wrapping herself in a *yukata*, she entered the room which contained nothing but a low table in the center, a hanging picture scroll, a vase in the alcove with a branch of sea pine, a pile of tasseled cushions and a floor mirror. It was all so simple, so lonely. She had begun to feel scared to be alone so much. Etsu had shied away from acknowledging the fact that on the night of the rice riot she had become desperate, fighting not to be killed but to stay alive. Deep, deep in her being, she knew that she would always ignore, refuse to accept that she had played the coward.

She hoped that she was not an exception to the rule. Hoped that other women, and men also, had such unrecognized compartments which they were forced to live with. Of course, one would never know the answer to that question.

Taking up and tossing down a floor-cushion, Etsu sat upon it, unconsciously taking on the pose of a student, back erect, head rock-still, determined not to spare herself during a time of self-analysis.

If, she pondered, she was to live out a long, healthy life, it would behoove her to face up to the future cheerfully.

At present, she was living in a circle, which in certain ways she was excluded from, one wherein wives and husbands exchanged intimate, knowing glances not understood by outsiders. Certainly, she had no desire to enter the married state, but at times anger stabbed at her spirit when she was left out of discussions, and when her comments were accepted politely but treated like the flippant remarks of a precocious child.

Child she was not. She was a woman whose heart had flamed with an incestuous, unconsummated love. Nine years had gone by since that dark night when her brother had held her so close. For all that time she had kept those sacred moments alive, but that passionate love now lay like a quiet pool hidden away in a secret corner of her heart. No longer was she able to recall the sound of Shinichi's voice. Days would pass by when she did not think of him at all. It was as though a magician had waved his wand and wiped out Shinichi's identity, thus causing her to lose her own, leaving her to feel that she was living on a diet of air.

So—what of the future? She was no longer young, but it was only common sense to admit that she was still a beautiful woman who delighted in presenting herself to the world in some style. Should she be true to herself in every respect? Have people realize that she was not yet a nonentity?

Etsu's self-counseling was interrupted by morning bird song. She leapt up from her cramped position and flitted across the *tatami* to kneel before the low floor-mirror. Allowing her robe to slide down and expose her breasts, she examined her reflection critically, murmuring, "Frankly, maturity enhances in certain ways. . . . The years have passed over me quite kindly. . . ."

An American passenger liner was in port and the dining room of the Grand Hotel was crowded, alive with the chatter of many languages, aglow with flowers. Music of an American flavor was played by a group of elderly Russian musicians who sawed away with their bows on precious instruments that had been salvaged from the fearsome Bolsheviks they had fled from some six years before. The headwaiter, with a show of exaggerated concern, went to greet Etsu, who, just arrived, was waiting in the manner of one accustomed to service.

Learning that every table was occupied, she smiled and allowed her gaze to dart from table to table. Moving forward, she said firmly, "Excuse me, I wish to speak with a friend."

She wore a champagne-hued dress of fluttering crepe de Chine. Long pearl earrings dangled on either side of her exquisitely made up face, and as she wove her way through the maze of tables, there were murmurs of admiration.

Coming to a stop at one table, Etsu bowed. "Aunt Aiko, I've no wish to interrupt your party, but on catching a glimpse of you, I felt the urge to say hello."

Fumio Nomura rose to his feet immediately and Etsu, eyes glinting with amusement, murmured, "No, no, Nomura San. Be seated. I've no intention of staying."

He remained standing while Etsu greeted his widowed mother with great respect, and then turning her full attention to Mitsu Ogata, she exclaimed, "Mitsu, there's the delightful air of a schoolgirl about you today." Without a pause she added teasingly, "Aunt Aiko, how is it that you did not invite your one and only niece to lunch with you here? Never mind! No hard feelings! I've been on a shopping spree. Nothing makes me hungrier than trying on clothes. Please—Nomura San, I beg you to be seated. I'll be on my way, take my lunch in the Grill Room. That is, if I can be squeezed in . . ."

"Nonsense." Nomura spoke directly to Aiko. "Baroness, with your permission, may I request an extra chair be brought to the table?"

Aiko shrugged her agreement while Etsu, casually accepting the arrangement, seated herself, then said directly to the widow Nomura, "I've long wanted to meet someone who could identify for me the maker of a *netsuke* which I treasure. Am I correct in believing that you are an expert?"

Somewhat taken aback, the widow Nomura replied, "In no way do I consider myself an expert. However, from my childhood days *netsuke* have fascinated me."

"So," Etsu murmured, "it is with me. Is that not true, Aunt Aiko?"

All eyes turned to Aiko, who appeared to be lost for words but who, after gathering herself together, said calmly, "It's true, Etsu, that *all* your enthusiasms know no bounds. But may I suggest that we continue with our meal?" Turning to her elderly friend, she added, "Nomura Sama, if it would not inconvenience you, may my niece confer about your mutual hobby some other time?"

"Nothing," the woman replied earnestly, "would give me greater pleasure. How delightful to have a young woman interested in things from our past. Baroness, you must be pleased to have such an erudite niece. I congratulate you."

"Please, Nomura Sama," Etsu exclaimed, "congratulations are not exactly in order. Firstly, I'm no longer young. My reputation is stained by having been divorced when very, *very* young. My family has little reason to be proud of me. Isn't that so, Aunt Aiko?"

Aiko was prevented from voicing her opinion as the widow Nomura said firmly, "Etsu, hearing you speak so frankly is a profound emotional experience. I've heard that you tended our wounded soldiers during the Russo-Japanese War. Am I correct?"

"Don't mention it!" Etsu murmured. "It so happened that I was a nursing aide. I merely followed the example of my samurai forebears. Women in ancient days fought along with their men. *Every battle fought must be won. No matter the cost.*"

Fumio Nomura, casting a curious glance at Etsu, said with some irony, "That success-at-all-costs syndrome is increasing in Japan. The whole system is built on it. It arouses hostility in the West and could eventually lead us to disaster."

Etsu turned to Nomura. "So, *you* refuse to be trapped by ambition?"

"I do. I'll stay the easygoing, roving reporter."

"Obviously," Etsu stated, "you are just naturally lazy."

The baldness of that statement made him grin. "Well, I've no heavy commitment to my employers. Shall we leave it at that?"

Aiko, intent on throwing cold water upon the discussion, remarked trenchantly, "Etsu, kindly give your attention to . . ." She gestured to the waiter, who was hovering over a trolley that held a tableau of culinary wonders. All eyes went to Etsu, who spoke to the gathering at large. "How unpredictable one's appetite can be! A glass of champagne will now more than satisfy my needs."

Taking but one delicate sip from the glass, Etsu rose to her feet with the air of one who led a dazzlingly busy life. Refusing to recognize Aiko's frosty, lingering stare, she bowed and wove her way slowly and gracefully toward the exit of the dining room.

That evening Etsu, obeying a telephoned summons from Aiko, sat with her aunt in a secluded corner of the hotel lounge. Both were drinking coffee and smoking gold-tipped cigarettes.

"Well, here I am," Etsu said. "Obedient as always, Aunt. May I learn the reason for your somewhat terse telephone call?"

Aiko, looking at her niece as one looks at a weather forecast map which is difficult to understand, said, "Etsu, you created an intolerable atmosphere at my luncheon party. Have you no apology to make?"

"No apology, Aunt. In fact, I hoped to receive one from you."

"Indeed."

"Indeed. Yes. Your attitude toward me of late has been very cold." Gesturing for silence, she went on, speaking rapidly. "For some time I've felt like a phantom creature of no interest to anybody. Suddenly I yearned, I wanted to be *noticed*." Etsu smiled. "Maybe my behavior during lunch *was* slightly outrageous."

An answering smile broke over Aiko's face. "Slightly?" she replied admiringly. "You were diabolical. You had me dumbfounded. Playing up to my old friend, gaining her interest, her sympathy. Yes, and causing young Mitsu to pale into insignificance. Really,

Etsu, I felt that you were acting as your own enterprising marriage broker."

"Was I as degenerate as that? You think I shocked the young woman and her patron?"

"Yes. But you didn't shock Fumio Nomura. I fear he's gallivanted about in the West for too long. He became a widower some ten years ago. His was a love marriage. The next union will be to ease his mother's mind. He has already told her so."

"Truly a good son!" Etsu then said with a smile, "Aunt Aiko, are you aware of a new spirit in me?"

"How could I not? What has aroused it?"

"A longing to express myself fully and freely."

"Have you not always done so?"

"No. Not always. Have you?"

"No." Aiko spoke sharply. "Kindly remember that I was married at sixteen. Need I elaborate?"

"Kindly remember," Etsu countered, "I also became a wife at that age. All that seems like a hundred years ago. Aunt, did I tell you that I met up with my ex-husband, Gen Ohara, in Tokyo during the winter?"

"You did not."

"Roly-poly, jolly as ever, he was walking in Ueno Park with his wife and their, I must admit, three delightful sons. We chatted about the weather. Silly things like that."

"Do I detect a note of regret."

"How astute of you! Yes. But only because at times I regret not having a child."

"You could. Etsu, why not marry again?" Aiko, intent on flicking a tiny bit of ash from her silken lap, hesitated for a long moment before speaking, then said, "Et-chan, woman to woman, tell me, does no man ever attract you?"

"What are you hinting at?" Etsu began to laugh. "No, no, Aunt, I'm a boringly normal person. But, woman to woman, I dislike, I *strongly object* to any talk concerning the marriage market."

"Say no more!" Aiko spoke abruptly. "So—at least it's good to know that you have womanly thoughts. Now, let's chat of other things."

Late that same night, Aiko was much put out when Yuichi arrived, announcing, "Here at this hotel I shall stay until my wife returns home."

"I intend to linger here until—" Aiko hesitated, then said firmly, "until I am ready to leave."

"Is that so, Baroness? Well, I dislike hotel life. So, I'll stay with Renzō."

"No, no. Think of poor Tama! Stay here. Yuichi, I assure you that you are more than welcome."

"Excuse me, Baroness. Who pays for these luxurious lodgings?"

There was a silence. Finally, Aiko, determined to keep her dignity, said cheerfully, "Tell me, how is Kentaro?"

"Extremely annoyed."

"Kentaro annoyed? Why?"

"Well, Maya, your daughter-in-law, has become enamored of Renzō's old shack at Nihombashi. To my son's ire, she has made up her mind to purchase it and turn it into a museum."

"How exotic!"

"Kentaro had other plans for the place."

Aiko stared coldly at her husband, who responded with a knowing wink. "It's said the marriage game can become boring and needs a little embellishment now and then. But I never had the chance to follow that road." He peered at Aiko over the top of his gold-rimmed spectacles, saying forlornly, "No offense meant. Tell me, Aiko, have I missed much because of my malady?"

His question put Aiko at a complete loss. With no wish to embarrass herself, and an even greater desire not to hurt him, she muttered, "Sad, how we humans fret and fuss. Yuichi, I believe you've no reason to envy any man."

Looking her full in the face, Yuichi, in a voice of gratitude and teasing admiration, said, "You are an excellent actress."

"But you're the better actor."

"How nice this is. Complimenting each other."

"Very nice." Aiko, struck by an inspiring thought, cried out enthusiastically, "Yuichi, on second thought, your idea of staying with Renzō is admirable."

"Why?" he asked suspiciously. "Exactly what is going on here at the hotel?"

Aiko threw her arms out wide and laughed. "Oh, you never fail to entertain me. Thanks for the compliment. But seriously, Etsu needs taking out of herself. She listens to you. Please take her in hand again. Renzō pays her little attention. Tama even less. There she is, stuck in that cottage. In all probability, lying sleepless listening to the monotonous sound of waves lapping on the shore."

Yuichi burst out impatiently, "I'll have a few scathing words to say to Renzō. He's become a very thick-headed old chap. Without doubt my visit to Yokohama is not ill timed. And the sea breezes will help to clear some recent traumas from my mind."

Several days later, Yuichi, unashamed of his scrawny physique, sat cross-legged on the sand wearing only a bright red loincloth. He was in his element, waving his arms, gesticulating in the accomplished style of a professional teller of tales and grinning when outbursts of laughter interrupted his story, of how old Kawabata had been trying out seductive ways on him. The ouija board, she declared, had conjured up a spirit who instructed her to give full rein to all her suppressed desires. He, Yuichi declared, had fled away to safety.

"So, Uncle Yuichi," Haru was shouting, "is all you say true?"

Yuichi placed a finger on his lips and glanced at his audience.

"Send the little girls away, Aunt Maya," Haru said. "Continue, Uncle. Don't tell us you *refused* her generous offers? Keep going. Aunt Aiko is not present."

Maya, shepherding her daughters away from the unseemly tale-telling, called out over her shoulder, "Tama, it would behoove you to follow my lead."

Tama replied, laughing. "Maya, I'm not as squeamish as you." She added, "I just wish that Renzō were here."

"Renzō?" Yuichi stared around the beach. "Where exactly *is* my cousin?"

"Never mind about my father," Haru cried out. "He and Aunt Aiko sneaked away to take lunch somewhere or other."

Yuichi slumped to the sand, saying moodily, "Haru, please get your uncle a glass of brandy."

"Only if you will finish the story when I return."

"If you so wish," Yuichi replied, but no sooner had the youth scampered off than he turned to Tama. "I'm indignant to learn that Aiko has *sneaked* off with *your* husband," he said. "Let me warn you, we should keep our eyes on them for the remainder of this summer."

Tama, withholding her amusement, said, "Ah, Baron Fukuda, shall we not agree to trust them implicitly?"

Yuichi, as though not having heard her, took up a handful of sand as if he wanted to count every single grain. Haru returned with the requested drink, but Yuichi did not notice him.

"Can it be, Mother," he asked curiously, "that the old man has gone into one of his mysterious trances?"

"Maybe," Tama replied quietly. "Haru, take me for a sail in your boat?"

"Nice idea, Mother. Just you and me. Let's go."

To Tama's frustration, no sooner had the craft slid from the shore than Yuichi's voice shouted, "Hold on! Hold on! Here I come. All ready to enjoy a little boat trip."

The woodlands crowning the bluff above Yokohama were at their summer's best, ringing with the songs of birds and cicadas. The air was hot, though cooling breezes blew off the ocean. Among those invited to Lenia Marakov's picnic lunch, only Renzō and Etsu were reminded of their past. As a youth Renzō had stood on the cliff's edge, buffeted by savage winds, blinded by grief, calling to his father's departed spirit. Those, and many other memories, came and went as he trudged along over springy turf shaded by cedar, pine, and maple trees, at times emerging into brilliant sunshine, then into shade again. He was aware of Etsu, who walked close to his side, but unaware that his daughter had once trod the same path intent on taking her life.

Etsu, respecting her father's thoughtful mood, breathed in the scent of fallen pine needles, humming to herself, the hum scarcely audible, giving herself up to the pleasure of being alive with no inner torment.

Renzō, rather out of breath, feigned interest in a giant cedar tree. Leaning heavily on his sturdy walking stick, he said, "Society appears to have become picnic-obsessed. Why couldn't Madame Marakov have invited us to her home instead of dragging us into the wilds. Tell me that?"

"Because, Father, Lenia lives in but two dingy rooms, in a not very salubrious part of town."

"She does? Hardly an address to coerce customers to. Poor woman. She'll be bankrupt before too long."

"I think not. The hideaway address is quite a plus. Certain of her clients demand privacy. They willingly pay high prices for her dressmaking services."

"Ah, yes!" Renzō laughed heartily. "Tama told me of those foreign chaps. Etsu, best warn Lenia that our government is about to outlaw male homosexuality in the community...." Cupping one ear, he listened carefully as a murmur of voices marked the approach of people. Pulling a face, he muttered, "Quickly, give me a rundown on the guest list."

"Aunt Aiko. The young woman Mitsu . . ."

"So! Plus the Nomuras and Katō, a colleague of the journalist."

"I wasn't aware of the latter."

The newcomers arrived and time was taken to bow and to express gratitude for past courtesies.

That time-consuming exercise completed, Renzō waved his stick aloft and declared, "Forward march!" Soon the group emerged from the dense woods into bright sunlight, where Lenia, with five kimono-clad girls, stood waiting, calling, "Welcome! Welcome!"

Lenia Marakov's select group of guests beheld a white-clothed table surrounded by eight comfortable chairs set beneath the shade of an ancient oak tree, the whole al fresco scene etched in silhouette high on the cliff above the ocean.

"Lenia—how nice," murmured Aiko, admiring her friend's way of returning hospitality.

"I rejoice in the twist of fate that has brought us all together," Lenia replied, "here, on this summer's day." There was about the Russian woman a certain delicacy. She treated the grand surroundings as her home. It had been no easy matter training her sewing-machine girls to take on the onerous task of waiting on table, but they were well rehearsed and catered to the guests with panache, serving delicacies usually found in highly celebrated restaurants.

"I declare," Renzō rumbled out pleasurably, "this caviar is fit for the palates of the gods."

"I agree, Yamamoto Sama," the widow Nomura exclaimed, in her slow-paced manner. "I'm reminded of an exciting episode, when, back in 1899, I accompanied my husband on a journey to Vladivostok to celebrate the founding of the Academy of Sciences there."

Lenia, always so emotional, suppressed her tears, saying, "Ah, Madame Nomura, happy was Russia in those days when our beloved tsar ruled in place of wicked Bolsheviks."

"Lenia," Aiko interjected hurriedly, "I propose a toast to your dear motherland." It was the first of many toasts given during the luncheon.

Lenia had decided to serve *sake* and thin tea, prepared some little distance away from the table over *hibachi* crackling cheerily with burning charcoal. The newly introduced man, Teruo Katō, raised his *sake* bowl and exclaimed, "*My* philosophy is, 'Try not to do evil. If wind is to blow, let it blow.' Agreed?"

"Agreed!" was the chorus, and all bowls were raised in a salute to life.

Etsu admired Teruo Katō's handsome appearance. His confidant manner indicated that he was accustomed to giving orders. Plainly, there was good fellowship between him and Nomura, the easygoing journalist, who treated Katō, his editor in chief, in a jokingly affectionate fashion.

No two men could have been less alike, and Etsu, suspecting that she was caught in an ambiguous situation, made vain attempts to receive a signal from her aunt indicating that perhaps Katō had been included in the gathering for her, Etsu's, consideration. Filled with internal amusement, she sat by, seldom speaking, feeling unusually happy but not knowing why.

Aiko let it be known that Katō, a widower, the father of two boys in high school, was the great-grandson of Nakajima, a highly honored swordsmith who had taken his life when an edict proclaimed that samurai were forbidden to bear their weapons. "My father," she murmured, "Count Okura, and *his* father before him, carried swords made by the great master. . . ."

Renzō, extending a hand, broke in. "As did my own father, Kenichi. May I tell of how, more than half a century ago, those two men, your father, Aiko, and mine, came here—to this *exact* place—bearing their Nakajima-made swords . . . ?"

Renzō related how Kenichi had arrived at the fishing hamlet of Yokohama, together with Count Okura—he deliberately refrained from mentioning Ohara, from whose clan Etsu was divorced.

The narrative enraptured his audience. He ended it by saying dreamily, "Never shall I forget that final banquet in my childhood home. Dr. Yamamoto, my scholarly grandfather, was present. . . . My parents, yes, and your father, Aiko. Yes, a *koto* was playing. . . . I recall being requested to compose and recite a poem to the sophisticated personages. How I agonized with shyness. All so very long ago now . . ."

He fell silent and tears misted Aiko's and Etsu's eyes as they gazed at him.

Some moments later the somber tone of a bell tolled slowly and Renzō, gesturing languidly toward a heavily treed area, grunted, "There's an old monastery hidden away over there. The only point of historical interest in these parts."

As he spoke, a saffron-robed monk appeared and walked by, seemingly oblivious of their presence. He went to the cliff's edge and stood immobile.

There was a timeless quality about the stationary figure, an air of serenity that affected Renzō. A breeze stirred the branches of the sea pines and overhead sky hawks, their wings outstretched, floated seemingly without effort against the hazy blue sky.

Getting up and moving forward, standing on the high cliff, he gazed slowly over the wide sweep of the ocean, out toward the sharply etched horizon.

Perhaps because of the two journalists present, he suddenly recalled a verse written by the late Meiji emperor and he recited softly:

> *"In newspapers, all see*
> *the doings of the world,*
> *which lead nowhere:*
> *better never written."*

"Hmmm . . . yes," he mused. "Commonsense words from a clever man."

Behind Renzō the picnic was winding down, the guests were restless, needing diversion.

Katō, quickly on his feet, suggested, "Who's coming to see the monastery?"

Nomura and Mitsu agreed, but Etsu, her gaze fixed on her father who was returning now to join the group, said vaguely, "I shall join you in a while."

"Not in urgent need of spiritual food, eh?" Nomura included Etsu in the bow he made to the elders about the table, then the trio rambled off to see the ancient building.

Suddenly, Etsu felt depressed. Aiko and Lenia were gossiping about private matters. The widow Nomura and Renzō, probably both lost in their own thoughts, and already on the verge of dozing, were scarcely scintillating company. No one noticed her get to her feet, and when she eventually arrived at the monastery, her depression increased as she walked past row after row of crumbling stone lanterns. Instead of entering the temple, she sat down upon the worn stone step.

Engrossed in her own thoughts, she was hardly aware of the approach of another person until Teruo Katō sat beside her, saying rather too heartily, "Good! So! Here you are at last! It's out of date to waste time. Regrettably, I fumble when it comes to subtlety, but I'm a man of action."

As though to prove his point, he got to his feet and stood for an instant, sniffing at the incense fumes that permeated the air. Sitting down again, he exclaimed, "Have I your permission to speak frankly?"

Bemused by his rapid-fire manner, Etsu gave her assent.

"Right!" He now spoke rather awkwardly and with spartan brevity. "First! The statistics! Age—forty-two. Unblemished family background. Splendid academic credentials. Generous to a fault, and fine sense of humor. Good friend in times of trouble. Believes the essence of marriage is that of total trust. Sadly in need of wifely companionship. Never expected to find it again. Now, out of the blue, deeply attracted to you." Pausing, he added with a slight bow, "Nothing untoward about *that*. Now, may I know of *your* feelings? Excuse my unadroit manner. Come, what *are* your feelings?" Katō sat staring at Etsu with a fixed, embarrassed grin on his face.

Astounded, Etsu looked at him angrily. "But of course you are not being serious," she said coldy.

"Never more so."

Controlling her temper, Etsu paused before commenting ironically, "Katō San, your scenario is more intriguing than most fiction I've come across. You know nothing about me. . . ."

"Surely that's of no real import." Katō leaned close. "Well, tell me, does he appeal to you? He's an exceptionally fine man. I can vouch for that."

"He?" Etsu, her mind rushing forward with the speed of an express train, stared at Katō blankly. Just as blankly, he returned her stare.

As if on cue, Fumio Nomura's voice sounded. "May I join you?"

Embarrassed, in a predicament, Etsu turned to see him standing in the temple's doorway. Katō leapt to his feet, blurting out, "My friend, I bungled it. I've failed you badly."

Nomura, as if aware of everything at once, said quietly, "Not with intention, I'm certain. Katō, Mitsu Ogata needs help with her Kodak. . . ."

As Katō left, like a man escaping from a burning building, Nomura gazed down at Etsu. "Don't move," he said, and, as if he had all the time in the world at his disposal, added, "May I join you?"

Strangely at her ease, unable to speak, she smiled her reply, as he sat down, saying, "Etsu, I'm sorry about this faux pas. Truly sorry. Trouble is, I'm due to leave for London in three weeks. . . ." His gaze became fixed on something in the middle distance. Etsu noticed the clean, strong line of his jaw, and the wry smile on his face, as turning to her he said, "You have kept me so at arm's length. In desperation I requested my colleague to speak up on my behalf. I was wrong. Can you forgive me?"

His presence was awakening something in her which to this moment had never been stirred, something warm, enticing, which caused her heart to increase its beat.

"Etsu, can you forgive me?" he repeated. After deliberating for a moment, he added, "Maybe this is not the time or place, but I want you to know that after the loss of my young wife, I presumed that, to please my mother, I would remarry one day. But I had no *desire* to do so until I met you. My defenses broke down. I was smitten. Yes—just like that . . ." His voice trailed off, then he said, "I am in love with you! Etsu, will you be my wife?"

There was a soft, smoldering quality to his voice that further stirred and excited her emotions and to Etsu's mind, his proposal was also an invitation to enter the realms of social acceptance. For one brief moment she felt an urge to glance over her shoulder, certain that Shinichi's spirit was hovering nearby. Instead, looking directly into Nomura's eyes, her cheeks flamed as she murmured with the shadow of a grin, "You give me little time to gather my wits." Then, almost without thought but with complete confidence, Etsu held out a hand.

Nomura took Etsu's compliant hand in his, declaring warmly, "*Kekkō desu*—How marvelous! Etsu, are you quite sure?"

"*Hai*—yes. Quite sure."

Now Nomura, utterly content, with no shadow of doubt in his mind about the future, smiled as he listened to the distant drum of surf crashing against the rocks far below the cliffs. But Etsu, her thoughts going out to Aiko, pulled her hand free, whispering in consternation, "But—what of Mitsu? Of . . . ?"

"Mitsu?" Nomura stared at Etsu. "Now, what has that young woman to do with us?"

"Umm . . ." Etsu, her mind spinning, bit at her lower lip. "Am I to understand that my aunt has all along the way been playing go-between for you and me?"

"But of course! She, along with my mother. Surely, Etsu, sophisticated as you are, surely you knew that?"

Etsu, not admiring Aiko's artful trickery, nevertheless laughed spontaneously and said, "I'll answer that question at a later date."

"As you will," Nomura replied warmly. "Meantime, shall we go and inform those two ladies that they did not toil in vain?"

. . .

As a stone thrown into a still pond sends out ripple after ripple, the news of Etsu's betrothal to Fumio Nomura spread far and wide. A marriage between a widower in his forties and a divorcee of mature years was scarcely a union to cause outward excitement, but those who cared for Etsu took to gazing at her with hungry eyes, eager to hoard up stores of precious memories, feeling the need to touch her, as if inadvertently, at every given opportunity. She would sometimes burst into tears as people would say with wry humor, "So you will live in London for quite a while!"

"The same moon shines over every country."

"After all, you'll only be a few weeks' travel away."

Nomura was accepted warmly into the clan, except by Yuichi Fukuda. At a family gathering he exclaimed, with some hostility, "Nomura, my niece, Etsu, has grown up in the midst of a large, loving family. I insist on knowing what provisions are to be made to give her solace, when you, the journalist, go off to do your job."

Turning to Etsu, he murmured conspiratorially, "Tell me, what are your feelings toward the journalist chap's mother? Come on, speak up. Spare no one's feelings. Would you consider having her pack up her traps, travel abroad, and stay with you in London?"

With no hesitation, Etsu, speaking directly to the widow Nomura, cried out, "Selfish of me, I know, but I really love the idea of having your company. Could you bear to make such a sacrifice?"

When the elder woman's jubilant response left no doubt about her feelings, Yuichi, resembling a tiger on the prowl after new prey, settled his hovering gaze on Haru. "Haru shall go too. He's *greatly* in need of discipline. A few years in an English public school is exactly what's required."

Turning his attention to Tama, he said with a kindly air, "Of late you've taken on a weary look. You need a vacation. Yes. A sea voyage. Tama, you must accompany those London-bound. Settle the boy down. Come home refreshed and—"

"Stop!" Haru cried out wildly. "I won't go. Those English schools are ruled by brutes."

"Ignorant boy!" Yuichi intervened contemptuously. "As usual, speaking without knowledge."

"I've knowledge and *proof*," Haru shouted. "Mr. Bixby's bottom still bears scars from the cruel canings he received in one of those English establishments."

"Proof?" Yuichi sneered. "Have you actually *seen* Bixby San's bottom?"

"Enough, enough!" Renzō laughingly declared. "Yuichi, stop frightening my young son." Speaking to the gathering at large, he said, "I have a yearning to revisit London. In that splendid metropolis I once trod the light fantastic. Yes, Etsu, before you were even born . . ." Realizing that his musings were arousing little interest, he straightened up, saying briskly, "Let me state, here and now. When autumn is over, I—Tama and Haru—will pay our respects to the Nomura family, and to London."

Gasps of amazement and a flood of talk greeted his announcement, but Yuichi interrupted, saying, "Yes. Yes. Yes. But now we must discuss plans for the wedding. . . ."

As a fresh deluge of talk broke out, the two principals left the table unnoticed and went strolling along the beach. Fumio Nomura, Etsu was discovering, had a mind of his own and prolonged discussions about unessential matters bored him. "Etsu," he stated, "going through a ceremonial wedding with all its trappings has no appeal for me. How about you?"

"Absolutely no appeal."

"Then how about an elopement? No?"

"Yes," she said, then added firmly, "but we must allow my father the honor of knowing our intentions. And your mother. And Aunt Aiko . . ."

"Wait! Wait!" He began to laugh. "That's scarcely the scenario for an elopement. But, ruefully, I agree. When the present storm quiets down, let us take those three into our confidence."

During the conference that took place a few days later in the hotel's lobby, the would-be elopers' plans were shattered when Renzō declared, "My daughter's marriage must be solemnized in a fitting manner."

"Exactly," Aiko put in. "Nomura San, this marriage is certainly not the result of a youthful infatuation, but there's still reason for ceremony."

"I," the widow Nomura ventured, "believe you would regret it deeply if you prevent those who care from attending your wedding ceremony."

The discussion finally came to end with Nomura declaring adamantly, "Etsu and I bow to certain of your wishes. We, a second-time-around couple, insist on a private ceremony. Then we shall gladly go along with plans to celebrate our union at a banquet."

When the three elders—not entirely satisfied—bid the stubborn pair a rather cold farewell, Nomura and Etsu remained to celebrate their joint victory, ordering mint juleps, sipping at them leisurely between puffs of cigarettes.

There was an intimacy between them that grew deeper as the moments went by. Nomura, as if in response to her thoughts, smiled and said, "So, Etsu, here we are. You and I, two experienced people out to make a new beginning."

"Yes," Etsu said quietly. "Two mature people, soon to share the same pillow."

Nomura hesitated, then said uncertainly, "Dare I hope that you also lie awake at night dreaming of that shared pillow?" Looking into Etsu's eyes, so misty with unhidden desires, he murmured exultantly, "Why should we wait?"

Softly Etsu said, "Yes. Why should we wait?"

In the privacy of his hotel room, without any embarrassment or haste, they spent some hours together, and for Etsu, time and space ceased to exist as she willingly and gladly lay with the man who had rescued her from the cold, lonely world in which she had dwelt for so many years.

Nomura, an experienced lover, gave himself over to acting with great tenderness, uttering words of deep-felt passion, bent on coaxing her further until the ultimate moments of rapture. . . .

At peace in the aftermath of lovemaking, Etsu thinking momentarily of that past disallowed love, cried out spontaneously, softly, "Not forbidden fruit . . . Not forbidden fruit!"

Those heartfelt words, Nomura believed, came from Etsu having broken the moral code by sharing the same pillow with him before their marriage ceremony, and he was glad that she had no regrets about their having done so.

THAT EVENING THE MEAL WAS eaten by the entire family group on the terrace before Renzō's house by the light of the moon. For the first time Nomura saw Etsu robed in a traditional kimono, and a general laugh went up when he remarked admiringly, "You look so different, Etsu."

Aiko murmured, "Yes, you do. Your face positively radiates contentment."

"True," Yuichi said, peering at his niece closely. "Now, what exactly have you been up to?"

Etsu gestured restively toward Nomura, who came to her aid, drawling out, "This afternoon we made up our minds to marry without further delay. Tomorrow—to be exact! Isn't that so, Etsu?"

She, taken by surprise, nodded her head but said nothing, not for the lack of anything to say, but because she felt so protected.

In contrast, Yuichi, fired by enthusiasm, pointed an admonitory finger at Nomura, exclaiming with genuine consternation, "A hole-in-the-corner ceremony? No, no, not for Etsu." Turning to Renzō, he cried out, "Come, bring out your paternal objections."

"I have no objections," Renzō remarked without any great conviction. Then, rising, he spoke in a dreamy fashion, saying, "All I request is that Kentaro be a witness of the legalities."

Yuichi, knowing when he was beaten, yawned widely, then said, "Ah, well! So be it. It grows late. Time to retire. Come Aiko, let us go. . . ."

Following their departure, Renzō, feeding tidbits to Pandi, appeared to be more interested in the animal than the human beings surrounding the table. Tama, stifling a yawn, agreed that Haru had her permission to go up the hill to visit Victor and Maddy-chan Bixby. Etsu, all at once alert, cried out, "A lovely idea. We'll go with you, Haru." Turning to Nomura, she murmured, "You will be enchanted. The old house on the hill was built more than a century ago by one of my ancestors."

"So it was," Haru shouted. "And Nomura Sama, it was once a famous brothel. Now it's the happiest home in the entire world. Come on! Hurry up! Let's go!"

As Etsu walked up the hill between Nomura and her young brother, she had the feeling that she was making a pilgrimage, not to visit the Bixby family, but to the house where her grandmother, Masa, had lived when but a bride of fourteen years. She felt that Lady Masa's spirit was traversing the road with her, sighing sadly, *"So—you discard me? Go your way? Leaving my life locked up in those old chests. Never mind—never mind . . ."*

Halting abruptly, Etsu shivered slightly, then murmured, "Do you believe in ghosts?"

"Absolutely not," Nomura stated. "Do you?"

"Maybe not. But I like the idea of them," she replied, and they walked on, upward through the wistful beauty of the night.

The following day Etsu and Nomura, accompanied by Kentaro and Teruo Katō, were legally married.

. . .

A week of glittering sun-filled days and incredibly lovely star-splashed nights followed that ceremony.

The newly married couple, quartered in the cottage, were given no respite. Gifts poured in, presented with love and generosity.

In every heart a lonely feeling flickered. Etsu leaving ... Etsu going far away ... "She must," Yuichi had insisted, "be surrounded by things Japanese while in that foreign land." After days of fret and countless discussions with Aiko, he exclaimed, "My decision is made."

"What a relief," Aiko responded. "May I be made privy to it?"

"Yes. Money. A sizable amount."

"As—a gift?" Aiko tensed her nostrils to express her distaste.

"What is wrong with money? Tell me that, Baroness?"

Aiko, knowing Etsu's love of luxury, threw away her objections. "I stand corrected. Yuichi, it's a splendid idea. In order to soothe away your vulgarity, I shall present Etsu with a simple gift."

"Such as?"

"I have in mind that *Koi netsuke* your mother set such store by. Am I correct in believing that it was gifted from her to Lady Masa?"

"I don't know. Maybe it was. But tell Etsu that anyway. It has a nice sentimental ring to it."

On receiving the *netsuke*, Etsu, deeply moved, showed it to Renzō, who, even more deeply moved, spent an enjoyable time relating in detail how he, with his aunt Sumiko had, after purchasing the little toggle, been caught up into the horrific holocaust caused by the arrival of Commodore Perry's American gunboats to Japan's shores.

Haru, his eyes a-goggle, cried out, "Father, that's all ancient history now."

"To me," Renzō said huskily, "it seems but yesterday. . . ."

Gazing at his father in some wonderment, Haru murmured, "How does it feel, Puppa, to be so old?"

"Remarkably pleasant," Renzō replied, adding, "My deep wish is, Haru, that you yourself will live to find out."

Kentaro's gift caused the raising of some eyebrows and comments such as: "But surely these scrolls—ancient though they be—are too erotic to hang on the walls of a house in London?"

"Nonsense," Kentaro said with confidence. "They will arouse envy, much discussion."

Nomura said stoutly, "They shall decorate my study, be enjoyed by my *gaijin* colleagues."

From the Bixby family came a Chinese long-rug, vividly colored, breathtakingly lovely, its dark red background covered with blue butterflies. "Our favorite rug," Bixby confided to Tama. "Tomiko and I sacrifice it gladly for Renzō's daughter."

From Katō, who now firmly believed that he had coerced Etsu into marrying his friend, came a paneled screen depicting the four seasons painted against a background of pale gold.

The widow Nomura, entirely captivated by her daughter-in-law, presented Etsu with a casket abrim with *obi*-brooches, rare clasps, some of lapis lazuli, of coral, amethysts, and pure gold.

Etsu, moved by all the attention, was more than content to spend days in Yokohama, clinging closely to her father. Her husband, now occupied with business and travel arrangements, spent most days in Tokyo.

Renzō had spared no expense and had given much thought to the hastily arranged wedding banquet that took place in the ballroom of Yokohama's finest hotel. One hundred people gathered to honor the occasion. On the following morning he was taking his usual early morning stroll along the beach, accompanied by Pandi, who, unleashed, was endeavoring to get within at least sniffing distance of just one sea gull.

Walking slowly, Renzō was reviewing the banquet. All in all, the affair had been a success. A grin spread over his face as he murmured, "In life there are certain situations which can be covered by the term *embarrassment*. Hmmm, yes. Locked hotel doors. Misunderstood introductions, and, yes, mistaken identities."

A chuckle escaped his lips as he recalled the sight of Aiko mingling at her ease in a group that had included Tomiko Bixby. Both women, gowned in ceremonial black kimono, were in accord, smiling together at some comment from Etsu, then, some moments later, Aiko, her eyes spitting angry gleams had wafted to his side, murmuring, "What an affront! *That* woman being here! Renzō, tell me, I notice that Sato, your ricksha puller, is not present. I presume he had a previous social engagement?"

Giving him no opportunity to reply, she had moved off in high dudgeon to join Yuichi, who, after inclining his ear to her whispered complaints, nodded sympathetically, then dashed off to spend time chatting with Tomiko, the despised woman. It had taken some effort from Tama to coerce Baroness Fukuda from doing a disappearing act, but her good spirits had been revived and she lingered on.

Apart from that small contretemps, the only other hitch had been

Nomura's and Kentaro's lack of sobriety. The two men had been a little too jovial at the commencement, but as champagne flowed and spirits rose generally, no harm had been done, and, as Tama had wisely said, "Rather a comfort to know that Nomura San is not altogether too serious. Etsu enjoys being stimulated. . . ."

Etsu! Halting, Renzō's eyes misted over. "Only natural," he said, addressing Pandi. "My daughter is going afar off. Leaving an echoing, an empty space behind . . ."

How comely she had looked at the reception. Surprising how she, so *à la mode*, had chosen to wear conventional Japanese garb . . .

How well behaved young Haru had been. Tama was an easygoing mother. Maybe Yuichi had been correct in suggesting that the boy was in need of discipline, but recalling his own childhood years spent under the watchful eyes of those stern instructors at the school, he had taken pleasure in observing Haru's carefree life. . . .

All at once Renzō became aware of a frisky Alsatian dog bounding along the beach, coming in his direction. At once, on the alert, he prepared to do battle. Fending the great brute off, he whacked it several times with his trusty English walking stick. As the dog slunk off, Renzō gazed around and about, muttering with just a touch of guilt, "Let's hope no one saw that little fracas." Hefting his treasured pet up into his arms, he continued on his way.

T AMA STOOD IN THE SHUTTERED garden cottage, glad that it no longer housed a guest. Pushing aside the heavy wooden shutters, her eyes adjusted to the brilliant sunshine that flooded in. Etsu and Nomura's wedding had been the highlight of recent weeks. The lavish banquet provided by Renzō had enraptured all present. The Nomura trio then departed for London and the beach lay deserted, no longer a popular picnic ground.

Maya and her covey of daughters had left to join her parents in their villa at Karuizawa. "To give the girls the benefit of pure mountain air," Kentaro had exclaimed.

Haru, secure in the knowledge that the forthcoming journey to London was to be only a vacation, had given in graciously. Tama had no complaints to make about her son's character. He was intelligent, loving, and loyal.

She knew only a little of Renzō's early days, but the loneliness of her own childhood was softened as she watched Haru growing up in the easygoing Hommoku Bay home. She delighted in his close relationship with the Bixby family.

Tama gasped as four unsaddled horses swept into sight, galloping across the sand. Astride the splendid creatures were Victor Bixby, Haru, Anna Dreyer—a red cloth tied about her forehead—and Maddy-chan, her long black hair flying free. All so young and full of life as they headed their mounts into the watery depths and slipped from the animals' backs. Humans and horses went swimming together.

"Lovely! Lovely!" she cried out.

At that moment a serving-maid entered, saying, "The master says that Baron and Baroness Fukuda are to be luncheon guests."

"Is that so!" she replied pleasantly, but her spirit dropped. The idea of taking the midday meal in the cottage, tête-à-tête with Renzō, had appealed greatly. Frowning, she exclaimed, "The meal is to be taken here as arranged. The same menu, if you please."

Sometime later, the four adults sat about the low table, wielding chopsticks, commenting on the fine quality of the raw tuna which they dipped in a spicy sauce. Words were few during the meal and Tama, feeling that she was expendable, spent time attending to the needs of the others. Blue steam curled wispily from the spout of an ornate iron kettle that rested above the glowing charcoal in the *hibachi*.

Seated on a floor-cushion, Aiko made a wonderfully elegant picture with her lips puffing out thin streams of smoke while her eyes, but half open, seemed to be gazing into eternity.

"I'm ready for tea now, Tama," Yuichi stated sweetly.

"Certainly," she replied, and while preparing the beverage wondered why Renzō was so strangely guarded. There was a wary expression in his eyes, even when he smiled.

Yuichi accepted his bowl of tea, saying casually, "Tama, thank you for being so kind to my family this summer. We gave you a busy time."

"Don't mention it!" she replied. "I find your family and friends all most interesting."

"*Interesting?* What a splendidly diplomatic term that is! Tama, tell me, do you have hopes for Etsu's future happiness with Nomura?"

Suppressing indifference in going over ground that had been covered too many times already, Tama murmured, "Etsu has made an excellent match."

"You think it wise that I sent the old mother away with the couple?"

"A perfect arrangement."

"Good! Yes, but I still insist that you and Haru should have gone with them."

Tama began to laugh. "Baron Fukuda, you seem to have a passion for arranging other people's lives for them."

"You think so!" Yuichi grinned. "Maybe that's the general effect. What's *your* opinion, Renzō?"

"What's that, Yuichi? Excuse me, my mind was wandering," he went on to say. "Yuichi, do you recall when it was discovered during Madame Marakov's picnic that Katō is the great-grandson of Nakajima Sensei, the master swordmaker?"

"How could I? *I* was not at that elite luncheon."

"Of course. Neither were you, Tama . . ."

Aiko, eyes flickering, said with contrived innocence, "What exactly are you leading up to?"

After a long pause Renzō spoke directly to Yuichi Fukuda, saying gravely, "My father, Kenichi Yamamoto, was possessed of two Nakajima-forged swords. Before leaving for London, it's my intention to present one of them, ceremoniously, to my young son, Haru." He broke off in mid-speech as some unknown water-bird flitted past the open *shōji*, shrieking out a strange, nerve-wrenching cry.

Tama shivered, not disturbed by the bird but by the odd blend of emotions permeating the room. She glanced at Aiko, so mysterious, so devious. At Yuichi, disconcerted, yet so perspicacious. At Renzō, whose eyes held an expression of unspeakable sadness. She felt that something incomprehensible, even dangerous, was going on among the three people who sat unmoving in the strange hush.

Finally, she said tremulously, "Renzō, Haru will be so proud, *so* honored." Her comment, although ignored, vanquished the mysterious shadows that her vivid imagination had summoned.

Renzō, as though no hiatus had occurred, now said, "Yuichi, the strings of kinship are strong. Your mother, my aunt Sumiko, was a Yamamoto daughter. Yamamoto blood flows in Kentaro's veins. Have I your permission to present that other family sword to him?"

During the moments that followed it seemed to Tama that she was witnessing a ruthless battle—one that had nothing to do with swords or the presentation of gifts.

Aiko gazed at her husband, her expression stony yet demanding. Or, Tama wondered, was she pleading with him? Deeply embarrassed, preferring not to look at their three faces, her eyes focused on their hands. Six hands, all tightly clenched. Hands marked by the passage of times that had nothing to do with her. She saw Yuichi's hands unclench. He laid his palms flat on the table, fingers fanning out, lying stiffly, then drumming indecisively as if he were toying with the keys of a piano, trying to work out a complicated musical score.

Finally Yuichi bowed to Renzō and said with the utmost courtesy, "Renzō. Cousin. Your thoughtfulness knows no bounds. In the name of my mother, your aunt Sumiko, I thank you."

Renzō, his face impassive, returned the bow.

Yuichi, turning to Aiko, said indulgently, "Have *you* anything to say?"

She executed a neat shrug, intimating that the matter was of little interest to her. Tama—not believing Aiko—was under the impression that apart from herself, everyone in the room believed that he—or she—had achieved a personal victory.

One week later, just before dusk had darkened the summer sky, Tama, in the company of Aiko and Yuichi, witnessed the ceremony of Renzō passing the Yamamoto swords—those emblems of his family's honor—into the keeping of Haru and Kentaro.

Nothing untoward happened. The recipients, both of them dressed in formal Japanese attire, accepted the honor bestowed upon them most courteously. She was immensely proud of Haru when he bowed, paying obeisance to his father and then to his elder cousin, Kentaro.

Acknowledging those bows Renzō's expression was that of a man whose heart was at peace.

Yuichi bowed, saying complacently, "Ah, Renzō! This must be a most *gratifying* occasion to you."

"Yes," Kentaro agreed. "Surely it must be accompanied by a toast to Haru's and my Yamamoto ancestors."

Sake was drunk all around. Aiko became extraordinarily merry. Her merriment was infectious and the entire group drove in a parade of ricksha to dine at the Grand Hotel. During the meal Yuichi announced that he and Aiko were to spend the remainder of the summer at Karuizawa. "It's cool. Far from the city. Haru, *you* will accompany us."

"Thank you, Uncle, but no." Haru spoke with the confidence of one who had a sword of his own. "I wouldn't miss being at the Bixbys' annual garden party for *anything*."

"Understandable," Renzō put in mildly, then teasingly exclaimed, "Haru, I believe, has secretly betrothed himself to young Maddy-chan Bixby."

Aiko interposed with some arrogance, addressing Renzō, "Your son must fly higher than *that* in the matrimonial stakes."

Haru was overcome by laughter, and as the party had broken up, Aiko rather sadly asked Renzō, "When does your ship sail?"

"September the fifth."

"Exactly one week to go!" Yuichi said. "Naturally I will return to farewell you."

"Not I." Aiko smiled directly into Renzō's eyes. "I dislike farewells so."

Returning her smile, Renzō said, bowing ceremoniously, "Then—*sayōnara*—since it must be so!"

Returning home, Renzō moved about restlessly. Eventually he said, "Tama, there is one other sword in the old chest. Would you care to see it?"

He brought forth a toy sword wrapped in a scrap of sky-blue velvet. Delighted she exclaimed, "How did you come by it?"

"I can't recall exactly. I put it in with some of my father's antique swords on my seventh birthday." With a gleam in his eye, he added, "That was quite a day! Yes, that was the day my grandfather took me in hand. The end of my childhood, one might say."

A moment later he said, "For some time I've been meaning to destroy certain love poems written by my father, Kenichi. All are much too intimate for other eyes to see. I shall also burn this useless little weapon."

She watched as he collected a small package from the drawer and took it, along with the velvet-wrapped toy, out into the night.

Following at a distance she stood by watching the odd little ceremony taking place on the sand at the water's edge.

The sight of the old samurai burning a toy sword, and bent on sending his long-gone father's love poems off into the spirit world, caused a bittersweet ache in Tama's heart.

Renzō waited until the last wisp of smoke had wafted away. Then, heaving a long sigh, he returned to the house. Half an hour later he was asleep. His deep snores and his peaceful expression were those of a man at the end of a perfect day.

Unable to sleep, Tama slipped out of bed. Feeling her way cautiously, she went down to the damp sand and found what she was searching for. Renzō had inadvertently dropped one of those love poems, but she had not told him so at the time. Overcome with curiosity, she crept back into the house with the stolen treasure.

The candle shed a flickering light over the faded characters of a love poem brushed so long ago with scholarly style by Kenichi Yamamoto:

> *With my wife I*
> *Share a pillow of ice*
> *Duty!*
> *Ah—Osen . . .*

So, Tama thought, the great love of Kenichi Yamamoto's life had been the courtesan, not the Lady Masa. "Too intimate for other eyes to see," Renzō had said. Guilt-stricken, she ran from the house down to the water, where she tore the delicate paper into confetti and cast the pieces into the waves. . . .

ANNA DREYER HAD LIVED THROUGH the past six years always nagged by the dread of being sent to Germany to live under the care of a distant relative in Berlin. She, like many other foreign children, alluded to herself as a "BIJ—a born in Japan person." She, like most others of that select group, had a jealously possessive attitude toward the land they lived in. They were "special," greatly admired by their Japanese friends, praised for their skill in their understanding the customs and the language.

Hans Dreyer, lost in the world of Buddhist codes and meditation, had finally settled permanently in the monastery, intending to remain there for the rest of his life, giving little thought to his daughter, who, at the end of the war had returned to live in the shabby old Dreyer house at Hommoku.

When Anna learned that her father had died, she went running to Tomiko Bixby, who, knowing the girl's character, had not been shocked when the orphan's tears had turned into hysterical laughter. The idea of Anna's laughter being genuine would be preposterous, and she had shown great compassion for the girl.

A short family consultation followed, and when Bixby put forward the plan to take Anna back into their midst, his proposal was accepted. When told of the decision, Anna cried out anxiously, "Do you mean for always and *always*?"

Bixby replied firmly, "Yes. If that is what you wish."

Unable to speak, to express her feelings of joy and relief, she ran into the garden where flocks of Tomiko's pigeons wheeled and fluttered against the sky of stainless blue. "My home," she whispered rapturously, "A real home forever . . ."

As she gazed at the house Tomiko came to her side, to speak with compassion, explaining that the passing of time would help Anna to recover from her sad loss.

Her homily was cut short by the arrival of Bixby, who came to join them and oversee the preparations for the annual garden party.

Just as Anna had done, he looked upward into the blue vault above their home. "Perfection," he muttered, "perfection."

Anna agreed, and, though she knew she should feel grief at the death of her father, whom she had seen so little of during her life, her heart soared in gladness as she watched Bixby and Tomiko saunter off, arm in arm. Truly, she thought, they were her real family.

Granite rocks around the fountains and lily ponds were being polished. The lawns beneath gingko, maple, and pine trees were being coaxed to perfection. Rose bushes, imported from England many years before, were in bloom and filled the air with a sweetness that enticed bees and small, colorful butterflies to the garden.

Bixby and Tomiko wandered about together, overseeing the preparations. They passed behind the sturdy bamboo thicket that had flourished long before the arrival of Commodore Perry and stood watching three carpenters building swings and slides to delight the children who were to attend the party.

After giving the workers unwanted instructions, Bixby and Tomiko left the grove to sit on a bench beneath the immense persimmon tree, its branches laden with golden globes of fruit. "A splendid tree," Tomiko murmured softly. "I've often wondered who planted it and how long it has stood here braving the seasons."

"*I*," Bixby replied, half teasingly, "often wonder how it is that *you*, Tomiko, become more lovely and dearer to me as the seasons go by."

PART VI

ARCHIE AND NATASHA BIXBY THOUGHT of the annual garden party as a double celebration. It was Archie's birthday and it was also the anniversary of their first meeting.

The servants rose shortly after dawn and immediately set to work. Maid-servants, proud of the new, bright-colored kimono they were wearing, prepared for the coming onslaught by drinking copious bowls of hot tea.

Victor had on a brand-new outfit, and he wondered why Archie and Bixby were content merely with new cravats which they wore with their formal frock coats and pinstripe trousers. He thought it a bit strange that his grandmother, Tomiko, wore the same dove-gray kimono every year. On her sash was a flute-shaped *obi*-brooch made of jade. It may, he assumed, have some significance, but if so, only she would understand it. At times, she placed a hand over the brooch and caressed it.

Lenia Marakov, exotically dressed, was one of the first to arrive. She stood on the gently curved old bridge spanning the iris garden and gazed down and about at the festive scene. She watched the other guests arrive. The women, intent on outdoing one another, wore flowery gowns and beribboned hats. Tama and Anna Dreyer, each wearing creations made in Lenia's Yokohama salon, Tama's of moss green, the other of black taffeta sashed by a crimson ribbon, stood out most pleasingly.

Maddy-chan, Kimono-clad, came running up to her, saying, "Madam Marakov, you look *so* happy."

"Why should I not, darling? So does everyone."

"Perhaps all for quite different reasons?"

"Wise child!" Lenia murmured. "Happiness is so personal. It can't be explained. I can *show* you an apricot, but I can't tell you how it tastes."

"I *know* how it tastes." Maddy-chan grinned, then cried out, "Lovely, lovely! *Kekkō desu*. The musicians are about to play! Come, Aunt Lenia, let's dance together."

As the small string orchestra broke into music, guests gazed with delight at the stout Russian woman and the young girl who, with no inhibitions, joined hands and swayed to the strains of a well-known melody.

The party was under way! Happiness was in the air. Voices were raised in talk, and laughter was heard against the sweetness of the music.

At times Renzō's mind wandered back to the days when no foreigner had dwelt freely in Japan, when the old bridge had curved over a sparkling pond where Lady Masa's colorful fish had swum leisurely. The sight of Tama chatting with two Japanese nuns from the Sacred Heart Convent caused him to smile wryly. He found the women's medieval garments pleasing, but during his youth any Japanese person daring to admit a Christian faith would have been decapitated. That unpleasant thought faded as peals of silvery laughter came wafting from the ancient bamboo grove where small children were playing. He concentrated his gaze on Tomiko Bixby, who stood with the Episcopalian cleric, obviously discussing the rare beauty of Bixby's English roses.

Bixby came to his side and Renzō exclaimed, "This is a happy occasion. You and Tomiko have created another masterpiece. I congratulate you."

"All thanks to you, my good friend," Bixby replied, not quite able to hide his emotions. "Need I say more?" After a pause he repeated, "Renzō, need I say more?"

"Enough! Enough!" Renzō gestured upward where the pine trees were dark against the sky. "I'm glad you've learned to care for my country. Shall I give your regards to that wonderful land, England, when I finally get there?"

Bixby's reply was lost as the orchestra began a rendition of his favorite—*Greensleeves*.

Voices were raised to sing along, and the old folk beat time while the young began to dance.

Anna Dreyer bowed before Renzō and Bixby, crying out coaxingly, "Let us three dance together? Let's all dance. . . . "

Tomiko watched as the trio joined hands to circle around in stately fashion. Catching up the hem of her kimono, she moved forward, calling gaily, "Please! Make room for me." The musicians gave of their best and the music played on until Wang appeared, crashing his gong, announcing that the time for feasting had arrived. . . .

The guests lingered until the first star appeared. Then Tomiko and Bixby, surrounded by their family, including Anna Dreyer, together with Renzō, Tama, and Haru, stood on the lawn before the house. There was a radiant atmosphere about the place as their ecstatic voices wafted into the still night air.

"Too perfect! Perhaps we dreamed it?"

"Was the champagne as good as last year?"

"Wasn't the garden a *picture*?"

"It was never so beautiful. . . ."

"Yes, the entire affair *was* more like a dream than reality."

"Could it be," Maddy-chan asked, "that *we* are not real but just figures in someone else's dream?"

"What about *this*?" Victor pinched her arm firmly.

"Now, Maddy-chan," Archie laughed, "no vengeance. No tears to spoil this happy occasion. Come, stand here, between Tashie and me. . . ."

"No party is complete without children and their laughter. . . ." Tama stated softly.

"A pity all the champagne went," said Renzō with regret.

"But I put a magnum aside—Veuve Clicquot to boot!" Bixby announced triumphantly.

To cap the glorious day, a series of toasts were made to one another, to old Wang, to faithful Tanaka, to the housemaids. Finally, all glasses were raised in a special toast to the old house on the hill.

It was a subdued gathering around the Bixbys' breakfast table. Wang, in an ugly mood, had upset Bixby by brewing the coffee badly. Everyone was suffering a letdown after the feasting and merriment of the previous day.

The carpenters, much too rowdy, were dismantling swings and slides as gardeners repaired the damage caused by tramping feet. "My lawns may never recover," Bixby complained moodily. "My belladonna lilies were crushed. Yes, and whose wretched child cut those initials into Tomiko's favorite birch? Such *vandalism*."

"Never mind," comforted Natasha. "No harm has come to your roses."

She fell silent as Tomiko and Bixby stared at her coldly. Archie took his wife's hand in his, saying protectively, "Tashie is right. No real harm has been done. Victor! *Please*, don't tilt your chair. It's *most* irritating. . . ." He stopped speaking as a ship's siren sent out a series of mournful hoots.

"That's the French liner in the docks due to sail this morning,"

Bixby announced as he strode toward the kitchen to confer with his cook. He came back to the table, grinning, saying, "The old rascal just needed a bit of smooching up to. Wang's brewing a fresh pot. About that document, Arch. I'm too exhausted to go down to the office."

"And *Archie* is exhausted too," Natasha cried out defensively.

"That's true," Archie replied lazily. "So, Victor, *you* shall trot down to the warehouse."

"Not I!" Victor cringed low in his chair. "I've a sick head from all that champagne."

"Nonsense!" Archie spoke callously. "A brisk walk will do you good. On your feet. You too, Maddy-chan."

"I don't want to." She ran to Bixby and collapsed limply on his lap, murmuring pathetically, "Do I have to, Grandpa?"

Cuddling her close, he barked out, "Come, Victor. Be a man! Do as you're told."

Anna, certain that an argument was about to break out, declared hastily, "I'll be glad to offer my services."

Her offer was thankfully accepted, and she stood proudly while being given all-important instructions. Never had she felt more needed—more loved.

Following custom, she bowed to the mistress of the house, saying, "I now leave my home."

Tomiko in response, replied—as was customary—"We await your safe return."

"Be back in time for lunch, Anna," Bixby warned.

"I'll be on time, I promise not to be late." Smiling cheerfully, she then ran down the long graveled driveway.

The September morning was cloyingly hot, the sky was overcast, and as Anna made her way through the familiar streets, a drizzling rain began to fall. Wind veering toward the south blew into a heavy gale. She loved the excitements, the inconsistencies of the climate and felt let down when the wind abated and the clouds cleared away, leaving the sky blue.

In the vicinity of the huge gasworks Anna halted impatiently for a few minutes in order to chat with Lenia Marakov, who stood by her gate buying yellow chrysanthemums from a cheerful peddler. She then hurried on and finally arrived at her destination. The old wooden warehouse had survived for more than half a century, and there were rumors floating around suggesting that it would soon be demolished.

To Anna the very thought of pulling down the ramshackle building was sacrilegious. She, Haru, Victor, and Maddy-chan knew every nook and cranny of its dim interior. Countless games of hide-and-seek had been played there among the motley collections of goods stored in dark corners where spiders wove webs and where rats scuttled about. Anna loved the strange, musty odor that pervaded the building. Passing through a maze of narrow corridors, she sniffed deeply before calling out, "*Gomen nasai*—Excuse me!"

Renzō's old retainer, Jutei San, came out of his document-filled cubbyhole. He treated the girl with great respect. Politely, she inquired after his well-being. "How," she asked, "does business go, Jutei San?"

"Picking up. Picking up!"

"Excellent. And can we expect a boom?"

"Perhaps." The old man, who had known Anna for so long, smiled and said, "May I have the pleasure of rewarding you for your kindness?"

"No, no!" she cried out. "I'm just doing my duty as a family member, Jutei San."

"Please, young lady," he gestured, "come with me."

Anna entered a windowless room lit only by the oil lamp that swayed in the old man's hand. It was like being in a curiosity shop full of cheap trinkets and valuable articles. "From this collection," her aged companion explained, "please honor me by choosing something."

Anna gasped with delight. Never before had she found herself in such a powerful position. Wandering around and about her gaze swept lingeringly over hundreds of objects. Time went by but still she could not make up her mind. "It's so difficult to choose," she said. "Won't you advise me Jutei San?"

A lengthy discussion took place all to no avail, then finally, all at once Anna made her choice, settling on a minute ivory brooch carved in the shape of a frog.

"Are you sure?" Jutei murmured. "Quite certain?"

"Yes. I'll treasure it always." Anna, confident that she had made a modest choice, had no idea that unwittingly she had chosen a valuable article. The ivory brooch had been carved with consummate skill some hundreds of years ago.

With great nicety Jutei bowed farewell, giving Anna no intimation of the anxiety of his heart. Having made the gift of his own volition, he would have to pay the price. "*Dōmo dōmo*—a tricky problem!" he muttered. "Never mind, never mind. Somehow I'll manage." Laughing silently, he settled down to his duties.

Back again in the street, the gift tucked safely in her pocket, Anna stood aside as a drove of ricksha swept by in single file. The sweating, shouting pullers were eager to find good trade at the nearby docks, for the gigantic French passenger liner had already been cut loose from the hawsers and was hooting out its heartrending siren-warnings.

The departing ship was of no interest to Anna, but as she drew close to the docks she halted, astonished to see that thousands of sea gulls were massed, floating on the water. Gazing skyward, she noticed that not one bird was on the wing. "Strange!" she exclaimed. *"How strange . . ."*

"What, may I ask," a pleasant male voice said, "is so strange?" Kentaro Fukuda, immaculate in his formal morning suit, smiled at the fragile, fair girl. "Don't you recognize me, Anna?"

"Yes, of course I do, Fukuda San." Anna smiled shyly. "But you took me by surprise."

"Well," he countered teasingly, "I'm surprised too. I've been farewelling a colleague who is sailing off to live in Paris, and my heart is consumed by jealousy. But—may I ask what you find so strange in these mundane surroundings?"

Strange . . . ? She shook her head as though to clear it, then she pointed, saying, "Look! Sea gulls! Floating! Not one in the air. Is it not strange?"

"It is a bit weird," Kentaro agreed casually. "Anna, my car is nearby. May I give you a lift?"

"Thank you, but I prefer to walk." Examining her blue enameled wristwatch, she announced, "I've plenty of time. It's just two minutes to midday. To the *second* . . ." Even as she spoke there was a weak seismic vibration. Accustomed to earth tremors, she and Kentaro were not perturbed. Then—almost in a moment—came an upheaval, quickly gaining in strength and violence. In an instant buildings surrounding them were leveled to the ground. Nature, with unbridled fury and savagery, was ravaging their world.

The spectacle struck terror into their hearts, rendering them speechless, deafening them as the great oil-storage tanks and their contents exploded into flames. Rivers of oil began to flow into the harbor, turning it into a sea of fire.

"*Jishin! Jishin!* Earthquake! Earthquake. . . ."

There were screams of fear and agony as fierce rains of sparks turned bodies into human torches.

The earth swayed, and tilted. The fire spread, eating up houses and buildings. The smoke billowed up in great suffocating clouds.

The world turned into a nightmare of destruction.

Then the earth was still.

A great echoing sound came.

The sky darkened as a furious tornado swept in lifting Anna and her companion up like chaff. They fell into a mass of screaming, burning men, women, and children, all wild, panic-stricken, heaving, shrieking, moving back and forth, trampling fallen victims to death.

Back and forth, terror beyond terror, then more terror—Kentaro, her protector, was gone.

Anna clawed out of the seething mob, screaming out his name again and again. Kentaro was with her once more.

Blood streamed from a gash in his forehead. She scarcely recognized his scorched face. He ripped the sash from her waist and tied her right arm tightly to his left arm. Bound together, they pushed their way, frantically fighting for life.

On they struggled. Amid people enveloped in flames, past piles of blackened corpses, through streets blockaded by fallen stores and houses, always with the sound of explosions and falling timbers, and the continuous roar of the fires.

"Faster!" screamed Anna. "Run faster. . . ."

She stumbled. They fell to the road. They struggled up. "Run!" Kentaro commanded, but she was no longer able to run. A wall of fire raged toward them.

"*You* go on, go on!" she screamed. "Set me loose!"

With maniacal strength, Kentaro ran on, dragging her along, away from the menacing flames, toward the water canal of the Nakayama spinning mill.

The great brick building lay in ruins. The canal had burst its banks and its swirling waters had escaped. They stumbled into the muddy ditch. Anna's world blacked out. . . .

Anna became aware of the scorching rays of the sun as it blazed down through the clouds of cinder-filled smoke. She became aware

that she lay in a pond of yellow mud, her head pillowed in someone's arms.

A voice was repeating over and over, "Get up! Run! Anna! *Run
to safety!*"

She remembered everything.

Yes, yes, she must run home. Slowly, she tried to get up.

"Hurry, be strong." Kentaro was covered in blood and ash. "Run,
run for your life. The wind is sending the fire our way!"

Deafening explosions came unceasingly. "The gasworks are exploding!" shouted terrified voices from the mob that swept past,
away from the furious fires.

Great columns of smoke shot high into the air. Anna screamed
out her terror as she fell back upon Kentaro and clung to him.

He pushed her off roughly and struck at her face, shouting, "Fool!
Fool! Run!"

Confused, she struggled up and scrambled from the mud-filled
ditch. Kentaro, she saw, was doomed, held captive by a jagged beam
of heavy timber that lay across his legs.

Could she desert him—leave him to die?"

"Move!" he shouted. "Move off . . ."

She tried to heave the timber off. "Go on, *go on* . . ." He kept
pushing her away, hampering her.

"Shut up! Shut up!" she screamed. "Help me free you!"

All about them people, horribly burned, fell into the swampy
canal, plastering mud over blistering flesh. . . . "Help us . . ." Anna
called out passionately, knowing that her words could not be heard
in the roar of the inferno.

"*God* help us!" she screamed, and, as if in answer to her prayer,
the ground shook violently.

"*Jishin!*—earthquake!" came moans of hopelessness from many
voices, but Anna, laughing wildly, cried out triumphantly. "Kentaro! Move . . . *now!*"

The new tremor had shifted the great beam. Kentaro heaved himself slowly out from under it. Together they struggled from the
ditch, only to be drawn into a seething mass attempting to reach the
safety of the ocean at Hommoku Bay which lay less than a mile
away.

They, and the crazed mob, running onward, were not aware that
the wind's direction had changed and the flames no longer pursued
them.

. . .

A saffron sun shone down upon the great hoard of refugees congregating in the Hommoku Bay area. The beachfront, once so peaceful, had taken on a nightmarish atmosphere, but Anna Dreyer gave no heed to the collapsed houses bordering the waterfront, or to the horrible sight of human and animal corpses floating among the debris on the still, sullen water.

Her gaze went up to the high bluff. Those ancient sea pines were no longer etched against the sky. The contours of the hill were not recognizable. The house—her home—had disappeared forever. . . .

Kentaro, no longer mindful of the young girl, pushed his way through the burned and bleeding but silent throng.

On reaching the beachfront, a shudder ran through his body as he beheld the sight of young Haru Yamamoto, his blood-spattered garment torn, his face a grimace of agony as he gestured toward his parents' shattered house.

Kentaro caught at the youth's arm. "Haru! *What?* Speak, *tell me!*"

The distraught boy was unable to communicate, but from beneath the piles of broken tiles and timbers came Renzō Yamamoto's voice, calling harshly, "*Tasukete kure . . . Tasukete kure*—help! Help if you please . . ."

When the new day arrived, barges and small craft arrived. Troops and Red Cross orderlies came ashore. People were to be unscrambled, classified, marshalled into a semblance of order.

Most anxious about the fate of his own family, Kentaro's mind was filled with foreboding, but he waited, attempting to comfort Renzō and Haru.

Tama was dead, crushed by a falling beam. She had died instantly. Her grief-stricken husband and son were inconsolable in the nightmarish atmosphere which increased as voices of officials blared out through loudspeakers, "*Yokohama is completely destroyed. Obey the imperial edicts. Be brave. Courteous. Calm.*

"*You must not try to return to your homes. Move toward the boats on the water.*

"*Disease and the spread of disease must be prevented.*

"*Move toward the boats on the water . . .*"

Renzō became entangled in a brief, fierce argument with officialdom. But Kentaro finally persuaded him that orders must be obeyed. Only the living were allowed on the rescue vessels.

As the trio joined the long queue moving slowly to the waiting boats, Haru broke into a dreadful fit of weeping as he attempted to run back to where his mother's body lay, but Renzō grasped the boy's arm and muttered harshly, "No. Haru. No. Move forward. *Don't look back. . . .*"

I N FAR-OFF LONDON NEWS of the earthquake had left Etsu and her mother-in-law both shocked and grief-stricken. To Fumio Nomura, it gave the opportunity to use his journalistic skills, translating Teruo Katō's flow of cables sent from Japan into English for the world press.

Putting his own emotions aside, Nomura gave vent to his love of drama, writing his reports in staccato fashion, attempting to give truthful, vivid pictures of the disastrous, world-shaking occurrences of the earthquake followed by tidal waves and fires:

> Tokyo, Japan's capital city, and Yokohama, the most flourishing seaport of the Far East, have been turned into veritable deserts of hot ashes. Along the coast whole villages have been swept away by tidal waves. . . .
>
> Bridges, roads, and railway lines have been demolished. Some six thousand vessels that had been moored in the rivers and along the bays have been destroyed. . . .
>
> It was clearly understood that many people would have survived had the earthquake not occurred at noon, when every firebox in every small home had been filled with live coals for the midday meal. Thousands of people, penned in alleys between their fragile dwellings, have been incinerated by the flames. Countless others fled to parks and open spaces, only to be roasted to their deaths, standing upright, so closely had they been packed. . . .
>
> Inmates from prisons and lunatic asylums roamed about. Macabre rumors spread through the cities. . . .
>
> In Tokyo alone more than a hundred thousand people have been annihilated. Thousands more are seriously injured. . . .
>
> In both cities corpses in tens of thousands are heaped in funeral pyres awaiting cremation. From other pyres the gray ashes of the dead are heaped into macabre piles before which makeshift altars have been constructed. Priests chant, mourners cast offerings of flowers which grow into mounds as high as the ghastly mountains of ashes. . . .
>
> During this time of national disaster, masses of country people,

their minds in disarray, crowd into the afflicted metropolis, adding to the confusion as they search for missing relatives. . . .

It was a relief to Nomura when Katō's reports became less horrific:

> People had lost all sense of time and space, but gradually minds have been calmed. It is as though millions of citizens, on a rampage of sorrow and fear, have gradually stopped in their tracks, becoming orderly, moving forward with a blend of zeal and arrogance into the future. . . .

Katō's reports were stringently exact, but Nomura, with a sense of guilt, held back on certain incidents, especially he did not mention crazed Japanese citizens' vicious attacks and treatment of the always despised Korean workers in the land. He also neglected to mention that directly after the catastrophe, when American destroyers sped into the waters of Tokyo Bay, mind-weakened officials were afraid that a foreign foe was out to fill the bitter bowl with a new terror. Rumors arose then faded away with embarrassing speed when it became evident that those rushing destroyers had been speeded up only by generosity, that they had arrived loaded with relief stores and with offers of much-needed practical help. . . .

Not proud of his reticence, Nomura wrote glowing reports, praising the extent of the world's concern, and the immediate help that had begun to flow in from many other countries. Writing how relief hutments and tent hospitals had been set up by the United States army, how foreign engineers were assisting in the building of bridges and in clearing foul-smelling clogged waterways . . .

Etsu's husband had few regrets when further reports of the earthquake's aftermath were no longer called for. Other world events had become more newsworthy, so, in need of some light relief, he escorted his wife and mother to Paris, hoping that fresh fields might give surcease to their grief-stricken hearts.

At times Nomura's thoughts went out to Yuichi Fukuda in great gusts of thankfulness for having put forward the idea of having his mother accompany them to London. There was a sweet rapport between the two women, and together they had achieved a kind of miracle in turning his casually run apartment into a delightful home. He was thus able to spend time, whenever he so wished, congregating with colleagues, untroubled by his conscience.

When a cable from Yuichi Fukuda arrived announcing that Etsu's bereaved young brother, Haru, was on his way to England for an unstated length of time, Etsu rejoiced and both Nomura and his mother responded to the plan with heartfelt cordiality.

SAFE IN THE VILLAGE OF Karuizawa, far away from the center of the earthquake, Aiko Fukuda had waited in anguish for news of her son. Kentaro's well-being, his happiness, was all-important to her. On learning that he had come through the holocaust alive, un-harmed but for a wound on his forehead, her joy and relief was in itself a kind of anguish. Following his arrival at the family villa, she had been unable to take her eyes off him as he sat surrounded by his wife and daughters, relating tales of terror, carnage, and of val-iant actions.

Baron Fukuda, on learning that his old family home stood un-scathed, had returned to Tokyo posthaste. But Aiko, sick at heart, had no wish to witness the results of nature's sabotage, no wish to endure the turbulence of reconstruction and the vulgarism of modern-day life. For her, a life without the sweet companionship of women friends would be dismal. So few had been left in her life, and now, to her sorrow, her last-made confidante, Lenia Marakov, had met a cruel death.

Renzō's loss of his young wife, Tama, gained her deep sympa-thies, but she could not bear the thought of seeing him a broken man bereaved and bowed down.

For quite some time the decline of the conservative tastes of earlier days had been bruising her spirit, and now she felt a longing, a positive need to experience an austere, mannerly way of living. With apologies to no one, she entered a religious retreat, one set beneath the shadow of volcanic Mount Asama. The nunnery's buildings were ancient, of classical design; the surrounding scenery was not rugged but of undulating beauty, that reacted dramatically to the change of seasons.

There, in the mountain sanctuary, Aiko hoped to dwell for the remainder of her days.

The national tragedy had aroused all Yuichi Fukuda's managerial talents. "I have," he told himself, "virtually to all intents and purposes, been reborn." Spry, energetic, he took command of his own life and the affairs of those around and about him.

On learning of Renzō's tragic circumstances, Yuichi had brought him, together with Haru, to stay in the mansion, settling them into old Sumiko's small sanctum, saying, "Here, Renzō, in this familiar room, your spirit will revive." Paying no attention to his cousin's lackluster response, he had convinced Renzō of the need to send his young son to London. "The boy," he had insisted, "will soon recover from his traumas when away from the turmoil and confusion."

Although busy and involved in myriad schemes, Yuichi became aware that Haru was in dire need of care and understanding. The boy had been so cherished. Nothing had prepared him for hardship, let alone for the macabre onslaught of death and wholesale destruction.

He had lost his adoring mother. Had been forced to leave her crushed, lifeless body lying in the open alongside a row of dead strangers.

The grand old house looked upon as Haru's second home had disappeared from the face of the earth, taking with it an entire family, people who had been central in his life. It was all too much, too dreadful to take in. Haru spent his time sitting rigidly in quiet corners holding a book, staring blankly at its pages.

Yuichi's heart went out to Haru in a flood of tenderness, but he spoke to him flatly, saying, "Haru, a memorial service is to be held in the Catholic church for your mother. You know that?"

"Yes, Uncle."

"Good! Haru, now about your friends, the Bixby family. Should we have a church service for them too? Were they all of the Christian faith?"

"I think so Uncle."

"Only think? You must know. Tell me all about them."

"I'd rather not."

"You must. I insist."

"I don't want to. I can't."

"Yes you can. You cared so much for them. I know that. Tell me, were they all present in the old house when it was buried beneath the landslide? All of them? Even the cook and the servants? Tell me . . . Let us talk about your friends. Their spirits will be lonely, we should comfort them . . ."

Haru began to weep and Yuichi was relieved, knowing that by

openly expressing the pain, the ache, and the grief, Haru was facing up to life.

After a long time the weeping ceased and from then on Haru, avoiding his father, followed his uncle about like a shadow.

Yuichi was deeply moved and shocked by the horrendous death-toll of the Englishman's household. In all, including the servants, twelve people had been buried alive. It just did not bear thinking of.

Having been told of Anna Dreyer's plight, he contacted the German consul, and without any ado the girl, in a state of shock, had been escorted on board a departing ship, told that she was on her way to live with a distant relative in Berlin. With speed and dexterity Yuichi took charge of and arranged the lives of many people, always modestly pleased with his success.

With sweeping generosity, he offered his home as a safe haven for orphaned and lost children. Before a week was up, the place was turned into a shambles of scared, bewildered small fry. Parents, decimated by grief, desperate, even suspicious, came crowding into the mansion, hoping to find that special child they searched for.

Dismayed by their unruly behavior, but refusing to succumb, Yuichi called on the services of the widow Kawabata, who, with verve and enthusiasm took command. Pleased with his acumen in having read the woman's capabilities, Yuichi turned his attention to more personal affairs.

To Kentaro's annoyance, Yuichi was not at all perturbed when his wife of many years donned the habit of a nun. "Typical of Aiko," he declared briskly. "Her fastidious nature will relish the break from harsh reality. Let's remember, she's free to come and go from the convent as she wishes. Her grandmother, the old Countess Okura, also became a nun when widowed."

"But, Father, my mother still has years of life ahead. And she is— not yet a widow."

"True, true," Yuichi agreed complacently. "Who should know that better than I? Never mind! Kentaro, each of us, in our own way, should have the privilege of adapting ourselves to unexpected conditions. Stop fretting about your mother. Was she not happy when you visited her new domain?"

"She appeared just as usual."

"Good. Does the religious raiment become her?"

"It does. She wears it with confidence and style."

"Say no more!" Yuichi chortled. "Aiko has always embraced

avant-garde styles. It's another legacy inherited from her aristocratic fop of a father. Actually, Kentaro, you have a touch of it yourself."

"Maybe I do. Certainly, I bear no resemblance in any way to you, Father."

"Now, never you mind about all that." Yuichi placed a hand on Kentaro's shoulder, saying hastily but with pride and affection, "I'd have you no different from how you are. By the way, I'm concerned about my old cousin. Without doubt he needs taking out of himself. Give me your opinion of Renzō? How would you describe his state of mind?"

With a stab of guilt, Kentaro realized that he had not seen his uncle for many weeks.

ONE BLUE-SKIED DAY, SOME six weeks after the catastrophic earthquake, Kentaro, accompanied by Renzō, was present at a mass meeting being held at the music stand in Hibiya Park. They were there to give expression to the popular feelings of gratitude for the assistance extended to Japan so freely and liberally by foreign nations.

As the speeches and formalities continued, Renzō was finding it difficult to concentrate. His mind was in a parlous state. He regretted having given in to Kentaro's pleadings that he should pluck up courage, leave the refuge of Sumiko's room, and step out into the world for a while.

The magnified voice of Tokyo's lord mayor ringing out reminded Renzō of those other voices of officialdom calling out, on that terrible day . . . *"Be orderly. Calm—brave . . ."*

Calm . . . ? Brave . . . ?

Tama . . . Tama . . . His dear, dear young wife . . . An involuntary groan came from Renzō. The sound caused Kentaro to murmur, "Uncle, better, perhaps, that we take our leave?"

"No, no. We should conform to the conventions of protocol."

Kentaro, who was representing one section of the Foreign Office, agreed that protocol should be upheld, but he deeply regretted having encouraged Renzō to attend the meeting. He felt that his uncle had come to the end of his active life.

A foreign dignitary was holding forth in praise of Japan's people, exhorting the nation to rejoice, because every member of the imperial family remained unharmed. Kentaro, bowing in accordance, rejoiced even more that every member of *his* family was also unharmed.

His close shave with death had aroused in him a new lust for life. The deep gash on his forehead was healing and would leave an impressive warriorlike scar. He seldom glimpsed that scar in the mirror without thinking of Anna Dreyer. She had saved his life. Regrettably, the young girl had left Japan before he had been able to contact her. Without doubt, that was blunting the edge of his inner happiness. In the not too distant future, he would make inquiries, make certain that she lacked for nothing while living in her native land.

He regretted the destruction of his Tokyo home and the recently acquired old house at Nihombashi. After much argument with his overly patriotic wife, and some string-pulling, he had obtained berths on an overcrowded Dollar Line steamer. Now Maya and his daughters were on the high seas. Later he would join them in the United States for a well-deserved vacation. . . .

As the British ambassador replied to the mayor's drawn-out speech on behalf of the *Corps Diplomatique*, Kentaro paid him full attention. Then there came a burst of loud, enthusiastic applause.

At long last, the meeting was over. . . .

T OKYO'S IMPERIAL HOTEL HAD COME through the disaster with very little damage, a tribute to its architect Frank Lloyd Wright, who had battled much opposition to build it this way. It now resembled a beckoning oasis in the center of unsightly wreckage. Always a popular watering hole for travelers the world over, myriad tales were to be told of multitudinous matters that had taken place within its massive gray stone walls—matters to do with business contracts, wedding banquets, romances, and as a rendezvous for illicit lovers of many nationalities, or, just as a pleasant place to meet a friend or to sit and watch the world go by.

Following the meeting in Ueno Park, Kentaro, fearing that Renzō might collapse unless given succor, directed their steps towards the hotel.

Depositing his uncle in an easy chair with a stiff whiskey and water close to hand, Kentaro excused himself and made for the basement bar. Relaxing among friends, he decided to linger on, one hope being that his charge might indulge in a much-needed nap.

Renzō sat very still. The glass on the table remained untouched. Someone, he pondered, perhaps Confucius, had decreed, *"Let mourning stop after full expression of our grief."*

Easy to preach such an edict. He would grieve for Tama to the final hour of his life. He hoped that time was not too far off. Certainly, he would be mannerly, moderate outward signs of bereavement. Show a polite face to society.

After some deliberation, Renzō raised his glass, not attempting to drink but holding it clutched in his hand. No matter how great his endeavors, his heart remained sodden, heavy with grief.

A somewhat tremulous smile touched his lips as he thought of Haru. The boy, suddenly bereft of his adoring mother, of young friends and all things familiar, had quietly bent to the suggestion that he should now travel, and join his sister in England. A cable had come from Etsu telling of her brother's safe arrival. Surely, over there, in new surroundings, Haru's laughter would ring out again?

Renzō tossed his whiskey down in one swallow. In an instant a waitress was by his side, bowing, saying, "Yamamoto Sama, may I assist you?"

The girl recognized him! Ah, well, his books, such as they were, had made him rather well known. From force of habit he ordered another whiskey, then took out his pipe, fondling it as he allowed his thoughts to wander. . . .

A vast sadness came over Renzō as he recalled his final farewell to the family who had dwelt for so long and so happily in the old house on the hill. Gone now. Every one of them. Tragic? Yes. But from an aesthetic point of view, one could see the Bixby saga as a bittersweet, lovely vignette. He had no regrets in having played his part in that much discussed marriage between East and West. Since then there had been many such unions. Society no longer considered them to be so scandalous. That romance between Bixby and Tomiko would always leave him nonplussed. She had been such an ordinary wisp of a girl. But her heart had remained focused on the man she loved. Yes, and his love on her.

Here he was, his life empty, his spirit bruised beyond repair. There was no virtue left in him. His grieving was not just for Tama but also for the good friends and acquaintances he had lost. And how desperately he missed that tiny, demanding dog of his . . .

His yearning for the companionship of old friends hurt like the twist of a knife in a wound. He needed those of his own ilk. Especially Aiko. She alone remained privy to his past. Her companionship would have lightened the darkness in his heart. He felt that she had betrayed him.

He was too old, too weary to bear what now seemed unbearable. His sword had rusted over. Gradually, he would become wholly dependent on others. . . .

Wholly dependent? Gradually? Was he not already so? Waiting to be escorted back to the old house at Yoyogi was scarcely the conduct of the complete man, and yes, for all Kentaro's punctiliousness, he had shown signs of impatience during that foot-dragging trek through the ravaged streets.

He was fully in sympathy with the vigorous young man, who, out to grab a brief reprieve from an old man's clingings, had made a hasty retreat to the hotel's bar.

Filled with self-disdain, Renzō became aware of his slumped shoulders. Correcting his posture, he gazed about the lobby. How crowded the place was. So many people standing here and there in groups. Others, at tables, drinking, eating, and chatting. Music from a string quartet blended in with snatches of laughter and the buzz of voices.

Truly, his senses were deeply offended. Yes, but the convivial atmosphere was oddly soothing to his ravaged heart. Sighing deeply, he began to wonder if, in fact, he might be able to experience at least a modicum of enjoyment during the short span left to him.

Could he dredge up enough vitality to free Kentaro of obligations?

Decamp, break free from Yuichi's generous but cloying attentions? Escape from that tiny room in the rambunctious Fukuda household?

Memories of the homes he had dwelt in throughout his life flickered through his mind's eye. Not one of those houses was left standing. He had become a displaced person. What an extraordinary situation to be in. Yes, but he had never been content to take the goods that the gods provided if the goods were not to his liking.

All at once Renzō became determined to take charge of his life. Somehow he would manage. Be independent, run his own affairs.

But how? Where? He was done with houses and domesticity. He was much too old for all that.

Then he knew. Renzō rose to his feet and went with slow-paced, steady steps toward the hotel's reception desk.

. . .

Reseating himself in the easy chair, Renzō gave a nod of satisfaction. He felt revitalized. And no wonder. It had required a touch of whip-in-hand diplomacy to have put the belligerent hotel manager in his proper place. For all the new aspects of modern day society, the differences between the classes still held sway. "Regrettably," he had been told, "no accommodation will be available for months to come . . ." But a samurai was still a samurai . . .

Kentaro was certainly over-staying his time at the bar. Well, the young chap had a surprise coming his way when he learned that his seemingly decrepit old charge had booked himself into the hotel. Period of residence? Indefinite.

He was feeling rather smug. And why not? He would be his own man again. Self-sufficient, with pleasant quarters and excellent service. This hotel's lobby was a world in itself, a place in which to relax. To meet people. Maybe even make new acquaintances? He might live on for quite some years. Only time would tell. Time? How would he be spending his time?

The thought of leading an indolent life began to worry him. He must take care, be wary, for he knew too well that surcease from his lasting grief would only come from work of some kind.

Could he perhaps begin another lightweight novel to occupy himself? That idea elicited no enthusiasm. Even the idea in itself seemed disgraceful. Disgraceful? Renzō sensed that he was being coerced into a spate of self-criticism. Always a realist, he had no need to gaze into a mirror to know that he had smothered his feelings of guilt over not producing a serious work derived from those years of grueling study. But perhaps it was not too late?

The ranks of men and women who had known life during the reign of the Meiji were diminishing, their miraculous endeavors through periods of strife and strain unrecognized, perhaps to be written down at some later date in history books—in all probability incorrectly by persons who had not experienced the times.

He had lived through those years of devastating changes. There were so many aspects of the terrors—the bloodletting, the strife and misunderstandings following the arrival of Commodore Perry. Those American battleships, their guns loaded, their decks cleared for action, had brought about a time of unbearable humiliation. No one spoke of those times anymore. Young people, his own son included, had little knowledge of and no interest in that past. Just as the earthquake destroyed the house on the hill, so it had put an end to the Japan of old.

Much had happened during his lifetime. But—where to begin such a challenging work?

All at once Renzō felt as though his spirit were rushing backward, passing swiftly before a series of convex mirrors that projected distorted images of events, places, and of people he had known.

The sensation was alarming. His breath came in gasps. Then he relaxed to sit with his eyes closed, his lips thrust out in an expression of satisfaction. He knew exactly where the chronicle was to begin. All he would need was time. Already, in his mind, he was composing the opening paragraph. . . .

> I clearly recall the hot, bright day that heralded in my seventh year. I awakened early, brimming over with energy . . .

Kentaro, slightly tipsy, having lingered at the bar longer than he intended, stood gazing down at Renzō, who appeared to be dozing. "Dear old man," he murmured softly. "It's a pity to disturb him. . . ."